EPIC

VIKING FOLK & FAIRY TALES

ANTHOLOGY OF CLASSIC TALES

Foreword by Dagrún Ósk Jónsdóttir

FLAME TREE PUBLISHING

TALES

This is a FLAME TREE Book

Publisher & Creative Director: Nick Wells
Editorial Director: Catherine Taylor
Special thanks to Tim Leng, Dawn Laker and Jocelyn Pontes

Publisher's Note: Due to the historical nature of the classic text, we're aware that there may be some language used which has the potential to cause offence to the modern reader. However, wishing overall to preserve the integrity of the text, rather than imposing contemporary sensibilities, we have left it unaltered.

FLAME TREE PUBLISHING
6 Melbray Mews, Fulham,
London SW6 3NS, United Kingdom
www.flametreepublishing.com

First published 2023

25 27 26 24
3 5 7 9 10 8 6 4

ISBN: 978-1-80417-591-0
Special ISBN: 978-1-80417-343-5

The cover image is created by Flame Tree Studio based on artwork by Slava Gerj, Gabor Ruszkai and Bourbon-88. Internal images are courtesy Shutterstock.com and the following artists: Morphart Creation (page 4), RedKoala, Victory1103 and Karlionau (story headers).

A copy of the CIP data for this book is available from the British Library.

Printed and bound in China

EPIC

VIKING FOLK & FAIRY TALES

ANTHOLOGY OF CLASSIC TALES

Foreword by Dagrún Ósk Jónsdóttir

FLAME TREE PUBLISHING

TALES

Contents

Tales of Trolls & Giants

Tales of Wind, Snow & Sea

Foreword

I HAVE ALWAYS LOVED STORIES. As a child, hearing them, and as I grew older, telling them. I remember driving around Iceland with my family as a child; I was bored and had already asked my parents too many times if we were 'there yet'. To escape my relentless questioning, my mother decided to tell me a story. She told me the story of the 'Tinder Box' by H.C. Andersen. She told it well, and as the story unfolded, I found myself transported from the car to a tower, guarded by three enormous dogs. She continued her storytelling and before I knew it, we had arrived. The story of the Tinder Box became a favourite of mine, but I would also encounter other stories in this book later in life.

Stories are magical; they possess the ability to transport us to another place and time, allowing us to forget our surroundings and become fully immersed in the narrative. Their influence can inspire, inform and even transform us. When listening to stories, we can experience joy or sadness, and they can spark fear or curiosity within us. They were told by those who ventured out to sea, as well as farmers, fishermen, workers and the many other classes that made up Nordic society of the past. Stories continued to be told through the ages, by regular people, storytellers, authors and even later, filmmakers.

Stories can work as windows into the past, through them we can see the worldviews of the people who told them, their hopes and dreams as well as their fears and prejudices. Stories are both shaped by society and they also shape it back, as they teach those who listen what is expected of them, about good morals and how one should behave (or not behave). They were told for entertainment or to mediate certain ideas. Good stories would travel and be told in different places of the world. Good storytellers would then adjust their stories to their audience. While many stories build on old themes or motifs from oral tradition, it is impossible to say how far back some truly date, as stories can only reflect the time in which they were collected or written down.

In this book the editors seek to show both the old myths and fairy tales of Scandinavia and the work of modern writers who continued to build on this tradition of storytelling. Some of these stories date back to the thirteenth century, such as the ones found in the *Prose Edda* which are believed to have their origin in oral tradition. The same applies for the folktales collected by folktale collectors such as the brothers' Grimm in Germany, Asbjørnssen and Moe in Norway and Jón Árnason in Iceland in the nineteenth century.

In this book you will also find stories written by famous Scandinavian fairy-tale authors such as Hans Christian Andersen in Denmark. Those fairy tales, although they are authored works and not collected from oral tradition, draw inspiration from the various folk and fairy tales. They also reflect the values, beliefs and struggles of the people of their time. All these stories have been told and retold and still hold relevance today.

I hope this book will also spark your interest in stories, that you will find enchantment within these pages and be transported to a different time and place, like I was in the family car so many years ago.

Dagrún Ósk Jónsdóttir
University of Iceland

Publisher's Note

THE FOLK AND FAIRY TALES contained here represent a broad tradition of Scandinavian storytelling that stretches back to ancient Norse mythology but which has blossomed and developed into the modern era across the northern lands that Viking culture touched. Thus, we have tales of the gods and from the Norse sagas alongside stories written by modern authors such as Hans Christian Andersen and Hjalmar Hjorth Boyesen. The tales originate in Norway, Iceland, Denmark and Sweden, with some hailing from Finland and Russia – and even Germany, via the Brothers Grimm who wrote about characters with Scandinavian cognates, such as Frau Holle. The collection aims to present an enjoyable and fascinating snapshot of the range and evolution of Nordic storytelling: from the legendary and epic, through the magic and wonder of the natural world to the common sense and faithfulness of the everyday in treasured fairy tales.

EPIC

VIKING FOLK & FAIRY TALES

ANTHOLOGY OF CLASSIC TALES

Foreword by Dagrún Ósk Jónsdóttir

FLAME TREE PUBLISHING

TALES

VIKING FOLK & FAIRY TALES

Introduction

SOME STORIES are centuries old. From their first narrations over camp fires, many have drifted on the breeze of time until they reach and envelop us, carrying us back to their own faraway pasts. For their magical, extraordinary characters, their breathtaking settings, and their inventive actions and conclusions, these stories can still capture and absorb us.

Some of the oldest stories and legends in this book may have first been told verbally over a thousand years ago, but not written down until much later; and many were written in the nineteenth century, building on elements of earlier oral traditions. Here is a melding of stories from Norse and Scandinavian myth, folklore and fairy tale, and they include heroic sagas, accounts of some of the earliest seafarers, magic, fantastic creatures, fables, histories and myths of adventure and daring. They are exciting and thought-provoking, alarming and inspiring. They explain the world and they add mystery to it. Originally, they may have been recited as people sat together around camp fires, each staring into the flickering tongues of flame, individually forming their own imaginative images. Deep into the night, the stories came to their conclusions as the glowing embers died away into the darkness. Later, poets recounted them in shadowy halls after great feasts, as the guests sat back to listen and dream, and later still, parents told the tales to their children as they gathered around crackling hearths on cold winter nights. In the modern era, these tales were collected and inspired further original stories. They are grand tales of magic, love, treachery, conquest and defeat, and remain eternal and universal human stories that continue to have resonance for us all.

Viking Foundations

The Norsemen spoke Old Norse, which they called *dönsk tunga* (the Danish tongue). With minor variations, this language was spoken throughout the Norse lands during the Viking period. The Vikings did not develop a written culture, but used runes to record short works, and long works were remembered using poetry. In its vehemence to implement Christianity in Europe, the Church did not authorize the recording of Viking myths, so once the Vikings had integrated with Christian society, most of the stories were either not written down, or were recorded by Christian priests who kept historical records, but lacked understanding of their original meanings. This meant that much of our knowledge of the Viking people has come from scant or obscure sources.

The Vikings and Norse people were strong, energetic and resourceful, originally from Norway, Sweden and Denmark, who existed from approximately 790 to 1100. They were originally traders, farmers, craftworkers and seafarers who took to the seas to raid, trade or explore, while Norsemen (Northmen) were traders and seafarers, but not fighters or warriors. Norse also refers to the language spoken by the Vikings and Norse people. By the eleventh century, many Vikings and Norsemen had settled across Northern and Western Europe and were becoming assimilated into those cultures.

Forward-Thinking

For about 300 years, the Vikings and Norsemen travelled to Europe, and they hugely influenced the cultures they settled amongst, particularly those in parts of Scotland, England, France and Ireland. Some founded Dublin, colonized Normandy in France, formed the area of the Danelaw in Britain, and became established in various communities throughout Scotland. Some settled in Iceland and Greenland and others travelled to North America. In the late 980s, the explorer Erik 'the Red' (*c.* 950–*c.* 1003) set up the first Viking settlement in Greenland. In *c.* 1000, his son, Leif 'the Lucky' (*c.* 970–*c.* 1020) arrived in North America. Influences went two ways, as eventually, Christianity was adopted by many of the Scandinavian settlers.

Although Vikings are now perceived to have been solely fierce warriors who undertook violent and deadly raids in their quests for treasure and slaves, they were also a highly developed civilization, who greatly valued the arts – including storytelling. They farmed and traded, created elaborate craftwork and they undertook daring voyages of discovery. Their society was divided into three classes; the Jarls (aristocracy), the Karls (lower classes) and the Thralls (slaves). However, rather than being ferocious and filthy as popular history suggests, in general, Vikings addressed their personal hygiene and their appearance. They braided their hair and the Jarls in particular wore fine cloaks, often silk robes, and intricately crafted jewellery. Women may not have been treated with full equality and respect, but they could inherit property, represent themselves in legal cases, own their own businesses and, if they were unmarried, choose where to live.

The Norse Universe

Viking religious beliefs included a universe that was full of gods, goddesses, spirits and supernatural energies. Like other pagan religions, each god or goddess had his or her own personality, abilities and specialisms, each explained aspects of the mysteries of the world, made things happen and generally helped mortals. However, each god also had his or her own failings and faults.

There were different types of gods. The Aesir gods represented power and combat. In maintaining order in the cosmos, they fought the Frost Giants – who represented darkness and confusion. These Frost Giants – called jötunns – were not necessarily huge. They had magical powers, and while some were ugly, others were beautiful. Although they were the enemies of the gods, they were also sometimes their lovers or spouses. The Aesir gods included Baldr, Bragi, Idun, Odin, Sif and Thor. The Vanir gods were gentler. They could see into the future and were associated with such benefits as health, fertility, nature and knowledge. They included Freya, Loki, Njord, Vili and Ve.

Several of these gods have become famous beyond the folklore, such as the hammer-wielding thunder-god Thor and one-eyed Odin, who carried his spear and pursued knowledge. In an act of self-sacrifice, Odin hanged himself upside-down for nine days and nights to gain knowledge of the runic alphabet, which he passed on to humanity. He was associated closely with death, wisdom and poetry; Loki was 'the author of all fraud and mischief,' and beautiful, sensual Freyja wore a feathered cloak and rode into battles to look for her missing husband Óðr. Her brother Freyr was associated with the weather, royalty, human sexuality and agriculture, and he brought peace and pleasure to humanity. Some women, known as Volva, could hear and understand the gods' language and they translated it for other mortals. With their origins in the Germanic gods of Northern Europe, Norse gods were believed to bestow life, and so it was up to every human to prove him or herself worthy of such a gift.

Four of our days of the week are named after these gods. They are: Tuesday – from Tyr, the bravest god of war and the lawgiver; Wednesday – from Odin (known in Old English as Wōden) who was married to Frigg; Thursday – from Thor, Odin's son, the god of thunder among many other attributes; and Friday – from Frigg, the goddess of marriage, families and motherhood, married to Odin and stepmother to Thor.

The Norse creation story explains that before the world began there was only the world of Muspelheim, that was a world of fire. Ages passed and then Niflheim was made; a world of ice – although Niflheim translates as 'World of Fog.' Between the two worlds was the void of Ginnungagap. Eventually, life emerged in Ginnungagap – a giant named Ymir – and soon he was joined by a cow called Audhumla. Audhumla fed Ymir milk from her udders. Meanwhile, she also licked the ice and this freed the trapped god Búri, who then produced a son, Borr. Borr married Bestla, the daughter of Bolthorn, a Frost Giant, and Bestla gave birth to the gods Odin, Vili and Ve. Together, these three gods killed Ymir and used his body to create the world – a sacred tree called Yggdrasil. Ymir's bones became rocks, his skull, the sky. The first humans to live in part of Yggdrasil were Ask and Embla, who had neither spirit nor form until Odin breathed life into them, and other gods gave them reason and passion. Because of Ymir's murder, all giants were a constant threat to both humans and gods.

Creation and Destruction

Before the creation of the cosmos, the freezing winds and ice of Niflheim met with the searing heat and fire from Muspelheim. Sparks flew and the gods, led by Odin, made the world from Ymir's body. This world was an enormous ash tree called Yggdrasil that had nine planes of existence. These planes were Midgard (Middle Earth – where mortals live), Asgard (where the Aesir gods live), Vanaheim (home to the Vanir gods), Jotunheim (land of the giants – the arch enemies of the gods), Alfheim (home to the fair elves), Svartalfaheim (home to the dark elves) and Nidavellir (where the dwarfs live and work). Niflheim was situated in the north, Muspelheim in the south. Women who died in childbirth went to the Hall of Frigg in Asgard, where they lived for eternity with Odin's wife, while men who died heroically in battle went to Odin's Hall of Valhalla.

Yggdrasil was nourished by three wells; the Well of Urd (the meeting place of the gods), the Well of Mimir (that gives wisdom to anyone who drinks from it) and the Well of Hvergelmir (where snakes and dragons live). Also living on and around Yggdrasil were several creatures; a wise eagle, a hawk called Veðrfölnir, four stags, a dragon, and a squirrel called Ratatosk. Sol drove the golden sun's chariot across the sky, pursued by the wolf Sköll. Sol's brother Mani drove the silver moon's chariot, chased by the wolf Hati. Jörð was the goddess of the Earth, Dagr was the god of day and Nótt was a jötunn of night.

Midgard was surrounded by water, where the World Serpent lived, and it was connected to Asgard by the Rainbow Bridge. Meanwhile, the whole of Yggdrasil was cared for by the Norns; three wise women who made mud with water from the Well of Urd each day and smeared it on to the tree's bark to keep it strong. Without the Norns, Yggdrasil would die. Travel between the worlds happens often in the myths, and the gods and other beings interact directly with humanity.

Fact and Fiction Intertwined

Feared across Northern Europe, the Vikings undertook sudden raids on ordinary people, killing many, stealing goods and treasures and capturing people as slaves. With spears, axes, bows, knives and hammers, they fought to the death. Their captives were put to work on farms or in Viking fortified towns called ring forts.

The Viking beliefs underpinned their lives. For example, men, women and children all worked hard – a fact that was echoed in some of the stories, such as *The Mead of Poetry*, in which Odin works the fields. Viking craftworkers included weavers, metalworkers, carvers and blacksmiths, and dwarfs of their beliefs were the best craftworkers, alleged to have made, among other things, Thor's hammer, Mjölnir and Odin's spear, Gungnir. The legend of the dragon-slaying hero Sigurd includes real historical figures.

The Vikings believed in two opposite ways of living: innangard, meaning 'within the enclosure', and utangard, meaning 'outside the enclosure.' Humans and civilized gods lived innangard, while the dark elves, dwarfs, trolls and giants lived utangard. The giants were the greatest adversaries of the Norse gods and goddesses. Unlike giants in other tales, Viking giants were not slow-witted, nor even huge. Like the gods, the giants had positive and negative aspects to their personalities. Some were beautiful or capable of kindnesses. Some were clever, astute or sporty, and some were cunning, vicious and full of malice. They included Ymir, the first giant; Surtr, the savage leader of the Fire Giants who brandished a blazing sword; and Aegir and Rán, who lived under the sea with their nine children. Giant animals include the serpent Jörmungandr (who encircled Midgard and who especially hated Thor), the malevolent serpent-dragon Nidhogg, the wolf Fenrir – who would ravage Yggdrasil during Ragnarök – and the Kraken, a giant squid-like creature that was said to measure more than a mile long and that lay in wait in deep waters, rising up only when disturbed by boats. Sailors often mistook the Kraken for land and headed straight for it, only realizing their mistake when they were pulled down to the bottom of the sea.

Other strange and supernatural beings existed, who, while not as powerful as the gods or giants, were capable of changing events or outcomes, usually working surreptitiously.

These included dwarfs, elves, trolls and spirits. Some were kind and helpful, but most were not. For instance, in their underground maze of tunnels in Svartalfheim, dwarfs created Sif's golden hair, Odin's magical ring Draupnir and Freyr's ship, as well as other wonderful treasures. Elves could similarly be good or bad – the good elves helped the Vanir gods, and like the dwarfs, the dark elves lived underground. Closely related to the giants, the trolls were ugly and evil and they lurked in dark places. Additionally, the Vikings believed that unseen spirits hovered over them during many important moments of life and just after death, such as on battlefields, at every child's birth and on distant voyages. Spirits were often female and generally protective. They included the Norns, who as well as caring for Yggdrasil, were present at every baby's birth; the landvættir who protected nature, and the Valkyries, who flew over battlefields and carried valorous fallen warriors to Valhalla. Animal spirits included the eight-legged horse Sleipnir, and two ravens owned by Odin: Hugin (or Huginn), who oversaw thoughts, and Munin (or Muninn), who oversaw memory. Odin used them to keep an eye on his people and to gain wisdom.

As with most religions, life after death was important to the Vikings. Warriors were told that if they fell bravely, they would be taken to Valhalla by Valkyries. This was a vast hall, owned by Odin, with a roof made of shields, wolves guarding its 540 doors, and eagles encircling the roof. Hel, Loki's daughter, ruled Niflheim, where many of the dead were believed to go, or they might be chosen by the goddess Freyja to live in her field Fólkvangr. The goddess Rán claimed those who died at sea.

From Belief to Book

Although these beliefs were well-established in Viking lore, and for years, most Vikings viewed Christianity with suspicion and scepticism, by 1100, Christianity had almost completely eclipsed Norse philosophies. For a while, many Vikings observed the two religions concurrently. For instance, some prayed to both Jesus and Thor, while others perceived Odin as being interchangeable with Jesus. Niflheim became exchanged with Heaven, and Muspelheim became assimilated with Hell. Gradually, Viking beliefs were disregarded. Some aspects of some of the tales had been carved on to stone and wood in runes, such as the story of Sigurd and the Dragon that was carved into a church doorway in Norway, but there were few written records or reliable sources.

Christianity eventually pushed away Viking paganism, old gods and deities were discarded – but they still appeared in tales, as fantastic characters and magical creatures. Christianity fitted with their outlook; Norse morality was based on personal accountability, and there was a sense of social responsibility, which is often apparent in the stories. Most of these are now known from two books: The Poetic Edda and The Prose Edda. The Poetic Edda was a collection of Old Norse poems that revealed information about the gods and heroes of pre-Christian Vikings and Norse people, their unique vision of the beginning and end of the world and more. The Poetic Edda includes eddic verse that includes stories of the gods, and skaldic verse, a form of bloodthirsty heroic poetry that was popular in the Viking Age. The Poetic Edda comes from an Icelandic medieval manuscript known as the Codex Regius, which contains thirty-one poems, and many later poets and writers have acknowledged their debt to them, including, for instance, English writer, poet and academic, J.R.R. Tolkien (1892–1973). Although the Codex Regius was written during the thirteenth century, it remained in obscurity until 1643, when it came into the possession of the Bishop of Skálholt. He sent it to the

Danish king as a gift and for centuries it was stored in the Royal Library in Copenhagen. In 1971, it was returned to Iceland.

During the early thirteenth century, the Icelandic historian, chieftain and poet Snorri Sturluson (1179–1241) was concerned that the tradition of composing poetry to commemorate stories and events was dying, and he researched Norse mythology – including The Poetic Edda. He wrote The Prose Edda, a four-part book that includes both prose and poetry. While most of Snorri's sources are unknown, he aimed for The Prose Edda to be a handbook for composing skaldic verse. He also sought to represent the stories unambiguously and impartially, but his perspective was quite male-oriented and although much is written about the importance of gods, there is less about the goddesses. There are some, for example, Frigg, the goddess of marriage, motherhood and the sky, who knows everyone's destiny; the merciless skiing goddess Skaði; Iðunn, who keeps apples that grant eternal youth; and Sif, the golden-haired goddess of the Earth, crops, fertility and farming. However, it is likely that there were more tales about the females than we now know.

Old to Modern

The stories in this book focus on the fairy and folk tales. Some are old, but some are relatively modern, yet they grew from older oral traditions, or borrowed narrative elements from the ancient myths. Since the seventeenth century, many of them have attracted the attention of European scholars, and during the Romantic period (approximately 1800–50), a revival of interest in much of the subject matter increased. Later still, these stories were copied, edited, translated and reinterpreted, and with their widespread publication, the stories spread into European literary culture. Many remain timeless and compelling, and aspects have been retold by others, such as the Danish children's author Hans Christian Andersen (1805–75) and the Norwegian authors Peter Christen Asbjørnsen (1812–55) and Jørgen Moe (1813–82). Several of these and those by other writers feature in this book.

Among the tales here are 'Why the Sea Is Salt', a Norwegian fairy tale collected by Asbjørnsen and Moe about a poor man and his rich brother. Ultimately, in strong fairy tale tradition, the story gives an imaginative reason why the sea became salty. 'The Little Match Seller' by Hans Christian Andersen tells of a poor little girl in the bitter winter, dreaming of warmth and food as she tries to earn money for her family. The moral of the tale is to behave charitably towards those who are less fortunate. 'The Seven Foals' is another story collected by Asbjørnsen and Moe, reminiscent of 'Cinderella', but about a boy known as Cinder-lad, while also by them is 'East of the Sun and West of the Moon', in which a young girl breaks her promise and has to travel east of the sun and west of the moon.

The folk-tales contained here have not only stood the test of time, but have shown an understanding of and empathy with the natural world and human nature. These stories have been endlessly reinvented, instilling moral values while retaining their original brilliance and vitality.

S. Hodge

Tales of Bravery

Introduction

THE SIGHT of the legendary warrior Holger Danske is an inspiring one. 'Clad in iron and steel', he sleeps – down endless centuries – in a deep, dark dungeon. In Denmark's hour of need, we're told, he'll rouse himself to save his people. It's an unsettling image too, however, hinting as it does at the existence of another dimension, an underworld of fears we feel can't quite fathom – and certainly aren't equipped to deal with all that well.

His destiny as his country's sleeping guardian clearly recalls that of King Arthur's as protector of Britain (another story being constantly retold at this point in the nineteenth century). This only underlines the extent to which Holger Danske was seen, not specifically as a soldier but as a defender against the more universal anxieties of the age. How were ancient qualities to be retooled for the modern world? What did Viking virtues of loyalty and valour have to offer in a here and now beset by very different challenges and problems?

Heroism has been harder to define since the age of the warrior ended. Perhaps it has been harder to attain as well.

Holger Danske

(Danish)

IN DENMARK THERE STANDS AN OLD CASTLE named Kronenburg, close by the Sound of Elsinore, where large ships, both English, Russian, and Prussian, pass by hundreds every day. And they salute the old castle with cannons, "Boom, boom," which is as if they said, "Good day." And the cannons of the old castle answer "Boom," which means "Many thanks." In winter no ships sail by, for the whole Sound is covered with ice as far as the Swedish coast, and has quite the appearance of a high-road. The Danish and the Swedish flags wave, and Danes and Swedes say, "Good day," and "Thank you" to each other, not with cannons, but with a friendly shake of the hand; and they exchange white bread and biscuits with each other, because foreign articles taste the best.

But the most beautiful sight of all is the old castle of Kronenburg, where Holger Danske sits in the deep, dark cellar, into which no one goes. He is clad in iron and steel, and rests his head on his strong arm; his long beard hangs down upon the marble table, into which it has become firmly rooted; he sleeps and dreams, but in his dreams he sees everything that happens in Denmark. On each Christmas Eve an angel comes to him and tells him that all he has dreamed is true, and that he may go to sleep again in peace, as Denmark is not yet in any real danger; but should danger ever come, then Holger Danske will rouse himself, and the table will burst asunder as he draws out his beard. Then he will come forth in his strength, and strike a blow that shall sound in all the countries of the world.

An old grandfather sat and told his little grandson all this about Holger Danske, and the boy knew that what his grandfather told him must be true. As the old man related this story, he was carving an image in wood to represent Holger Danske, to be fastened to the prow of a ship; for the old grandfather was a carver in wood, that is, one who carved figures for the heads of ships, according to the names given to them. And now he had carved Holger Danske, who stood there erect and proud, with his long beard, holding in one hand his broad battle-axe, while with the other he leaned on the Danish arms. The old grandfather told the little boy a great deal about Danish men and women who had distinguished themselves in olden times, so that he fancied he knew as much even as Holger Danske himself, who, after all, could only dream; and when the little fellow went to bed, he thought so much about it that he actually pressed his chin against the counterpane, and imagined that he had a long beard which had become rooted to it. But the old grandfather remained sitting at his work and carving away at the last part of it, which was the Danish arms. And when he had finished he looked at the whole figure, and thought of all he had heard and read, and what he had that evening related to his little grandson. Then he nodded his head, wiped his spectacles and put them on, and said, "Ah, yes; Holger Danske will not appear in my lifetime, but the boy who is in bed there may very likely live to see him when the event really comes to pass." And the old grandfather nodded again; and the more he looked at Holger Danske, the more satisfied he felt that he had carved a good image of him. It seemed to glow with the colour of life;

the armour glittered like iron and steel. The hearts in the Danish arms grew more and more red; while the lions, with gold crowns on their heads, were leaping up. "That is the most beautiful coat of arms in the world," said the old man. "The lions represent strength; and the hearts, gentleness and love." And as he gazed on the uppermost lion, he thought of King Canute, who chained great England to Denmark's throne; and he looked at the second lion, and thought of Waldemar, who untied Denmark and conquered the Vandals. The third lion reminded him of Margaret, who united Denmark, Sweden, and Norway. But when he gazed at the red hearts, their colours glowed more deeply, even as flames, and his memory followed each in turn. The first led him to a dark, narrow prison, in which sat a prisoner, a beautiful woman, daughter of Christian the Fourth, Eleanor Ulfeld, and the flame became a rose on her bosom, and its blossoms were not more pure than the heart of this noblest and best of all Danish women. "Ah, yes; that is indeed a noble heart in the Danish arms," said the grandfather, and his spirit followed the second flame, which carried him out to sea, where cannons roared and the ships lay shrouded in smoke, and the flaming heart attached itself to the breast of Hvitfeldt in the form of the ribbon of an order, as he blew himself and his ship into the air in order to save the fleet. And the third flame led him to Greenland's wretched huts, where the preacher, Hans Egede, ruled with love in every word and action. The flame was as a star on his breast, and added another heart to the Danish arms. And as the old grandfather's spirit followed the next hovering flame, he knew whither it would lead him. In a peasant woman's humble room stood Frederick the Sixth, writing his name with chalk on the beam. The flame trembled on his breast and in his heart, and it was in the peasant's room that his heart became one for the Danish arms. The old grandfather wiped his eyes, for he had known King Frederick, with his silvery locks and his honest blue eyes, and had lived for him, and he folded his hands and remained for some time silent. Then his daughter came to him and said it was getting late, that he ought to rest for a while, and that the supper was on the table.

"What you have been carving is very beautiful, grandfather," said she. "Holger Danske and the old coat of arms; it seems to me as if I have seen the face somewhere."

"No, that is impossible," replied the old grandfather; "but I have seen it, and I have tried to carve it in wood, as I have retained it in my memory. It was a long time ago, while the English fleet lay in the roads, on the second of April, when we showed that we were true, ancient Danes. I was on board the Denmark, in Steene Bille's squadron; I had a man by my side whom even the cannon balls seemed to fear. He sung old songs in a merry voice, and fired and fought as if he were something more than a man. I still remember his face, but from whence he came, or whither he went, I know not; no one knows. I have often thought it might have been Holger Danske himself, who had swam down to us from Kronenburg to help us in the hour of danger. That was my idea, and there stands his likeness."

The wooden figure threw a gigantic shadow on the wall, and even on part of the ceiling; it seemed as if the real Holger Danske stood behind it, for the shadow moved; but this was no doubt caused by the flame of the lamp not burning steadily. Then the daughter-in-law kissed the old grandfather, and led him to a large arm-chair by the table; and she, and her husband, who was the son of the old man and the father of the little boy who lay in bed, sat down to supper with him. And the old grandfather talked of the Danish lions and the Danish hearts, emblems of strength and gentleness, and explained quite clearly that there is another strength than that which lies in a sword, and he pointed to a shelf where lay a number of old books, and amongst them a collection of Holberg's plays, which are much read and are so clever and amusing that it is easy to fancy we have known the people of those days, who are described in them.

"He knew how to fight also," said the old man; "for he lashed the follies and prejudices of people during his whole life."

Then the grandfather nodded to a place above the looking-glass, where hung an almanac, with a representation of the Round Tower upon it, and said "Tycho Brahe was another of those who used a sword, but not one to cut into the flesh and bone, but to make the way of the stars of heaven clear, and plain to be understood. And then he whose father belonged to my calling, – yes, he, the son of the old image-carver, he whom we ourselves have seen, with his silvery locks and his broad shoulders, whose name is known in all lands; – yes, he was a sculptor, while I am only a carver. Holger Danske can appear in marble, so that people in all countries of the world may hear of the strength of Denmark. Now let us drink the health of Bertel."

But the little boy in bed saw plainly the old castle of Kronenburg, and the Sound of Elsinore, and Holger Danske, far down in the cellar, with his beard rooted to the table, and dreaming of everything that was passing above him.

And Holger Danske did dream of the little humble room in which the image-carver sat; he heard all that had been said, and he nodded in his dream, saying, "Ah, yes, remember me, you Danish people, keep me in your memory, I will come to you in the hour of need."

The bright morning light shone over Kronenburg, and the wind brought the sound of the hunting-horn across from the neighboring shores. The ships sailed by and saluted the castle with the boom of the cannon, and Kronenburg returned the salute, "Boom, boom." But the roaring cannons did not awake Holger Danske, for they meant only "Good morning," and "Thank you." They must fire in another fashion before he awakes; but wake he will, for there is energy yet in Holger Danske.

The Legend of Thorgunna

(Icelandic)

A SHIP FROM ICELAND chanced to winter in a haven near Helgafels. Among the passengers was a woman named Thorgunna, a native of the Hebrides, who was reported by the sailors to possess garments and household furniture of a fashion far surpassing those used in Iceland. Thurida, sister of the pontiff Snorro, and wife of Thorodd, a woman of a vain and covetous disposition, attracted by these reports, made a visit to the stranger, but could not prevail upon her to display her treasures. Persisting, however, in her inquiries, she pressed Thorgunna to take up her abode at the house of Thorodd. The Hebridean reluctantly assented, but added, that as she could labour at every usual kind of domestic industry, she trusted in that manner to discharge the obligation she might lie under to the family, without giving any part of her property in recompense of her lodging. As Thurida continued to urge her request, Thorgunna accompanied her to Froda, the house of Thorodd, where the seamen deposited a huge chest and cabinet, containing the property of her new guest, which Thurida viewed with curious and covetous eyes. So soon as they had pointed out to Thorgunna the place assigned for her bed, she opened the chest, and took forth such an embroidered bed coverlid, and such a splendid and complete set of tapestry hangings, and bed furniture of English linen, interwoven with silk, as had never been seen in Iceland.

"Sell to me," said the covetous matron, "this fair bed furniture."

"Believe me," answered Thorgunna, "I will not lie upon straw in order to feed thy pomp and vanity"; an answer which so greatly displeased Thurida that she never again repeated her request. Thorgunna, to whose character subsequent events added something of a mystical solemnity, is described as being a woman of a tall and stately appearance, of a dark complexion, and having a profusion of black hair. She was advanced in age; assiduous in the labours of the field and of the loom; a faithful attendant upon divine worship; grave, silent, and solemn in domestic society. She had little intercourse with the household of Thorodd, and showed particular dislike to two of its inmates. These were Thorer, who, having lost a leg in the skirmish between Thorbiorn and Thorarin the Black, was called Thorer-Widlegr (wooden-leg), from the substitute he had adopted; and his wife, Thorgrima, called Galldra-Kinna (wicked sorceress), from her supposed skill in enchantments. Kiartan, the son of Thurida, a boy of excellent promise, was the only person of the household to whom Thorgunna showed much affection; and she was much vexed at times when the childish petulance of the boy made an indifferent return to her kindness.

After this mysterious stranger had dwelt at Froda for some time, and while she was labouring in the hay-field with other members of the family, a sudden cloud from the northern mountain led Thorodd to anticipate a heavy shower. He instantly commanded the hay-workers to pile up in ricks the quantity which each had been engaged in turning to the wind. It was afterwards remembered that Thorgunna did not pile up her portion, but left it spread on the field. The cloud approached with great celerity, and sank so heavily around the farm, that it was scarce possible to see beyond the limits of the field. A heavy shower next descended, and so soon as the clouds broke away and the sun shone forth it was observed that it had rained blood. That which fell upon the ricks of the other labourers soon dried up, but what Thorgunna had wrought upon remained wet with gore. The unfortunate Hebridean, appalled at the omen, betook herself to her bed, and was seized with a mortal illness. On the approach of death she summoned Thorodd, her landlord, and intrusted to him the disposition of her property and effects.

"Let my body," said she, "be transported to Skalholt, for my mind presages that in that place shall be founded the most distinguished church in this island. Let my golden ring be given to the priests who shall celebrate my obsequies, and do thou indemnify thyself for the funeral charges out of my remaining effects. To thy wife I bequeath my purple mantle, in order that, by this sacrifice to her avarice, I may secure the right of disposing of the rest of my effects at my own pleasure. But for my bed, with its coverings, hangings, and furniture, I entreat they may be all consigned to the flames. I do not desire this because I envy anyone the possession of these things after my death, but because I wish those evils to be avoided which I plainly foresee will happen if my will be altered in the slightest particular."

Thorodd promised faithfully to execute this extraordinary testament in the most exact manner. Accordingly, so soon as Thorgunna was dead, her faithful executor prepared a pile for burning her splendid bed. Thurida entered, and learned with anger and astonishment the purpose of these preparations. To the remonstrances of her husband she answered that the menaces of future danger were only caused by Thorgunna's selfish envy, who did not wish anyone should enjoy her treasures after her decease. Then, finding Thorodd inaccessible to argument, she had recourse to caresses and blandishments, and at length extorted permission to separate from the rest of the bed-furniture the tapestried curtains and coverlid; the rest was consigned to the flames, in obedience to the will of the testator. The body of Thorgunna, being wrapped in new linen and placed in a coffin, was next to be transported through the precipices and morasses of Iceland to the distant district she had assigned for her place of sepulture. A remarkable incident occurred on the way. The transporters of the body arrived at evening, late, weary, and drenched with rain, in a house called Nether-Ness, where the niggard hospitality of the proprietor only afforded them house-room, without any supply of food or fuel. But, so soon as they entered, an unwonted noise was heard in the kitchen of the mansion, and the figure of a woman, soon recognized to be the deceased Thorgunna, was seen busily employed in preparing victuals. Their inhospitable landlord, being made acquainted with this frightful circumstance, readily agreed to supply every refreshment which was necessary, on which the vision instantly disappeared. The apparition having become public, they had no reason to ask twice for hospitality as they proceeded on their journey, and they came to Skalholt, where Thorgunna, with all due ceremonies of religion, was deposited quietly in the grave. But the consequences of the breach of her testament were felt severely at Froda.

The dwelling at Froda was a simple and patriarchal structure, built according to the fashion used by the wealthy among the Icelanders. The apartments were very large, and a part boarded off contained the beds of the family. On either side was a sort of storeroom, one of which contained meal, the other dried fish. Every evening large fires were lighted in this apartment for dressing the victuals; and the domestics of the family usually sat around them for a considerable time, until supper was prepared. On the night when the conductors of Thorgunna's funeral returned to Froda, there appeared, visible to all who were present, a meteor, or spectral appearance, resembling a half-moon, which glided around the boarded walls of the mansion in an opposite direction to the course of the sun, and continued to perform its revolutions until the domestics retired to rest. This apparition was renewed every night during a whole week, and was pronounced by Thorer with the wooden leg to presage pestilence or mortality. Shortly after a herdsman showed signs of mental alienation, and gave various indications of having sustained the persecution of evil demons. This man was found dead in his bed one morning, and then commenced a scene of ghost-seeing unheard of in the annals of superstition. The first victim was Thorer, who had presaged the calamity. Going out of doors one evening, he was grappled by the spectre of the deceased shepherd as he attempted to re-enter the house. His wooden leg stood him in poor stead in such an encounter; he was hurled to the earth, and so fearfully beaten, that he died in consequence of the bruises. Thorer was no sooner dead than his ghost associated itself to that of the herdsman, and joined him in pursuing and assaulting the inhabitants of Froda. Meantime an infectious disorder spread fast among them, and several of the bondsmen died one after the other. Strange portents were seen within-doors, the meal was displaced and mingled, and the dried fish flung about in a most alarming manner, without any visible agent. At length, while the servants were forming their evening circle round the fire, a spectre, resembling the head of a seal-fish, was seen to emerge out of the pavement of the room, bending its round black eyes full on the tapestried bed-curtains of Thorgunna. Some of the domestics ventured to strike at this figure, but, far from giving way, it rather erected itself further from the floor, until Kiartan, who seemed to have a natural predominance over these supernatural prodigies, seizing a huge forge-hammer, struck the seal repeatedly on the head, and compelled it to disappear, forcing it down into the floor, as if he had driven a stake into the earth. This prodigy was found to intimate a new calamity. Thorodd, the master of the family, had some time before set forth on a voyage to bring home a cargo of dried fish; but in crossing the river Enna the skiff was lost and he perished with the servants who attended him. A solemn funeral feast was held at Froda, in memory of the deceased, when, to the astonishment of the guests, the apparition of Thorodd and his followers seemed to enter the apartment dripping with water. Yet this vision excited less horror than might have been expected, for the Icelanders, though nominally Christians, retained, among other pagan superstitions, a belief that the spectres of such drowned persons as had been favourably received by the goddess Rana were wont to show themselves at their funeral feast. They saw, therefore, with some composure, Thorodd and his dripping attendants plant themselves by the fire, from which all mortal guests retreated to make room for them. It was supposed this apparition would not be renewed after the conclusion of the festival. But so far were their hopes disappointed, that, so soon as the mourning guests had departed, the fires being lighted, Thorodd and his comrades marched in on one side, drenched as before with water; on the other entered Thorer, heading all those who had died in the pestilence, and who appeared covered with dust. Both parties seized the seats by the fire, while the half-frozen and terrified domestics spent the night without either light or warmth. The same phenomenon took place the next night, though the fires had been lighted in a separate house, and at length Kiartan was obliged to compound matters with the spectres by kindling a large fire for them in the principal apartment, and one for the family and domestics in a separate hut. This prodigy continued during the whole feast of Jol. Other portents also happened to appal this devoted family: the contagious disease again broke forth, and when anyone fell a sacrifice to it his spectre was sure to join the troop of persecutors, who had now almost full possession of the mansion of Froda. Thorgrima Galldrakinna, wife of Thorer, was one of these victims, and, in short, of thirty servants belonging to the household, eighteen died, and five fled for fear of the apparitions, so that only seven remained in the service of Kiartan.

Kiartan had now recourse to the advice of his maternal uncle Snorro, in consequence of whose counsel, which will perhaps appear surprising to the reader, judicial measures were instituted against the spectres. A Christian priest was, however, associated with Thordo Kausa, son of Snorro, and with Kiartan, to superintend and sanctify the proceedings. The inhabitants were regularly summoned to attend upon the inquest, as in a cause between man and man, and the assembly was constituted before the gate of the mansion, just as the spectres had assumed their wonted station by the fire. Kiartan boldly ventured to approach them, and, snatching a brand from the fire, he commanded the tapestry belonging to Thorgunna to be carried out of doors, set fire to it, and reduced it to ashes with all the other ornaments of her bed, which had been so inconsiderately preserved at the request of Thurida. A tribunal being then constituted with the usual legal solemnities, a charge was preferred by Kiartan against Thorer with the wooden leg, by Thordo Kausa against Thorodd, and by others chosen as accusers against the individual spectres present, accusing them of molesting the mansion, and introducing death and disease among its inhabitants. All the solemn rites of judicial procedure were observed on this singular occasion; evidence was adduced, charges given, and the cause formally decided. It does not appear that the ghosts put themselves on their defence, so that sentence of ejectment was pronounced against them individually in due and legal form. When Thorer heard the judgement, he arose, and saying –

"I have sat while it was lawful for me to do so," left the apartment by the door opposite to that at which the judicial assembly was constituted. Each of the spectres, as it heard its individual sentence, left the place, saying something which indicated its unwillingness to depart, until Thorodd himself was solemnly called on to leave.

"We have here no longer," said he, "a peaceful dwelling, therefore will we remove."

Kiartan then entered the hall with his followers, and the priest, with holy water, and celebration of a solemn mass, completed the conquest over the goblins, which had been commenced by the power and authority of the Icelandic law.

Tales From the Prose Edda

(Norse)

The Gods and the Wolf

AMONG THE ÆSIR, OR GODS, is reckoned one named Loki or Loptur. By many he is called the reviler of the gods, the author of all fraud and mischief, and the shame of gods and men alike. He is the son of the giant Farbauti, his mother being Laufey or Nal, and his brothers Byleist and Helblindi. He is of a goodly appearance and elegant form, but his mood is changeable, and he is inclined to all wickedness. In cunning and perfidy he excels everyone, and many a time has he placed the gods in great danger, and often has he saved them again by his cunning. He has a wife named Siguna, and their son is called Nari.

Loki had three children by Angurbodi, a giantess of Jotunheim (the giants' home). The first of these was Fenris, the wolf; the second was Jörmungand, the Midgard serpent; and the third was Hela, death. Very soon did the gods become aware of this evil progeny which was being reared in Jotunheim, and by divination they discovered that they must receive great injury from them. That they had such a mother spoke bad for them, but their coming of such a sire was a still worse presage. All-father therefore despatched certain of the gods to bring the children to him, and when they were brought before him he cast the serpent down into the ocean which surrounds the world. There the monster waxed so large that he wound himself round the whole globe, and that with such ease that he can with his mouth lay hold of his tail. Hela All-father cast into Niflheim, where she rules over nine worlds. Into these she distributes all those who are sent to her, – that is to say, all who die through sickness or old age. She has there an abode with very thick walls, and fenced with strong gates. Her hall is Elvidnir; her table is Hunger; her knife, Starvation; her man-servant, Delay; her maid-servant, Sloth; her threshold, Precipice; her bed, Care; and her curtains, Anguish of Soul. The one half of her body is livid, the other half is flesh-colour. She has a terrible look, so that she can be easily known.

As to the wolf, Fenris, the gods let him grow up among themselves, Tyr being the only one of them who dare give him his food. When, however, they perceived how he every day increased prodigiously in size, and that the oracles warned them that he would one day prove fatal to them, they determined to make very strong iron fetters for him which they called Loeding. These they presented to the wolf, and desired him to put them on to show his strength by endeavouring to break them. The wolf saw that it would not be difficult for him to burst them, so he let the gods put the fetters on him, then violently stretching himself he broke the fetters asunder, and set himself free.

Having seen this, the gods went to work, and prepared a second set of fetters, called Dromi, half as strong again as the former, and these they persuaded the wolf to put on, assuring him that if he broke them he would then furnish them with an undeniable proof of his power. The wolf saw well enough that it would not be easy to break this set, but he considered that he had himself increased in strength since he broke the others, and he knew that without running some risk he could never become celebrated. He therefore allowed the gods to place the fetters on him. Then Fenris shook himself, stretched his limbs, rolled on the ground, and at length burst the fetters, which he made fly in all directions. Thus did he free himself the second time from his chains, and from this has arisen the saying, "To get free from Loeding, or to burst from Dromi," meaning to perform something by strong exertion.

The gods now despaired of ever being able to secure the wolf with any chain of their own making. All-father, however, sent Skirnir, the messenger of the god Frey, into the country of the Black Elves, to the dwarfs, to ask them to make a chain to bind Fenris with. This chain was composed of six things – the noise made by the fall of a cat's foot, the hair of a woman's beard, the roots of stones, the nerves of bears, the breath of fish, and the spittle of birds.

The fetters were as smooth and as soft as silk, and yet, as you will presently see, of great strength. The gods were very thankful for them when they were brought to them, and returned many thanks to him who brought them. Then they took the wolf with them on to the island Lyngvi, which is in the lake Amsvartnir, and there they showed him the chain, desiring him to try his strength in breaking it. At the same time they told him that it was a good deal stronger than it looked. They took it in their own hands and pulled at it, attempting in vain to break it, and then they said to Fenris –

"No one else but you, Fenris, can break it."

"I don't see," replied the wolf, "that I shall gain any glory by breaking such a slight string, but if any artifice has been employed in the making of it, you may be sure, though it looks so fragile, it shall never touch foot of mine."

The gods told him he would easily break so slight a bandage, since he had already broken asunder shackles of iron of the most solid make.

"But," said they, "if you should not be able to break the chain, you are too feeble to cause us any anxiety, and we shall not hesitate to loose you again."

"I very much fear," replied the wolf, "that if you once tie me up so fast that I cannot release myself, you will be in no haste to unloose me. I am, therefore, unwilling to have this cord wound around me; but to show you I am no coward, I will agree to it, but one of you must put his hand in my mouth, as a pledge that you intend me no deceit."

The gods looked on one another wistfully, for they found themselves in an embarrassing position.

Then Tyr stepped forward and bravely put his right hand in the monster's mouth. The gods then tied up the wolf, who forcibly stretched himself, as he had formerly done, and exerted all his powers to disengage himself; but the more efforts he made the tighter he drew the chain about him, and then all the gods, except Tyr, who lost his hand, burst out into laughter at the sight. Seeing that he was so fast tied that he would never be able to get loose again, they took one end of the chain, which was called Gelgja, and having drilled a hole for it, drew it through the middle of a large broad rock, which they sank very deep in the earth. Afterwards, to make all still more secure, they tied the end of the chain, which came through the rock to a great stone called Keviti, which they sank still deeper. The wolf used his utmost power to free himself, and, opening his mouth, tried to bite them. When the gods saw that they took a sword and thrust it into his mouth, so that it entered his under jaw right up to the hilt, and the point reached his palate. He howled in the most terrible manner, and since then the foam has poured from his mouth in such abundance that it forms the river called Von. So the wolf must remain until Ragnarök.

Such a wicked race has Loki begot. The gods would not put the wolf to death because they respected the sanctity of the place, which forbade blood being shed there.

Thor's Journey to the Land of the Giants

One day the god Thor set out with Loki in his chariot drawn by two he-goats. Night coming on they were obliged to put up at a peasant's cottage, when Thor slew his goats, and having skinned them, had them put into the pot. When this had been done he sat down to supper and invited the peasant and his children to take part in the feast. The peasant had a son named Thjalfi, and a daughter, Röska. Thor told them to throw the bones into the goatskins, which were spread out near the hearth, but young Thjalfi, in order to get at the marrow, broke one of the shank bones with his knife. Having passed the night in this place, Thor rose early in the morning, and having dressed himself, held up his hammer, Mjolnir, and thus consecrating the goatskins; he had no sooner done it than the two goats took again their usual form, only one of them was now lame in one of its hind legs. When Thor saw this he at once knew that the peasant or one of his family had handled the bones of the goat too roughly, for one was broken. They were terribly afraid when Thor knit his brows, rolled his eyes, seized his hammer, and grasped it with such force that the very joints of his fingers were white again. The peasant, trembling, and fearful that he would be struck down by the looks of the god, begged with his family for pardon, offering whatever they possessed to repair the damage they might have done. Thor allowed them to appease him, and contented himself with taking with him Thjalfi and Röska, who became his servants, and have since followed him.

Leaving his goats at that place, Thor set out to the east, to the country of the giants. At length they came to the shore of a wide and deep sea which Thor, with Loki, Thjalfi, and Röska passed over. Then they came to a strange country, and entered an immense forest in which they journeyed all day. Thjalfi was unexcelled by any man as a runner, and he carried Thor's bag, but in the forest they could find nothing eatable to put in it. As night came on they searched on all sides for a place where they might sleep, and at last they came to what appeared to be a large hall, the gate of which was so large that it took up the whole of one side of the building. Here they lay down to sleep, but about the middle of the night they were alarmed by what seemed to be an earthquake which shook the whole of the building. Thor, rising, called his companions to seek with him some safer place. Leaving the apartment they were in, they found on their right hand an adjoining chamber into which they entered, but while the others, trembling with fear, crept to the farthest corner of their retreat, Thor, armed with his mace, remained at the entrance ready to defend himself, happen what might. Throughout the night they heard a terrible groaning, and when the morning came, Thor, going out, observed a man of enormous size, lying near, asleep and snoring heavily. Then Thor knew that this was the noise he had heard during the night. He immediately girded on his belt of prowess which had the virtue of increasing his strength. The giant awoke and stood up, and it is said that for once Thor was too frightened to use his hammer, and he therefore contented himself with inquiring the giant's name.

"My name," replied the giant, "is Skrymir. As for you it is not necessary I should ask your name. You are the god Thor. Tell me, what have you done with my glove?"

Then Skrymir stretched out his hand and took it up, and Thor saw that what he and his companions had taken for a hall in which they had passed the night, was the giant's glove, the chamber into which they had retreated being only the thumb.

Skrymir asked whether they might not be friends, and Thor agreeing, the giant opened his bag and took out something to eat. Thor and his companions also made their morning meal, but eat in another place. Then Skrymir, proposing that they should put their provisions together, and Thor assenting to it, put all into one bag, and laying it on his shoulder marched before them, with huge strides, during the whole day. At night he found a place where Thor and his companions might rest under an oak. There, he said, he would lie down and sleep.

"You take the bag," said he, "and make your supper."

He was soon asleep, and, strange as it may seem, when Thor tried to open the bag he could not untie a single knot nor loose the string. Enraged at this he seized his hammer, swayed it in both his hands, took a step forward, and hurled it at the giant's head. This awoke the giant, who asked him if a leaf had not fallen on his head, and whether they had finished their supper. Thor said they were just about to lie down to sleep, and went to lie under another oak tree. About midnight, observing that Skrymir was snoring so loudly that the forest re-echoed the din, Thor grasped his hammer and hurled it with such force at him that it sank up to the handle in his head.

"What is the matter?" asked he, awakening. "Did an acorn fall on my head? How are you going on, Thor?"

Thor departed at once, saying that it was only midnight and that he hoped to get some more sleep yet. He resolved, however, to have a third blow at the giant, hoping that with this he might settle everything. Seizing his hammer, he, with all his force, threw it at the giant's cheek, into which it buried itself up to the handle. Skrymir, awaking, put his hand to his cheek, and said –

"Are there any birds perched on this tree? I thought some moss fell upon me. How! art thou awake, Thor? It is time, is it not, for us to get up and dress ourselves? You have not far, however, to go before you arrive at the city Utgard. I have heard you whispering together that I am a very tall fellow, but there you will see many larger than me. Let me advise you then when you get there not to take too much upon yourselves, for the men of Utgard-Loki will not bear much from such little folk as you. I believe your best way would even be to turn back again, but if you are determined to proceed take the road that goes towards the east, as for me mine now lies to the north."

After he had said this, he put his bag upon his shoulder and turned away into a forest; and I could never hear that Thor wished him a good journey.

Proceeding on his way with his companions, Thor saw towards noon a city situated in the middle of a vast plain. The wall of the city was so lofty that one could not look up to the top of it without throwing one's head quite back upon the shoulder. On coming to the wall, they found the gateway closed with bars, which Thor never could have opened, but he and his companions crept in between them, and thus entered the place. Before them was a large palace, and as the door of it was open, they entered and found a number of men of enormous size, seated on benches. Going on they came into the presence of the king, Utgard-Loki, whom they saluted with great respect, but he, looking upon them for a time, at length cast a scornful glance at them, and burst into laughter.

"It would take up too much time," said he, "to ask you concerning the long journey you have made, but if I am not mistaken that little man there is Aku-Thor. You may," said he to Thor, "be bigger than you seem to be. What are you and your companions skilled in that we may see what they can do, for no one may remain here unless he understands some art and excels in it all other men?"

"I," said Loki, "can eat quicker than anyone else, and of that I am ready to give proof if there is here anyone who will compete with me."

"It must, indeed, be owned," replied the king, "that you are not wanting in dexterity, if you are able to do what you say. Come, let us test it."

Then he ordered one of his followers who was sitting at the further end of the bench, and whose name was Logi (Flame) to come forward, and try his skill with Loki. A great tub or trough full of flesh meat was placed in the hall, and Loki having placed himself at one end of the trough, and Logi having set himself at the other end, the two commenced to eat. Presently they met in the middle of the trough, but Loki had only devoured the flesh of his portion, whereas the other had devoured both flesh and bones. All the company therefore decided that Loki was beaten.

Then Utgard-Loki asked what the young man could do who accompanied Thor. Thjalfi said that in running he would compete with anyone. The king admitted that skill in running was something very good, but he thought Thjalfi must exert himself to the utmost to win in the contest. He rose and, accompanied by all the company, went to a plain where there was a good place for the match, and then calling a young man named Hugi (Spirit or Thought), he ordered him to run with Thjalfi. In the first race Hugi ran so fast away from Thjalfi that on his returning to the starting-place he met him not far from it. Then said the king –

"If you are to win, Thjalfi, you must run faster, though I must own no man has ever come here who was swifter of foot."

In the second trial, Thjalfi was a full bow-shot from the boundary when Hugi arrived at it.

"Very well do you run, Thjalfi," said Utgard-Loki; "but I do not think you will gain the prize. However, the third trial will decide."

They ran a third time, but Hugi had already reached the goal before Thjalfi had got halfway. Then all present cried out that there had been a sufficient trial of skill in that exercise.

Then Utgard-Loki asked Thor in what manner he would choose to give them a proof of the dexterity for which he was so famous. Thor replied that he would contest the prize for drinking with anyone in the court. Utgard-Loki consented to the match, and going into the palace, ordered his cup-bearer to bring the large horn out of which his followers were obliged to drink when they had trespassed in any way against the customs of the court. The cup-bearer presented this to Thor, and Utgard-Loki said –

"Whoever is a good drinker will empty that horn at a draught. Some men make two draughts of it, but the most puny drinker of all can empty it in three."

Thor looked at the horn, which seemed very long, but was otherwise of no extraordinary size. He put it to his mouth, and, without drawing breath, pulled as long and as deeply as he could, that he might not be obliged to make a second draught of it. When, however, he set the horn down and looked in it he could scarcely perceive that any of the liquor was gone.

"You have drunk well," said Utgard-Loki; "but you need not boast. Had it been told me that Asu-Thor could only drink so little, I should not have credited it. No doubt you will do better at the second pull."

Without a word, Thor again set the horn to his lips and exerted himself to the utmost. When he looked in it seemed to him that he had not drunk quite so much as before, but the horn could now be carried without danger of spilling the liquor. Then Utgard-Loki said –

"Well, Thor, you should not spare yourself more than befits you in such drinking. If now you mean to drink off the horn the third time it seems to me you must drink more than you have done. You will never be reckoned so great a man amongst us as the Æsir make you out to be if you cannot do better in other games than it appears to me you will do in this."

Thor, angry, put the horn to his mouth and drank the best he could and as long as he was able, but when he looked into the horn the liquor was only a little lower. Then he gave the horn to the cup-bearer, and would drink no more.

Then said Utgard-Loki –

"It is plain that you are not so mighty as we imagined. Will you try another game? It seems to me there is little chance of your taking a prize hence."

"I will try more contests yet," answered Thor. "Such draughts as I have drunk would not have seemed small to the Æsir. But what new game have you?"

Utgard-Loki answered –

"The lads here do a thing which is not much. They lift my cat up from the ground. I should not have thought of proposing such a feat to Asu-Thor, had I not first seen that he is less by far than we took him to be."

As he spoke there sprang upon the hall floor a very large grey cat. Thor went up to it and put his hand under its middle and tried to lift it from the floor. The cat bent its back as Thor raised his hands, and when Thor had exerted himself to the utmost the cat had only one foot off the floor. Then Thor would make no further trial.

"I thought this game would go so," said Utgard-Loki. "The cat is large and Thor is little when compared with our men."

"Little as you call me," answered Thor, "let anyone come here and wrestle with me, for now I am angry."

Utgard-Loki looked along the benches, and said –

"I see no man here who would not think it absurd to wrestle with you, but let someone call here the old woman, my nurse, Elli, and let Thor wrestle with her, if he will. She has cast to the ground many a man who seemed to me to be as strong as Thor."

Then came into the hall a toothless old woman, and Utgard-Loki told her to wrestle with Asu-Thor. The story is not a long one. The harder Thor tightened his hold, the firmer the old woman stood. Then she began to exert herself, Thor tottered, and at last, after a violent tussle, he fell on one knee. On this Utgard-Loki told them to stop, adding that Thor could not desire anyone else to wrestle with him in the hall, and the night had closed in. He showed Thor and his companions to seats, and they passed the night, faring well.

At daybreak the next morning, Thor and his companions rose, dressed themselves, and prepared to leave at once. Then Utgard-Loki came to them and ordered a table to be set for them having on it plenty of meat and drink. Afterwards he led them out of the city, and on parting asked Thor how he thought his journey had prospered, and whether he had met with any stronger than himself. Thor said he must own he had been much shamed.

"And," said he, "I know you will call me a man of little might, and I can badly bear that."

"Shall I tell you the truth?" said Utgard-Loki. "We are now out of the city, and while I live and have my own way, you will never again enter it. By my word you had never come in had I known before you had been so strong and would bring us so near to great misfortune. I have deluded thee with vain shows; first in the forest, where I met you, and where you were unable to untie the wallet because I had bound it with iron-thread so that you could not discover where the knot could be loosened. After that you gave me three blows with your hammer. The first blow, though the lightest, would have killed me had it fallen on me, but I put a rock in my place which you did not see. In that rocky mountain you will find three dales, one of which is very deep, those are the dints made by your hammer. In the other games, I have deceived you with illusions. The first one was the match with Loki. He was hungry and eat fast, but Logi was Flame, and he consumed not only the flesh but the trough with it. When Thjalfi contended with Hugi in running, Hugi was my thought, and it was not possible for Thjalfi to excel that in swiftness. When you drank of the horn and the liquor seemed to get lower so slowly, you did, indeed, so well that had I not seen it, I should never have believed it. You did not see that one end of the horn was in the sea, but when you come to the shore you will see how much the sea has shrunk in consequence of your draughts, which have caused what is called the ebb. Nor did you do a less wondrous thing when you lifted up the cat, and I can assure you all were afraid when you raised one of its paws off the ground. The cat was the great Midgard serpent which lies stretched round the whole earth, and when you raised it so high then did its length barely suffice to enclose the earth between its head and tail. Your wrestling match with Elli was, too, a great feat, for no one has there been yet, and no one shall there be whom old age does not come and trip up, if he but await her coming. Now we must part, and let me say that it will be better for both of us if you never more come to seek me, for I shall always defend my city with tricks, so that you will never overcome me."

When Thor heard that he grasped his mace in a rage, and raised it to hurl it at Utgard-Loki, but he had disappeared. Then Thor wanted to return to the city, but he could see nothing but a wide fair plain. So he turned, and went on his way till he came to Thrudvang, resolving if he had an opportunity to attack the Midgard serpent.

The Death of Baldur

Baldur the Good had dreams which forewarned him that his life was in danger, and he told the gods of them. The gods took counsel together what should be done, and it was agreed that they should conjure away all danger that might threaten him. Frigga took an oath of fire, water, iron, and all other metals, stones, earth, trees, sicknesses, beasts, birds, poisons, and worms, that these would none of them hurt Baldur. When this had been done the gods used to divert themselves, Baldur standing up in the assembly, and all the others throwing at him, hewing at him, and smiting him with stones, for, do all they would, he received no hurt, and in this sport all enjoyed themselves.

Loki, however, looked on with envy when he saw that Baldur was not hurt. So he assumed the form of a woman, and set out to Fensalir to Frigga. Frigga asked if the stranger knew what the gods did when they met. He answered that they all shot at Baldur and he was not hurt.

"No weapon, nor tree may hurt Baldur," answers Frigga, "I have taken an oath of them all not to do so."

"What," said the pretended woman, "have all things then sworn to spare Baldur?"

"There is only one little twig which grows to the east of Valhalla, which is called the mistletoe. Of that I took no oath, for it seemed to me too young and feeble to do any hurt."

Then the strange woman departed, and Loki having found the mistletoe, cut it off, and went to the assembly. There he found Hodur standing apart by himself, for he was blind. Then said Loki to him –

"Why do you not throw at Baldur?"

"Because," said he, "I am blind and cannot see him, and besides I have nothing to throw."

"Do as the others," said Loki, "and honour Baldur as the rest do. I will direct your aim. Throw this shaft at him."

Hodur took the mistletoe and, Loki directing him, aimed at Baldur. The aim was good. The shaft pierced him through, and Baldur fell dead upon the earth. Surely never was there a greater misfortune either among gods or men.

When the gods saw that Baldur was dead then they were silent, aghast, and stood motionless. They looked on one another, and were all agreed as to what he deserved who had done the deed, but out of respect to the place none dared avenge Baldur's death. They broke the silence at length with wailing, words failing them with which to express their sorrow. Odin, as was right, was more sorrowful than any of the others, for he best knew what a loss the gods had sustained.

At last when the gods had recovered themselves, Frigga asked –

"Who is there among the gods who will win my love and goodwill? That shall he have if he will ride to Hel, and seek Baldur, and offer Hela a reward if she will let Baldur come home to Asgard."

Hermod the nimble, Odin's lad, said he would make the journey. So he mounted Odin's horse, Sleipner, and went his way.

The gods took Baldur's body down to the seashore, where stood Hringhorn, Baldur's vessel, the biggest in the world. When the gods tried to launch it into the water, in order to make on it a funeral fire for Baldur, the ship would not stir. Then they despatched one to Jotunheim for the sorceress called Hyrrokin, who came riding on a wolf with twisted serpents by way of reins. Odin called for four Berserkir to hold the horse, but they could not secure it till they had thrown it to the ground. Then Hyrrokin went to the stem of the ship, and set it afloat with a single touch, the vessel going so fast that fire sprang from the rollers, and the earth trembled. Then Thor was so angry that he took his hammer and wanted to cast it at the woman's head, but the gods pleaded for her and appeased him. The body of Baldur being placed on the ship, Nanna, the daughter of Nep, Baldur's wife, seeing it, died of a broken heart, so she was borne to the pile and thrown into the fire.

Thor stood up and consecrated the pile with Mjolnir. A little dwarf, called Litur, ran before his feet, and Thor gave him a push, and threw him into the fire, and he was burnt. Many kinds of people came to this ceremony. With Odin came Frigga and the Valkyrjor with his ravens. Frey drove in a car drawn by the boar, Gullinbursti or Slidrugtanni. Heimdall rode the horse Gulltopp, and Freyja drove her cats. There were also many of the forest-giants and mountain-giants there. On the pile Odin laid the gold ring called Draupnir, giving it the property that every ninth night it produces eight rings of equal weight. In the same pile was also consumed Baldur's horse.

For nine nights and days Hermod rode through deep valleys, so dark that he could see nothing. Then he came to the river Gjöll which he crossed by the bridge which is covered with shining gold. The maid who keeps the bridge is called Modgudur. She asked Hermod his name and family, and told him that on the former day there had ridden over the bridge five bands of dead men.

"They did not make my bridge ring as you do, and you have not the hue of the dead. Why ride you thus on the way to Hel?"

He said –

"I ride to Hel to find Baldur. Have you seen him on his way to that place?"

"Baldur," answered she, "has passed over the bridge, but the way to Hel is below to the north."

Hermod rode on till he came to the entrance of Hel, which was guarded by a grate. He dismounted, looked to the girths of his saddle, mounted, and clapping his spurs into the horse, cleared the grate easily. Then he rode on to the hall and, dismounting, entered it. There he saw his brother, Baldur, seated in the first place, and there Hermod stopped the night.

In the morning he saw Hela, and begged her to let Baldur ride home with him, telling her how much the gods had sorrowed over his death. Hela told him she would test whether it were true that Baldur was so much loved.

"If," said she, "all things weep for him, then he shall return to the gods, but if any speak against him or refuse to weep, then he shall remain in Hel."

Then Hermod rose to go, and Baldur, leading him out of the hall, gave him the ring, Draupnir, which he wished Odin to have as a keepsake. Nanna also sent Frigga a present, and a ring to Fulla.

Hermod rode back, and coming to Asgard related all he had seen and heard. Then the gods sent messengers over all the world seeking to get Baldur brought back again by weeping. All wept, men and living things, earth, stones, trees, and metals, all weeping as they do when they are subjected to heat after frost. Then the messengers came back again, thinking they had done their errand well. On their way they came to a cave wherein sat a hag named Thaukt. The messengers prayed her to assist in weeping Baldur out of Hel.

"I will weep dry tears," answered she, "over Baldur's pyre. What gain I by the son of man, be he live or dead? Let Hela hold what she has."

It was thought that this must have been Loki, Laufey's son, he who has ever wrought such harm to the gods.

The Punishment of Loki

The gods were so angry with Loki that he had to run away and hide himself in the mountains, and there he built a house which had four doors, so that he could see around him on every side. He would often in the day-time change himself into a salmon and hide in the water called Franangursfors, and he thought over what trick the gods might devise to capture him there. One day while he sat in his house, he took flax and yarn, and with it made meshes like those of a net, a fire burning in front of him. Then he became aware that the gods were near at hand, for Odin had seen out of Hlidskjalf where he was. Loki sprang up, threw his work into the fire, and went to the river. When the gods came to the house, the first that entered was Kvasir, who was the most acute of them all. In the hot embers he saw the ashes of a net, such as is used in fishing, and he told the gods of it, and they made a net like that which they saw in the ashes. When it was ready they went to the river and cast the net in, Thor holding one end and the rest of the gods the other, and so they drew it. Loki travelled in front of it and lay down between two stones so that the net went over him, but the gods felt that something living had been against the net. Then they cast the net a second time, binding up in it a weight so that nothing could pass under it. Loki travelled before it till he saw the sea in front of him. Then he leapt over the top of the net and again made his way up the stream. The gods saw this, so they once more dragged the stream, while Thor waded in the middle of it. So they went to the sea.

Then Loki saw in what a dangerous situation he was. He must risk his life if he swam out to sea. The only other alternative was to leap over the net. That he did, jumping as quickly as he could over the top cord.

Thor snatched at him, and tried to hold him, but he slipped through his hand, and would have escaped, but for his tail, and this is the reason why salmon have their tails so thin.

Loki being captured, they took him to a certain cavern, and they took three rocks, through each of which they bored a hole. Then they took Loki's sons Vali and Nari, and having changed Vali into a wolf, he tore his brother Nari into pieces. Then the gods took his intestines and bound Loki with them to the three stones, and they changed the cord into bands of iron. Skadi then took a serpent and suspended it over Loki's head so that the venom drops from it on to his face. Siguna, Loki's wife, stands near him, and holds a dish receiving the venom as it falls, and when the dish is full she goes out and pours its contents away. While she is doing this, however, the venom falls on Loki, and causes him such intense pain that he writhes so that the earth is shaken as if by an earthquake.

There he lies till Ragnarök (the twilight of the gods).

Harald the Viking

(Norwegian)

ERIK THE RED, the most famous of all Vikings, had three sons, and once when they were children the king came to visit Erik and passed through the playground where the boys were playing. Leif and Biorn, the two oldest, were building little houses and barns and were making believe that they were full of cattle and sheep, while Harald, who was only four years old, was sailing chips of wood in a pool. The king asked Harald what they were, and he said, "Ships of war." King Olaf laughed and said, "The time may come when you will command ships, my little friend." Then he asked Biorn what he would like best to have. "Corn-land," he said; "ten farms." "That would yield much corn," the king replied. Then he asked Leif the same question, and he answered, "Cows." "How many?" "So many that when they went to the lake to be watered, they would stand close round the edge, so that not another could pass." "That would be a large housekeeping," said the king, and he asked the same question of Harald. "What would you like best to have?" "Servants and followers," said the child, stoutly. "How many would you like?" "Enough," said the child, "to eat up all the cows and crops of my brothers at a single meal." Then the king laughed, and said to the mother of the children, "You are bringing up a king."

As the boys grew, Leif and Harald were ever fond of roaming, while Biorn wished to live on the farm at peace. Their sister Freydis went with the older boys and urged them on. She was not gentle and amiable, but full of energy and courage: she was also quarrelsome and vindictive. People said of her that even if her brothers were all killed, yet the race of Erik the Red would not end while she lived; that "she practised more of shooting and the handling of sword and shield than of sewing or embroidering, and that as she was able, she did evil oftener than good; and that when she was hindered she ran into the woods and slew men to get their property." She was always urging her brothers to deeds of daring and adventure. One day they had been hawking, and when they let slip the falcons, Harald's falcon killed two blackcocks in one flight and three in another. The dogs ran and brought the birds, and he said proudly to the others, "It will be long before most of you have any such success," and they all agreed to this. He rode home in high spirits and showed his birds to his sister Freydis. "Did any king," he asked, "ever make so great a capture in so short a time?" "It is, indeed," she said, "a good morning's hunting to have got five blackcocks, but it was still better when in one morning a king of Norway took five kings and subdued all their kingdoms." Then Harald went away very humble and besought his father to let him go and serve on the Varangian Guard of King Otho at Constantinople, that he might learn to be a warrior.

So Harald was brought from his Norwegian home by his father Erik the Red, in his galley called the *Sea-serpent*, and sailed with him through the Mediterranean Sea, and was at last made a member of the Emperor Otho's Varangian Guard at Constantinople. This guard will be well remembered by the readers of Scott's novel, *Count Robert of Paris*, and was maintained by successive emperors and drawn largely from the Scandinavian races. Erik the Red had no hesitation in leaving his son among them, as the young man was stout and strong, very self-willed, and quite able to defend himself. The father knew also that the Varangian Guard, though hated by the people, held to one another like a band of brothers; and that anyone brought up among them would be sure of plenty of fighting and plenty of gold, – the two things most prized by early Norsemen. For ordinary life, Harald's chief duties would be to lounge about the palace, keeping guard, wearing helmet and buckler and bearskin, with purple underclothes and golden clasped hose; and bearing as armour a mighty battle-axe and a small scimitar. Such was the life led by Harald, till one day he had a message from his father, through a new recruit, calling him home to join an expedition to the western seas. "I hear, my son," the message said, "that your good emperor, whom may the gods preserve, is sorely ill and may die any day. When he is dead, be prompt in getting your share of the plunder of the palace and come back to me."

The emperor died, and the order was fulfilled. It was the custom of the Varangians to reward themselves in this way for their faithful services of protection; and the result is that, to this day, Greek and Arabic gold crosses and chains are to be found in the houses of Norwegian peasants and may be seen in the museums of Christiania and Copenhagen. No one was esteemed the less for this love of spoil, if he was only generous in giving. The

Norsemen spoke contemptuously of gold as 'the serpent's bed,' and called a generous man 'a hater of the serpent's bed,' because such a man parts with gold as with a thing he hates.

When the youth came to his father, he found Erik the Red directing the building of one of the great Norse galleys, nearly eighty feet long and seventeen wide and only six feet deep. The boat had twenty ribs, and the frame was fastened together by withes made of roots, while the oaken planks were held by iron rivets. The oars were twenty feet long, and were put through oar holes, and the rudder, shaped like a large oar, was not at the end, but was attached to a projecting beam on the starboard (originally steer-board) side. The ship was to be called a Dragon, and was to be painted so as to look like one, having a gilded dragon's head at the bow and a gilded tail on the stern; while the moving oars would look like legs, and the row of red and white shields, hung along the side of the boat, would resemble the scales of a dragon, and the great square sails, red and blue, would look like wings. This was the vessel which young Harald was to command.

He had already made trips in just such vessels with his father; had learned to attack the enemy with arrow and spear; also with stones thrown down from above, and with grappling-irons to clutch opposing boats. He had learned to swim, from early childhood, even in the icy northern waters, and he had been trained in swimming to hide his head beneath his floating shield, so that it could not be seen. He had learned also to carry tinder in a walnut shell, enclosed in wax, so that no matter how long he had been in the water he could strike a light on reaching shore. He had also learned from his father acts of escape as well as attack. Thus he had once sailed on a return trip from Denmark after plundering a town; the ships had been lying at anchor all night in a fog, and at sunlight in the morning lights seemed burning on the sea. But Erik the Red said, "It is a fleet of Danish ships, and the sun strikes on the gilded dragon crests; furl the sail and take to the oars." They rowed their best, yet the Danish ships were overtaking them, when Erik the Red ordered his men to throw wood overboard and cover it with Danish plunder. This made some delay, as the Danes stopped to pick it up, and in the same way Erik the Red dropped his provisions, and finally his prisoners; and in the delay thus caused he got away with his own men.

But now Harald was not to go to Denmark, but to the new western world, the Wonderstrands which Leif had sought and had left without sufficient exploration. First, however, he was to call at Greenland, which his father had first discovered. It was the custom of the Viking explorers, when they reached a new country, to throw overboard their 'seat posts,' or *setstokka*, – the curved part of their doorways, – and then to land where they floated ashore. But Erik the Red had lent his to a friend and could not get them back, so that he sailed in search of them, and came to a new land which he called Greenland, because, as he said, people would be attracted thither if it had a good name. Then he established a colony there, and then Leif the Lucky, as he was called, sailed still farther, and came to the Wonderstrand, or Magic Shores. These he called Vinland or Wineland, and now a rich man named Karlsefne was to send a colony thither from Greenland, and the young Harald was to go with it and take command of it.

Now as Harald was to be presented to the rich Karlsefne, he thought he must be gorgeously arrayed. So he wore a helmet on his head, a red shield richly inlaid with gold and iron, and a sharp sword with an ivory handle wound with golden thread. He had also a short spear, and wore over his coat a red silk short cloak on which was embroidered, both before and behind, a yellow lion. We may well believe that the sixty men and five women who composed the expedition were ready to look on him with admiration, especially as one of the women was his own sister, Freydis, now left to his peculiar care, since Erik the Red had died. The sturdy old hero had died still a heathen, and it was only just after his death that Christianity was introduced into Greenland, and those numerous churches were built there whose ruins yet remain, even in regions from which all population has gone.

So the party of colonists sailed for Vinland, and Freydis, with the four older women, came in Harald's boat, and Freydis took easily the lead among them for strength, though not always, it must be admitted, for amiability.

The boats of the expedition having left Greenland soon after the year 1000, coasted the shore as far as they could, rarely venturing into open sea. At last, amidst fog and chilly weather, they made land at a point where a river ran through a lake into the sea, and they could not enter from the sea except at high tide. It was once believed that this was Narragansett Bay in Rhode Island, but this is no longer believed. Here they landed and called the place Hóp, from the Icelandic word *hópa*, meaning an inlet from the ocean. Here they found grapevines growing and fields of wild wheat; there were fish in the lake and wild animals in the woods. Here they landed the cattle and the provisions which they had brought with them; and here they built their huts. They went in the spring, and during that summer the natives came in boats of skin to trade with them – men described as black, and ill favoured, with large eyes and broad cheeks and with coarse hair on their heads. These, it is thought, may have been the Esquimaux. The first time they came, these visitors held up a white shield as a sign of peace, and were so frightened by the bellowing of the bull that they ran away. Then returning, they brought furs to sell and wished to buy weapons, but Harald tried another plan: he bade the women bring out milk, butter, and cheese from their dairies, and when the Skraelings saw that, they wished for nothing else, and, the legend says, "the Skraelings carried away their wares in their stomachs, but the Norsemen had the skins they had purchased." This happened yet again, but at the second visit one of the Skraelings was accidentally killed or injured.

The next time the Skraelings came they were armed with slings, and raised upon a pole a great blue ball and attacked the Norsemen so furiously that they were running away when Erik's sister, Freydis, came out before them with bare arms, and took up a sword, saying, "Why do you run, strong men as you are, from these miserable dwarfs whom I thought you would knock down like cattle? Give me weapons, and I will fight better than any of you." Then the rest took courage and began to fight, and the Skraelings were driven back. Once more the strangers came, and one of them took up an axe, a thing which he had not before seen, and struck at one of his companions, killing him. Then the leader took the axe and threw it into the water, after which the Skraelings retreated, and were not seen again.

The winter was a mild one, and while it lasted, the Norsemen worked busily at felling wood and house-building. They had also many amusements, in most of which Harald excelled. They used to swim in all weathers. One of their feats was to catch seals and sit on them while swimming; another was to pull one another down and remain as long as possible under water. Harald could swim for a mile or more with his armour on, or with a companion on his shoulder. Indoors they used to play the tug of war, dragging each other by a walrus hide across the fire. Harald was good at this, and was also the best archer, sometimes aiming at something placed on a boy's head, the boy having a cloth tied around his head, and held by two men, that he might not move at all on hearing the whistling of the arrow. In this way Harald could even shoot an arrow under a nut placed on the head, so that the nut would roll down and the head not be hurt. He could plant a spear in the ground and then shoot an arrow upward so skilfully that it would turn in the air and fall with the point in the end of the spear-shaft. He could also shoot a blunt arrow through the thickest ox-hide from a cross-bow. He could change weapons from one hand to the other during a fencing match, or fence with either hand, or throw two spears at the same time, or catch a spear in motion. He could run so fast that no horse could overtake him, and play the rough games with bat and ball, using a ball of the hardest wood. He could race on snowshoes, or wrestle when bound by a belt to his antagonist. Then when he and his companions wished a rest, they amused themselves with harp-playing or riddles or chess. The Norsemen even played chess on board their vessels, and there are still to be seen, on some of these, the little holes that were formerly used for the sharp ends of the chessmen, so that they should not be displaced.

They could not find that any European had ever visited this place; but some of the Skraelings told them of a place farther south, which they called 'the Land of the Whiteman,' or 'Great Ireland.' They said that in that place there were white men who clothed themselves in long white garments, carried before them poles to which white cloths were hung, and called with a loud voice. These, it was thought by the Norsemen, must be Christian processions, in which banners were borne and hymns were chanted. It has been thought from this that some expedition from Ireland – that of St. Brandan, for instance – may have left a settlement there, long before, but this has never been confirmed. The Skraelings and the Northmen were good friends for a time; until at last one of Erik's own warriors killed a Skraeling by accident, and then all harmony was at an end.

They saw no hope of making a lasting settlement there, and, moreover, Freydis who was very grasping, tried to deceive the other settlers and get more than her share of everything, so that Harald himself lost patience with her and threatened her. It happened that one of the men of the party, Olaf, was Harald's foster-brother. They had once had a fight, and after the battle had agreed that they would be friends for life and always share the same danger. For this vow they were to walk under the turf; that is, a strip of turf was cut and held above their heads, and they stood beneath and let their blood flow upon the ground whence the turf had been cut. After this they were to own everything by halves and either must avenge the other's death. This was their brotherhood; but Freydis did not like it; so she threatened Olaf, and tried to induce men to kill him, for she did not wish to bring upon herself the revenge that must come if she slew him.

This was the reason why the whole enterprise failed, and why Olaf persuaded Harald, for the sake of peace, to return to Greenland in the spring and take a load of valuable timber to sell there, including one stick of what was called massur wood, which was as valuable as mahogany, and may have been at some time borne by ocean currents to the beach. It is hardly possible that, as some have thought, the colonists established a regular trade in this wood for no such wood grows on the northern Atlantic shores. However this may be, the party soon returned, after one winter in Vinland the Good; and on the way back Harald did one thing which made him especially dear to his men.

A favourite feat of the Norsemen was to toss three swords in the air and catch each by the handle as it came down. This was called the *handsax* game. The young men used also to try the feat of running along the oar-blades of the rowers as they were in motion, passing around the bow of the vessel with a spring and coming round to the stern over the oars on the other side. Few could accomplish this, but no one but Harald could do it and play the handsax game as he ran; and when he did it, they all said that he was the most skilful man at *idrottie* ever seen. That was their word for an athletic feat. But presently came a time when not only his courage but his fairness and justice were to be tried.

It happened in this way. There was nothing of which the Norsemen were more afraid than of the teredo, or shipworm, which gnaws the wood of ships. It was observed in Greenland and Iceland that pieces of wood often floated on shore which were filled with holes made by this animal, and they thought that in certain places the seas were full of this worm, so that a ship would be bored and sunk in a little while. It is said that on this return voyage Harald's vessel entered a worm-sea and presently began to sink. They had, however, provided a smaller boat smeared with sea-oil, which the worms would not attack. They went into the boat, but found that it would not hold more than half of them all. Then Harald said, "We will divide by lots, without regard to the rank; each taking his chance with the rest." This they thought, the Norse legend says, "a high-minded offer." They drew lots, and Harald was among those assigned to the safer boat. He stepped in, and when he was there a man called from the other boat and said, "Dost thou intend, Harald, to separate from me here?" Harald answered, "So it turns out," and the man said, "Very different was thy promise to my father when we came from Greenland, for the promise was that we should share the same fate."

Then Harald said, "It shall not be thus. Go into the boat, and I will go back into the ship, since thou art so anxious to live." Then Harald went back to the ship, while the man took his place in the boat, and after that Harald was never heard of more.

The Dwarf-Sword Tirfing

(Norse)

EUAFORLAMI, THE SECOND IN DESCENT FROM ODIN, was king over Gardarike (Russia). One day he rode a-hunting, and sought long after a hart, but could not find one the whole day. When the sun was setting, he found himself plunged so deep in the forest that he knew not where he was. On his right hand he saw a hill, and before it he saw two dwarfs. He drew his sword against them, and cut off their retreat by getting between them and the rock. They offered him ransom for their lives, and he asked them their names, and they said that one of them was called Dyren and the other Dualin. Then he knew that they were the most ingenious and the most expert of all the dwarfs, and he therefore demanded that they should make for him a sword, the best that they could form. Its hilt was to be of gold, and its belt of the same metal. He moreover commanded that the sword should never miss a blow, should never rust, that it should cut through iron and stone as through a garment, and that it should always be victorious in war and in single combat. On these conditions he granted the dwarfs their lives.

At the time appointed he came, and the dwarfs appearing, they gave him the sword. When Dualin stood at the door, he said –

"This sword shall be the bane of a man every time it is drawn, and with it shall be perpetrated three of the greatest atrocities, and it will also prove thy bane."

Suaforlami, when he heard that, struck at the dwarf, so that the blade of the sword penetrated the solid rock. Thus Suaforlami became possessed of this sword, and he called it Tirfing. He bore it in war and in single combat, and with it he slew the giant Thiasse, whose daughter Fridur he took.

Suaforlami was soon after slain by the Berserker Andgrim, who then became master of the sword. When the twelve sons of Andgrim were to fight with Hialmar and Oddur for Ingaborg, the beautiful daughter of King Inges, Angantyr bore the dangerous Tirfing, but all the brethren were slain in the combat, and were buried with their arms.

Angantyr left an only daughter, Hervor, who, when she grew up, dressed herself in man's attire, and took the name of Hervardar, and joined a party of Vikinger, or pirates. Knowing that Tirfing lay buried with her father, she determined to awaken the dead, and obtain the charmed blade. She landed alone, in the evening, on the Island of Sams, where her father and uncles lay in their sepulchral mounds, and ascending by night to their tombs, that were enveloped in flame, she, by the force of entreaty, obtained from the reluctant Angantyr the formidable Tirfing.

Hervor proceeded to the court of King Gudmund, and there one day, as she was playing at tables with the king, one of the servants chanced to take up and draw Tirfing, which shone like a sunbeam. But Tirfing was never to see the light but for the bane of men, and Hervor, by a sudden impulse, sprang from her seat, snatched the sword, and struck off the head of the unfortunate man.

After this she returned to the house of her grandfather, Jarl Biartmar, where she resumed her female attire, and was married to Haufud, the son of King Gudmund. She bore him two sons, Angantyr and Heidreker; the former of a mild and gentle disposition, the latter violent and fierce. Haufud would not permit Heidreker to remain at his court, and as he was departing, his mother, among other gifts, presented him with Tirfing.

His brother accompanied him out of the castle. Before they parted, Heidreker drew out his sword to look at and admire it, but scarcely did the rays of light fall on the magic blade, when the Berserker rage came on its owner, and he slew his gentle brother.

After this he joined a body of Vikinger, and became so distinguished that King Harold, for the aid he lent him, gave him his daughter Helga in marriage. But it was the destiny of Tirfing to commit crime, and Harold fell by the sword of his son-in-law. Heidreker was afterwards in Russia, and the son of the king was his foster-son. One day as they were out hunting, Heidreker and his foster-son happened to be separated from the rest of the party, when a wild boar appeared before them.

Heidreker ran at him with his spear, but the beast caught it in his mouth and broke it across. Then he alighted and drew Tirfing, and killed the boar. On looking round him, he saw no one but his foster-son, and Tirfing could only be appeased with warm human blood, so Heidreker slew the poor youth.

In the end Heidreker was murdered in his bed by his Scottish slaves, who carried off Tirfing. His son Angantyr, who succeeded him, discovered the thieves and put them to death, and recovered the magic blade. He made great slaughter in battle against the Huns, but among the slain was discovered his own brother, Landur.

So ends the history of the Dwarf-Sword Tirfing.

The Master-Maid

(Norwegian)

ONCE UPON A TIME there was a king who had many sons. I do not exactly know how many there were, but the youngest of them could not stay quietly at home, and was determined to go out into the world and try his luck, and after a long time the King was forced to give him leave to go. When he had travelled about for several days, he came to a giant's house, and hired himself to the giant as a servant. In the morning the giant had to go out to pasture his goats, and as he was leaving the house he told the King's son that he must clean out the stable. "And after you have done that," he said, "you need not do any more work today, for you have come to a kind master, and that you shall find. But what I set you to do must be done both well and thoroughly, and you must on no account go into any of the rooms which lead out of the room in which you slept last night. If you do, I will take your life."

"Well to be sure, he is an easy master!" said the Prince to himself as he walked up and down the room humming and singing, for he thought there would be plenty of time left to clean out the stable; "but it would be amusing to steal a glance into his other rooms as well," thought the Prince, "for there must be something that he is afraid of my seeing, as I am not allowed to enter them." So he went into the first room. A cauldron was hanging from the walls; it was boiling, but the Prince could see no fire under it. "I wonder what is inside it," he thought, and dipped a lock of his hair in, and the hair became just as if it were all made of copper. "That's a nice kind of soup. If anyone were to taste that his throat would be gilded," said the youth, and then he went into the next chamber. There, too, a cauldron was hanging from the wall, bubbling and boiling, but there was no fire under this either. "I will just try what this is like too," said the Prince, thrusting another lock of his hair into it, and it came out silvered over. "Such costly soup is not to be had in my father's palace," said the Prince; "but everything depends on how it tastes," and then he went into the third room. There, too, a cauldron was hanging from the wall, boiling, exactly the same as in the two other rooms, and the Prince took pleasure in trying this also, so he dipped a lock of hair in, and it came out so brightly gilded that it shone again. "Some talk about going from bad to worse," said the Prince; "but this is better and better. If he boils gold here, what can he boil in there?" He was determined to see, and went through the door into the fourth room. No cauldron was to be seen there, but on a bench someone was seated who was like a king's daughter, but, whosoever she was, she was so beautiful that never in the Prince's life had he seen her equal.

"Oh! in heaven's name what are you doing here?" said she who sat upon the bench.

"I took the place of servant here yesterday," said the Prince.

"May you soon have a better place, if you have come to serve here!" said she.

"Oh, but I think I have got a kind master," said the Prince. "He has not given me hard work to do today. When I have cleaned out the stable I shall be done."

"Yes, but how will you be able to do that?" she asked again. "If you clean it out as other people do, ten pitchforksful will come in for every one you throw out. But I will teach you how to do it; you must turn your pitchfork upside-down, and work with the handle, and then all will fly out of its own accord."

"Yes, I will attend to that," said the Prince, and stayed sitting where he was the whole day, for it was soon settled between them that they would marry each other, he and the King's daughter; so the first day of his service with the giant did not seem long to him. But when evening was drawing near she said that it would now be better for him to clean out the stable before the giant came home. When he got there he had a fancy to try if what she had said were true, so he began to work in the same way that he had seen the stable-boys doing in his father's stables, but he soon saw that he must give up that, for when he had worked a very short time he had scarcely any room left to stand. So he did what the Princess had taught him, turned the pitchfork round, and worked with the handle, and in the twinkling of an eye the stable was as clean as if it had been scoured. When he had done that, he went back again into the room in which the giant had given him leave to stay, and there he walked backward and forward on the floor, and began to hum and sing.

Then came the giant home with the goats. "Have you cleaned the stable?" asked the giant.

"Yes, now it is clean and sweet, master," said the King's son.

"I shall see about that," said the giant, and went round to the stable, but it was just as the Prince had said.

"You have certainly been talking to my Master-maid, for you never got that out of your own head," said the giant.

"Master-maid! What kind of a thing is that, master?" said the Prince, making himself look as stupid as an ass; "I should like to see that."

"Well, you will see her quite soon enough," said the giant.

On the second morning the giant had again to go out with his goats, so he told the Prince that on that day he was to fetch home his horse, which was out on the mountainside, and when he had done that he might rest himself for the remainder of the day, "for you have come to a kind master, and that you shall find," said the giant once more. "But do not go into any of the rooms that I spoke of yesterday, or I will wring your head off," said he, and then went away with his flock of goats.

"Yes, indeed, you are a kind master," said the Prince; "but I will go in and talk to the Master-maid again; perhaps before long she may like better to be mine than yours."

So he went to her. Then she asked him what he had to do that day.

"Oh! not very dangerous work, I fancy," said the King's son. "I have only to go up the mountainside after his horse."

"Well, how do you mean to set about it?" asked the Master-maid.

"Oh! there is no great art in riding a horse home," said the King's son. "I think I must have ridden friskier horses before now."

"Yes, but it is not so easy a thing as you think to ride the horse home," said the Master-maid; "but I will teach you what to do. When you go near it, fire will burst out of its nostrils like flames from a pine torch; but be very careful, and take the bridle which is hanging by the door there, and fling the bit straight into his jaws, and then it will become so tame that you will be able to do what you like with it." He said he would bear this in mind, and then he again sat in there the whole day by the Master-maid, and they chatted and talked of one thing and another, but the first thing and the last now was, how happy and delightful it would be if they could but marry each other, and get safely away from the giant; and the Prince would have forgotten both the mountainside and the horse if the Master-maid had not reminded him of them as evening drew near, and said that now it would be better if he went to fetch the horse before the giant came. So he did this, and took the bridle which was hanging on a crook, and strode up the mountainside, and it was not long before he met with the horse, and fire and red flames streamed forth out of its nostrils. But the youth carefully watched his opportunity, and just as it was rushing at him with open jaws he threw the bit straight into its mouth, and the horse stood as quiet as a young lamb, and there was no difficulty at all in getting it home to the stable. Then the Prince went back into his room again, and began to hum and to sing.

Toward evening the giant came home. "Have you fetched the horse back from the mountainside?" he asked.

"That I have, master; it was an amusing horse to ride, but I rode him straight home, and put him in the stable too," said the Prince.

"I will see about that," said the giant, and went out to the stable, but the horse was standing there just as the Prince had said. "You have certainly been talking with my Master-maid, for you never got that out of your own head," said the giant again.

"Yesterday, master, you talked about this Master-maid, and today you are talking about her; ah, heaven bless you, master, why will you not show me the thing? for it would be a real pleasure to me to see it," said the Prince, who again pretended to be silly and stupid.

"Oh! you will see her quite soon enough," said the giant.

On the morning of the third day the giant again had to go into the wood with the goats. "Today you must go underground and fetch my taxes," he said to the Prince. "When you have done this, you may rest for the remainder of the day, for you shall see what an easy master you have come to," and then he went away.

"Well, however easy a master you may be, you set me very hard work to do," thought the Prince; "but I will see if I cannot find your Master-maid; you say she is yours, but for all that she may be able to tell me what to do now," and he went back to her. So, when the Master-maid asked him what the giant had set him to do that day, he told her that he was to go underground and get the taxes.

"And how will you set about that?" said the Master-maid.

"Oh! you must tell me how to do it," said the Prince, "for I have never yet been underground, and even if I knew the way I do not know how much I am to demand."

"Oh! yes, I will soon tell you that; you must go to the rock there under the mountain-ridge, and take the club that is there, and knock on the rocky wall," said the Master-maid. "Then someone will come out who will sparkle with fire; you shall tell him your errand, and when he asks you how much you want to have you are to say: 'As much as I can carry.'"

"Yes, I will keep that in mind," said he, and then he sat there with the Master-maid the whole day, until night drew near, and he would gladly have stayed there till now if the Master-maid had not reminded him that it was time to be off to fetch the taxes before the giant came.

So he set out on his way, and did exactly what the Master-maid had told him. He went to the rocky wall, and took the club, and knocked on it. Then came one so full of sparks that they flew both out of his eyes and his nose. "What do you want?" said he.

"I was to come here for the giant, and demand the tax for him," said the King's son.

"How much are you to have then?" said the other.

"I ask for no more than I am able to carry with me," said the Prince.

"It is well for you that you have not asked for a horse-load," said he who had come out of the rock. "But now come in with me."

This the Prince did, and what a quantity of gold and silver he saw! It was lying inside the mountain like heaps of stones in a waste place, and he got a load that was as large as he was able to carry, and with that he went his way. So in the evening, when the giant came home with the goats, the Prince went into the chamber and hummed and sang again as he had done on the other two evenings.

"Have you been for the tax?" said the giant.

"Yes, that I have, master," said the Prince.

"Where have you put it then?" said the giant again.

"The bag of gold is standing there on the bench," said the Prince.

"I will see about that," said the giant, and went away to the bench, but the bag was standing there, and it was so full that gold and silver dropped out when the giant untied the string.

"You have certainly been talking with my Master-maid!" said the giant, "and if you have I will wring your neck."

"Master-maid?" said the Prince; "yesterday my master talked about this Master-maid, and today he is talking about her again, and the first day of all it was talk of the same kind. I do wish I could see the thing myself," said he.

"Yes, yes, wait till tomorrow," said the giant, "and then I myself will take you to her."

"Ah! master, I thank you – but you are only mocking me," said the King's son.

Next day the giant took him to the Master-maid. "Now you shall kill him, and boil him in the great big cauldron you know of, and when you have got the broth ready give me a call," said the giant; then he lay down on the bench to sleep, and almost immediately began to snore so that it sounded like thunder among the hills.

So the Master-maid took a knife, and cut the Prince's little finger, and dropped three drops of blood upon a wooden stool; then she took all the old rags, and shoe-soles, and all the rubbish she could lay hands on, and put them in the cauldron; and then she filled a chest with gold dust, and a lump of salt, and a water-flask which was hanging by the door, and she also took with her a golden apple, and two gold chickens; and then she and the Prince went away with all the speed they could, and when they had gone a little way they came to the sea, and then they sailed, but where they got the ship from I have never been able to learn.

Now, when the giant had slept a good long time, he began to stretch himself on the bench on which he was lying. "Will it soon boil?" said he.

"It is just beginning," said the first drop of blood on the stool.

So the giant lay down to sleep again, and slept for a long, long time. Then he began to move about a little again. "Will it soon be ready now?" said he, but he did not look up this time any more than he had done the first time, for he was still half asleep.

"Half done!" said the second drop of blood, and the giant believed it was the Master-maid again, and turned himself on the bench, and lay down to sleep once more. When he had slept again for many hours, he began to move and stretch himself. "Is it not done yet?" said he.

"It is quite ready," said the third drop of blood. Then the giant began to sit up and rub his eyes, but he could not see who it was who had spoken to him, so he asked for the Master-maid, and called her. But there was no one to give him an answer.

"Ah! well, she has just stolen out for a little," thought the giant, and he took a spoon, and went off to the cauldron to have a taste; but there was nothing in it but shoe-soles, and rags, and such trumpery as that, and all was boiled up together, so that he could not tell whether it was porridge or milk pottage. When he saw this, he understood what had happened, and fell into such a rage that he hardly knew what he was doing. Away he went after the Prince and the Master-maid so fast that the wind whistled behind him, and it was not long before he came to the water, but he could not get over it. "Well, well, I will soon find a cure for that; I have only to call my river-sucker," said the giant, and he did call him. So his river-sucker came and lay down, and drank one, two, three draughts, and with that the water in the sea fell so low that the giant saw the Master-maid and the Prince out on the sea in their ship. "Now you must throw out the lump of salt," said the Master-maid, and the Prince did so, and it grew up into such a great high mountain right across the sea that the giant could not come over it, and the river-sucker could not drink any more water. "Well, well, I will soon find a cure for that," said the giant, so he called to his hill-borer to come and bore through the mountain so that the river-sucker might be able to drink up the water again. But just as the hole was made, and the river-sucker was beginning to drink, the Master-maid told the Prince to throw one or two drops out of the flask, and when he did this the sea instantly became full of water again, and before the river-sucker could take one drink they reached the land and were in safety. So they determined to go home to the Prince's father, but the Prince would on no account permit the Master-maid to walk there, for he thought that it was unbecoming either for her or for him to go on foot.

"Wait here the least little bit of time, while I go home for the seven horses which stand in my father's stable," said he; "it is not far off, and I shall not be long away, but I will not let my betrothed bride go on foot to the palace."

"Oh! no, do not go, for if you go home to the King's palace you will forget me, I foresee that."

"How could I forget you? We have suffered so much evil together, and love each other so much," said the Prince; and he insisted on going home for the coach with the seven horses, and she was to wait for him there, by the seashore. So at last the Master-maid had to yield, for he was so absolutely determined to do it. "But when you get there you must not even give yourself time to greet anyone, but go straight into the stable, and take the horses, and put them in the coach, and drive back as quickly as you can. For they will all come round about you; but you must behave just as if you did not see them, and on no account must you taste anything, for if you do it will cause great misery both to you and to me," said she; and this he promised.

But when he got home to the King's palace one of his brothers was just going to be married, and the bride and all her kith and kin had come to the palace; so they all thronged round him, and questioned him about this and that, and wanted him to go in with them; but he behaved as if he did not see them, and went straight to the stable, and got out the horses and began to harness them. When they saw that they could not by any means prevail on him to go in with them, they came out to him with meat and drink, and the best of everything that they had prepared for the wedding; but the Prince refused to touch anything, and would do nothing but put the horses in as quickly as he could. At last, however, the bride's sister rolled an apple across the yard to him, and said: "As you won't eat anything else, you may like to take a bite of that, for you must be both hungry and thirsty after your long journey." And he took up the apple and bit a piece out of it. But no sooner had he got the piece of apple in his mouth than he forgot the Master-maid and that he was to go back in the coach to fetch her.

"I think I must be mad! what do I want with this coach and horses?" said he; and then he put the horses back into the stable, and went into the King's palace, and there it was settled that he should marry the bride's sister, who had rolled the apple to him.

The Master-maid sat by the seashore for a long, long time, waiting for the Prince, but no Prince came. So she went away, and when she had walked a short distance she came to a little hut which stood all alone in a small wood, hard by the King's palace. She entered it and asked if she might be allowed to stay there. The hut belonged to an old crone, who was also an ill-tempered and malicious troll. At first she would not let the Master-maid remain with her; but at last, after a long time, by means of good words and good payment, she obtained leave. But the hut was as dirty and black inside as a pigsty, so the Master-maid said that she would smarten it up a little, that it might look a little more like what other people's houses looked inside. The old crone did not like this either. She scowled, and was very cross, but the Master-maid did not trouble herself about that. She took out her chest of gold, and flung a handful of it or so into the fire, and the gold boiled up and poured out over the whole of the hut, until every part of it both inside and out was gilded. But when the gold began to bubble up the old hag grew so terrified that she fled as if the Evil One himself were pursuing her, and she did not remember to stoop down as she went through the doorway, and so she split her head and died. Next morning the sheriff came traveling by there. He was greatly astonished when he saw the gold hut shining and glittering there in the copse, and he was still more astonished when he went in and caught sight of the beautiful young maiden who was sitting there; he fell in love with her at once, and straightaway on the spot he begged her, both prettily and kindly, to marry him.

"Well, but have you a great deal of money?" said the Master-maid.

"Oh! yes; so far as that is concerned, I am not ill off," said the sheriff. So now he had to go home to get the money, and in the evening he came back, bringing with him a bag with two bushels in it, which he set down on the bench. Well, as he had such a fine lot of money, the Master-maid said she would have him, so they sat down to talk.

But scarcely had they sat down together before the Master-maid wanted to jump up again. "I have forgotten to see to the fire," she said.

"Why should you jump up to do that?" said the sheriff; "I will do that!" So he jumped up, and went to the chimney in one bound.

"Just tell me when you have got hold of the shovel," said the Master-maid.

"Well, I have hold of it now," said the sheriff.

"Then you may hold the shovel, and the shovel you, and pour red-hot coals over you, till day dawns," said the Master-maid. So the sheriff had to stand there the whole night and pour red-hot coals over himself, and, no matter how much he cried and begged and entreated, the red-hot coals did not grow the colder for that. When the day began to dawn, and he had power to throw down the shovel, he did not stay long where he was, but ran away as fast as he possibly could; and everyone who met him stared and looked after him, for he was flying as if he were mad, and he could not have looked worse if he had been both flayed and tanned, and everyone wondered where he had been, but for very shame he would tell nothing.

The next day the attorney came riding by the place where the Master-maid dwelt. He saw how brightly the hut shone and gleamed through the wood, and he too went into it to see who lived there, and when he entered and saw the beautiful young maiden he fell even more in love with her than the sheriff had done, and began to woo her at once. So the Master-maid asked him, as she had asked the sheriff, if he had a great deal of money, and the attorney said he was not ill off for that, and would at once go home to get it; and at night he came with a great big sack of money – this time it was a four-bushel sack – and set it on the bench by the Master-maid. So she promised to have him, and he sat down on the bench by her to arrange about it, but suddenly she said that she had forgotten to lock the door of the porch that night, and must do it.

"Why should you do that?" said the attorney; "sit still, I will do it."

So he was on his feet in a moment, and out in the porch.

"Tell me when you have got hold of the door-latch," said the Master-maid.

"I have hold of it now," cried the attorney.

"Then you may hold the door, and the door you, and may you go between wall and wall till day dawns."

What a dance the attorney had that night! He had never had such a waltz before, and he never wished to have such a dance again. Sometimes he was in front of the door, and sometimes the door was in front of him, and it went from one side of the porch to the other, till the attorney was well-nigh beaten to death. At first he began to abuse the Master-maid, and then to beg and pray, but the door did not care for anything but keeping him where he was till break of day.

As soon as the door let go its hold of him, off went the attorney. He forgot who ought to be paid off for what he had suffered, he forgot both his sack of money and his wooing, for he was so afraid lest the house door should come dancing after him. Everyone who met him stared and looked after him, for he was flying like a madman, and he could not have looked worse if a herd of rams had been butting at him all night long.

On the third day the bailiff came by, and he too saw the gold house in the little wood, and he too felt that he must go and see who lived there; and when he caught sight of the Master-maid he became so much in love with her that he wooed her almost before he greeted her.

The Master-maid answered him as she had answered the other two, that if he had a great deal of money, she would have him. "So far as that is concerned, I am not ill off," said the bailiff; so he was at once told to go home and fetch it, and this he did. At night he came back, and he had a still larger sack of money with him than the attorney had brought; it must have been at least six bushels, and he set it down on the bench. So it was settled that he was to have the Master-maid. But hardly had they sat down together before she said that she had forgotten to bring in the calf, and must go out to put it in the byre.

"No, indeed, you shall not do that," said the bailiff; "I am the one to do that." And, big and fat as he was, he went out as briskly as a boy.

"Tell me when you have got hold of the calf's tail," said the Master-maid.

"I have hold of it now," cried the bailiff.

"Then may you hold the calf's tail, and the calf's tail hold you, and may you go round the world together till day dawns!" said the Master-maid. So the bailiff had to bestir himself, for the calf went over rough and smooth, over hill and dale, and, the more the bailiff cried and screamed, the faster the calf went. When daylight began to appear, the bailiff was half dead; and so glad was he to leave loose of the calf's tail, that he forgot the sack of money and all else. He walked now slowly – more slowly than the sheriff and the attorney had done, but, the slower he went, the more time had everyone to stare and look at him; and they used it too, and no one can imagine how tired out and ragged he looked after his dance with the calf.

On the following day the wedding was to take place in the King's palace, and the elder brother was to drive to church with his bride, and the brother who had been with the giant with her sister. But when they had seated themselves in the coach and were about to drive off from the palace one of the trace-pins broke, and, though they made one, two, and three to put in its place, that did not help them, for each broke in turn, no matter what kind of wood they used to make them of. This went on for a long time, and they could not get away from the palace, so they were all in great trouble. Then the sheriff said (for he too had been bidden to the wedding at Court): "Yonder away in the thicket dwells a maiden, and if you can get her to lend you the handle of the shovel that she uses to make up her fire I know very well that it will hold fast." So they sent off a messenger to the thicket, and begged so prettily that they might have the loan of her shovel-handle of which the sheriff had spoken that they were not refused; so now they had a trace-pin which would not snap in two.

But all at once, just as they were starting, the bottom of the coach fell in pieces. They made a new bottom as fast as they could, but, no matter how they nailed it together, or what kind of wood they used, no sooner had they got the new bottom into the coach and were about to drive off than it broke again, so that they were still worse off than when they had broken the trace-pin. Then the attorney said, for he too was at the wedding in the palace: "Away there in the thicket dwells a maiden, and if you could but get her to lend you one-half of her porch-door I am certain that it will hold together." So they again sent a messenger to the thicket, and begged so prettily for the loan of the gilded porch-door of which the attorney had told them that they got it at once. They were just setting out again, but now the horses were not able to draw the coach. They had six horses already, and now they put in eight, and then ten, and then twelve, but the more they put in, and the more the coachman whipped them, the less good it did; and the coach never stirred from the spot. It was already beginning to be late in the day, and to church they must and would go, so everyone who was in the palace was in a state of distress. Then the bailiff spoke up and said: "Out there in the gilded cottage in the thicket dwells a girl, and if you could but get her to lend you her calf I know it could draw the coach, even if it were as heavy as a mountain." They all thought that it was ridiculous to be drawn to church by a calf, but there was nothing else for it but to send a messenger once more, and beg as prettily as they could, on behalf of the King, that she would let them have the loan of the calf that the bailiff had told them about. The Master-maid let them have it immediately – this time also she would not say "no."

Then they harnessed the calf to see if the coach would move; and away it went, over rough and smooth, over stock and stone, so that they could scarcely breathe, and sometimes they were on the ground, and sometimes up in the air; and when they came to the church the coach began to go round and round like a spinning-wheel, and it was with the utmost difficulty and danger that they were able to get out of the coach and into the church. And when they went back again the coach went quicker still, so that most of them did not know how they got back to the palace at all.

When they had seated themselves at the table the Prince who had been in service with the giant said that he thought they ought to have invited the maiden who had lent them the shovel-handle, and the porch-door, and the calf up to the palace, "for," said he, "if we had not got these three things, we should never have got away from the palace."

The King also thought that this was both just and proper, so he sent five of his best men down to the gilded hut, to greet the maiden courteously from the King, and to beg her to be so good as to come up to the palace to dinner at midday.

"Greet the King, and tell him that, if he is too good to come to me, I am too good to come to him," replied the Master-maid.

So the King had to go himself, and the Master-maid went with him immediately, and, as the King believed that she was more than she appeared to be, he seated her in the place of honour by the youngest bridegroom. When they had sat at the table for a short time, the Master-maid took out the cock, and the hen, and the golden apple which she had brought away with her from the giant's house, and set them on the table in front of her, and instantly the cock and the hen began to fight with each other for the golden apple.

"Oh! look how those two there are fighting for the golden apple," said the King's son.

"Yes, and so did we two fight to get out that time when we were in the mountain," said the Master-maid.

So the Prince knew her again, and you may imagine how delighted he was. He ordered the troll-witch who had rolled the apple to him to be torn in pieces between four-and-twenty horses, so that not a bit of her was left, and then for the first time they began really to keep the wedding, and, weary as they were, the sheriff, the attorney, and the bailiff kept it up too.

Grettir the Outlaw

(Icelandic)

Chapter I: Winter Tales

IT WAS NIGHT – drawing on to midnight – in summer, that I who write this book arrived at the little lonely farm of Biarg, on the Middle River, in the north of Iceland. It was night, near on midnight, and yet I could hardly call it night, for the sky overhead was full of light of the clearest amethyst, and every stock and stone was distinctly visible. Across the valley rose a rugged moor, and above its shoulder a snow-clad mountain, turned to rosy gold by the night sun. As I stood there watching the mist form on the cold river in the vale below, all at once I heard a strange sound like horns blowing far away in the sky, and looking up, I saw a train of swans flying from west to east, bathed in sunlight, their wings of silver, and their feathers as gold.

I had come all the way from England to see Biarg, for there was born, about the year AD 997, a man called Grettir, whose history I had read, and which interested me so much that I was resolved to see his native home, and the principal scenes where his stormy life was passed.

The landscape was the same as that on which Grettir's childish eyes had looked more than eight hundred and fifty years ago. The same outline of dreary moor, the same snowy ridge of mountain standing above it, catching the midnight summer sun, the same mist forming over the river; but the house was altogether different. Now there stood only a poor heap of farm-buildings, erected of turf and wood, where had once been a noble hall of wood, with carved gable-ends, surrounded by many out-houses.

Before we begin on the story of Grettir, it will be well to say a few words about its claim to be history.

Iceland never was, and it is not now, a much-peopled island. The farmhouses are for the most part far apart, and the farms are of very considerable extent, because, owing to the severity of the climate, very little pasturage is obtained over a wide extent of country for the sheep and cattle. The population lives round the coast, on the fiords or creeks of the sea, or on the rivers that flow into these fiords. The centre of the island is occupied by a vast waste of ice-covered mountain, and desert black as ink strewn with volcanic ash and sand, or else with a region of erupted lava that is impassable, because in cooling it has exploded, and forms a country of bristling spikes and gulfs and sharp edges, very much like the wreck of a huge ginger-beer bottle factory.

What are now farmhouses were the halls and mansions of families of noble descent. Indeed, the original settlers in Iceland were the nobles of Norway who left their native land to avoid the tyranny of Harold Fairhair, who tried to crush their power so as to make himself a despotic king in the land.

These Norse nobles came in their boats to Iceland, bringing with them their wives, children, their thralls or slaves, and their cattle; and they settled all round the coast. The present Icelanders are descended from these first colonists.

Now, the history of Iceland for a few hundred years consists of nothing but the history of the quarrels of these great families. Iceland was without any political organization, but it had an elected lawman or judge, and every year the heads of the families rode to Thingvalla, a plain in the south-west, where they brought their complaints, carried on their lawsuits, and had them settled by the judge. There was no army, no navy, no government in Iceland for a long time; also no foreign wars, and no internal revolutions.

These noble families settled in the valleys and upon the fiords thought a good deal of themselves, and they carefully preserved, at first orally then in writing, the record of their pedigrees, and also the tradition of the famous deeds of their great men.

In summer there is no night; in winter, no day. In winter there is little or nothing to be done but sit over the fire, sing songs, and tell yarns. Now, in winter the Icelanders told the tales of the brave men of old in their families, and so the tradition was handed on from father to son, the same stories told every winter, till all the particulars became well known. At the same time there can be no doubt that little embellishments were added, some exaggerations were indulged in, and here and there the grand deed of some other man was grafted into the story of the family hero. About two hundred or two hundred and fifty years after the death of Grettir, his history was committed to writing, and then it became fixed – nothing further was added to it, and we have his story after having travelled down over two hundred years as a tradition. That was plenty of time for additions and emendations, and the hobgoblin and ghost stories that come into his life are some of these embellishments. But the main facts of his life are true history. We are able to decide this by comparing his story with those of other families in the same part of the island, and to see whether they agree as to dates, and as to the circumstances narrated in them.

In the north-west of Iceland is an immense bay called the Huna-floi, which branches off into several creeks, the largest of which is called the Ramsfirth, and the next to that is the Middlefiord. Into this flows a river that has its rise in the central desert, in a perfect tangle of lakes. Three rivers issuing from these lakes unite just above Biarg, and pour their waters a short morning's ride lower through sands into the Middlefirth.

The valley is not cheerful, running from north to south. Biarg lies on the east side, and faces the western sun. The moor which lies behind it, and forms the hill on the other side of the river, is not broken and picturesque, and if it were not for the peak of Burfell, covered with snow a good part of the year, the view from Biarg would be as uninteresting as any to be found in the land. But then, when one rides down to the coast, or ascends the moor, what a splendid view bursts on the sight! The great Polar Sea is before one, intensely blue, not with the deep ultramarine of the Mediterranean, but with the blue of the nemophyla or forget-me-not, rolling in from the mysterious North; and across the mighty bay of the Huna-floi can be seen the snowy mountains of that extraordinary peninsula which runs out to the north-west of Iceland, and is only just not converted into an island because [it is] connected with Iceland by a narrow strip of land. That great projection is like a hand with fiords between the fingers of land, and glacier-mountains where are the knuckles; but the wrist is very narrow indeed, only about one English mile across, and there lies a trough along this junction, with a little stream and a lake in it. Now, at this wrist, as we may call it, lies the farm of Eyre, where, somewhat later, lived the sister of Grettir, who married a man that farmed there, named Glum.

Looking away across the great blue bay, the mountains of the hand may be seen rising out of the sea, and looking like icebergs.

Grettir the Strong was the son of a well-to-do bonder, or yeoman, who lived at Biarg, and was descended from some of the great nobles of Norway. His father's name was Asmund with the Greyhead, and his mother's name was Asdis.

He had a brother called Atli, a gentle, kindly young fellow, who never wittingly quarrelled with anyone, and was liked by all with whom he had to do. He had also two sisters – one was called Thordis, and she was married to Glum of Eyre – but neither come into the story; and he had another sister called Rannveig, who was married to Gamli of Melar, at the head of Ramsfirth. He had also a little brother called Illugi, of whom more hereafter. Grettir was not a good-looking boy; he had reddish hair, a pale face full of freckles, and light blue eyes. He was broad-built, not tall as a boy, though in the end he grew to be a very big man.

He was not considered a good-tempered or sociable boy. He seemed lazy and sullen; he liked to sit by the fire without speaking to anyone, listening to what was said, and brooding over what he had heard.

If his father set him a task, he did it so unwillingly, and so badly that Asmund Greyhead regretted having set him to do anything.

Now, during the winter, as we have already seen, when there is but a very little daylight, and the nights are vastly long, when, moreover, the whole land is deep in snow, so that there is no farm-work that can be done, and no travelling about to visit neighbours, it was, and is still, usual in Iceland for those in the house to tell tales, or sagas, as they are called. Some of these sagas relate to the old gods of the Norsemen, some are fabulous stories of old heroes who never existed, or, if they did exist, have had all sorts of fantastic legends tacked on to their histories; but other sagas are the tales of the doings of ancestors of the family.

Now, among the sagas that Grettir used to hearken to with greatest delight was that of old Onund Treefoot, his great-grandfather, who first settled in Iceland. And this was the tale:

* * *

Onund, the son of Ufeigh Clubfoot, son of Ivar the Smiter, was a mighty Viking in Norway; that is, he went about every summer harrying the coasts of England, Ireland,

and Scotland. He joined with three friends, and they had five ships together, and one summer they sailed to the Hebrides – which were then called the Sudereys, or southern isles. The Bishop of the Isle of Man is still called Bishop of Sodor and Man, because his diocese originally included the Sudereys. Then out against them came Kiarval, king of the Hebrides, with five ships, and they gave him battle, and there was a hard fray. But the men of Onund were the mightiest warriors. On each side many fell, but the end of the battle was that the king fled with only one ship. So Onund took the four vessels and great spoil, and he wrought great havoc on the coast, plundering and burning, and so in the fall of the year returned to Norway. In the history of England, and in that of Scotland and of Ireland, we read of the terrible annoyance given to the natives of Great Britain and Ireland by the northern pirates; and, indeed, they conquered Dublin, and established a kingdom there, and also took to themselves Orkney. Well, when Onund returned to Norway he did not find that matters were pleasant there; for King Harald the Unshorn had begun to establish himself sole king in Norway. Hitherto there had been many small kings and earls; but Harald had taken an oath that he would not cut or trim his hair till he had subdued all under his power, and made himself supreme throughout the land.

A great many bonders and all the little kings united against him, and there was a great battle fought at Hafrsfiord – the greatest battle that had as yet been fought in Norway. Onund was in the battle along with his friend, King Thorir Longchin, and he set his ship alongside of that of King Longchin. King Harald ran his ship up alongside of that of Longchin, grappled it, and boarded it. There was a furious fight, and Harald sent on board his Bearsarks, a set of half-mad ruffians, who wore not bear but wolf skins, and who were said to lead charmed lives, so that no weapon would wound them. Thorir Longchin and all his men were killed; and then King Harald cut away the ship and ran up against that of Onund. Onund was in the fore part, and he fought manfully. As the grappling-irons of Harald caught his ship, Onund made a sweep with his longsword at the man who threw the irons, and in so doing he put his leg over the bulwark. Then one on the king's ship threw a spear at Onund. He saw it flung, and leaned his head back to let it fly over him, and as he did so one on the king's ship smote at him with a battle-axe, and the axe fell on his leg below the knee and shore his leg off. Then Onund fell back on board his own vessel, and his men carried him across into that of a friend named Thrand, who lay alongside of him on the other board. And Thrand had a great cauldron there of pitch boiled, and Onund set his knee in the boiling pitch, and never blinked nor uttered a cry. That staunched the blood. If he had not done this he would have bled to death.

Now, Thrand saw that King Harald was gaining the mastery everywhere, so he fled away with his ship and sailed west.

Onund was healed of his wound, but ever after he walked with a wooden leg, and that is why he got the name of Onund Treefoot.

After the battle of Hafrsfiord, Onund could only return to Norway by stealth, and he could not recover his lands there, so he deemed it wisest for him to sail away and seek a home elsewhere. That is how he left Norway and settled in Iceland.

And when King Harald saw himself lord and master through all the land, then he had his hair trimmed and combed, and it was so long and so beautiful, that ever after he who had been called 'The Unshorn' went by the name of 'Fairhair,' and in history he is known as King Harald Fairhair.

The Story of Audunn and the Bear

(Icelandic)

I

THERE WAS A MAN CALLED AUDUNN; he came of a family of the Western Firths, and was not well off. Audunn left Iceland from the Western Firths with the assistance of Thorsteinn, a substantial farmer, and of Thorir, a ship's captain, who had stayed with Thorsteinn during the winter. Audunn had been on the same farm, working for Thorir, and as his reward he got his passage to Norway under Thorir's care.

Audunn had set aside the greater part of his property, such as it was, for his mother, before he took ship, and it was determined that this should support her for three years.

Now they sailed to Norway and had a prosperous voyage, and Audunn spent the following winter with the skipper Thorir, who had a farm in Moérr. The summer after that, they sailed out to Greenland, where they stayed for the winter.

It is told that in Greenland, Audunn bought a white bear, a magnificent beast, and paid for him all he had. Next summer they returned to Norway, and their voyage was without mishap. Audunn brought his bear with him, intending to go south to Denmark to visit King Sveinn, and to present the beast to him. When he reached due south of Norway and came to the place where the King was in residence, Audunn went ashore, leading his bear, and hired lodgings.

King Haraldr was soon told that a bear had been brought to the place, a magnificent creature, belonging to an Icelander. The King immediately sent men to fetch Audunn, and when he entered the King's presence, Audunn saluted him as was proper. The King acknowledged the salute suitably and then asked:

Is it true that you have a great treasure, a white bear?

Audunn answered and said that he had got a bear of some sort.

The King said: Will you sell him to us for the price you paid for him?

Audunn answered: I would not care to do that, my Lord.

Will you then, said the King, have me pay twice the price? That would be fairer if you gave all you had for him.

I would not care to do that, my Lord, answered Audunn, but the King said:

Will you give him to me then?

No, my Lord, answered Audunn.

The King asked: What do you mean to do with him then? – and Audunn answered: I mean to go south to Denmark and give him to King Sveinn.

Can it be that you are such a fool, said King Haraldr, that you have not heard about the war between these two countries? Or do you think your luck so good that you will be able to bring valuable possessions to Denmark, while others cannot get there unmolested, even though they have pressing business?

Audunn answered: My Lord, that is for you to decide, but I shall agree to nothing other than that which I had already planned.

Then the King said: Why should we not have it like this, that you go your own way, just as you choose, and then visit me on your way back, and tell me how King Sveinn rewards you for the bear? It may be that luck will go with you.

I will promise you to do that, said Audunn.

Audunn now followed the coast southward and eastward into the Vik, and from there to Denmark, and by that time every penny of his money had been spent, and he had to beg food for himself as well as for the bear. He called on one of King Sveinn's stewards, a man named Aki, and asked him for some provisions, both for himself and for his bear – I intend, said he, to give the bear to King Sveinn.

Aki said that he would sell him some provisions if he liked, but Audunn answered that he had nothing to pay for them – but yet, said he, I would like to carry out my plan, and to take the beast to the King.

Aki answered: I will supply such provisions as the two of you need until you go before the King, but in exchange I will have half the bear. You can look at it in this way: the beast will die on your hands, since you need a lot of provisions and your money is spent, and it will come to this, that you will have nothing out of the bear.

When Audunn considered this, it seemed to him that there was some truth in what the steward had said, and they agreed on these terms: he gave Aki half the bear, and the King was then to set a value on the whole.

Now they were both to visit the King, and so they did. They went into his presence and stood before his table. The King wondered who this man could be, whom he did not recognize, and then said to Audunn: Who are you?

Audunn answered: I am an Icelander, my Lord, and I came lately from Greenland, and now from Norway, intending to bring you this white bear. I gave all I had for him, but I have had a serious setback, so now I only own half of the beast – then Audunn told the King what had happened between him and the steward, Aki.

The King asked: Is that true, what he says, Aki?

True it is, said Aki.

The King said: And did you think it proper, seeing that I had placed you in a high position, to let and hinder a man who had taken it on himself to bring me a precious gift, for which he had given all he had? King Haraldr saw fit to let him go his way in peace, and he is no friend of ours. Think, then, how far this was honest on your part. It would be just to have you put to death, but I will not do that now; you must rather leave this land at once, and never come into my sight again. But to you, Audunn, I owe the same gratitude as if you were giving me the whole of the bear, so now stay here with me.

Audunn accepted the invitation and stayed with King Sveinn for a while.

II

After some time had passed Audunn said to the King: I desire to go away now, my Lord.

The King answered rather coldly: What do you want to do then, since you do not wish to stay with us?

Audunn answered: I wish to go south on a pilgrimage.

If you had not such a good end before you, said the King, I should be vexed at your desire to go away.

Now the King gave Audunn a large sum of silver, and he travelled south with pilgrims bound for Rome. The King arranged for his journey, asking him to visit him when he came back.

Audunn went on his way until he reached the city of Rome in the south. When he had stayed there as long as he wished, he turned back, and a severe illness attacked him, and he grew terribly emaciated. All the money which the King had given him for his pilgrimage was now spent, and so he took up his staff and begged his food. By now his hair had fallen out and he looked in a bad way. He got back to Denmark at Easter, and went to the place where the King was stationed. He dared not let the King see him, but stayed in a side-aisle of the church, intending to approach the King when he went to church for Nones. But when Audunn beheld the King and his courtiers splendidly arrayed, he did not dare to show himself.

When the King went to drink in his hall, Audunn ate his meal out of doors, as is the custom of Rome pilgrims, so long as they have not laid aside their staff and scrip. In the evening, when the King went to Vespers, Audunn intended to meet him, but shy as he was before, he was much more so now that the courtiers were merry with drink. As they were going back, the King noticed a man, and thought he could see that he had not the confidence to come forward and meet him. But as the courtiers walked in, the King turned back and said:

Let the man who wants to meet me come forward; I think there must be someone who does.

Then Audunn came forward and fell at the feet of the King, but the King hardly recognized him. As soon as he knew who he was, he took Audunn by the hand and welcomed him: You have changed a lot since we met last, he said, and then he led Audunn into the hall after him. When the courtiers saw Audunn they laughed at him, but the King said:

There is no need for you to laugh at this man, for he has provided better for his soul than you have.

The King had a bath prepared for Audunn and then gave him clothes, and now he stayed with the King.

III

It is told that one day in the spring the King invited Audunn to stay with him for good, and said he would make him his cup-bearer, and do him great honour.

Audunn answered: May God reward you, my Lord, for all the favours you would show me, but my heart is set on sailing out to Iceland.

The King said: This seems a strange choice to me – but Audunn answered: My Lord, I cannot bear to think that I should be enjoying high honour here with you, while my mother is living the life of a beggar out in Iceland. For by now, all that I contributed for her subsistence before I left Iceland has been used up.

The King answered: That is well spoken and like a man, and good fortune will go with you. This was the one reason for your departure which would not have offended me. So stay with me until the ships are made ready for sea.

And this Audunn did.

One day towards the end of spring King Sveinn walked down to the quay, where men were getting ships ready to sail to various lands, to the Baltic lands and Germany, to

Sweden and Norway. The King and Audunn came to a fine vessel, and there were some men busy fitting her out. The King asked:

How do you like this ship, Audunn?

Audunn answered: I like her well, my Lord.

The King said: I will give you this ship and reward you for the white bear.

Audunn thanked the King for his gift as well as he knew how.

After a time, when the ship was quite ready to sail, King Sveinn said to Audunn:

If you wish to go now, I shall not hinder you, but I have heard that you are badly off for harbours in your country, and that there are many shelterless coasts, dangerous to shipping. Now, supposing you are wrecked, and lose your ship and your goods, there will be little to show that you have visited King Sveinn and brought him a precious gift.

Then the King handed him a leather purse full of silver: You will not be altogether penniless, said he, even if you wreck your ship, so long as you can hold on to this. But yet it may be, said the King, that you will lose this money, and then it will be of little use to you that you have been to see King Sveinn and given him a precious gift.

Then the King drew a ring from his arm and gave it to Audunn, saying: Even if it turns out so badly that you wreck your ship and lose your money, you will still not be a pauper if you reach land, for many men have gold about them in a shipwreck, and if you keep this ring there will be something to show that you have been to see King Sveinn. But I will give you this advice, said the King, do not give this ring away, unless you should feel yourself so much indebted to some distinguished man – then give the ring to him, for it is a fitting gift for a man of rank. And now farewell.

IV

After this Audunn put to sea and made Norway, and had his merchandise brought ashore, and that was a more laborious task than it had been last time he was in Norway. Then he went into the presence of King Haraldr, wishing to fulfil the promise he had given him before he went to Denmark. Audunn gave the King a friendly greeting, which he accepted warmly.

Sit down, said the King, and drink with us, and so Audunn did. Then King Haraldr asked: What reward did King Sveinn give you for the bear?

Audunn answered: This, my Lord, that he accepted him from me.

I would have given you that, said the King, but what else did he give you?

Audunn said: He gave me silver to make a pilgrimage to Rome, but King Haraldr said: King Sveinn gives many people silver for pilgrimages and for other things, even if they do not bring him valuable gifts. What more did he do for you?

He offered to make me his cup-bearer and to give me great honours.

That was a good offer, said the King, but he must have given you still more.

Audunn said: He gave me a merchantman with a cargo of wares most profitable for the Norway trade.

That was generous, said the King, but I would have rewarded you as well as that. Did he give you anything else?

Audunn said: He gave me a leather purse full of silver, and said that I would still not be penniless if I kept it, even if my ship were wrecked off Iceland.

The King said: That was magnificent, and more than I should have done. I would have thought my debt discharged if I had given you the ship. Did he give you anything else?

Certainly he gave me something else, my Lord, said Audunn; he gave me this ring which I am wearing on my arm, and said that I might chance to lose all my property, and yet not be destitute if I had this ring. But he advised me not to part with it unless I were under such an obligation to some noble man that I wished to give it to him. And now I have come to the right man, for it was in your power to take from me both my bear and my life, but you allowed me to go to Denmark in peace when others could not go there.

The King received the gift graciously and gave Audunn fine presents in exchange before they parted. Audunn laid out his merchandise on his voyage to Iceland, and sailed out that same summer, and people thought him the luckiest of men.

The Story of Sigurd

(Danish)

ONCE UPON A TIME there was a King in the North who had won many wars, but now he was old. Yet he took a new wife, and then another Prince, who wanted to have married her, came up against him with a great army. The old King went out and fought bravely, but at last his sword broke, and he was wounded and his men fled. But in the night, when the battle was over, his young wife came out and searched for him among the slain, and at last she found him, and asked whether he might be healed. But he said, "No," his luck was gone, his sword was broken, and he must die. And he told her that she would have a son, and that son would be a great warrior, and would avenge him on the other King, his enemy. And he bade her keep the broken pieces of the sword, to make a new sword for his son, and that blade should be called Gram.

Then he died. And his wife called her maid to her and said, "Let us change clothes, and you shall be called by my name, and I by yours, lest the enemy finds us."

So this was done, and they hid in a wood, but there some strangers met them and carried them off in a ship to Denmark. And when they were brought before the King, he thought the maid looked like a Queen, and the Queen like a maid. So he asked the Queen, "How do you know in the dark of night whether the hours are wearing to the morning?"

And she said:

"I know because, when I was younger, I used to have to rise and light the fires, and still I waken at the same time."

"A strange Queen to light the fires," thought the King.

Then he asked the Queen, who was dressed like a maid, "How do you know in the dark of night whether the hours are wearing near the dawn?"

"My father gave me a gold ring," said she, "and always, ere the dawning, it grows cold on my finger."

"A rich house where the maids wore gold," said the King. "Truly you are no maid, but a King's daughter."

So he treated her royally, and as time went on she had a son called Sigurd, a beautiful boy and very strong. He had a tutor to be with him, and once the tutor bade him go to the King and ask for a horse.

"Choose a horse for yourself," said the King; and Sigurd went to the wood, and there he met an old man with a white beard, and said, "Come! Help me in horse-choosing."

Then the old man said, "Drive all the horses into the river, and choose the one that swims across."

So Sigurd drove them, and only one swam across. Sigurd chose him: his name was Grani, and he came of Sleipnir's breed, and was the best horse in the world. For Sleipnir was the horse of Odin, the God of the North, and was as swift as the wind.

But a day or two later his tutor said to Sigurd, "There is a great treasure of gold hidden not far from here, and it would become you to win it."

But Sigurd answered, "I have heard stories of that treasure, and I know that the dragon Fafnir guards it, and he is so huge and wicked that no man dares to go near him."

"He is no bigger than other dragons," said the tutor, "and if you were as brave as your father you would not fear him."

"I am no coward," says Sigurd; "why do you want me to fight with this dragon?"

Then his tutor, whose name was Regin, told him that all this great hoard of red gold had once belonged to his own father. And his father had three sons – the first was Fafnir, the Dragon; the next was Otter, who could put on the shape of an otter when he liked; and the next was himself, Regin, and he was a great smith and maker of swords.

Now there was at that time a dwarf called Andvari, who lived in a pool beneath a waterfall, and there he had hidden a great hoard of gold. And one day Otter had been fishing there, and had killed a salmon and eaten it, and was sleeping, like an otter, on a stone. Then someone came by, and threw a stone at the otter and killed it, and flayed off the skin, and took it to the house of Otter's father. Then he knew his son was dead, and to punish the person who had killed him he said he must have the Otter's skin filled with gold, and covered all over with red gold, or it should go worse with him. Then the person who had killed Otter went down and caught the Dwarf who owned all the treasure and took it from him.

Only one ring was left, which the Dwarf wore, and even that was taken from him.

Then the poor Dwarf was very angry, and he prayed that the gold might never bring any but bad luck to all the men who might own it, for ever.

Then the otter skin was filled with gold and covered with gold, all but one hair, and that was covered with the poor Dwarf's last ring.

But it brought good luck to nobody. First Fafnir, the Dragon, killed his own father, and then he went and wallowed on the gold, and would let his brother have none, and no man dared go near it.

When Sigurd heard the story he said to Regin:

"Make me a good sword that I may kill this Dragon."

So Regin made a sword, and Sigurd tried it with a blow on a lump of iron, and the sword broke.

Another sword he made, and Sigurd broke that too.

Then Sigurd went to his mother, and asked for the broken pieces of his father's blade, and gave them to Regin. And he hammered and wrought them into a new sword, so sharp that fire seemed to burn along its edges.

Sigurd tried this blade on the lump of iron, and it did not break, but split the iron in two. Then he threw a lock of wool into the river, and when it floated down against the sword it was cut into two pieces. So Sigurd said that sword would do. But before he went against the Dragon he led an army to fight the men who had killed his father, and he slew their King, and took all his wealth, and went home.

When he had been at home a few days, he rode out with Regin one morning to the heath where the Dragon used to lie. Then he saw the track which the Dragon made when he went to a cliff to drink, and the track was as if a great river had rolled along and left a deep valley.

Then Sigurd went down into that deep place, and dug many pits in it, and in one of the pits he lay hidden with his sword drawn. There he waited, and presently the earth began to shake with the weight of the Dragon as he crawled to the water. And a cloud of venom flew before him as he snorted and roared, so that it would have been death to stand before him.

But Sigurd waited till half of him had crawled over the pit, and then he thrust the sword Gram right into his very heart.

Then the Dragon lashed with his tail till stones broke and trees crashed about him.

Then he spoke, as he died, and said:

"Whoever thou art that hast slain me this gold shall be thy ruin, and the ruin of all who own it."

Sigurd said:

"I would touch none of it if by losing it I should never die. But all men die, and no brave man lets death frighten him from his desire. Die thou, Fafnir," and then Fafnir died.

And after that Sigurd was called Fafnir's Bane, and Dragonslayer.

Then Sigurd rode back, and met Regin, and Regin asked him to roast Fafnir's heart and let him taste of it.

So Sigurd put the heart of Fafnir on a stake, and roasted it. But it chanced that he touched it with his finger, and it burned him. Then he put his finger in his mouth, and so tasted the heart of Fafnir.

Then immediately he understood the language of birds, and he heard the woodpeckers say:

"There is Sigurd roasting Fafnir's heart for another, when he should taste of it himself and learn all wisdom."

The next bird said:

"There lies Regin, ready to betray Sigurd, who trusts him."

The third bird said:

"Let him cut off Regin's head, and keep all the gold to himself."

The fourth bird said:

"That let him do, and then ride over Hindfell, to the place where Brynhild sleeps."

When Sigurd heard all this, and how Regin was plotting to betray him, he cut off Regin's head with one blow of the sword Gram.

Then all the birds broke out singing:

"We know a fair maid,
A fair maiden sleeping;
Sigurd, be not afraid,
Sigurd, win thou the maid Fortune is keeping.

"High over Hindfell
Red fire is flaming,
There doth the maiden dwell
She that should love thee well,
Meet for thy taming.

"There must she sleep till thou
Comest for her waking
Rise up and ride, for now
Sure she will swear the vow
Fearless of breaking."

Then Sigurd remembered how the story went that somewhere, far away, there was a beautiful lady enchanted. She was under a spell, so that she must always sleep in a castle surrounded by flaming fire; there she must sleep for ever till there came a knight who would ride through the fire and waken her. There he determined to go, but first he rode right down the horrible trail of Fafnir. And Fafnir had lived in a cave with iron doors, a cave dug deep down in the earth, and full of gold bracelets, and crowns, and rings; and there, too, Sigurd found the Helm of Dread, a golden helmet, and whoever wears it is invisible. All these he piled on the back of the good horse Grani, and then he rode south to Hindfell.

Now it was night, and on the crest of the hill Sigurd saw a red fire blazing up into the sky, and within the flame a castle, and a banner on the topmost tower. Then he set the horse Grani at the fire, and he leaped through it lightly, as if it had been through the heather. So Sigurd went within the castle door, and there he saw someone sleeping, clad all in armour. Then he took the helmet off the head of the sleeper, and behold, she was a most beautiful lady. And she wakened and said, "Ah! is it Sigurd, Sigmund's son, who has broken the curse, and comes here to waken me at last?"

This curse came upon her when the thorn of the tree of sleep ran into her hand long ago as a punishment because she had displeased Odin the God. Long ago, too, she had vowed never to marry a man who knew fear, and dared not ride through the fence of flaming fire. For she was a warrior maid herself, and went armed into the battle like a man. But now she and Sigurd loved each other, and promised to be true to each other, and he gave her a ring, and it was the last ring taken from the dwarf Andvari. Then Sigurd rode away, and he came to the house of a King who had a fair daughter. Her name was Gudrun, and her mother was a witch. Now Gudrun fell in love with Sigurd, but he was always talking of Brynhild, how beautiful she was and how dear. So one day Gudrun's witch mother put poppy and forgetful drugs in a magical cup, and bade Sigurd drink to her health, and he drank, and instantly he forgot poor Brynhild and he loved Gudrun, and they were married with great rejoicings.

Now the witch, the mother of Gudrun, wanted her son Gunnar to marry Brynhild, and she bade him ride out with Sigurd and go and woo her. So forth they rode to her father's house, for Brynhild had quite gone out of Sigurd's mind by reason of the witch's wine, but she remembered him and loved him still. Then Brynhild's father told Gunnar that she would marry none but him who could ride the flame in front of her enchanted tower, and thither they rode, and Gunnar set his horse at the flame, but he would not face it. Then Gunnar tried Sigurd's horse Grani, but he would not move with Gunnar on his back. Then Gunnar remembered witchcraft that his mother had taught him, and by his magic he made Sigurd look exactly like himself, and he looked exactly like Sigurd. Then Sigurd, in the shape of Gunnar and in his mail, mounted on Grani, and Grani leaped the fence of fire, and Sigurd went in and found Brynhild, but he did not remember her yet, because of the forgetful medicine in the cup of the witch's wine.

Now Brynhild had no help but to promise she would be his wife, the wife of Gunnar as she supposed, for Sigurd wore Gunnar's shape, and she had sworn to wed whoever should ride the flames. And he gave her a ring, and she gave him back the ring he had given her before in his own shape as Sigurd, and it was the last ring of that poor dwarf Andvari. Then he rode out again, and he and Gunnar changed shapes, and each was himself again, and they went home to the witch Queen's, and Sigurd gave the dwarf's ring to his wife, Gudrun. And Brynhild went to her father, and said that a King had come called Gunnar, and had ridden the fire, and she must marry him. "Yet I thought," she said, "that no man could have done this deed but Sigurd, Fafnir's bane, who was my true love. But he has forgotten me, and my promise I must keep."

So Gunnar and Brynhild were married, though it was not Gunnar but Sigurd in Gunnar's shape, that had ridden the fire.

And when the wedding was over and all the feast, then the magic of the witch's wine went out of Sigurd's brain, and he remembered all. He remembered how he had freed Brynhild from the spell, and how she was his own true love, and how he had forgotten and had married another woman, and won Brynhild to be the wife of another man.

But he was brave, and he spoke not a word of it to the others to make them unhappy. Still he could not keep away the curse which was to come on everyone who owned the treasure of the dwarf Andvari, and his fatal golden ring.

And the curse soon came upon all of them. For one day, when Brynhild and Gudrun were bathing, Brynhild waded farthest out into the river, and said she did that to show she was Gudrun's superior. For her husband, she said, had ridden through the flame when no other man dared face it.

Then Gudrun was very angry, and said that it was Sigurd, not Gunnar, who had ridden the flame, and had received from Brynhild that fatal ring, the ring of the dwarf Andvari.

Then Brynhild saw the ring which Sigurd had given to Gudrun, and she knew it and knew all, and she turned as pale as a dead woman, and went home. All that evening she never spoke. Next day she told Gunnar, her husband, that he was a coward and a liar, for he had never ridden the flame, but had sent Sigurd to do it for him, and pretended that he had done it himself. And she said he would never see her glad in his hall, never drinking wine, never playing chess, never embroidering with the golden thread, never speaking words of kindness. Then she rent all her needlework asunder and wept aloud, so that everyone in the house heard her. For her heart was broken, and her pride was broken in the same hour. She had lost her true love, Sigurd, the slayer of Fafnir, and she was married to a man who was a liar.

Then Sigurd came and tried to comfort her, but she would not listen, and said she wished the sword stood fast in his heart.

"Not long to wait," he said, "till the bitter sword stands fast in my heart, and thou will not live long when I am dead. But, dear Brynhild, live and be comforted, and love Gunnar thy husband, and I will give thee all the gold, the treasure of the dragon Fafnir."

Brynhild said:

"It is too late."

Then Sigurd was so grieved and his heart so swelled in his breast that it burst the steel rings of his shirt of mail.

Sigurd went out and Brynhild determined to slay him. She mixed serpent's venom and wolf's flesh, and gave them in one dish to her husband's younger brother, and when he had tasted them he was mad, and he went into Sigurd's chamber while he slept and pinned him to the bed with a sword. But Sigurd woke, and caught the sword Gram into his hand, and threw it at the man as he fled, and the sword cut him in twain. Thus died Sigurd, Fafnir's bane, whom no ten men could have slain in fair fight. Then Gudrun wakened and saw him dead, and she moaned aloud, and Brynhild heard her and laughed; but the kind horse Grani lay down and died of very grief. And then Brynhild fell a-weeping till her heart broke. So they attired Sigurd in all his golden armour, and built a great pile of wood on board his ship, and at night laid on it the dead Sigurd and the dead Brynhild, and the good horse, Grani, and set fire to it, and launched the ship. And the wind bore it blazing out to sea, flaming into the dark. So there were Sigurd and Brynhild burned together, and the curse of the dwarf Andvari was fulfilled.

The Isle of Udröst

(Norwegian)

ONCE UPON A TIME there lived at Vaerö, not far from Röst, a poor fisherman, named Isaac. He had nothing but a boat and a couple of goats, which his wife fed as well as she could with fish leavings, and with the grass she was able to gather on the surrounding hills; but his whole hut was full of hungry children. Yet he was always satisfied with what God sent him. The only thing that worried him was his inability to live at peace with his neighbour. The latter was a rich man, thought himself entitled to far more than such a beggarly fellow as Isaac, and wanted to get him out of the way, in order to take for himself the anchorage before Isaac's hut.

One day Isaac had put out a few miles to sea to fish, when suddenly a dark fog fell, and in a flash such a tremendous storm broke, that he had to throw all his fish overboard in order to lighten the ship and save his life. Even then it was very hard to keep the boat afloat; but he steered a careful course between and across the mountainous waves, which seemed ready to swallow him from moment to moment.

After he had kept on for five or six hours in this manner, he thought that he ought to touch land somewhere. But time went by, and the storm and fog grew worse and worse. Then he began to realize that either he was steering out to sea, or that the wind had veered, and at last he made sure the latter was the case; for he sailed on and on without a sight of land. Suddenly he heard a hideous cry from the stern of the boat, and felt certain that it was the *drang*, who was singing his death-song. Then he prayed God to guard his wife and children, for he thought his last hour had come. As he sat there and prayed, he made out something black; but when his boat drew nearer, he noticed that it was only three cormorants, sitting on a piece of driftwood and – *swish*! he had passed them. Thus he sailed for a long time, and grew so hungry, so thirsty and so weary that he did not know what to do; for the most part he sat with the rudder in his hand and slept. But all of a sudden the boat ran up on a beach and stopped. Then Isaac opened his eyes. The sun broke through the fog, and shone on a beautiful land. Its hills and mountains were green to their very tops, fields and meadows lay among their slopes, and he seemed to breathe a fragrance of flowers and grass sweeter than any he had ever known before.

"God be praised, now I am safe, for this is Udröst!" said Isaac to himself. Directly ahead of him lay a field of barley, with ears so large and heavy that he had never seen their like, and through the barley-field a narrow path led to a green turf-roofed cottage of clay, that rose above the field, and on the roof of the cottage grazed a white goat with gilded horns, and an udder as large as that of the largest cow. Before the door sat a little man clad in blue, puffing away at a little pipe. He had a beard so long and so large that it hung far down upon his breast.

"Welcome to Udröst, Isaac!" said the man.

"Good day to you, father," said Isaac, "and do you know me?"

"It might be that I do," said the man. "I suppose you want to stay here overnight?"

"That would suit me very well, father," was Isaac's reply.

"The trouble is with my sons, for they cannot bear the smell of a Christian," answered the man. "Did you meet them?"

"No, I only met three cormorants, who were sitting on a piece of driftwood and croaking," was Isaac's reply.

"Well, those were my sons," said the man, and emptied his pipe, "and now come into the house, for I think you must be hungry and thirsty."

"I'll take that liberty, father," said Isaac.

When the man opened the door, everything within was so beautiful that Isaac could not get over his admiration. He had never seen anything like it. The table was covered with the finest dishes, bowls of cream, and salmon and game, and liver dumplings with syrup, and cheese as well, and there were whole piles of doughnuts, and there was mead, and everything else that is good. Isaac ate and drank bravely, and yet his plate was never empty; and no matter how much he drank, his glass was always full. The man neither ate much nor said much; but suddenly they heard a noise and clamour before the house, and the man went out. After a time he returned with his three sons, and Isaac trembled inwardly when they came through the door; but their father must have quieted them, for they were very friendly and amiable, and told Isaac he must use his guest-right, and sit down and drink with them; for Isaac had risen to leave the table, saying he had satisfied his hunger. But he gave in to them, and they drank mead together, and became good friends. And they said that Isaac must go fishing with them, so that he would have something to take with him when he went home.

The first time they put out a great storm was raging. One of the sons sat at the rudder, the second at the bow, and the third in the middle; and Isaac had to work with the bailing-can until he dripped perspiration. They sailed as though they were mad. They never reefed a sail, and when the boat was full of water, they danced on the crests of the waves, and slid down them so that the water in the stern spurted up like a fountain. After a time the storm subsided, and they began to fish. And the sea was so full of fish that they could not even put out an anchor, since mountains of fish were piled up beneath them. The sons of Udröst drew up one fish after another. Isaac knew his business; but he had taken along his own fishing-tackle, and as soon as a fish bit he let go again, and at last he had caught not a single one. When the boat was filled, they sailed home again to Udröst, and the sons cleaned the fish, and laid them on the stands. Meanwhile Isaac had complained to their father of his poor luck. The man promised that he should do better next time, and gave him a couple of hooks; and the next time they went out to fish, Isaac caught just as many as the others, and when they reached home, he was given three stands of fish as his share.

At length Isaac began to get homesick, and when he was about to leave, the man made him a present of a new fishing-boat, full of meal, and tackle and other useful things. Isaac thanked him repeatedly, and the man invited him to come back when the season opened again, since he himself was going to take a cargo to Bergen, in the second *stevne*, and Isaac could go along and sell his fish there himself. Isaac was more than willing, and asked him what course he should set when he again wanted to reach Udröst. "All you need do is to follow the cormorant when he heads for the open sea, then you will be on the right course," said the man. "Good luck on your way!"

But when Isaac got underway, and looked around, there was no Udröst in sight; far and wide, all around him, he saw no more than the ocean.

When the time came, Isaac sailed to join the man of Udröst's fishing-craft. But such a craft he had never seen before. It was two hails long, so that when the steersman, who was on lookout in the stern, wanted to call out something to the rower, the latter could not hear him. So they had stationed another man in the middle of the ship, close by the mast, who had to relay the steersman's call to the rower, and even he had to shout as loudly as he could in order to make himself heard.

Isaac's share was laid down in the forepart of the boat; and he himself took down the fish from the stands; yet he could not understand how it was that the stands were continually filled with fresh fish, no matter how many he took away, and when he sailed away they were still as full as ever. When he reached Bergen, he sold his fish, and got so much money for them that he was able to buy a new schooner, completely fitted out, and with a cargo to boot, as the man of Udröst had advised him. Late in the evening, when he was about to sail for home, the man came aboard and told him never to forget those who survived his neighbour, for his neighbour himself had died; and then he wished Isaac all possible success and good fortune for his schooner, in advance. "All is well, and all stands firm that towers in the air," said he, and what he meant was that there was one aboard whom none could see, but who would support the mast on his back, if need be.

Since that time fortune was Isaac's friend. And well he knew why this was so, and never forgot to prepare something good for whoever held the winter watch, when the schooner was drawn up on land in the fall. And every Christmas night there was the glow and shimmer of light, the sound of fiddles and music, of laughter and merriment, and of dancing on the deserted schooner.

Tales of Beasts & Animals

Introduction

IN 'DAPPLEGRIM', a dapple-grey foal asks a young man to sacrifice twelve other foals for three years in a row so that their mares can nurse him. In the process, he grows into a giant, gleaming steed like no other, and guides the young man as they undertake several perilous trials to free a princess from a troll and win her hand in marriage.

This story is one of many tales collected by Peter Christen Asbjørnsen and Jørgen Engebretsen Moe, and reminiscent of many tales found throughout the Eddas and Sagas, in which the hero shares a deep, even sacred, bond with his trusted steed.

The reality is that birds and animals speak to us in so many different ways, even if we don't literally understand the words they say. Living amongst thick forests at home; pursued by the plaintive seagull's cry as they made their way along the 'whale's road', the early Vikings had learned this lesson very well. Wildlife figures prominently in the mythological legacy they left behind: Nature speaks very clearly in these stories.

Dapplegrim

(Norwegian)

THERE WAS ONCE UPON A TIME a couple of rich folks who had twelve sons, and when the youngest was grown up he would not stay at home any longer, but would go out into the world and seek his fortune. His father and mother said that they thought he was very well off at home, and that he was welcome to stay with them; but he could not rest, and said that he must and would go, so at last they had to give him leave. When he had walked a long way, he came to a King's palace. There he asked for a place and got it.

Now the daughter of the King of that country had been carried off into the mountains by a Troll, and the King had no other children, and for this cause both he and all his people were full of sorrow and affliction, and the King had promised the Princess and half his kingdom to anyone who could set her free; but there was no one who could do it, though a great number had tried. So when the youth had been there for the space of a year or so, he wanted to go home again to pay his parents a visit; but when he got there his father and mother were dead, and his brothers had divided everything that their parents possessed between themselves, so that there was nothing at all left for him.

"Shall I, then, receive nothing at all of my inheritance?" asked the youth.

"Who could know that you were still alive – you who have been a wanderer so long?" answered the brothers. "However, there are twelve mares upon the hills which we have not yet divided among us, and if you would like to have them for your share, you may take them."

So the youth, well pleased with this, thanked them, and at once set off to the hill where the twelve mares were at pasture. When he got up there and found them, each mare had her foal, and by the side of one of them was a big dapple-grey foal as well, which was so sleek that it shone again.

"Well, my little foal, you are a fine fellow!" said the youth.

"Yes, but if you will kill all the other little foals so that I can suck all the mares for a year, you shall see how big and handsome I shall be then!" said the Foal.

So the youth did this – he killed all the twelve foals, and then went back again.

Next year, when he came home again to look after his mares and the foal, it was as fat as it could be, and its coat shone with brightness, and it was so big that the lad had the greatest difficulty in getting on its back, and each of the mares had another foal.

"Well, it's very evident that I have lost nothing by letting you suck all my mares," said the lad to the yearling; "but now you are quite big enough, and must come away with me."

"No," said the Colt, "I must stay here another year; kill the twelve little foals, and then I can suck all the mares this year also, and you shall see how big and handsome I shall be by summer."

So the youth did it again, and when he went up on the hill next year to look after his colt and the mares, each of the mares had her foal again; but the dappled colt was so big that when the lad wanted to feel its neck to see how fat it was, he could not reach up to it, it was so high? and it was so bright that the light glanced off its coat.

"Big and handsome you were last year, my colt, but this year you are ever so much handsomer," said the youth; "in all the King's court no such horse is to be found. But now you shall come away with me."

"No," said the dappled Colt once more; "here I must stay for another year. Just kill the twelve little foals again, so that I can suck the mares this year also, and then come and look at me in the summer."

So the youth did it – he killed all the little foals, and then went home again.

But next year, when he returned to look after the dappled colt and the mares, he was quite appalled. He had never imagined that any horse could become so big and overgrown, for the dappled horse had to lie down on all fours before the youth could get on his back, and it was very hard to do that even when it was lying down, and it was so plump that its coat shone and glistened just as if it had been a looking-glass. This time the dappled horse was not unwilling to go away with the youth, so he mounted it, and when he came riding home to his brothers they all smote their hands together and crossed themselves, for never in their lives had they either seen or heard tell of such a horse as that.

"If you will procure me the best shoes for my horse, and the most magnificent saddle and bridle that can be found," said the youth, "you may have all my twelve mares just as they are standing out on the hill, and their twelve foals into the bargain." For this year also each mare had her foal. The brothers were quite willing to do this; so the lad got such shoes for his horse that the sticks and stones flew high up into the air as he rode away over the hills, and such a gold saddle and such a gold bridle that they could be seen glittering and glancing from afar.

"And now we will go to the King's palace," said Dapplegrim – that was the horse's name, "but bear in mind that you must ask the King for a good stable and excellent fodder for me."

So the lad promised not to forget to do that. He rode to the palace, and it will be easily understood that with such a horse as he had he was not long on the way.

When he arrived there, the King was standing out on the steps, and how he did stare at the man who came riding up!

"Nay," said he, "never in my whole life have I seen such a man and such a horse."

And when the youth inquired if he could have a place in the King's palace, the King was so delighted that he could have danced on the steps where he was standing, and there and then the lad was told that he should have a place.

"Yes; but I must have a good stable and most excellent fodder for my horse," said he.

So they told him that he should have sweet hay and oats, and as much of them as the dappled horse chose to have, and all the other riders had to take their horses out of the stable that Dapplegrim might stand alone and really have plenty of room.

But this did not last long, for the other people in the King's Court became envious of the lad, and there was no bad thing that they would not have done to him if they had but dared. At last they bethought themselves of telling the King that the youth had said that, if he chose, he was quite able to rescue the Princess who had been carried off into the mountain a long time ago by the Troll.

The King immediately summoned the lad into his presence, and said that he had been informed that he had said that it was in his power to rescue the Princess, so he was now to do it. If he succeeded in this, he no doubt knew that the King had promised his daughter and half the kingdom to anyone who set her free, which promise should be faithfully and honourably kept, but if he failed he should be put to death. The youth denied that he had said this, but all to no purpose, for the King was deaf to all his words; so there was nothing to be done but say that he would make the attempt.

He went down into the stable, and very sad and full of care he was. Then Dapplegrim inquired why he was so troubled, and the youth told him, and said that he did not know what to do, "for as to setting the Princess free, that was downright impossible."

"Oh, but it might be done," said Dapplegrim. "I will help you; but you must first have me well shod. You must ask for ten pounds of iron and twelve pounds of steel for the shoeing, and one smith to hammer and one to hold."

So the youth did this, and no one said him nay. He got both the iron and the steel, and the smiths, and thus was Dapplegrim shod strongly and well, and when the youth went out of the King's palace a cloud of dust rose up behind him. But when he came to the mountain into which the Princess had been carried, the difficulty was to ascend the precipitous wall of rock by which he was to get on to the mountain beyond, for the rock stood right up on end, as steep as a house side and as smooth as a sheet of glass. The first time the youth rode at it he got a little way up the precipice, but then both Dapplegrim's fore legs slipped, and down came horse and rider with a sound like thunder among the mountains. The next time that he rode at it he got a little farther up, but then one of Dapplegrim's fore legs slipped, and down they went with the sound of a landslip. But the third time Dapplegrim said: "Now we must show what we can do," and went at it once more till the stones sprang up sky high, and thus they got up. Then the lad rode into the mountain cleft at full gallop and caught up the Princess on his saddle-bow, and then out again before the Troll even had time to stand up, and thus the Princess was set free.

When the youth returned to the palace the King was both happy and delighted to get his daughter back again, as may easily be believed, but somehow or other the people about the Court had so worked on him that he was angry with the lad too. "Thou shalt have my thanks for setting my Princess free," he said, when the youth came into the palace with her, and was then about to go away.

"She ought to be just as much my Princess as she is yours now, for you are a man of your word," said the youth.

"Yes, yes," said the King. "Have her thou shalt, as I have said it; but first of all thou must make the sun shine into my palace here."

For there was a large and high hill outside the windows which overshadowed the palace so much that the sun could not shine in.

"That was no part of our bargain," answered the youth. "But as nothing that I can say will move you, I suppose I shall have to try to do my best, for the Princess I will have."

So he went down to Dapplegrim again and told him what the King desired, and Dapplegrim thought that it might easily be done; but first of all he must have new shoes, and ten pounds of iron and twelve pounds of steel must go to the making of them, and two smiths were also necessary, one to hammer and one to hold, and then it would be very easy to make the sun shine into the King's palace.

The lad asked for these things and obtained them instantly, for the King thought that for very shame he could not refuse to give them, and so Dapplegrim got new shoes, and they were good ones. The youth seated himself on him, and once more they went their way, and for each hop that Dapplegrim made, down went the hill fifteen ells into the earth, and so they went on until there was no hill left for the King to see.

When the youth came down again to the King's palace he asked the King if the Princess should not at last be his, for now no one could say that the sun was not shining into the palace. But the other people in the palace had again stirred up the King, and he answered that the youth should have her, and that he had never intended that he should not; but first of all he must get her quite as good a horse to ride to the wedding on as that which he had himself. The youth said that the King had never told him he was to do that, and it seemed to him that he had now really earned the Princess; but the King stuck to what he had said, and if the youth were unable to do it he was to lose his life, the King said. The youth went down to the stable again, and very sad and sorrowful he was, as anyone may well imagine. Then he told Dapplegrim that the King had now required that he should get the Princess as good a bridal horse as that which the bridegroom had, or he should lose his life. "But that will be no easy thing to do," said he, "for your equal is not to be found in all the world."

"Oh yes, there is one to match me," said Dapplegrim. "But it will not be easy to get him, for he is underground. However, we will try. Now you must go up to the King and ask for new shoes for me, and for them we must again have ten pounds of iron, twelve pounds of steel, and two smiths, one to hammer and one to hold, but be very particular to see that the hooks are very sharp. And you must also ask for twelve barrels of rye, and twelve slaughtered oxen must we have with us, and all the twelve ox-hides with twelve hundred spikes set in each of them; all these things must we have, likewise a barrel of tar with twelve tons of tar in it. The youth went to the King and asked for all the things that Dapplegrim had named, and once more, as the King thought that it would be disgraceful to refuse them to him, he obtained them all.

So he mounted Dapplegrim and rode away from the Court, and when he had ridden for a long, long time over hills and moors, Dapplegrim asked: "Do you hear anything?"

"Yes; there is such a dreadful whistling up above in the air that I think I am growing alarmed," said the youth.

"That is all the wild birds in the forest flying about; they are sent to stop us," said Dapplegrim. "But just cut a hole in the corn sacks, and then they will be so busy with the corn that they will forget us."

The youth did it. He cut holes in the corn sacks so that barley and rye ran out on every side, and all the wild birds that were in the forest came in such numbers that they darkened the sun. But when they caught sight of the corn they could not refrain from it, but flew down and began to scratch and pick at the corn and rye, and at last they began to fight among themselves, and forgot all about the youth and Dapplegrim, and did them no harm.

And now the youth rode onwards for a long, long time, over hill and dale, over rocky places and morasses, and then Dapplegrim began to listen again, and asked the youth if he heard anything now.

"Yes; now I hear such a dreadful crackling and crashing in the forest on every side that I think I shall be really afraid," said the youth.

"That is all the wild beasts in the forest," said Dapplegrim; "they are sent out to stop us. But just throw out the twelve carcasses of the oxen, and they will be so much occupied with them that they will quite forget us." So the youth threw out the carcasses of the oxen, and then all the wild beasts in the forest, both bears and wolves, and lions, and grim beasts of all kinds, came. But when they caught sight of the carcasses of the oxen they began to fight for them till the blood flowed, and they entirely forgot Dapplegrim and the youth.

So the youth rode onwards again, and many and many were the new scenes they saw, for travelling on Dapplegrim's back was not travelling slowly, as may be imagined, and then Dapplegrim neighed.

"Do you hear anything?" he said.

"Yes; I heard something like a foal neighing quite plainly a long, long way off," answered the youth.

"That's a full-grown colt," said Dapplegrim, "if you hear it so plainly when it is so far away from us."

So they travelled onwards a long time, and saw one new scene after another once more. Then Dapplegrim neighed again.

"Do you hear anything now?" said he.

"Yes; now I heard it quite distinctly, and it neighed like a full-grown horse," answered the youth.

"Yes, and you will hear it again very soon," said Dapplegrim; "and then you will hear what a voice it has." So they travelled on through many more different kinds of country, and then Dapplegrim neighed for the third time; but before he could ask the youth if he heard anything, there was such a neighing on the other side of the heath that the youth thought that hills and rocks would be rent in pieces.

"Now he is here!" said Dapplegrim. "Be quick, and fling over me the ox-hides that have the spikes in them, throw the twelve tons of tar over the field, and climb up into that great spruce fir tree. When he comes, fire will spurt out of both his nostrils, and then the tar will catch fire. Now mark what I say – if the flame ascends I conquer, and if it sinks I fail; but if you see that I am winning, fling the bridle, which you must take off me, over his head, and then he will become quite gentle."

Just as the youth had flung all the hides with the spikes over Dapplegrim, and the tar over the field, and had got safely up into the spruce fir, a horse came with flame spouting from his nostrils, and the tar caught fire in a moment; and Dapplegrim and the horse began to fight until the stones leapt up to the sky. They bit, and they fought with their fore legs and their hind legs, and sometimes the youth looked at them. And sometimes he looked at the tar, but at last the flames began to rise, for wheresoever the strange horse bit or wheresoever he kicked he hit upon the spikes in the hides, and at length he had to yield. When the youth saw that, he was not long in getting down from the tree and flinging the bridle over the horse's head, and then he became so tame that he might have been led by a thin string.

This horse was dappled too, and so like Dapplegrim that no one could distinguish the one from the other. The youth seated himself on the dappled horse which he had captured, and rode home again to the King's palace, and Dapplegrim ran loose by his side. When he got there, the King was standing outside in the courtyard.

"Can you tell me which is the horse I have caught, and which is the one I had before?" said the youth. "If you can"t, I think your daughter is mine."

The King went and looked at both the dappled horses; he looked high and he looked low, he looked before and he looked behind, but there was not a hair's difference between the two.

"No," said the King; "that I cannot tell thee, and as thou hast procured such a splendid bridal horse for my daughter thou shalt have her; but first we must have one more trial, just to see if thou art fated to have her. She shall hide herself twice, and then thou shalt hide thyself twice. If thou canst find her each time that she hides herself, and if she cannot find thee in thy hiding places, then it is fated, and thou shalt have the Princess."

"That, too, was not in our bargain," said the youth. "But we will make this trial since it must be so."

So the King's daughter was to hide herself first.

Then she changed herself into a duck, and lay swimming in a lake that was just outside the palace. But the youth went down into the stable and asked Dapplegrim what she had done with herself.

"Oh, all that you have to do is to take your gun, and go down to the water and aim at the duck which is swimming about there, and she will soon discover herself," said Dapplegrim.

The youth snatched up his gun and ran to the lake. "I will just have a shot at that duck," said he, and began to aim at it.

"Oh, no, dear friend, don't shoot! It is I," said the Princess. So he had found her once.

The second time the Princess changed herself into a loaf, and laid herself on the table among four other loaves; and she was so like the other loaves that no one could see any difference between them.

But the youth again went down to the stable to Dapplegrim, and told him that the Princess had hidden herself again, and that he had not the least idea what had become of her.

"Oh, just take a very large bread-knife, sharpen it, and pretend that you are going to cut straight through the third of the four loaves which are lying on the kitchen table in the King's palace – count them from right to left – and you will soon find her," said Dapplegrim.

So the youth went up to the kitchen, and began to sharpen the largest bread-knife that he could find; then he caught hold of the third loaf on the left-hand side, and put the knife to it as if he meant to cut it straight in two. "I will have a bit of this bread for myself," said he.

"No, dear friend, don't cut, it is I!" said the Princess again; so he had found her the second time.

And now it was his turn to go and hide himself; but Dapplegrim had given him such good instructions that it was not easy to find him. First he turned himself into a horse-fly, and hid himself in Dapplegrim's left nostril. The Princess went poking about and searching everywhere, high and low, and wanted to go into Dapplegrim's stall too, but he began to bite and kick about so that she was afraid to go there, and could not find the youth. "Well," said she, "as I am unable to find you, you must show yourself; "whereupon the youth immediately appeared standing there on the stable floor.

Dapplegrim told him what he was to do the second time, and he turned himself into a lump of earth, and stuck himself between the hoof and the shoe on Dapplegrim's left fore foot. Once more the King's daughter went and sought everywhere, inside and outside, until at last she came into the stable, and wanted to go into the stall beside Dapplegrim. So this time he allowed her to go into it, and she peered about high and low, but she could not look under his hoofs, for he stood much too firmly on his legs for that, and she could not find the youth.

"Well, you will just have to show where you are yourself, for I can't find you," said the Princess, and in an instant the youth was standing by her side on the floor of the stable.

"Now you are mine!" said he to the Princess.

"Now you can see that it is fated that she should be mine," he said to the King.

"Yes, fated it is," said the King. "So what must be, must."

Then everything was made ready for the wedding with great splendour and promptitude, and the youth rode to church on Dapplegrim, and the King's daughter on the other horse. So everyone must see that they could not be long on their way thither.

Prince Lindworm

(Norwegian)

ONCE UPON A TIME, there was a fine young King who was married to the loveliest of Queens. They were exceedingly happy, all but for one thing – they had no children. And this often made them both sad, because the Queen wanted a dear little child to play with, and the King wanted an heir to the kingdom.

One day the Queen went out for a walk by herself, and she met an ugly old woman. The old woman was just like a witch: but she was a nice kind of witch, not the cantankerous sort. She said, "Why do you look so doleful, pretty lady?" "It's no use my telling you," answered the Queen, "nobody in the world can help me." "Oh, you never know," said the old woman. "Just you let me hear what your trouble is, and maybe I can put things right."

"My dear woman, how can you?" said the Queen: and she told her, "The King and I have no children: that's why I am so distressed." "Well, you needn't be," said the old witch. "I can set that right in a twinkling, if only you will do exactly as I tell you. Listen. Tonight, at sunset, take a little drinking-cup with two ears" (that is, handles), "and put it bottom upwards on the ground in the northwest corner of your garden. Then go and lift it up tomorrow morning at sunrise, and you will find two roses underneath it, one red and one white. If you eat the red rose, a little boy will be born to you: if you eat the white rose, a little girl will be sent. But, whatever you do, you mustn't eat *both* the roses, or you'll be sorry, – that I warn you! Only one: remember that!" "Thank you a thousand times," said the Queen, "this is good news indeed!" And she wanted to give the old woman her gold ring; but the old woman wouldn't take it.

So the Queen went home and did as she had been told: and next morning at sunrise she stole out into the garden and lifted up the little drinking-cup. She was surprised, for indeed she had hardly expected to see anything. But there were the two roses underneath it, one red and one white. And now she was dreadfully puzzled, for she did not know which to choose. "If I choose the red one," she thought, "and I have a little boy, he may grow up and go to the wars and get killed. But if I choose the white one, and have a little girl, she will stay at home awhile with us, but later on she will get married and go away and leave us. So, whichever it is, we may be left with no child after all."

However, at last she decided on the white rose, and she ate it. And it tasted so sweet, that she took and ate the red one too: without ever remembering the old woman's solemn warning.

Some time after this, the King went away to the wars: and while he was still away, the Queen became the mother of twins. One was a lovely baby boy, and the other was a Lindworm, or Serpent. She was terribly frightened when she saw the Lindworm, but he wriggled away out of the room, and nobody seemed to have seen him but herself: so that she thought it must have been a dream. The baby Prince was so beautiful and so healthy, the Queen was full of joy: and likewise, as you may suppose, was the King when he came home and found his son and heir. Not a word was said by anyone about the Lindworm: only the Queen thought about it now and then.

Many days and years passed by, and the baby grew up into a handsome young Prince, and it was time that he got married. The King sent him off to visit foreign kingdoms, in the Royal coach, with six white horses, to look for a Princess grand enough to be his wife. But at the very first crossroads, the way was stopped by an enormous Lindworm, enough to frighten the bravest. He lay in the middle of the road with a great wide open mouth, and cried, "A bride for me before a bride for you!" Then the Prince made the coach turn round and try another road: but it was all no use. For, at the first cross-ways, there lay the Lindworm again, crying out, "A bride for me before a bride for you!" So the Prince had to turn back home again to the Castle, and give up his visits to the foreign kingdoms. And his mother, the Queen, had to confess that what the Lindworm said was true. For he was really the eldest of her twins: and so he ought to have a wedding first.

There seemed nothing for it but to find a bride for the Lindworm, if his younger brother, the Prince, were to be married at all. So the King wrote to a distant country, and asked for a Princess to marry his son (but, of course, he didn't say which son), and presently a Princess arrived. But she wasn't allowed to see her bridegroom until he stood by her side in the great hall and was married to her, and then, of course, it was too late for her to say she wouldn't have him. But next morning the Princess had disappeared. The Lindworm lay sleeping all alone: and it was quite plain that he had eaten her.

A little while after, the Prince decided that he might now go journeying again in search of a Princess. And off he drove in the Royal chariot with the six white horses. But at the first cross-ways, there lay the Lindworm, crying with his great wide open mouth, "A bride for me before a bride for you!" So the carriage tried another road, and the same thing happened, and they had to turn back again this time, just as formerly. And the King wrote to several foreign countries, to know if anyone would marry his son. At last another Princess arrived, this time from a very far distant land. And, of course, she was not allowed to see her future husband before the wedding took place, – and then, lo and behold! it was the Lindworm who stood at her side. And next morning the Princess had disappeared: and the Lindworm lay sleeping all alone; and it was quite clear that he had eaten her.

By and by the Prince started on his quest for the third time: and at the first crossroads there lay the Lindworm with his great wide open mouth, demanding a bride as before. And the Prince went straight back to the castle, and told the King: "You must find another bride for my elder brother."

"I don't know where I am to find her," said the King, "I have already made enemies of two great Kings who sent their daughters here as brides: and I have no notion how I can obtain a third lady. People are beginning to say strange things, and I am sure no Princess will dare to come."

Now, down in a little cottage near a wood, there lived the King's shepherd, an old man with his only daughter. And the King came one day and said to him, "Will you give me your daughter to marry my son the Lindworm? And I will make you rich for the rest of your life."

– "No, sire," said the shepherd, "that I cannot do. She is my only child, and I want her to take care of me when I am old. Besides, if the Lindworm would not spare two beautiful Princesses, he won't spare her either. He will just gobble her up: and she is much too good for such a fate."

But the King wouldn't take "No" for an answer: and at last the old man had to give in.

Well, when the old shepherd told his daughter that she was to be Prince Lindworm's bride, she was utterly in despair. She went out into the woods, crying and wringing her hands and bewailing her hard fate. And while she wandered to and fro, an old witch-woman suddenly appeared out of a big hollow oak tree, and asked her, "Why do you look so doleful, pretty lass?" The shepherd-girl said, "It's no use my telling you, for nobody in the world can help me." – "Oh, you never know," said the old woman. "Just you let me hear what your trouble is, and maybe I can put things right." – "Ah, how can you?" said the girl, "For I am to be married to the King's eldest son, who is a Lindworm. He has already married two beautiful Princesses, and devoured them: and he will eat me too! No wonder I am distressed."

"Well, you needn't be," said the witch-woman. "All that can be set right in a twinkling: if only you will do exactly as I tell you." So the girl said she would.

"Listen, then," said the old woman. "After the marriage ceremony is over, and when it is time for you to retire to rest, you must ask to be dressed in ten snow-white shifts. And you must then ask for a tub full of lye," (that is, washing water prepared with wood-ashes) "and a tub full of fresh milk, and as many whips as a boy can carry in his arms, – and have all these brought into your bedchamber. Then, when the Lindworm tells you to shed a shift, do you bid him slough a skin. And when all his skins are off, you must dip the whips in the lye and whip him; next, you must wash him in the fresh milk; and, lastly, you must take him and hold him in your arms, if it's only for one moment."

"The last is the worst notion – ugh!" said the shepherd's daughter, and she shuddered at the thought of holding the cold, slimy, scaly Lindworm.

"Do just as I have said, and all will go well," said the old woman. Then she disappeared again in the oak tree.

When the wedding-day arrived, the girl was fetched in the Royal chariot with the six white horses, and taken to the castle to be decked as a bride. And she asked for ten snow-white shifts to be brought her, and the tub of lye, and the tub of milk, and as many whips as a boy could carry in his arms. The ladies and courtiers in the castle thought, of course, that this was some bit of peasant superstition, all rubbish and nonsense. But the King said, "Let her have whatever she asks for." She was then arrayed in the most wonderful robes, and looked the loveliest of brides. She was led to the hall where the wedding ceremony was to take place, and she saw the Lindworm for the first time as he came in and stood by her side. So they were married, and a great wedding-feast was held, a banquet fit for the son of a king.

When the feast was over, the bridegroom and bride were conducted to their apartment, with music, and torches, and a great procession. As soon as the door was shut, the Lindworm turned to her and said, "Fair maiden, shed a shift!" The shepherd's daughter answered him, "Prince Lindworm, slough a skin!" – "No one has ever dared tell me to do that before!" said he. – "But I command you to do it now!" said she. Then he began to moan and wriggle: and in a few minutes a long snake-skin lay upon the floor beside him. The girl drew off her first shift, and spread it on top of the skin.

The Lindworm said again to her, "Fair maiden, shed a shift."

The shepherd's daughter answered him, "Prince Lindworm, slough a skin."

"No one has ever dared tell me to do that before," said he. – "But I command you to do it now," said she. Then with groans and moans he cast off the second skin: and she covered it with her second shift. The Lindworm said for the third time, "Fair maiden, shed a shift." The shepherd's daughter answered him again, "Prince Lindworm, slough a skin." – "No one has ever dared tell me to do that before," said he, and his little eyes rolled furiously. But the girl was not afraid, and once more she commanded him to do as she bade.

And so this went on until nine Lindworm skins were lying on the floor, each of them covered with a snow-white shift. And there was nothing left of the Lindworm but a huge thick mass, most horrible to see. Then the girl seized the whips, dipped them in the lye, and whipped him as hard as ever she could. Next, she bathed him all over in the fresh milk. Lastly, she dragged him on to the bed and put her arms round him. And she fell fast asleep that very moment.

Next morning very early, the King and the courtiers came and peeped in through the keyhole. They wanted to know what had become of the girl, but none of them dared enter the room. However, in the end, growing bolder, they opened the door a tiny bit. And there they saw the girl, all fresh and rosy, and beside her lay – no Lindworm, but the handsomest prince that anyone could wish to see.

The King ran out and fetched the Queen: and after that, there were such rejoicings in the castle as never were known before or since. The wedding took place all over again, much finer than the first, with festivals and banquets and merrymakings for days and weeks. No bride was ever so beloved by a King and Queen as this peasant maid from the shepherd's cottage. There was no end to their love and their kindness towards her: because, by her sense and her calmness and her courage, she had saved their son, Prince Lindworm.

The Seven Foals

(Norwegian)

THERE WAS ONCE UPON A TIME a couple of poor folks who lived in a wretched hut, far away from everyone else, in a wood. They only just managed to live from hand to mouth, and had great difficulty in doing even so much as that, but they had three sons, and the youngest of them was called Cinderlad, for he did nothing else but lie and poke about among the ashes.

One day the eldest lad said that he would go out to earn his living; he soon got leave to do that, and set out on his way into the world. He walked on and on for the whole day, and when night was beginning to fall he came to a royal palace. The King was standing outside on the steps, and asked where he was going.

"Oh, I am going about seeking a place, my father," said the youth.

"Wilt thou serve me, and watch my seven foals?" asked the King. "If thou canst watch them for a whole day and tell me at night what they eat and drink, thou shalt have the Princess and half my kingdom, but if thou canst not, I will cut three red stripes on thy back."

The youth thought that it was very easy work to watch the foals, and that he could do it well enough.

Next morning, when day was beginning to dawn, the King's Master of the Horse let out the seven foals; and they ran away, and the youth after them just as it chanced, over hill and dale, through woods end bogs. When the youth had run thus for a long time he began to be tired, and when he had held on a little longer he was heartily weary of watching at all, and at the same moment he came to a cleft in a rock where an old woman was sitting spinning with her distaff in her hand.

As soon as she caught sight of the youth, who was running after the foals till the perspiration streamed down his face, she cried:

"Come hither, come hither, my handsome son, and let me comb your hair for you."

The lad was willing enough, so he sat down in the cleft of the rock beside the old hag, and laid his head on her knees, and she combed his hair all day while he lay there and gave himself up to idleness.

When evening was drawing near, the youth wanted to go.

"I may just as well go straight home again," said he, "for it is no use to go to the King's palace."

"Wait till it is dusk," said the old hag, "and then the King's foals will pass by this place again, and you can run home with them; no one will ever know that you have been lying here all day instead of watching the foals."

So when they came she gave the lad a bottle of water and a bit of moss, and told him to show these to the King and say that this was what his seven foals ate and drank.

"Hast thou watched faithfully and well the whole day long?" said the King, when the lad came into his presence in the evening.

"Yes, that I have!" said the youth.

"Then you are able to tell me what it is that my seven foals eat and drink," said the King.

So the youth produced the bottle of water and the bit of moss which he had got from the old woman, saying:

"Here you see their meat, and here you see their drink."

Then the King knew how his watching had been done, and fell into such a rage that he ordered his people to chase the youth back to his own home at once; but first they were to cut three red stripes in his back, and rub salt into them.

When the youth reached home again, anyone can imagine what a state of mind he was in. He had gone out once to seek a place, he said, but never would he do such a thing again.

Next day the second son said that he would now go out into the world to seek his fortune. His father and mother said "No," and bade him look at his brother's back, but the youth would not give up his design, and stuck to it, and after a long, long time he got leave to go, and set forth on his way. When he had walked all day he too came to the King's palace, and the King was standing outside on the steps, and asked where he was going; and when the youth replied that he was going about in search of a place, the King said that he might enter into his service and watch his seven foals. Then the King promised him the same punishment and the same reward that he had promised his brother.

The youth at once consented to this and entered into the King's service, for he thought he could easily watch the foals and inform the King what they ate and drank.

In the grey light of dawn the Master of the Horse let out the seven foals, and off they went again over hill and dale, and off went the lad after them. But all went with him as it had gone with his brother. When he had run after the foals for a long, long time and was hot and tired, he passed by a cleft in the rock where an old woman was sitting spinning with a distaff, and she called to him:

"Come hither, come hither, my handsome son, and let me comb your hair."

The youth liked the thought of this, let the foals run where they chose, and seated himself in the cleft of the rock by the side of the old hag. So there he sat with his head on her lap, taking his ease the livelong day.

The foals came back in the evening, and then he too got a bit of moss and a bottle of water from the old hag, which things he was to show to the King. But when the King asked the youth: "Canst thou tell me what my seven foals eat and drink?" and the youth showed him the bit of moss and the bottle of water, and said: "Yes here may you behold their meat, and here their drink," the King once more became wroth, and commanded that three red stripes should be cut on the lad's back, that salt should be strewn upon them, and that he should then be instantly chased back to his own home. So when the youth got home again he too related all that had happened to him, and he too said that he had gone out in search of a place once, but that never would he do it again.

On the third day Cinderlad wanted to set out. He had a fancy to try to watch the seven foals himself, he said.

The two others laughed at him, and mocked him. "What I when all went so ill with us, do you suppose that you are going to succeed? You look like succeeding – you who have never done anything else but lie and poke about among the ashes!" said they.

"Yes, I will go too," said Cinderlad, "for I have taken it into my head."

The two brothers laughed at him, and his father and mother begged him not to go, but all to no purpose, and Cinderlad set out on his way. So when he had walked the whole day, he too came to the King's palace as darkness began to fall.

There stood the King outside on the steps, and he asked whither he was bound.

"I am walking about in search of a place," said Cinderlad.

"From whence do you come, then?" inquired the King, for by this time he wanted to know a little more about the men before he took any of them into his service.

So Cinderlad told him whence he came, and that he was brother to the two who had watched the seven foals for the King, and then he inquired if he might be allowed to try to watch them on the following day.

"Oh, shame on them!" said the King, for it enraged him even to think of them. "If thou art brother to those two, thou too art not good for much. I have had enough of such fellows."

"Well, but as I have come here, you might just give me leave to make the attempt," said Cinderlad.

"Oh, very well, if thou art absolutely determined to have thy back flayed, thou may'st have thine own way if thou wilt," said the King.

"I would much rather have the Princess," said Cinderlad.

Next morning, in the grey light of dawn, the Master of the Horse let out the seven foals again, and off they set over hill and dale, through woods and bogs, and off went Cinderlad after them. When he had run thus for a long time, he too came to the cleft in the rock. There the old hag was once more sitting spinning from her distaff, and she cried to Cinderlad;

"Come hither, come hither, my handsome son, and let me comb your hair for you."

"Come to me, then; come to me!" said Cinderlad, as he passed by jumping and running, and keeping tight hold of one of the foals' tails.

When he had got safely past the cleft in the rock, the youngest foal said:

"Get on my back, for we have still a long way to go." So the lad did this.

And thus they journeyed onwards a long, long way.

"Dost thou see anything now?" said the Foal.

"No," said Cinderlad.

So they journeyed onwards a good bit farther.

"Dost thou see anything now?" asked the Foal.

"Oh, no," said the lad.

When they had gone thus for a long, long way, the Foal again asked:

"Dost thou see anything now?"

"Yes, now I see something that is white," said Cinderlad. "It looks like the trunk of a great thick birch tree."

"Yes, that is where we are to go in," said the Foal.

When they got to the trunk, the eldest foal broke it down on one side, and then they saw a door where the trunk had been standing, and inside this there was a small room, and in the room there was scarcely anything but a small fireplace and a couple of benches, but behind the door hung a great rusty sword and a small pitcher.

"Canst thou wield that sword?" asked the Foal.

Cinderlad tried, but could not do it; so he had to take a draught from the pitcher, and then one more, and after that still another, and then he was able to wield the sword with perfect ease.

"Good," said the Foal; "and now thou must take the sword away with thee, and with it shalt thou cut off the heads of all seven of us on thy wedding-day, and then we shall become princes again as we were before. For we are brothers of the Princess whom thou art to have when thou canst tell the King what we eat and drink, but there is a mighty Troll who has cast a spell over us. When thou hast cut off our heads, thou must take the greatest care to lay each head at the tail of the body to which it belonged before, and then the spell which the Troll has cast upon us will lose all its power."

Cinderlad promised to do this, and then they went on farther.

When they had travelled a long, long way, the Foal said:

"Dost thou see anything?"

"No," said Cinderlad.

So they went on a great distance farther.

"And now?" inquired the Foal, "seest thou nothing now?"

"Alas! no," said Cinderlad.

So they travelled onwards again, for many and many a mile, over hill and dale.

"Now, then," said the Foal, "dost thou not see anything now?"

"Yes," said Cinderlad; "now I see something like a bluish streak, far, far away."

"That is a river," said the Foal, "and we have to cross it."

There was a long, handsome bridge over the river, and when they had got to the other side of it they again travelled on a long, long way, and then once more the Foal inquired if Cinderlad saw anything. Yes, this time he saw something that looked black, far, far away, and was rather like a church tower.

"Yes," said the Foal, "we shall go into that."

When the Foals got into the churchyard they turned into men and looked like the sons of a king, and their clothes were so magnificent that they shone with splendour, and they went into the church and received bread and wine from the priest, who was standing before the altar, and Cinderlad went in too. But when the priest had laid his hands on the princes and read the blessing, they went out of the church again, and Cinderlad went out too, but he took with him a flask of wine and some consecrated bread. No sooner had the seven princes come out into the churchyard than they became foals again, and Cinderlad got upon the back of the youngest, and they returned by the way they had come, only they went much, much faster.

First they went over the bridge, and then past the trunk of the birch tree, and then past the old hag who sat in the cleft of the rock spinning, and they went by so fast that Cinderlad could not hear what the old hag screeched after him, but just heard enough to understand that she was terribly enraged.

It was all but dark when they got back to the King at nightfall, and he himself was standing in the courtyard waiting for them.

"Hast thou watched well and faithfully the whole day?" said the King to Cinderlad.

"I have done my best," replied Cinderlad.

"Then thou canst tell me what my seven foals eat and drink?" asked the King.

So Cinderlad pulled out the consecrated bread and the flask of wine, and showed them to the King. "Here may you behold their meat, and here their drink," said he.

"Yes, diligently and faithfully hast thou watched," said the King, "and thou shalt have the Princess and half the kingdom."

So all was made ready for the wedding, and the King said that it was to be so stately and magnificent that everyone should hear of it, and everyone inquire about it.

But when they sat down to the marriage-feast, the bridegroom arose and went down to the stable, for he said that he had forgotten something which he must go and look to. When he got there, he did what the foals had bidden him, and cut off the heads of all the seven. First the eldest, and then the second, and so on according to their age, and he was extremely careful to lay each head at the tail of the foal to which it had belonged, and when that was done, all the foals became princes again. When he returned to the marriage-feast with the seven princes, the King was so joyful that he both kissed Cinderlad and clapped him on the back, and his bride was still more delighted with him than she had been before.

"Half my kingdom is thine already," said the King, "and the other half shall be thine after my death, for my sons can get countries and kingdoms for themselves now that they have become princes again."

Therefore, as all may well believe, there was joy and merriment at that wedding.

The Fir Tree

(Danish)

FAR DOWN IN THE FOREST, where the warm sun and the fresh air made a sweet resting-place, grew a pretty little fir tree; and yet it was not happy, it wished so much to be tall like its companions – the pines and firs which grew around it. The sun shone, and the soft air fluttered its leaves, and the little peasant children passed by, prattling merrily, but the fir tree heeded them not. Sometimes the children would bring a large basket of raspberries or strawberries, wreathed on a straw, and seat themselves near the fir tree, and say, "Is it not a pretty little tree?" which made it feel more unhappy than before. And yet all this while the tree grew a notch or joint taller every year; for by the number of joints in the stem of a fir tree we can discover its age. Still, as it grew, it complained, "Oh! how I wish I were as tall as the other trees, then I would spread out my branches on every side, and my top would over-look the wide world. I should have the birds building their nests on my boughs, and when the wind blew, I should bow with stately dignity like my tall companions." The tree was so discontented, that it took no pleasure in the warm sunshine, the birds, or the rosy clouds that floated over it morning and evening. Sometimes, in winter, when the snow lay white and glittering on the ground, a hare would come springing along, and jump right over the little tree; and then how mortified it would feel! Two winters passed, and when the third arrived, the tree had grown so tall that the hare was obliged to run round it. Yet it remained unsatisfied, and would exclaim, "Oh, if I could but keep on growing tall and old! There is nothing else worth caring for in the world!" In the autumn, as usual, the woodcutters came and cut down several of the tallest trees, and the young fir tree, which was now grown to its full height, shuddered as the noble trees fell to the earth with a crash. After the branches were lopped off, the trunks looked so slender and bare, that they could scarcely be recognized. Then they were placed upon wagons, and drawn by horses out of the forest. "Where were they going? What would become of them?" The young fir tree wished very much to know; so in the spring, when the swallows and the storks came, it asked, "Do you know where those trees were taken? Did you meet them?"

The swallows knew nothing, but the stork, after a little reflection, nodded his head, and said, "Yes, I think I do. I met several new ships when I flew from Egypt, and they had fine masts that smelt like fir. I think these must have been the trees; I assure you they were stately, very stately."

"Oh, how I wish I were tall enough to go on the sea," said the fir tree. "What is the sea, and what does it look like?"

"It would take too much time to explain," said the stork, flying quickly away.

"Rejoice in thy youth," said the sunbeam; "rejoice in thy fresh growth, and the young life that is in thee."

And the wind kissed the tree, and the dew watered it with tears; but the fir tree regarded them not.

Christmastime drew near, and many young trees were cut down, some even smaller and younger than the fir tree who enjoyed neither rest nor peace with longing to leave its forest home. These young trees, which were chosen for their beauty, kept their branches, and were also laid on wagons and drawn by horses out of the forest.

"Where are they going?" asked the fir tree. "They are not taller than I am: indeed, one is much less; and why are the branches not cut off? Where are they going?"

"We know, we know," sang the sparrows; "we have looked in at the windows of the houses in the town, and we know what is done with them. They are dressed up in the most splendid manner. We have seen them standing in the middle of a warm room, and adorned with all sorts of beautiful things, – honey cakes, gilded apples, playthings, and many hundreds of wax tapers."

"And then," asked the fir tree, trembling through all its branches, "and then what happens?"

"We did not see any more," said the sparrows; "but this was enough for us."

"I wonder whether anything so brilliant will ever happen to me," thought the fir tree. "It would be much better than crossing the sea. I long for it almost with pain. Oh! when will Christmas be here? I am now as tall and well grown as those which were taken away last year. Oh! that I were now laid on the wagon, or standing in the warm room, with all that brightness and splendour around me! Something better and more beautiful is to come after, or the trees would not be so decked out. Yes, what follows will be grander and more splendid. What can it be? I am weary with longing. I scarcely know how I feel."

"Rejoice with us," said the air and the sunlight. "Enjoy thine own bright life in the fresh air."

But the tree would not rejoice, though it grew taller every day; and, winter and summer, its dark-green foliage might be seen in the forest, while passers by would say, "What a beautiful tree!"

A short time before Christmas, the discontented fir tree was the first to fall. As the axe cut through the stem, and divided the pith, the tree fell with a groan to the earth, conscious of pain and faintness, and forgetting all its anticipations of happiness, in sorrow at leaving its home in the forest. It knew that it should never again see its dear old companions, the trees, nor the little bushes and many-coloured flowers that had grown by its side; perhaps not even the birds. Neither was the journey at all pleasant. The tree first recovered itself while being unpacked in the courtyard of a house, with several other trees; and it heard a man say, "We only want one, and this is the prettiest."

Then came two servants in grand livery, and carried the fir tree into a large and beautiful apartment. On the walls hung pictures, and near the great stove stood great china vases, with lions on the lids. There were rocking chairs, silken sofas, large tables, covered with pictures, books, and playthings, worth a great deal of money, – at least, the children said so. Then the fir tree was placed in a large tub, full of sand; but green baize hung all around it, so that no one could see it was a tub, and it stood on a very handsome carpet. How the fir tree trembled! "What was going to happen to him now?" Some young ladies came, and the servants helped them to adorn the tree. On one branch they hung little bags cut out of coloured paper, and each bag was filled with sweetmeats; from other branches hung gilded apples and walnuts, as if they had grown there; and above, and all round, were hundreds of red, blue, and white tapers, which were fastened on the branches. Dolls, exactly like real babies, were placed under the green leaves, – the tree had never seen such things before, – and at the very top was fastened a glittering star, made of tinsel. Oh, it was very beautiful!

"This evening," they all exclaimed, "how bright it will be!" "Oh, that the evening were come," thought the tree, "and the tapers lighted! then I shall know what else is going to happen. Will the trees of the forest come to see me? I wonder if the sparrows will peep in at the windows as they fly? shall I grow faster here, and keep on all these ornaments summer and winter?" But guessing was of very little use; it made his bark ache, and this pain is as bad for a slender fir tree, as headache is for us. At last the tapers were lighted, and then what a glistening blaze of light the tree presented! It trembled so with joy in all its branches, that one of the candles fell among the green leaves and burnt some of them. "Help! help!" exclaimed the young ladies, but there was no danger, for they quickly extinguished the fire. After this, the tree tried not to tremble at all, though the fire frightened him; he was so anxious not to hurt any of the beautiful ornaments, even while their brilliancy dazzled him. And now the folding doors were thrown open, and a troop of children rushed in as if they intended to upset the tree; they were followed more silently by their elders. For a moment the little ones stood silent with astonishment, and then they shouted for joy, till the room rang, and they danced merrily round the tree, while one present after another was taken from it.

"What are they doing? What will happen next?" thought the fir. At last the candles burnt down to the branches and were put out. Then the children received permission to plunder the tree.

Oh, how they rushed upon it, till the branches cracked, and had it not been fastened with the glistening star to the ceiling, it must have been thrown down. The children then danced about with their pretty toys, and no one noticed the tree, except the children's maid who came and peeped among the branches to see if an apple or a fig had been forgotten.

"A story, a story," cried the children, pulling a little fat man towards the tree.

"Now we shall be in the green shade," said the man, as he seated himself under it, "and the tree will have the pleasure of hearing also, but I shall only relate one story; what shall it be? 'Ivede-Avede,' or 'Humpty Dumpty,' who fell downstairs, but soon got up again, and at last married a princess."

"'Ivede-Avede,'" cried some. "'Humpty Dumpty,'" cried others, and there was a fine shouting and crying out. But the fir tree remained quite still, and thought to himself, "Shall I have anything to do with all this?" but he had already amused them as much as they wished. Then the old man told them the story of 'Humpty Dumpty,' how he fell downstairs, and was raised up again, and married a princess. And the children clapped their hands and cried, "Tell another, tell another," for they wanted to hear the story of 'Ivede-Avede'; but they only had 'Humpty Dumpty.' After this the fir tree became quite silent and thoughtful; never had the birds in the forest told such tales as 'Humpty Dumpty,' who fell downstairs, and yet married a princess.

"Ah! yes, so it happens in the world," thought the fir tree; he believed it all, because it was related by such a nice man. "Ah! well," he thought, "who knows? perhaps I may fall down too, and marry a princess"; and he looked forward joyfully to the next evening, expecting to be again decked out with lights and playthings, gold and fruit. "Tomorrow I will not tremble," thought he; "I will enjoy all my splendour, and I shall hear the story of 'Humpty Dumpty' again, and perhaps 'Ivede-Avede.'" And the tree remained quiet and thoughtful all night. In the morning the servants and the housemaid came in. "Now," thought the fir, "all my splendour is going to begin again." But they dragged him out of the room and upstairs to the garret, and threw him on the floor, in a dark corner, where no daylight shone, and there they left him. "What does this mean?" thought the tree, "what am I to do here? I can hear nothing in a place like this," and he had time enough to think, for days and nights passed and no one came near him, and when at last somebody did come, it was only to put away large boxes in a corner. So the tree was completely hidden from sight as if it had never existed. "It is winter now," thought the tree, "the ground is hard and covered with snow, so that people cannot plant me. I shall be sheltered here, I dare say, until spring comes. How thoughtful and kind everybody is to me! Still I wish this place were not so dark, as well as lonely, with not even a little hare to look at. How pleasant it was out in the forest while the snow lay on the ground, when the hare would run by, yes, and jump over me too, although I did not like it then. Oh! it is terrible lonely here."

"Squeak, squeak," said a little mouse, creeping cautiously towards the tree; then came another; and they both sniffed at the fir tree and crept between the branches.

"Oh, it is very cold," said the little mouse, "or else we should be so comfortable here, shouldn't we, you old fir tree?"

"I am not old," said the fir tree, "there are many who are older than I am."

"Where do you come from? and what do you know?" asked the mice, who were full of curiosity. "Have you seen the most beautiful places in the world, and can you tell us all about them? and have you been in the storeroom, where cheeses lie on the shelf, and hams hang from the ceiling? One can run about on tallow candles there, and go in thin and come out fat."

"I know nothing of that place," said the fir tree, "but I know the wood where the sun shines and the birds sing." And then the tree told the little mice all about its youth. They had never heard such an account in their lives; and after they had listened to it attentively, they said, "What a number of things you have seen? you must have been very happy."

"Happy!" exclaimed the fir tree, and then as he reflected upon what he had been telling them, he said, "Ah, yes! after all those were happy days." But when he went on and related all about Christmas Eve, and how he had been dressed up with cakes and lights, the mice said, "How happy you must have been, you old fir tree."

"I am not old at all," replied the tree, "I only came from the forest this winter, I am now checked in my growth."

"What splendid stories you can relate," said the little mice. And the next night four other mice came with them to hear what the tree had to tell. The more he talked the more he remembered, and then he thought to himself, "Those were happy days, but they may come again. Humpty Dumpty fell downstairs, and yet he married the princess; perhaps I may marry a princess too." And the fir tree thought of the pretty little birch tree that grew in the forest, which was to him a real beautiful princess.

"Who is Humpty Dumpty?" asked the little mice. And then the tree related the whole story; he could remember every single word, and the little mice was so delighted with it, that they were ready to jump to the top of the tree. The next night a great many more mice made their appearance, and on Sunday two rats came with them; but they said, it was not a pretty story at all, and the little mice were very sorry, for it made them also think less of it.

"Do you know only one story?" asked the rats.

"Only one," replied the fir tree; "I heard it on the happiest evening of my life; but I did not know I was so happy at the time."

"We think it is a very miserable story," said the rats. "Don't you know any story about bacon, or tallow in the storeroom."

"No," replied the tree.

"Many thanks to you then," replied the rats, and they marched off.

The little mice also kept away after this, and the tree sighed, and said, "It was very pleasant when the merry little mice sat round me and listened while I talked. Now that is all passed too. However, I shall consider myself happy when someone comes to take me out of this place." But would this ever happen? Yes; one morning people came to clear out the garret, the boxes were packed away, and the tree was pulled out of the corner, and thrown roughly on the garret floor; then the servant dragged it out upon the staircase where the daylight shone. "Now life is beginning again," said the tree, rejoicing in the sunshine and fresh air. Then it was carried downstairs and taken into the courtyard so quickly, that it forgot to think of itself, and could only look about, there was so much to be seen. The court was close to a garden, where everything looked blooming. Fresh and fragrant roses hung over the little palings. The linden trees were in blossom; while the swallows flew here and there, crying, "Twit, twit, twit, my mate is coming," – but it was not the fir tree they meant. "Now I shall live," cried the tree, joyfully spreading out its branches; but alas! they were all withered and yellow, and it lay in a corner amongst weeds and nettles. The star of gold paper still stuck in the top of the tree and glittered in the sunshine. In the same courtyard two of the merry children were playing who had danced round the tree at Christmas, and had been so happy. The youngest saw the gilded star, and ran and pulled it off the tree. "Look what is sticking to the ugly old fir tree," said the child, treading on the branches till they crackled under his boots. And the tree saw all the fresh bright flowers in the garden, and then looked at itself, and wished it had remained in the dark corner of the garret. It thought of its fresh youth in the forest, of the merry Christmas evening, and of the little mice who had listened to the story of 'Humpty Dumpty.' "Past! past!" said the old tree; "Oh, had I but enjoyed myself while I could have done so! but now it is too late." Then a lad came and chopped the tree into small pieces, till a large bundle lay in a heap on the ground. The pieces were placed in a fire under the copper, and they quickly blazed up brightly, while the tree sighed so deeply that each sigh was like a pistol-shot. Then the children, who were at play, came and seated themselves in front of the fire, and looked at it and cried, "Pop, pop." But at each "pop," which was a deep sigh, the tree was thinking of a summer day in the forest; and of Christmas evening, and of "Humpty Dumpty," the only story it had ever heard or knew how to relate, till at last it was consumed. The boys still played in the garden, and the youngest wore the golden star on his breast, with which the tree had been adorned during the happiest evening of its existence. Now all was past; the tree's life was past, and the story also, – for all stories must come to an end at last

The Tinderbox

(Danish)

A SOLDIER CAME MARCHING along the high road: "Left, right – left, right." He had his knapsack on his back, and a sword at his side; he had been to the wars, and was now returning home.

As he walked on, he met a very frightful-looking old witch in the road. Her under-lip hung quite down on her breast, and she stopped and said, "Good evening, soldier; you have a very fine sword, and a large knapsack, and you are a real soldier; so you shall have as much money as ever you like."

"Thank you, old witch," said the soldier.

"Do you see that large tree," said the witch, pointing to a tree which stood beside them. "Well, it is quite hollow inside, and you must climb to the top, when you will see a hole, through which you can let yourself down into the tree to a great depth. I will tie a rope round your body, so that I can pull you up again when you call out to me."

"But what am I to do, down there in the tree?" asked the soldier.

"Get money," she replied; "for you must know that when you reach the ground under the tree, you will find yourself in a large hall, lighted up by three hundred lamps; you will then see three doors, which can be easily opened, for the keys are in all the locks. On entering the first of the chambers, to which these doors lead, you will see a large chest, standing in the middle of the floor, and upon it a dog seated, with a pair of eyes as large as teacups. But you need not be at all afraid of him; I will give you my blue checked apron, which you must spread upon the floor, and then boldly seize hold of the dog, and place him upon it. You can then open the chest, and take from it as many pence as you please, they are only copper pence; but if you would rather have silver money, you must go into the second chamber. Here you will find another dog, with eyes as big as mill-wheels; but do not let that trouble you. Place him upon my apron, and then take what money you please. If, however, you like gold best, enter the third chamber, where there is another chest full of it. The dog who sits on this chest is very dreadful; his eyes are as big as a tower, but do not mind him. If he also is placed upon my apron, he cannot hurt you, and you may take from the chest what gold you will."

"This is not a bad story," said the soldier; "but what am I to give you, you old witch? for, of course, you do not mean to tell me all this for nothing."

"No," said the witch; "but I do not ask for a single penny. Only promise to bring me an old tinder-box, which my grandmother left behind the last time she went down there."

"Very well; I promise. Now tie the rope round my body."

"Here it is," replied the witch; "and here is my blue checked apron."

As soon as the rope was tied, the soldier climbed up the tree, and let himself down through the hollow to the ground beneath; and here he found, as the witch had told him, a large hall, in which many hundred lamps were all burning. Then he opened the first door. "Ah!" there sat the dog, with the eyes as large as teacups, staring at him.

"You're a pretty fellow," said the soldier, seizing him, and placing him on the witch's apron, while he filled his pockets from the chest with as many pieces as they would hold. Then he closed the lid, seated the dog upon it again, and walked into another chamber, And, sure enough, there sat the dog with eyes as big as mill-wheels.

"You had better not look at me in that way," said the soldier; "you will make your eyes water"; and then he seated him also upon the apron, and opened the chest. But when he saw what a quantity of silver money it contained, he very quickly threw away all the coppers he had taken, and filled his pockets and his knapsack with nothing but silver.

Then he went into the third room, and there the dog was really hideous; his eyes were, truly, as big as towers, and they turned round and round in his head like wheels.

"Good morning," said the soldier, touching his cap, for he had never seen such a dog in his life. But after looking at him more closely, he thought he had been civil enough, so he placed him on the floor, and opened the chest. Good gracious, what a quantity of gold there was! enough to buy all the sugar-sticks of the sweet-stuff women; all the tin soldiers, whips, and rocking-horses in the world, or even the whole town itself There was, indeed, an immense quantity. So the soldier now threw away all the silver money he had taken, and filled his pockets and his knapsack with gold instead; and not only his pockets and his knapsack, but even his cap and boots, so that he could scarcely walk.

He was really rich now; so he replaced the dog on the chest, closed the door, and called up through the tree, "Now pull me out, you old witch."

"Have you got the tinder-box?" asked the witch.

"No; I declare I quite forgot it." So he went back and fetched the tinderbox, and then the witch drew him up out of the tree, and he stood again in the high road, with his pockets, his knapsack, his cap, and his boots full of gold.

"What are you going to do with the tinder-box?" asked the soldier.

"That is nothing to you," replied the witch; "you have the money, now give me the tinder-box."

"I tell you what," said the soldier, "if you don't tell me what you are going to do with it, I will draw my sword and cut off your head."

"No," said the witch.

The soldier immediately cut off her head, and there she lay on the ground. Then he tied up all his money in her apron, and slung it on his back like a bundle, put the tinderbox in his pocket, and walked off to the nearest town. It was a very nice town, and he put up at the best inn, and ordered a dinner of all his favourite dishes, for now he was rich and had plenty of money.

The servant, who cleaned his boots, thought they certainly were a shabby pair to be worn by such a rich gentleman, for he had not yet bought any new ones. The next day, however, he procured some good clothes and proper boots, so that our soldier soon became known as a fine gentleman, and the people visited him, and told him all the wonders that were to be seen in the town, and of the king's beautiful daughter, the princess.

"Where can I see her?" asked the soldier.

"She is not to be seen at all," they said; "she lives in a large copper castle, surrounded by walls and towers. No one but the king himself can pass in or out, for there has been a prophecy that she will marry a common soldier, and the king cannot bear to think of such a marriage."

"I should like very much to see her," thought the soldier; but he could not obtain permission to do so. However, he passed a very pleasant time; went to the theatre, drove in the king's garden, and gave a great deal of money to the poor, which was very good of him; he remembered what it had been in olden times to be without a shilling. Now he was rich, had fine clothes, and many friends, who all declared he was a fine fellow and a real gentleman, and all this gratified him exceedingly. But his money would not last forever; and as he spent and gave away a great deal daily, and received none, he found himself at last with only two shillings left. So he was obliged to leave his elegant rooms, and live in a little garret under the roof, where he had to clean his own boots, and even mend them with a large needle. None of his friends came to see him, there were too many stairs to mount up. One dark evening, he had not even a penny to buy a candle; then all at once he remembered that there was a piece of candle stuck in the tinder-box, which he had brought from the old tree, into which the witch had helped him.

He found the tinder-box, but no sooner had he struck a few sparks from the flint and steel, than the door flew open and the dog with eyes as big as teacups, whom he had seen while down in the tree, stood before him, and said, "What orders, master?"

"Hallo," said the soldier; "well this is a pleasant tinderbox, if it brings me all I wish for."

"Bring me some money," said he to the dog.

He was gone in a moment, and presently returned, carrying a large bag of coppers in his month. The soldier very soon discovered after this the value of the tinder-box. If he struck the flint once, the dog who sat on the chest of copper money made his appearance; if twice, the dog came from the chest of silver; and if three times, the dog with eyes like towers, who watched over the gold. The soldier had now plenty of money; he returned to his elegant rooms, and reappeared in his fine clothes, so that his friends knew him again directly, and made as much of him as before.

After a while he began to think it was very strange that no one could get a look at the princess. "Everyone says she is very beautiful," thought he to himself; "but what is the use of that if she is to be shut up in a copper castle surrounded by so many towers. Can I by any means get to see her. Stop! where is my tinder-box?" Then he struck a light, and in a moment the dog, with eyes as big as teacups, stood before him.

"It is midnight," said the soldier, "yet I should very much like to see the princess, if only for a moment."

The dog disappeared instantly, and before the soldier could even look round, he returned with the princess. She was lying on the dog's back asleep, and looked so lovely, that everyone who saw her would know she was a real princess. The soldier could not help kissing her, true soldier as he was. Then the dog ran back with the princess; but in the morning, while at breakfast with the king and queen, she told them what a singular dream she had had during the night, of a dog and a soldier, that she had ridden on the dog's back, and been kissed by the soldier.

"That is a very pretty story, indeed," said the queen. So the next night one of the old ladies of the court was set to watch by the princess's bed, to discover whether it really was a dream, or what else it might be.

The soldier longed very much to see the princess once more, so he sent for the dog again in the night to fetch her, and to run with her as fast as ever he could. But the old lady put on water boots, and ran after him as quickly as he did, and found that he carried the princess into a large house. She thought it would help her to remember the place if she made a large cross on the door with a piece of chalk. Then she went home to bed, and the dog presently returned with the princess. But when he saw that a cross had been made on the door of the house, where the soldier lived, he took another piece of chalk and made crosses on all the doors in the town, so that the lady-in-waiting might not be able to find out the right door.

Early the next morning the king and queen accompanied the lady and all the officers of the household, to see where the princess had been.

"Here it is," said the king, when they came to the first door with a cross on it.

"No, my dear husband, it must be that one," said the queen, pointing to a second door having a cross also.

"And here is one, and there is another!" they all exclaimed; for there were crosses on all the doors in every direction.

So they felt it would be useless to search any farther. But the queen was a very clever woman; she could do a great deal more than merely ride in a carriage. She took her large gold scissors, cut a piece of silk into squares, and made a neat little bag. This bag she filled with buckwheat flour, and tied it round the princess's neck; and then she cut a small hole in the bag, so that the flour might be scattered on the ground as the princess went along. During the night, the dog came again and carried the princess on his back, and ran with her to the soldier, who loved her very much, and wished that he had been a prince, so that he might have her for a wife. The dog did not observe how the flour ran out of the bag all the way from the castle wall to the soldier's house, and even up to the window, where he had climbed with the princess. Therefore in the morning the king and queen found out where their daughter had been, and the soldier was taken up and put in prison.

Oh, how dark and disagreeable it was as he sat there, and the people said to him, "Tomorrow you will be hanged." It was not very pleasant news, and besides, he had left the tinder-box at the inn. In the morning he could see through the iron grating of the little window how the people were hastening out of the town to see him hanged; he heard the drums beating, and saw the soldiers marching. Everyone ran out to look at them, and a shoemaker's boy, with a leather apron and slippers on, galloped by so fast, that one of his slippers flew off and struck against the wall where the soldier sat looking through the iron grating. "Hallo, you shoemaker's boy, you need not be in such a hurry," cried the soldier to him. "There will be nothing to see till I come; but if you will run to the house where I have been living, and bring me my tinder-box, you shall have four shillings, but you must put your best foot foremost."

The shoemaker's boy liked the idea of getting the four shillings, so he ran very fast and fetched the tinder-box, and gave it to the soldier. And now we shall see what happened. Outside the town a large gibbet had been erected, round which stood the soldiers and several thousands of people. The king and the queen sat on splendid thrones opposite to the judges and the whole council. The soldier already stood on the ladder; but as they were about to place the rope around his neck, he said that an innocent request was often granted to a poor criminal before he suffered death. He wished very much to smoke a pipe, as it would be the last pipe he should ever smoke in the world. The king could not refuse this request, so the soldier took his tinder-box, and struck fire, once, twice, thrice, – and there in a moment stood all the dogs; – the one with eyes as big as teacups, the one with eyes as large as mill-wheels, and the third, whose eyes were like towers. "Help me now, that I may not be hanged," cried the soldier.

And the dogs fell upon the judges and all the councillors; seized one by the legs, and another by the nose, and tossed them many feet high in the air, so that they fell down and were dashed to pieces.

"I will not be touched," said the king. But the largest dog seized him, as well as the queen, and threw them after the others. Then the soldiers and all the people were afraid, and cried, "Good soldier, you shall be our king, and you shall marry the beautiful princess."

So they placed the soldier in the king's carriage, and the three dogs ran on in front and cried "Hurrah!" and the little boys whistled through their fingers, and the soldiers presented arms. The princess came out of the copper castle, and became queen, which was very pleasing to her. The wedding festivities lasted a whole week, and the dogs sat at the table, and stared with all their eyes.

Faithful and Unfaithful

(Swedish/German)

ONCE UPON A TIME there was a couple of humble cottagers who had no children until, at last, the man's wife was blessed with a boy, which made both of them very happy. They named him Faithful and when he was christened a *huldra* came to the hut, seated herself beside the child's cradle, and foretold that he would meet with good fortune. "What is more," she said, "when he is fifteen years of age, I will make him a present of a horse with many rare qualities, a horse that has the gift of speech!" And with that the *huldra* turned and went away.

The boy grew up and became strong and powerful. And when he had passed his fifteenth year, a strange old man came up to their hut one day, knocked, and said that the horse he was leading had been sent by his queen, and that henceforward it was to belong to Faithful, as she had promised. Then the ancient man departed; but the beautiful horse was admired by all, and Faithful learned to love it more with every passing day.

At length he grew weary of home. "I must away and try my fortune in the world," said he, and his parents did not like to object; for there was not much to wish for at home. So he led his dear horse from the stable, swung himself into the saddle, and rode hurriedly into the wood. He rode on and on, and had already covered a good bit of ground, when he saw two lions engaged in a struggle with a tiger, and they were well-nigh overcome. "Make haste to take your bow," said the horse, "shoot the tiger and deliver the two lions!" "Yes, that's what I will do," said the youth, fitted an arrow to the bow-string, and in a moment the tiger lay prone on the ground. The two lions drew nearer, nuzzled their preserver in a friendly and grateful manner, and then hastened back to their cave.

Faithful now rode along for a long time among the great trees until he suddenly spied two terrified white doves fleeing from a hawk who was on the point of catching them. "Make haste to take your bow," said the horse, "shoot the hawk and save the two doves!" "Yes, that's what I'll do," said the youth. He fitted an arrow to the bow-string, and in a moment the hawk lay prone on the ground. But the two doves flew nearer, fluttered about their deliverer in a tame and grateful manner, and then hurried back to their nest.

The youth pressed on through the wood and by now was far, far from home. But his horse did not tire easily, and ran on with him until they came to a great lake. There he saw a gull rise up from the water, holding a pike in its claws. "Make haste to take your bow," said the horse, "shoot the gull and save the pike!" "Yes, that's what I'll do," answered the youth, fitted an arrow to his bow-string, and in a moment the gull was threshing the ground with its wings, mortally wounded. But the pike who had been saved swam nearer, gave his deliverer a friendly, grateful glance, and then dove down to join his fellows beneath the waves.

Faithful rode on again, and before evening came to a great castle. He at once had himself announced to the king, and begged that the latter would take him into his service. "What kind of a place do you want?" asked the king, who was inclined to look with favour on the bold horseman.

"I should like to be a groom," was Faithful's answer, "but first of all I must have stable-room and fodder for my horse." "That you shall have," said the king, and the youth was taken on as a groom, and served so long and so well, that everyone in the castle liked him, and the king in particular praised him highly.

But among the other servitors was one named Unfaithful who was jealous of Faithful, and did what he could to harm him; for he thought to himself:

"Then I would be rid of him, and need not see him continue to rise in my lord's favour." Now it happened that the king was very sad, for he had lost his queen, whom a troll had stolen from the castle. It is true that the queen had not taken pleasure in the king's society, and that she did not love him. Still the king longed for her greatly, and often spoke of it to Unfaithful his servant. So one day Unfaithful said: "My lord need distress himself no longer, for Faithful has been boasting to me that he could rescue your beautiful queen from the hands of the troll." "If he has done so," replied the king, "then he must keep his word."

He straightaway ordered Faithful to be brought before him, and threatened him with death if he did not at once hurry into the hill and bring back the wife of whom he had been robbed. If he were successful great honour should be his reward. In vain Faithful denied what Unfaithful had said of him. The king stuck to his demand, and the youth withdrew, convinced that he had not long to live. Then he went to the stable to bid farewell to his beautiful horse, and stood beside him and wept. "What grieves you so?" asked the horse. Then the youth told him of all that had happened, and said that this was probably the last time he would be able to visit him. "If it be no more than that," said the horse, "there is a way to help you. Up in the garret of the castle there is an old fiddle, take it with you and play it when you come to the place where the queen is kept. And fashion for yourself armour of steel wire, and set knives into it everywhere, and then, when you see the troll open his jaws, descend into his maw, and thus slay him. But you must have no fear, and must trust me to show you the way." These words filled the youth with fresh courage. He went to the king and received permission to leave, secretly fashioned his steel armour, took the old fiddle from the garret of the castle, led his dear horse out of the stable, and without delay set forth for the troll's hill.

Before long he saw it, and rode directly to the troll's abode. When he came near, he saw the troll, who had crept out of his castle, lying stretched out at the entrance to his cave, fast asleep, and snoring so powerfully that the whole hill shook. But his mouth was wide open, and his maw was so tremendous that it was easy for the youth to crawl into it. He did so, for he was not afraid, and made his way into the troll's innards where he was so active that the troll was soon killed. Then Faithful crept out again, laid aside his armour, and entered the troll's castle. Within the great golden hall sat the captive queen, fettered with seven strong chains of gold. Faithful could not break the strong chains; but he took up his fiddle and played such tender music on it, that the golden chains were moved, and one after another, fell from the queen, until she was able to rise and was free once more. She looked at the courageous youth with joy and gratitude, and felt very kindly toward him, because he was so handsome and courteous. And the queen was perfectly willing to return with him to the king's castle.

The return of the queen gave rise to great joy, and Faithful received the promised reward from the king. But now the queen treated her husband with even less consideration than before. She would not exchange a word with him, she did not laugh, and locked herself up in her room with her gloomy thoughts. This greatly vexed the king, and one day he asked the queen why she was so sad: "Well," said she, "I cannot be happy unless I have the beautiful golden hall which I had in the hill at the troll's; for a hall like that is to be found nowhere else."

"It will be no easy matter to obtain it for you," said the king, "and I cannot promise you that anyone will be able to do it." But when he complained of his difficulty to his servant Unfaithful, the latter answered: "The chances of success are not so bad, for Faithful said he could easily bring the troll's golden hall to the castle." Faithful was at once sent for, and the king commanded him, as he loved his life, to make good his word and bring the golden hall from the troll's hill. It was in vain that Faithful denied Unfaithful's assertions: go he must, and bring back the golden hall.

Inconsolable, he went to his beautiful horse, wept and wanted to say farewell to him forever. "What troubles you?" asked the horse. And the youth replied: "Unfaithful has again been telling lies about me, and if I do not bring the troll's golden hall to the queen, my life will be forfeited." "Is it nothing more serious than that?" said the horse. "See that you obtain a great ship, take your fiddle with you and play the golden hall out of the hill, then hitch the troll's horses before it, and you will be able to bring the glistening hall here without trouble."

Then Faithful felt somewhat better, did as the horse had told him, and was successful in reaching the great hill. And as he stood there playing the fiddle, the golden hall heard him, and was drawn to the sounding music, and it moved slowly, slowly, until it stood outside the hill. It was built of virgin gold, like a house by itself, and under it were many wheels. Then the youth took the troll's horses, put them to the golden hall, and thus brought it aboard his ship. Soon he had crossed the lake, and brought it along safely so that it reached the castle without damage, to the great joy of the queen. Yet despite the fact, she was as weary of everything as she had been before, never spoke to her husband, the king, and no one ever saw her laugh.

Now the king grew even more vexed than he had been, and again asked her why she seemed so sad. "Ah, how can I be happy unless I have the two colts that used to belong to me, when I stayed at the troll's! Such handsome steeds are to be seen nowhere else!" "It will be anything but easy to obtain for you what you want," declared the king, "for they were untamed, and long ago must have run far away into the wild wood." Then he left her, sadly, and did not know what to do. But Unfaithful said: "Let my lord give himself no concern, for Faithful has declared he could easily secure both of the troll's colts." Faithful was at once sent for, and the king threatened him with death, if he did not show his powers in the matter of the colts. But should he succeed in catching them, then he would be rewarded.

Now Faithful knew quite well that he could not hope to catch the troll's wild colts, and he once more turned to the stable in order to bid farewell to the *huldra*'s gift. "Why do you weep over such a trifle?" said the horse. "Hurry to the wood, play your fiddle, and all will be well!" Faithful did as he was told, and after a while the two lions whom he had rescued came leaping toward him, listened to his playing and asked him whether he was in distress. "Yes, indeed," said Faithful, and told them what he had to do. They at once ran back into the wood, one to one side and the other to the other, and returned quickly, driving the two colts before them. Then Faithful played his fiddle and the colts followed him, so that he soon reached the king's castle in safety, and could deliver the steeds to the queen.

The king now expected that his wife would be gay and happy. But she did not change, never addressed a word to him, and only seemed a little less sad when she happened to speak to the daring youth.

Then the king asked her to tell him what she lacked, and why she was so discontented. She answered: "I have secured the colts of the troll, and I often sit in the glittering hall of gold; but I can open none of the handsome chests that are filled to the brim with my valuables, because I have no keys. And if I do not get the keys again, how can I be happy?" "And where may the keys be?" asked the king. "In the lake by the troll's hill," said the queen, "for that is where I threw them when Faithful brought me here." "This is a ticklish affair, this business of those keys you want!" said the king. "And I can scarcely promise that you will ever see them again." In spite of this, however, he was willing to make an attempt, and talked it over with his servant Unfaithful. "Why, that is easily done," said the latter, "for Faithful boasted to me that he could get the queen's keys without any difficulty if he wished." "Then I shall compel him to keep his word," said the king. And he at once ordered Faithful, on pain of death, to get the queen's keys out of the lake by the troll's hill without delay.

This time the youth was not so depressed, for he thought to himself: "My wise horse will be able to help me." And so he was, for he advised him to go along playing his fiddle, and to wait for what might happen. After the youth had played for a while, the pike he had saved thrust his head out of the water, recognized him, and asked whether he could be of any service to him. "Yes, indeed!" said the youth, and told him what it was he wanted. The pike at once dived, quickly rose to the surface of the water with the golden keys in his mouth, and gave them to his deliverer. The latter hastened back with them, and now the queen could open the great chests in the golden hall to her heart's content.

Notwithstanding, the king's wife was as sorrowful as ever, and when the king complained about it to Unfaithful, the latter said: "No doubt it is because she loves Faithful. I would therefore advise that my lord have him beheaded. Then there will be a change." This advice suited the king well, and he determined to carry it out shortly. But one day Faithful's horse said to him: "The king is going to have your head chopped off. So hurry to the wood, play your fiddle, and beg the two doves to bring you a bottle of the water of life. Then go to the queen and ask her to set your head on your body and to sprinkle you with the water when you have been beheaded." Faithful did so. He went to the wood that very day with his fiddle, and before long the two doves were fluttering around him, and shortly after brought back the bottle filled with the water of life. He took it back home with him and gave it to the queen, so that she might sprinkle him with it after he had been beheaded. She did so, and at once Faithful rose again, as full of life as ever; but far better looking. The king was astonished at what he had seen, and told the queen to cut off his own head and then sprinkle him with the water. She at once seized the sword, and in a moment the king's head rolled to the ground. But she sprinkled none of the water of life upon it, and the king's body was quickly carried out and buried. Then the queen and Faithful celebrated their wedding with great pomp; but Unfaithful was banished from the land and went away in disgrace. The wise horse dwelt contentedly in a wonderful chamber, and the king and queen kept the magic fiddle, the golden hall, and the troll's other valuables, and lived in peace and happiness day after day.

Helge-Hal in the Blue Hill

(Norwegian)

ONCE UPON A TIME there was a sinister old couple, who lived out under the open sky. All that they had were three sons, an old cook-pot, an old frying-pan, and an old cat. Then the man died, and after a time his wife died, too. Now their estate was to be divided. So the oldest took the old cook-pot, and the second took the old frying-pan, and Ebe Ashpeter had no choice. He had to take the old cat, and they did not ask him whether he wanted to or not.

"Brother Peter can scrape out the cook-pot after he has loaned it out," said Ebe. "Brother Paul gets a crust of bread when he lends out his frying-pan; but what am I to do with this wretched cat?" And he was angry and envious. Yet he scratched the cat and stroked it, and this pleased the cat so that she began to purr, and raised her tail in the air.

"Wait, wait, I'll help you yet," said the cat, "wait, wait, I'll help you yet!"

There was nothing to bite or break in the hut. Brother Peter and Brother Paul had each of them gone off in a different direction. So Ebe set out, too, with the cat in the lead, himself following; but after a time he turned and went home again, to see whether the floor had been swept, and the cat tripped on alone. After she had gone her way, tipp, tapp, tipp, tapp, for a while, she came to a great rock, and there she met an enormous herd of reindeer. The cat crept softly around the herd, and then with one leap sprang between the horns of the finest buck.

"If you do not go where I want you to, I'll scratch out your eyes, and drive you over rock and precipice!" said she. So the buck did not dare do anything save what the cat wished, and off they went over stick and stone, from cliff to cliff, close by Ebe, who was just polishing the door-sill of his house, and with one bound right into the castle.

"I am to deliver a kind greeting from Ebe, and ask whether my lord king might care to have this buck reindeer to drive," said the cat. Yes, he could make good use of such a young, handsome animal, some time, when he had occasion to drive out to visit a neighbouring king.

"This Ebe must be a proud and powerful lord," said the king, "if he can make me such presents."

"Yes, he is the greatest lord in all your land and kingdom," said the cat, but no matter how many questions the king asked, he learned nothing more.

"Tell him that I am much obliged," said the king, and he sent him a whole cartload of handsome presents. But Ebe looked past them and paid no attention to them.

"Brother Peter can scrape out his cook-pot when he has loaned it out, and Brother Paul gets a crust of bread when he lends out his frying-pan; but what am I to do with this wretched cat!" said he, and felt angry and envious; but still he scratched the cat, and stroked her, and this pleased her so much that she began to purr, and raised her tail in the air.

"Wait, wait, I will help you yet," said the cat, "wait, wait, I will help you yet!"

The next day they both set out again, the cat in the lead, and Ebe following. After a while he turned back to see whether the folding-table at home had been scoured. And the cat tripped on alone. After she had gone her way, tipp, tapp, tipp, tapp, for a while, she came to a dense forest slope. There she found an enormous herd of elk. The cat crept softly up, and suddenly there she sat between the horns of one of the stateliest of the bull elks.

"If you do not go where I want you to, I will scratch out your eyes, and drive you over rock and precipice!" said the cat. The elk did not dare do anything save what the cat wished, and so off they went, like lightning, over stick and stone, from cliff to cliff, right past Ebe, who stood before the house scouring the shutters, and with one bound into the king's castle.

"I am to deliver a kind greeting from Ebe, and ask whether my lord king might not care to have this bull elk for courier service." It was quite clear that, should the king want a swift messenger, some time, he could not find a swifter in all his kingdom.

"This Ebe must be a most distinguished lord, since he finds such presents for me," said the king.

"Yes, indeed, one might call him a distinguished lord," said the cat, "his wealth is without end or limit." But no matter how many other questions the king asked, he received no more explicit information.

"Tell him that I am much obliged, and to do me the honour to call when he is passing here some time," said the king, and sent him a robe as handsome as the one he himself was wearing, and three cartloads of handsome presents. But Ebe did not even want to put on the royal robe, and hardly looked at the other presents.

"Brother Peter can scrape out his cook-pot when he has loaned it out, Brother Paul gets a crust of bread when he lends out his frying-pan; but of what use is this wretched cat to me!" he said, in spite of all. Yet he stroked the cat, and pressed her to his cheek, and scratched her, and this pleased the cat so very much that she purred more than on the other occasions, and stuck her tail up into the air as straight as a rod.

"Wait, wait, I will help you yet," said the cat, "wait, wait, I will help you yet!"

On the third day they set out again, the cat in the lead, and Ebe following. After a time it occurred to him to go back and let the mice out of the house, so that they would not be altogether starved in the old hut; and the cat tripped on alone. After she had gone her way, tipp, tapp, tipp, tapp, for a while, she came to a dense pine forest, and there she met a father bear, a mother bear and a baby bear. The cat crept softly up to them, and all at once she was hanging by her claws to the father bear's head.

"If you do not go where I want you to, I will scratch out your eyes, and drive you over rock and precipice!" said the cat, and spat and arched her back. Then the father bear did not dare do anything save what the cat wished, and now they dashed past Ebe, who had just carried all the young mice over the threshold, like a storm, over stick and stone, from cliff to cliff, so that the earth trembled and shook. The king was just standing in the hallway, and was not a little surprised to see such guests arriving.

"I am to deliver a kind greeting from Ebe, and ask whether my lord king might not care to have this bear for a general or royal counsellor," said the cat. The king was more than pleased to secure such a creature for his nearest adviser, who could doubt it.

"Tell him that I am much obliged, but that I do not at all know how to show my appreciation," said the king.

"Well, he would like to marry your youngest daughter!" said the cat.

"Yes, but that is asking a good deal," said the king. "He really ought to pay me a visit."

"Ebe does not enter such plain houses," said the cat.

"Has he a handsomer castle than this?" asked the king.

"Handsomer? Why, your castle seems like the shabbiest hut in comparison with his!" was the cat's reply.

"You dare come into my presence, and tell me that there is someone living in my kingdom who is more handsomely housed than I, the king!" shouted the king, beside himself with rage. He came near wringing the cat's neck.

"You might wait until you see it," said the cat. And the king said yes, he would wait. "But if you have told me a falsehood, you shall die, and though you had seven lives," said he.

In the morning the king and the whole court set out to travel to Ebe Ashpeter's castle. The cat was in the little hut, and called for Ebe, thinking it would be best if both of them got underway an hour earlier. After they had gone a while, they met some folk who were herding sheep; and the sheep were bleating and grazing over the whole plain. They were as large as full-grown calves, and their wool was so long that it dragged along the ground after them. "To whom do the sheep belong?" asked the cat. "To Helge-Hal in the Blue Hill," said the shepherds.

"The court is coming past in a moment," said the cat, "and if then you do not at once say that they belong to Ebe, I will scratch out your eyes, and drive you over rock and precipice!" said the cat, and spat and arched her back, and showed her teeth. Then the shepherds were so frightened that they at once promised to do as the cat had ordered.

"But to whom do all these sheep belong?" asked the king, when he came by with the court somewhat later. "They are every bit as handsome as my own!"

"They belong to Ebe," said the shepherds.

Then the cat and Ebe wandered on for a while, and came to a dense forest slope. There they met folk who were tending goats. The goats skipped and leaped about everywhere, and gave such fine milk that better could nowhere be found.

"To whom do the goats belong?" asked the cat.

"To Helge-Hal in the Blue Hill," said the herdsmen. Then the cat again went through her ferocious preparations, and the herdsmen were so frightened that they did not dare oppose her wishes.

"Now who in the world can be the owner of so many goats?" asked the king. "I myself have none finer!"

"They belong to Ebe," said the herdsmen.

Then they wandered on for a while, and met folk who were tending cows: wherever one looked the cows lowed and glistened, and each yielded milk enough for three. When the cat heard that these herdsmen were also in the service of Helge-Hal of the Blue Hill, she spat once more, and arched her back, and then all the herdsmen were ready that moment to say what she wished.

"But in heaven's name, to whom do all these beautiful cattle belong?" asked the king. "There are no such cattle in my whole kingdom!"

"They belong to Lord Ebe," said the herdsmen.

Then they wandered on for a long, long time. At last they came to a great plain, and there they met horse-herders; and horses whinnied and disported themselves over the whole plain, and their coats were so fine that they glistened as though gilded, and each horse was worth a whole castle.

"For whom do you herd these horses?" asked the cat.

"For Helge-Hal in the Blue Hill," the herders replied.

"Well, the court will come by here in a little while," said the cat, "and if you do not say you are herding them for Ebe, I will scratch out your eyes, and drive you over rock and precipice!" And she spat, and showed her teeth and claws, and grew so angry her hair stood up all along her back. Then the herders were terribly frightened, and did not dare do anything but what the cat wished.

"But in the name of heaven, to whom do all these horses belong?" asked the king, when he came by with his court.

"They belong to Ebe," said the herders.

"I never have seen or heard anything like it in all my life!" cried the king. "This Ebe is such a distinguished lord that it is past my understanding!"

The cat and Ebe had long since gone on their way, and had wandered far and ever farther over hill and rock. In the evening, at dusk, they came to a royal castle that glittered and shimmered as though it were of the purest silver and gold – which it was.

Yet it was gloomy and depressing, and lonely and barren there, and nowhere was there a sign of life.

Here they went in, and the cat stood with a cake of rye meal just below the door. Suddenly there came a thundering and a thumping so that the earth trembled, and the whole castle shook, and that was the troll who was coming home. And suddenly all was quiet again, and before they knew it, Helge-Hal in the Blue Hill had thrust his three great horrible heads in at the door.

"Let me in! Let me in!" he cried, so that everyone shivered. "Wait, wait a bit while I tell you what the rye had to go through before he was made into this cake," said the cat, and spoke to him in the sweetest way. "First he was threshed, and then he was beaten, and then he was pounded, and then he was thumped, and then he was thrown from one wall to another, and then he was sifted through a sieve..."

"Let me in! Let me in, you chatterbox!" cried the troll, and he was so furious that sparks flew from him.

"Wait a bit, wait a bit. I will tell you what the rye had to go through before he was made into this cake!" said the cat, and he spoke to him still more sweetly.

"First he was threshed, and then he was beaten, and then he was pounded, and then he was thumped, and then he was thrown from one wall to another, and then he was sifted through a sieve, and shaken here and there, and then he was put on the drying-board, and then in the stove, until it grew so hot that he puffed up more and more, and wanted to get out, but could not," said the cat, and took her time.

"Get out of the way and let me in!" cried the troll once more, and nearly burst with rage; but the cat acted as though she did not hear him, and talked down the blue from the sky, and went up and down the while, and whenever the troll tried to come in, she met him beneath the door with the cake.

"O, but do take a look at the shining maiden coming up there behind the mountain!" said the cat, after she had talked at length about the sufferings of the rye. And Helge-Hal in the Blue Hill turned his three heads around in order to see the beautiful maiden, too. Then the sun rose, and the troll stiffened into stone. Now Ebe obtained all the riches that the troll had possessed, the sheep and goats, the cows and all the spirited horses, and the handsome golden castle, and some big bags of money besides.

"Here come the king and all his court," said the cat. "Just go out before the door and receive them!" So Ebe got up and went to meet them.

"You are indeed a very distinguished lord!" said the king to him. "So far as I am concerned you may have the youngest princess!"

Then they started brewing and baking on a large scale in the greatest haste, and everything was made ready for the wedding. On the first day of the feast the cat came and begged the bridegroom to cut off her head. This he did not at all want to do; but the cat spat and showed her teeth, and then Ebe did not dare disobey her. But when the head fell to the ground, the cat turned into a most handsome prince. He married the second princess, and as the wedding procession was on its way to church, they met a third prince who was looking for a wife, and he took the oldest princess. Then they all three celebrated their weddings so that the story went the rounds in twelve kingdoms.

"Spin, span, spun,
Now our tale is done!"

The Cooper and the Wolves

(Norwegian)

TOLLEF KOLSTAD WAS A COOPER, and a very skilful cooper he was said to be. He had a little son named Thor, who was as fond of his father as his father was of him. Whatever Tollef did or said, Thor was sure to imitate; if Tollef was angry and flung a piece of wood at the dog who used to come into the shop and bother him, Thor, thinking it was a manly thing to do, flung another piece at poor Hector, who ran out whimpering through the door.

Thor, of course, was not very old before he had a corner in his father's shop, where, with a small set of tools which had been especially bought for him, he used to make little pails and buckets and barrels, which he sold for five or ten cents apiece to the boys of the neighbourhood. All the money earned in this way he put into a bank of tin, made like a drum, of which his mother kept the key. When he grew up, he thought, he would be a rich man.

The last weeks before Christmas are, in Norway, always the briskest season in all trades; then the farmer wants his horses shod, so that he may take his wife and children to church in his fine, swan-shaped sleigh; he wants bread and cakes made to last through the holidays, so that his servants may be able to amuse themselves, and his guests may be well entertained when they call; and, above all, he wants large tubs and barrels, stoutly made of beech staves, for his beer and mead, with which he pledges every stranger who, during the festival, happens to pass his door. You may imagine, then, that at Christmastime coopers are much in demand, and that it is not to be wondered at if sometimes they are behind-hand with their orders. This was unfortunately the case with Tollef Kolstad at the time when the strange thing happened which I am about to tell you. He had been at work since the early dawn, upon a huge tub or barrel, which had been ordered by Grim Berglund, the richest peasant in the parish. Grim was to give a large party on the following day (which was Christmas Eve), and he had made Tollef promise to bring the barrel that same night, so that he might pour the beer into it, and have all in readiness for the holidays, when it would be wrong to do any work. It was about ten o'clock at night when Tollef made the last stroke with his hatchet on the large hollow thing, upon which every blow resounded as on a drum. He went to a neighbour and hired from him his horse and flat sleigh, and was about to start on his errand, when he heard a tiny voice calling behind him:

"Father, do take me along, too!"

"I can't, my boy. There may be wolves on the lake, tonight, and they might like to eat up little boys who stay out of bed so late."

"But I am not afraid of them, father. I have my whip and my hatchet, and I'll whip them and cut them."

Thor here made some threatening flourishes with his weapons in the air, indicating how he would give it to the wolves in case they should venture to molest him.

"Well, come along, you little rascal," said his father, laughing, and feeling rather proud of his boy's dauntless spirit. "You and I are not to be trifled with when we get mad, are we, Thor?"

"No, indeed, father," said Thor, and clenched his little mittened fist.

Tollef then lifted him up, wrapped him warmly in his sheepskin jacket, and put him between his knees, while he himself seized the reins and urged the horse on.

It was a glorious winter night. The snow sparkled and shone as if sprinkled with starry diamonds, the aurora borealis flashed in pale, shifting colours along the horizon, and the moon sailed calmly through a vast, dark-blue sea of air. Little Thor shouted with delight as he saw the broad expanse of glittering ice, which they were about to cross, stretching out before them like a polished shield of steel.

"Oh, father, I wish we had taken our skates along, and pulled your barrel across on a sled," cried the boy, ecstatically.

"That I might have done, if I had had a sled large enough for the barrel," replied the father. "But then we should have been obliged to pull it up the hills on the other side."

The sleigh now struck the ice and shot forward, swinging from side to side, as the horse pulled a little unevenly. Whew! how the cold air cut in their faces. How it whizzed and howled in the treetops! Hark! What was that? Tollef instinctively pressed his boy more closely to him. Hush! – his heart stood still, while that of the boy, who merely felt the reflex shock of his father's agitation, hammered away the more rapidly. A terrible, long-drawn howl, as from a chorus of wild, far-away voices, came floating away over the crowns of the pine trees.

"What was that, father?" asked Thor, a little tremulously.

"It was wolves, my child," said Tollef, calmly.

"Are you afraid, father?" asked the boy again.

"No, child, I am not afraid of one wolf, nor of ten wolves; but if they are in a flock of twenty or thirty, they are dangerous. And if they scent our track, as probably they will, they will be on us in five minutes."

"How will they scent our track, father?"

"They smell us in the wind; and the wind is from us and to them, and then they howl to notify their comrades, so that they may attack us in sufficient force."

"Why don't we return home, then?" inquired the boy, still with a tolerably steady voice, but with sinking courage.

"They are behind us. Our only chance is to reach the shore before they overtake us."

The horse, sniffing the presence of wild beasts, snorted wildly as it ran, but, electrified as it were, with the sense of danger, strained every nerve in its efforts to reach the farther shore. The howls now came nearer and nearer, and they rose with a frightful distinctness in the clear, wintry air, and resounded again from the border of the forest.

"Why don't you throw away the barrel, father?" said Thor, who, for his father's sake, strove hard to keep brave. "Then the sleigh will run so much the faster."

"If we are overtaken, our safety is in the barrel. Fortunately, it is large enough for two, and it has no ears and will fit close to the ice."

Tollef was still calm; but, with his one disengaged arm, hugged his little son convulsively.

"Now, keep brave, my boy," he whispered in his ear. "They will soon be upon us. Give me your whip."

It just occurred to Tollef that he had heard that wolves were very suspicious, and that men had often escaped them by dragging some small object on the ground behind them. He therefore broke a chip from one of the hoops of the barrel, and tied it to the lash of the whip; just then he heard a short, hungry bark behind him, and, turning his head, saw a pack of wolves, numbering more than a dozen, the foremost of which was within a few yards of the sleigh. He saw the red, frothy tongue hanging out of its mouth, and he smelt that penetrating, wild smell with which everyone is familiar who has met a wild beast in its native haunts. While encouraging the reeking, foam-flecked horse, Tollef, who had only half faith in the experiment with the whip, watched anxiously the leader of the wolves, and observed to his astonishment that it seemed to be getting no nearer. One moment it seemed to be gaining upon them, but invariably, as soon as it reached the little chip which was dragging along the ice, this suddenly arrested its attention and immediately its speed slackened. The cooper's hope began to revive, and he thought that perhaps there was yet a possibility that they might see the morrow's sun. But his courage again began to ebb when he discovered in the distance a second pack of wolves, larger than the first, and which, with terrific speed, came running, leaping, and whirling toward them from another direction. And while this terrible discovery was breaking through his almost callous sense, he forgot, for an instant, the whip, the lash of which swung under the runners of the sleigh and snapped. The horse, too, was showing signs of exhaustion, and Tollef, seeing that only one chance was left, rose up with his boy in his arms, and upsetting the barrel on the ice, concealed himself and the child under it. Hardly had he had time to brace himself against its sides, pressing his feet against one side and his back against the other, when he heard the horse giving a wild scream, while the short, whining bark of the wolves told him that the poor beast was selling its life dearly. Then there was a desperate scratching and scraping of horseshoes, and all of a sudden the sound of galloping hoof-beats on the ice, growing fainter and fainter. The horse had evidently succeeded in breaking away from the sleigh, and was testing his speed in a race for life. Some of the wolves were apparently pursuing him, while the greater number remained to investigate the contents of the barrel. The howling and barking of these furious creatures without was now incessant. Within the barrel it was dark as pitch.

"Now, keep steady!" said Tollef, feeling a sudden shock, as if a wolf had leaped against their improvised house with a view to upsetting it. He felt himself and the boy gliding a foot or two over the smooth ice, but there was no further result from the attack. A minute passed: again there came a shock, and a stronger one than the first. A long, terrible howl followed this second failure. The little boy, clutching his small cooper's hatchet in one hand, sat pale but determined in the dark, while with the other he clung to his father's arm.

"Oh, father!" he cried, in terror, "I feel something on my back."

The father quickly struck a light, for he fortunately had a supply of matches in his pocket, and saw a wolf's paw wedged in between the ice and the rim of the barrel; and in the same instant he tore the hatchet from his son's hand and buried its edge in the ice. Then he handed the amputated paw to Thor, and said:

"Put that into your wallet, and the sheriff will pay you a reward for it. For a wolf without paws couldn't do much harm."

While he was yet speaking, a third assault upon the barrel lifted one side of it from the ice, and almost overturned it. Instead of pushing against the part nearest the ice, a wolf, more cunning than the rest, had leaped against the upturned bottom.

You can imagine what a terrible night father and son spent together in this constant struggle with the voracious beasts, that never grew weary of attacking their hiding place. The father was less warmly clad than the son, and, moreover, was obliged to sit on the ice, while Thor could stand erect without knocking against the bottom of the barrel; and if it had not been for the excitement of the situation, which made Tollef's blood course with unwonted rapidity, it is more than probable that the intense cold would have made him drowsy, and thus lessened his power of resistance. The warmth of his body had made a slight cavity where he was sitting, and whenever he remained a moment still, his trousers froze fast to the ice. It was only the presence of his boy that inspired him with fresh courage, whenever hope seemed about to desert him.

About an hour after the flight of the horse, when five or six wolves' paws had been cut off in the same manner as the first, there was a lull in the attack, but a sudden increase of the howling, whining, yelping, and barking noise without. Tollef concluded that the wolves, maddened by the smell of blood, were attacking their wounded fellows; and as their howls seemed to come from a short distance, he cautiously lifted one side of the barrel and peered forth; but in the same instant a snarling bark rang right in his ear, and two paws were thrust into the opening. Then came a howl of pain, and another paw was put into Thor's wallet.

But hark! What is that? It sounds like a song, or rather like a hymn. The strain comes nearer and nearer, resounding from mountain to mountain, floating peacefully through the pure and still air:

"Who knows how near I am mine ending;
So quickly time doth pass away."

Tollef, in whose breast hope again was reviving, put his ear to the ice, and heard distinctly the tread of horses and of many human feet. He listened for a minute or more, but could not discover whether the sound was coming any nearer. It occurred to him that in all probability the people, being unarmed, would have no desire to cope with a large pack of wolves, especially as to them there could be no object in it. If they saw the barrel, how could they know that there was anybody under it? He comprehended instantly that his only chance of life was in joining those people before they were too far away. And, quickly resolved, he lifted the boy on his left arm, and grasped the hatchet in his disengaged hand. Then, with a violent thrust, he flung the barrel from over him, and ran in the direction of the sound. The wolves, as he had inferred, were lacerating their bleeding comrades; but the moment they saw him, a pack of about a dozen immediately started in pursuit. They leaped up against him on all sides, while he struck furiously about him with his small weapon. Fortunately, he had sharp steel pegs on his boots, and kept his footing well; otherwise the combat would have been a short one. His voice, too, was powerful, and his shouts rose high above the howling of the beasts. He soon perceived that he had been observed, and he saw in the bright moonlight six or eight men running toward him. Just then, as perhaps in his joy his vigilance was for a fraction of a second relaxed, he felt a pull in the fleshy part of his right arm. He was not conscious of any sharp pain, and was astonished to see the blood flowing from an ugly wound. But he only held his boy the more tightly, while he fought and ran with the strength of despair.

Now the men were near. He could hear their voices. But his brain was dizzy, and he saw but dimly.

"Hello, friend; don't crack my skull for my pains!" someone was shouting close to his ear, and he let his hatchet fall, and he fell himself, too, prostrate on the ice.

The wolves, at the sight of the men, had retired to a safe distance, from which they watched the proceedings, as if uncertain whether to return.

As soon as Tollef had recovered somewhat from his exhaustion and his loss of blood, he and his boy were placed upon a sleigh, and his wound was carefully bandaged. He now learned that his rescuers were on their way to a funeral, which was to take place on the next day, but, on account of the distance to the church, they had been obliged to start during the night. Hence their solemn mood, and their singing of funeral hymns.

After an hour's ride they reached the cooper's cottage, and were invited to rest and to share such hospitality as the house could afford. But when they were gone, Tollef clasped his sleeping boy in his arms and said to his wife: "If it had not been for him, you might have had no husband today. It was his little whip and toy hatchet that saved our lives."

Eleven wolves' paws were found in Thor's wallet, and, on Christmas Eve, he went to the sheriff with them and received a reward which nearly burst his old savings-bank, and compelled his mother to buy a new one.

Mikkel

(Norwegian)

I
How Mikkel Was Found

YOU MAY FIND IT HARD TO BELIEVE what I am going to tell you, but it is, nevertheless, strictly true. I knew the boy who is the hero of this story. His name was Thor Larsson, and a very clever boy he was. Still I don't think he would have amounted to much in the world, if it had not been for his friend Michael, or, as they write it in Norwegian, Mikkel. Mikkel, strange to say, was not a boy, but a fox. Thor caught him, when he was a very small lad, in a den under the roots of a huge tree. It happened in this way. Thor and his elder brother, Lars, and still another boy, named Ole Thomlemo, were up in the woods gathering faggots, which they tied together in large bundles to carry home on their backs; for their parents were poor people, and had no money to buy wood with. The boys rather liked to be sent on errands of this kind, because delicious raspberries and blueberries grew in great abundance in the woods, and gathering faggots was, after all, a much manlier occupation than staying at home minding the baby.

Thor's brother Lars and Ole Thomlemo were great friends, and they had a disagreeable way of always plotting and having secrets together and leaving Thor out of their councils. One of their favourite tricks, when they wished to get rid of him, was to pretend to play hide-and-seek; and when he had hidden himself, they would run away from him and make no effort to find him. It was this trick of theirs which led to the capture of Mikkel, and to many things besides.

It was on a glorious day in the early autumn that the three boys started out together, as frisky and gay as a company of squirrels. They had no luncheon-baskets with them, although they expected to be gone for the whole day; but they had hooks and lines in their pockets, and meant to have a famous dinner of brook-trout up in some mountain glen, where they could sit like pirates around a fire, conversing in mysterious language, while the fish was being fried upon a flat stone. Their tolle knives were hanging, sheathed, from their girdles, and the two older ones carried, besides, little hatchets wherewith to cut off the dry twigs and branches. Lars and Ole Thomlemo, as usual, kept ahead and left Thor to pick his way over the steep and stony road as best he might; and when he caught up with them, they started to run, while he sat down panting on a stone. Thus several hours passed, until they came to a glen in which the blueberries grew so thickly that you couldn't step without crushing a handful. The boys gave a shout of delight and flung themselves down, heedless of their clothes, and began to eat with boyish greed. As far as their eyes could reach between the mossy pine trunks, the ground was blue with berries, except where bunches of ferns or clusters of wild flowers intercepted the view. When they had dulled the edge of their hunger, they began to cut the branches from the trees which the lumbermen had felled, and Ole Thomlemo, who was clever with his hands, twisted withes, which they used instead of ropes for tying their bundles together. They had one bundle well secured and another under way, when Ole, with a mischievous expression, ran over to Lars and whispered something in his ear.

"Let us play hide-and-seek," said Lars aloud, glancing over toward his little brother, who was working like a Trojan, breaking the faggots so as to make them all the same length.

Thor, who in spite of many exasperating experiences had not yet learned to be suspicious, threw down an armful of dry boughs and answered: "Yes, let us, boys. I am in for anything."

"I'll blind first," cried Ole Thomlemo; "now, be quick and get yourselves hidden."

And off the two brothers ran, while Ole turned his face against a big tree and covered his eyes with his hands. But the very moment Thor was out of sight, Lars stole back again to his friend, and together they slipped away under cover of the bushes, until they reached the lower end of the glen. There, they pulled out their fish-lines, cut rods with their hatchets, and went down to the tarn, or brook, which was only a short distance off; the fishing was excellent, and when the large speckled trout began to leap out of the water to catch their flies, the two boys soon ceased to trouble themselves about little Thor, who, they supposed, was hiding under some bush and waiting to be discovered.

In this supposition they were partly right and partly wrong.

No sooner had Ole Thomlemo given the signal for hiding, than Thor ran up the hillside, stumbling over the moss-grown stones, pushing the underbrush aside with his hands, and looking eagerly for a place where he would be least likely to be found. He was full of the spirit of the game, and anticipated with joyous excitement the wonder of the boys when they should have to give up the search and call to him to reveal himself. While these thoughts were filling his brain, he caught sight of a huge old fir tree, which was leaning down the mountainside as if ready to fall. The wind had evidently given it a pull in the top, strong enough to loosen its hold on the ground, and yet not strong enough to overthrow it. On the upper side, for a dozen yards or more, the thick, twisted roots, with the soil and turf still clinging to them, had been lifted, so as to form a little den about two feet wide at the entrance. Here, thought Thor, was a wonderful hiding place. Chuckling to himself at the discomfiture of his comrades, he threw himself down on his knees and thrust his head into the opening. To his surprise the bottom felt soft to his hands, as if it had been purposely covered with moss and a layer of feathers and eiderdown. He did not take heed of the peculiar wild smell which greeted his nostrils, but fearlessly pressed on, until nearly his whole figure, with the exception of the heels of his boots, was hidden. Then a sharp little bark startled him, and raising his head he saw eight luminous eyes staring at him from a dark recess, a few feet beyond his nose. It is not to be denied that he was a little frightened; for it instantly occurred to him that he had unwittingly entered the den of some wild beast, and that, in case the old ones were at home, there was small chance of his escaping with a whole skin. It could hardly be a bear's den, for the entrance was not half big enough for a gentleman of Bruin's size. It might possibly be a wolf's premises he was trespassing upon, and the idea made his blood run cold. For Mr. Graylegs, as the Norwegians call the wolf, is not to be trifled with; and a small boy armed only with a knife was hardly a match for such an antagonist. Thor concluded, without much reflection, that his safest plan would be to beat a hasty retreat. Digging his hands into the mossy ground, he tried to push himself backward, but, to his unutterable dismay, he could not budge an inch. The feathers, interspersed with the smooth pine-needles, slipped away under his fingers, and the roots caught in his clothes and held him as in a vice. He tried to force his way, but the more he wriggled the more he realized how small was his chance of escape. To turn was impossible, and to pull off his coat and trousers was a scarcely less difficult task. It was fortunate that the four inhabitants of the den, to whom the glaring eyes belonged, seemed no less frightened than himself; for they remained huddled together in their corner, and showed no disposition to fight. They only stared wildly at the intruder, and seemed anxious to know what he intended to do next. And Thor stared at them in return, although the darkness was so dense that he could discern nothing except the eight luminous eyes, which were fixed upon him with an uncanny and highly uncomfortable expression. Unpleasant as the situation was, he began to grow accustomed to it, and he collected his scattered thoughts sufficiently to draw certain conclusions. The size of the den, as well as the feathers which everywhere met his fumbling hands, convinced him that his hosts were young foxes, and that probably their respected parents, for the moment, were on a raid in search of rabbits or stray poultry. That reflection comforted him, for he had never known a fox to use any other weapon of defence than its legs, unless it was caught in a trap and had to fight for bare life. He was just dismissing from his mind all thought of danger from that source, when a sudden sharp pain in his heel put an end to his reasoning. He gave a scream, at which the eight eyes leaped apart in pairs and distributed themselves in a row along the curving wall of the den. Another bite in his ankle convinced him that he was being attacked from behind, and he knew no other way of defence than to kick with all his might, screaming at the same time so as to attract the attention of the boys, who, he supposed, could hardly be far off. But his voice sounded choked and feeble in the close den, and he feared that no one would be able to hear it ten yards away. The strong odour, too, began to stifle him, and a strange dizziness wrapped his senses, as it were, in a grey, translucent veil. He made three or four spasmodic efforts to rouse himself, screamed feebly, and kicked; but probably he struck his wounded ankle against a root or a stone, for the pain shot up his leg and made him clench his teeth to keep the tears from starting. He thought of his poor mother, whom he feared he should never see again, and how she would watch for his return through the long night and cry for him, as it said in the Bible that Jacob cried over Joseph when he supposed that a wild beast had torn him to pieces and killed him. Curious lights, like shooting stars, began to move before his eyes; his tongue felt dry and parched, and his throat seemed burning hot. It occurred to him that certainly God saw his peril and might yet help him, if he only prayed for help; but the only prayer which he could remember was the one which the minister repeated every Sunday for "our most gracious sovereign, Oscar II., and the army and navy of the United Kingdoms." Next he stumbled upon "the clergy, and the congregations committed to their charge"; and he was about to finish with "sailors in distress at sea," when his words, like his thoughts, grew more and more hazy, and he drifted away into unconsciousness.

Lars and Ole Thomlemo in the meanwhile had enjoyed themselves to the top of their bent, and when they had caught a dozen trout, among which was one three-pounder, they reeled up their lines, threaded the fish on withes, and began to trudge leisurely up the glen. When they came to the place where they had left their bundles of faggots, they stopped to shout for Thor, and when they received no reply, they imagined that, being tired of waiting, he had gone home alone, or fallen in with someone who was on his way down to the valley. The only thing that troubled them was that Thor's bundle had not been touched since they left him, and they knew that the boy was not lazy, and that, moreover, he would be afraid to go home without the faggots. They therefore concluded to search the copse and the surrounding underbrush, as it was just possible that he might have fallen asleep in his hiding place while waiting to be discovered.

"I think Thor is napping somewhere under the bushes," cried Ole Thomlemo, swinging his hatchet over his head like an Indian tomahawk. "We shall have to halloo pretty loud, for you know he sleeps like a top."

And they began scouring the underbrush, traversing it in all directions, and hallooing lustily, both singly and in chorus. They were just about giving up the quest, when Lars's attention was attracted by two foxes which, undismayed by the noise, were running about a large fir tree, barking in a way which betrayed anxiety, and stopping every minute to dig up the ground with their forepaws. When the boys approached the tree, the foxes ran only a short distance, then stopped, ran back, and again fled, once more to return.

"Those fellows act very queerly," remarked Lars, eyeing the foxes curiously; "I'll wager there are young un's under the tree here, but" – Lars gasped for breath – "Ole – Ole – Oh, look! What is this?"

Lars had caught sight of a pair of heels, from which a little stream of blood had been trickling, colouring the stones and pine-needles. Ole Thomlemo, hearing his comrade's exclamation of fright, was on the spot in an instant, and he comprehended at once how everything had happened.

"Look here, Lars," he said, resolutely, "this is no time for crying. If Thor is dead, it is we who have killed him; but if he isn't dead, we've got to save him."

"Oh, what shall we do, Ole?" sobbed Lars, while the tears rolled down over his cheeks, "what shall we do? I shall never dare go home again if he is dead. We have been so very bad to him!"

"We have got to save him, I tell you," repeated Ole, tearless and stern: "we must pull him out; and if we can't do that, we must cut through the roots of this fir tree; then it'll plunge down the mountainside, without hurting him. A few roots that have burrowed into the rocks are all that keep the tree standing. Now, act like a man. Take hold of him by one heel and I'll take the other."

Lars, who looked up to his friend as a kind of superior being, dried his tears and grasped his brother's foot, while Ole carefully handled the wounded ankle. But their combined efforts had no perceptible effect, except to show how inextricably the poor lad's clothes were intertangled with the tree-roots, which, growing all in one direction, made entrance easy, but exit impossible.

"That won't do," said Ole, after three vain trials. "We might injure him without knowing it, driving the sharp roots into his eyes and ears, as likely as not. We've got to use the hatchets. You cut that root and I'll manage this one."

Ole Thomlemo was a lumberman's son, and since he was old enough to walk had spent his life in the forest. He could calculate with great nicety how a tree would fall, if cut in a certain way, and his skill in this instance proved valuable. With six well-directed cuts he severed one big root, while Lars laboured at a smaller one. Soon with a great crash the mighty tree fell down the mountainside, crushing a dozen birches and smaller pines under its weight. The moss-grown sod around about was torn up with the remaining roots, and three pretty little foxes, blinded and stunned by the rush of daylight, sprang out from their hole and stared in bewilderment at the sudden change of scene. Through the cloud of flying dust and feathers the boys discerned, too, Thor's insensible form, lying outstretched, torn and bleeding, his face resting upon his hands, as if he were asleep. With great gentleness they lifted him up, brushed the moss and earth from his face and clothes, and placed him upon the grass by the side of the brook which flowed through the bottom of the glen. Although his body was warm, they could hardly determine whether he was dead or alive, for he seemed scarcely to be breathing, and it was not until Ole put a feather before his mouth and perceived its faint inward and outward movement, that they felt reassured and began to take heart. They bathed his temples with the cool mountain water and rubbed and chafed his hands, until at last he opened his eyes wonderingly and moved his lips, as if endeavouring to speak.

"Where am I?" he whispered at last, after several vain efforts to make himself heard.

"Why, cheer up, old fellow," answered Ole, encouragingly; "you have had a little accident, that's all, but you'll be all right in a minute."

"Unbutton my vest," whispered Thor again; "there is something scratching me here."

He put his hand over his heart, and the boys quickly tore his waistcoat open, but to their unutterable astonishment a little fox, the image of the three that had escaped, put his head out and looked about him with his alert eyes, as if to say: "Here am I; how do you like me?" He evidently felt so comfortable where he was, that he had no desire to get away. No doubt the little creature, prompted either by his curiosity or a desire to escape from the den, had crept into Thor's bosom while he was insensible, and, finding his quarters quite to his taste, had concluded to remain. Lars picked him up, tied a string about his neck, and put him in the side pocket of his jacket. Then, as it was growing late, Ole lifted Thor upon his back, and he and Lars took turns in carrying him down to the valley.

Thor's ankle gave him some trouble, as the wound was slow in healing. With that exception, he was soon himself again; and he and Mikkel (for that was the name he gave to the little fox) grew to be great friends and had many a frolic together.

But the little fox was not a model of deportment, as you will see when I tell you, in the next chapter, how Mikkel disgraced himself.

II
How Mikkel Disgraced Himself

When Thor was twelve years old, he had to go out into the world to make his own living; for his parents were poor, and they had half a dozen younger children, who also had to be fed and clothed. As it happened, Judge Nannestad, who lived on a large estate down at the fiord, wanted an office-boy, and as Thor was a bright and active lad, he had no difficulty in obtaining the situation. The only question was, how to dispose of Mikkel; for, to be frank, Mikkel (in spite of his many admirable traits) was not a general favourite, and Thor suspected that when his protector was away Mikkel would have a hard time of it. He well knew that Mikkel was of a peculiar temperament, which required to be studied in order to be appreciated, and as there was no one but himself who took this trouble, he did not wonder that his friend was generally misunderstood. Mikkel's was not a nature to invite confidences; he scrupulously kept his own counsel, and was always alert and on his guard. There was a bland expression on his face, a kind of lurking smile, which never varied, and which gave absolutely no clue to his thoughts. When he had skimmed the cream off the milk-pans on the top shelf in the kitchen, he returned, licking his chops, with the same inscrutable smile, as if his conscience were as clean as a new-born babe's; and when he had slipped his collar over his head and dispatched the kitten, burying its remains in the backyard, he betrayed no more remorse than if he had been cracking a nut. Sultan, the dog, strange to say, had private reasons for being afraid of him, and always slank away in a shamefaced manner, whenever Mikkel gave him one of his quiet sidelong glances. And yet the same Mikkel would roll on his back, and jump and play with the baby by the hour, seize her pudgy little hands gently with his teeth, never inflicting a bite or a scratch. He would nestle on Thor's bosom inside of his coat, while Thor was learning his lesson, or he would sit on his shoulder and look down on the book with his superior smile. It was not to be denied that Mikkel had a curious character – an odd mixture of good and bad qualities; but as, in Thor's judgement, the good were by far the more prominent, he would not listen to his father's advice and leave his friend behind him, when he went down to the judge's at the grand estate.

It was the day after New Year's that Thor left the cottage up under the mountain, and, putting on his *skees*, slid down the steep hillside to the fiord. Mikkel was nestling, according to his wont, in the bosom of his master's coat, while his pretty head, with the clean dark snout and dark moustache, was sticking out above the boy's collar, just under his chin. Mikkel had never been so far away from home before, and he concluded that the world was a bigger affair than he had been aware of.

It was with a loudly thumping heart that Thor paused outside the door of the judge's office, for he greatly feared that the judge might share the general prejudice against

Mikkel, and make difficulties about his board and lodgings. Instead of entering, he went to the pump in the yard and washed his friend's face carefully and combed his hair with the fragment of a comb with which his mother had presented him at parting. It was important that Mikkel should appear to advantage, so as to make a good impression upon the judge. And really he did look irresistible, Thor thought, with his bright, black eyes, his dainty paws, and his beautiful red skin. He felt satisfied that if the judge had not a heart of stone he could not help being captivated at the sight of so lovely a creature. Thor took courage and knocked at the door.

"Ah, you are our new office-boy," said the judge, as he entered; "but what is that you have under your coat?"

"It is Mikkel, sir, please your Honour," stammered Thor, putting the fox on the floor, so as to display his charms. But hardly had he taken his hands off him, when a sudden scrambling noise was heard in the adjoining office, and a large hound came bounding with wild eyes and drooping tongue through the open door. With lightning speed Mikkel leaped up on the judge's writing-desk, scattering his writing materials, upsetting an inkstand by an accidental whisk of his tail, and bespattering the honourable gentleman's face and shirt-front with the black fluid. To perform a similar service on the next desk, where a clerk was writing, to jump from there to the shoulder of a marble bust, which fell from its pedestal down on the hound's head and broke into a dozen pieces, and to reach a place of safety on the top of a tall bookcase were all a moment's work. The hound lay howling, with a wounded nose, on the floor. The judge stood scowling at his desk, rubbing the ink all over his face with his handkerchief, and Mikkel sat smiling on the top of the bookcase, surveying calmly the ruin which he had wrought. But the most miserable creature in the room was neither the judge, with his black face, nor the hound, with the bleeding nose; it was Thor, who stood trembling at the door, expecting that something still more terrible would happen. And knowing that, after having caused such a commotion, his place was forfeited, he held out his arms to Mikkel, who accepted the invitation, and with all speed at their disposal they rushed out through the door and away over the snowy fields, scarcely knowing whither their feet bore them.

After half an hour's run, when he had no more breath left, Thor seated himself on a tree-stump and tried to collect his thoughts. What should he now do? Where should he turn? Go home he could not; and if he did, it would be the end of Mikkel. The only thing he could think of was to go around in the parish, from farm to farm, until he found somebody who would give him something to do.

"I hope you will appreciate, my dear Mikkel," he said to his fox, "that it is on your account I have all this trouble. It was very naughty of you to behave so badly, and if you do it again I shall have to whip you! Do you understand that, Mikkel?"

Mikkel looked sheepish, which plainly showed that he understood.

"Now, Mikkel," Thor continued, "we will go to the parson; perhaps he may have some use for us. What do you think of trying the parson?"

Mikkel apparently thought well of the parson, for he licked his master behind his ear and rubbed his snout against his cheek. Accordingly, by noon they reached the parsonage, and after a long parley with the parson's wife, he was engaged as a sort of errand-boy, whose duty it should be to do odd jobs about the house. Mikkel was to have a kennel provided for him in the stable, but was under no circumstances to enter the house. Thor had to vouch for his good behaviour, and the moment he made himself in any way obnoxious it was decided that he should be killed. Poor Thor had nominally to accept these hard conditions, but in his own mind he determined to run away with Mikkel the moment he was caught in any kind of mischief. It seemed very hard for Mikkel, too, who had been accustomed to sleep in Thor's arms in his warm bed, to be chained, and to spend the long, dark nights in the stable in a miserable kennel. Nevertheless, there was no help for it; so Thor went to work that same afternoon and made Mikkel as comfortable a kennel as he could, taking care to make the hole which served for entrance no bigger than it had to be, so that no dog or other enemy should be able to enter.

For about four months all went well at the parsonage. So long as Mikkel was confined in the stable he behaved himself with perfect propriety, and, occasionally, when he was (by special permission) taken into the house to play with the children, he won golden opinions for himself by his cunning tricks, and became, in fact, a great favourite in the nursery. When the spring came and the sun grew warm, his kennel was, at Thor's request, moved out into the yard, where he could have the benefit of the fine spring weather. There he could be seen daily, lying in the sun, with half-closed eyes, resting his head on his paws, seeming too drowsy and comfortable to take notice of anything. The geese and hens, which were at first a trifle suspicious, gradually grew accustomed to his presence, and often strayed within range of Mikkel's chain, and even within reach of his paws; but it always happened that on such occasions either the parson or his wife was near, and Mikkel knew enough to be aware that goose was forbidden fruit. But one day (it was just after dinner, when the parson was taking his nap), it happened that a great fat gander, prompted by a pardonable curiosity, stretched his neck a little too far toward the sleeping Mikkel; when, quick as a wink and wide-awake, Mr. Mikkel jumped up, and before he knew it, the gander found himself minus his head. Very cautiously the culprit peered about, and seeing no one near, he rapidly dug a hole under his kennel and concealed his victim there, covering it well with earth, until a more favourable opportunity should present itself for making a meal of it. Then he lay down, and stretched himself in the sun as before, and seemed too sleepy even to open his eyes; and when, on the following day, the gander was missed, the innocent demeanour of Mikkel so completely imposed upon everyone, that he was not even suspected. Not even when the second and the third goose disappeared could any reasonable charge be brought against Mikkel.

When the summer vacation came, however, the even tenor of Mikkel's existence was rudely interrupted by the arrival of the parson's oldest son, Finn, who was a student in Christiania, and his dog Achilles. Achilles was a handsome brown pointer, who, having been brought up in the city, had never been accustomed to look upon the fox as a domestic animal. He, therefore, spent much of his time in harassing Mikkel, making sudden rushes for him when he thought him asleep; but always returning from these exploits shamefaced and discomfited, for Mikkel was always a great deal too clever to be taken by surprise. He would lie perfectly still until Achilles was within a foot of him, and then, with remarkable alertness, he would slip into the kennel, through his door, where the dog's size would not permit him to follow; and the moment his enemy turned his tail to him, Mikkel's face would appear bland and smiling, at the door, as if to say:

"Goodbye! Call again whenever you feel like it. Now, don't you wish you were as clever as I am?"

And yet in spite of his daily defeats, Achilles could never convince himself that his assaults upon Mikkel brought him no glory. Perhaps his master, who did not like Mikkel any too well, encouraged him in his enmity, for it is certain that the assaults grew fiercer daily. And at last, one day when the young student was standing in the yard, holding his dog by the collar, while exciting him against the half-sleeping fox, Achilles ran with such force against the kennel that he upset it. Alas! For then the evidence of Mikkel's misdemeanours came to light. From the door-hole of the rolling kennel a heap of goose-feathers flew out, and were scattered in the air; and, what was worse, a little 'dug-out' became visible, filled with bones and bills and other indigestible articles, unmistakably belonging to the goose's anatomy. Mikkel, who was too wise to leave the kennel so long as it was in motion, now peeped cautiously out, and he took in the situation at a glance. Mr. Finn, the student, who thought that Mikkel's skin would look charming as a rug before his fireplace in the city, was overjoyed to find out what a rascal this innocent-looking creature had been; for he knew well enough that his father would now no longer oppose his desire for the crafty little creature's skin. So he went into the house, loaded his rifle, and prepared himself as executioner.

But at that very moment, Thor chanced to be coming home from an errand; and he had hardly entered the yard, when he sniffed danger in the air. He knew, without asking, that Mikkel's doom was sealed. For the parson was a great poultry-fancier and was said to be more interested in his ganders than he was in his children. Therefore, without waiting for further developments, Thor unhooked Mikkel's chain, lifted the culprit in his arms, and slipped him into the bosom of his waistcoat. Then he stole up to his garret, gathered his clothes in a bundle, and watched his chance to escape from the house unnoticed. And while Master Finn and his dog were hunting high and low for Mikkel in the barns and stables, Thor was hurrying away over the fields, every now and then glancing anxiously behind him, and nearly smothering Mikkel in his efforts to keep him concealed, lest Achilles should catch his scent. But Mikkel had his own views on that subject, and was not to be suppressed; and just as his master was congratulating himself on their happy escape, they heard the deep baying of a dog, and saw Achilles, followed by the student with his gun, tracking them in fierce pursuit. Thor, whose only hope was to reach the fiord, redoubled his speed, skipped across fences, hedges, and stiles, and ran so fast that earth and stones seemed to be flying in the other direction. Yet Achilles' baying was coming nearer and nearer, and was hardly twenty feet distant by the time the boy had flung himself into a boat, and with four vigorous oar-strokes had shot out into the water. The dog leaped after him, but was soon beyond his depth, and the high breakers flung him back upon the beach.

"Come back at once," cried Finn, imperiously. "It is not your boat. If you don't obey, I'll have you arrested."

Thor did not answer, but rowed with all his might.

"If you take another stroke," shouted the student furiously, levelling his gun, "I'll shoot both you and your thievish fox."

It was meant only for intimidation; but where Mikkel's life was at stake, Thor was not easily frightened.

"Shoot away!" he cried, thinking that he was now at a safe distance, and that the student's marksmanship was none of the best. But before he realized what he had said, whiz! went a bullet over his head. A stiff gale was blowing, and the little boat was tossed like a football on the incoming and the outgoing waves; but the plucky lad struggled on bravely, until he hove alongside a fishing schooner, which was to sail the next morning for Drontheim. Fortunately the skipper needed a deck hand, and Thor was promptly engaged. The boat which had helped him to escape was found later and towed back to shore by a fisherman.

III
How Mikkel Makes His Fortune

In Drontheim, which is a large commercial city on the western coast of Norway, Thor soon found occupation as office-boy in a bank, which did business under the name of C.P. Lyng & Co. He was a boy of an open, fearless countenance, and with a frank and winning manner. Mr. Lyng, at the time when Thor entered his employ, had just separated from his partner, Mr. Tulstrup, because the latter had defrauded the firm and several of its customers. Mr. Lyng had papers in his safe which proved Mr. Tulstrup's guilt, but he had contented himself with dismissing him from the firm, and had allowed him to take the share of the firm's property to which he was legally entitled. The settlement, however, had not satisfied Mr. Tulstrup, and he had, in order to revenge himself, gone about to the various customers, whom he had himself defrauded, and persuaded them to commence suit against Mr. Lyng, whom he represented as being the guilty party. He did not, at that time, know that Mr. Lyng had gained possession of the papers which revealed the real author of the fraud. On the contrary, he flattered himself that he had destroyed every trace of his own dishonest transactions.

The fact that Mr. Lyng belonged to a family which had always been distinguished, in business and social circles, for its integrity and honour only whetted Tulstrup's desire to destroy his good name, and having laid his plans carefully, he anticipated an easy triumph over honest Mr. Lyng. His dismay, therefore, was very great when, after the suit had been commenced in the courts, he learned that it was his own name and liberty which were in danger, and not those of his former partner. Mr. Tulstrup, in spite of the position he had occupied, was a desperate man, and was capable, under such circumstances, of resorting to desperate remedies. But, like most Norwegians, he had a streak of superstition in his nature, and cherished an absurd belief in signs and omens, in lucky and unlucky days, and in spectres and apparitions, foreboding death or disaster. Mr. Tulstrup's father had believed in such things, and it had been currently reported among the peasantry that he had been followed by a spectral fox, which some asserted to be his wraith, or double. This fox, it was said, had frequently been seen during the old man's lifetime, and when he once saw it himself, he was frightened nearly out of his wits. Superstitious stories of this kind are so common in Norway that one can hardly spend a month in any country district without hearing dozens of them. The belief in a *fylgia*, or wraith in the shape of an animal, dates far back into antiquity, and figures largely in the sagas, or ancient legends of the Northland.

It has already been told that Thor had obtained a position as office-boy in Mr. Lyng's bank; and it was more owing to the boy's winning appearance than to any fondness for foxes, on Mr. Lyng's part, that Mikkel also was engaged. It was arranged that a cushion whereupon Mikkel might sleep should be put behind the stove in the back office. At first Mikkel endured his captivity here with great fortitude; but he did not like it, and it was plain that he was pining for the parsonage and his kennel in the free air, and the pleasant companionship of the geese and the stupid Achilles. Thor then obtained permission to have him walk about unchained, and the clerks, who admired his graceful form and dainty ways, soon grew very fond of him, and stroked him caressingly, as he promenaded along the counter or seated himself on their shoulders, inspecting their accounts with critical eyes. Thor was very happy to see his friend petted, though he had an occasional twinge of jealousy when Mikkel made himself too agreeable to old Mr. Barth, the cashier, or kissed young Mr. Dreyer, the assistant bookkeeper. Such faithlessness on Mikkel's part was an ill return for all the sacrifices Thor had made for him; and yet, hard as it was, it had to be borne. For an office-boy cannot afford to have emotions, or, if he has them, cannot afford the luxury of giving way to them.

C.P. Lyng & Co.'s bank was a solid, old-fashioned business-house which the clerks entered as boys and where they remained all their lives. Mr. Barth, the cashier, had occupied his present desk for twenty-one years, and had spent nine years more in inferior positions. He was now a stout little man of fifty, with close cropped, highly-respectable side-whiskers and thin grey hair, which was made to cover his crown by the aid of a small comb. This comb, which was fixed above his right ear and held the straggling locks together, was a source of great amusement to the clerks, who made no end of witticisms about it. But Mr. Barth troubled himself very little about their poor puns, and sat serenely poring over his books and packages of bank-bills from morning till night. He prided himself above all on his regularity, and it was said that he had never been one minute too late or too early during the thirty years he had been in Mr. Lyng's bank; accordingly, he had little patience with the shortcomings of his subordinates, and fined and punished them in various ways, if they were but a moment tardy; for the most atrocious of all crimes, in Mr. Barth's opinion, was tardiness. The man who suffered most from his severity was Mr. Dreyer, the assistant bookkeeper. Mr. Dreyer was a good-looking young man, and very fond of society; and it happened sometimes that, on the morning after a ball, he would sleep rather late. He had long rebelled in silence against Mr. Barth's tyranny, and when he found that his dissatisfaction was shared by many of the other clerks, he conceived a plan to revenge himself on his persecutor. To this end a conspiracy was formed among the younger clerks, and it was determined to make Mikkel the agent of their vengeance.

It was well known by the clerks that Mr. Barth was superstitious and afraid in the dark; and it was generally agreed that it would be capital fun to give him a little fright. Accordingly the following plan was adopted: A bottle of the oil of phosphorus was procured and Mikkel's fur was thoroughly rubbed with it, so that in the dark the whole animal would be luminous. At five minutes before five, someone should go down in the cellar and turn off the gas, just as the cashier was about to enter the back office to lock up the safe. Then, when the illuminated Mikkel glared out on him from a dark corner, he would probably shout or faint or cry out, and then all the clerks should rush sympathetically to him and render him every assistance.

Thus the plan was laid, and there was a breathless, excited stillness in the bank when the hour of five approached. It had been dark for two hours, and the clerks sat on their high stools, bending silently over their desks, scribbling away for dear life. Promptly at seven minutes before five, up rose Mr. Barth and gave the signal to have the books closed; then, to the unutterable astonishment of the conspirators, he handed the key of the safe to Mr. Dreyer (who knew the combination), and told him to lock the safe and return the key. At that very instant, out went the gas; and Mr. Dreyer, although he was well prepared, could himself hardly master his fright at Mikkel's terrible appearance. He struck a match, lighted a wax taper (which was used for sealing letters), and tremblingly locked the safe; then, abashed and discomfited, he advanced to the cashier's desk and handed him the key.

"Perhaps you would have the kindness, Mr. Dreyer," said Mr. Barth, calmly, "to write a letter of complaint to the gas company before you go home. It will never do in the world to have such things happen. I suppose there must be water in the pipes."

The old man buttoned his overcoat up to his chin and marched out; whereupon a shout of laughter burst forth, in which Mr. Dreyer did not join. He could not see what they found to laugh at, he said. It took him a long while to compose his letter of complaint to the gas company.

Mikkel in the meanwhile was feeling very uncomfortable. He could not help marvelling at his extraordinary appearance. He rubbed himself against chairs and tables, and found to his astonishment that he made everything luminous that he touched. He had never known any respectable fox which possessed this accomplishment, and he felt sure that in some way something was wrong with him. He could not sleep, but walked restlessly about on the desks and counters, bristled with anger at the slightest sound, and was miserable and excited. He could not tell how far the night had advanced, when he heard a noise in the back office (which fronted upon the courtyard) as if a window was being opened. His curiosity was aroused and he walked sedately across the floor; then he stopped for a moment to compose himself, for he was well aware that what he saw was something extraordinary. A man with a dark-lantern in his hand was kneeling before the safe with a key in his hand. Mikkel advanced a little farther and paused in a threatening attitude on the threshold of the door. With his luminous face and body, and a halo of phosphorescent light round about him, he was terrible to behold. He gave a little snort, at which the man turned quickly about. But no sooner had he caught sight of the illuminated Mikkel than he flung himself on his knees before the little animal, and with clasped hands and a countenance wild with fear exclaimed: "Oh, I know who thou art! Pardon me, pardon me! Thou art my father's spectral fox! I know thee, I know thee!"

Mikkel had never suspected that he was anything so terrible; but, as he saw that the man was bent on mischief, he did not think it worthwhile to contradict him. He only curved his back and bristled, until the man, beside himself with fear, made a rush for the window and leaped out into the courtyard. Then Mikkel, thinking that he had had excitement enough for one night, curled himself up on his cushion behind the stove and went to sleep.

The next morning, when Mr. Barth arrived, he found a window in the back office broken, and the door of the safe wide open. On the floor lay a bundle of papers, all relating to the transactions of Tulstrup while a member of the firm, and, moreover, a hat, marked on the inside with Tulstrup's name, was found on a chair.

On the same day Mr. Lyng was summoned to the bedside of his former partner, who made a full confession, and offered to return through him the money which he had fraudulently acquired. His leg was broken, and he seemed otherwise shattered in body and mind. It had been his purpose, he said, to drive Mr. Lyng from the firm in disgrace, and he was sure he could have accomplished it, if Providence itself had not interfered. But, incredible as it seemed, he had seen a luminous animal in the bank, and he felt convinced that it was his father's spectral fox. It was well enough to smile at such things and call them childish, but he had certainly seen, he said, a wonderful, shining fox.

Mr. Lyng did not attempt to convince Mr. Tulstrup that he was wrong. He took the money and distributed it among those who had suffered by Mr. Tulstrup's frauds, and thus many needy people – widows and industrious labourers – regained their hard-earned property, and all because Mikkel's skin was luminous. When Mr. Lyng heard the whole story from Mr. Dreyer, he laughed heartily and long. But from that day he took a warm interest in Thor and his fox, and sent the former to school and, later, to the university, where he made an honourable name for himself by his talents and industry.

Poor Mikkel is now almost grey, and his teeth are so blunt that he has to have his food minced before he can eat it. But he still occupies a soft rug behind the stove in the student's room, and Thor hopes he will live long enough to be introduced to his master's wife. For it would be a pity if she were not to know him to whom her husband owes his position, and she, accordingly, hers.

Magnie's Dangerous Ride

(Norwegian)

I

MAGNIE WAS CONSUMED with the hunting fever. He had been away to school since he was ten years old, and had never had the chance of doing anything remarkable. While his brother, Olaf, who was a midshipman in the navy, roamed about the world, and had delightful adventures with Turks and Arabs, and all sorts of outlandish people, Magnie had to scan Virgil and Horace and torment his soul with algebraic problems. It was not at all the kind of life he had sketched out for himself, and if it had not been his father who had imposed it upon him, he would have broken away from all restraints and gone to Turkey or China, or some place where exciting things happened. In the meanwhile, as he lacked money for such an enterprise, he would content himself with whatever excitement there was in hunting, and as his brothers, Olaf and little Edwin (who was fourteen years old), were also at home for the vacation, there was a prospect of many delightful expeditions by sea and by land. Moreover, their old friend Grim Hering-Luck, who was their father's right-hand man, had promised to be at their disposal and put them on the track of exciting experiences. They had got each a gun, and had practised shooting at a target daily since their return from the city. Magnie, or Magnus Birk, as his real name was, had once (though Olaf stoutly maintained that it was mere chance) hit the bull's-eye at a hundred yards, and he was now eager to show his skill on something more valuable than a painted target. It was therefore decided that Grim and the boys should go reindeer-hunting. They were to be accompanied by the professional hunter, Bjarne Sheepskin.

It was a glorious morning. The rays of the sun shot from the glacier peaks in long radiant shafts down into the valley. The calm mirror of the fiord glittered in the light and fairly dazzled the eye, and the seabirds drifted in noisy companies about the jutting crags, plunged headlong into the sea, and scattered the spray high into the air. The blue smoke rose perpendicularly from the chimneys of the fishermen's cottages along the beach, and the housewives, still drowsy with sleep, came out, rubbed their eyes and looked toward the sun to judge of the hour. One boat after another was pushed out upon the water, and the ripples in their wakes spread in long diverging lines toward either shore. The fish leaped in the sun, heedless of the gulls which sailed in wide circles under the sky, keeping a sharp lookout for the movements of the finny tribe. The three boys could only stand and gaze in dumb astonishment upon the splendid sights which the combined heavens, earth, and sea afforded. Their father, who was much pleased with their determination and enterprise, had readily given his consent to the reindeer hunt, on condition that Grim should take command and be responsible for their safety. They were now mounted upon three sturdy ponies, while their provisions, guns, and other commodities were packed upon a fourth beast – a shaggy little monster named Bruno, who looked more like a hornless goat than a horse. Bjarne Sheepskin, a long, round-shouldered fellow, with a pair of small, lively eyes, was leading this heavily laden Bruno by the bridle, and the little caravan, being once set in motion, climbed the steep slopes toward the mountains with much persistence and dexterity. The ponies, which had been especially trained for mountain climbing, planted their hoofs upon the slippery rocks with a precision which was wonderful to behold, jumped from stone to stone, slipped, scrambled up and down, but never fell. As they entered the pine forest, where the huge trunks grew in long, dark colonnades, letting in here and there stray patches of sunshine, partridges and ptarmigan often started under the very noses of the horses, and Magnie clamoured loudly for his gun, and grew quite angry with Bjarne, who would allow "no fooling with tomtits and chipmunks, when they were in search of big game." Even hares were permitted to go unmolested; and it was not until a fine capercailzie cock tumbled out of the underbrush close to the path, that Bjarne flung his gun to his cheek and fired. The capercailzie made a somersault in the air, and the feathers flew about it as it fell. Bjarne picked it up quietly, tied its legs together, and hung it on the pommel of Edwin's saddle. "That will make a dinner for gentlefolks," he said, "if the dairymaids up on the *saeters* should happen to have nothing in the larder."

Gradually, as they mounted higher, the trees became more stunted in their growth, and the whole character of the vegetation changed. The low dwarf birch stretched its long, twisted branches along the earth, the silvery-white reindeer-moss clothed in patches the barren ground, and a few shivering alpine plants lifted their pale, pink flowers out of the general desolation. As they reached the ridge of the lower mountain range the boys saw before them a scene the magnificence of which nearly took their breath away. Before them lay a wide mountain plain, in the bottom of which two connected lakes lay coldly glittering. Round about, the plain was settled with rude little log-houses, the so-called *saeter*s, or mountain dairies, where the Norse peasants spend their brief summers, pasturing their cattle.

They started at a lively trot down the slope toward this highland plain, intending to reach the Hasselrud *saeter*, where they expected to spend the night; for it was already several hours past noon, and there could be no thought of hunting reindeer so late in the day. Judging by appearances, the boys concluded that fifteen or twenty minutes would bring them to the *saeter*; but they rode on for nearly two hours, and always the cottages seemed to recede, and the distance showed no signs of diminishing. They did not know how deceptive all distances are in this wondrously clear mountain air, whose bright transparency is undimmed by the dust and exhalations of the lower regions of the earth. They would scarcely have believed that those huge glacier peaks, which seemed to be looming up above their very heads, were some eight to twelve miles away, and that the eagle which soared above them was far beyond the range of their rifles.

It was about five o'clock when they rode in upon the *saeter* green, where the dairymaids were alternately blowing their horns and yodelling. Their long flaxen braids hung down their backs, and their tight-fitting scarlet bodices and white sleeves gave them a picturesque appearance. The cattle were lowing against the sky, answering the call of the horn. The bells of cows, goats, and sheep were jangled in harmonious confusion; and the noise of the bellowing bulls, the bleating sheep, and the neighing horses was heard from all sides over the wide plain.

The three brothers were received with great cordiality by the maids, and they spent the evening, after the supper was finished, in listening to marvellous stories about the ogres who inhabited the mountains, and the hunting adventures with which Bjarne Sheepskin's life had been crowded, and which he related with a sportsman's usual exaggerations. The beds in one of the *saeter* cottages were given up to the boys, and they slept peacefully until about four o'clock in the morning, when Grim aroused them and told them that everything was ready for their departure. They swallowed their breakfast hastily, and started in excited silence across the plateau. Edwin and the horses they left behind in charge of the dairymaids, but took with them an old staghound who had some good blood in him, and a finer scent than his sedate behaviour and the shape of his nose would have led one to suppose.

Light clouds hovered under the sky; the mist lay like a white sheet over the mountain, and drifted in patches across the plain. Bjarne and Grim were carrying the guns, while Olaf led the hound, and Magnus trotted briskly along, stopping every now and then to examine every unfamiliar object that came in his way. The wind blew toward them, so that there was no chance that their scent could betray them, in case there were herds of deer toward the north at the base of the glaciers. They had not walked very far, when Bjarne put his hand to his lips and stooped down to examine the ground. The dog lifted his nose and began to snuff the air, wag his tail, and whine impatiently.

"Hush, Yutul," whispered Bjarne; "down! down, and keep still!"

The dog crouched down obediently and held his peace.

"Here is a fresh track," the hunter went on, pointing to a hardly perceptible depression in the moss. "There has been a large herd here – one buck and at least a dozen cows. Look, here is a stalk that has just been bitten off, and the juice is not dry yet."

"How long do you think it will be before we shall meet them?" asked Magnus, breathlessly. The hunting-fever was throbbing in his veins, and he crawled cautiously among the boulders with his rifle cocked.

"Couldn't tell; may be an hour, may be three. Hand me your field-glass, Lieutenant, and I will see if I can catch sight of 'em. A grey beast ain't easily seen agin the grey stone. It was fer the same reason I wanted ye to wear grey clothes; we don't want to give the game any advantage, fer the sentinels be allers on the lookout fer the herd, and at the least bit of unfamiliar colour, they give their warnin' snort, and off starts the flock, scudding away like a drift of mist before the wind."

Crouching down among the lichen-clad rocks, all listened in eager expectation.

"Down!" whispered Bjarne, "and cock rifles! A pair of antlers agin the snow! Hallo! it is as I thought – a big herd. One, two, three – five – seven – ten – fourteen! One stunnin' buck, worth his forty dollars at least. Now follow me slowly. Look out for your guns! You, Grim, keep the dog muzzled."

The boys strained their eyes above the edge of the stones, but could see nothing. Their hearts hammered against their sides, and the blood throbbed in their temples. As far as their eyes could reach they saw only the grey waste of boulders, interrupted here and there by patches of snow or a white glacier-stream, which plunged wildly over a precipice, while a hovering moke indicated its further progress through the plain. Nevertheless, trusting the experience of their leader, they made no remark, but crept after him, choosing like him every available stone for cover. After half an hour of this laborious exercise, Bjarne suddenly stretched himself flat upon the ground, and the others, though seeing no occasion for such a manœuvre, promptly followed his example. But the next moment enlightened them. Looming up against the white snow, some sixty or a hundred feet from them, they saw a magnificent pair of antlers, and presently the whole body of a proud animal was distinctly visible against the glacier. In the ravine below a dozen or more cows with their calves were nibbling the moss between the stones, but with great deliberateness, lifting their heads every minute and snuffing the air suspiciously; they presently climbed up on the hard snow and began a frolic, the like of which the boys had never seen before. The great buck raised himself on his hind legs, shook his head, and made a leap, kicking the snow about him with great vehemence. Several of the cows took this as an invitation for a general jollification, and they began to frisk about, kicking their heels against the sky and shaking their heads, not with the wanton grace of their chief, but with half-pathetic attempts at imitation. This, Magnus thought, was evidently a reindeer ball; and very sensible they were to have it early in the morning, when they felt gay and frisky, rather than in the night, when they ought to be asleep. What troubled him, however, was that Bjarne did not shoot; he himself did not venture to send a bullet into the big buck, although it seemed to him he had an excellent aim. The slightest turn in the wind would inevitably betray them, and then they would have had all their toil for nothing. He would have liked to suggest this to Bjarne; but in order to do this, he would have to overtake him, and Bjarne was still wriggling himself cautiously forward among the stones, pushing himself on with his elbows, as a seal does with his flippers. In his eagerness to impart his counsel to Bjarne, Magnus began to move more rapidly; raising himself on his knees he quite inadvertently showed his curly head above a boulder. The buck lifted his superb head with a snort, and with incredible speed the whole herd galloped away; but in the same moment two bullets whistled after them, and the buck fell flat upon the snow. The cow which had stood nearest to him reared on her hind legs, made a great leap, and plunged headlong down among the stones. With a wild war-whoop, the boys jumped up, and Magnus, who had come near ruining the whole sport, seized, in order to make up for his mishap, a long hunting-knife and rushed forward to give the buck the *coup de grâce*, in accordance with the rules of the chase. Bounding forward with reckless disregard of all obstacles, he was the first down on the snow. In one instant he was astride of the animal, and had just raised his knife, when up leaped the buck and tore away along the edge of the snow like a gust of wind. The long-range shot, hitting him in the head, had only stunned him, but had not penetrated the skull. And, what was worse, in his bewilderment at the unexpected manœuvre, Magnus dropped his knife, seizing instinctively the horns of the reindeer to keep from falling. Away they went with a terrific dizzying speed. The frightened boy clung convulsively to the great antlers; if he should fall off, his head would be crushed against the boulders. The cold glacier-wind whistled in his ears, and stung his face like a multitude of tiny needles. He had to turn his head in order to catch his breath; and he strained his eyes to see if anything was being done by his companions for his rescue. But he could see nothing except a great expanse of grey and white lines, which ran into each other and climbed and undulated toward him and sloped away, but seemed associated with no tangible object. He thought, for a moment, that he saw Grim Hering-Luck aiming his gun, but he seemed to be up in the sky, and to be growing huger and huger until he looked more like a fantastic cloud than a man. The thought suddenly struck him that he might be fainting, and it sent a thrill of horror through him. With a vehement effort he mastered his fear and resolved that, whatever happened, he would not give way to weakness. If he was to lose his life, he would, at all events, make a hard fight for it; it was, on the whole, quite a valuable life, he concluded, and he did not mean to sell it cheaply.

Troubling himself little about the direction his steed was taking, he shut his eyes, and began to meditate upon his chances of escape; and after some minutes, he was forced to admit that they seemed very slim. When the buck should have exhausted his strength, as in the course of time he must, he would leave his rider somewhere in this vast trackless wilderness, where the biting wind swept down from the eternal peaks of ice, where wolves roamed about in great hungry companies, and where, beside them, the reindeer and the ptarmigan were the only living things amid the universal desolation. When he opened his eyes again, Magnus discovered that the buck had overtaken the fleeing herd, which, however, were tearing away madly at his approach, being evidently frightened at the sight and the scent of the unfamiliar rider. The animal was still galloping on, though with a less dizzying rapidity, and Magnus could distinguish the general outline of the objects which seemed to be rushing against him, as if running a race in the opposite direction. The herd were evidently betaking themselves into the upper glacier region, where no foot less light and swift than theirs could find safety among the terrible ravines and crevasses.

Fully an hour had passed, possibly two, and it seemed vain to attempt to measure the distance which he had passed over in this time. At all events, the region did not present one familiar object, and of Olaf and his companions Magnie saw no trace. The only question was, what chance had they of finding him, if they undertook to search for him, as, of course, they would. If he could only leave some sign or mark by which they might know the direction he had taken, their search might perhaps be rewarded with success. He put one hand in his pocket, but could find nothing that he could spare except a red silk handkerchief. That had the advantage of being bright, and would be sure to attract attention. The dog would be likely to detect it or to catch the scent of it. But he must have something heavy to tie up in the handkerchief, or it might blow 'all over creation.' The only thing he could find was a silver matchbox which he had obtained by a trade with Olaf, and which bore the latter's initials. He carefully emptied it, and put the matches (which he foresaw might prove useful) in his vest-pocket; then tied up the box securely and dropped it, with the handkerchief, upon a conspicuous rock, where its bright colour might appear striking and unnatural. He was just on the ridge of what proved to be a second and higher mountain plateau, the wild grandeur of which far transcended that of the first. Before him lay a large sheet of water of a cool green tint, and so clear that the bottom was visible as far as the eye could reach. A river had made its way from the end of this lake and plunged, in a series of short cataracts, down the slope to the lower plain.

It made Magnus shiver with dread to look at this coldly glittering surface, and what was his horror when suddenly his reindeer, in his pursuit of the herd, which were already in the water, rushed in, and began, with loud snorts, to swim across to the farther shore! This was an unforeseen stratagem which extinguished his last hope of rescue; for how could Bjarne track him through the water, and what means would he find of crossing, in case he should guess that the herd had played this dangerous trick on him? He began to dread also that the endurance of the buck would be exhausted before he reached dry land again, and that they might both perish miserably in the lake. In this horrible distress nothing occurred to him except to whisper the Lord's Prayer; but as his terror increased, his voice grew louder and louder, until he fairly shouted the words, "And deliver us from evil," and the echoes from the vast solitudes repeated, first clearly and loudly, then with fainter and fainter accents: "And deliver us from evil – and deliver us from evil." His despairing voice rang strangely under the great empty sky, and rumbled among the glaciers, which flung it back and forth until it died away in the blue distance. It was as if the vast silent wilderness, startled at the sound of a human voice, were wonderingly repeating the strange and solemn words.

A vague sense of security stole over him when he had finished his prayer. But the chill of the icy water had nearly benumbed his limbs, and he feared that the loss of heat would conquer his will, and make him unconscious before the buck should reach the shore. He felt distinctly his strength ebbing away, and he knew of nothing that he could do to save himself. Then suddenly a daring thought flashed through his brain. With slow and cautious movements he drew his legs out of the water, and, standing for a moment erect on the buck's back, he crawled along his neck and climbed up on the great antlers, steadying himself carefully and clinging with all his might. His only fear was that the animal would shake him off and send him headlong into the icy bath from which he was endeavouring to escape. But, after two futile efforts, during which the boy had held on only by desperate exertion, the buck would probably have resigned himself to his fate, if he had not been in imminent danger of drowning. Magnus was, therefore, much against his will, forced to dip his limbs into the chilly water, and resume his former position. It was a strange spectacle, to see all the horned heads round about sticking out of the water, and Magnus, though he had always had a thirst for adventures, had never expected to find himself in such an incredible situation. Fortunately, they were now approaching the shore, and whatever comfort there was in having *terra firma* under his feet would not be wanting to him. The last minutes were indeed terribly long, and again and again the buck, overcome with fatigue, dipped his nose under the water, only to raise it again with a snort, and shake his head as if impatient to rid himself of his burden. But the boy, with a spark of reviving hope, clung only the more tenaciously to the antlers, and remained unmoved.

At last – and it seemed a small eternity since he had left his brother and companions – Magnus saw the herd scramble up on the stony beach. The buck he rode was soon among the foremost, and, having reached the land, shook his great body and snorted violently.

"Now's my chance," thought Magnus; "now I can slide off into the snow before he takes to his heels again."

But, odd as it may seem, he had a reluctance to part company with the only living creature (except the wolves) that inhabited this awful desert. There was a vague chance of keeping from freezing to death as long as he clung to the large, warm animal; while, seated alone upon this bleak shore, with his clothes wringing wet, and the cold breath of the glacier sweeping down upon him, he would die slowly and miserably with hunger and cold. He was just contemplating this prospect, seeing himself in spirit lying dead upon the shore of the lake, and picturing to himself the grief of his brother and father, when suddenly his glance was arrested by what seemed a faint column of smoke rising from among the boulders. The herd of reindeer had evidently made the same discovery, for they paused, in a startled manner, and wheeled about toward the easterly shore, past which a branch of the glacier was pushing downward into the lower fiord-valley.

Magnie, who had by this time made up his mind not to give up his present place except for a better one, strained his eye in the opposite direction, to make sure that he was not deceived; and having satisfied himself that what he saw was really smoke, he determined to leap from his seat at the very first opportunity. But as yet the speed of the buck made such a venture unsafe. With every step, however, the territory was becoming more irregular, and made the progress even of a reindeer difficult.

Magnus drew up his feet, and was about to slide off, having planned to drop with as slight a shock as possible upon a flat moss-grown rock, when, to his utter amazement, he saw a human figure standing at the edge of the glacier, and aiming a rifle, as it appeared, straight at his head. He tried to scream, but terror choked his voice. He could not bring forth a sound. And before even the thought had taken shape in his bewildered brain he saw a flash, and heard the report of a shot which rumbled away with tremendous reverberations among the glaciers. There was a surging sound in his ears, and strange lights danced before his eyes. He thought he must be dead.

II

Magnie never knew how long he was unconscious. The first thing he remembered was a delicious sense of warmth and comfort stealing through him, and strange, unintelligible sounds buzzing in the air about him. Somebody was talking kindly to him, and a large, warm hand was gliding over his forehead and cheeks. The peace and warmth were grateful to him after the intense strain of his dangerous ride. He was even loth to open his eyes when his reviving memory began to make the situation clear to him.

"It was a reckless shot, Harry," he heard someone say in a foreign tongue, which he soon recognized as English, "even if it did turn out well. Suppose you had sent your bullet crashing through the young fellow instead of the buck. How would you have felt then?"

"I should have felt very badly, I am sure," answered a younger voice, which obviously belonged to Magnie's rescuer; "but I followed my usual way of doing things. If I didn't act that way, I shouldn't act at all. And you will admit, Uncle, it is a queer sort of thing to see a fellow come riding on a reindeer buck, in the midst of a wild herd, and in a trackless wilderness like this, where nobody but wolves or geologists would be apt to discover any attractions. Now, I saw by the young man's respectable appearance that he couldn't be a geologist; and if he was a wolf, I didn't mind much if I did shoot him."

At this point Magnie opened his eyes and stared wonderingly about him. He found himself in a small, cramped room, the walls of which were draped with canvas, and scarcely high enough under the ceiling to allow a man to stand erect. Against the walls a number of shining brass instruments were leaning, and in a corner there was a hearth, the smoke of which escaped through a hole in the roof. Two bunks filled with moss, with a sheet and a blanket thrown over each, completed the outfit of the primitive dwelling. But Magnie was more interested in the people than in the looks of the room. A large, blond, middle-aged man, inclined to stoutness, was holding Magnie's hand as if counting his pulse-beat, and a very good-looking young fellow, of about his own age, was standing at the hearth, turning a spit upon which was a venison steak.

"Hallo! Our young friend is returning from the land of Nod," said the youth who had been addressed as Harry. "I am glad you didn't start on a longer journey, young chap, when I fired at you; for if you had you would have interfered seriously with my comfort."

Magnie, who was a fair English scholar, understood perfectly what was said to him, but several minutes elapsed before he could collect himself sufficiently to answer. In order to gain time, he made an effort to raise himself and take a closer look at his surroundings, but was forced by the older man to abandon the attempt.

"Not so fast, my dear, not so fast"; he said, stooping over him, and gently pushing him back into a reclining position. "You must remember that you have a big lump on your head from your fall, and it won't do to be frisky just yet. But before conversing further, it might be well to ascertain whether we understand each other."

"Yes, I think – I think – I do," stammered Magnie. "I know some English."

"Ah, then we shall get along charmingly," the man remarked, with an encouraging smile. "And I think Harry's venison steak is done by this time; and dinner, as you know, affords the most delightful opportunity for getting acquainted. Gunnar, our guide, who is outside skinning your reindeer buck, will soon present himself and serve the dinner. Here he is, and he is our cook, butler, chambermaid, laundress, beast of burden, and interpreter, all in one."

The man to whom the professor alluded was at this moment seen crawling on his hands and knees through the low doorway, which his bulky figure completely filled. He was a Norwegian peasant of the ordinary sort, with a square, rudely cut face, dull blue eyes, and a tuft of towy hair hanging down over his forehead. With one hand he was dragging the skin of the buck, and between his teeth he held an ugly-looking knife.

"Ve haf got to bury him," he said.

"Bury him!" cried Harry. "Why, you blood-thirsty wretch, don't you see he is sitting there, looking as bright as a sixpence?"

"I mean de buck," replied Gunnar, imperturbably.

"And why do you wish to bury the buck? I would much rather eat him. This steak here has a most tempting flavour, and I am quite tired of canned abominations by this time."

"De volves vill be sure to scent de meat, now dat it is flayed, and before an hour ve might haf a whole congregation of dem here."

"Well, then, we will shoot them down," insisted the cheerful Harry. "Come, now, Uncle, and let us have a civilized dinner. I don't pretend to be an expert in the noble art of cookery; but if this tastes as good as it smells, I wouldn't exchange it for a Delmonico banquet. And if the wolves, as Gunnar says, can smell a dead reindeer miles away, they would be likely to smell a venison steak from the ends of creation. Perhaps, if we don't hurry, all the wolves of the earth may invite themselves to our dinner."

Gunnar, upon whom this fanciful raillery was lost, was still standing on all fours in the door, with his front half in the warm room and his rearward portion in the arctic regions without. He was gazing helplessly from one to another, as if asking for an explanation of all this superfluous talk. "Vill you cawme and help me, Mester Harry?" he asked at last, stolidly.

"Yes, when I have had my dinner I will, Mester Gunnar," answered Harry, gayly.

"Vel, I haf notting more to say, den," grumbled the guide; "but it vould vonder me much if, before you are troo, you von't have some unbidden guests."

"All right, Gunnar – the more the merrier," retorted Harry as, with exaggerated imitation of a waiter's manner, he distributed plates, knives, and napkins to Magnie and his uncle.

They now fell to chatting, and Magnie learned, after having given a brief account of himself, that his entertainers were Professor Winchester, an American geologist, and his nephew, Harry Winchester, who was accompanying his uncle, chiefly for the fun of the thing, and also for the purpose of seeing the world and picking up some crumbs of scientific knowledge. The professor was especially interested in glaciers and their action in ages past upon the surface of the earth, and, as the Norwegian glaciers had never been thoroughly studied, he had determined to devote a couple of months to observations and measurements, with a view to settling some mooted geological questions upon which he had almost staked his reputation.

They had just finished the steak, which would perhaps have been tenderer if it had not been so fresh, and were helping themselves to the contents of a jar of raspberry preserves, when Harry suddenly dropped his spoon and turned, with a serious face, to his uncle.

"Did you hear that?" he said.

"No; what was it?"

Harry waited for a minute; then, as a wild, doleful howl was heard, he laid his hand on the professor's arm, and remarked: "The old fellow was right. We shall have unbidden guests."

"But they are hardly dangerous in these regions, so far as I can learn," said the professor, reassuringly.

"That depends upon their number. We could tackle a dozen; but two dozen we might find troublesome. At any rate, they have spoiled my appetite for raspberry jam, and that is something I shan't soon forgive them."

Three or four howls sounding nearer, and echoing with terrible distinctness from the glaciers, seemed to depress Harry's spirits still further, and he put the jar away and began to examine the lock of his rifle.

"They are evidently summoning a mass-meeting," remarked the professor, as another chorus of howls re-echoed from the glacier. "I wish we had more guns."

"And I wish mine were a Remington or a springfield breech-loader, with a dozen cartridges in it!" Harry exclaimed. "These double-barrelled Norwegian machines, with two shots in them, are really good for nothing in an emergency. They are antediluvian both in shape and construction."

He had scarcely finished this lament, when Gunnar's huge form reappeared in the door, quadruped fashion, and made an attempt to enter. But his great bulk nearly filled the narrow room, and made it impossible for the others to move. He examined silently first Harry's rifle, then his own, cut off a slice of steak with his pocket-knife, and was about to crawl out again, when the professor, who could not quite conceal his anxiety, asked him what he had done with the reindeer.

"Oh!" he answered, triumphantly, "I haf buried him among de stones, vhere he vill be safe from all de volves in de vorld."

"But, my dear fellow," ejaculated the professor, hotly, "why didn't you rather let the wolves have it? Then, at least, they would spare us."

"You surely vouldn't gif a goot fresh reindeer, legs and all, to a pack of skountrelly volves, vould you?"

"I would much rather give them that than give them myself."

"But it is vort tventy dollars, if you can get it down fresh and sell it to de English yachts," protested Gunnar, stolidly.

"Yes, yes; but you great stupid," cried the professor in despair, "what do you think my life is worth? And Master Harry's? And this young fellow's?" (pointing to Magnie). "Now go as quick as you can and dig the deer out again."

Gunnar, scarcely able to comprehend such criminal wastefulness, was backing out cautiously with his feet foremost, when suddenly he gave a scream and a jump which nearly raised the roof from the hut. It was evident that he had been bitten. In the same moment a fresh chorus of howls resounded without, mingled with sharp, whining barks, expressive of hunger and ferocity. There was something shudderingly wild and mournful in these long-drawn discords, as they rose toward the sky in this lonely desert; and brave as he was, Magnie could not restrain the terror which he felt stealing upon him. Weakened by his icy bath, moreover, and by the nervous strain of his first adventure, he had no great desire to encounter a pack of ravenous wolves. Still, he manned himself for the occasion and, in as steady a voice as he could command, begged the professor to hand him some weapon. Harry, who had instinctively taken the lead, had just time to reach him a long hunting-knife, and arm his uncle with an ax, when, through the door which Gunnar had left open, two wolves came leaping in and paused in bewilderment at the sight of the fire on the hearth. They seemed dazed by the light, and stood panting and blinking, with their trembling red tongues lolling out of their mouths. Harry, whose gun was useless at such close range, snatched the axe away from the professor, and at one blow split the skull of one of the intruders, while Magnie ran his knife up to the very hilt in the neck of the other. The beast was, however, by no means dead after that, but leaped up on his assailant's chest, and would have given him an ugly wound in the neck had not the professor torn it away and flung it down upon the fire, where, with a howling whine, it expired. The professor had also found time to bolt the door before more visitors could enter; and two successive shots without seemed to indicate that Gunnar was holding his own against the pack. But the question was, how long would he succeed in keeping them at bay? He had fired both his shots, and he would scarcely have a chance to load again, with the hungry beasts leaping about him. This they read in one another's faces, but no one was anxious to anticipate the other in uttering his dread.

"Help, help!" cried Gunnar, in dire need.

"Take your hand away, Uncle!" demanded Harry. "I am going out to help him."

"For your life's sake, Harry," implored the professor, "don't go! Let me go! What would your mother say to me if I should return without you?"

"I'll come back again, Uncle, don't you fear," said the youth, with feigned cheerfulness; "but I won't let this poor fellow perish before my very eyes, even though he is a fool."

"It was his foolishness which brought this danger upon us," remonstrated the professor.

"He knew no better," cried Harry, tearing the door open, and with axe uplifted rushing out into the twilight. What he saw seemed merely a dark mass, huddled together and swaying sideways, from which now and then a black figure detached itself with a howl, jumped wildly about, and again joined the dark, struggling mass. He could distinguish Gunnar's head, and his arms fighting desperately, and, from the yelps and howls of the wolves, he concluded that he had thrown away the rifle and was using his knife with good effect.

"Help!" he yelled, "help!"

"You shall have it, old fellow," cried Harry, plunging forward and swinging his axe about him; and the professor, who had followed close at his heels, shouting at the top of his voice, pressed in Harry's wake right into the centre of the furious pack. But, at that very instant, there came a long "Hallo-o!" from the lake below, and a rifle-bullet flew whistling above their heads and struck a rock scarcely a yard above the professor's hat. Several wolves lay gasping and yelping on the ground, and the rest slunk aside. Another shot followed, and a large beast made a leap and fell dead among the stones. Gunnar, who was lying bleeding upon the ground, was helped to his feet, and supported by Harry and the professor to the door of the cottage.

"Hallo, there!" shouted Harry, in response to the call from below.

"Hallo!" someone shouted back.

The figures of three men were now seen looming up in the dusk, and Magnie, who instinctively knew who they were, sprang to meet them, and in another moment lay sobbing in his brother's arms. The poor lad was so completely unnerved by the prolonged suspense and excitement, that he had to be carried back into the hut, and his brother, after having hurriedly introduced himself to the professor, came very near giving way to his feelings, too. Gunnar's wounds, which were numerous, though not serious, were washed and bandaged by Grim Hering-Luck; and having been wrapped in a horse-blanket, to keep out the cold, he was stowed away in a bunk and was soon asleep. As the hut was too small to admit all the company at once, Grim and Bjarne remained outside, and busied themselves in skinning the seven wolves which had fallen on the field of battle. Harry, who had got a bad bite in his arm, which he refused to regard as serious, consented with reluctance to his uncle's surgery, and insisted upon sitting up and conversing with Olaf Birk, to whom he had taken a great liking. But after a while the conversation began to lag, and tired heads began to droop; and when, about midnight, Grim crept in to see how his invalid was doing, he found the professor reclining on some loose moss upon the floor, while Harry was snoring peacefully in a bunk, using Olaf's back for a pillow. And Olaf, in spite of his uncomfortable attitude, seemed also to have found his way to the land of Nod. Grim, knowing the danger of exposure in this cold glacier air, covered them all up with skins and horse-blankets, threw a few dry sticks upon the fire, and resumed his post as sentinel at the door.

The next morning Professor Winchester and his nephew accepted Olaf's invitation to spend a few days at Hasselrud, and without further adventures the whole caravan descended into the valley, calling on their way at the *saeter* where Edwin had been left. It appeared, when they came to discuss the strange incidents of the preceding day, that it was Magnie's silk handkerchief which had enabled them to track him to the edge of the lake, and, by means of a raft, which Bjarne kept hidden among the stones in a little bay, they had been enabled to cross, leaving their horses in charge of a shepherd boy whom they had found tending goats close by.

The reindeer cow which Olaf had killed was safely carried down to the valley, and two wolf-skins were presented to Magnie by Harry Winchester. The other wolf-skins, as well as the skin of the reindeer buck, Bjarne prepared in a special manner, and Harry looked forward with much pleasure to seeing them as rugs upon the floor of his room at college; and he positively swelled with pride when he imagined himself relating to his admiring fellow students the adventures which had brought him these precious possessions.

Big Hans and Little Hans

(Norwegian)

I

ON THE NORTHWESTERN COAST OF NORWAY the mountains hide their heads in the clouds and dip their feet in the sea. In fact, the cliffs are in some places so tall and steep that streams, flowing from the inland glaciers and plunging over their sides, vanish in the air, being blown in a misty spray out over the ocean. In other places there may be a narrow slope, where a few potatoes, some garden vegetables, and perhaps even a patch of wheat, may be induced to grow by dint of much coaxing; for the summer, though short, is mild and genial in those high latitudes, and has none of that fierce intensity which, with us, forces the vegetation into sudden maturity, and sends our people flying toward all the points of the compass during the first weeks in June.

It was on such a sunny little slope, right under the black mountain-wall, that Halvor Myrbraaten had built his cottage. Halvor was a merry fellow, who went about humming snatches of hymns and old songs and dance-melodies all day long, and sometimes mixed up both words and tune woefully; and when his memory failed him, sang anything that popped into his head. Some people said they had heard him humming the multiplication table to the tune of 'Old Norway's Lion,' and whole pages out of Luther's Catechism to jolly dance-tunes. Not that he ever meant to be irreverent; it was just his way of amusing himself. He was an odd stick, people thought, and not of much use to his family. Whatever he did, 'luck' went against him. But it affected his temper very little. Halvor was still light-hearted and good-natured, and went about humming as usual. If he went out hunting, and came home with an empty pouch, it did not interfere in the least with his gayety; but knowing well the reception which was in store for him; it did occasionally happen that he paused with a quizzical look before opening the door, and perhaps, after a minute's reflection, concluded to spend the night in the barn; for Turid, his wife, had a mind of her own, and knew how to express herself with emphasis. She was, as everyone admitted, a very worthy and competent woman, and accomplished more in a day than her husband did in a fortnight. But worthy and competent people are not invariably the pleasantest people to associate with, and the gay and genial good-for-nothing Halvor, with his bright irresponsible smile and his pleasant ways, was a far more popular person in the parish than his austere, estimable, over-worked wife. For one thing, with all her poverty, she had a great deal of pride; and people who had never suspected that one so poor could have any objection to receiving alms had been much offended by her curt way of refusing their proffered gifts.

Halvor, they said, showed a more realizing sense of his position: he had the humble and contrite heart which was becoming in an unsuccessful man, and accepted with equal cheerfulness and gratitude whatever was offered him, from a dollar bill to a pair of worn-out mittens. It was, in fact, this extreme readiness to accept things which first made difficulty between Halvor and his wife. It seemed to him a pure waste of labour to work for a thing which he could get for nothing; and it seemed to her a waste of something still more precious to accept as a gift what one might have honestly earned by work. But as she could never hope to have Halvor agree with her on this point, she comforted herself by impressing her own horror of alms-taking upon her children; and the children, in their turn, impressed the same sound principles upon their pet kid and the pussy cat.

There were five children at Myrbraaten. Hans, the eldest, was ten years old, and Dolly, the youngest, was one, and the rest were scattered between. It was a pretty sight to see them of a summer afternoon on the grass plot before the house, rolling over one another and gambolling like a sportive family of kittens; only you could hardly help feeling vaguely uneasy about the mountain, the steep, black wall of which, sparsely clad with pines, rose so threateningly above them. It seemed as if it must, some day, swoop down upon them and crush them. The mother, it must be admitted, was occasionally oppressed by some such fear; but when she reflected that the mountain had stood there from time immemorial, and had never yet moved, or harmed anyone, she felt ashamed of her apprehension, and blamed herself for her distrust of God's providence.

Besides the children there was another young inhabitant of the Myrbraaten cottage, and surely a very important one. He, too, was named Hans, but, in order to distinguish him from the son of the house, the word 'Little' was prefixed, and the latter, although he was really the smaller of the two, was called, by way of distinction, Big Hans. The most remarkable thing about Little Hans was that he had, in spite of his youth, a very well-developed beard. Big Hans, who had not a hair on his chin, rather envied him this manly ornament. Then, again, Little Hans was a capital fighter, and could knock you down in one round with great coolness and sweet-tempered seriousness, as if he were acting entirely from a sense of duty. He never used any hard words; but the moment his adversary attempted to rise, Little Hans quietly gave him another knock, and winked wickedly at him, as if warning him to lie still. He never bragged of his victories, but showed a modest self-appreciation to which very few of his age ever attain. Big Hans, who valued his friend and namesake above others, and had a hearty admiration for his many fine qualities, declared himself utterly unable to rival him in combativeness, modesty, and coolness of temper. For Big Hans, I am sorry to say, was sometimes given to bragging of his muscle and of his skill in turning hand-springs and standing on his head, and he could easily be teased into a furious temper. Now, Little Hans could not turn hand-springs, nor could he stand on his head; but, though he promptly resented any trifling with his dignity, I never once knew him to lose his temper. He never laughed when anything struck him as being funny; in fact, he seemed to regard every boisterous exhibition of feeling as undignified. He only turned his head away and stood chewing a piece of paper or a straw, with his usual look of comical gravity in his eye.

Many people wondered at the fast friendship which bound Big Hans and Little Hans together. Their tastes, people said, were dissimilar; in temperament, too, they had few points of resemblance. And yet they were absolutely inseparable. Wherever Big Hans went, Little Hans was sure to follow. Often they were seen racing along the beach or climbing up the mountainside; and, as Little Hans was a capital hand (or ought I to say foot?) at climbing, Big Hans often had hard work to keep up with him. Sometimes Little Hans would leap up a rock which was so steep that it was impossible for his friend to climb it, and then he would grin comically down at Big Hans, who would stand below calling tearfully to his companion until he descended, which usually was very soon. For Little Hans was very fond of Big Hans, and could never bear to see him cry. And that is not in the least to be wondered at, as Big Hans had saved him from starvation and death when Little Hans was really in the sorest need. Their acquaintance began in the following manner: one day when Big Hans was up in the mountains trapping hares, he heard a feeble voice in a cleft of the rocks nearby, and hurrying to the spot, he found Little Hans wedged in between two great stones, and his leg caught in so distressing a manner that it cost Big Hans nearly an hour's work to set it free. Then he dressed the bruised foot with a rag torn from the lining of his coat, and carried Little Hans home in his arms. And as Little Hans' parents had never claimed him, and he himself could give no satisfactory account of them, he had thenceforth remained at Myrbraaten, where all the children were very fond of him. Turid, their mother, on the other hand, had no great liking for him, especially after he had devoured her hymn book (which was her most precious property) and eaten with much appetite a piece of Dolly's dress. For, as I intimated, Little Hans' tastes were very curious, and nothing came amiss when he was hungry. He had a trick of pulling off Dolly's stockings when she was sitting out on the green, and if he were not discovered in time, he was sure to make his breakfast off of them. With these tastes, you will readily understand, Big Hans could have no sympathy, and the only thing which could induce him to forgive Little Hans' eccentricities was the fact that Little Hans was a goat.

II

In the winter of 187—, a great deal of snow fell on the northwestern coast of Norway. The old pines about the Myrbraaten cottage were laden down with it; the children had to be put to work with snow-shovels early in the morning, in order to hollow out a tunnel to the cow-stable where the cow stood bellowing with hunger. The mother, too, worked bravely, and sometimes when the thin roof of snow caved in and fell down upon them, they laughed heartily, and their mother, too, could not help laughing because they were so happy. Little Hans also made a pretence of working, but only succeeded in being in everybody's way, and when the cold snow drizzled down upon his nose he grinned and made faces so queer that the children shouted with merriment.

Day after day, and week after week, the snow continued to descend. Big Hans and his friend sat at the window watching the large feathery flakes, as they whirled slowly and silently through the air and covered the earth far and near with a white pall. Soon there was a scarcity of wood at the Myrbraaten cottage, and Halvor was obliged to get into his *skees* and go to the forest. Humming the multiplication table (so far as he knew it) to the tune of a hymn, he pulled on his warmest jacket, took his axe from its hiding place under the eaves, and went in a slanting line up the mountainside; but before he had gone many rods it struck him that it was useless to go so far for wood, when the whole mountain-slope was covered with pines. Fresh pine would be a little hard to burn, to be sure, but then pine was full of pitch and would burn anyhow. He therefore took off his *skees*, dug a hole in the snow, and felled three or four trees only a few hundred rods above the cottage. When his wife heard the sound of his axe so near the house, she rushed out and cried to him:

"Halvor, Halvor, don't cut down the trees on the slope! They are all that keep the snow from coming down upon us in an avalanche, and sweeping us into the ocean!"

"Oh, the Lord will look out for his own," sang Halvor, cheerily.

"The Lord put the pine trees there to protect us," replied his wife.

But the end was that, in spite of his wife's protests, Halvor continued to fell the trees.

The heavy fall of snow was followed in the course of a week by a sudden thaw.

Strange creaking and groaning sounds stole through the forest. Sometimes when a large load of snow fell, it rolled and grew as it rolled, until it dashed against a huge trunk and nearly broke it with its weight.

Then, one night, there came down a great load which fell with a dull thud and rolled down and down, pushing a growing wall of snow before it, until it reached the clearing where Halvor had cut his wood; there, meeting with no obstructions, it gained a tremendous headway, sweeping all the snow and the felled trunks with it, and rushed down in a great mass, carrying along stones, shrubs, huge trees, and the very soil itself, leaving nothing but the bare rock behind it. How terrible was the sight! A smoke-like cloud rose in the darkness, and a sound as of a thousand thundering cataracts filled the night. On it swept, onward, with a wild, resistless speed! At the jutting rock, where the juniper stood, the avalanche divided, tearing up the old spruces and the birches by the roots and hurling them down, but leaving the juniper standing alone on its barren peak. It was but a moment's work. The avalanche shot downward with increased speed – hark! – a sharp shriek, a smothered groan, then a fierce hissing sound of waves that rose toward the sky and returned with a long thundering cannonade to the strand! The night was darker and the silence deeper than before.

III

Where the Myrbraaten cottage had stood, the bare rock now stares black and dismal against the sun. The rumour of the calamity spread like wildfire through the valley, and the folk of the whole parish came to gaze upon the ruin which the avalanche had wrought. All that was left of Myrbraaten was the cow-stable, where the cow and Little Hans and Big Hans had slept. Little Hans had been very ill-behaved the night before, so Turid had sent him to sleep with the cow; and Big Hans, who thought it would be cruel to ask his companion to spend the night in that dark stable, with only a cow for company, had gone with him and slept with him in the hay. Thus it happened that Little Hans and Big Hans both were saved. It was pitiful to see them shivering in the wet snow. Big Hans was crying as if his heart would break; and the women who crowded about him were unable to comfort him. What should he, a small boy of ten, do alone in this wide world? His father and his mother and his little brothers and sisters were all gone, and there was no one left who cared for him. Just then Little Hans, who was anxious to express his sympathy, put his nose close to Big Hans' face and rubbed it against his cheek.

"Yes, you are right, Little Hans," sobbed the boy, embracing his faithful friend; "you do care for me. You are the only one I have left now, in all the world. You and I will stand by each other always."

Little Hans then said, "Ma-a-a," which in his language meant, "Yes."

The question soon arose in the parish – what was to be done with Big Hans? He had no relatives except a brother of his mother, who had emigrated many years before to Minnesota; and there was no one else who seemed disposed to assume the burden of his support. It was finally decided that he should be hired out as a pauper to the lowest bidder, and that the parish should pay for his board. But when the people who bid for him refused to take Little Hans too, the boy determined, after some altercation with the authorities, to seek his uncle in America. One thing he was sure of, and that was that he would not part from Little Hans. But there was no one in the parish who would board Little Hans without extra pay. Accordingly, the cow and the barn were sold for the boy's benefit, and he and his comrade went on foot to the city, where they bought a ticket for New York.

Thus it happened that Big Hans and Little Hans became Americans. But before they reached the United States some rather curious things happened to them. The captain of the steamship, Big Hans found, was not willing to take a goat as a passenger, and Big Hans was forced to return with his friend to the pier, while the other emigrants thronged on board. He was nearly at his wits' end, when it suddenly occurred to him to put Little Hans in a bag and smuggle him on board as baggage. This was a lucky thought. Little Hans was quite heavy, to be sure, but he seemed to comprehend the situation perfectly, and kept as still as a mouse in his bag while Big Hans, with the assistance of a benevolent fellow passenger, lugged him up the gangplank. And when he emerged from his retirement some time after the steamer was well under way, none of the officers even thought of throwing the poor goat overboard; for Little Hans became a great favourite with both crew and passengers, although he played various mischievous pranks, in his quiet, unostentatious way, and ate some shirts which had been hung out to dry.

It was early in April when the two friends arrived in New York. They attracted considerable attention as they walked up Broadway together; and many people turned around to laugh at the little emigrant boy, in his queer Norwegian costume, who led a full-grown goat after him by a halter. The bootblacks and the newsboys pointed their fingers at them, and, when that had no effect, made faces at them, and pulled Big Hans by his short jacket and Little Hans by his short tail. Big Hans was quite frightened when he saw how many of them there were, but, perceiving that Little Hans was not in the least ruffled, he felt ashamed of himself, and took heart again. Thus they marched on for several blocks, while the crowd behind them grew more and more boisterous and importunate. Suddenly, one big boy, who seemed to be the leader of the gang, sprang forward with a yell and knocked off Big Hans' hat, while all the rest cheered loudly; but just as he was turning around to enjoy his triumph, Little Hans turned around too, and gave him a bump from behind which sent him headlong into the gutter. Then, rising on his hind legs, Little Hans leaped forward again and again, and despatched the second and third boy in the same manner, whereupon all the rest ran away, helter-skelter, scattering through the side streets. It was all done in so quiet and gentlemanly a manner that not one of the grown-up spectators who had gathered on the sidewalk thought of interfering. Big Hans, however, who had intended to see something of the city before starting for the West, was so discouraged at the inhospitable reception the United States had given him, that he gave up his purpose, and returned disconsolately to Castle Garden. There he spent the rest of the day, and when the night came, he went to sleep on the floor, with his little bundle under his head; while Little Hans, who did not seem to be sleepy, lay down at his side, quietly munching a piece of pie which he had stolen from somebody's luncheon-basket.

Early the next morning Big Hans was awakened by a gentle pulling at his coat-collar; and, looking up, he saw that it was Little Hans. He jumped up as quickly as he could, and he found that it was high time, for all the emigrants had formed into a sort of a procession and were filing through the gate on their way to the railway station. There were some seven or eight hundred of them – toil-worn, sad-faced men and women, and queer-looking children in all sorts of outlandish costumes. Big Hans and his friend ran to take their places at the very end of the procession, and just managed to slip through the gate before it was closed. At the railway station the boy exhibited his ticket which he had bought at the steamship office in Norway, and was just about to board the train, when the conductor cried out:

"Hold on, there! This is not a cattle-train! You can't take your goat into the passenger-car!"

Big Hans did not quite comprehend what was said, but from the expression of the conductor's voice and face, he surmised that there was some objection to his comrade.

"I think I have money enough to buy a ticket for Little Hans, too," he said, in his innocent Norwegian way, as he pulled a five-dollar bill from his pocket.

"I don't want your money," cried the conductor, who knew as little of Norwegian as Big Hans did of English.

"Get out of the way there with your billy goat!"

And he hustled the boy roughly out of the way to make room for the other emigrants, who were thronging up to the platform.

"Well, then," said Big Hans, "since they don't want us on the train, Little Hans, we shall have to walk to Minnesota. And as this railroad is going that way, I suppose we shall get there if we follow the track."

Little Hans seemed to think that this was a good plan; for, as soon as the train had steamed off, he started at a brisk rate along the track, so that his master had great difficulty in keeping up with him. For several hours they trudged along cheerfully, and both were in excellent spirits. Minnesota, Big Hans supposed, might, perhaps, be a day's journey off, and if he walked fast he thought he would probably be there at nightfall. When once he was there, he did not doubt but that everybody would know his Uncle Peter. He was somewhat puzzled, however, when he came to a place where no less than three railroad tracks branched off in different directions; and, as there was no one to ask, he sat down patiently in the shade of a tree and determined to wait. Presently a man came along with a red flag.

"Perhaps you would kindly tell me if this is the way to Minnesota," said Big Hans, taking off his cap and bowing politely to the man.

The man shook his head sullenly, but did not answer; he did not understand the boy's language.

"And you don't happen to know my uncle, Peter Volden?" essayed the boy, less confidently, making another respectful bow to the flagman.

"You are a queer loon of a chap," grumbled the man; "but if you don't jump off the track with your goat, the train will run over both of you."

He had hardly spoken, when the train was seen rounding the curve, and the boy had just time to pull Little Hans over into the ditch when the locomotive came thundering along, sending out volumes of black smoke, which scattered slowly in the warm air, making the sunlight for awhile seem grey and dingy. Big Hans was almost stunned, but picked himself up, with a little fainter heart than before, perhaps; but whispering a snatch of a prayer which his mother had taught him, he seized Little Hans by the halter, and started once more upon his weary way after the train.

"Minnesota must be a great way off, I am afraid," he said, addressing himself, as was his wont, to his companion; "but if we keep on walking, it seems to me we must, in the end, get there; or, what do you think, Little Hans?"

Little Hans did not choose to say what he thought, just then, for his attention had been called to some tender grass at the roadside which he knew tasted very sweet. Big Hans was then reminded that he, too, was hungry, and he sat down on a stone and ate a piece of bread which he had brought with him from Castle Garden. The sun rose higher in the sky and the heat grew more and more oppressive. Still the emigrant boy trudged on patiently. Whenever he came to a station he stopped, and read the sign, and shook his head sadly when he saw some unfamiliar name.

"Not Minnesota yet, Little Hans," he sighed; "I am afraid we shall have to take lodgings somewhere for the night. I am so footsore and tired."

It was then about six o'clock in the evening, and the two friends had walked about twenty miles. At the next station they met a hand-organ man, who was sitting on a truck, feeding his monkey.

Big Hans, who had never seen so funny an animal before, was greatly delighted. He went close up to the man, and put out his hand cautiously to touch the monkey.

"Are you going to Minnesota, too?" he asked, in a tone of great friendliness; "if so, we might bear each other company. I like that hairy little fellow of yours very much."

The hand-organ man, who, like most men of his calling, was an Italian, shook his head, and the monkey shook his head, too, as if to say, "All that may be very fine, but I don't understand it."

The boy, however, was too full of delight to notice whether he was understood or not; and when the monkey took off his little red hat and offered to shake hands with him, he laughed until the tears rolled down his cheeks. He seemed to have entirely forgotten Little Hans, who was standing by, glowering at the monkey with a look which was by no means friendly. The fact was, Little Hans had never been accustomed to any rival in his master's affection, and he didn't enjoy in the least the latter's interest in the monkey. He kept his jealousy to himself, however, as long as he could; but when Big Hans, after having giving ten cents to the organ-man, took the monkey on his lap and patted and stroked it, Little Hans' heart was ready to burst. He could not endure seeing his affections so cruelly trifled with. Bending his head and rising on his hind legs, he darted forward and gave his rival a knock on the head that sent him tumbling in a heap at Big Hans' feet. The Italian jumped up with a terrible shout and seized his treasure in his arms. The monkey made an effort to open its eyes, gave a little shiver, and – was dead. The boy stood staring in mute despair at the tiny stiffened body; he felt like a murderer. Hardly knowing what he did, he seized Little Hans' halter; but in the same moment the enraged owner of the monkey rushed at the goat with the butt end of his whip uplifted. Little Hans, who was dauntless as ever, dexterously dodged the blow, but the instant his antagonist had turned to vent his wrath upon his master, he gave him an impetus from behind which sent him headlong out upon the railroad track. A crowd of men and boys (of the class who always lounge about railroad stations) had now collected to see the fight, and goaded both combatants on with their jeering cries. The Italian, who was maddened with anger, had just picked himself up, and was plunging forward for a second attack upon Little Hans, when Big Hans, seeing the danger, flung himself over his friend's back, clasping his arms about his neck. The loaded end of the whip struck Big Hans in the back of the head; without a sound, the boy fell senseless upon the track.

Then a policeman arrived, and Little Hans, the Italian, and the insensible boy were taken to the police station. A doctor was summoned, and he declared that Big Hans' wound was very dangerous, and that he must be taken to the hospital. And there the emigrant boy lay for six weeks, hovering between life and death; but when, at the end of that time, he was permitted to go out, he heard with dread that he was to testify at the Italian's trial. A Norwegian interpreter was easily found, and when Hans told his simple story to the judge, there were many wet eyes in the courtroom. And he himself cried, too, for he thought that Little Hans was lost. But just as he had finished his story, he heard a loud "Ba-a-a" in his ear; he jumped down from the witness-stand and flung his arms about Little Hans' neck and laughed and cried as if he had lost his wits.

It is safe to say that such a scene had never before been witnessed in an American courtroom.

The next day Big Hans and Little Hans were both sent by rail, at the expense of some kind-hearted citizens, to their uncle in Minnesota. And it was there I made their acquaintance.

Tales of Transformation & Trickery

Introduction

IN 'THE WONDERFUL BIRCH', a girl's mother is transformed into a black sheep by a wicked witch, who subsequently slaughters her to make a soup. But her daughter lovingly gathers up her bones and buries them. She springs up out of the ground renewed, a living tree.

Mythic transformation can be for good or ill; it can be done in malevolence or spite, in a spirit of revenge or punishment, or kindly, to help someone out of a tight spot. It can hint ominously that the apparently benign may not be all it seems or reassure us that bad situations might yet end well. For better or worse, in other words, things can always change. At a still deeper level, tales of transformation exemplify the magical power of literature itself, the ability of metaphor to make one thing into another.

Trickery transforms situations. It makes appearances even more deceptive than they already were and finds solutions where there seem to be only problems. In so doing, it reminds us of the power of human ingenuity and resourcefulness. Our ability to make things better than they are.

The Wonderful Birch

(Finnish/Russian)

ONCE UPON A TIME there were a man and a woman, who had an only daughter. Now it happened that one of their sheep went astray, and they set out to look for it, and searched and searched, each in a different part of the wood. Then the good wife met a witch, who said to her:

"If you spit, you miserable creature, if you spit into the sheath of my knife, or if you run between my legs, I shall change you into a black sheep."

The woman neither spat, nor did she run between her legs, but yet the witch changed her into a sheep. Then she made herself look exactly like the woman, and called out to the good man:

"Ho, old man, halloa! I have found the sheep already!"

The man thought the witch was really his wife, and he did not know that his wife was the sheep; so he went home with her, glad at heart because his sheep was found. When they were safe at home the witch said to the man:

"Look here, old man, we must really kill that sheep lest it run away to the wood again."

The man, who was a peaceable quiet sort of fellow, made no objections, but simply said:

"Good, let us do so."

The daughter, however, had overheard their talk, and she ran to the flock and lamented aloud:

"Oh, dear little mother, they are going to slaughter you!"

"Well, then, if they do slaughter me," was the black sheep's answer, "eat you neither the meat nor the broth that is made of me, but gather all my bones, and bury them by the edge of the field."

Shortly after this they took the black sheep from the flock and slaughtered it. The witch made pease-soup of it, and set it before the daughter. But the girl remembered her mother's warning. She did not touch the soup, but she carried the bones to the edge of the field and buried them there; and there sprang up on the spot a birch tree – a very lovely birch tree.

Some time had passed away – who can tell how long they might have been living there? – when the witch, to whom a child had been born in the meantime, began to take an ill-will to the man's daughter, and to torment her in all sorts of ways.

Now it happened that a great festival was to be held at the palace, and the King had commanded that all the people should be invited, and that this proclamation should be made:

"Come, people all!
Poor and wretched, one and all!
Blind and crippled though ye be,
Mount your steeds or come by sea."

And so they drove into the King's feast all the outcasts, and the maimed, and the halt, and the blind. In the good man's house, too, preparations were made to go to the palace. The witch said to the man:

"Go you on in front, old man, with our youngest; I will give the elder girl work to keep her from being dull in our absence."

So the man took the child and set out. But the witch kindled a fire on the hearth, threw a potful of barleycorns among the cinders, and said to the girl:

"If you have not picked the barley out of the ashes, and put it all back in the pot before nightfall, I shall eat you up!"

Then she hastened after the others, and the poor girl stayed at home and wept. She tried to be sure to pick up the grains of barley, but she soon saw how useless her labour was; and so she went in her sore trouble to the birch tree on her mother's grave, and cried and cried, because her mother lay dead beneath the sod and could help her no longer. In the midst of her grief she suddenly heard her mother's voice speak from the grave, and say to her:

"Why do you weep, little daughter?"

"The witch has scattered barleycorns on the hearth, and bid me pick them out of the ashes," said the girl; "that is why I weep, dear little mother."

"Do not weep," said her mother consolingly. "Break off one of my branches, and strike the hearth with it crosswise, and all will be put right." The girl did so. She struck the hearth with the birchen branch, and lo! the barleycorns flew into the pot, and the hearth was clean. Then she went back to the birch tree and laid the branch upon the grave. Then her mother bade her bathe on one side of the stem, dry herself on another, and dress on the third. When the girl had done all that, she had grown so lovely that no one on earth could rival her. Splendid clothing was given to her, and a horse, with hair partly of gold, partly of silver, and partly of something more precious still. The girl sprang into the saddle, and rode as swift as an arrow to the palace. As she turned into the courtyard of the castle the King's son came out to meet her, tied her steed to a pillar, and led her in. He never left her side as they passed through the castle rooms; and all the people gazed at her, and wondered who the lovely maiden was, and from what castle she came; but no one knew her – no one knew anything about her. At the banquet the Prince invited her to sit next him in the place of honour; but the witch's daughter gnawed the bones under the table. The Prince did not see her, and thinking it was a dog, he gave her such a push with his foot that her arm was broken. Are you not sorry for the witch's daughter? It was not her fault that her mother was a witch.

Towards evening the good man's daughter thought it was time to go home; but as she went, her ring caught on the latch of the door, for the King's son had had it smeared with tar. She did not take time to pull it off, but, hastily unfastening her horse from the pillar, she rode away beyond the castle walls as swift as an arrow. Arrived at home, she took off her clothes by the birch tree, left her horse standing there, and hastened to her place behind the stove. In a short time the man and the woman came home again too, and the witch said to the girl:

"Ah! you poor thing, there you are to be sure! You don't know what fine times we have had at the palace! The King's son carried my daughter about, but the poor thing fell and broke her arm."

The girl knew well how matters really stood, but she pretended to know nothing about it, and sat dumb behind the stove.

The next day they were invited again to the King's banquet.

"Hey! old man," said the witch, "get on your clothes as quick as you can; we are bidden to the feast. Take you the child; I will give the other one work, lest she weary."

She kindled the fire, threw a potful of hemp seed among the ashes, and said to the girl:

"If you do not get this sorted, and all the seed back into the pot, I shall kill you!"

The girl wept bitterly; then she went to the birch tree, washed herself on one side of it and dried herself on the other; and this time still finer clothes were given to her, and a very beautiful steed. She broke off a branch of the birch tree, struck the hearth with it, so that the seeds flew into the pot, and then hastened to the castle.

Again the King's son came out to meet her, tied her horse to a pillar, and led her into the banqueting hall. At the feast the girl sat next him in the place of honour, as she had done the day before. But the witch's daughter gnawed bones under the table, and the Prince gave her a push by mistake, which broke her leg – he had never noticed her crawling about among the people's feet. She was VERY unlucky!

The good man's daughter hastened home again betimes, but the King's son had smeared the door-posts with tar, and the girl's golden circlet stuck to it. She had not time to look for it, but sprang to the saddle and rode like an arrow to the birch tree. There she left her horse and her fine clothes, and said to her mother:

"I have lost my circlet at the castle; the door-post was tarred, and it stuck fast."

"And even had you lost two of them," answered her mother, "I would give you finer ones."

Then the girl hastened home, and when her father came home from the feast with the witch, she was in her usual place behind the stove. Then the witch said to her:

"You poor thing! what is there to see here compared with what WE have seen at the palace? The King's son carried my daughter from one room to another; he let her fall, 'tis true, and my child's foot was broken.'

The man's daughter held her peace all the time, and busied herself about the hearth.

The night passed, and when the day began to dawn, the witch awakened her husband, crying:

"Hi! get up, old man! We are bidden to the royal banquet."

So the old man got up. Then the witch gave him the child, saying:

"Take you the little one; I will give the other girl work to do, else she will weary at home alone."

She did as usual. This time it was a dish of milk she poured upon the ashes, saying:

"If you do not get all the milk into the dish again before I come home, you will suffer for it."

How frightened the girl was this time! She ran to the birch tree, and by its magic power her task was accomplished; and then she rode away to the palace as before. When she got to the courtyard she found the Prince waiting for her. He led her into the hall, where she was highly honoured; but the witch's daughter sucked the bones under the table, and crouching at the people's feet she got an eye knocked out, poor thing! Now no one knew any more than before about the good man's daughter, no one knew whence she came; but the Prince had had the threshold smeared with tar, and as she fled her gold slippers stuck to it. She reached the birch tree, and laying aside her finery, she said:

"Alas I dear little mother, I have lost my gold slippers!"

"Let them be," was her mother's reply; "if you need them I shall give you finer ones."

Scarcely was she in her usual place behind the stove when her father came home with the witch. Immediately the witch began to mock her, saying:

"Ah! you poor thing, there is nothing for you to see here, and WE – ah: what great things we have seen at the palace! My little girl was carried about again, but had the ill-luck to fall and get her eye knocked out. You stupid thing, you, what do you know about anything?"

"Yes, indeed, what can I know?" replied the girl; "I had enough to do to get the hearth clean."

Now the Prince had kept all the things the girl had lost, and he soon set about finding the owner of them. For this purpose a great banquet was given on the fourth day, and all the people were invited to the palace. The witch got ready to go too. She tied a wooden beetle on where her child's foot should have been, a log of wood instead of an arm, and stuck a bit of dirt in the empty socket for an eye, and took the child with her to the castle. When all the people were gathered together, the King's son stepped in among the crowd and cried:

"The maiden whose finger this ring slips over, whose head this golden hoop encircles, and whose foot this shoe fits, shall be my bride."

What a great trying on there was now among them all! The things would fit no one, however.

"The cinder wench is not here," said the Prince at last; "go and fetch her, and let her try on the things."

So the girl was fetched, and the Prince was just going to hand the ornaments to her, when the witch held him back, saying:

"Don't give them to her; she soils everything with cinders; give them to my daughter rather."

Well, then the Prince gave the witch's daughter the ring, and the woman filed and pared away at her daughter's finger till the ring fitted. It was the same with the circlet and the shoes of gold. The witch would not allow them to be handed to the cinder wench; she worked at her own daughter's head and feet till she got the things forced on. What was to be done now? The Prince had to take the witch's daughter for his bride whether he would or no; he sneaked away to her father's house with her, however, for he was ashamed to hold the wedding festivities at the palace with so strange a bride. Some days passed, and at last he had to take his bride home to the palace, and he got ready to do so. Just as they were taking leave, the kitchen wench sprang down from her place by the stove, on the pretext of fetching something from the cowhouse, and in going by she whispered in the Prince's ear as he stood in the yard:

"Alas! dear Prince, do not rob me of my silver and my gold."

Thereupon the King's son recognized the cinder wench; so he took both the girls with him, and set out. After they had gone some little way they came to the bank of a river, and the Prince threw the witch's daughter across to serve as a bridge, and so got over with the cinder wench. There lay the witch's daughter then, like a bridge over the river, and could not stir, though her heart was consumed with grief. No help was near, so she cried at last in her anguish:

"May there grow a golden hemlock out of my body! perhaps my mother will know me by that token."

Scarcely had she spoken when a golden hemlock sprang up from her, and stood upon the bridge.

Now, as soon as the Prince had got rid of the witch's daughter he greeted the cinder wench as his bride, and they wandered together to the birch tree which grew upon the mother's grave. There they received all sorts of treasures and riches, three sacks full of gold, and as much silver, and a splendid steed, which bore them home to the palace. There they lived a long time together, and the young wife bore a son to the Prince. Immediately word was brought to the witch that her daughter had borne a son – for they all believed the young King's wife to be the witch's daughter.

"So, so," said the witch to herself; "I had better away with my gift for the infant, then."

And so saying she set out. Thus it happened that she came to the bank of the river, and there she saw the beautiful golden hemlock growing in the middle of the bridge, and when she began to cut it down to take to her grandchild, she heard a voice moaning:

"Alas! dear mother, do not cut me so!"

"Are you here?" demanded the witch.

"Indeed I am, dear little mother," answered the daughter "They threw me across the river to make a bridge of me."

In a moment the witch had the bridge shivered to atoms, and then she hastened away to the palace. Stepping up to the young Queen's bed, she began to try her magic arts upon her, saying:

"Spit, you wretch, on the blade of my knife; bewitch my knife's blade for me, and I shall change you into a reindeer of the forest."

"Are you there again to bring trouble upon me?" said the young woman.

She neither spat nor did anything else, but still the witch changed her into a reindeer, and smuggled her own daughter into her place as the Prince's wife. But now the child grew restless and cried, because it missed its mother's care. They took it to the court, and tried to pacify it in every conceivable way, but its crying never ceased.

"What makes the child so restless?" asked the Prince, and he went to a wise widow woman to ask her advice.

"Ay, ay, your own wife is not at home," said the widow woman; "she is living like a reindeer in the wood; you have the witch's daughter for a wife now, and the witch herself for a mother-in-law."

"Is there any way of getting my own wife back from the wood again?" asked the Prince.

"Give me the child," answered the widow woman. "I'll take it with me tomorrow when I go to drive the cows to the wood. I'll make a rustling among the birch leaves and a trembling among the aspens – perhaps the boy will grow quiet when he hears it."

"Yes, take the child away, take it to the wood with you to quiet it," said the Prince, and led the widow woman into the castle.

"How now? you are going to send the child away to the wood?" said the witch in a suspicious tone, and tried to interfere.

But the King's son stood firm by what he had commanded, and said:

"Carry the child about the wood; perhaps that will pacify it."

So the widow woman took the child to the wood. She came to the edge of a marsh, and seeing a herd of reindeer there, she began all at once to sing –

"Little Bright-eyes, little Redskin,
Come nurse the child you bore!
That bloodthirsty monster,
That man-eater grim,
Shall nurse him, shall tend him no more.
They may threaten and force as they will,
He turns from her, shrinks from her still,"

and immediately the reindeer drew near, and nursed and tended the child the whole day long; but at nightfall it had to follow the herd, and said to the widow woman:

"Bring me the child tomorrow, and again the following day; after that I must wander with the herd far away to other lands."

The following morning the widow woman went back to the castle to fetch the child. The witch interfered, of course, but the Prince said:

"Take it, and carry it about in the open air; the boy is quieter at night, to be sure, when he has been in the wood all day."

So the widow took the child in her arms, and carried it to the marsh in the forest. There she sang as on the preceding day –

"Little Bright-eyes, little Redskin,
Come nurse the child you bore!
That bloodthirsty monster,
That man-eater grim,
Shall nurse him, shall tend him no more.
They may threaten and force as they will,
He turns from her, shrinks from her still,"

and immediately the reindeer left the herd and came to the child, and tended it as on the day before. And so it was that the child throve, till not a finer boy was to be seen anywhere. But the King's son had been pondering over all these things, and he said to the widow woman:

"Is there no way of changing the reindeer into a human being again?"

"I don't rightly know," was her answer. "Come to the wood with me, however; when the woman puts off her reindeer skin I shall comb her head for her; whilst I am doing so you must burn the skin."

Thereupon they both went to the wood with the child; scarcely were they there when the reindeer appeared and nursed the child as before. Then the widow woman said to the reindeer:

"Since you are going far away tomorrow, and I shall not see you again, let me comb your head for the last time, as a remembrance of you."

Good; the young woman stript off the reindeer skin, and let the widow woman do as she wished. In the meantime the King's son threw the reindeer skin into the fire unobserved.

"What smells of singeing here?" asked the young woman, and looking round she saw her own husband. "Woe is me! you have burnt my skin. Why did you do that?"

"To give you back your human form again."

"Alack-a-day! I have nothing to cover me now, poor creature that I am!" cried the young woman, and transformed herself first into a distaff, then into a wooden beetle, then into a spindle, and into all imaginable shapes. But all these shapes the King's son went on destroying till she stood before him in human form again.

"Alas! wherefore take me home with you again," cried the young woman, "since the witch is sure to eat me up?"

"She will not eat you up," answered her husband; and they started for home with the child.

But when the witch wife saw them she ran away with her daughter, and if she has not stopped she is running still, though at a great age. And the Prince, and his wife, and the baby lived happy ever afterwards.

Lasse, My Thrall!

(Swedish)

ONCE UPON A TIME there was a prince or a duke or whatever you choose to call him, but at any rate a noble tremendously high-born, who did not want to stay at home. And so he travelled about the world, and wherever he went he was well received, and hobnobbed with the very finest people; for he had an unheard of amount of money. He at once found friends and acquaintances, no matter where he came; for whoever has a full trough can always find pigs to thrust their snouts into it. But since he handled his money as he did, it grew less and less, and at last he was left high and dry, without a red cent. And there was an end to all his many friends; for they did just as the pigs do. When he had been well fleeced, they began to snivel and grunt, and soon scattered, each about his own business. And there he stood, after having been led about by the nose, abandoned by all. All had been glad to help him get rid of his money; but none were willing to help him regain it, so there was nothing left for him to do but to wander back home again like a journeyman apprentice, and beg his way as he went.

Late one evening he found himself in a big forest, without any idea as to where he might spend the night. And as he was looking around, his glance happened to fall on an old hut, peeping out from among the bushes. Of course an old hut was no lodging for such a fine gentleman; but when we cannot have what we want, we must take what we can get, and since there was no help for it, he went into the hut. There was not even a cat in it, not even a stool to sit on. But against one wall there was a great chest. What might there be in the chest? Suppose there were a few mouldy crusts of bread in it? They would taste good to him, for he had not been given a single thing all day long, and he was so hungry that his inwards stuck to his ribs. He opened the chest. But within the chest was another chest, and in that chest still another chest, and so it went, one always smaller than the other, until they were nothing but little boxes. And the more there were of them the more trouble he took to open them; for whatever was hidden away so carefully must be something exceptionally beautiful, thought he.

At last he came to a tiny box, and in the tiny box was a slip of paper – and that was all he had for his pains! At first he was much depressed. But all at once, he saw that something was written on the piece of paper, and on closer examination he was even able to spell out the words, though they had a strange appearance. And he read:

"Lasse, my thrall!"

No sooner had he spoken these words than something answered, close to his ear:

"What does my master command?"

He looked around, but saw no one. That's strange, thought he, and once more read aloud:

"Lasse, my thrall!"

And just as before came the answer:

"What does my master command?"

"If there be someone about who hears what I say, he might be kind enough to get me a little something to eat," said he; and at that very moment a table, covered with all the good things to eat that one could imagine, was standing in the hut. He at once began to eat and drink and did well by himself. I have never had a better meal in my life, thought he. And when his hunger was completely satisfied, he grew sleepy and took up his scrap of paper again.

"Lasse, my thrall!"

"What does my master command?"

"Now that you have brought me food and drink, you must also bring me a bed in which to sleep. But it must be a very fine bed," said he; for as you may well imagine, his ideas were more top-lofty now that he had eaten well. His command was at once obeyed; and a bed so fine and handsome stood in the hut, that a king might have been glad to have found such sleeping accommodations. Now this was all very well and good; but the good can always be bettered, and when he had lain down, he decided that, after all, the hut was far too wretched for such a fine bed. He took up the scrap of paper:

"Lasse, my thrall!"

"What does my master command?"

"If you can produce such a meal, and such a bed here in the wild wood, you must surely be able to give me a better room; for you know I am one of those who are used to sleeping in a castle, with golden mirrors and rugs of gold brocade and luxuries and conveniences of every kind," said he. And no sooner had he spoken the words, than he was lying in the most magnificent room he had ever seen.

Now matters were arranged to suit him, and he was quite content as he turned his face to the wall and closed his eyes.

But the room he had slept in was not the end of his magnificence. When he woke the following morning and looked around, he saw that he had been sleeping in a great castle. There was one room after another, and wherever he went walls and ceilings were covered with ornaments and decorations of every kind, all glittering so splendidly when the rays of the sun fell on them that he had to put his hand to his eyes; for wherever he looked everything sparkled with gold and silver. Then he glanced out of the window and first began to realize how really beautiful everything was. Gone were the fir trees and juniper bushes, and in their place showed the loveliest garden one might wish to see, filled with beautiful trees and roses of every variety, in bush and tree form. But there was not a human being in sight, not even a cat. Yet he found it quite natural that everything should be so fine, and that he should once more have become a great lord.

He took up the scrap of paper:

"Lasse, my thrall!"

"What does my master command?"

"Now that you have provided me with food and a castle in which to dwell, I am going to stay here, because it suits me," said he, "but I cannot live here all alone in this fashion. I must have serving-men and serving-maids, at my command." And so it was. Servants and lackeys and maids and serving-women of every description arrived, and some of them bowed and others courtseyed, and now the duke really began to feel content.

Now it happened that another great castle lay on the opposite side of the forest, in which dwelt a king who owned the forest, and many broad acres of field and meadow round about. And when the king came and happened to look out of his window, he saw the new castle, on whose roof the golden weathercocks were swinging to and fro, from time to time, shining in his eyes.

"This is very strange," thought he, and sent for his courtiers. They came without delay, bowing and scraping.

"Do you see the castle yonder?" said the king.

Their eyes grew as large as saucers and they looked.

Yes, indeed, they saw the castle.

"Who has dared to build such a castle on my ground?"

The courtiers bowed and scraped, but did not know. So the king sent for his soldiers. They came tramping in and presented arms.

"Send out all my soldiers and horsemen," said the king, "tear down the castle instantly, hang whoever built it, and see to this at once."

The soldiers assembled in the greatest haste and set forth. The drummers beat their drums and the trumpeters blew their trumpets, and the other musicians practiced their art, each in his own way; so that the duke heard them long before they came in sight. But this was not the first time he had heard music of this sort, and he knew what it meant, so once more he took up the scrap of paper:

"Lasse, my thrall!"

"What does my master command?"

"There are soldiers coming," said he, "and now you must provide me with soldiers and horsemen until I have twice as many as the folk on the other side of the forest. And sabres and pistols and muskets and cannon, and all that goes with them – but you must be quick about it!"

Quick it was, and when the duke looked out there was a countless host of soldiers drawn up around the castle.

When the king's people arrived, they stopped and did not dare advance. But the duke was by no means shy. He went at once to the king's captain and asked him what he wanted.

The captain repeated his instructions.

"They will not gain you anything," said the duke. "You can see how many soldiers I have, and if the king chooses to listen to me, we can agree to become friends, I will aid him against all his enemies, and what we undertake will succeed." The captain was pleased with this proposal, so the duke invited him to the castle, together with all his officers, and his soldiers were given a swallow or two of something wet and plenty to eat along with it. But while the duke and the officers were eating and drinking, there was more or less talk, and the duke learned that the king had a daughter, as yet unmarried and so lovely that her like had never been seen. And the more they brought the king's officers to eat, the stronger they inclined to the opinion that the king's daughter would make a good wife for the duke. And as they talked about it, the duke himself began to think it over. The worst of it was, said the officers, that she was very haughty, and never even deigned to look at a man. But the duke only laughed. "If it be no worse than that," he said, "it is a trouble that may be cured."

When at last the soldiers had stowed away as much as they could hold, they shouted hurrah until they woke the echoes in the hills, and marched away. One may imagine what a fine parade march it was, for some of them had grown a little loose-jointed in the knees. The duke charged them to carry his greetings to the king, and say that he would soon pay him a visit.

When the duke was alone once more, he began to think of the princess again, and whether she were really as beautiful as the soldiers had said. He decided he would like to find out for himself. Since so many strange things had happened that day, it was quite possible, thought he.

"Lasse, my thrall!"

"What does my master command?"

"Only that you bring the king's daughter here, as soon as she has fallen asleep," said he. "But mind that she does not wake up, either on her way here, or on her way back." And before long there lay the princess on the bed. She was sleeping soundly, and looked charming as she lay there asleep. One had to admit that she was as sweet as sugar. The duke walked all around her; but she appeared just as beautiful from one side as from the other, and the more the duke looked at her, the better she pleased him.

"Lasse, my thrall!"

"What does my master command?"

"Now you must take the princess home again," said he, "because now I know what she looks like and tomorrow I shall sue for her hand."

The following morning the king stepped to the window. "Now I shall not have to see that castle across the way," he thought to himself. But the evil one must have had a hand in the matter – there stood the castle just as before, and the sun was shining brightly on its roof, and the weather-vanes were sending beams into his eyes.

The king once more fell into a rage, and shouted for all his people, who hurried to him with more than usual rapidity. The courtiers bowed and scraped and the soldiers marched in parade step and presented arms.

"Do you see that castle there?" roared the king.

They stretched their necks, their eyes grew large as saucers and they looked.

Yes, indeed, they saw it.

"Did I not order you to tear down that castle and hang its builder?" he said.

This they could not deny; but now the captain himself stepped forward and told what had occurred, and what an alarming number of soldiers the duke had, and how magnificent his castle was.

Then he also repeated what the duke had said, and that he had sent his greetings to the king.

All this made the king somewhat dizzy, and he had to set his crown on the table and scratch his head. It was beyond his comprehension – for all that he was a king; since he could have sworn that it had all come to pass in the course of a single night, and if the duke were not the devil himself, he was at least a magician.

And as he sat there and thought, the princess came in.

"God greet you, father," she said, "I had a most strange and lovely dream last night."

"And what did you dream, my girl?" said the king.

"O, I dreamt that I was in the new castle over yonder, and there was a duke, handsome and so splendid beyond anything I could have imagined, and now I want a husband."

"What, you want a husband, and you have never even deigned to look at a man; that is very strange!" said the king.

"Be that as it may," said the princess, "but that is how I feel now; and I want a husband, and the duke is the husband I want," she concluded.

The king simply could not get over the astonishment the duke had caused him.

Suddenly he heard an extraordinary beating of drums, and sounding of trumpets and other instruments of every kind. And a message came that the duke had arrived with a great retinue, all so magnificently attired that every seam of their dresses was sparkling with gold and silver. The king, in his crown and finest robe of state, stood looking down the stairway, and the princess was all the more in favour of carrying out her idea as quickly as possible.

The duke greeted the king pleasantly, and the king returned his greeting in the same way, and discussing their affairs together they became good friends. There was a great banquet, and the duke sat beside the princess at the table. What they said to each other I do not know, but the duke knew so well how to talk that, no matter what he said, the princess could not say no, and so he went to the king and begged for her hand. The king could not exactly refuse it, for the duke was the kind of a man whom it was better to have for a friend than for an enemy; but he could not give his answer out of hand, either. First he wished to see the duke's castle, and know how matters stood with regard to this, that and the other – which was natural.

So it was agreed that they should pay the duke a visit and bring the princess with them, in order that she might examine his possessions, and with that they parted.

When the duke reached home, Lasse had a lively time of it, for he was given any number of commissions. But he rushed about, carrying them out, and everything was arranged so satisfactorily that when the king arrived with his daughter, a thousand pens could not have described it. They went through all the rooms and looked around, and everything was as it should be, and even better thought the king, who was very happy. Then the wedding was celebrated and when it was over, and the duke returned home with his young wife, he, too, gave a splendid banquet, and that is how it went.

After some time had passed, the duke one evening heard the words:

"Is my master content now?" It was Lasse, though the duke could not see him.

"I am well content," answered the duke, "for you have brought me all that I have."

"But what did I get for it?" said Lasse.

"Nothing," replied the duke, "but, heaven above, what was I to give you, who are not flesh and blood, and whom I cannot even see," said he. "Yet if there be anything I can do for you, why let me know what it is, and I will do it."

"I would very much like to have the little scrap of paper that you keep in the box," said Lasse.

"If that is all you want, and if such a trifle is of any service to you, your wish shall be granted, for I believe I know the words by heart now," said the duke.

Lasse thanked him, and said all the duke need do, would be to lay the paper on the chair beside his bed, when he went to sleep, and that he would fetch it during the night.

This the duke did, and then he went to bed and fell asleep.

But toward morning the duke woke up, freezing so that his teeth chattered, and when he had fully opened his eyes, he saw that he had been stripped of everything, and had scarcely a shirt to his name. And instead of lying in the handsome bed in the handsome bed-room in the magnificent castle, he lay on the big chest in the old hut. He at once called out:

"Lasse, my thrall!" But there was no answer.

Then he cried again:

"Lasse, my thrall!" Again there was no answer. So he called out as loudly as he could:

"Lasse, my thrall!" But this third call was also in vain.

Now he began to realize what had happened, and that Lasse, when he obtained the scrap of paper, no longer had to serve him, and that he himself had made this possible. But now things were as they were, and there stood the duke in the old hut, with scarcely a shirt to his name. The princess herself was not much better off, though she had kept her clothes; for they had been given her by her father, and Lasse had no power over them.

Now the duke had to explain everything to the princess, and beg her to leave him, since it would be best if he tried to get along as well as he could himself, said he. But this the princess would not do. She had a better memory for what the pastor had said when he married them, she told him, and that she was never, never to leave him.

At length the king awoke in his castle, and when he looked out of the window, he saw not a single stone of the other castle in which his son-in-law and his daughter lived. He grew uneasy and sent for his courtiers.

They came in, bowing and scraping.

"Do you see the castle there, on the other side of the forest?" he asked. They stretched their necks and opened their eyes. But they could see nothing.

"What has become of it?" said the king. But this question they were unable to answer.

In a short time the king and his entire court set out, passed through the forest, and when they came to the place where the castle, with its great gardens, should have been standing, they saw nothing but juniper bushes and scrub pines. And then they happened to see the little hut amid the brush. He went in and – O the poor king! – what did he see?

There stood his son-in-law, with scarcely a shirt to his name, and his daughter, and she had none too much to wear, and was crying and snivelling at a fearful rate. "For heaven's sake, what is the trouble here?" said the king. But he received no answer; for the duke would rather have died than have told him the whole story.

The king urged and pressed him, first amiably, then in anger; but the duke remained obstinate and would have nothing to say. Then the king fell into a rage, which is not very surprising, for now he realized that this fine duke was not what he purported to be, and he therefore ordered him to be hung, and hung on the spot. It is true that the princess pleaded earnestly for him, but tears and prayers were useless now, for he was a rascal and should die a rascal's death – thus spake the king.

And so it was. The king's people set up a gallows and put a rope around the duke's neck. But as they were leading him to the gallows, the princess got hold of the hangman and gave him a gratuity, for which they were to arrange matters in such wise that the duke need not die. And toward evening they were to cut him down, and he and the princess would disappear. So the bargain was made. In the meantime they strung him up and then the king, together with his court and all the people, went away.

Now the duke was at the end of his rope. Yet he had time enough to reflect about his mistake in not contenting himself with an inch instead of reaching out at once for an ell; and that he had so foolishly given back the scrap of paper to Lasse annoyed him most of all. If I only had it again, I would show everyone that adversity has made me wise, he thought to himself. But when the horse is stolen we close the stable door. And that is the way of the world.

And then he dangled his legs, since for the time being there was nothing else for him to do.

It had been a long, hard day for him, and he was not sorry when he saw the sun sinking behind the forest. But just as the sun was setting he suddenly heard a most tremendous Yo ho! and when he looked down there were seven carts of worn-out shoes coming along the road, and atop the last cart was a little old man in grey, with a night-cap on his head. He had the face of some horrible spectre, and was not much better to look at in other respects.

He drove straight up to the gallows, and stopped when he was directly beneath them, looked up at the duke and laughed – the horrible old creature!

"And is this the measure of your stupidity?" he said, "but then what is a fellow of your sort to do with his stupidity, if he does not put it to some use?" – and then he laughed again. "Yes, there you hang, and here I am carting off all the shoes I wore out going about on your silly errands. I wonder, sometimes, whether you can actually read what is written on that scrap of paper, and whether you recognize it," said he, laughing again, indulging in all sorts of horse-play, and waving the scrap of paper under the duke's nose.

But all who are hanging on the gallows are not dead, and this time Lasse was the greater fool of the two.

The duke snatched – and tore the scrap of paper from his hand!

"Lasse, my thrall!"

"What does my master command?"

"Cut me down from the gallows at once, and restore the castle and everything else just as it was before, then when it is dark, bring the princess back to it."

Everything was attended to with alarming rapidity, and soon all was exactly as it had been before Lasse had decamped.

When the king awoke the following morning, he looked out of the window as usual, and there the castle was standing as before, with its weathercocks gleaming handsomely in the sunlight. He sent for his courtiers, and they came in bowing and scraping.

"Do you see the castle over yonder?" asked the king.

They stretched their necks, and gazed and stared. Yes, indeed, they could see the castle.

Then the king sent for the princess; but she was not there. Thereupon the king set off to see whether his son-in-law was hanging in the appointed spot; but no, there was not a sign of either son-in-law or gallows.

Then he had to take off his crown and scratch his head. Yet that did not change matters, and he could not for the life of him understand why things should be as they were. Finally he set out with his entire court, and when they reached the spot where the castle should have been standing, there it stood.

The gardens and the roses were just as they had been, and the duke's servitors were to be seen in swarms beneath the trees. His son-in-law in person, together with his daughter, dressed in the finest clothes, came down the stairs to meet him.

The devil has a hand in it, thought the king; and so strange did all seem to him that he did not trust the evidence of his own eyes.

"God greet you and welcome, father!" said the duke. The king could only stare at him. "Are you, are you my son-in-law?" he asked.

"Why, of course," said the duke, "who else am I supposed to be?"

"Did I not have you strung up yesterday as a thief and a vagabond?" inquired the king.

"I really believe father has gone out of his mind on the way over to us," said the duke and laughed.

"Does father think that I would allow myself to be hanged so easily? Or is there anyone present who dare suppose such a thing?" he said, and looked them straight in the eye, so that they knew he was looking at them. They bent their backs and bowed and scraped.

"And who can imagine any such thing? How could it be possible? Or should there be anyone present who dare say that the king wishes me ill, let him speak out," said the duke, and gazed at them with even greater keenness than before. All bent their backs and bowed and scraped.

How should any of them come to any such conclusion? No, none of them were foolish to such a degree, they said.

Now the king was really at a loss to know what to think. When he looked at the duke he felt sure that he could never have wished to harm him, and yet – he was not quite sure.

"Was I not here yesterday, and was not the whole castle gone, and had not an old hut taken its place, and did I not enter the hut and see you standing there with scarcely a shirt to your name?" he asked.

"How father talks," said the duke. "I am afraid, very much afraid, that trolls have blinded you, and led you astray in the forest. What do you think?" he said and turned to the courtiers.

They at once bowed and cringed fifty times in succession, and took the duke's side, as stands to reason.

The king rubbed his eyes and looked around.

"It must be as you say," he told the duke, "and I believe that I have recovered my reason, and have found my eyes again. And it would have been a sin and shame had I had you hung," said he. Then he grew joyful and no one gave the matter further thought.

But adversity teaches one to be wise, so people say, and the duke now began to attend to most things himself, and to see to it that Lasse did not have to wear out so many pairs of shoes. The king at once bestowed half the kingdom upon him, which gave him plenty to do, and people said that one would have to look far in order to find a better ruler.

Then Lasse came to the duke one day, and though he did not look much better than before, he was more civil and did not venture to grin and carry on.

"You no longer need my help," said he, "for though formerly I used to wear out all my shoes, I now cannot even wear out a single pair, and I almost believe my legs are moss-grown. Will you not discharge me?"

The duke thought he could. "I have taken great pains to spare you, and I really believe that I can get along without you," he replied. "But the castle here and all the other things I could not well dispense with, since I never again could find an architect like yourself, and you may take for granted that I have no wish to ornament the gallows-tree a second time. Therefore I will not, of my own free will, give you back the scrap of paper," said he.

"While it is in your possession I have nothing to fear," answered Lasse.

"But should the paper fall into other hands, then I should have to begin to run and work all over again and that, just that, is what I would like to prevent. When a fellow has been working a thousand years, as I have, he is bound to grow weary at last."

So they came to the conclusion that the duke should put the scrap of paper in its little box and bury it seven ells underground, beneath a stone that had grown there and would remain there as well. Then they thanked each other for pleasant comradeship and separated. The duke did as he had agreed to do, and no one saw him hide the box.

He lived happily with his princess, and was blessed with sons and daughters. When the king died, he inherited the whole kingdom and, as you may imagine, he was none the worse off thereby, and no doubt he is still living and ruling there, unless he has died.

As to the little box containing the scrap of paper, many are still digging and searching for it.

Katie Woodencloak

(Norwegian)

ONCE ON A TIME there was a King who had become a widower. By his Queen he had one daughter, who was so clever and lovely, there wasn't a cleverer or lovelier Princess in all the world. So the King went on a long time sorrowing for the Queen, whom he had loved so much, but at last he got weary of living alone, and married another Queen, who was a widow, and had, too, an only daughter; but this daughter was just as bad and ugly as the other was kind, and clever, and lovely, The stepmother and her daughter were jealous of the Princess, because she was so lovely; but so long as the King was at home, they daredn't do her any harm, he was so fond of her.

Well, after a time, he fell into war with another King, and went out to battle with his host, and then the stepmother thought she might do as she pleased; and so she both starved and beat the Princess, and was after her in every hole and corner of the house. At last she thought everything too good for her, and turned her out to herd cattle. So there she went about with the cattle, and herded them in the woods and on the fells. As for food, she got little or none, and she grew thin and wan, and was always sobbing and sorrowful. Now in the herd there was a great dun bull, which always kept himself so neat and sleek, and often and often he came up to the Princess, and let her pat him. So one day when she sat there, sad, and sobbing, and sorrowful, he came up to her and asked her outright why she was always in such grief. She answered nothing, but went on weeping.

"Ah!" said the Bull, "I know all about it quite well, though you won't tell me; you weep because the Queen is bad to you, and because she is ready to starve you to death. But food you've no need to fret about, for in my left ear lies a cloth, and when you take and spread it out, you may have as many dishes as you please."

So she did that, took the cloth and spread it out on the grass, and lo! it served up the nicest dishes one could wish to have; there was wine too, and mead, and sweet cake. Well, she soon got up her flesh again, and grew so plump, and rosy, and white, that the Queen and her scrawny chip of a daughter turned blue and yellow for spite. The Queen couldn't at all make out how her stepdaughter got to look so well on such bad fare, so she told one of her maids to go after her in the wood, and watch and see how it all was, for she thought some of the servants in the house must give her food. So the maid went after her, and watched in the wood, and then she saw how the stepdaughter took the cloth out of the Bull's ear, and spread it out, and how it served up the nicest dishes, which the stepdaughter ate and made good cheer over. All this the maid told the Queen when she went home.

And now the King came home from war, and had won the fight against the other king with whom he went out to battle. So there was great joy throughout the palace, and no one was gladder than the King's daughter. But the Queen shammed sick, and took to her bed, and paid the doctor a great fee to get him to say she could never be well again unless she had some of the Dun Bull's flesh to eat. Both the king's daughter and the folk in the palace asked the doctor if nothing else would help her, and prayed hard for the Bull, for everyone was fond of him, and they all said there wasn't that Bull's match in all the land. But, no; he must and should be slaughtered, nothing else would do. When the king's daughter heard that, she got very sorrowful, and went down into the byre to the Bull. There, too, he stood and hung down his head, and looked so downcast that she began to weep over him.

"What are you weeping for?" asked the Bull.

So she told him how the King had come home again, and how the Queen had shammed sick and got the doctor to say she could never be well and sound again unless she got some of the Dun Bull's flesh to eat, and so now he was to be slaughtered.

"If they get me killed first", said the Bull, "they'll soon take your life too. Now, if you're of my mind, we'll just start off, and go away tonight."

Well, the Princess thought it bad, you may be sure, to go and leave her father, but she thought it still worse to be in the house with the Queen; and so she gave her word to the Bull to come to him.

At night, when all had gone to bed, the Princess stole down to the byre to the Bull, and so he took her on his back, and set off from the homestead as fast as ever he could. And when the folk got up at cockcrow next morning to slaughter the Bull, why, he was gone; and when the King got up and asked for his daughter, she was gone too. He sent out messengers on all sides to hunt for them, and gave them out in all the parish churches; but there was no one who had caught a glimpse of them. Meanwhile, the Bull went through many lands with the King's daughter on his back, and so one day they came to a great copper wood, where both the trees, and branches, and leaves, and flowers, and everything, were nothing but copper.

But before they went into the wood, the Bull said to the King's daughter:

"Now, when we get into this wood, mind you take care not to touch even a leaf of it, else it's all over both with me and you, for here dwells a Troll with three heads who owns this wood."

No, bless her, she'd be sure to take care not to touch anything. Well, she was very careful, and leant this way and that to miss the boughs, and put them gently aside with her hands; but it was such a thick wood, 'twas scarce possible to get through; and so, with all her pains, somehow or other she tore off a leaf, which she held in her hand.

"AU! AU! what have you done now?" said the Bull; "there's nothing for it now but to fight for life or death; but mind you keep the leaf safe."

Soon after they got to the end of the wood, and a Troll with three heads came running up:

"Who is this that touches my wood?" said the Troll.

"It's just as much mine as yours", said the Bull.

"Ah!" roared the Troll, "we'll try a fall about that."

"As you choose", said the Bull.

So they rushed at one another, and fought; and the Bull he butted, and gored, and kicked with all his might and main; but the Troll gave him as good as he brought, and it lasted the whole day before the Bull got the mastery; and then he was so full of wounds, and so worn out, he could scarce lift a leg. Then they were forced to stay there a day to rest, and then the Bull bade the King's daughter to take the horn of ointment which hung at the Troll's belt, and rub him with it. Then he came to himself again, and the day after they trudged on again. So they travelled many, many days, until, after a long, long time, they came to a silver wood, where both the trees, and branches, and leaves, and flowers, and everything, were silvern.

Before the Bull went into the wood, he said to the King's daughter:

"Now, when we get into this wood, for heaven's sake mind you take good care; you mustn't touch anything, and not pluck off so much as one leaf, else it is all over both with me and you; for here is a Troll with six heads who owns it, and him I don't think I should be able to master."

"No", said the King's daughter; "I'll take good care and not touch anything you don't wish me to touch."

But when they got into the wood, it was so close and thick, they could scarce get along. She was as careful as careful could be, and leant to this side and that to miss the boughs, and put them on one side with her hands, but every minute the branches struck her across the eyes, and in spite of all her pains, it so happened she tore off a leaf.

"AU! AU! what have you done now?" said the Bull. "There's nothing for it now but to fight for life and death, for this Troll has six heads, and is twice as strong as the other, but mind you keep the leaf safe, and don't lose it."

Just as he said that, up came the Troll:

"Who is this", he said, "that touches my wood?"

"It's as much mine as yours", said the Bull.

"That we'll try a fall about", roared the Troll.

"As you choose", said the Bull, and rushed at the Troll, and gored out his eyes, and drove his horns right through his body, so that the entrails gushed out; but the Troll was almost a match for him, and it lasted three whole days before the Bull got the life gored out of him. But then he, too, was so weak and wretched, it was as much as he could do to stir a limb, and so full of wounds, that the blood streamed from him. So he said to the King's daughter she must take the horn of ointment that hung at the Troll's belt, and rub him with it. Then she did that, and he came to himself; but they were forced to stay there a week to rest before the Bull had strength enough to go on.

At last they set off again, but the Bull was still poorly, and they went rather slowly at first. So, to spare time, the King's daughter said, as she was young and light of foot, she could very well walk, but she couldn't get leave to do that. No; she must seat herself up on his back again. So on they travelled through many lands a long time, and the King's daughter did not know in the least whither they went; but after a long, long time they came to a gold wood. It was so grand, the gold dropped from every twig, and all the trees, and boughs, and flowers, and leaves, were of pure gold. Here, too, the same thing happened as had happened in the silver wood and copper wood. The Bull told the King's daughter she mustn't touch it for anything, for there was a Troll with nine heads who owned it, and he was much bigger and stouter than both the others put together; and he didn't think he could get the better of him. No; she'd be sure to take heed not to touch it; that he might know very well. But when they got into the wood, it was far thicker and closer than the silver wood, and the deeper they went into it, the worse it got. The wood went on, getting thicker and thicker, and closer and closer; and at last she thought there was no way at all to get through it. She was in such an awful fright of plucking off anything, that she sat, and twisted, and turned herself this way and that, and hither and thither, to keep clear of the boughs, and she put them on one side with her hands; but every moment the branches struck her across the eyes, so that she couldn't see what she was clutching at; and lo! before she knew how it came about, she had a gold apple in her hand. Then she was so bitterly sorry, she burst into tears, and wanted to throw it away; but the Bull said, she must keep it safe and watch it well, and comforted her as well as he could; but he thought it would be a hard tussle, and he doubted how it would go.

Just then up came the Troll with the nine heads, and he was so ugly, the King's daughter scarcely dared to look at him.

"WHO IS THIS THAT TOUCHES MY WOOD?" he roared.

"It's just as much mine as yours", said the Bull.

"That we'll try a fall about", roared the Troll again.

"Just as you choose", said the Bull; and so they rushed at one another, and fought, and it was such a dreadful sight, the King's daughter was ready to swoon away. The Bull gored out the Troll's eyes, and drove his horns through and through his body, till the entrails came tumbling out; but the Troll fought bravely; and when the Bull got one head gored to death, the rest breathed life into it again, and so it lasted a whole week before the Bull was able to get the life out of them all. But then he was utterly worn out and wretched. He couldn't stir a foot, and his body was all one wound. He couldn't so much as ask the King's daughter to take the horn of ointment which hung at the Troll's belt, and rub it over him. But she did it all the same, and then he came to himself by little and little; but they had to lie there and rest three weeks before he was fit to go on again.

Then they set off at a snail's pace, for the Bull said they had still a little further to go, and so they crossed over many high hills and thick woods. So after awhile they got upon the fells.

"Do you see anything?" asked the Bull.

"No, I see nothing but the sky, and the wild fell", said the King's daughter.

So when they climbed higher up, the fell got smoother, and they could see further off.

"Do you see anything now?" asked the Bull.

"Yes, I see a little castle far, far away", said the Princess.

"That's not so little though", said the Bull.

After a long, long time, they came to a great cairn, where there was a spur of the fell that stood sheer across the way.

"Do you see anything now?" asked the Bull.

"Yes, now I see the castle close by", said the King's daughter, "and now it is much, much bigger."

"Thither you're to go", said the Bull. "Right underneath the castle is a pigsty, where you are to dwell. When you come thither you'll find a wooden cloak, all made of strips of lath; that you must put on, and go up to the castle and say your name is 'Katie Woodencloak', and ask for a place. But before you go, you must take your penknife and cut my head off, and then you must flay me, and roll up the hide, and lay it under the wall of rock yonder, and under the hide you must lay the copper leaf, and the silver leaf, and the golden apple. Yonder, up against the rock, stands a stick; and when you want anything, you've only got to knock on the wall of rock with that stick."

At first she wouldn't do anything of the kind; but when the Bull said it was the only thanks he would have for what he had done for her, she couldn't help herself. So, however much it grieved her heart, she hacked and cut away with her knife at the big beast till she got both his head and his hide off, and then she laid the hide up under the wall of rock, and put the copper leaf, and the silvern leaf, and the golden apple inside it.

So when she had done that, she went over to the pigsty, but all the while she went she sobbed and wept. There she put on the wooden cloak, and so went up to the palace. When she came into the kitchen she begged for a place, and told them her name was Katie Woodencloak. Yes, the cook said she might have a place – she might have leave to be there in the scullery, and wash up, for the lassie who did that work before had just gone away.

"But as soon as you get weary of being here, you'll go your way too, I'll be bound."

No; she was sure she wouldn't do that.

So there she was, behaving so well, and washing up so handily. The Sunday after there were to be strange guests at the palace, so Katie asked if she might have leave to carry up water for the Prince's bath; but all the rest laughed at her, and said:

"What should you do there? Do you think the Prince will care to look at you, you who are such a fright!"

But she wouldn't give it up, and kept on begging and praying; and at last she got leave. So when she went up the stairs, her wooden cloak made such a clatter, the Prince came out and asked:

"Pray who are you?"

"Oh! I was just going to bring up water for your Royal Highness's bath", said Katie.

"Do you think now", said the Prince, "I'd have anything to do with the water you bring?" and with that he threw the water over her.

So she had to put up with that, but then she asked leave to go to church; well, she got that leave too, for the church lay close by. But, first of all, she went to the rock, and knocked on its face with the stick which stood there, just as the Bull had said. And straightaway out came a man, who said:

"What's your will?"

So the Princess said she had got leave to go to church and hear the priest preach, but she had no clothes to go in. So he brought out a kirtle, which was as bright as the copper wood, and she got a horse and saddle beside. Now, when she got to the church she was so lovely and grand, all wondered who she could be, and scarce one of them listened to what the priest said, for they looked too much at her. As for the Prince, he fell so deep in love with her, he didn't take his eyes off her for a single moment.

So, as she went out of church, the Prince ran after her, and held the church door open for her; and so he got hold of one of her gloves, which was caught in the door. When she went away and mounted her horse, the Prince went up to her again, and asked whence she came.

"Oh! I'm from Bath", said Katie; and while the Prince took out the glove to give it to her, she said:

Bright before and dark behind,
Clouds come rolling on the wind;
That this Prince may never see
Where my good steed goes with me.

The Prince had never seen the like of that glove, and went about far and wide asking after the land whence the proud lady, who rode off without her glove, said she came; but there was no one who could tell where "Bath" lay.

Next Sunday someone had to go up to the Prince with a towel.

"Oh! may I have leave to go up with it?" said Katie.

"What's the good of your going?" said the others; "you saw how it fared with you last time."

But Katie wouldn't give in; she kept on begging and praying, till she got leave; and then she ran up the stairs, so that her wooden cloak made a great clatter. Out came the Prince, and when he saw it was Katie, he tore the towel out of her hand, and threw it into her face.

"Pack yourself off, you ugly Troll", he cried; "do you think I'd have a towel which you have touched with your smutty fingers?"

After that the Prince set off to church, and Katie begged for leave to go too. They all asked what business she had at church – she who had nothing to put on but that wooden cloak, which was so black and ugly. But Katie said the priest was such a brave man to preach, what he said did her so much good; and so she at last got leave. Now she went again to the rock and knocked, and so out came the man, and gave her a kirtle far finer than the first one; it was all covered with silver, and it shone like the silver wood; and she got besides a noble steed, with a saddle-cloth broidered with silver, and a silver bit.

So when the King's daughter got to the church, the folk were still standing about in the churchyard. And all wondered and wondered who she could be, and the Prince was soon on the spot, and came and wished to hold her horse for her while she got off. But she jumped down, and said there was no need, for her horse was so well broke, it stood still when she bid it, and came when she called it. So they all went into church; but there was scarce a soul that listened to what the priest said, for they looked at her a deal too much; and the Prince fell still deeper in love than the first time.

When the sermon was over, and she went out of church and was going to mount her horse, up came the Prince again, and asked her whence she came.

"Oh! I'm from Towelland", said the King's daughter; and as she said that, she dropped her riding-whip, and when the Prince stooped to pick it up, she said:

Bright before and dark behind,
Clouds come rolling on the wind;
That this Prince may never see
Where my good steed goes with me.

So away she was again; and the Prince couldn't tell what had become of her. He went about far and wide asking after the land whence she said she came, but there was no one who could tell him where it lay; and so the Prince had to make the best he could of it.

Next Sunday someone had to go up to the Prince with a comb. Katie begged for leave to go up with it, but the others put her in mind how she had fared the last time, and scolded her for wishing to go before the Prince – such a black and ugly fright as she was in her wooden cloak. But she wouldn't leave off asking till they let her go up to the Prince with his comb. So, when she came clattering up the stairs again, out came the Prince, and took the comb, and threw it at her, and bade her be off as fast as she could. After that the Prince went to church, and Katie begged for leave to go too. They asked again what business she had there, she who was so foul and black, and who had no clothes to show herself in. Might be the Prince or someone else would see her, and then both she and all the others would smart for it; but Katie said they had something else to do than to look at her; and she wouldn't leave off begging and praying till they gave her leave to go.

So the same thing happened now as had happened twice before. She went to the rock and knocked with the stick, and then the man came out and gave her a kirtle which was far grander than either of the others. It was almost all pure gold, and studded with diamonds; and she got besides a noble steed, with a gold broidered saddle-cloth and a golden bit.

Now when the King's daughter got to the church, there stood the priest and all the people in the churchyard waiting for her. Up came the Prince running, and wanted to hold her horse, but she jumped off, and said:

"No; thanks – there's no need, for my horse is so well broke, it stands still when I bid him."

So they all hastened into church, and the priest got into the pulpit, but no one listened to a word he said; for they all looked too much at her, and wondered whence she came; and the Prince, he was far deeper in love than either of the former times. He had no eyes, or ears, or sense for anything, but just to sit and stare at her.

So when the sermon was over, and the King's daughter was to go out of the church, the Prince had got a firkin of pitch poured out in the porch, that he might come and help her over it; but she didn't care a bit – she just put her foot right down into the midst of the pitch, and jumped across it; but then one of her golden shoes stuck fast in it, and as she got on her horse, up came the Prince running out of the church, and asked whence she came.

"I'm from Combland", said Katie. But when the Prince wanted to reach her the gold shoe, she said,

Bright before and dark behind,
Clouds come rolling on the wind;
That this Prince may never see
Where my good steed goes with me.

So the Prince couldn't tell still what had become of her, and he went about a weary time all over the world asking for "Combland"; but when no one could tell him where it lay, he ordered it to be given out everywhere that he would wed the woman whose foot could fit the gold shoe.

So many came of all sorts from all sides, fair and ugly alike; but there was no one who had so small a foot as to be able to get on the gold shoe. And after a long, long time, who should come but Katie's wicked stepmother, and her daughter, too, and her the gold shoe fitted; but ugly she was, and so loathly she looked, the Prince only kept his word sore against his will. Still they got ready the wedding-feast, and she was dressed up and decked out as a bride; but as they rode to church, a little bird sat upon a tree and sang:

A bit off her heel,
And a bit off her toe;
Katie Woodencloak's tiny shoe
Is full of blood – that's all I know.

And, sure enough, when they looked to it the bird told the truth, for blood gushed out of the shoe.

Then all the maids and women who were about the palace had to go up to try on the shoe, but there was none of them whom it would fit at all.

"But where's Katie Woodencloak?" asked the Prince, when all the rest had tried the shoe, for he understood the song of birds very well, and bore in mind what the little bird had said.

"Oh! she think of that!" said the rest; "it's no good her coming forward. Why, she's legs like a horse."

"Very true, I daresay", said the Prince; "but since all the others have tried, Katie may as well try too."

"Katie", he bawled out through the door; and Katie came trampling upstairs, and her wooden cloak clattered as if a whole regiment of dragoons were charging up.

"Now, you must try the shoe on, and be a Princess, you too," said the other maids, and laughed and made game of her.

So Katie took up the shoe, and put her foot into it like nothing, and threw off her wooden cloak; and so there she stood in her gold kirtle, and it shone so that the sunbeams glistened from her; and, lo! on her other foot she had the fellow to the gold shoe.

So when the Prince knew her again, he grew so glad, he ran up to her and threw his arms round her, and gave her a kiss; and when he heard she was a King's daughter, he got gladder still, and then came the wedding feast; and so,

Snip, snip, snover,
This story's over.

Mother Holle

(German)

THERE WAS ONCE A WIDOW who had two daughters – one of whom was pretty and industrious, whilst the other was ugly and idle. But she was much fonder of the ugly and idle one, because she was her own daughter; and the other, who was a stepdaughter, was obliged to do all the work, and be the Cinderella of the house. Every day the poor girl had to sit by a well, in the highway, and spin and spin till her fingers bled.

Now it happened that one day the shuttle was marked with her blood, so she dipped it in the well, to wash the mark off; but it dropped out of her hand and fell to the bottom. She began to weep, and ran to her stepmother and told her of the mishap. But she scolded her sharply, and was so merciless as to say, "Since you have let the shuttle fall in, you must fetch it out again."

So the girl went back to the well, and did not know what to do; and in the sorrow of her heart she jumped into the well to get the shuttle. She lost her senses; and when she awoke and came to herself again, she was in a lovely meadow where the sun was shining and many thousands of flowers were growing. Along this meadow she went, and at last came to a baker's oven full of bread, and the bread cried out, "Oh, take me out! take me out! or I shall burn; I have been baked a long time!" So she went up to it, and took out all the loaves one after another with the bread-shovel. After that she went on till she came to a tree covered with apples, which called out to her, "Oh, shake me! shake me! we apples are all ripe!" So she shook the tree till the apples fell like rain, and went on shaking till they were all down, and when she had gathered them into a heap, she went on her way.

At last she came to a little house, out of which an old woman peeped; but she had such large teeth that the girl was frightened, and was about to run away.

But the old woman called out to her, "What are you afraid of, dear child? Stay with me; if you will do all the work in the house properly, you shall be the better for it. Only you must take care to make my bed well, and shake it thoroughly till the feathers fly – for then there is snow on the earth. I am Mother Holle.

As the old woman spoke so kindly to her, the girl took courage and agreed to enter her service. She attended to everything to the satisfaction of her mistress, and always shook her bed so vigorously that the feathers flew about like snow-flakes. So she had a pleasant life with her; never an angry word; and boiled or roast meat every day.

She stayed some time with Mother Holle, and then she became sad. At first she did not know what was the matter with her, but found at length that it was home-sickness: although she was many thousand times better off here than at home, still she had a longing to be there. At last she said to the old woman, "I have a longing for home; and however well off I am down here, I cannot stay any longer; I must go up again to my own people." Mother Holle said, "I am pleased that you long for your home again, and as you have served me so truly, I myself will take you up again." Thereupon she took her by the hand, and led her to a large door. The door was opened, and just as the maiden was standing beneath the doorway, a heavy shower of golden rain fell, and all the gold remained sticking to her, so that she was completely covered over with it.

"You shall have that because you have been so industrious," said Mother Holle, and at the same time she gave her back the shuttle which she had let fall into the well. Thereupon the door closed, and the maiden found herself up above upon the earth, not far from her mother's house.

And as she went into the yard the cock was standing by the well-side, and cried –

"Cock-a-doodle-doo!
Your golden girl's come back to you!"

So she went in to her mother, and as she arrived thus covered with gold, she was well received, both by her and her sister.

The girl told all that had happened to her; and as soon as the mother heard how she had come by so much wealth, she was very anxious to obtain the same good luck for the ugly and lazy daughter. She had to seat herself by the well and spin; and in order that her shuttle might be stained with blood, she stuck her hand into a thorn bush and pricked her finger. Then she threw her shuttle into the well, and jumped in after it.

She came, like the other, to the beautiful meadow and walked along the very same path. When she got to the oven the bread again cried, "Oh, take me out! take me out! or I shall burn; I have been baked a long time!" But the lazy thing answered, "As if I had any wish to make myself dirty?" and on she went. Soon she came to the apple tree, which cried, "Oh, shake me! shake me! we apples are all ripe!" But she answered, "I like that! one of you might fall on my head," and so went on.

When she came to Mother Holle's house she was not afraid, for she had already heard of her big teeth, and she hired herself to her immediately.

The first day she forced herself to work diligently, and obeyed Mother Holle when she told her to do anything, for she was thinking of all the gold that she would give her. But on the second day she began to be lazy, and on the third day still more so, and then she would not get up in the morning at all. Neither did she make Mother Holle's bed as she ought, and did not shake it so as to make the feathers fly up. Mother Holle was soon tired of this, and gave her notice to leave. The lazy girl was willing enough to go, and thought that now the golden rain would come. Mother Holle led her also to the great door; but while she was standing beneath it, instead of the gold a big kettleful of pitch was emptied over her. "That is the reward for your service," said Mother Holle, and shut the door.

So the lazy girl went home; but she was quite covered with pitch, and the cock by the well-side, as soon as he saw her, cried out –

"Cock-a-doodle-doo!
Your pitchy girl's come back to you!"

But the pitch stuck fast to her, and could not be got off as long as she lived.

East of the Sun and West of the Moon

(Norwegian)

ONCE ON A TIME there was a poor husbandman who had so many children that he hadn't much of either food or clothing to give them. Pretty children they all were, but the prettiest was the youngest daughter, who was so lovely there was no end to her loveliness.

So one day, 'twas on a Thursday evening late at the fall of the year, the weather was so wild and rough outside, and it was so cruelly dark, and rain fell and wind blew, till the walls of the cottage shook again. There they all sat round the fire, busy with this thing and that. But just then, all at once something gave three taps on the windowpane. Then the father went out to see what was the matter; and, when he got out of doors, what should he see but a great big White Bear.

"Good-evening to you!" said the White Bear.

"The same to you!" said the man.

"Will you give me your youngest daughter? If you will, I'll make you as rich as you are now poor," said the Bear.

Well, the man would not be at all sorry to be so rich; but still he thought he must have a bit of a talk with his daughter first; so he went in and told them how there was a great

White Bear waiting outside, who had given his word to make them so rich if he could only have the youngest daughter.

The lassie said "No!" outright. Nothing could get her to say anything else; so the man went out and settled it with the White Bear that he should come again the next Thursday evening and get an answer. Meantime he talked his daughter over, and kept on telling her of all the riches they would get, and how well off she would be herself; and so at last she thought better of it, and washed and mended her rags, made herself as smart as she could, and was ready to start. I can't say her packing gave her much trouble.

Next Thursday evening came the White Bear to fetch her, and she got upon his back with her bundle, and off they went. So, when they had gone a bit of the way, the White Bear said:

"Are you afraid?"

"No," she wasn't.

"Well! mind and hold tight by my shaggy coat, and then there's nothing to fear," said the Bear.

So she rode a long, long way, till they came to a great steep hill. There, on the face of it, the White Bear gave a knock, and a door opened, and they came into a castle where there were many rooms all lit up; rooms gleaming with silver and gold; and there, too, was a table ready laid, and it was all as grand as grand could be. Then the White Bear gave her a silver bell; and when she wanted anything, she was only to ring it, and she would get it at once.

Well, after she had eaten and drunk, and evening wore on, she got sleepy after her journey, and thought she would like to go to bed, so she rang the bell; and she had scarce taken hold of it before she came into a chamber where there was a bed made, as fair and white as anyone would wish to sleep in, with silken pillows and curtains and gold fringe. All that was in the room was gold or silver; but when she had gone to bed and put out the light, a man came and laid himself alongside her. That was the White Bear, who threw off his beast shape at night; but she never saw him, for he always came after she had put out the light, and before the day dawned he was up and off again. So things went on happily for a while, but at last she began to get silent and sorrowful; for there she went about all day alone, and she longed to go home to see her father and mother and brothers and sisters. So one day, when the White Bear asked what it was that she lacked, she said it was so dull and lonely there, and how she longed to go home to see her father and mother and brothers and sisters, and that was why she was so sad and sorrowful, because she couldn't get to them.

"Well, well!" said the Bear, "perhaps there's a cure for all this; but you must promise me one thing, not to talk alone with your mother, but only when the rest are by to hear; for she'll take you by the hand and try to lead you into a room alone to talk; but you must mind and not do that, else you'll bring bad luck on both of us."

So one Sunday the White Bear came and said, now they could set off to see her father and mother. Well, off they started, she sitting on his back; and they went far and long. At last they came to a grand house, and there her brothers and sisters were running about out of doors at play, and everything was so pretty, 'twas a joy to see.

"This is where your father and mother live now," said the White Bear; "but don't forget what I told you, else you'll make us both unlucky."

"No! bless her, she'd not forget"; – and when she had reached the house, the White Bear turned right about and left her.

Then, when she went in to see her father and mother, there was such joy, there was no end to it. None of them thought they could thank her enough for all she had done for them. Now, they had everything they wished, as good as good could be, and they all wanted to know how she got on where she lived.

Well, she said, it was very good to live where she did; she had all she wished. What she said beside I don't know, but I don't think any of them had the right end of the stick, or that they got much out of her. But so, in the afternoon, after they had done dinner, all happened as the White Bear had said. Her mother wanted to talk with her alone in her bedroom; but she minded what the White Bear had said, and wouldn't go upstairs.

"Oh! what we have to talk about will keep!" she said, and put her mother off. But, somehow or other, her mother got round her at last, and she had to tell her the whole story. So she said, how every night when she had gone to bed a man came and lay down beside her as soon as she had put out the light; and how she never saw him, because he was always up and away before the morning dawned; and how she went about woeful and sorrowing, for she thought she should so like to see him; and how all day long she walked about there alone; and how dull and dreary and lonesome it was.

"My!" said her mother; "it may well be a Troll you slept with! But now I'll teach you a lesson how to set eyes on him. I'll give you a bit of candle, which you can carry home in your bosom; just light that while he is asleep, but take care not to drop the tallow on him."

Yes! she took the candle and hid it in her bosom, and as night drew on, the White Bear came and fetched her away.

But when they had gone a bit of the way, the White Bear asked if all hadn't happened as he had said.

"Well, she couldn't say it hadn't."

"Now, mind," said he, "if you have listened to your mother's advice, you have brought bad luck on us both, and then, all that has passed between us will be as nothing."

"No," she said, "she hadn't listened to her mother's advice."

So when she reached home, and had gone to bed, it was the old story over again. There came a man and lay down beside her; but at dead of night, when she heard he slept, she got up and struck a light, lit the candle, and let the light shine on him, and so she saw that he was the loveliest Prince one ever set eyes on, and she fell so deep in love with him on the spot, that she thought she couldn't live if she didn't give him a kiss there and then. And so she did; but as she kissed him, she dropped three hot drops of tallow on his shirt, and he woke up.

"What have you done?" he cried; "now you have made us both unlucky, for had you held out only this one year, I had been freed. For I have a stepmother who has bewitched me, so that I am a White Bear by day, and a Man by night. But now all ties are snapt between us; now I must set off from you to her. She lives in a Castle which stands East of the Sun and West of the Moon, and there, too, is a Princess, with a nose three ells long, and she's the wife I must have now."

She wept and took it ill, but there was no help for it; go he must.

Then she asked if she mightn't go with him.

No, she mightn't.

"Tell me the way, then," she said, "and I'll search you out; that surely I may get leave to do."

"Yes," she might do that, he said; "but there was no way to that place. It lay East of the Sun and West of the Moon, and thither she'd never find her way."

So next morning, when she woke up, both Prince and castle were gone, and then she lay on a little green patch, in the midst of the gloomy thick wood, and by her side lay the same bundle of rags she had brought with her from her old home.

So when she had rubbed the sleep out of her eyes, and wept till she was tired, she set out on her way, and walked many, many days, till she came to a lofty crag. Under it sat an old hag, and played with a gold apple which she tossed about. Here the lassie asked if she knew the way to the Prince, who lived with his stepmother in the Castle, that lay East of the Sun and West of the Moon, and who was to marry the Princess with a nose three ells long.

"How did you come to know about him?" asked the old hag; "but maybe you are the lassie who ought to have had him?"

Yes, she was.

"So, so; it's you, is it?" said the old hag. "Well, all I know about him is, that he lives in the castle that lies East of the Sun and West of the Moon, and thither you'll come, late or never; but still you may have the loan of my horse, and on him you can ride to my next neighbour. Maybe she'll be able to tell you; and when you get there, just give the horse a switch under the left ear, and beg him to be off home; and, stay, this gold apple you may take with you."

So she got upon the horse, and rode a long, long time, till she came to another crag, under which sat another old hag, with a gold carding-comb. Here the lassie asked if she knew the way to the castle that lay East of the Sun and West of the Moon, and she answered, like the first old hag, that she knew nothing about it, except it was east of the sun and west of the moon.

"And thither you'll come, late or never, but you shall have the loan of my horse to my next neighbour; maybe she'll tell you all about it; and when you get there, just switch the horse under the left ear, and beg him to be off home."

And this old hag gave her the golden carding-comb; it might be she'd find some use for it, she said. So the lassie got up on the horse, and rode a far, far way, and a weary time; and so at last she came to another great crag, under which sat another old hag, spinning with a golden spinning-wheel. Her, too, she asked if she knew the way to the Prince, and where the castle was that lay East of the Sun and West of the Moon. So it was the same thing over again.

"Maybe it's you who ought to have had the Prince?" said the old hag.

Yes, it was.

But she, too, didn't know the way a bit better than the other two. "East of the sun and west of the moon it was," she knew – that was all.

"And thither you'll come, late or never; but I'll lend you my horse, and then I think you'd best ride to the East Wind and ask him; maybe he knows those parts, and can blow you thither. But when you get to him, you need only give the horse a switch under the left ear, and he'll trot home of himself."

And so, too, she gave her the gold spinning-wheel. "Maybe you'll find a use for it," said the old hag.

Then on she rode many many days, a weary time, before she got to the East Wind's house, but at last she did reach it, and then she asked the East Wind if he could tell her the way to the Prince who dwelt east of the sun and west of the moon. Yes, the East Wind had often heard tell of it, the Prince and the castle, but he couldn't tell the way, for he had never blown so far.

"But, if you will, I'll go with you to my brother the West Wind, maybe he knows, for he's much stronger. So, if you will just get on my back, I'll carry you thither."

Yes, she got on his back, and I should just think they went briskly along.

So when they got there, they went into the West Wind's house, and the East Wind said the lassie he had brought was the one who ought to have had the Prince who lived in the castle East of the Sun and West of the Moon; and so she had set out to seek him, and how he had come with her, and would be glad to know if the West Wind knew how to get to the castle.

"Nay," said the West Wind, "so far I've never blown; but if you will, I'll go with you to our brother the South Wind, for he's much stronger than either of us, and he has flapped his wings far and wide. Maybe he'll tell you. You can get on my back, and I'll carry you to him."

Yes! she got on his back, and so they travelled to the South Wind, and weren't so very long on the way, I should think.

When they got there, the West Wind asked him if he could tell her the way to the castle that lay East of the Sun and West of the Moon, for it was she who ought to have had the Prince who lived there.

"You don't say so! That's she, is it?" said the South Wind.

"Well, I have blustered about in most places in my time, but so far have I never blown; but if you will, I'll take you to my brother the North Wind; he is the oldest and strongest of the whole lot of us, and if he don't know where it is, you'll never find anyone in the world to tell you. You can get on my back, and I'll carry you thither."

Yes! she got on his back, and away he went from his house at a fine rate. And this time, too, she wasn't long on her way.

So when they got to the North Wind's house, he was so wild and cross, cold puffs came from him a long way off.

"BLAST YOU BOTH, WHAT DO YOU WANT?" he roared out to them ever so far off, so that it struck them with an icy shiver.

"Well," said the South Wind, "you needn't be so foul-mouthed, for here I am, your brother, the South Wind, and here is the lassie who ought to have had the Prince who dwells in the castle that lies East of the Sun and West of the Moon, and now she wants to ask you if you ever were there, and can tell her the way, for she would be so glad to find him again."

"YES, I KNOW WELL ENOUGH WHERE IT IS," said the North Wind; "once in my life I blew an aspen leaf thither, but, I was so tired I couldn't blow a puff for ever so many days, after. But if you really wish to go thither, and aren't afraid to come along with me, I'll take you on my back and see if I can blow you thither."

Yes! with all her heart; she must and would get thither if it were possible in any way; and as for fear, however madly he went, she wouldn't be at all afraid.

"Very well, then," said the North Wind, "but you must sleep here tonight, for we must have the whole day before us, if we're to get thither at all."

Early next morning the North Wind woke her, and puffed himself up, and blew himself out, and made himself so stout and big, 'twas gruesome to look at him; and so off they went high up through the air, as if they would never stop till they got to the world's end.

Down here below there was such a storm; it threw down long tracts of wood and many houses, and when it swept over the great sea, ships foundered by hundreds.

So they tore on and on – no one can believe how far they went – and all the while they still went over the sea, and the North Wind got more and more weary, and so out of breath he could scarce bring out a puff, and his wings drooped and drooped, till at last he sunk so low that the crests of the waves dashed over his heels.

"Are you afraid?" said the North Wind.

"No!" she wasn't.

But they weren't very far from land; and the North Wind had still so much strength left in him that he managed to throw her up on the shore under the windows of the castle which lay East of the Sun and West of the Moon; but then he was so weak and worn out, he had to stay there and rest many days before he could get home again.

Next morning the lassie sat down under the castle window, and began to play with the gold apple; and the first person she saw was the Long-nose who was to have the Prince.

"What do you want for your gold apple, you lassie?" said the Long-nose, and threw up the window.

"It's not for sale, for gold or money," said the lassie.

"If it's not for sale for gold or money, what is it that you will sell it for? You may name your own price," said the Princess.

"Well! if I may get to the Prince, who lives here, and be with him tonight, you shall have it," said the lassie whom the North Wind had brought.

Yes! she might; that could be done. So the Princess got the gold apple; but when the lassie came up to the Prince's bed-room at night he was fast asleep; she called him and shook him, and between whiles she wept sore; but all she could do she couldn't wake him up. Next morning, as soon as day broke, came the Princess with the long nose, and drove her out again.

So in the daytime she sat down under the castle windows and began to card with her carding-comb, and the same thing happened. The Princess asked what she wanted for it; and she said it wasn't for sale for gold or money, but if she might get leave to go up to the Prince and be with him that night, the Princess should have it. But when she went up she found him fast asleep again, and all she called, and all she shook, and wept, and prayed, she couldn't get life into him; and as soon as the first grey peep of day came, then came the Princess with the long nose, and chased her out again.

So, in the daytime, the lassie sat down outside under the castle window, and began to spin with her golden spinning-wheel, and that, too, the Princess with the long nose wanted to have. So she threw up the window and asked what she wanted for it. The lassie said, as she had said twice before, it wasn't for sale for gold or money; but if she might go up to the Prince who was there, and be with him alone that night, she might have it.

Yes! she might do that and welcome. But now you must know there were some Christian folk who had been carried off thither, and as they sat in their room, which was next the Prince, they had heard how a woman had been in there, and wept and prayed, and called to him two nights running, and they told that to the Prince.

That evening, when the Princess came with her sleepy drink, the Prince made as if he drank, but threw it over his shoulder, for he could guess it was a sleepy drink. So, when the lassie came in, she found the Prince wide awake; and then she told him the whole story how she had come thither.

"Ah," said the Prince, "you've just come in the very nick of time, for tomorrow is to be our wedding-day; but now I won't have the Long-nose, and you are the only woman in the world who can set me free. I'll say I want to see what my wife is fit for, and beg her to wash the shirt which has the three spots of tallow on it; she'll say yes, for she doesn't know 'tis you who put them there; but that's a work only for Christian folk, and not for such a pack of Trolls, and so I'll say that I won't have any other for my bride than the woman who can wash them out, and ask you to do it."

So there was great joy and love between them all that night. But next day, when the wedding was to be, the Prince said:

"First of all, I'd like to see what my bride is fit for."

"Yes!" said the stepmother, with all her heart.

"Well," said the Prince, "I've got a fine shirt which I'd like for my wedding shirt, but somehow or other it has got three spots of tallow on it, which I must have washed out; and I have sworn never to take any other bride than the woman who's able to do that. If she can't, she's not worth having."

Well; that was no great thing they said, so they agreed, and she with the long-nose began to wash away as hard as she could, but the more she rubbed and scrubbed, the bigger the spots grew.

"Ah!" said the old hag, her mother, "you can't wash; let me try."

But she hadn't long taken the shirt in hand before it got far worse than ever, and with all her rubbing, and wringing, and scrubbing, the spots grew bigger and blacker, and the darker and uglier was the shirt.

Then all the other Trolls began to wash, but the longer it lasted, the blacker and uglier the shirt grew, till at last it was as black all over as if it had been up the chimney.

"Ah!" said the Prince, "you're none of you worth a straw; you can't wash. Why there, outside, sits a beggar lassie, I'll be bound she knows how to wash better than the whole lot of you. COME IN, LASSIE!" he shouted.

Well, in she came.

"Can you wash this shirt clean, lassie you?" said he.

"I don't know," she said, "but I think I can."

And almost before she had taken it and dipped it in the water, it was as white as driven snow, and whiter still.

"Yes; you are the lassie for me," said the Prince.

At that the old hag flew into such a rage, she burst on the spot, and the Princess with the long nose after her, and the whole pack of Trolls after her – at least I've never heard a word about them since.

As for the Prince and Princess, they set free all the poor Christian folk who had been carried off and shut up there; and they took with them all the silver and gold, and flitted away as far as they could from the Castle that lay East of the Sun and West of the Moon.

The Emperor's New Suit

(Danish)

MANY, MANY YEARS AGO lived an emperor, who thought so much of new clothes that he spent all his money in order to obtain them; his only ambition was to be always well dressed. He did not care for his soldiers, and the theatre did not amuse him; the only thing, in fact, he thought anything of was to drive out and show a new suit of clothes. He had a coat for every hour of the day; and as one would say of a king "He is in his cabinet," so one could say of him, "The emperor is in his dressing-room."

The great city where he resided was very gay; every day many strangers from all parts of the globe arrived. One day two swindlers came to this city; they made people believe that they were weavers, and declared they could manufacture the finest cloth to be imagined. Their colours and patterns, they said, were not only exceptionally beautiful, but the clothes made of their material possessed the wonderful quality of being invisible to any man who was unfit for his office or unpardonably stupid.

"That must be wonderful cloth," thought the emperor. "If I were to be dressed in a suit made of this cloth I should be able to find out which men in my empire were unfit for their places, and I could distinguish the clever from the stupid. I must have this cloth woven for me without delay." And he gave a large sum of money to the swindlers, in advance, that they should set to work without any loss of time. They set up two looms, and pretended to be very hard at work, but they did nothing whatever on the looms. They asked for the finest silk and the most precious gold-cloth; all they got they did away with, and worked at the empty looms till late at night.

"I should very much like to know how they are getting on with the cloth," thought the emperor. But he felt rather uneasy when he remembered that he who was not fit for his office could not see it. Personally, he was of opinion that he had nothing to fear, yet he thought it advisable to send somebody else first to see how matters stood. Everybody in the town knew what a remarkable quality the stuff possessed, and all were anxious to see how bad or stupid their neighbours were.

"I shall send my honest old minister to the weavers," thought the emperor. "He can judge best how the stuff looks, for he is intelligent, and nobody understands his office better than he."

The good old minister went into the room where the swindlers sat before the empty looms. "Heaven preserve us!" he thought, and opened his eyes wide, "I cannot see anything at all," but he did not say so. Both swindlers requested him to come near, and asked him if he did not admire the exquisite pattern and the beautiful colours, pointing to the empty looms. The poor old minister tried his very best, but he could see nothing, for there was nothing to be seen. "Oh dear," he thought, "can I be so stupid? I should never have thought so, and nobody must know it! Is it possible that I am not fit for my office? No, no, I cannot say that I was unable to see the cloth."

"Now, have you got nothing to say?" said one of the swindlers, while he pretended to be busily weaving.

"Oh, it is very pretty, exceedingly beautiful," replied the old minister looking through his glasses. "What a beautiful pattern, what brilliant colours! I shall tell the emperor that I like the cloth very much."

"We are pleased to hear that," said the two weavers, and described to him the colours and explained the curious pattern. The old minister listened attentively, that he might relate to the emperor what they said; and so he did.

Now the swindlers asked for more money, silk and gold-cloth, which they required for weaving. They kept everything for themselves, and not a thread came near the loom, but they continued, as hitherto, to work at the empty looms.

Soon afterwards the emperor sent another honest courtier to the weavers to see how they were getting on, and if the cloth was nearly finished. Like the old minister, he looked and looked but could see nothing, as there was nothing to be seen.

"Is it not a beautiful piece of cloth?" asked the two swindlers, showing and explaining the magnificent pattern, which, however, did not exist.

"I am not stupid," said the man. "It is therefore my good appointment for which I am not fit. It is very strange, but I must not let anyone know it"; and he praised the cloth, which he did not see, and expressed his joy at the beautiful colours and the fine pattern. "It is very excellent," he said to the emperor.

Everybody in the whole town talked about the precious cloth. At last the emperor wished to see it himself, while it was still on the loom. With a number of courtiers, including the two who had already been there, he went to the two clever swindlers, who now worked as hard as they could, but without using any thread.

"Is it not magnificent?" said the two old statesmen who had been there before. "Your Majesty must admire the colours and the pattern." And then they pointed to the empty looms, for they imagined the others could see the cloth.

"What is this?" thought the emperor, "I do not see anything at all. That is terrible! Am I stupid? Am I unfit to be emperor? That would indeed be the most dreadful thing that could happen to me."

"Really," he said, turning to the weavers, "your cloth has our most gracious approval"; and nodding contentedly he looked at the empty loom, for he did not like to say that he saw nothing. All his attendants, who were with him, looked and looked, and although they could not see anything more than the others, they said, like the emperor, "It is very beautiful." And all advised him to wear the new magnificent clothes at a great procession which was soon to take place. "It is magnificent, beautiful, excellent," one heard them say; everybody seemed to be delighted, and the emperor appointed the two swindlers "Imperial Court weavers."

The whole night previous to the day on which the procession was to take place, the swindlers pretended to work, and burned more than sixteen candles. People should see that they were busy to finish the emperor's new suit. They pretended to take the cloth from the loom, and worked about in the air with big scissors, and sewed with needles without thread, and said at last: "The emperor's new suit is ready now."

The emperor and all his barons then came to the hall; the swindlers held their arms up as if they held something in their hands and said: "These are the trousers!" "This is the coat!" and "Here is the cloak!" and so on. "They are all as light as a cobweb, and one must feel as if one had nothing at all upon the body; but that is just the beauty of them."

"Indeed!" said all the courtiers; but they could not see anything, for there was nothing to be seen.

"Does it please your Majesty now to graciously undress," said the swindlers, "that we may assist your Majesty in putting on the new suit before the large looking-glass?"

The emperor undressed, and the swindlers pretended to put the new suit upon him, one piece after another; and the emperor looked at himself in the glass from every side.

"How well they look! How well they fit!" said all. "What a beautiful pattern! What fine colours! That is a magnificent suit of clothes!"

The master of the ceremonies announced that the bearers of the canopy, which was to be carried in the procession, were ready.

"I am ready," said the emperor. "Does not my suit fit me marvellously?" Then he turned once more to the looking-glass, that people should think he admired his garments.

The chamberlains, who were to carry the train, stretched their hands to the ground as if they lifted up a train, and pretended to hold something in their hands; they did not like people to know that they could not see anything.

The emperor marched in the procession under the beautiful canopy, and all who saw him in the street and out of the windows exclaimed: "Indeed, the emperor's new suit is incomparable! What a long train he has! How well it fits him!" Nobody wished to let others know he saw nothing, for then he would have been unfit for his office or too stupid. Never emperor's clothes were more admired.

"But he has nothing on at all," said a little child at last. "Good heavens! listen to the voice of an innocent child," said the father, and one whispered to the other what the child had said. "But he has nothing on at all," cried at last the whole people. That made a deep impression upon the emperor, for it seemed to him that they were right; but he thought to himself, "Now I must bear up to the end." And the chamberlains walked with still greater dignity, as if they carried the train which did not exist.

The Master-Thief

(German)

ONE DAY AN OLD MAN AND HIS WIFE were sitting in front of a miserable house resting a while from their work. Suddenly a splendid carriage with four black horses came driving up, and a richly-dressed man descended from it. The peasant stood up, went to the great man, and asked what he wanted, and in what way he could be useful to him? The stranger stretched out his hand to the old man, and said, "I want nothing but to enjoy for once a country dish; cook me some potatoes, in the way you always have them, and then I will sit down at your table and eat them with pleasure." The peasant smiled and said, "You are a count or a prince, or perhaps even a duke; noble gentlemen often have such fancies, but you shall have your wish." The wife went into the kitchen, and began to wash and rub the potatoes, and to make them into balls, as they are eaten by the country-folks. Whilst she was busy with this work, the peasant said to the stranger, "Come into my garden with me for a while, I have still something to do there." He had dug some holes in the garden, and now wanted to plant some trees in them. "Have you no children," asked the stranger, "who could help you with your work?" "No," answered the peasant, "I had a son, it is true, but it is long since he went out into the world. He was a ne'er-do-well; sharp, and knowing, but he would learn nothing and was full of bad tricks, at last he ran away from me, and since then I have heard nothing of him."

The old man took a young tree, put it in a hole, drove in a post beside it, and when he had shovelled in some earth and had trampled it firmly down, he tied the stem of the tree above, below, and in the middle, fast to the post by a rope of straw. "But tell me," said the stranger, "why you don't tie that crooked knotted tree, which is lying in the corner there, bent down almost to the ground, to a post also that it may grow straight, as well as these?" The old man smiled and said, "Sir, you speak according to your knowledge, it is easy to see that you are not familiar with gardening. That tree there is old, and misshapen, no one can make it straight now. Trees must be trained while they are young." "That is how it was with your son," said the stranger, "if you had trained him while he was still young, he would not have run away; now he too must have grown hard and misshapen." "Truly it is a long time since he went away," replied the old man, "he must have changed." "Would you know him again if he were to come to you?" asked the stranger. "Hardly by his face," replied the peasant, "but he has a mark about him, a birth-mark on his shoulder, that looks like a bean." When he had said that the stranger pulled off his coat, bared his shoulder, and showed the peasant the bean. "Good God!" cried the old man, "Thou art really my son!" and love for his child stirred in his heart. "But," he added, "how canst thou be my son, thou hast become a great lord and livest in wealth and luxury? How hast thou contrived to do that?" "Ah, father," answered the son, "the young tree was bound to no post and has grown crooked, now it is too old, it will never be straight again. How have I got all that? I have become a thief, but do not be alarmed, I am a master-thief. For me there are neither locks nor bolts, whatsoever I desire is mine. Do not imagine that I steal like a common thief, I only take some of the superfluity of the rich. Poor people are safe, I would rather give to them than take anything from them. It is the same with anything which I can have without trouble, cunning and dexterity I never touch it." "Alas, my son," said the father, "it still does not please me, a thief is still a thief, I tell thee it will end badly." He took him to his mother, and when she heard that was her son, she wept for joy, but when he told her that he had become a master-thief, two streams flowed down over her face. At length she said, "Even if he has become a thief, he is still my son, and my eyes have beheld him once more." They sat down to table, and once again he ate with his parents the wretched food which he had not eaten for so long. The father said, "If our Lord, the count up there in the castle, learns who thou art, and what trade thou followest, he will not take thee in his arms and cradle thee in them as he did when he held thee at the font, but will cause thee to swing from a halter." "Be easy, father, he will do me no harm, for I understand my trade. I will go to him myself this very day." When evening drew near, the master-thief seated himself in his carriage, and drove to the castle. The count received him civilly, for he took him for a distinguished man. When, however, the stranger made himself known, the count turned pale and was quite silent for some time. At length he said, "Thou art my godson, and on that account mercy shall take the place of justice, and I will deal leniently with thee. Since thou pridest thyself on being a master-thief, I will put thy art to the proof, but if thou dost not stand the test, thou must marry the rope-maker's daughter, and the croaking of the raven must be thy music on the occasion." "Lord count," answered the master-thief, "Think of three things, as difficult as you like, and if I do not perform your tasks, do with me what you will." The count reflected for some minutes, and then said, "Well, then, in the first place, thou shalt steal the horse I keep for my own riding, out of the stable; in the next, thou shalt steal the sheet from beneath the bodies of my wife and myself when we are asleep, without our observing it, and the wedding-ring of my wife as well; thirdly and lastly, thou shalt steal away out of the church, the parson and clerk. Mark what I am saying, for thy life depends on it."

The master-thief went to the nearest town; there he bought the clothes of an old peasant woman, and put them on. Then he stained his face brown, and painted wrinkles on it as well, so that no one could have recognized him. Then he filled a small cask with old Hungary wine in which was mixed a powerful sleeping-drink. He put the cask in a basket, which he took on his back, and walked with slow and tottering steps to the count's castle. It was already dark when he arrived. He sat down on a stone in the courtyard and began to cough, like an asthmatic old woman, and to rub his hands as if he were cold. In front of the door of the stable some soldiers were lying round a fire; one of them observed the woman, and called out to her, "Come nearer, old mother, and warm thyself beside us. After all, thou hast no bed for the night, and must take one where thou canst find it." The old woman tottered up to them, begged them to lift the basket from her back, and sat down beside them at the fire. "What hast thou got in thy little cask, old lady?" asked one. "A good mouthful of wine," she answered. "I live by trade, for money and fair words I am quite ready to let you have a glass." "Let us have it here, then," said the soldier, and when he had tasted one glass he said, "When wine is good, I like another glass," and had another poured out for himself, and the rest followed his example. "Hallo, comrades," cried one of them to those who were in the stable, "here is an old goody who has wine that is as old as herself; take a draught, it will warm your stomachs far better than our fire." The old woman carried her cask into the stable. One of the soldiers had seated himself on the saddled riding-horse, another held its bridle in his hand, a third had laid hold of its tail. She poured out as much as they wanted until the spring ran dry. It was not long before the bridle fell from the hand of the one, and he fell down and began to snore, the other left hold of the tail, lay down and snored still louder. The one who was sitting in the saddle, did remain sitting, but bent his head almost down to the horse's neck, and slept and blew with his mouth like the bellows of a forge. The soldiers outside had already been asleep for a long time, and were lying on the ground motionless, as if dead. When the master-thief saw that he had succeeded, he gave the first a rope in his hand instead of the bridle, and the other who had been holding the tail, a wisp of straw, but what was he to do with the one who was sitting on the horse's back? He did not want to throw him down, for he might have awakened and have uttered a cry. He had a good idea, he unbuckled the girths of the saddle, tied a couple of ropes which were hanging to a ring on the wall fast to the saddle, and drew the sleeping rider up into the air on it, then he twisted the rope round the posts, and made it fast. He soon unloosed the horse from the chain, but if he had ridden over the stony pavement of the yard they would have heard the noise in the castle. So he wrapped the horse's hoofs in old rags, led him carefully out, leapt upon him, and galloped off.

When day broke, the master galloped to the castle on the stolen horse. The count had just got up, and was looking out of the window. "Good morning, Sir Count," he cried to him, "here is the horse, which I have got safely out of the stable! Just look, how beautifully your soldiers are lying there sleeping; and if you will but go into the stable, you will see how comfortable your watchers have made it for themselves." The count could not help laughing, then he said, "For once thou hast succeeded, but things won't go so well the second time, and I warn thee that if thou comest before me as a thief, I will handle thee as I would a thief." When the countess went to bed that night, she closed her hand with the wedding-ring tightly together, and the count said, "All the doors are locked and bolted, I will keep awake and wait for the thief, but if he gets in by the window, I will shoot him." The master-thief, however, went in the dark to the gallows, cut a poor sinner who was hanging there down from the halter, and carried him on his back to the castle. Then he set a ladder up to the bedroom, put the dead body on his shoulders, and began to climb up. When he had got so high that the head of the dead man showed at the window, the count, who was watching in his bed, fired a pistol at him, and immediately the master let the poor sinner fall down, and hid himself in one corner. The night was sufficiently lighted by the moon, for the master to see distinctly how the count got out of the window on to the ladder, came down, carried the dead body into the garden, and began to dig a hole in which to lay it. "Now," thought the thief, "the favourable moment has come," stole nimbly out of his corner, and climbed up the ladder straight into the countess's bedroom. "Dear wife," he began in the count's voice, "the thief is dead, but, after all, he is my godson, and has been more of a scape-grace than a villain. I will not put him to open shame; besides, I am sorry for the parents. I will bury him myself before daybreak, in the garden that the thing may not be known, so give me the sheet, I will wrap up the body in it, and bury him as a dog burries things by scratching." The countess gave him the sheet. "I tell you what," continued the thief, "I have a fit of magnanimity on me, give me the ring too, – the unhappy man risked his life for it, so he may take it with him into his grave." She would not gainsay the count, and although she did it unwillingly she drew the ring from her finger, and gave it to him. The thief made off with both these things, and reached home safely before the count in the garden had finished his work of burying.

What a long face the count did pull when the master came next morning, and brought him the sheet and the ring. "Art thou a wizard?" said he, "Who has fetched thee out of the grave in which I myself laid thee, and brought thee to life again?" "You did not bury me," said the thief, "but the poor sinner on the gallows," and he told him exactly how everything had happened, and the count was forced to own to him that he was a clever, crafty thief. "But thou hast not reached the end yet," he added, "thou hast still to perform the third task, and if thou dost not succeed in that, all is of no use." The master smiled and returned no answer. When night had fallen he went with a long sack on his back, a bundle under his arms, and a lantern in his hand to the village-church. In the sack he had some crabs, and in the bundle short wax-candles. He sat down in the churchyard, took out a crab, and stuck a wax-candle on his back. Then he lighted the little light, put the crab on the ground, and let it creep about. He took a second out of the sack, and treated it in the same way, and so on until the last was out of the sack. Hereupon he put on a long black garment that looked like a monk's cowl, and stuck a grey beard on his chin. When at last he was quite unrecognizable, he took the sack in which the crabs had been, went into the church, and ascended the pulpit. The clock in the tower was just striking twelve; when the last stroke had sounded, he cried with a loud and piercing voice, "Hearken, sinful men, the end of all things has come! The last day is at hand! Hearken! Hearken! Whosoever wishes to go to heaven with me must creep into the sack. I am Peter, who opens and shuts the gate of heaven. Behold how the dead outside there in the churchyard, are wandering about collecting their bones. Come, come, and creep into the sack; the world is about to be destroyed!" The cry echoed through the whole village. The parson and clerk who lived nearest to the church, heard it first, and when they saw the lights which were moving about the churchyard, they observed that something unusual was going on, and went into the church. They listened to the sermon for a while, and then the clerk nudged the parson and said, "It would not be amiss if we were to use the opportunity together, and before the dawning of the last day, find an easy way of getting to heaven." "To tell the truth," answered the parson, "that is what I myself have been thinking, so if you are inclined, we will set out on our way." "Yes," answered the clerk, "but you, the pastor, have the precedence, I will follow." So the parson went first, and ascended the pulpit where the master opened his sack. The parson crept in first, and then the clerk. The master immediately tied up the sack tightly, seized it by the middle, and dragged it down the pulpit-steps, and whenever the heads of the two fools bumped against the steps, he cried, "We are going over the mountains." Then he drew them through the village in the same way, and when they were passing through puddles, he cried, "Now we are going through wet clouds." And when at last he was dragging them up the steps of the castle, he cried, "Now we are on the steps of heaven, and will soon be in the outer court." When he had got to the top, he pushed the sack into the pigeon-house, and when the pigeons fluttered about, he said, "Hark how glad the angels are, and how they are flapping their wings!" Then he bolted the door upon them, and went away.

Next morning he went to the count, and told him that he had performed the third task also, and had carried the parson and clerk out of the church. "Where hast thou left them?" asked the lord. "They are lying upstairs in a sack in the pigeon-house, and imagine that they are in heaven." The count went up himself, and convinced himself that the master had told the truth. When he had delivered the parson and clerk from their captivity, he said, "Thou art an arch-thief, and hast won thy wager. For once thou escapest with a whole skin, but see that thou leavest my land, for if ever thou settest foot on it again, thou may'st count on thy elevation to the gallows." The arch-thief took leave of his parents, once more went forth into the wide world, and no one has ever heard of him since.

The Icelandic Sorceresses

(Icelandic)

"TELL ME," SAID KATLA, a handsome and lively widow, to Gunlaugar, an accomplished and gallant young warrior, "tell me why thou goest so oft to Mahfahlida? Is it to caress an old woman?"

"Thine own age, Katla," answered the youth inconsiderately, "might prevent thy making that of Geirrida a subject of reproach."

"I little deemed," replied the offended matron, "that we were on an equality in that particular – but thou, who supposest that Geirrida is the sole source of knowledge, mayst find that there are others who equal her in science."

It happened in the course of the following winter that Gunlaugar, in company with Oddo, the son of Katla, had renewed one of those visits to Geirrida with which Katla had upbraided him.

"Thou shalt not depart tonight," said the sage matron; "evil spirits are abroad, and thy bad destiny predominates."

"We are two in company," answered Gunlaugar, "and have therefore nothing to fear."

"Oddo," replied Geirrida, "will be of no aid to thee; but go, since thou wilt go, and pay the penalty of thy own rashness."

In their way they visited the rival matron, and Gunlaugar was invited to remain in her house that night. This he declined, and, passing forward alone, was next morning found lying before the gate of his father Thorbiorn, severely wounded and deprived of his judgement. Various causes were assigned for this disaster; but Oddo, asserting that they had parted in anger that evening from Geirrida, insisted that his companion must have sustained the injury through her sorcery. Geirrida was accordingly cited to the popular assembly and accused of witchcraft. But twelve witnesses, or compurgators, having asserted upon their oath the innocence of the accused party, Geirrida was honourably freed from the accusation brought against her. Her acquittal did not terminate the rivalry between the two sorceresses, for, Geirrida belonging to the family of Kiliakan, and Katla to that of the pontiff Snorro, the animosity which still subsisted between these septs became awakened by the quarrel.

It chanced that Thorbiorn, called Digri (or the corpulent), one of the family of Snorro, had some horses which fed in the mountain pastures, near to those of Thorarin, called the Black, the son of the enchantress Geirrida. But when autumn arrived, and the horses were to be withdrawn from the mountains and housed for the winter, those of Thorbiorn could nowhere be found, and Oddo, the son of Katla, being sent to consult a wizard, brought back a dubious answer, which seemed to indicate that they had been stolen by Thorarin. Thorbiorn, with Oddo and a party of armed followers, immediately set forth for Mahfahlida, the dwelling of Geirrida and her son Thorarin. Arrived before the gate, they demanded permission to search for the horses which were missing. This Thorarin refused, alleging that neither was the search demanded duly authorised by law, nor were the proper witnesses cited to be present, nor did Thorbiorn offer any sufficient pledge of security when claiming the exercise of so hazardous a privilege. Thorbiorn replied, that as Thorarin declined to permit a search, he must be held as admitting his guilt; and constituting for that purpose a temporary court of justice, by choosing out six judges, he formally accused Thorarin of theft before the gate of his own house. At this the patience of Geirrida forsook her.

"Well," said she to her son Thorarin, "is it said of thee that thou art more a woman than a man, or thou wouldst not bear these intolerable affronts."

Thorarin, fired at the reproach, rushed forth with his servants and guests; a skirmish soon disturbed the legal process which had been instituted, and one or two of both parties were wounded and slain before the wife of Thorarin and the female attendants could separate the fray by flinging their mantles over the weapons of the combatants.

Thorbiorn and his party retreating, Thorarin proceeded to examine the field of battle. Alas! among the reliques of the fight was a bloody hand too slight and fair to belong to any of the combatants. It was that of his wife Ada, who had met this misfortune in her attempts to separate the foes. Incensed to the uttermost, Thorarin threw aside his constitutional moderation, and, mounting on horseback, with his allies and followers, pursued the hostile party, and overtook them in a hay-field, where they had halted to repose their horses, and to exult over the damage they had done to Thorarin. At this moment he assailed them with such fury that he slew Thorbiorn upon the spot, and killed several of his attendants, although Oddo, the son of Katla, escaped free from wounds, having been dressed by his mother in an invulnerable garment. After this action, more blood being shed than usual in an Icelandic engagement, Thorarin returned to Mahfahlida, and, being questioned by his mother concerning the events of the skirmish, he answered in the improvisatory and enigmatical poetry of his age and country –

"From me the foul reproach be far,
With which a female waked the war,
From me, who shunned not in the fray
Through foemen fierce to hew my way
(Since meet it is the eagle's brood
On the fresh corpse should find their food);
Then spared I not, in fighting field,
With stalwart hand my sword to wield;

And well may claim at Odin's shrine
The praise that waits this deed of mine."

To which effusion Geirrida answered –

"Do these verses imply the death of Thorbiorn?"

And Thorarin, alluding to the legal process which Thorbiorn had instituted against him, resumed his song –

"Sharp bit the sword beneath the hood
Of him whose zeal the cause pursued,
And ruddy flowed the stream of death,
Ere the grim brand resumed the sheath;
Now on the buckler of the slain
The raven sits, his draught to drain,
For gore-drenched is his visage bold,
That hither came his courts to hold."

As the consequence of this slaughter was likely to be a prosecution at the instance of the pontiff Snorro, Thorarin had now recourse to his allies and kindred, of whom the most powerful were Arnkill, his maternal uncle, and Verimond, who readily premised their aid both in the field and in the Comitia, or popular meeting, in spring, before which it was to be presumed Snorro would indict Thorarin for the slaughter of his kinsman. Arnkill could not, however, forbear asking his nephew how he had so far lost his usual command of temper. He replied in verse –

"Till then, the master of my mood,
Men called me gentle, mild, and good;
But yon fierce dame's sharp tongue might wake
In wintry den the frozen snake."

While Thorarin spent the winter with his uncle Arnkill, he received information from his mother Geirrida that Oddo, son of her old rival Katla, was the person who had cut off the hand of his wife Ada, and that he gloried in the fact. Thorarin and Arnkill determined on instant vengeance, and, travelling rapidly, surprised the house of Katla. The undismayed sorceress, on hearing them approach, commanded her son to sit close beside her, and when the assailants entered they only beheld Katla, spinning coarse yarn from what seemed a large distaff, with her female domestics seated around her.

"My son," she said, "is absent on a journey"; and Thorarin and Arnkill, having searched the house in vain, were obliged to depart with this answer. They had not, however, gone far before the well-known skill of Katla, in optical delusion occurred to them, and they resolved on a second and stricter search. Upon their return they found Katla in the outer apartment, who seemed to be shearing the hair of a tame kid, but was in reality cutting the locks of her son Oddo. Entering the inner room, they found the large distaff flung carelessly upon a bench. They returned yet a third time, and a third delusion was prepared for them; for Katla had given her son the appearance of a hog, which seemed to grovel upon the heap of ashes. Arnkill now seized and split the distaff, which he had at first suspected, upon which Kalta tauntingly observed, that if their visits had been frequent that evening, they could not be said to be altogether ineffectual, since they had destroyed a distaff. They were accordingly returning completely baffled, when Geirrida met them, and upbraided them with carelessness in searching for their enemy.

"Return yet again," she said, "and I will accompany you."

Katla's maidens, still upon the watch, announced to her the return of the hostile party, their number augmented by one who wore a blue mantle.

"Alas!" cried Katla, "it is the sorceress Geirrida, against whom spells will be of no avail."

Immediately rising from the raised and boarded seat which she occupied, she concealed Oddo beneath it, and covered it with cushions as before, on which she stretched herself complaining of indisposition. Upon the entrance of the hostile party, Geirrida, without speaking a word, flung aside her mantle, took out a piece of sealskin, in which she wrapped up Katla's head, and commanded that she should be held by some of the attendants, while the others broke open the boarded space, beneath which Oddo lay concealed, seized upon him, bound him, and led him away captive with his mother. Next morning Oddo was hanged, and Katla stoned to death; but not until she had confessed that, through her sorcery, she had occasioned the disaster of Gunlaugar, which first led the way to these feuds.

The Evil One and Kitta Grau

(Swedish)

ONE DAY THE DEVIL met Kitta Grau:

"Where have you been, old man?" asked Kitta Grau, for she recognized him.

"Well," said the evil one, "I have been out on the farmstead where the newly wedded couple live. This is the third time I have tried to sow dissension between them; but they think so much of each other that it is a sheer impossibility."

"You talk like a real stupid. That is something I could bring about the very first time I went there," said Kitta Grau.

"If you can do that, you shall have a splendid pair of shoes," was the evil one's reply.

"Mind you keep your word!" said Kitta, and turned toward the farmstead.

There the woman was home alone; for her husband had gone to the forest. Kitta said to the young wife:

"You really have a splendid husband."

"And that is the truth," the woman replied, "for he grants my every wish before it is spoken."

"But take my word for it," said Kitta, "there is still a bit of deceit in him. He has a pair of long hairs under his chin – if you could get at them with a razor, and cut them off while he is asleep, then he would be altogether without malice."

"Well," said the woman, "if that will help, I will be sure to keep an eye open after dinner and attend to it, for then he always takes a little noonday nap."

Then Kitta Grau went out into the forest to the husband and bade him good day.

"You really have a very good wife," said Kitta.

"She could not be bettered," replied the husband.

"Well you might be mistaken for all that," said Kitta. "When you come home, be on your guard, for when you go to take your noonday nap, she has in mind to cut your throat. So be sure not to go to sleep."

The husband did not think much of the matter; but still he thanked Kitta Grau for her trouble.

Then he went home and ate his dinner, laid down and pretended to fall asleep at once.

Thereupon his wife went to his shaving-kit, took out his razor, went softly up to him and took hold of his chin with her hand.

Up flew the man.

"Do you want to murder me?" he cried, and gave his wife such a thump that she measured her full length on the floor.

And from that day forward there was no peace in the house. Now Kitta Grau was to receive her reward from the evil one. But he was so afraid of her that he did not venture to give her the shoes until he stood on one side of a stream, while she stood on the other, and then he passed them over to her on a long pole.

"You are ever so much worse than I am," he told Kitta Grau.

The black man had made a bargain with a merchant. He had promised him that all goods which he might buy he should sell again within three weeks' time at a handsome profit. But, if he had prospered, after seven years had passed he was to be the devil's own. And he did prosper; for no matter what manner of old trash the merchant bought, and if it were no more than an old worn-out fur coat, he was always able to sell it again, and always at a profit.

Kitta Grau came into his shop and showed him the handsome shoes the evil one had given her.

So the merchant said:

"May heaven keep me from him! He will surely fetch me when the time comes; for I have made a pact with him; and I have been unable to buy anything without selling it again in three weeks' time."

Then Kitta Grau said: "Buy me, for I am sure no one will buy me from you!" And that is what the merchant did. He bought Kitta, had her disrobe and cover herself with tar, and roll in a pile of feathers. Then he put her in a glass cage as though she were a bird.

Now the first week went by, and the second week went by, and the third week went by, and no one appeared who wanted to buy the curious bird. And then, in due time, came the evil one, and wanted to fetch his merchant.

"Have patience," said the merchant, "I still have something I have bought, but have not been able to sell again in three weeks' time."

"That is something I'd like to see," said the black man. Then the merchant showed him Kitta Grau, sitting in her glass cage. But no sooner had the evil one seen the handsome bird than he cried:

"Oh, I see! It is you Kitta Grau! No one who knows you would buy you!"

And with that he hurried on his way.

Thus Kitta Grau could help do evil, and help do good.

The Twelve Wild Ducks

(Norwegian)

ONCE ON A TIME there was a Queen who was out driving, when there had been a new fall of snow in the winter; but when she had gone a little way, she began to bleed at the nose, and had to get out of her sledge. And so, as she stood there, leaning against the fence, and saw the red blood on the white snow, she fell a-thinking how she had twelve sons and no daughter, and she said to herself,

"If I only had a daughter as white as snow and as red as blood, I shouldn't care what became of all my sons."

But the words were scarce out of her mouth before an old witch of the Trolls came up to her.

"A daughter you shall have," she said, "and she shall be as white as snow, and as red as blood; and your sons shall be mine, but you may keep them till the babe is christened."

So when the time came the Queen had a daughter, and she was as white as snow, and as red as blood, just as the Troll had promised, and so they called her 'Snow-white and Rosy-red'. Well, there was great joy at the King's court, and the Queen was as glad as glad could be; but when what she had promised to the old witch came into her mind, she sent for a silversmith, and bade him make twelve silver spoons, one for each prince, and after that she bade him make one more, and that she gave to Snow-white and Rosy-red. But as soon as ever the Princess was christened, the Princes were turned into twelve wild ducks, and flew away. They never saw them again – away they went, and away they stayed.

So the Princess grew up, and she was both tall and fair, but she was often so strange and sorrowful, and no one could understand what it was that ailed her. But one evening the Queen was also sorrowful, for she had many strange thoughts when she thought of her sons. She said to Snow-white and Rosy-red,

"Why are you so sorrowful, my daughter? Is there anything you want? If so, only say the word, and you shall have it."

"Oh, it seems so dull and lonely here," said Snow-white and Rosy-red; "everyone else has brothers and sisters, but I am all alone; I have none; and that's why I'm so sorrowful."

"But you *had* brothers, my daughter," said the Queen; "I had twelve sons who were your brothers, but I gave them all away to get you"; and so she told her the whole story.

So when the Princess heard that, she had no rest; for, in spite of all the Queen could say or do, and all she wept and prayed, the lassie would set off to seek her brothers, for she thought it was all her fault; and at last she got leave to go away from the palace. On and on she walked into the wide world, so far, you would never have thought a young lady could have strength to walk so far.

So, once, when she was walking through a great, great wood, one day she felt tired, and sat down on a mossy tuft and fell asleep. Then she dreamt that she went deeper and deeper into the wood, till she came to a little wooden hut, and there she found her brothers; just then she woke, and straight before her she saw a worn path in the green moss, and this path went deeper into the wood; so she followed it, and after a long time she came to just such a little wooden house as that she had seen in her dream.

Now, when she went into the room there was no one at home, but there stood twelve beds, and twelve chairs, and twelve spoons – a dozen of everything, in short. So when she saw that, she was so glad, she hadn't been so glad for many a long year, for she could guess at once that her brothers lived here, and that they owned the beds, and chairs, and spoons. So she began to make up the fire, and sweep the room, and make the beds, and cook the dinner, and to make the house as tidy as she could; and when she had done all the cooking and work, she ate her own dinner, and crept under her youngest brother's bed, and lay down there, but she forgot her spoon upon the table.

So she had scarcely laid herself down before she heard something flapping and whirring in the air, and so all the twelve wild ducks came sweeping in; but as soon as ever they crossed the threshold they became Princes.

"Oh, how nice and warm it is in here," they said. "Heaven bless him who made up the fire, and cooked such a good dinner for us."

And so each took up his silver spoon, and was going to eat. But when each had taken his own, there was one still left lying on the table, and it was so like the rest that they couldn't tell it from them.

"This is our sister's spoon," they said; "and if her spoon be here, she can't be very far off herself."

"If this be our sister's spoon, and she be here," said the eldest, "she shall be killed, for she is to blame for all the ill we suffer."

And this she lay under the bed and listened to.

"No," said the youngest; "'twere a shame to kill her for that. She has nothing to do with our suffering ill; for if anyone's to blame, it's our own mother."

So they set to work hunting for her both high and low, and at last they looked under all the beds, and so when they came to the youngest Prince's bed, they found her, and dragged her out. Then the eldest Prince wished again to have her killed, but she begged and prayed so prettily for herself.

"Oh! gracious goodness! don't kill me, for I've gone about seeking you these three years, and if I could only set you free, I'd willingly lose my life."

"Well!" said they, "if you will set us free, you may keep your life; for you can if you choose."

"Yes; only tell me," said the Princess; "how it can be done, and I'll do it, whatever it be."

"You must pick thistledown," said the Princes, "and you must card it, and spin it, and weave it; and after you have done that, you must cut out and make twelve coats, and twelve shirts, and twelve neckerchiefs, one for each of us, and while you do that, you must neither talk, nor laugh, nor weep. If you can do that, we are free."

"But where shall I ever get thistledown enough for so many neckerchiefs, and shirts, and coats?" asked Snow-white and Rosy-red.

"We'll soon shew you," said the Princes; and so they took her with them to a great wide moor, where there stood such a crop of thistles, all nodding and nodding in the breeze, and the down all floating and glistening like gossamers through the air in the sunbeams. The Princess had never seen such a quantity of thistledown in her life, and she began to pluck and gather it as fast and as well as she could; and when she got home at night she set to work carding and spinning yarn from the down. So she went on a long, long time, picking, and carding, and spinning, and all the while keeping the Princes' house, cooking and making their beds. At evening home they came, flapping and whirring like wild ducks, and all night they were Princes, but in the morning off they flew again, and were wild ducks the whole day.

But now it happened once, when she was out on the moor to pick thistledown – and if I don't mistake, it was the very last time she was to go thither – it happened that the young King who ruled that land was out hunting, and came riding across the moor and saw her. So he stopped there and wondered who the lovely lady could be that walked along the moor picking thistledown, and he asked her her name, and when he could get no answer, he was still more astonished; and at last he liked her so much, that nothing would do but he must take her home to his castle and marry her. So he ordered his servants to take her and put her upon his horse. Snow-white and Rosy-red, she wrung her hands, and made signs to them, and pointed to the bags in which her work was, and when the King saw she wished to have them with her, he told his men to take up the bags behind them. When they had done that the Princess came to herself little by little, for the King was both a wise man and a handsome man too, and he was as soft and kind to her as a doctor. But when they got home to the palace, and the old Queen, who was his stepmother, set eyes on Snow-white and Rosy-red, she got so cross and jealous of her because she was so lovely, that she said to the King –

"Can't you see now, that this thing whom you have picked up, and whom you are going to marry, is a witch. Why? She can't either talk, or laugh, or weep!"

But the King didn't care a pin for what she said, but held on with the wedding, and married Snow-white and Rosy-red, and they lived in great joy and glory; but she didn't forget to go on sewing at her shirts.

So when the year was almost out Snow-white and Rosy-red brought a Prince into the world; and then the old Queen was more spiteful and jealous than ever, and at dead of night, she stole in to Snow-white and Rosy-red, while she slept, and took away her babe, and threw it into a pit full of snakes. After that she cut Snow-white and Rosy-red in her finger, and smeared the blood over her mouth, and went straight to the King.

"Now come and see," she said, "what sort of a thing you have taken for your Queen; here she has eaten up her own babe."

Then the King was so downcast, he almost burst into tears, and said –

"Yes, it must be true, sure I see it with my own eyes; but she'll not do it again, I'm sure, and so this time I'll spare her life."

So before the next year was out she had another son, and the same thing happened. The King's stepmother got more and more jealous and spiteful. She stole in to the young Queen at night while she slept, took away the babe, and threw it into a pit full of snakes, cut the young Queen's finger, and smeared the blood over her mouth, and then went and told the King she had eaten up her own child. Then the King was so sorrowful, you can't think how sorry he was, and he said –

"Yes, it must be true, since I see it with my own eyes; but she'll not do it again, I'm sure, and so this time too I'll spare her life."

Well! before the next year was out, Snow-white and Rosy-red brought a daughter into the world, and her, too, the old Queen took and threw into the pit full of snakes, while the young Queen slept. Then she cut her finger, smeared the blood over her mouth, and went again to the King and said –

"Now you may come and see if it isn't as I say; she's a wicked, wicked witch, for here she has gone and eaten up her third babe too."

Then the King was so sad, there was no end to it, for now he couldn't spare her any longer, but had to order her to be burnt alive on a pile of wood. But just when the pile was all ablaze, and they were going to put her on it, she made signs to them to take twelve boards and lay them round the pile, and on these she laid the neckerchiefs, and the shirts, and the coats for her brothers, but the youngest brother's shirt wanted its left arm, for she hadn't had time to finish it. And as soon as ever she had done that, they heard such a flapping and whirring in the air, and down came twelve wild ducks flying over the forest, and each of them snapped up his clothes in his bill and flew off with them.

"See now!" said the old Queen to the King, "wasn't I right when I told you she was a witch; but make haste and burn her before the pile burns low."

"Oh!" said the King, "we've wood enough and to spare, and so I'll wait a bit, for I have a mind to see what the end of all this will be."

As he spoke, up came the twelve Princes riding along, as handsome well-grown lads as you'd wish to see; but the youngest Prince had a wild duck's wing instead of his left arm.

"What's all this about?" asked the Princes.

"My Queen is to be burnt," said the King, "because she's a witch, and because she has eaten up her own babes."

"She hasn't eaten them at all," said the Princes. "Speak now, sister; you have set us free and saved us, now save yourself."

Then Snow-white and Rosy-red spoke, and told the whole story; how every time she was brought to bed, the old Queen, the King's stepmother, had stolen in to her at night, had taken her babes away, and cut her little finger, and smeared the blood over her mouth; and then the Princes took the King, and shewed him the snake-pit where three babes lay playing with adders and toads, and lovelier children you never saw.

So the King had them taken out at once, and went to his stepmother, and asked her what punishment she thought that woman deserved who could find it in her heart to betray a guiltless Queen and three such blessed little babes.

"She deserves to be fast bound between twelve unbroken steeds, so that each may take his share of her," said the old Queen.

"You have spoken your own doom," said the King, "and you shall suffer it at once."

So the wicked old Queen was fast bound between twelve unbroken steeds, and each got his share of her. But the King took Snow-white and Rosy-red, and their three children, and the twelve Princes; and so they all went home to their father and mother, and told all that had befallen them, and there was joy and gladness over the whole kingdom, because the Princess was saved and set free, and because she had set free her twelve brothers.

Bushy Bride

(Norwegian)

THERE WAS ONCE ON A TIME a widower who had a son and a daughter by his first wife. They were both good children, and loved each other with all their hearts. After some time had gone by the man married again, and he chose a widow with one daughter who was ugly and wicked, and her mother was ugly and wicked too. From the very day that the new wife came into the house there was no peace for the man's children, and not a corner to be found where they could get any rest; so the boy thought that the best thing he could do was to go out into the world and try to earn his own bread.

When he had roamed about for some time he came to the King's palace, where he obtained a place under the coachman; and very brisk and active he was, and the horses that he looked after were so fat and sleek, that they shone again.

But his sister, who was still at home, fared worse and worse. Both her stepmother and her stepsister were always finding fault with her, whatsoever she did and whithersoever she went, and they scolded her and abused her so that she never had an hour's peace. They made her do all the hard work, and hard words fell to her lot early and late, but little enough food accompanied them.

One day they sent her to the brook to fetch some water home, and an ugly and horrible head rose up out of the water, and said, "Wash me, girl!"

"Yes, I will wash you with pleasure," said the girl, and began to wash and scrub the ugly face, but she couldn't help thinking that it was a very unpleasant piece of work. When she had done it, and done it well, another head rose up out of the water, and this one was uglier still.

"Brush me, girl!" said the head.

"Yes, I will brush you with pleasure," said the girl, and set to work with the tangled hair, and, as may be easily imagined, this too was by no means pleasant work.

When she had got it done, another and a much more ugly and horrible-looking head rose up out of the water.

"Kiss me, girl!" said the head.

"Yes, I will kiss you," said the man's daughter, and she did it, but she thought it was the worst bit of work that she had ever had to do in her life.

So the heads all began to talk to each other, and to ask what they should do for this girl who was so full of kindliness.

"She shall be the prettiest girl that ever was, and fair and bright as the day," said the first head.

"Gold shall drop from her hair whenever she brushes it," said the second.

"Gold shall drop from her mouth whenever she speaks," said the third head.

So when the man's daughter went home, looking as beautiful and bright as day, the stepmother and her daughter grew much more ill-tempered, and it was worse still when she began to talk, and they saw that golden coins dropped from her mouth. The stepmother fell into such a towering passion that she drove the man's daughter into the pigsty – she might stay there with her fine show of gold, the stepmother said, but she should not be permitted to set foot in the house.

It was not long before the mother wanted her own daughter to go to the stream to fetch some water.

When she got there with her pails, the first head rose up out of the water close to the bank. "Wash me, girl!" it said.

"Wash yourself!" answered the woman's daughter.

Then the second head appeared.

"Brush me, girl!" said the head.

"Brush yourself!" said the woman's daughter.

So down it went to the bottom, and the third head came up.

"Kiss me, girl!" said the head.

"As if I would kiss your ugly mouth!" said the girl.

So again the heads talked together about what they should do for this girl who was so ill-tempered and full of her own importance, and they agreed that she should have a nose that was four ells long, and a jaw that was three ells, and a fir bush in the middle of her forehead, and every time she spoke ashes should fall from her mouth.

When she came back to the cottage door with her pails, she called to her mother who was inside, "Open the door!"

"Open the door yourself, my own dear child!" said the mother.

"I can't get near, because of my nose," said the daughter.

When the mother came and saw her you may imagine what a state of mind she was in, and how she screamed and lamented, but neither the nose nor the jaw grew any the less for that.

Now the brother, who was in service in the King's palace, had taken a portrait of his sister, and he had carried the picture away with him, and every morning and evening he knelt down before it and prayed for his sister, so dearly did he love her.

The other stable-boys had heard him doing this, so they peeped through the keyhole into his room, and saw that he was kneeling there before a picture; so they told everyone that every morning and evening the youth knelt down and prayed to an idol which he had; and at last they went to the King himself, and begged that he too would peep through the keyhole, and see for himself what the youth did. At first the King would not believe this, but after a long, long time, they prevailed with him, and he crept on tip-toe to the door, peeped through, and saw the youth on his knees, with his hands clasped together before a picture which was hanging on the wall.

"Open the door!" cried the King, but the youth did not hear.

So the King called to him again, but the youth was praying so fervently that he did not hear him this time either.

"Open the door, I say!" cried the King again. "It is I! I want to come in."

So the youth sprang to the door and unlocked it, but in his haste he forgot to hide the picture.

When the King entered and saw it, he stood still as if he were in fetters, and could not stir from the spot, for the picture seemed to him so beautiful.

"There is nowhere on earth so beautiful a woman as this!" said the King.

But the youth told him that she was his sister, and that he had painted her, and that if she was not prettier than the picture she was at all events not uglier.

"Well, if she is as beautiful as that, I will have her for my Queen," said the King, and he commanded the youth to go home and fetch her without a moment's delay, and to lose no time in coming back. The youth promised to make all the haste he could, and set forth from the King's palace.

When the brother arrived at home to fetch his sister, her stepmother and stepsister would go too. So they all set out together, and the man's daughter took with her a casket in which she kept her gold, and a dog which was called Little Snow. These two things were all that she had inherited from her mother. When they had travelled for some time they had to cross the sea, and the brother sat down at the helm, and the mother and the two half-sisters went to the forepart of the vessel, and they sailed a long, long way. At last they came in sight of land.

"Look at that white strand there; that is where we shall land," said the brother, pointing across the sea.

"What is my brother saying?" inquired the man's daughter.

"He says that you are to throw your casket out into the sea," answered the stepmother.

"Well, if my brother says so, I must do it," said the man's daughter, and she flung her casket into the sea.

When they had sailed for some time longer, the brother once more pointed over the sea. "There you may see the palace to which we are bound," said he.

"What is my brother saying?" asked the man's daughter.

"Now he says that you are to throw your dog into the sea," answered the stepmother.

The man's daughter wept, and was sorely troubled, for Little Snow was the dearest thing she had on earth, but at last she threw him overboard.

"If my brother says that, I must do it, but Heaven knows how unwilling I am to throw thee out, Little Snow!" said she.

So they sailed onwards a long way farther.

"There may'st thou see the King coming out to meet thee," said the brother, pointing to the seashore.

"What is my brother saying?" asked his sister again.

"Now he says that you are to make haste and throw yourself overboard," answered the stepmother.

She wept and she wailed, but as her brother had said that, she thought she must do it; so she leaped into the sea.

But when they arrived at the palace, and the King beheld the ugly bride with a nose that was four ells long, a jaw that was three ells, and a forehead that had a bush in the middle of it, he was quite terrified; but the wedding feast was all prepared, as regarded brewing and baking, and all the wedding guests were sitting waiting, so, ugly as she was, the King was forced to take her.

But he was very wroth, and none can blame him for that; so he caused the brother to be thrown into a pit full of snakes.

On the first Thursday night after this, a beautiful maiden came into the kitchen of the palace, and begged the kitchen-maid, who slept there, to lend her a brush. She begged very prettily, and got it, and then she brushed her hair, and the gold dropped from it.

A little dog was with her, and she said to it, "Go out, Little Snow, and see if it will soon be day!"

This she said thrice, and the third time that she sent out the dog to see, it was very near dawn. Then she was forced to depart, but as she went she said:

"Out on thee, ugly Bushy Bride,
Sleeping so soft by the young King's side,
On sand and stones my bed I make,
And my brother sleeps with the cold snake,
Unpitied and unwept."

"I shall come twice more, and then never again," said she.

In the morning the kitchen-maid related what she had seen and heard, and the King said that next Thursday night he himself would watch in the kitchen and see if this were true, and when it had begun to grow dark he went out into the kitchen to the girl. But though he rubbed his eyes and did everything he could to keep himself awake it was all in vain, for the Bushy Bride crooned and sang till his eyes were fast closed, and when the beautiful young maiden came he was sound asleep and snoring.

This time also, as before, she borrowed a brush and brushed her hair with it, and the gold dropped down as she did it; and again she sent the dog out three times, and when day dawned she departed, but as she was going she said as she had said before, "I shall come once more, and then never again."

On the third Thursday night the King once more insisted on keeping watch. Then he set two men to hold him; each of them was to take an arm, and shake him and jerk him by the arm whenever he seemed to be going to fall asleep; and he set two men to watch his Bushy Bride. But as the night wore on the Bushy Bride again began to croon and to sing, so that his eyes began to close and his head to droop on one side. Then came the lovely maiden, and got the brush and brushed her hair till the gold dropped from it, and then she sent her Little Snow out to see if it would soon be day, and this she did three times. The third time it was just beginning to grow light, and then she said:

"Out on thee, ugly Bushy Bride,
Sleeping so soft by the young King's side,
On sand and stones my bed I make,
And my brother sleeps with the cold snake,
Unpitied and unwept."

"Now I shall never come again," she said, and then she turned to go. But the two men who were holding the King by the arms seized his hands and forced a knife into his grasp, and then made him cut her little finger just enough to make it bleed.

Thus the true bride was freed. The King then awoke, and she told him all that had taken place, and how her stepmother and stepsister had betrayed her. Then the brother was at once taken out of the snake-pit – the snakes had never touched him – and the stepmother and stepsister were flung down into it instead of him.

No one can tell how delighted the King was to get rid of that hideous Bushy Bride, and get a Queen who was bright and beautiful as day itself.

And now the real wedding was held, and held in such a way that it was heard of and spoken about all over seven kingdoms. The King and his bride drove to church, and Little Snow was in the carriage too. When the blessing was given they went home again, and after that I saw no more of them.

The Magic Pipe

(Norse)

THERE WERE ONCE THREE BROTHERS, all the sons of the same father and mother.

The two elder were hard-working, thrifty lads, who had no care except as to how they might better themselves in the world. But the youngest, whose name was Boots, was not thrifty at all. He was a do-nothing and was quite content to sit in the chimney corner and warm his shins and think about things.

One day the eldest son came to his father and said, "I have it in mind to go over yonder to the King's castle and take service there, for I hear the King has need of a herdsman to take care of his hares for him. The wages are six dollars a week, and if anyone can keep the herd together and bring them safe home every night without losing one of them the King will give him the Princess for a wife."

The father was pleased when he heard this. Six dollars a week was fair pay, and it would be a fine thing if the lad could win the Princess for his wife. At any rate it was worth trying for.

So the eldest son cocked his hat over one ear, and off he set for the palace.

He had not gone so very far when he came to the edge of a forest, and there was an old crone with a green nose a yard long, and it was caught in a crack of a log. She was dancing and hopping about, but for all her dancing and hopping she got no farther than that one spot, for her nose held her there.

The lad stopped and stared at her, and she looked so funny to his mind that he laughed and laughed till his sides ached.

"You gawk!" screamed the old hag. "Come and drive a wedge in the crack so I can get my nose out. Here I have stood for twice a hundred years, and no Christian soul has come to set me free."

"If you have stood there twice a hundred years you might as well stay a while longer. As for me, I'm expected at the King's palace, and I have no time to waste driving wedges," said the lad, and away he went, one foot before the other, leaving the old crone with her nose still in the crack.

When the lad came to the palace, he knocked at the door and told the man who opened it that he had come to see about the place of herdsman. When the man heard this he brought the lad straight to the King, and told him what the lad had come for.

The King listened and nodded his head. Yes, he was in need of a herdsman and would be glad to take the lad into his service, and the wages were just as the youth thought, with a chance of winning the Princess to boot. But there was one part of the bargain that had been left out. If the lad failed to keep the herd together and lost so much as even one small leveret, he was to receive such a beating as would turn him black and blue.

That part of the bargain was not such pleasant hearing as the rest of it. Still the lad had a mind to try for the Princess. So he was taken out to the paddock where the hares were, and a pretty sight it was to see them hopping and frisking about, hundreds and hundreds of them, big and little.

All morning the hares were kept there in the paddock with the new herdsman watching them, and as long as that was the case everything went well. But later on the hares had to be driven out on the hills for a run and a bite of fresh grass, and then the trouble began. The lad could no more keep them together than if they had been sparks from a fire. Away they sped, some one way and some another, into the woods and over the hills – there was no keeping track of them. The lad shouted and ran and ran and shouted till the sweat poured down his face, but he could not herd them back. By the time evening came he had scarce a score of them to drive home to the palace.

And there on the steps stood the King with a stout rod in his hands, all ready to give the lad a beating. And a good beating it was, I can tell you. When the King had finished with him he could hardly stand. Home he went with only his sore bones for wages.

Then it was the second brother's turn. He also had a mind to try his hand at keeping the King's hares, with the chance of winning the Princess for a wife. Off he set along the same road his brother had taken, and after a while he came to the place where the old crone was dancing about with her long, green nose still caught in the crack of a log. He was just as fond of a good laugh as his brother was, and he stood for a while to watch her, for he thought it a merry sight. He laughed and laughed till the tears ran down his cheeks, and the old hag was screaming with rage.

"You gawk! Come and drive a wedge into the crack so that I can get my nose out," she bawled. "Here I have been for twice a hundred years and no Christian soul has come to set me free."

"If you have been there that long it will not hurt to stay a bit longer," said the youth. "I'm no woodsman, and besides that I'm on my way to the King's palace to win a Princess for a wife." And away he went, leaving the old woman screaming after him.

After a while the second brother came to the palace, and when the servants heard why he had come they were not slow in bringing him before the King. Yes, the King was as much in need of a herdsman for his hares as ever, but was the lad willing to run the risk of having only a beating for his pains?

Yes, the lad was willing to run that risk, for he was almost sure he could keep the herd together, and it was not every day one had a chance of winning a Princess for a wife.

So they took him out to the paddock where the hares were. All morning he herded them there as his brother had done before him, and that was an easy task. But it was in the afternoon that the trouble began. For no sooner did the fresh wind of the hillside ruffle up their fur than away they fled, this way and that, kicking up their heels behind them. It was in vain the lad chased after them and shouted and sweated; he could not keep them together. In the end he had scarcely threescore of them to drive back to the palace in the evening.

And the King was waiting for him with a cudgel in his hands, and if the lad did not get a good drubbing that day, then nobody ever did. When the King finished with him he was black and blue from his head to his heels, and that is all he got for trying to win a Princess for a wife.

Now after the second son had come home again with his doleful tale, Boots sat and thought and thought about what had happened. After a while, however, he rose up and shook the ashes from his clothes and said that now it was his turn to have a try at winning the Princess for his wife.

When the elder brothers heard that they scoffed and hooted. Boots was no better than a numskull anyway, and how could he hope to succeed where they had failed.

Well, all that might be true or it might not, but at any rate he was for having a try at this business, so off he set, just as the other two had before him.

After a while he came to the log where his brothers had seen the hag with her nose caught in the crack, and there she was still, for no one had come by in the meantime to set her free. He stood and stared and stared, for it was a curious sight.

"Oh, you gawk! Why do you stand there staring?" cried the old hag. "Here I have been for twice a hundred years, and no Christian soul will take the trouble to set me free. Drive a wedge into the crack so that I may get my nose out."

"That I will and gladly, good mother," said the youth. "Two hundred years is a long time for one to have one's nose pinched in a crack."

Quickly he found a wedge and drove it into the crack with a stone, and then the old hag pulled her nose out.

"Now you have done me a good turn, and I have it in mind to do the same for you," she said. With that she took a pretty little pipe out of the pocket of her skirt. "Do you take this," she said, "and it will come in handy if you're on your way to the King's palace. If you blow on the right end of the whistle the things around you will be blown every which way as if a strong wind had struck them, and if you blow on the wrong end of it they will be gathered together again. And those are not the only tricks the pipe has, for if anyone takes it from you, you have only to wish for it, and you can wish it back into your fingers again."

Boots took the pipe and thanked the old hag kindly, and then he bade her goodbye and went on his way to the King's palace.

When the King heard what Boots had come for, he was no less ready to take him for a herdsman than he had been to take his brothers. "But, mind you, you shall have a drubbing that will make your bones ache if you come back in the evening with even the smallest leveret missing from the herd," said the King.

Yes, that was all right. The lad was ready to take the risk, so all morning Boots herded the hares in the paddock, and in the afternoon he took them out to the hills, as the bargain was. There the hares could no longer be kept in a herd. They kicked up their heels and away they went, every which way.

So that was the game, was it? Boots was very willing to play it, too. He took out his pipe and blew a tune on the right end of it, and away the hares flew faster than they had intended, as though a strong wind had blown them. Presently there was not one left on the hill. Then the lad lay down in the sun and fell asleep.

When he awoke it was toward evening and time to be bringing the hares back to the castle, but not one of them was in sight.

Then Boots sat up, and shook the hair out of his eyes and blew on the wrong end of the pipe. Immediately there was the whole herd before him, drawn up in ranks just like soldiers. Not even one of the smallest leverets was missing.

"That is well," said Boots. "And now we'll be going home again."

Off he set for the palace, driving the hares before him, and as soon as he came near enough he could see the King standing on the steps waiting for him with a stout cudgel in his hand – for he had no thought but that Boots would fail in his task.

When he saw the whole herd come hopping home, as tame as sheep, and turning into the paddock, he could hardly believe his eyes. He hurried after and began to count them. He counted them over and over again, and not one was missing.

Well, Boots had brought them all back safely that time, but the question was whether he could do it again.

Boots thought he could. Indeed, he was sure he could. So the next afternoon he set out for the hills, whistling merrily as he tramped along with the hares hopping before him.

That day things happened just as they had before. As soon as the hares began to stray Boots took his pipe and blew them away as though they were so much chaff. He lay down and slept until it was time to take them home again, and then he blew them together with the wrong end of the pipe.

When the King found the lad had brought the whole herd home again for the second time he was greatly troubled, for he had no mind to give the Princess to Boots for a bride. So the third day he bade the Princess go out to the hills and hide herself among the bushes and watch and see how it was that Boots managed to keep the hares together.

This the Princess did. She hid at the back of the bushes; she saw Boots come tramping up the hill with the hares frisking before him; she saw him blow them away with his pipe as though they had been so many dry leaves in the wind, and then, after he had had a nap, she saw him blow them together again.

Then the Princess must and would have that pipe. She came out from the bushes and offered to buy it. She offered ten dollars for it.

"No."

"Fifty!"

"No!"

"A hundred!"

"No." Boots had no wish to sell, but as it was the Princess, and as she seemed so set and determined on having it, he would tell her what he would do; he would sell the pipe for a hundred dollars if she would give him a kiss for every dollar she paid.

The Princess did not know what to say to that. It was not becoming that a Princess should kiss a herdsman; still she wanted the pipe and as that was the only way to get it she at last agreed. She paid the lad a hundred bright silver dollars, and she also gave him a hundred kisses out there on the hillside, with no one to look on but the hares.

Then she took the pipe and hastened home with it.

But small good the pipe did her. Just as she reached the palace steps the pipe slipped out of her fingers as though it had been buttered, and look as she might she could not find it again.

That was because the lad had wished it back to himself. At that very moment he was on his way home with the pipe in his pocket and the hares hopping before him in lines like soldiers.

When the King heard the story he thought and pondered. The Princess had told him nothing of the kisses. He thought she had bought the pipe for a hundred dollars, so the next day he sent the Queen out to the hillside with two hundred dollars in her pocket.

"The Princess is young and foolish," said he. "She must have lost the pipe on the hillside, and no doubt the lad has it back by this time. Do you go out and see if you can buy it from him and if you once have your fingers on it you'll not lose it, I'll wager."

So the Queen went out to the hillside and hid herself in the bushes, and she saw Boots blow the hares away and lie down to sleep and afterward blow them together again in a twinkling.

Then she came out from the bushes and offered to buy the pipe. At first the lad said no, and again no, and then no for the third time, but in the end he sold the pipe to the Queen for two hundred dollars and fifty kisses to go with them, and the Queen hoped the King would never hear of it. She took the pipe and hastened home with it, but she fared no better than the Princess, for just before she reached the palace the pipe disappeared from her fingers, and what had become of it she did not know.

When the King heard that he was a wroth and angry man. Now he himself would go out to the hill and buy the pipe, for there was no trusting the womenfolk. If he once had the pipe in his hands there would be no losing it again, and of that he felt very sure. So he mounted his old mare Whitey and rode over to the hillside. There he hid himself among the bushes, and he hid old Whitey there with him, and he watched until he had seen all that the others had told him about. Then he came out and tried to strike a bargain with the lad. But this time it seemed as though Boots would not sell the pipe – neither for love nor money. The King offered him three hundred dollars, and four hundred dollars, and five hundred dollars for it, and still Boots said no.

"Listen!" said Boots suddenly. "If you'll go over there in the bushes and kiss old Whitey on the mouth five-and-twenty times, I'll sell you the pipe for five hundred dollars, but not otherwise."

That was a thing the King was loath to do, for it ill befitted a king to kiss an old horse, but have the pipe he must and would; and besides there was nobody there to see him do it but Boots, and he did not count. "May I spread a handkerchief between old Whitey's mouth and mine before I do it?" asked the King.

Yes, he might do that.

So the King went back into the bushes and spread his handkerchief over old Whitey's mouth and kissed her through it five-and-twenty times. Then he came back and the lad gave him the pipe, and the King mounted and rode away with it, and he was well pleased with himself for his cleverness, and he held the pipe tight in one hand and the bridle in the other. "No danger of my losing it as the Queen and the Princess did," thought he. But scarcely had the King reached the palace steps when the pipe slipped through his fingers like water, and what became of it he did not know.

But when Boots drove the hares home that evening he had the pipe safely hidden away up his sleeve, though nobody knew it.

And now how about the Princess? Would the King keep his promise and give her to the herdsman for a wife?

But that was a thing the King and Queen could not bear to think of.

They put their heads together and talked and talked, and the more they talked the more unwilling they were to have a herdsman in the family. So in the end this is what they said. The Princess was a very clever girl, and she must have a clever lad for a husband. If Boots could tell bigger stories than the Princess then he should have her for a wife, but if she could tell bigger stories than he, then he should have three red strips cut from his back and be beaten all the way home.

To this Boots agreed.

Then the Princess began. "I looked out of my window," said she, "and there was a tree that grew straight up to the sky, and the fruit of it was diamonds and pearls and rubies. I reached out and picked them and made myself such a necklace as never was, and I might have it yet only I leaned over the well to look at myself in the waters, and the necklace fell off, and there it lies still at the bottom of the well for anyone who cares to dive for it."

"That is a pretty story!" said Boots; "but I can tell a better. When I was herding hares the Princess came up on the hill and gave me a hundred bright silver dollars and a hundred kisses as well, one for every dollar."

Then the King scowled till his brows met, and the Princess grew as red as fire. "Oh, what a story!" cried she.

Then it was her turn again.

"I went to see my godmother, and she took me for a ride in a golden coach drawn by six fleas, and the fleas were as big as horses, and they went so fast we were back again a day before we started."

"That's a good story," said Boots, "but here's a better. The Queen came out on the hillside and made me a present of two hundred dollars, and she kissed me over and over again; fifty kisses she gave me."

"Is that true?" said the King to the Queen; and his face was as black as thunder.

"It's a great wicked story," cried the Queen, "and you must know it is."

Then the Princess tried again. "I had six suitors, and I cared for one no more than another, but the seventh one was a demon, and he would have had me whether or no. He would have flown away with me before this, but I caught his tail in the crack of the door, and he howled most horribly. There he is still, if you care to look, unless he has vanished in a puff of smoke."

"Now it is my turn," said Boots, "and you may believe this or not, but it's mostly true. The King came up on the hillside and kissed the old white mare twenty-five times. I was there and I saw. He kissed her twenty-five times, and he gave me five hundred dollars not to tell."

When Boots told this right out before everyone, the King was so ashamed he did not know which way to look. "There's not a word of it true. It's the biggest story I ever heard," said he.

"Very well, then I have won the Princess," said Boots. "And when shall we be married?"

And married they were that day week, for the King and Queen could no longer refuse to give Boots the Princess for a wife.

The Princess was willing, too, for Boots was a handsome, fine-looking lad. They had a great feast at the wedding, with plenty of cake and ale flowing like water. I was there, and I ate and drank with the best of them.

Pfst! There goes a mouse. Catch it and you may make a fine big cloak of its skin – and that's a story, too.

Torre Jeppe

(Swedish)

IN A CHURCH NAVE a spectre sat night by night, and the spectre's name was Torre Jeppe. He was a dried-up corpse that could not decay. One night three tailors were working at a farmstead in the neighbourhood. They were laughing and joking, and among other things they asked the girl in the house, who was known to be brave, what they would have to give her to go to church and fetch back Torre Jeppe. She could trust herself to do it, was her answer; but they must give her a dress of home-spun wool for her trouble. That she should surely have, said the tailors, for they did not believe the girl would dare such a venture. Yet she took the tailors at their word and really went.

When she reached the church, she took Torre Jeppe on her back, carried him home and sat him down on the bench beside the tailors. They timidly moved away; but Torre Jeppe moved after them, and looked at them with his big eyes until they nearly lost their reason. In their terror they begged the girl in the name of God to deliver them from the spectre. They would gladly give her another dress if she would only carry the dead man away again. They had no need to tell her twice, for she took Torre Jeppe on her back, and dragged him away again.

But when she tried to set him down in the place where she had found him, he did not want to let her go; but clasped his arms firmly about her neck. In vain she said to him several times: "Torre Jeppe, let me go!" At last he said: "I will not let you go until you promise me that you will go this very night to the brook and ask three times: 'Anna Perstochter, do you forgive Torre Jeppe?'" The girl promised to do as he said, and he at once released her. The brook was a good mile off; but she went there and asked three times in a loud voice, as she had promised: "Anna Perstochter, do you forgive Torre Jeppe?" And when she had called the third time a woman's voice replied from out of the water: "If God has forgiven him, then I, too, forgive him!"

When the girl came back to the church Torre Jeppe asked eagerly: "What did she say?" "Well, if God has forgiven you, then she, too, will forgive you!" Then Torre Jeppe thanked her and said: "Come back again before sunrise, and you shall receive your reward for the service you have done me." The girl went back at sunrise, and in the place where the phantom had been sitting she found a bushel of silver coin. In addition she received the two dresses promised her by the tailors. But Torre Jeppe was never seen again.

Murmur Goose-Egg

(Norwegian)

ONCE UPON A TIME there were five women who were standing in a field, mowing. Heaven had not given a single one of them a child, and each of them wanted to have one. And suddenly they saw a goose-egg of quite unheard-of size, well-nigh as large as a man's head. "I saw it first," said the one. "I saw it at the same time that you did," insisted another. "But I want it, for I saw it first of all," maintained a third. And thus they went on, and fought so about the egg that they nearly came to blows. Finally they agreed that it should belong to all five of them, and that all of them should sit on it, as a goose would do, and hatch out the little gosling. The first remained sitting on the egg for eight days, and hatched, and did not move or do a thing; and during this time the rest had to feed her and themselves as well. One of them grew angry because of this and scolded her.

"You did not crawl out of the egg either before you could cry peep!" said the one who was sitting on the egg and hatching. "Yet I almost believe that a human child is going to slip out of the egg, for something is murmuring inside it without ever stopping: 'Herring and mush, porridge and milk,'" said she. "And now you can sit on it for eight days, while we bring you food."

When the fifth day of the eight had passed, it was plain to her that there was a child in the egg, which kept on calling: "Herring and mush, porridge and milk," and so she punched a hole in the egg, and instead of a gosling out came a child, and it was quite disgustingly homely, with a big head and a small body, and no sooner had it crawled out than it began to cry: "Herring and mush, porridge and milk!" So they named the child Murmur Goose-Egg.

In spite of the child's homeliness, the women at first took a great deal of pleasure in him; but before long he grew so greedy that he devoured everything they had. When they cooked a dish of mush or a potful of porridge that was to do for all six of them, the child swallowed it all by himself. So they did not want to keep him any longer. "I have not had a single full meal since the changling crawled out," said one of them; and when Murmur Goose-Egg heard that, and the rest agreed, he said that he would gladly go his own gait, for "if they had no need of him, then he had no need of them," and with that he went off. Finally he came to a farmstead that lay in a rocky section, and asked for work. Yes, they needed a workman, and the master told him to gather up the stones in the field. Then Murmur Goose-Egg gathered up the stones in the field; he picked up some that were so large that a number of horses could not have dragged them, and large and small, one and all, he put them in his pocket. Before long he had finished his work, and wanted to know what he was to do next.

"You have picked up the stones in the field?" said his master. "You cannot possibly have finished before you have really begun!"

But Murmur Goose-Egg emptied his pockets, and threw the stones on a pile. Then his master saw that he had finished his work, and that one would have to handle such a strong fellow with kid gloves. So he told him to come in and eat. That suited Murmur Goose-Egg, and he ate up everything that was to have supplied the master and his family, and the help, and then he was only half satisfied.

He was really a splendid worker; but a dangerous eater, like a bottomless cask, said the peasant. "Such a serving-man could eat up a poor peasant, house and ground, before he noticed it," said he. He had no more work for him, and the best thing to do would be to go to the king's castle.

So Murmur Goose-Egg went to the king, and was at once given a place, and there was enough to eat and drink in the castle. He was to be the errand-boy, and help the maids fetch wood and water, and do other odd jobs. So he asked what he was to do first.

For the time being he could chop firewood, said they. So Murmur Goose-Egg began to chop firewood, and hewed to the line in such fashion that the chips fairly flew. Before long he had chopped up all that there was, kindling wood and building wood, beams and boards, and when he was through with it, he came and asked what he was to do now.

"You can finish chopping the firewood," said they.

"There is none left," said Murmur Goose-Egg.

That could not be possible, said the superintendent, and looked into the wood-bin. Yes, indeed, Murmur Goose-Egg had chopped up everything, large and small, beams and boards. That was very bad, and therefore the superintendent said that Murmur Goose-Egg should have nothing to eat until he had chopped down just as much wood in the forest as he had just chopped up for firewood.

Then Murmur Goose-Egg went into the smithy, and had the smith make an iron axe of five hundredweights. With that he went into the forest and began to chop. He chopped down big pine and fir trees, as thick as masts, and all that he found on the king's ground, as well as what he found on that of his neighbours. But he cut off neither the branches nor the treetops, so that all lay there as though felled by the storm. Then he loaded a sizable stack on the sled, and put to the horses. But they could not move the load from the spot, and when he took them by the heads, in order to pull them forward, he tore off their heads. So he unharnessed them, and left them lying in the field, and put himself to the sled, and went off alone with the load. When he came to the king's castle, there stood the king with the master carpenter in the entrance, and they were ready to give him a warm reception, because of the destruction he had wrought in the forest. For the master carpenter had been there and seen the havoc he had made. But when Murmur Goose-Egg came along with half the forest, the king grew frightened as well as angry, and he thought that if Murmur was so strong, it would be best to handle him with care.

"Why, you are a splendid workman," said the king, "but tell me, how much do you really eat at once," he continued, "for I am sure you are hungry?"

If he were to have enough porridge, they would have to take twelve tons of meal to make it; but after he had eaten that, then he could wait a while, said Murmur Goose-Egg.

It took some time before so much porridge could be prepared, and in the meantime Murmur was to carry wood into the kitchen. So he piled the whole load of wood on a sled, but when he drove it through the door, he did not go to work about it very gently. The house nearly broke from its joints, and he well-nigh tore down the entire castle. When at last dinner was ready, they sent him out into the field, to call the help. He called so loudly that hill and vale re-echoed the sound. But still the people did not come quick enough to suit him. So he picked a quarrel with them, and killed twelve.

"You kill twelve of my people, and you eat for twelve times twelve of them, but how many men's work can you do?" asked the king.

"I do the work of twelve times twelve, too," said Murmur. When he had eaten, he was to go to the barn and thresh. So he pulled the beam out of the roof tree, and made a flail out of it, and when the roof threatened to fall in, he took a pine tree with all its boughs and branches, and set it up in place of the roof-beam. Then he threshed corn and hay and straw, all together, and it seemed as though a cloud hung over the royal castle.

When Murmur Goose-Egg had nearly finished threshing, the enemy broke into the land, and war began. Then the king told him to gather people about him, and go to meet the foe, and do battle with him, for he thought the enemy would probably kill him.

No, said Murmur Goose-Egg, he did not want to have the king's people killed, he would see that he dealt with the enemy himself.

All the better, thought the king, then I am sure to get rid of him. But he would need a proper club, said Murmur.

So they sent to the smith, and he forged a club of two hundredweights. That would only do for a nut-cracker, said Murmur Goose-Egg. So he forged another that weighed six hundredweights, and that would do to hammer shoes with, said Murmur Goose-Egg. But the smith told him that he and all his workmen together could not forge a larger one.

Then Murmur Goose-Egg went into the smithy himself, and forged himself a club of thirty hundredweights, and it would have taken a hundred men just to turn it around on the anvil. This might do at a pinch, said Murmur. Then he wanted a knapsack with provisions. It was sewn together out of fifteen ox-skins, and stuffed full of provisions, and then Murmur wandered down the hill with the knapsack on his back, and the club over his shoulder.

When he came near enough for the soldiers to see him, they sent to ask whether he had a mind to attack them.

"Just wait until I have eaten," said Murmur, and sat him down behind his knapsack to eat. But the enemy would not wait, and began to fire at him. And it fairly rained and hailed musket-balls all around Murmur.

"I don't care a fig for these blueberries," said Murmur Goose-Egg, and feasted on quite at ease. Neither lead nor iron could wound him, and his knapsack stood before him, and caught the bullets like a wall.

Then the enemy began to throw bombs at him, and shoot at him with cannon. He hardly moved when he was struck. "O, that's of no account!" said he.

But then a bomb flew into his windpipe. "Faugh!" said he, and spat it out again, and then came a chain-bullet and fell into his butter-plate, and another tore away the bit of bread from between his fingers.

Then he grew angry, stood up, took his club, pounded the ground with it, and asked whether they wanted to take the food from his mouth with the blueberries they were blowing out at him from their clumsy blowpipes. Then he struck a few more blows, so that the hills and valleys round about trembled, and all the enemy flew up into the air like chaff, and that was the end of the war.

When Murmur came back and asked for more work, the king was at a loss, for he had felt sure that now he was rid of him. So he knew of nothing better to do than to send him to the devil's place.

"Now you can go to the devil, and fetch the tribute from him," said the king. Murmur Goose-Egg went off with his knapsack on his back, and his club over his shoulder. He had soon reached the right spot; but when he got there the devil was away at a trial. There was no one home but his grandmother, and she said she had never yet heard anything about a tribute, and that he was to come back some other time.

"Yes, indeed, come again tomorrow," said he. "I know that old excuse!" But since he was there, he would stay there, for he had to take home the tribute, and he had plenty of time to wait. But when he had eaten all his provisions, he grew weary, and again demanded the tribute from the grandmother.

"You will get nothing from me, and that's as flat as the old fir tree outside is fast," said the devil's grandmother. The fir tree stood in front of the gate to the devil's place, and was so large that fifteen men could hardly girdle it with their arms. But Murmur climbed up into its top and bent and shook it to and fro as though it were a willow wand, and then asked the devil's grandmother once more whether she would now pay him the tribute.

So she did not dare to refuse any longer, and brought out as much money as he could possibly carry in his knapsack. Then he set out for home with the tribute, and now no sooner had he gone than the devil came home, and when he learned that Murmur had taken along a big bag of money, he first beat his grandmother, and then hurried after Murmur. And he soon caught up to him, for he ran over sticks and stones, and sometimes flew in between; while Murmur had to stick to the highway with his heavy knapsack. But with the devil at his heels, he began to run as fast as he could, and stretched out the club behind him, to keep the devil from coming to close quarters. And thus they ran along, one behind the other; while Murmur held the shaft and the devil the end of the club, until they reached a deep valley. There Murmur jumped from one mountaintop to another, and the devil followed him so hotly that he ran into the club, fell down into the valley and broke his foot – and there he lay.

"There's your tribute!" said Murmur Goose-Egg, when he had reached the royal castle, and he flung down the knapsack full of money before the king, so that the whole castle tottered. The king thanked him kindly, and promised him a good reward, and a good character, if he wanted it; but Murmur only wanted more work to do.

"What shall I do now?" he asked. The king reflected for a while, and then he said Murmur should travel to the hill-troll, who had robbed him of the sword of his ancestors. He lived in a castle by the sea, where no one ventured to go.

Murmur was given a few cartloads of provisions in his big knapsack, and once more set out. Long he wandered, though, over field and wood, over hills and deep valleys, till he came to a great mountain where the troll lived who had robbed the king of the sword.

But the troll was not out in the open, and the mountain was closed, so Murmur could not get it. So he joined a party of stone-breakers, who were working at a mountainside, and worked along with them. They had never had such a helper, for Murmur hewed away at the rocks till they burst, and stone boulders as large as houses came rolling down. But when he was about to rest and eat up the first cartload of his provisions, it had already been eaten up. "I have a good appetite myself," said Murmur, "but whoever got hold of it has an even better one, for he has eaten up the bones as well!"

Thus it went the first day, and the second was no better. On the third day he went to work again, and took along the third cartload, lay down behind it, and pretended to be sleeping.

Then a troll with seven heads came out of the hill, began to smack his lips, and eat of his provisions.

"Now the table is set, so now I am going to eat," said he.

"First we'll see about that," said Murmur, and hewed away at the troll so that the heads flew from his body.

Then he went into the hill out of which the troll had come, and inside stood a horse eating out of a barrel of glowing ashes, while behind him stood a barrel filled with oats.

"Why don't you eat out of the barrel of oats?" asked Murmur Goose-Egg.

"Because I cannot turn around," said the horse.

"I will turn you around," said Murmur Goose-Egg.

"Tear my head off instead," pleaded the horse.

Murmur did so, and then the horse turned into a fine-looking man. He said that he had been enchanted, and turned into a horse by the troll. Then he helped Murmur look for the sword, which the troll had hidden under the bed. But in the bed lay the troll's grandmother, and she was snoring.

They went home by water, and just as they sailed off the old troll grandmother came after them; but she could not get at them, hence she commenced to drink, so that the water went down and grew lower. But at last she could not drink up the whole sea, and so she burst.

When they came ashore, Murmur sent to the king, and had him told to have the sword fetched; but though the king sent four horses, they could not move it from the spot. He sent eight, he sent twelve, but the sword remained where it was, and could not be moved from the spot by any means. Then Murmur Goose-Egg took it up, and carried it alone.

The king could not believe his eyes when he saw Murmur once more; but he was very friendly and promised him gold and green forests. But when Murmur asked for more work, he told him to travel to his troll's castle, where no one dared go, and to remain there until he had built a bridge across the sound, so that people could cross. If he could do that, he would reward him well, yes, he would even give him his daughter, said the king. He would attend to it, said Murmur.

Yet no human being had ever returned thence alive; all who had gotten so far, lay on the ground dead, and crushed to a jelly, and the king thought, when sending him there, that he would never see him again.

But Murmur set out. He took with him his knapsack full of provisions, and a properly turned and twisted block of pine wood, as well as an ax, a wedge and some wooden chips.

When he reached the sound, the river was full of drifting ice, and it roared like a waterfall. But he planted his legs firmly on the ground, and waded along until he got across. When he had warmed himself and satisfied his hunger, he wanted to sleep; but a tumult and rumbling started, as though the whole castle were to be turned upside-down. The gate flew wide open, and Murmur saw nothing but a pair of yawning jaws that reached from the threshold to the top of the door.

"Let's see who you may be? Perhaps you are an old friend of mine," said Murmur. And sure enough, it was Master Devil. Then they played cards together. The devil would gladly have won back some of the tribute Murmur had forced from his grandmother for the king. Yet, no matter how he played, Murmur always won; for he made a cross on the cards. And after he had won all the devil had with him, the latter had to give him some of the gold and silver that was in the castle.

In the midst of their game the fire went out, so that they could no longer tell the cards apart.

"Now we must split wood," said Murmur. He hewed into the block of pine wood with his ax, and drove in the wedge, but the tree-stump was tough, and would not split at once, though Murmur gave himself all manner of pains.

"You are supposed to be strong," he said to the devil. "Spit on your hands, slap in your claws here, and pull the block apart, so that I can see what you can do!"

The devil obediently thrust both hands into the split, and tore and clawed with all his might; but suddenly Murmur Goose-Egg knocked out the wedge, and there the devil was caught in a vice, while Murmur belaboured his back with the ax. The devil wailed, and begged Murmur to let him go; but Murmur would hear nothing of it until he had promised never to come back and make a nuisance of himself again. Besides that, he had to promise to build a bridge over the sound, on which one could go back and forth at all seasons of the year. And the bridge was to be completed immediately after the breaking up of the ice-drift.

"Alas!" said the devil, but there was nothing for it but to promise if he wished to go free. Yet he made one condition, that he was to have the first soul that crossed the bridge as sound-toll.

He could have it, said Murmur. Then he let the devil out, and he ran straight home. But Murmur lay down and slept until far into the following day.

Then the king came to see whether Murmur Goose-Egg were lying crushed on the ground, or had merely been badly beaten. He had to wade through piles of money before he could reach the bed. The money was stacked up high along the walls in heaps and in bags, and Murmur lay in the bed and snored.

"May heaven help me and my daughter!" cried the king, when he saw that Murmur Goose-Egg was in the best of health. Yes, and no one could deny that everything had been well and thoroughly done, said the king; but there could be no talk of marriage as long as the bridge had not been built.

Then one day the bridge was finished; and on it stood the devil, ready to collect the toll promised him.

Murmur Goose-Egg wanted the king to be the first to try the bridge with him; but the king had no mind to do so, therefore Murmur himself mounted a horse, and swung up the fat dairymaid from the castle before him on the saddle-bow – she looked almost like a gigantic block of wood – and dashed across the bridge with her so that the planks fairly thundered.

"Where is my sound-toll? Where is the soul?" cried the devil. "Sitting in this block of wood! If you want her, you must spit on your hands and catch hold of her," said Murmur Goose-Egg. "No, thank you! If she does not catch hold of me, then I'll certainly not catch hold of her," said the devil. "You caught me in a vice once, but you can't fool me a second time," said he, and flew straight home to his grandmother, and since then nothing more has been heard or seen of him.

But Murmur Goose-Egg hurried back to the castle and asked for the reward the king had promised him. And when the king hesitated and began to make all sorts of excuses, in order not to have to keep his promise, Murmur said it would be best to have a substantial knapsackful of provisions made ready, since now he, Murmur, was going to take his reward himself. This the king did, and when the knapsack was ready, Murmur took the king along with him in front of the castle, and gave him a proper shove, so that he flew high up into the air. And he threw the knapsack up after him, so that he would not be left altogether without provisions; and if he has not come down yet, then he, together with the knapsack, is floating between heaven and earth to this very day.

The Witch in the Stone Boat

(Icelandic)

THERE WAS ONCE A KING AND QUEEN, and they had a son called Sigurd, who was very strong and active and good-looking. When the king came to be bowed down with the weight of years he spoke to his son, and said that now it was time for him to look out for a fitting match for himself, for he did not know how long he might last now, and he would like to see him married before he died.

Sigurd was not averse to this and asked his father where he thought it best to look for a wife. The king answered that in a certain country there was a king who had a beautiful daughter, and he thought it would be most desirable if Sigurd could get her. So the two parted, and Sigurd prepared for the journey and went to where his father had directed him.

He came to the king and asked his daughter's hand, which was readily granted him, but only on the condition that he should remain there as long as he could, for the king himself was not strong and not very able to govern his kingdom. Sigurd accepted this condition, but added that he would have to get leave to go home again to his own country when he heard news of his father's death. After that Sigurd married the princess and helped his father-in-law to govern the kingdom. He and the princess loved each other dearly, and after a year a son came to them, who was two years old when word came to Sigurd that his father was dead. Sigurd now prepared to return home with his wife and child and went on board ship to go by sea.

They had sailed for several days, when the breeze suddenly fell and there came a dead calm at a time when they needed only one day's voyage to reach home. Sigurd and his queen were one day on deck when most of the others on the ship had fallen asleep. There they sat and talked for a while, and had their little son along with them. After a time Sigurd became so heavy with sleep that he could no longer keep awake, so he went below and lay down, leaving the queen alone on the deck playing with her son.

A good while after Sigurd had gone below the queen saw something black on the sea which seemed to be coming nearer. As it approached she could make out that it was a boat and could see the figure of someone sitting in it and rowing it. At last the boat came alongside the ship, and now the queen saw that it was a stone boat, out of which there came on board the ship a fearfully ugly witch. The queen was more frightened than words can describe, and could neither speak a word nor move from the place so as to awaken the king or the sailors. The witch came right up to the queen, took the child from her, and laid it on the deck; then she took the queen and stripped her of all her fine clothes, which she proceeded to put on herself and looked then like a human being. Last of all she took the queen, put her into the boat and said:

"This spell I lay upon you, that you slacken not your course until you come to my brother in the underworld."

The queen sat stunned and motionless, but the boat at once shot away from the ship with her, and before long she was out of sight.

When the boat could no longer be seen the child began to cry, and though the witch tried to quiet it she could not manage it; so, with the child on her arm, she went below to where the king was sleeping, and awakened him, scolding him for leaving them alone on deck while he and all the crew were asleep. It was great carelessness of him, she said, to leave no one to watch the ship with her.

Sigurd was greatly surprised to hear his queen scold him so much, for she had never said an angry word to him before; but he thought it was quite excusable in this case, and tried to quiet the child along with her but it was no use. Then he went and wakened the sailors and bade them hoist the sails, for a breeze had sprung up and was blowing straight toward the harbour.

They soon reached the land which Sigurd was to rule over, and found all the people sorrowful for the old king's death, but they became glad when they got Sigurd back to the court, and made him king over them.

The king's son, however, hardly ever stopped crying from the time he had been taken from his mother on the deck of the ship, although he had always been such a good child before, so that at last the king had to get a nurse for him – one of the maids of the court. As soon as the child got into her charge he stopped crying and behaved as well as before.

After the sea voyage it seemed to the king that the queen had altered very much in many ways, and not for the better. He thought her much more haughty and stubborn and difficult to deal with than she used to be. Before long others began to notice this as well as the king. In the court there were two young fellows, one of eighteen years old, the other of nineteen, who were very fond of playing chess and often sat long inside playing at it. Their room was next the queen's, and often during the day they heard the queen talking.

One day they paid more attention than usual when they heard her talk, and put their ears close to a crack in the wall between the rooms, and heard the queen say quite plainly: "When I yawn a little, then I am a nice little maiden: when I yawn halfway, then I am half a troll; and when I yawn fully then I am a troll altogether."

As she said this she yawned tremendously, and in a moment had put on the appearance of a fearfully ugly troll. Then there came up through the floor of the room a three-headed giant with a trough full of meat, who saluted her as his sister and set down the trough before her. She began to eat out of it and never stopped till she had finished it. The young fellows saw all this going on, but did not hear the two of them say anything to each other. They were astonished, though, at how greedily the queen devoured the meat and how much she ate of it, and were no longer surprised that she took so little when she sat at table with the king. As soon as she had finished it the giant disappeared with the trough by the same way as he had come, and the queen returned to her human shape.

Now we must go back to the king's son after he had been put in charge of the nurse. One evening. after she had lit a candle and was holding the child, several planks sprang up in the floor of the room, and out at the opening came a beautiful woman dressed in white, with an iron belt round her waist, to which was fastened an iron chain that went down into the ground. The woman came up to the nurse, took the child from her, and pressed it to her breast; then she gave it back to the nurse and returned by the same way as she had come, and the floor closed over her again. Although the woman had not spoken a single word to her, the nurse was very much frightened, but told no one about it.

Next evening the same thing happened again, just as before, but as the woman was going away she said in a sad tone, "Two are gone and one only is left," and then disappeared as before. The nurse was still more frightened when she heard the woman say this, and thought that perhaps some danger was hanging over the child, though she had no ill opinion of the unknown woman, who, indeed, had behaved toward the child as if it were her own. The most mysterious thing was the woman saying "and only one is left"; but the nurse guessed that this must mean that only one day was left, since she had come for two days already.

At last the nurse made up her mind to go to the king. She told him the whole story and asked him to be present in person the next day about the time when the woman usually came. The king promised to do so, and came to the nurse's room a little before the time and sat down on a chair with his drawn sword in his hand. Soon after the planks in the floor sprang up as before, and the woman came up, dressed in white, with the iron belt and chain. The king saw at once that it was his own queen, and immediately hewed asunder the iron chain that was fastened to the belt. This was followed by such noises and crashings down in the earth that all the king's palace shook, so that no one expected anything else than to see every bit of it shaken to pieces. At last the noises and shaking stopped, and they began to come to themselves again.

The king and queen embraced each other, and she told him the whole story – how the witch came to the ship when they were all asleep and sent her off in the boat. After she had gone so far that she could not see the ship, she sailed on through darkness until she landed beside a three-headed giant. The giant wished her to marry him, but she refused; whereupon he shut her up by herself and told her she would never get free until she consented. After a time she began to plan how to get her freedom, and at last told him that she would consent if he would allow her to visit her son on earth three days on end. This he agreed to, but put on her this iron belt and chain, the other end of which he fastened around his own waist, and the great noises that were heard when the king cut the chain must have been caused by the giant's falling down the underground passage when the chain gave way so suddenly. The giant's dwelling, indeed, was right under the palace, and the terrible shakings must have been caused by him in his death throes.

The king now understood how the queen he had had for some time past had been so ill-tempered. He at once had a sack drawn over her head and made her be stoned to death, and after that torn in pieces by untamed horses. The two young fellows also told now what they had heard and seen in the queen's room, for before this they had been afraid to say anything about it, on account of the queen's power.

The real queen was now restored to all her dignity and was beloved by all. The nurse was married to a nobleman and the king and queen gave her splendid presents.

The Magician's Daughter

(Swedish)

JUST ON THE FINNISH FRONTIERS there is situated a high mountain, which, on the Swedish side, is covered with beautiful copsewood, and on the other with dark pine trees, so closely ranked together, and so luxuriant in shade, that one might almost say the smallest bird could not find its way through the thickets. Below the copsewood there stands a chapel with the image of St. George, as guardian of the land and as a defence against dragons, if there be such, and other monsters of paganism, while, on the other side, on the borders of the dark firwood, are certain cottages inhabited by wicked sorcerers, who have, moreover, a cave cut so deep into the mountain that it joins with the bottomless abyss, whence come all the demons that assist them. The Swedish Christians who dwelt in the neighbourhood of this mountain thought it would be necessary, besides the chapel and statue of St. George, to choose some living protector, and therefore selected an ancient warrior, highly renowned for his prowess on the battlefield, who had, in his old age, become a monk. When this man went to take up his abode upon the mountains, his only son (for he had formerly lived as a married man in the world) would on no account leave him, but lived there also, assisting his father in his duties as watcher, and in the exercises of prayer and penitence, fully equalling the example that was now afforded him as he had formerly done his example as a soldier.

The life led by those two valiant champions is said to have been most admirable and pious.

Once on a time it happened that the young hero went out to cut wood in the forest. He bore a sharp axe on his shoulders, and was besides girded with a great sword; for as the woods were not only full of wild beasts, but also haunted by wicked men, the pious hermits took the precaution of always going armed. While the good youth was forcing his way through the thickest of the copsewood, and already beheld over it the pointed tops of the fir trees (for he was close on the Finnish frontier), there rushed out against him a great white wolf, so that he had only just time enough to leap to one side, and not being able immediately to draw his sword, he flung his axe at his assailant. The blow was so well aimed that it struck one of the wolf's fore-legs, and the animal, being sorely wounded, limped back, with a yell of anguish, into the wood. The young hermit warrior, however, thought to himself –

"It is not enough that I am rescued, but I must take such measures that no one else may in future be injured, or even terrified by this wild beast."

So he rushed in as fast as possible among the fir trees, and inflicted such a vehement blow with his sword on the wolf's head, that the animal, groaning piteously, fell to the ground. Hereupon there came over the young man all at once a strange mood of regret and compassion for his poor victim. Instead of putting it immediately to death, he bound up the wounds as well as he could with moss and twigs of trees, placed it on a sort of canvas sling on which he was in the habit of carrying great faggots, and with much labour brought it home, in hopes that he might be able at last to cure and tame his fallen adversary. He did not find his father in the cottage, and it was not without some fear and anxiety that he laid the wolf on his own bed, which was made of moss and rushes, and over which he had nailed St. George and the Dragon. He then turned to the fireplace of the small hut, in order to prepare a healing salve for the wounds. While he was thus occupied, how much was he astonished to hear the moanings and lamentations of a human voice from the bed on which he had just before deposited the wolf. On returning thither his wonder was inexpressible on perceiving, instead of the frightful wild beast, a most beautiful damsel, on whose head the wound which he had inflicted was bleeding through her fine golden hair, and whose right arm, in all its grace and snow-white luxuriance, was stretched out motionless, for it had been broken by the blow from his axe.

"Pray," said she, "have pity, and do not kill me outright. The little life that I have still left is, indeed, painful enough, and may not last long; yet, sad as my condition is, it is yet tenfold better than death."

The young man then sat down weeping beside her, and she explained to him that she was the daughter of a magician, on the other side of the mountain, who had sent her out in the shape of a wolf to collect plants from places which, in her own proper form, she could not have reached. It was but in terror she had made that violent spring which the youth had mistaken for an attack on him, when her only wish had been to pass by him.

"But you directly broke my right arm," said she, "though I had no evil design against you."

How she had now regained her proper shape she could not imagine, but to the youth it was quite clear that the picture of St. George and the Dragon had broken the spell by which the poor girl had been transformed.

While the son was thus occupied, the old man returned home, and soon heard all that had occurred, perceiving, at the same time, that if the young pagan wanderer had been released from the spells by which she had been bound, the youth was, in his turn, enchanted and spellbound by her beauty and amiable behaviour.

From that moment he exerted himself to the utmost for the welfare of her soul, endeavouring to convert her to Christianity, while his son attended to the cure of her wounds; and, as their endeavours were on both sides successful, it was resolved that the lovers should be united in marriage, for the youth had not restricted himself by any monastic vows.

The magician's daughter was now restored to perfect health. A day had been appointed for her baptism and marriage. It happened that one evening the bride and bridegroom went to take a pleasure walk through the woods. The sun was yet high in the west, and shone so fervently through the beech trees on the green turf that they could never resolve on turning home, but went still deeper and deeper into the forest. Then the bride told him stories of her early life, and sang old songs which she had learned when a child, and which sounded beautifully amid the woodland solitude. Though the words were such that they could not be agreeable to the youth's ears (for she had learned them among her pagan and wicked relations), yet he could not interrupt her, first, because he loved her so dearly, and, secondly, because she sang in a voice so clear and sweet that the whole forest seemed to rejoice in her music. At last, however, the pointed heads of the pine trees again became visible, and the youth wished to turn back, in order that he might not come again too near the hated Finnish frontier. His bride, however, said to him –

"Dearest Conrad, why should we not walk on a little further? I would gladly see the very place where you so cruelly wounded me on the head and arm, and made me prisoner, all which has, in the end, contributed to my happiness. Methinks we are now very near the spot."

Accordingly they sought about here and there until at last the twilight fell dim and heavy on the dense woods. The sun had long since set. The moon, however, had risen, and, as a light broke forth, the lovers stood on the Finnish frontier, or rather they must have gone already some distance beyond it, for the bridegroom was exceedingly terrified when he found his cap lifted from his head, as if by human hand, though he saw only the branch of a fir tree. Immediately thereafter the whole air around them was filled with strange and supernatural beings – witches, devils, dwarfs, horned owls, fire-eyed cats, and a thousand other wretches that could not be named and described, whirled around them as if dancing to rapid music. When the bride had looked on for a while, she broke out into loud laughter, and at last began to dance furiously along with them. The poor bridegroom might shout and pray as much and as earnestly as he would, for she never attended to him, but at last transformed herself in a manner so extraordinary that he could not distinguish her from the other dancers. He thought, however, that he had kept his eyes upon her, and seized on one of the dancers; but alas! it was only a horrible spectre which held him fast, and threw its wide waving shroud around him, so that he could not make his escape, while, at the same time, some of the subterraneous black demons pulled at his legs, and wanted to bear him down along with them into their bottomless caves.

Fortunately he happened at that moment to cross himself and call on the name of the Saviour, upon which the whole of this vile assembly fell into confusion. They howled aloud and ran off in all directions, while Conrad in the meantime saved himself by recrossing the frontier, and getting under the protection of the Swedish copsewood. His beautiful bride, however, was completely lost; and by no endeavours could he ever obtain her again, though he often came to the Finnish border, called out her name aloud, wept and prayed, but all in vain. Many times, it is true, he saw her floating about through the pine trees, as if in chase, but she was always accompanied by a train of frightful creatures, and she herself also looked wild and disfigured. For the most part she never noticed Conrad, but if she could not help fixing her eyes upon him, she laughed so immoderately, and in a mood of merriment so strange and unnatural, that he was terrified and made the sign of the cross, whereupon she always fled away, howling, into one of the thickets.

Conrad fell more and more into melancholy abstraction, hardly ever spoke, and though he had given over his vain walks into the forest, yet if one asked him a question, the only answer he returned was –

"Ay, she is gone away beyond the mountains," so little did he know or remember of any other object in the world but the lost beauty.

At last he died of grief; and according to a request which he had once made, his father prepared a grave for him on the place where the bride was found and lost, though during the fulfilment of this duty he had enough to do – one while in contending with his crucifix against evil spirits, and at another, with his sword against wild beasts, which were no doubt sent thither by the magicians to attack and annoy him. At length, however, he brought his task to an end, and thereafter it seemed as if the bride mourned for the youth's untimely death, for there was heard often a sound of howling and lamentation at the grave. For the most part, indeed, this voice is like the voices of wolves, yet, at the same time, human accents are to be distinguished, and I myself have often listened thereto on dark winter nights.

Alas! that the poor maiden should have ventured again so near the accursed paths she had once renounced. A few steps in the backward course, and all is lost!

The Werewolf

(Swedish)

ONCE UPON A TIME there was a king, who reigned over a great kingdom. He had a queen, but only a single daughter, a girl. In consequence the little girl was the apple of her parents' eyes; they loved her above everything else in the world, and their dearest thought was the pleasure they would take in her when she was older. But the unexpected often happens; for before the king's daughter began to grow up, the queen her mother fell ill and died. It is not hard to imagine the grief that reigned, not alone in the royal castle, but throughout the land; for the queen had been beloved of all. The king grieved so that he would not marry again, and his one joy was the little princess.

A long time passed, and with each succeeding day the king's daughter grew taller and more beautiful, and her father granted her every wish. Now there were a number of women who had nothing to do but wait on the princess and carry out her commands. Among them was a woman who had formerly married and had two daughters. She had an engaging appearance, a smooth tongue and a winning way of talking, and she was as soft and pliable as silk; but at heart she was full of machinations and falseness. Now when the queen died, she at once began to plan how she might marry the king, so that her daughters might be kept like royal princesses. With this end in view, she drew the young princess to her, paid her the most fulsome compliments on everything she said and did, and was forever bringing the conversation around to how happy she would be were the king to take another wife. There was much said on this head, early and late, and before very long the princess came to believe that the woman knew all there was to know about everything. So she asked her what sort of a woman the king ought to choose for a wife. The woman answered as sweet as honey: "It is not my affair to give advice in this matter; yet he should choose for queen someone who is kind to the little princess. For one thing I know, and that is, were I fortunate enough to be chosen, my one thought would be to do all I could for the little princess, and if she wished to wash her hands, one of my daughters would have to hold the wash-bowl and the other hand her the towel." This and much more she told the king's daughter, and the princess believed it, as children will.

From that day forward the princess gave her father no peace, and begged him again and again to marry the good court lady. Yet he did not want to marry her. But the king's daughter gave him no rest; but urged him again and again, as the false court lady had persuaded her to do. Finally, one day, when she again brought up the matter, the king cried: "I can see you will end by having your own way about this, even though it be entirely against my will. But I will do so only on one condition." "What is the condition?" asked the princess. "If I marry again," said the king, "it is only because of your ceaseless pleading. Therefore you must promise that, if in the future you are not satisfied with your stepmother or your stepsisters, not a single lament or complaint on your part reaches my ears." This she promised the king, and it was agreed that he should marry the court lady and make her queen of the whole country.

As time passed on, the king's daughter had grown to be the most beautiful maiden to be found far and wide; the queen's daughters, on the other hand, were homely, evil of disposition, and no one knew any good of them. Hence it was not surprising that many youths came from East and West to sue for the princess's hand; but that none of them took any interest in the queen's daughters. This made the stepmother very angry; but she concealed her rage, and was as sweet and friendly as ever. Among the wooers was a king's son from another country.

He was young and brave, and since he loved the princess dearly, she accepted his proposal and they plighted their troth. The queen observed this with an angry eye, for it would have pleased her had the prince chosen one of her own daughters. She therefore made up her mind that the young pair should never be happy together, and from that time on thought only of how she might part them from each other.

An opportunity soon offered itself. News came that the enemy had entered the land, and the king was compelled to go to war. Now the princess began to find out the kind of stepmother she had. For no sooner had the king departed than the queen showed her true nature, and was just as harsh and unkind as she formerly had pretended to be friendly and obliging. Not a day went by without her scolding and threatening the princess; and the queen's daughters were every bit as malicious as their mother. But the king's son, the lover of the princess, found himself in an even worse position. He had gone hunting one day, had lost his way, and could not find his people. Then the queen used her black arts and turned him into a werewolf, to wander through the forest for the remainder of his life in that shape. When evening came and there was no sign of the prince, his people returned home, and one can imagine what sorrow they caused when the princess learned how the hunt had ended. She grieved, wept day and night, and was not to be consoled. But the queen laughed at her grief, and her heart was filled with joy to think that all had turned out exactly as she wished.

Now it chanced one day, as the king's daughter was sitting alone in her room, that she thought she would go herself into the forest where the prince had disappeared. She went to her stepmother and begged permission to go out into the forest, in order to forget her surpassing grief. The queen did not want to grant her request, for she always preferred saying no to yes. But the princess begged her so winningly that at last she was unable to say no, and she ordered one of her daughters to go along with her and watch her. That caused a great deal of discussion, for neither of the stepdaughters wanted to go with her; each made all sorts of excuses, and asked what pleasures were there in going with the king's daughter, who did nothing but cry. But the queen had the last word in the end, and ordered that one of her daughters must accompany the princess, even though it be against her will. So the girls wandered out of the castle into the forest. The king's daughter walked among the trees, and listened to the song of the birds, and thought of her lover, for whom she longed, and who was now no longer there. And the queen's daughter followed her, vexed, in her malice, with the king's daughter and her sorrow.

After they had walked a while, they came to a little hut, lying deep in the dark forest. By then the king's daughter was very thirsty, and wanted to go into the little hut with her stepsister, in order to get a drink of water. But the queen's daughter was much annoyed and said: "Is it not enough for me to be running around here in the wilderness with you? Now you even want me, who am a princess, to enter that wretched little hut. No, I will not step a foot over the threshold! If you want to go in, why, go in alone!" The king's daughter lost no time; but did as her stepsister advised, and stepped into the little hut. When she entered she saw an old woman sitting there on a bench, so enfeebled by age that her head shook. The princess spoke to her in her usual friendly way: "Good evening, motherkin. May I ask you for a drink of water?" "You are heartily welcome to it," said the old woman. "Who may you be, that step beneath my lowly roof and greet me in so winning a way?" The king's daughter told her who she was, and that she had gone out to relieve her heart, in order to forget her great grief. "And what may your great grief be?" asked the old woman. "No doubt it is my fate to grieve," said the princess, "and I can never be happy again. I have lost my only love, and God alone knows whether I shall ever see him again." And she also told her why it was, and the tears ran down her cheeks in streams, so that anyone would have felt sorry for her. When she had ended the old woman said: "You did well in confiding your sorrow to me. I have lived long and may be able to give you a bit of good advice. When you leave here you will see a lily growing from the ground. This lily is not like other lilies, however, but has many strange virtues. Run quickly over to it, and pick it. If you can do that then you need not worry, for then one will appear who will tell you what to do." Then they parted and the king's daughter thanked her and went her way; while the old woman sat on the bench and wagged her head. But the queen's daughter had been standing without the hut the entire time, vexing herself, and grumbling because the king's daughter had taken so long.

So when the latter stepped out, she had to listen to all sorts of abuse from her stepsister, as was to be expected. Yet she paid no attention to her, and thought only of how she might find the flower of which the old woman had spoken. They went through the forest, and suddenly she saw a beautiful white lily growing in their very path. She was much pleased and ran up at once to pick it; but that very moment it disappeared and reappeared somewhat further away.

The king's daughter was now filled with eagerness, no longer listened to her stepsister's calls, and kept right on running; yet each time when she stooped to pick the lily, it suddenly disappeared and reappeared somewhat further away. Thus it went for some time, and the princess was drawn further and further into the deep forest. But the lily continued to stand, and disappear and move further away, and each time the flower seemed larger and more beautiful than before. At length the princess came to a high hill, and as she looked toward its summit, there stood the lily high on the naked rock, glittering as white and radiant as the brightest star. The king's daughter now began to climb the hill, and in her eagerness she paid no attention to stones nor steepness. And when at last she reached the summit of the hill, lo and behold! the lily no longer evaded her grasp; but remained where it was, and the princess stooped and picked it and hid it in her bosom, and so heartfelt was her happiness that she forgot her stepsisters and everything else in the world.

For a long time she did not tire of looking at the beautiful flower. Then she suddenly began to wonder what her stepmother would say when she came home after having remained out so long. And she looked around, in order to find the way back to the castle. But as she looked around, behold, the sun had set and no more than a little strip of daylight rested on the summit of the hill. Below her lay the forest, so dark and shadowed that she had no faith in her ability to find the homeward path. And now she grew very sad, for she could think of nothing better to do than to spend the night on the hill-top. She seated herself on the rock, put her hand to her cheek, cried, and thought of her unkind stepmother and stepsisters, and of all the harsh words she would have to endure when she returned. And she thought of her father, the king, who was away at war, and of the love of her heart, whom she would never see again; and she grieved so bitterly that she did not even know she wept. Night came and darkness, and the stars rose, and still the princess sat in the same spot and wept. And while she sat there, lost in her thoughts, she heard a voice say: "Good evening, lovely maiden! Why do you sit here so sad and lonely?" She stood up hastily, and felt much embarrassed, which was not surprising. When she looked around there was nothing to be seen but a tiny old man, who nodded to her and seemed to be very humble. She answered: "Yes, it is no doubt my fate to grieve, and never be happy again. I have lost my dearest love, and now I have lost my way in the forest, and am afraid of being devoured by wild beasts." "As to that," said the old man, "you need have no fear. If you will do exactly as I say, I will help you." This made the princess happy; for she felt that all the rest of the world had abandoned her. Then the old man drew out flint and steel and said: "Lovely maiden, you must first build a fire." She did as he told her, gathered moss, brush and dry sticks, struck sparks and lit such a fire on the hill-top that the flame blazed up to the skies. That done the old man said: "Go on a bit and you will find a kettle of tar, and bring the kettle to me." This the king's daughter did. The old man continued: "Now put the kettle on the fire." And the princess did that as well. When the tar began to boil, the old man said: "Now throw your white lily into the kettle." The princess thought this a harsh command, and earnestly begged to be allowed to keep the lily. But the old man said: "Did you not promise to obey my every command? Do as I tell you or you will regret it." The king's daughter turned away her eyes, and threw the lily into the boiling tar; but it was altogether against her will, so fond had she grown of the beautiful flower.

The moment she did so a hollow roar, like that of some wild beast, sounded from the forest. It came nearer, and turned into such a terrible howling that all the surrounding hills re-echoed it. Finally there was a cracking and breaking among the trees, the bushes were thrust aside, and the princess saw a great grey wolf come running out of the forest and straight up the hill. She was much frightened and would gladly have run away, had she been able. But the old man said: "Make haste, run to the edge of the hill and the moment the wolf comes along, upset the kettle on him!" The princess was terrified, and hardly knew what she was about; yet she did as the old man said, took the kettle, ran to the edge of the hill, and poured its contents over the wolf just as he was about to run up. And then a strange thing happened: no sooner had she done so, than the wolf was transformed, cast off his thick grey pelt, and in place of the horrible wild beast, there stood a handsome young man, looking up to the hill. And when the king's daughter collected herself and looked at him, she saw that it was really and truly her lover, who had been turned into a werewolf.

It is easy to imagine how the princess felt. She opened her arms, and could neither ask questions nor reply to them, so moved and delighted was she. But the prince ran hastily up the hill, embraced her tenderly, and thanked her for delivering him. Nor did he forget the little old man, but thanked him with many civil expressions for his powerful aid. Then they sat down together on the hill-top, and had a pleasant talk. The prince told how he had been turned into a wolf, and of all he had suffered while running about in the forest; and the princess told of her grief, and the many tears she had shed while he had been gone. So they sat the whole night through, and never noticed it until the stars grew pale and it was light enough to see. When the sun rose, they saw that a broad path led from the hill-top straight to the royal castle; for they had a view of the whole surrounding country from the hill-top. Then the old man said: "Lovely maiden, turn around! Do you see anything out yonder?" "Yes," said the princess, "I see a horseman on a foaming horse, riding as fast as he can." Then the old man said: "He is a messenger sent on ahead by the king your father. And your father with all his army is following him." That pleased the princess above all things, and she wanted to descend the hill at once to meet her father. But the old man detained her and said: "Wait a while, it is too early yet. Let us wait and see how everything turns out."

Time passed and the sun was shining brightly, and its rays fell straight on the royal castle down below. Then the old man said: "Lovely maiden, turn around! Do you see anything down below?" "Yes," replied the princess, "I see a number of people coming out of my father's castle, and some are going along the road, and others into the forest." The old man said: "Those are your stepmother's servants. She has sent some to meet the king and welcome him; but she has sent others to the forest to look for you." At these words the princess grew uneasy, and wished to go down to the queen's servants. But the old man withheld her and said: "Wait a while, and let us first see how everything turns out."

More time passed, and the king's daughter was still looking down the road from which the king would appear, when the old man said: "Lovely maiden, turn around! Do you see anything down below?" "Yes," answered the princess, "there is a great commotion in my father's castle, and they are hanging it with black." The old man said: "That is your stepmother and her people. They will assure your father that you are dead." Then the king's daughter felt bitter anguish, and she implored from the depths of her heart: "Let me go, let me go, so that I may spare my father this anguish!" But the old man detained her and said: "No, wait, it is still too early. Let us first see how everything turns out."

Again time passed, the sun lay high above the fields, and the warm air blew over meadow and forest. The royal maid and youth still sat on the hill-top with the old man, where we had left them. Then they saw a little cloud rise against the horizon, far away in the distance, and the little cloud grew larger and larger, and came nearer and nearer along the road, and as it moved one could see it was agleam with weapons, and nodding helmets, and waving flags, one could hear the rattle of swords, and the neighing of horses, and finally recognize the banner of the king. It is not hard to imagine how pleased the king's daughter was, and how she insisted on going down and greeting her father. But the old man held her back and said: "Lovely maiden, turn around! Do you see anything happening at the castle?" "Yes," answered the princess, "I can see my stepmother and stepsisters coming out, dressed in mourning, holding white kerchiefs to their faces, and weeping bitterly." The old man answered: "Now they are pretending to weep because of your death. Wait just a little while longer. We have not yet seen how everything will turn out."

After a time the old man said again: "Lovely maiden, turn around! Do you see anything down below?" "Yes," said the princess, "I see people bringing a black coffin – now my father is having it opened. Look, the queen and her daughters are down on their knees, and my father is threatening them with his sword!" Then the old man said: "Your father wished to see your body, and so your evil stepmother had to confess the truth." When the princess heard that she said earnestly: "Let me go, let me go, so that I may comfort my father in his great sorrow!" But the old man held her back and said: "Take my advice and stay here a little while longer. We have not yet seen how everything will turn out."

Again time went by, and the king's daughter and the prince and the old man were still sitting on the hill-top. Then the old man said: "Lovely maiden, turn around! Do you see anything down below?" "Yes," answered the princess, "I see my father and my stepsisters and my stepmother with all their following moving this way." The old man said: "Now they have started out to look for you. Go down and bring up the wolf's pelt in the gorge." The king's daughter did as he told her. The old man continued: "Now stand at the edge of the hill." And the princess did that, too. Now one could see the queen and her daughters coming along the way, and stopping just below the hill. Then the old man said: "Now throw down the wolf's pelt!" The princess obeyed him, and threw down the wolf's pelt according to his command. It fell directly on the evil queen and her daughters. And then a most wonderful thing happened: no sooner had the pelt touched the three evil women than they immediately changed shape, and turning into three horrible werewolves, they ran away as fast as they could into the forest, howling dreadfully.

No more had this happened than the king himself arrived at the foot of the hill with his whole retinue. When he looked up and recognized the princess, he could not at first believe his eyes; but stood motionless, thinking her a vision. Then the old man cried: "Lovely maiden, now hasten, run down and make your father happy!" There was no need to tell the princess twice. She took her lover by the hand and they ran down the hill. When they came to the king, the princess ran on ahead, fell on her father's neck, and wept with joy. And the young prince wept as well, and the king himself wept; and their meeting was a pleasant sight for everyone. There was great joy and many embraces, and the princess told of her evil stepmother and stepsisters and of her lover, and all that she had suffered, and of the old man who had helped them in such a wonderful way. But when the king turned around to thank the old man he had completely vanished, and from that day on no one could say who he had been or what had become of him.

The king and his whole retinue now returned to the castle, where the king had a splendid banquet prepared, to which he invited all the able and distinguished people throughout the kingdom, and bestowed his daughter on the young prince. And the wedding was celebrated with gladness and music and amusements of every kind for many days. I was there, too, and when I rode through the forest I met a wolf with two young wolves, and they showed me their teeth and seemed very angry. And I was told they were none other than the evil stepmother and her two daughters.

The Secret Church

(Norwegian)

ONCE THE SCHOOLMASTER OF ETNEDAL was staying in the mountains to fish. He was very fond of reading, and so he always carried one book or another along with him, with which he could lie down, and which he read on holidays, or when the weather forced him to stay in the little fishing-hut. One Sunday morning, as he was lying there reading, it seemed as though he could hear church bells; sometimes they sounded faintly, as though from a great distance; at other times the sound was clear, as though carried by the wind. He listened long and with surprise; and did not trust his ears – for he knew that it was impossible to hear the bells of the parish church so far out among the hills – yet suddenly they sounded quite clearly on his ear. So he laid aside his book, stood up and went out. The sun was shining, the weather was fine, and one group of churchgoers after another passed him in their Sunday clothes, their hymn books in their hands. A little further on in the forest, where he had never before seen anything but trees and brush, stood an old wooden church. After a time the priest came by, and he was so old and decrepit that his wife and daughter led him. And when they came to the spot where the schoolmaster was standing, they stopped and invited him to come to church and hear mass. The schoolmaster thought for a moment; but since it occurred to him that it might be amusing to see how these people worshipped God, he said he would go along, if he did not thereby suffer harm. No, no harm should come to him, said they, but rather a blessing. In the church all went forward in a quiet and orderly manner, there were neither dogs nor crying children to disturb the service, and the singing was good – but he could not make out the words. When the priest had been led to the pulpit he delivered what seemed to the listening schoolmaster a really fine and edifying sermon – but one, it appeared to him, of quite a peculiar trend of thought, which he was not always able to follow. Nor did the 'Our Father in heaven…' sound just right, and the 'Deliver us from evil…' he did not hear at all. Nor was the name of Jesus uttered; and at the close no blessing was spoken.

When mass had been said, the schoolmaster was invited to the parsonage. He gave the same answer he had already returned, that he would be glad to go if he suffered no harm thereby. And as before, they assured him he would not lose; but rather gain thereby. So he went with them to the parsonage, just such an attractive and well-built parsonage like most in the neighbourhood. It had a garden with flowers and apple trees, with a neat lattice fence around it. They invited him to dinner, and the dinner was well cooked and carefully prepared. As before, he said that he would gladly accept their invitation, if he came to no harm thereby, and was given the same reply. So he ate with them, and said later that he had noticed no difference between this food and the Christian dinner he had received when, once or twice, he had been asked to dinner by the priest of the village church. When he had drunk his coffee, the wife and daughter drew him aside into another room, and the wife complained that her husband had grown so old and decrepit that he could not keep up much longer. Then she began to say that the schoolmaster was such a strong and able man, and finally, that she and her daughter would like to have him for priest, and whether he would not stay and succeed the old father. The schoolmaster objected that he was no scholar. But they insisted that he had more learning than was needed in their case, for they never had any visits from the bishop, nor did the dean ever hold a chapter, for of all such things they knew nothing. When the schoolmaster heard that, he said that even though he had the necessary scholarship, he doubted very much that he had the right vocation, and since this was a most important matter for him and for them, it would be unwise to act too hurriedly, so he would ask for a year to think it over. When he had said that, he found himself standing by a pond in the wood, and could see neither church nor parsonage. So he thought the matter was at an end. But a year later, just as the term he had set was up, he was working on a house, for during the school vacation he busied himself either with fishing or carpentering.

He was just straddling a wall when he saw the parson's daughter, the one whom he had seen in the mountains, coming straight toward him. She asked him if he had thought over the matter. "Yes," said he, "I have thought it over, but I cannot; since I cannot answer for it before God and my own conscience." That very moment the parson's daughter from underground vanished; but immediately after he cut himself in the knee with the axe in such wise that he remained a cripple for life.

The Charcoal Burner

(Norwegian)

ONCE ON A TIME there was a charcoal burner, who had a son, who was a charcoal burner too. When the father was dead, the son took him a wife; but he was lazy and would turn his hand to nothing. He was careless in minding his pits too, and the end was no one would have him to burn charcoal for them.

It so fell out that one day he had burned a pit full for himself, and set off to the town with a few loads and sold them; and when he had done selling, he loitered in the street and looked about him. On his way home he fell in with townsmen and neighbours, and made merry, and drank, and chattered of all he had seen in the town. "The prettiest thing I saw," he said, "was a great crowd of priests, and all the folks greeted them and took off their hats to them. I only wish I were a priest myself; then maybe they would take off their hats to me too. As it was they looked as though they did not even see me at all."

"Well, well!" said his friends, "if you are nothing else, you can't say you're not as black as a priest. And now we are about it, we can go to the sale of the old priest, who is dead, and have a glass, and meanwhile you can buy his gown and hood." That was what the neighbours said; and what they said he did, and when he got home he had not so much as a penny left.

"Now you have both means and money, I dare say," said his goody, when she heard he had sold his charcoal.

"I should think so. Means, indeed!" said the charcoal burner, "for you must know I have been ordained priest. Here you see both gown and hood."

"Nay, I'll never believe that," said the goody, "strong ale makes big words. You are just as bad, whichever end of you turns up. That you are," she said.

"You shall neither scold nor sorrow for the pit, for its last coal is quenched and cold," said the charcoal burner.

It fell out one day that many people in priests' robes passed by the charcoal burner's cottage on their way to the king's palace, so that it was easy to see there was something in the wind there. Yes! The charcoal burner would go too, and so he put on his gown and hood.

His goody thought it would be far better to stay at home; for even if he chanced to hold a horse for some great man, the drink-money he got would only go down his throat like so many before it.

"There are many, mother, who talk of drink," said the man, "who never think of thirst. All I know is, the more one drinks the more one thirsts;" and with that he set off for the palace. When he got there, all the strangers were bidden to come in, and the charcoal burner followed with the rest. So the king made them a speech, and said he had lost his costliest ring, and was quite sure it had been stolen. That was why he had summoned all the learned priests in the land, to see if there were one of them who could tell him who the thief was. And he made a vow there and then, and said what reward he would give to the man who found out the thief. If he were a curate, he should have a living; if he was a rector, he should be made a dean; if he were a dean, he should be made a bishop; and if he were a bishop, he should become the first man in the kingdom after the king.

So the king went round and round among them all, from one to the other, asking them if they could find the thief; and when he came to the charcoal burner, he said,

"Who are you?"

"I am the wise priest and the true prophet," said the charcoal burner.

"Then you can tell me," said the king, "who has taken my ring?"

"Yes!" said the charcoal burner; "it isn't so right against rhyme and reason that what has happened in darkness should come to light; but it isn't every year that salmon spawn in fir tree tops. Here have I been a curate for seven years, trying to feed myself and my children, and I haven't got a living yet. If that thief is to be found out, I must have lots of time and reams of paper; for I must write and reckon, and track him out through many lands."

"Yes! He should have as much time and paper as he chose, if he would only lay his finger on the thief."

So they shut him up by himself in a room in the king's palace, and it was not long before they found out that he must know much more than his Lord's Prayer; for he scribbled over so much paper that it lay in great heaps and rolls, and yet there was not a man who could make out a word of what he wrote, for it looked like nothing else than pot-hooks and hangers. But, as he did this, time went on, and still there was not a trace of the thief. At last the king got weary, and so he said, if the priest couldn't find the thief in three days he should lose his life.

"More haste, worse speed. You can't cart coal till the pit is cool," said the charcoal burner. But the king stuck to his word – that he did; and the charcoal burner felt his life wasn't worth much.

Now there were three of the king's servants who waited on the charcoal burner day by day, in turn, and these three fellows had stolen the ring between them. So when one of these servants came into the room and cleared the table when he had eaten his supper, and was going out again, the charcoal burner heaved a deep sigh as he looked after him, and said,

"There goes the first of them!" but he only meant the first of the three days he had still to live.

"That priest knows more than how to fill his mouth," said the servant, when he was alone with his fellows; for he said, "I was the first of them."

The next day, the second servant was to mark what the prisoner said when he waited on him, and sure enough when he went out, after clearing the table, the charcoal burner stared him full in the face and fetched a deep sigh, and said,

"There goes the second of them!"

So the third was to take heed to what the charcoal burner said on the third day, and it was all worse and no better; for when the servant had his hand on the door as he went out with the plates and dishes, the charcoal burner clasped his hands together, and said, with a sigh as though his heart would break,

"There goes the third of them!"

So the man went down to his fellows with his heart in his throat, and said it was clear as day the priest knew all about it; and so they all three went into his room and fell on their knees before him, and begged and prayed he would not say it was they who had stolen the ring. If he would do this, they were ready to give him, each of them, a hundred dollars, if he would not bring them into trouble.

Well, he gave his word, like a man, to do that and keep them harmless, if they would only give him the money and the ring and a great bowl of porridge. And what do you think he did with the ring when he got it? Why, he stuffed it well down into the porridge, and bade them go and give it to the biggest pig in the king's sty.

Next morning the king came, and was in no mood for jokes, and said he must know all about the thief.

"Well! well! Now I have written and reckoned all the world round," said the charcoal burner, "but it is no child of man that stole your majesty's ring."

"Pooh!" said the king; "who was it, then?"

"It was the biggest pig in your sty," said the charcoal burner.

Yes! They killed the pig, and there the ring was inside it; there was no mistake about that; and so the charcoal burner got a living, and the king was so glad he gave him a farm and a horse, and a hundred dollars into the bargain.

You may fancy the charcoal burner was not slow in flitting to the living, and the first Sunday after he got there he was going to church to read himself in; but before he left his house he was to have his breakfast, and so he took the king's letter and laid it on a bit of dry toast and then, by mistake, he dipped both toast and letter into his brose, and when he found it tough to chew, he gave the whole morsel to his dog Tray, and Tray gobbled up both toast and letter.

And now he scarce knew what to do, or how to turn. To church he must, for the people were waiting; and when he got there, he went straight up into the pulpit. In the pulpit he put on such a grave face that all thought he was a grand priest; but as the service went on, it was not so good after all. This was how he began:

"The words, my brethren, which you should have heard this day have gone, alas! to the dogs; but come next Sunday, dear parishioners, and you shall hear something else; and so this sermon comes to an end. Amen!"

All the parish thought they had got a strange priest, for they had never heard such a funny sermon before; but still they said to themselves, "He'll be better perhaps by-and-by, and if he isn't better we shall know how to deal with him."

Next Sunday, when there was service again, the church was so crowded full with folk who wished to hear the new priest that there was scarce standing-room. Well, he came again, and went straight up into the pulpit, and there he stood awhile and said never a word. But all at once he burst out, and bawled at the top of his voice –

"Hearken to me, old Nannygoat Bridget! Why in the world do you sit so far back in the church?"

"Oh, your reverence," said she, "if you must know, it's because my shoes are all in holes."

"That's no reason; for you might take an old bit of pig-skin and stitch yourself new shoes, and then you could also come far forward in the church, like the other fine ladies. For the rest, you all ought to bethink yourselves of the way you are going; for I see when ye come to church, some of you come from the north and some from the south, and it is the same when you go from church again. But sometimes ye stand and loiter on the way, and then it may well be asked, What will become of you? Yea! who can tell what will become of every one of us? By the way, I have to give notice of a black mare which has strayed from the old priest's widow. She has hair on her fetlocks and a falling mane, and other marks which I will not name in this place. Besides, I may tell you, I have a hole in my old breeches-pocket, and I know it, but you do not know it; and another thing you do not know, and which I do not know, is whether any of you has a bit of cloth to patch that hole. Amen."

Some few of the hearers were very well pleased with this sermon. They thought it sure he would make a brave priest in time; but, to tell the truth, most of them thought it too bad, and when the dean came they complained of the priest, and said no one had ever heard such sermons before, and there was even one of them who knew the last by heart, and wrote it down and read it to the dean.

"I call it a very good sermon," said the dean, "for it was likely that he spoke in parables as to seeking light and shunning darkness and its deeds, and as to those who were walking either on the broad or the strait path; but most of all," he said, "that wa a grand parable when he gave that notice about the priest's black mare, and how i would fare with us all at the last. The pocket with the hole in it was to show the nee of the church, and the piece of cloth to patch it was the gifts and offerings of th congregation." That was what the dean said.

As for the parish, what they said was, "Ay! ay!" so much we could understand that i was to go into the priest's pocket.

The end was, the dean said, he thought the parish had got such a good an understanding priest, there was no fault to find with him, and so they had to make th best of him; but after a while, as he got worse instead of better, they complained of hin to the bishop.

Well! Sooner or later the bishop came, and there was to be a visitation. But, the da before, the priest had gone into the church, unbeknown to anybody, and sawed th props of the pulpit all but in two, so that it would only just hang together if one went u into it very carefully. So when the people were gathered together and he was to preac before the bishop, he crept up into the pulpit and began to expound, as he was wont and when he had gone on a while, he got more in earnest, threw his arms about an bawled out:

"If there be any here who is wicked or given to ill deeds, it were better he left thi place; for this very day there shall be a fall, such as hath not been seen since th world began."

With that he struck the reading-desk like thunder, and lo! the desk and the pries and the whole pulpit tumbled down on the floor of the church with such a crash tha the whole congregation ran out of church, as if Doomsday were at their heels.

But then the bishop told the fault-finders he was amazed that they dared to complain o a priest who had such gifts in the pulpit, and so much wisdom that he could foresee thing about to happen. For his part, he thought he ought to be a dean at least, and it was no long either before he was a dean. So there was no help for it; they had to put up with him.

Now it so happened that the king and queen had no children; but when the kin heard that, perhaps, there was one coming, he was eager to know if it would be an hei to his crown and realm, or if it would only be a princess. So all the wise men in th land were gathered to the palace, that they might say beforehand what it would be. Bu when there was not a man of them that could say that, both the king and the bisho thought of the charcoal burner, and it was not long before they got him between them and asked him about it. "No!" he said, "that was past his power, for it was not good t guess at what no man alive could know."

"All very fine, I dare say," said the king. "It's all the same to me, of course, if you know it or if you don't know it; but, you know, you are the wise priest and the true prophe who can foretell things to come; and all I can say is if you don't tell it me, you shall los your gown. And now I think of it, I'll try you first."

So he took the biggest silver tankard he had and went down to the seashore, and, i a little while, called the priest.

"If you can tell me now what there is in this tankard," said the king, "you will be able to tell me the other also;" and as he said this, he held the lid of the tankard tight.

The charcoal burner only wrung his hands and bemoaned himself.

"Oh! you most wretched crab and cripple on this earth," he cried out, "this is what all your backslidings and sidelong tricks have brought on you."

"Ah!" cried out the king, "how could you say you did not know? For you must know he had a crab in the tankard." So the charcoal burner had to go into the parlour to the queen. He took a chair and sat down in the middle of the floor, while the queen walked up and down in the room.

"One should never count one's chickens before they are hatched, and never quarrel about a baby's name before it is born," said the charcoal burner; "but I never heard or saw such a thing before! When the queen comes toward me, I almost think it will be a prince, and when she goes away from me it looks as if it would be a princess."

Lo! when the time came, it was both a prince and a princess, for twins were born; and so the charcoal burner had hit the mark that time too. And because he could tell that which no man could know, he got money in carts full, and was the next man to the king in the realm.

Trip, trap, trill,
A man is often more than he will.

Tales of Trolls & Giants

Introduction

LYING IN WAIT beneath his bridge, the Troll in 'The Three Billy Goats Gruff' is not so much a character as a symbol. Ugly, outlandish and frighteningly fierce, he embodies the sort of destructive impulses that surge in our subconscious, ready to break the surface and upset our lives at any time. The Vikings never got to read the psychological theories of Sigmund Freud (1856–1939), but they understood the darker side of human nature. They also knew about life and the disagreeable surprises it could spring.

But they also appreciated that a vividly imagined monster or giant – the more bloodthirsty the better – could lend a welcome frisson to any tale. A troll with three, five or seven heads – especially if he's obligingly easy for a hero to outwit, and then dispatch with slapstick violence – makes for enjoyable entertainment every time. The monsters in these stories can be cartoonish creations, as comically inept as they are grotesque.

Trolls and giants in Nordic folk and fairy tale serve a paradoxical purpose, then. Though emblems of evil, they underline the triumph of good.

The Three Billy Goats Gruff

(Norwegian)

ONCE ON A TIME there were three Billy goats, who were to go up to the hillside to make themselves fat, and the name of all three was "Gruff".

On the way up was a bridge over a burn they had to cross; and under the bridge lived a great ugly Troll, with eyes as big as saucers, and a nose as long as a poker.

So first of all came the youngest billy goat Gruff to cross the bridge.

"Trip, trap; trip, trap!" went the bridge.

"WHO'S THAT tripping over my bridge?" roared the Troll.

"Oh! it is only I, the tiniest billy goat Gruff; and I'm going up to the hillside to make myself fat", said the billy goat, with such a small voice.

"Now, I'm coming to gobble you up", said the Troll.

"Oh, no! pray don't take me. I'm too little, that I am", said the billy goat; "wait a bit till the second billy goat Gruff comes, he's much bigger."

"Well! be off with you", said the Troll.

A little while after came the second billy goat Gruff to cross the bridge.

"TRIP, TRAP! TRIP, TRAP! TRIP, TRAP!" went the bridge.

"WHO'S THAT tripping over my bridge?" roared the Troll.

"Oh! it's the second billy goat Gruff, and I'm going up to the hillside to make myself fat", said the billy goat, who hadn't such a small voice.

"Now, I'm coming to gobble you up", said the Troll.

"Oh, no! don't take me, wait a little till the big billy goat Gruff comes, he's much bigger."

"Very well! be off with you", said the Troll.

But just then up came the big billy goat Gruff.

"TRIP, TRAP! TRIP, TRAP! TRIP, TRAP!" went the bridge, for the billy goat was so heavy that the bridge creaked and groaned under him.

"WHO'S THAT tramping over my bridge?" roared the Troll.

"IT'S I! THE BIG BILLY GOAT GRUFF", said the billy goat, who had an ugly hoarse voice of his own.

"Now, I'm coming to gobble you up", roared the Troll.

Well, come along! I've got two spears,
And I'll poke your eyeballs out at your ears;
I've got besides two curling-stones,
And I'll crush you to bits, body and bones.

That was what the big billy goat said; and so he flew at the Troll and poked his eyes out with his horns, and crushed him to bits, body and bones, and tossed him out into the burn, and after that he went up to the hillside. There the billy goats got so fat they were scarce able to walk home again; and if the fat hasn't fallen off them, why they're still fat; and so:

Snip, snap, snout,
This tale's told out.

Soria Moria Castle

(Norwegian)

THERE WAS ONCE UPON A TIME a couple of folks who had a son called Halvor. Ever since he had been a little boy he had been unwilling to do any work, and had just sat raking about among the ashes. His parents sent him away to learn several things, but Halvor stayed nowhere, for when he had been gone two or three days he always ran away from his master, hurried off home, and sat down in the chimney corner to grub among the ashes again.

One day, however, a sea captain came and asked Halvor if he hadn't a fancy to come with him and go to sea, and behold foreign lands. And Halvor had a fancy for that, so he was not long in getting ready.

How long they sailed I have no idea, but after a long, long time there was a terrible storm, and when it was over and all had become calm again, they knew not where they were, for they had been driven away to a strange coast of which none of them had any knowledge.

As there was no wind at all they lay there becalmed, and Halvor asked the skipper to give him leave to go on shore to look about him, for he would much rather do that than lie there and sleep.

"Dost thou think that thou art fit to go where people can see thee?" said the skipper; "thou hast no clothes but those rags thou art going about in!"

Halvor still begged for leave, and at last got it, but he was to come back at once if the wind began to rise.

So he went on shore, and it was a delightful country; whithersoever he went there were wide plains with fields and meadows, but as for people, there were none to be seen. The wind began to rise, but Halvor thought that he had not seen enough yet, and that he would like to walk about a little longer, to try if he could not meet somebody. So after a while he came to a great highway, which was so smooth that an egg might have been rolled along it without breaking. Halvor followed this, and when evening drew near he saw a big castle far away in the distance, and there were lights in it. So as he had now been walking the whole day and had not brought anything to eat away with him, he was frightfully hungry. Nevertheless, the nearer he came to the castle the more afraid he was.

A fire was burning in the castle, and Halvor went into the kitchen, which was more magnificent than any kitchen he had ever yet beheld. There were vessels of gold and silver, but not one human being was to be seen. When Halvor had stood there for some time, and no one had come out, he went in and opened a door, and inside a Princess was sitting at her wheel spinning.

"Nay!" she cried, "can Christian folk dare to come hither? But the best thing that you can do is to go away again, for if not the Troll will devour you. A Troll with three heads lives here."

"I should have been just as well pleased if he had had four heads more, for I should have enjoyed seeing the fellow," said the youth; "and I won't go away, for I have done no harm, but you must give me something to eat, for I am frightfully hungry."

When Halvor had eaten his fill, the Princess told him to try if he could wield the sword which was hanging on the wall, but he could not wield it, nor could he even lift it up.

"Well, then, you must take a drink out of that bottle which is hanging by its side, for that's what the Troll does whenever he goes out and wants to use the sword," said the Princess.

Halvor took a draught, and in a moment he was able to swing the sword about with perfect ease. And now he thought it was high time for the Troll to make his appearance, and at that very moment he came, panting for breath.

Halvor got behind the door.

"Hutetu!" said the Troll as he put his head in at the door. "It smells just as if there were Christian man's blood here!"

"Yes, you shall learn that there is!" said Halvor, and cut off all his heads.

The Princess was so rejoiced to be free that she danced and sang, but then she remembered her sisters, and said: "If my sisters were but free too!"

"Where are they?" asked Halvor.

So she told him where they were. One of them had been taken away by a Troll to his castle, which was six miles off, and the other had been carried off to a castle which was nine miles farther off still.

"But now," said she, "you must first help me to get this dead body away from here."

Halvor was so strong that he cleared everything away, and made all clean and tidy very quickly. So then they ate and drank, and were happy, and next morning he set off in the grey light of dawn. He gave himself no rest, but walked or ran the livelong day. When he came in sight of the castle he was again just a little afraid. It was much more splendid than the other, but here too there was not a human being to be seen. So Halvor went into the kitchen, and did not linger there either, but went straight in.

"Nay! do Christian folk dare to come here?" cried the second Princess. "I know not how long it is since I myself came, but during all that time I have never seen a Christian man. It will be better for you to depart at once, for a Troll lives here who has six heads."

"No, I shall not go," said Halvor; "even if he had six more I would not."

"He will swallow you up alive," said the Princess.

But she spoke to no purpose, for Halvor would not go; he was not afraid of the Troll, but he wanted some meat and drink, for he was hungry after his journey. So she gave him as much as he would have, and then she once more tried to make him go away.

"No," said Halvor, "I will not go, for I have not done anything wrong, and I have no reason to be afraid."

"He won't ask any questions about that," said the Princess, "for he will take you without leave or right; but as you will not go, try if you can wield that sword which the Troll uses in battle."

He could not brandish the sword; so the Princess said that he was to take a draught from the flask which hung by its side, and when he had done that he could wield the sword.

Soon afterwards the Troll came, and he was so large and stout that he was forced to go sideways to get through the door. When the Troll got his first head in he cried: "Hutetu! It smells of a Christian man's blood here!"

With that Halvor cut off the first head, and so on with all the rest. The Princess was now exceedingly delighted, but then she remembered her sisters, and wished that they too were free. Halvor thought that might be managed, and wanted to set off immediately; but first he had to help the Princess to remove the Troll's body, so it was not until morning that he set forth on his way.

It was a long way to the castle, and he both walked and ran to get there in time. Late in the evening he caught sight of it, and it was very much more magnificent than either of the others. And this time he was not in the least afraid, but went into the kitchen, and then straight on inside the castle. There a Princess was sitting, who was so beautiful that there was never anyone to equal her. She too said what the others had said, that no Christian folk had ever been there since she had come, and entreated him to go away again, or else the Troll would swallow him up alive. The Troll had nine heads, she told him.

"Yes, and if he had nine added to the nine, and then nine more still, I would not go away," said Halvor, and went and stood by the stove.

The Princess begged him very prettily to go lest the Troll should devour him; but Halvor said, "Let him come when he will."

So she gave him the Troll's sword, and bade him take a drink from the flask to enable him to wield it.

At that same moment the Troll came, breathing hard, and he was ever so much bigger and stouter than either of the others, and he too was forced to go sideways to get in through the door.

"Hutetu! what a smell of Christian blood there is here!" said he.

Then Halvor cut off the first head, and after that the others, but the last was the toughest of them all, and it was the hardest work that Halvor had ever done to get it off, but he still believed that he would have strength enough to do it.

And now all the Princesses came to the castle, and were together again, and they were happier than they had ever been in their lives; and they were delighted with Halvor, and he with them, and he was to choose the one he liked best; but of the three sisters the youngest loved him best.

But Halvor went about and was so strange and so mournful and quiet that the Princesses asked what it was that he longed for, and if he did not like to be with them. He said that he did like to be with them, for they had enough to live on, and he was very comfortable there; but he longed to go home, for his father and mother were alive, and he had a great desire to see them again.

They thought that this might easily be done.

"You shall go and return in perfect safety if you will follow our advice," said the Princesses.

So he said that he would do nothing that they did not wish.

Then they dressed him so splendidly that he was like a King's son; and they put a ring on his finger, and it was one which would enable him to go there and back again by wishing, but they told him that he must not throw it away, or name their names; for if he did, all his magnificence would be at an end, and then he would never see them more.

"If I were but at home again, or if home were but here!" said Halvor, and no sooner had he wished this than it was granted. Halvor was standing outside his father and mother's cottage before he knew what he was about. The darkness of night was coming on, and when the father and mother saw such a splendid and stately stranger walk in, they were so startled that they both began to bow and curtsey.

Halvor then inquired if he could stay there and have lodging for the night. No, that he certainly could not. "We can give you no such accommodation," they said, "for we have none of the things that are needful when a great lord like you is to be entertained. It will be better for you to go up to the farm. It is not far off, you can see the chimney-pots from here, and there they have plenty of everything."

Halvor would not hear of that, he was absolutely determined to stay where he was; but the old folks stuck to what they had said, and told him that he was to go to the farm, where he could get both meat and drink, whereas they themselves had not even a chair to offer him.

"No," said Halvor, "I will not go up there till early tomorrow morning; let me stay here tonight. I can sit down on the hearth."

They could say nothing against that, so Halvor sat down on the hearth, and began to rake about among the ashes just as he had done before, when he lay there idling away his time.

They chattered much about many things, and told Halvor of this and of that, and at last he asked them if they had never had any child.

"Yes," they said; they had had a boy who was called Halvor, but they did not know where he had gone, and they could not even say whether he were dead or alive.

"Could I be he?" said Halvor.

"I should know him well enough," said the old woman rising. "Our Halvor was so idle and slothful that he never did anything at all, and he was so ragged that one hole ran into another all over his clothes. Such a fellow as he was could never turn into such a man as you are, sir."

In a short time the old woman had to go to the fireplace to stir the fire, and when the blaze lit up Halvor, as it used to do when he was at home raking up the ashes, she knew him again.

"Good Heavens! is that you, Halvor?" said she, and such great gladness fell on the old parents that there were no bounds to it. And now he had to relate everything that had befallen him, and the old woman was so delighted with him that she would take him up to the farm at once to show him to the girls who had formerly looked down on him so. She went there first, and Halvor followed her. When she got there she told them how Halvor had come home again, and now they should just see how magnificent he was. "He looks like a prince," she said.

"We shall see that he is just the same ragamuffin that he was before," said the girls, tossing their heads.

At that same moment Halvor entered, and the girls were so astonished that they left their kirtles lying in the chimney corner, and ran away in nothing but their petticoats. When they came in again they were so shamefaced that they hardly dared to look at Halvor, towards whom they had always been so proud and haughty before.

"Ay, ay! you have always thought that you were so pretty and dainty that no one was equal to you," said Halvor, "but you should just see the eldest Princess whom I set free. You look like herds-women compared with her, and the second Princess is also much prettier than you; but the youngest, who is my sweetheart, is more beautiful than either sun or moon. I wish to Heaven they were here, and then you would see them."

Scarcely had he said this before they were standing by his side, but then he was very sorrowful, for the words which they had said to him came to his mind.

Up at the farm a great feast was made ready for the Princesses, and much respec paid to them, but they would not stay there.

"We want to go down to your parents," they said to Halvor, "so we will go out and loo about us."

He followed them out, and they came to a large pond outside the farmhouse. Very nea the water there was a pretty green bank, and there the Princesses said they would sit dow and while away an hour, for they thought that it would be pleasant to sit and look out ove the water, they said.

There they sat down, and when they had sat for a short time the youngest Princess saic "I may as well comb your hair a little, Halvor."

So Halvor laid his head down on her lap, and she combed it, and it was not lon before he fell asleep. Then she took her ring from him and put another in its place, an then she said to her sisters: "Hold me as I am holding you. I would that we were at Sori Moria Castle."

When Halvor awoke he knew that he had lost the Princesses, and began to weep an lament, and was so unhappy that he could not be comforted. In spite of all his father's an mother's entreaties, he would not stay, but bade them farewell, saying that he would neve see them more, for if he did not find the Princess again he did not think it worthwhil to live.

He again had three hundred dollars, which he put into his pocket and went on his wa When he had walked some distance he met a man with a tolerably good horse. Halvo longed to buy it, and began to bargain with the man.

"Well, I have not exactly been thinking of selling him," said the man, "but if we coul agree, perhaps—"

Halvor inquired how much he wanted to have for the horse.

"I did not give much for him, and he is not worth much; he is a capital horse to ride, bu good for nothing at drawing; but he will always be able to carry your bag of provisions an you too, if you walk and ride by turns." At last they agreed about the price, and Halvor lai his bag on the horse, and sometimes he walked and sometimes he rode. In the evenin he came to a green field, where stood a great tree, under which he seated himself. Ther he let the horse loose and lay down to sleep, but before he did that he took his bag of the horse. At daybreak he set off again, for he did not feel as if he could take any rest. Sc he walked and rode the whole day, through a great wood where there were many greer places which gleamed very prettily among the trees. He did not know where he was o whither he was going, but he never lingered longer in any place than was enough to let his horse get a little food when they came to one of these green spots, while he himself took out his bag of provisions.

So he walked and he rode, and it seemed to him that the wood would never come tc an end. But on the evening of the second day he saw a light shining through the trees.

"If only there were some people up there I might warm myself and get something tc eat," thought Halvor.

When he got to the place where the light had come from, he saw a wretched little cottage, and through a small pane of glass he saw a couple of old folks inside. They were very old, and as grey-headed as a pigeon, and the old woman had such a long nose that she sat in the chimney corner and used it to stir the fire.

"Good evening! good evening!" said the old hag; "but what errand have you that can bring you here? No Christian folk have been here for more than a hundred years."

So Halvor told her that he wanted to get to Soria Moria Castle, and inquired if she knew the way thither.

"No," said the old woman, "that I do not, but the Moon will be here presently, and I will ask her, and she will know. She can easily see it, for she shines on all things."

So when the Moon stood clear and bright above the treetops the old woman went out. "Moon! Moon!" she screamed. "Canst thou tell me the way to Soria Moria Castle?"

"No," said the Moon, "that I can't, for when I shone there, there was a cloud before me."

"Wait a little longer," said the old woman to Halvor, "for the West Wind will presently be here, and he will know it, for he breathes gently or blows into every corner."

"What! have you a horse too?" she said when she came in again. "Oh! let the poor creature loose in our bit of fenced-in pasture, and don't let it stand there starving at our very door. But won't you exchange him with me? We have a pair of old boots here with which you can go fifteen quarters of a mile at each step. You shall have them for the horse, and then you will be able to get sooner to Soria Moria Castle."

Halvor consented to this at once, and the old woman was so delighted with the horse that she was ready to dance. "For now I, too, shall be able to ride to church," she said. Halvor could take no rest, and wanted to set off immediately; but the old woman said that there was no need to hasten. "Lie down on the bench and sleep a little, for we have no bed to offer you," said she, "and I will watch for the coming of the West Wind."

Ere long came the West Wind, roaring so loud that the walls creaked.

The old woman went out and cried:

"West Wind! West Wind! Canst thou tell me the way to Soria Moria Castle? Here is one who would go thither."

"Yes, I know it well," said the West Wind. "I am just on my way there to dry the clothes for the wedding which is to take place. If he is fleet of foot he can go with me."

Out ran Halvor.

"You will have to make haste if you mean to go with me," said the West Wind; and away it went over hill and dale, and moor and morass, and Halvor had enough to do to keep up with it.

"Well, now I have no time to stay with you any longer," said the West Wind, "for I must first go and tear down a bit of spruce fir before I go to the bleaching-ground to dry the clothes; but just go along the side of the hill, and you will come to some girls who are standing there washing clothes, and then you will not have to walk far before you are at Soria Moria Castle."

Shortly afterwards Halvor came to the girls who were standing washing, and they asked him if he had seen anything of the West Wind, who was to come there to dry the clothes for the wedding.

"Yes," said Halvor, "he has only gone to break down a bit of spruce fir. It won't be long before he is here." And then he asked them the way to Soria Moria Castle. They put him in the right way, and when he came in front of the castle it was so full of horses and people that it swarmed with them. But Halvor was so ragged and torn with following the West Wind through bushes and bogs that he kept on one side, and would not go among the crowd until the last day, when the feast was to be held at noon.

So when, as was the usage and custom, all were to drink to the bride and the young girls who were present, the cup-bearer filled the cup for each in turn, both bride and bridegroom, and knights and servants, and at last, after a very long time, he came to Halvor. He drank their health, and then slipped the ring which the Princess had put on his finger when they were sitting by the waterside into the glass, and ordered the cup-bearer to carry the glass to the bride from him and greet her.

Then the Princess at once rose up from the table, and said, "Who is most worthy to have one of us – he who has delivered us from the Trolls or he who is sitting here as bridegroom?"

There could be but one opinion as to that, everyone thought, and when Halvor heard what they said he was not long in flinging off his beggar's rags and arraying himself as a bridegroom.

"Yes, he is the right one," cried the youngest Princess when she caught sight of him; so she flung the other out of the window and held her wedding with Halvor.

Charcoal Nils and the Troll-Woman

(Swedish)

IN THE OLD DAYS there lived on a headland that juts out into the northwestern corner of Lake Rasval, in the neighbourhood of the Linde mining-district, a charcoal burner named Nils, generally known as Charcoal Nils. He let a farm-hand attend to his little plot of land, and he himself made his home in the forest, where he chopped wood in the summer and burned it to charcoal in the winter. Yet no matter how hard he struggled, his work was unblessed with reward, and no one ever spoke of him save as poor Charcoal Nils.

One day, when he was on the opposite shore of the lake, near the gloomy Harsberg, a strange woman came up to him, and asked whether he needed someone to help him with his charcoal burning.

"Yes, indeed," said he, "help would be welcome." So she began to gather blocks of wood and tree-trunks, more than Charcoal Nils could have dragged together with his horse, and by noon there was enough wood for a new kiln. When evening came, she asked the charcoal burner whether he were satisfied with the day's work she had done, and if she were to come back the next day.

That suited the charcoal burner perfectly, and she came back the next day and all the following ones. And when the kiln had been burned out she helped Nils clear it, and never before had he had such a quantity of charcoal, nor charcoal of so fine a quality.

So she became his wife and lived with him in the wood for three years. They had three children, yet this worried Nils but little, seeing that she looked after them, and they gave him no trouble.

But when the fourth year came, she grew more exacting, and insisted on going back to his home with him, and living with him there. Nils wished to hear nothing about this; yet since she was so useful to him in his charcoal-burning, he did not betray his feelings, and said he would think it over.

It happened one Sunday that he went to church – where he had not been for many years, and what he heard there brought up thoughts he had not known since the innocent days of his childhood. He began to wonder whether there were not some hocus-pocus about the charcoal-burning, and whether it were not due to the forest woman, who aided him so willingly.

Preoccupied with this and other thoughts, he forgot while returning to his kiln, that he had promised the strange woman at the very beginning, when she had first helped him, that, whenever he had been home and was returning to the kiln, he would rap three times with his axe against an old pine tree not far from it. On this occasion, as we have said, he forgot the sign, and as a result he saw something that nearly robbed him of his wits.

As he drew near the kiln, he saw it all aflame, and around it stood the three children and their mother, and they were clearing out the kiln. They were pulling down and putting out so that flames, smoke and ashes whirled sky-high, but instead of the spruce branches that were generally used to put out the fire, *they had bushy tails which they dipped in the snow*!

When Charcoal Nils had looked on for a while, he slunk back to the old pine tree, and made its trunk echo to the sound of his three ax-strokes till one could hear them on the Harsberg. Then he went to the kiln, as though he had seen nothing, and all went on as before. The kiln was glowing with a handsome, even glow, and the tall woman was about and working as usual.

As soon as she saw Charcoal Nils, she came back with her pressing demand that he take her home to his little house, and that they live there.

"Yes, that shall come about," said Nils to console her, and turned back home to fetch a horse. But instead he went out on the headline of Kallernäs, on the eastern shore of Lake Rasval, where a wise man lived, and asked the latter what he should do.

The old man advised him to go home and hitch his horse to his charcoal-wagon, but to hitch the horse in such wise that there would be not a single loop either in the harness or traces. Then he was to mount the horse and ride back to the kiln without stopping, have the troll-woman and her children get into the wagon, and at once drive out on the ice with them.

The charcoal burner did as the old man told him, saddled his horse, paying strict attention that there were no loops in saddle or bridle, rode across the ice through the wood to his kiln, and told the troll-woman and her children to get in. Then he quickly turned back through the wood, out on the ice, and there let his horse run as fast as he could. When he reached the middle of the lake, he saw a pack of wolves running along in the direction of Aboda-land, at the northern end of the lake, and heading for the ice. Then he tore the saddle-harness from the traces, so that the wagon with the troll-folk was left standing on the bare ice, and rode as fast as his horse could carry him for the opposite shore. When the trolls saw the wolves they began to scream.

"Turn back, turn back!" cried the mother. "And if you will not for my sake, then at least do so for the sake of Vipa (Peewee), your youngest daughter!" But Charcoal Nils rode for the shore without looking back. Then he heard the troll-woman calling on others for aid.

"Brother in the Harsberg, Sister in Stripa, Cousin in Ringfels; Take the loop and pull!"

"There is no loop to pull!" came the answer from deep within the Harsberg. "Then catch him at Harkallarn." "He is not riding in that direction." The reply came from Ringfels.

And indeed Charcoal Nils did not ride in that direction; but over stick and stone straight to his own home. Yet when he reached his own courtyard, the horse fell, and a shot from the trolls tore away a corner of the stable. Nils shortly after fell sick, and had to lie a-bed for a number of weeks. When he was well again he sold his forest land, and worked the little farm by the cottage until his death. So that was one occasion when the troll-folk came off second best.

Origin of Tiis Lake

(Danish)

A TROLL HAD ONCE taken up his abode near the village of Kund, in the high bank on which the church now stands, but when the people about there had become pious, and went constantly to church, the troll was dreadfully annoyed by their almost incessant ringing of bells in the steeple of the church. He was at last obliged, in consequence of it, to take his departure, for nothing has more contributed to the emigration of the troll-folk out of the country, than the increasing piety of the people, and their taking to bell-ringing. The troll of Kund accordingly quitted the country, and went over to Funen, where he lived for some time in peace and quiet. Now it chanced that a man who had lately settled in the town of Kund, coming to Funen on business, met this same troll on the road.

"Where do you live?" asked the troll.

Now there was nothing whatever about the troll unlike a man, so he answered him, as was the truth –

"I am from the town of Kund."

"So?" said the troll, "I don't know you then. And yet I think I know every man in Kund. Will you, however," said he, "be so kind as to take a letter for me back with you to Kund?"

The man, of course, said he had no objection.

The troll put a letter into his pocket and charged him strictly not to take it out until he came to Kund church. Then he was to throw it over the churchyard wall, and the person for whom it was intended would get it.

The troll then went away in great haste, and with him the letter went entirely out of the man's mind. But when he was come back to Zealand he sat down by the meadow where Tiis lake now is, and suddenly recollected the troll's letter. He felt a great desire to look at it at least, so he took it out of his pocket and sat a while with it in his hands, when suddenly there began to dribble a little water out of the seal. The letter now unfolded itself and the water came out faster and faster, and it was with the utmost difficulty the poor man was able to save his life, for the malicious troll had enclosed a whole lake in the letter.

The troll, it is plain, had thought to avenge himself on Kund church by destroying it in this manner, but God ordered it so that the lake chanced to run out in the great meadow where it now stands.

Minnikin

(Norwegian)

THERE WAS ONCE UPON A TIME a couple of needy folk who lived in a wretched hut, in which there was nothing but black want; so they had neither food to eat nor wood to burn. But if they had next to nothing of all else they had the blessing of God so far as children were concerned, and every year brought them one more. The man was not overpleased at this. He was always going about grumbling and growling, and saying that it seemed to him that there might be such a thing as having too many of these good gifts; so shortly before another baby was born he went away into the wood for some firewood, saying that he did not want to see the new child; he would hear him quite soon enough when he began to squall for some food.

As soon as this baby was born it began to look about the room. "Ah, my dear mother!" said he, "give me some of my brothers' old clothes, and food enough for a few days, and I will go out into the world and seek my fortune, for, so far as I can see, you have children enough."

"Heaven help thee, my son!" said the mother, "that will never do; thou art still far too little."

But the little creature was determined to do it, and begged and prayed so long that the mother was forced to let him have some old rags, and tie up a little food for him, and then gaily and happily he went out into the world.

But almost before he was out of the house another boy was born, and he too looked about him, and said, "Ah, my dear mother! give me some of my brothers" old clothes, and food for some days, and then I will go out into the world and find my twin brother, for you have children enough."

"Heaven help thee, little creature! thou art far too little for that," said the woman; "it would never do."

But she spoke to no purpose, for the boy begged and prayed until he had got some old rags and a bundle of provisions, and then he set out manfully into the world to find his twin brother.

When the younger had walked for some time he caught sight of his brother a short distance in front of him, and called to him and bade him to stop.

"Wait a minute," he said; "you are walking as if for a wager, but you ought to have stayed to see your younger brother before you hurried off into the world."

So the elder stood still and looked back, and when the younger had got up to him, and had told him that he was his brother, he said: "But now, let us sit down and see what kind of food our mother has given us," and that they did.

When they had walked on a little farther they came to a brook which ran through a green meadow, and there the younger said that they ought to christen each other. 'As we had to make such haste, and had no time to do it at home, we may as well do it here," said he.

"What will you be called?" asked the elder.

"I will be called Minnikin," answered the second; "and you, what will you be called?"

"I will be called King Pippin," answered the elder.

They christened each other and then went onwards. When they had walked for some time they came to a crossway, and there they agreed to part, and each take his own road. This they did, but no sooner had they walked a short distance than they met again. So they parted once more, and each took his own road, but in a very short time the same thing happened again – they met each other before they were at all aware, and so it happened the third time also. Then they arranged with each other that each should choose his own quarter, and one should go east and the other west.

"But if ever you fall into any need or trouble," said the elder, "call me thrice, and I will come and help you; only you must not call me until you are in the utmost need."

"In that case we shall not see each other for some time," said Minnikin; so they bade farewell to each other, and Minnikin went east and King Pippin went west.

When Minnikin had walked a long way alone, he met an old, old crook-backed hag, who had only one eye. Minnikin stole it.

"Oh! oh!" cried the old hag, "what has become of my eye?"

"What will you give me to get your eye back?" said Minnikin.

"I will give thee a sword which is such a sword that it can conquer a whole army, let it be ever so great," replied the woman.

"Let me have it, then," said Minnikin.

The old hag gave him the sword, so she got her eye back. Then Minnikin went onwards, and when he had wandered on for some time he again met an old, old crook-backed hag, who had only one eye. Minnikin stole it before she was aware.

"Oh! oh! what has become of my eye?" cried the old hag.

"What will you give me to get your eye back?" said Minnikin.

"I will give thee a ship which can sail over fresh water and salt water, over high hills and deep dales," answered the old woman.

"Let me have it then," said Minnikin.

So the old woman gave him a little bit of a ship which was no bigger than he could put in his pocket, and then she got her eye back, and she went her way and Minnikin his. When he had walked on for a long time, he met for the third time an old, old crook-backed hag, who had only one eye. This eye also Minnikin stole, and when the woman screamed and lamented, and asked what had become of her eye, Minnikin said, "What will you give me to get your eye back?"

"I will give thee the art to brew a hundred lasts of malt in one brewing."

So, for teaching that art, the old hag got her eye back, and they both went away by different roads.

But when Minnikin had walked a short distance, it seemed to him that it might be worthwhile to see what his ship could do; so he took it out of his pocket, and first he put one foot into it, and then the other, and no sooner had he put one foot into the ship than it became much larger, and when he set the other foot into it, it grew as large as ships that sail on the sea.

Then Minnikin said: "Now go over fresh water and salt water, over high hills and deep dales, and do not stop until thou comest to the King's palace."

And in an instant the ship went away as swiftly as any bird in the air till it got just below the King's palace, and there it stood still.

From the windows of the King's palace many persons had seen Minnikin come sailing thither, and had stood to watch him; and they were all so astounded that they ran down to see what manner of man this could be who came sailing in a ship through the air. But while they were running down from the King's palace, Minnikin had got out of the ship and had put it in his pocket again; for the moment he got out of it, it once more became as small as it had been when he got it from the old woman, and those who came from the King's palace could see nothing but a ragged little boy who was standing down by the seashore. The King asked where he had come from, but the boy said he did not know, nor yet could he tell them how he had got there, but he begged very earnestly and prettily for a place in the King's palace. If there was nothing else for him to do, he said he would fetch wood and water for the kitchen-maid, and that he obtained leave to do.

When Minnikin went up to the King's palace he saw that everything there was hung with black both outside and inside, from the bottom to the top; so he asked the kitchen-maid what that meant.

"Oh, I will tell you that," answered the kitchen-maid. "The King's daughter was long ago promised away to three Trolls, and next Thursday evening one of them is to come to fetch her. Ritter Red has said that he will be able to set her free, but who knows whether he will be able to do it? so you may easily imagine what grief and distress we are in here."

So when Thursday evening came, Ritter Red accompanied the Princess to the seashore; for there she was to meet the Troll, and Ritter Red was to stay with her and protect her. He, however, was very unlikely to do the Troll much injury, for no sooner had the Princess seated herself by the seashore than Ritter Red climbed up into a great tree which was standing there, and hid himself as well as he could among the branches.

The Princess wept, and begged him most earnestly not to go and leave her; but Ritter Red did not concern himself about that. "It is better that one should die than two," said he.

In the meantime Minnikin begged the kitchen-maid very prettily to give him leave to go down to the strand for a short time.

"Oh, what could you do down at the strand?" said the kitchen-maid. "You have nothing to do there."

"Oh yes, my dear, just let me go," said Minnikin. "I should so like to go and amuse myself with the other children."

"Well, well, go then!" said the kitchen-maid, "but don't let me find you staying there over the time when the pan has to be set on the fire for supper, and the roast put on the spit; and mind you bring back a good big armful of wood for the kitchen."

Minnikin promised this, and ran down to the seashore.

Just as he got to the place where the King's daughter was sitting, the Troll came rushing up with a great whistling and whirring, and he was so big and stout that he was terrible to see, and he had five heads.

"Fire!" screeched the Troll.

"Fire yourself!" said Minnikin.

"Can you fight?" roared the Troll.

"If not, I can learn," said Minnikin.

So the Troll struck at him with a great thick iron bar which he had in his fist, till the sods flew five yards up into the air.

"Fie!" said Minnikin. "That was not much of a blow. Now you shall see one of mine."

So he grasped the sword which he had got from the old crook-backed woman, and slashed at the Troll so that all five heads went flying away over the sands.

When the Princess saw that she was delivered she was so delighted that she did not know what she was doing, and skipped and danced.

"Come and sleep a bit with your head in my lap," she said to Minnikin, and as he slept she put a golden dress on him.

But when Ritter Red saw that there was no longer any danger afoot, he lost no time in creeping down from the tree. He then threatened the Princess, until at length she was forced to promise to say that it was he who had rescued her, for he told her that if she did not he would kill her. Then he took the Troll's lungs and tongue and put them in his pocket-handkerchief, and led the Princess back to the King's palace; and whatsoever had been lacking to him in the way of honour before was lacking no longer, for the King did not know how to exalt him enough, and always set him on his own right hand at table.

As for Minnikin, first he went out on the Troll's ship and took a great quantity of gold and silver hoops away with him, and then he trotted back to the King's palace.

When the kitchen-maid caught sight of all this gold and silver she was quite amazed, and said: "My dear friend Minnikin, where have you got all that from?" for she was half afraid that he had not come by it honestly.

"Oh," answered Minnikin, "I have been home a while, and these hoops had fallen off some of our buckets, so I brought them away with me for you."

So when the kitchen-maid heard that they were for her, she asked no more questions about the matter. She thanked Minnikin, and everything was right again at once.

Next Thursday evening all went just the same, and everyone was full of grief and affliction, but Ritter Red said that he had been able to deliver the King's daughter from one Troll, so that he could very easily deliver her from another, and he led her down to the seashore. But he did not do much harm to this Troll either, for when the time came when the Troll might be expected, he said as he had said before: "It is better that one should die than two," and then climbed up into the tree again.

Minnikin once more begged the cook's leave to go down to the seashore for a short time.

"Oh, what can you do there?" said the cook.

"My dear, do let me go!" said Minnikin; "I should so like to go down there and amuse myself a little with the other children."

So this time also she said that he should have leave to go, but he must first promise that he would be back by the time the joint was turned and that he would bring a great armful of wood with him.

No sooner had Minnikin got down to the strand than the Troll came rushing along with a great whistling and whirring, and he was twice as big as the first Troll, and he had ten heads.

"Fire!" shrieked the Troll.

"Fire yourself!" said Minnikin.

"Can you fight?" roared the Troll.

"If not, I can learn," said Minnikin.

So the Troll struck at him with his iron club – which was still bigger than that which the first Troll had had – so that the earth flew ten yards up in the air.

"Fie!" said Minnikin. "That was not much of a blow. Now you shall see one of my blows."

Then he grasped his sword and struck at the Troll, so that all his ten heads danced away over the sands.

And again the King's daughter said to him, "Sleep a while on my lap," and while Minnikin lay there she drew some silver raiment over him.

As soon as Ritter Red saw that there was no longer any danger afoot, he crept down from the tree and threatened the Princess, until at last she was again forced to promise to say that it was he who had rescued her; after which he took the tongue and the lungs of the Troll and put them in his pocket-handkerchief, and then he conducted the Princess back to the palace. There was joy and gladness in the palace, as may be imagined, and the King did not know how to show enough honour and respect to Ritter Red.

Minnikin, however, took home with him an armful of gold and silver hoops from the Troll's ship. When he came back to the King's palace the kitchen-maid clapped her hands and wondered where he could have got all that gold and silver; but Minnikin answered that he had been home for a short time, and that it was only the hoops which had fallen off some pails, and that he had brought them away for the kitchen-maid.

When the third Thursday evening came, everything happened exactly as it had happened on the two former occasions. Everything in the King's palace was hung with black, and everyone was sorrowful and distressed; but Ritter Red said that he did not think that they had much reason to be afraid – he had delivered the King's daughter from two Trolls, so he could easily deliver her from the third as well.

He led her down to the strand, but when the time drew near for the Troll to come, he climbed up into the tree again and hid himself.

The Princess wept and entreated him to stay, but all to no purpose. He stuck to his old speech, "It is better that one life should be lost than two."

This evening also, Minnikin begged for leave to go down to the seashore.

"Oh, what can you do there?" answered the kitchen-maid.

However, he begged until at last he got leave to go, but he was forced to promise that he would be back again in the kitchen when the roast had to be turned.

Almost immediately after he had got down to the seashore the Troll came with a great whizzing and whirring, and he was much, much bigger than either of the two former ones, and he had fifteen heads.

"Fire!" roared the Troll.

"Fire yourself!" said Minnikin.

"Can you fight?" screamed the Troll.

"If not, I can learn," said Minnikin.

"I will teach you," yelled the Troll, and struck at him with his iron club so that the earth flew up fifteen yards high into the air.

"Fie!" said Minnikin. "That was not much of a blow. Now I will let you see one of my blows."

So saying he grasped his sword, and cut at the Troll in such a way that all his fifteen heads danced away over the sands.

Then the Princess was delivered, and she thanked Minnikin and blessed him for saving her.

"Sleep a while now on my lap," said she, and while he lay there she put a garment of brass upon him.

"But now, how shall we have it made known that it was you who saved me?" said the King's daughter.

"That I will tell you," answered Minnikin. "When Ritter Red has taken you home again, and given out that it was he who rescued you, he will, as you know, have you to wife, and half the kingdom. But when they ask you on your wedding-day whom you will have to be your cup-bearer, you must say, 'I will have the ragged boy who is in the kitchen, and carries wood and water for the kitchen-maid;' and when I am filling your cups for you, I will spill a drop upon his plate but none upon yours, and then he will be angry and strike me, and this will take place thrice. But the third time you must say, 'Shame on you thus to smite the beloved of mine heart. It is he who delivered me from the Troll, and he is the one whom I will have.'"

Then Minnikin ran back to the King's palace as he had done before, but first he went on board the Troll's ship and took a great quantity of gold and silver and other precious things, and out of these he once more gave to the kitchen-maid a whole armful of gold and silver hoops.

No sooner did Ritter Red see that all danger was over than he crept down from the tree, and threatened the King's daughter till he made her promise to say that he had rescued her. Then he conducted her back to the King's palace, and if honour enough had not been done him before it was certainly done now, for the King had no other thought than how to make much of the man who had saved his daughter from the three Trolls; and it was settled then that Ritter Red should marry her, and receive half the kingdom.

On the wedding-day, however, the Princess begged that she might have the little boy who was in the kitchen, and carried wood and water for the kitchen-maid, to fill the wine-cups at the wedding feast.

"Oh, what can you want with that dirty, ragged boy, in here?" said Ritter Red, but the Princess said that she insisted on having him as cup-bearer and would have no one else; and at last she got leave, and then everything was done as had been agreed on between the Princess and Minnikin. He spilt a drop on Ritter Red's plate but none upon hers, and each time that he did it Ritter Red fell into a rage and struck him. At the first blow all the ragged garments which he had worn in the kitchen fell from off Minnikin, at the second blow the brass garments fell off, and at the third the silver raiment, and there he stood in the golden raiment, which was so bright and splendid that light flashed from it.

Then the King's daughter said: "Shame on you thus to smite the beloved of my heart. It is he who delivered me from the Troll, and he is the one whom I will have."

Ritter Red swore that he was the man who had saved her, but the King said: "He who delivered my daughter must have some token in proof of it."

So Ritter Red ran off at once for his handkerchief with the lungs and tongue, and Minnikin went and brought all the gold and silver and precious things which he had taken out of the Trolls' ships; and they each of them laid these tokens before the King.

"He who has such precious things in gold and silver and diamonds," said the King, "must be the one who killed the Troll, for such things are not to be had anywhere else." So Ritter Red was thrown into the snake-pit, and Minnikin was to have the Princess, and half the kingdom.

One day the King went out walking with Minnikin, and Minnikin asked him if he had never had any other children.

"Yes," said the King, "I had another daughter, but the Troll carried her away because there was no one who could deliver her. You are going to have one daughter of mine, but if you can set free the other, who has been taken by the Troll, you shall willingly have her too, and the other half of the kingdom as well."

"I may as well make the attempt," said Minnikin, "but I must have an iron rope which is five hundred ells long, and then I must have five hundred men with me, and provisions for five weeks, for I have a long voyage before me."

So the King said he should have these things, but the King was afraid that he had no ship large enough to carry them all.

"But I have a ship of my own," said Minnikin, and he took the one which the old woman had given him out of his pocket. The King laughed at him and thought that it was only one of his jokes, but Minnikin begged him just to give him what he had asked for, and then he should see something. Then all that Minnikin had asked for was brought; and first he ordered them to lay the cable in the ship, but there was no one who was able to lift it, and there was only room for one or two men at a time in the little bit of a ship. Then Minnikin himself took hold of the cable, and laid one or two links of it into the ship, and as he threw the links into it the ship grew bigger and bigger, and at last it was so large that the cable, and the five hundred men, and provisions, and Minnikin himself, had room enough.

"Now go over fresh water and salt water, over hill and dale, and do not stop until thou comest to where the King's daughter is," said Minnikin to the ship, and off it went in a moment over land and water till the wind whistled and moaned all round about it.

When they had sailed thus a long, long way, the ship stopped short in the middle of the sea.

"Ah, now we have got there," said Minnikin, "but how we are to get back again is a very different thing."

Then he took the cable and tied one end of it round his body. "Now I must go to the bottom," he said, "but when I give a good jerk to the cable and want to come up again, you must all pull like one man, or there will be an end of all life both for you and for me." So saying he sprang into the water, and yellow bubbles rose up all around him. He sank lower and lower, and at last he came to the bottom. There he saw a large hill with a door in it, and in he went. When he had got inside he found the other Princess sitting sewing, but when she saw Minnikin she clapped her hands.

"Ah, heaven be praised!" she cried, "I have not seen a Christian man since I came here."

"I have come for you," said Minnikin.

"Alas! you will not be able to get me," said the King's daughter. "It is no use even to think of that; if the Troll catches sight of you he will take your life."

"You had better tell me about him," said Minnikin. "Where is he gone? It would be amusing to see him."

So the King's daughter told Minnikin that the Troll was out trying to get hold of someone who could brew a hundred lasts of malt at one brewing, for there was to be a feast at the Troll's, at which less than that would not be drunk.

"I can do that," said Minnikin.

"Ah! if only the Troll were not so quick-tempered I might have told him that," answered the Princess, "but he is so ill-natured that he will tear you to pieces, I fear, as soon as he comes in. But I will try to find some way of doing it. Can you hide yourself here in the cupboard? and then we will see what happens."

Minnikin did this, and almost before he had crept into the cupboard and hidden himself, came the Troll.

"Huf! What a smell of Christian man's blood!" said the Troll.

"Yes, a bird flew over the roof with a Christian man's bone in his bill, and let it fall down our chimney," answered the Princess. "I made haste enough to get it away again, but it must be that which smells so, notwithstanding."

"Yes, it must be that," said the Troll.

Then the Princess asked if he had got hold of anyone who could brew a hundred lasts of malt at one brewing.

"No, there is no one who can do it," said the Troll.

"A short time since there was a man here who said he could do it," said the King's daughter.

"How clever you always are!" said the Troll. "How could you let him go away? You must have known that I was just wanting a man of that kind."

"Well, but I didn't let him go, after all," said the Princess; "but father is so quick-tempered, so I hid him in the cupboard, but if father has not found anyone then the man is still here."

"Let him come in," said the Troll.

When Minnikin came, the Troll asked if it were true that he could brew a hundred lasts of malt at one brewing.

"Yes," said Minnikin, "it is."

"It is well then that I have lighted on thee," said the Troll. "Fall to work this very minute, but Heaven help thee if thou dost not brew the ale strong."

"Oh, it shall taste well," said Minnikin, and at once set himself to work to brew.

"But I must have more trolls to help to carry what is wanted," said Minnikin; "these that I have are good for nothing."

So he got more and so many that there was a swarm of them, and then the brewing went on. When the sweet-wort was ready they were all, as a matter of course, anxious to taste it, first the Troll himself and then the others; but Minnikin had brewed the wort so strong that they all fell down dead like so many flies as soon as they had drunk any of it. At last there was no one left but one wretched old hag who was lying behind the stove.

"Oh, poor old creature!" said Minnikin, "you shall have a taste of the wort too like the rest." So he went away and scooped up a little from the bottom of the brewing vat in a milk pan, and gave it to her, and then he was quit of the whole of them.

While Minnikin was now standing there looking about him, he cast his eye on a large chest. This he took and filled it with gold and silver, and then he tied the cable round himself and the Princess and the chest, and tugged at the rope with all his might, whereupon his men drew them up safe and sound.

As soon as Minnikin had got safely on his ship again, he said: "Now go over salt water and fresh water, over hill and dale, and do not stop until thou comest unto the King's palace." And in a moment the ship went off so fast that the yellow foam rose up all round about it.

When those who were in the King's palace saw the ship, they lost no time in going to meet him with song and music, and thus they marched up towards Minnikin with great rejoicings; but the gladdest of all was the King, for now he had got his other daughter back again.

But now Minnikin was not happy, for both the Princesses wanted to have him, and he wanted to have none other than the one whom he had first saved, and she was the younger. For this cause he was continually walking backwards and forwards, thinking how he could contrive to get her, and yet do nothing that was unkind to her sister. One day when he was walking about and thinking of this, it came into his mind that if he only had his brother, King Pippin, with him, who was so like himself that no one could distinguish the one from the other, he could let him have the elder Princess and half the kingdom; as for himself, he thought, the other half was quite enough. As soon as this thought occurred to him he went outside the palace and called for King Pippin, but no one came. So he called a second time, and a little louder, but no! still no one came. So Minnikin called for the third time, and with all his might, and there stood his brother by his side.

"I told you that you were not to call me unless you were in the utmost need," he said to Minnikin, "and there is not even so much as a midge here who can do you any harm!" and with that he gave Minnikin such a blow that he rolled over on the grass.

"Shame on you to strike me!" said Minnikin. "First have I won one Princess and half the kingdom, and then the other Princess and the other half of the kingdom; and now, when I was just thinking that I would give you one of the Princesses and one of the halves of the kingdom, do you think you have any reason to give me such a blow?"

When King Pippin heard that he begged his brother's pardon, and they were reconciled at once and became good friends.

"Now, as you know," said Minnikin, "we are so like each other that no one can tell one of us from the other; so just change clothes with me and go up to the palace, and then the Princesses will think that I am coming in, and the one who kisses you first shall be yours, and I will have the other." For he knew that the elder Princess was the stronger, so he could very well guess how things would go.

King Pippin at once agreed to this. He changed clothes with his brother, and went into the palace. When he entered the Princess's apartments they believed that he was Minnikin, and both of them ran up to him at once; but the elder, who was bigger and stronger, pushed her sister aside, and threw her arms round King Pippin's neck and kissed him; so he got her to wife, and Minnikin the younger sister. It will be easy to understand that two weddings took place, and they were so magnificent that they were heard of and talked about all over seven kingdoms.

The Giant Who Had No Heart in His Body

(Norwegian)

ONCE ON A TIME there was a king who had seven sons, and he loved them so much that he could never bear to be without them all at once, but one must always be with him. Now, when they were grown up, six were to set off to woo, but as for the youngest, his father kept him at home, and the others were to bring back a princess for him to the palace. So the king gave the six the finest clothes you ever set eyes on, so fine that the light gleamed from them a long way off, and each had his horse, which cost many, many hundred dollars, and so they set off. Now, when they had been to many palaces, and seen many princesses, at last they came to a king who had six daughters; such lovely king's daughters they had never seen, and so they fell to wooing them, each one, and when they had got them for sweethearts, they set off home again, but they quite forgot that they were to bring back with them a sweetheart for Boots, their brother, who stayed at home, for they were over head and ears in love with their own sweethearts.

But when they had gone a good bit on their way, they passed close by a steep hillside, like a wall, where the giant's house was, and there the giant came out, and set his eyes upon them, and turned them all into stone, princes and princesses and all. Now the king waited and waited for his six sons, but the more he waited, the longer they stayed away; so he fell into great trouble, and said he should never know what it was to be glad again.

"And if I had not you left", he said to Boots, "I would live no longer, so full of sorrow am I for the loss of your brothers."

"Well, but now I've been thinking to ask your leave to set out and find them again; that's what I'm thinking of", said Boots.

"Nay, nay!" said his father; "that leave you shall never get, for then you would stay away too."

But Boots had set his heart upon it; go he would; and he begged and prayed so long that the king was forced to let him go. Now, you must know the king had no other horse to give Boots but an old broken-down jade, for his six other sons and their train had carried off all his horses; but Boots did not care a pin for that, he sprang up on his sorry-old-steed.

"Farewell, father", said he; "I'll come back, never fear, and like enough I shall bring my six brothers back with me"; and with that he rode off.

So, when he had ridden a while, he came to a Raven, which lay in the road and flapped its wings, and was not able to get out of the way, it was so starved.

"Oh, dear friend", said the Raven, "give me a little food, and I'll help you again at your utmost need."

"I haven't much food", said the Prince, "and I don't see how you'll ever be able to help me much; but still I can spare you a little. I see you want it."

So he gave the raven some of the food he had brought with him.

Now, when he had gone a bit further, he came to a brook, and in the brook lay a great Salmon, which had got upon a dry place and dashed itself about, and could not get into the water again.

"Oh, dear friend", said the Salmon to the Prince; "shove me out into the water again, and I'll help you again at your utmost need."

"Well!" said the Prince, "the help you'll give me will not be great, I daresay, but it's a pity you should lie there and choke"; and with that he shot the fish out into the stream again.

After that he went a long, long way, and there met him a Wolf, which was so famished that it lay and crawled along the road on its belly.

"Dear friend, do let me have your horse", said the Wolf; "I'm so hungry the wind whistles through my ribs; I've had nothing to eat these two years."

"No", said Boots, "this will never do; "first I came to a raven, and I was forced to give him my food; next I came to a salmon, and him I had to help into the water again; and now you will have my horse. It can't be done, that it can't, for then I should have nothing to ride on."

"Nay, dear friend, but you can help me", said Graylegs the wolf; "you can ride upon my back, and I'll help you again in your utmost need."

"Well! the help I shall get from you will not be great, I'll be bound", said the Prince; "but you may take my horse, since you are in such need."

So when the wolf had eaten the horse, Boots took the bit and put it into the wolf's jaw, and laid the saddle on his back; and now the wolf was so strong, after what he had got inside, that he set off with the Prince like nothing. So fast he had never ridden before.

"When we have gone a bit farther", said Graylegs; "I'll show you the Giant's house."

So after a while they came to it.

"See, here is the Giant's house", said the Wolf; "and see, here are your six brothers, whom the Giant has turned into stone; and see here are their six brides, and away yonder is the door, and in at that door you must go."

"Nay, but I daren't go in", said the Prince; "he'll take my life."

"No! no!" said the Wolf; "when you get in you'll find a Princess, and she'll tell you what to do to make an end of the Giant. Only mind and do as she bids you."

Well! Boots went in, but, truth to say, he was very much afraid. When he came in the Giant was away, but in one of the rooms sat the Princess, just as the wolf had said, and so lovely a princess Boots had never yet set eyes on.

"Oh! heaven help you! whence have you come?" said the Princess, as she saw him; "it will surely be your death. No one can make an end of the Giant who lives here, for he has no heart in his body."

"Well! well!" said Boots; "but now that I am here, I may as well try what I can do with him; and I will see if I can't free my brothers, who are standing turned to stone out of doors; and you, too, I will try to save, that I will."

"Well, if you must, you must", said the Princess; "and so let us see if we can't hit on a plan. Just creep under the bed yonder, and mind and listen to what he and I talk about. But, pray, do lie as still as a mouse."

So he crept under the bed, and he had scarce got well underneath it, before the Giant came.

"Ha!" roared the Giant, "what a smell of Christian blood there is in the house!"

"Yes, I know there is", said the Princess, "for there came a magpie flying with a man's bone, and let it fall down the chimney. I made all the haste I could to get it out, but all one can do, the smell doesn't go off so soon."

So the Giant said no more about it, and when night came, they went to bed. After they had lain awhile, the Princess said:

"There is one thing I'd be so glad to ask you about, if I only dared."

"What thing is that?" asked the Giant.

"Only where it is you keep your heart, since you don't carry it about you", said the Princess.

"Ah! that's a thing you've no business to ask about; but if you must know, it lies under the door-sill", said the Giant.

"Ho! ho!" said Boots to himself under the bed, "then we'll soon see if we can't find it."

Next morning the Giant got up cruelly early, and strode off to the wood; but he was hardly out of the house before Boots and the Princess set to work to look under the door-sill for his heart; but the more they dug, and the more they hunted, the more they couldn't find it.

"He has baulked us this time", said the Princess, "but we'll try him once more."

So she picked all the prettiest flowers she could find, and strewed them over the door-sill, which they had laid in its right place again; and when the time came for the Giant to come home again, Boots crept under the bed. Just as he was well under, back came the Giant.

Snuff – snuff, went the Giant's nose. "My eyes and limbs, what a smell of Christian blood there is in here", said he.

"I know there is", said the Princess, "for there came a magpie flying with a man's bone in his bill, and let it fall down the chimney. I made as much haste as I could to get it out, but I daresay it's that you smell."

So the Giant held his peace, and said no more about it. A little while after, he asked who it was that had strewed flowers about the door-sill.

"Oh, I, of course", said the Princess.

"And, pray, what's the meaning of all this?" said the Giant.

"Ah!" said the Princess, "I'm so fond of you that I couldn't help strewing them, when I knew that your heart lay under there."

"You don't say so", said the Giant; "but after all it doesn't lie there at all."

So when they went to bed again in the evening, the Princess asked the Giant again where his heart was, for she said she would so like to know.

"Well", said the Giant, "if you must know, it lies away yonder in the cupboard against the wall."

"So, so!" thought Boots and the Princess; "then we'll soon try to find it."

Next morning the Giant was away early, and strode off to the wood, and so soon as he was gone Boots and the Princess were in the cupboard hunting for his heart, but the more they sought for it, the less they found it.

"Well", said the Princess, "we'll just try him once more."

So she decked out the cupboard with flowers and garlands, and when the time came for the Giant to come home, Boots crept under the bed again.

Then back came the Giant.

Snuff-snuff! "My eyes and limbs, what a smell of Christian blood there is in here!"

"I know there is", said the Princess; "for a little while since there came a magpie flying with a man's bone in his bill, and let it fall down the chimney. I made all the haste I could to get it out of the house again; but after all my pains, I daresay it's that you smell."

When the Giant heard that, he said no more about it; but a little while after, he saw how the cupboard was all decked about with flowers and garlands; so he asked who it was that had done that? Who could it be but the Princess.

"And, pray, what's the meaning of all this tom-foolery?" asked the Giant.

"Oh, I'm so fond of you, I couldn't help doing it when I knew that your heart lay there", said the Princess.

"How can you be so silly as to believe any such thing?" said the Giant.

"Oh yes; how can I help believing it, when you say it", said the Princess.

"You're a goose", said the Giant; "where my heart is, you will never come."

"Well", said the Princess"; but for all that, 'twould be such a pleasure to know where it really lies."

Then the poor Giant could hold out no longer, but was forced to say:

"Far, far away in a lake lies an island; on that island stands a church; in that church is a well; in that well swims a duck; in that duck there is an egg, and in that egg there lies my heart, – you darling!"

In the morning early, while it was still grey dawn, the Giant strode off to the wood.

"Yes! now I must set off too", said Boots; "if I only knew how to find the way." He took a long, long farewell of the Princess, and when he got out of the Giant's door, there stood the Wolf waiting for him. So Boots told him all that had happened inside the house, and said now he wished to ride to the well in the church, if he only knew the way. So the Wolf bade him jump on his back, he'd soon find the way; and away they went, till the wind whistled after them, over hedge and field, over hill and dale. After they had travelled many, many days, they came at last to the lake. Then the Prince did not know how to get over it, but the Wolf bade him only not be afraid, but stick on, and so he jumped into the lake with the Prince on his back, and swam over to the island. So they came to the church; but the church keys hung high, high up on the top of the tower, and at first the Prince did not know how to get them down.

"You must call on the raven", said the Wolf.

So the Prince called on the raven, and in a trice the raven came, and flew up and fetched the keys, and so the Prince got into the church. But when he came to the well, there lay the duck, and swam about backwards and forwards, just as the Giant had said. So the Prince stood and coaxed it and coaxed it, till it came to him, and he grasped it in his hand; but just as he lifted it up from the water the duck dropped the egg into the well, and then Boots was beside himself to know how to get it out again.

"Well, now you must call on the salmon to be sure", said the Wolf; and the king's son called on the salmon, and the salmon came and fetched up the egg from the bottom of the well.

Then the Wolf told him to squeeze the egg, and as soon as ever he squeezed it the Giant screamed out.

"Squeeze it again", said the Wolf; and when the Prince did so, the Giant screamed still more piteously, and begged and prayed so prettily to be spared, saying he would do all that the Prince wished if he would only not squeeze his heart in two.

"Tell him, if he will restore to life again your six brothers and their brides, whom he has turned to stone, you will spare his life", said the Wolf. Yes, the Giant was ready to do that, and he turned the six brothers into king's sons again, and their brides into king's daughters.

"Now, squeeze the egg in two", said the Wolf. So Boots squeezed the egg to pieces, and the Giant burst at once.

Now, when he had made an end of the Giant, Boots rode back again on the wolf to the Giant's house, and there stood all his six brothers alive and merry, with their brides. Then Boots went into the hillside after his bride, and so they all set off home again to their father's house. And you may fancy how glad the old king was when he saw all his seven sons come back, each with his bride – "But the loveliest bride of all is the bride of Boots, after all", said the king, "and he shall sit uppermost at the table, with her by his side."

So he sent out, and called a great wedding-feast, and the mirth was both loud and long, and if they have not done feasting, why, they are still at it.

Finn, the Giant, and the Minster of Lund

(Swedish)

THERE STANDS IN THE UNIVERSITY TOWN OF SCHONEN, the town of Lund, the seat of the first archbishopric in all Scandinavia, a stately Romanic minster, with a large, handsome crypt beneath the choir. The opinion is universal that the minster will never be altogether finished, but that something will always be lacking about the structure. The reason is said to be as follows:

When St. Lawrence came to Lund to preach the Gospel, he wanted to build a church; but did not know how he was to obtain the means to do so.

While he was cudgelling his brains about it, a giant came to him and offered to build the church on condition that St. Lawrence tell him his name before the church was completed. But should St. Lawrence be unable to do so, the giant was to receive either the sun, the moon or St. Lawrence's eyes. The saint agreed to his proposal.

The building of the church made rapid progress, and ere long it was nearly finished. St. Lawrence thought ruefully about his prospects, for he did not know the giant's name; yet at the same time he did not relish losing his eyes. And it happened that while he was walking without the town, much concerned about the outcome of the affair, he grew weary, and sat down on a hill to rest. As he sat there he heard a child crying within the hill, and a woman's voice began to sing:

"Sleep, sleep, my baby dear,
Tomorrow your father, Finn, will be here;
Then sun and moon you shall have from the skies
To play with, or else St. Lawrence's eyes."

When St. Lawrence heard that he was happy; for now he knew the giant's name. He ran back quickly to town, and went to the church. There sat the giant on the roof, just about to set the last stone in place, when at that very moment the saint called out:

"Finn, Finn,
Take care how you put the stone in!"

Then the giant flung the stone from him, full of rage, said that the church should never be finished, and with that he disappeared. Since then something has always been missing from the church.

Others say that the giant and his wife rushed down into the crypt in their rage, and each seizing a column were about to tear down the church, when they were turned into stone, and may be seen to this day standing beside the columns they had grasped

Knös

(Swedish)

ONCE UPON A TIME there was a poor widow, who found an egg under a pile of brush as she was gathering kindlings in the forest. She took it and placed it under a goose, and when the goose had hatched it, a little boy slipped out of the shell. The widow had him baptized Knös, and such a lad was a rarity; for when no more than five years old he was grown, and taller than the tallest man. And he ate in proportion, for he would swallow a whole batch of bread at a single sitting, and at last the poor widow had to go to the commissioners for the relief of the poor in order to get food for him. But the town authorities said she must apprentice the boy at a trade, for he was big enough and strong enough to earn his own keep.

So Knös was apprenticed to a smith for three years. For his pay he asked a suit of clothes and a sword each year: a sword of five hundredweights the first year, one of ten hundredweights the second year, and one of fifteen hundredweights the third year. But after he had been in the smithy only a few days, the smith was glad to give him all three suits and all three swords at once; for he smashed all his iron and steel to bits.

Knös received his suits and swords, went to a knight's estate, and hired himself out as a serving-man. Once he was told to go to the forest to gather firewood with the rest of the men, but sat at the table eating long after the others had driven off and when he had at last satisfied his hunger and was ready to start, he saw the two young oxen he was to drive waiting for him. But he let them stand and went into the forest, seized the two largest trees growing there, tore them out by the roots, took one tree under each arm, and carried them back to the estate. And he got there long before the rest, for they had to chop down the trees, saw them up and load them on the carts.

On the following day Knös had to thresh. First he hunted up the largest stone he could find, and rolled it around on the grain, so that all the corn was loosened from the ears. Then he had to separate the grain from the chaff. So he made a hole in each side of the roof of the barn, and stood outside the barn and blew, and the chaff and straw flew out into the yard, and the corn remained lying in a heap on the floor. His master happened to come along, laid a ladder against the barn, climbed up and looked down into one of the holes. But Knös was still blowing, and the wind caught his master, and he fell down and was nearly killed on the stone pavement of the court.

"He's a dangerous fellow," thought his master. It would be a good thing to be rid of him, otherwise he might do away with all of them; and besides, he ate so that it was all one could do to keep him fed. So he called Knös in, and paid him his wages for the full year, on condition that he leave. Knös agreed, but said he must first be decently provisioned for his journey.

So he was allowed to go into the storehouse himself, and there he hoisted a flitch of bacon on each shoulder, slid a batch of bread under each arm, and took leave. But his master loosed the vicious bull on him. Knös, however, grasped him by the horns, and flung him over his shoulder, and thus he went off. Then he came to a thicket where he slaughtered the bull, roasted him and ate him together with a batch of bread. And when he had done this he had about taken the edge off his hunger.

Then he came to the king's court, where great sorrow reigned because, once upon a time, when the king was sailing out at sea, a sea troll had called up a terrible tempest, so that the ship was about to sink. In order to escape with his life, the king had to promise the sea troll to give him whatever first came his way when he reached shore. The king thought his hunting dog would be the first to come running to meet him, as usual; but instead his three young daughters came rowing out to meet him in a boat. This filled the king with grief, and he vowed that whoever delivered his daughters should have one of them for a bride, whichever one he might choose. But the only man who seemed to want to earn the reward was a tailor, named Red Peter.

Knös was given a place at the king's court, and his duty was to help the cook. But he asked to be let off on the day the troll was to come and carry away the oldest princess, and they were glad to let him go; for when he had to rinse the dishes he broke the king's vessels of gold and silver; and when he was told to bring firewood, he brought in a whole wagon-load at once, so that the doors flew from their hinges.

The princess stood on the seashore and wept and wrung her hands; for she could see what she had to expect. Nor did she have much confidence in Red Peter, who sat on a willow-stump, with a rusty old sabre in his hand. Then Knös came and tried to comfort the princess as well as he knew how, and asked her whether she would comb his hair. Yes, he might lay his head in her lap, and she combed his hair. Suddenly there was a dreadful roaring out at sea. It was the troll who was coming along, and he had five heads. Red Peter was so frightened that he rolled off his willow-stump. "Knös, is that you?" cried the troll. "Yes," said Knös. "Haul me up on the shore!" said the troll. "Pay out the cable!" said Knös. Then he hauled the troll ashore; but he had his sword of five hundredweights at his side, and with it he chopped off all five of the troll's heads, and the princess was free. But when Knös had gone off, Red Peter put his sabre to the breast of the princess, and told her he would kill her unless she said he was her deliverer.

Then came the turn of the second princess. Once more Red Peter sat on the willow-stump with his rusty sabre, and Knös asking to be let off for the day, went to the seashore and begged the princess to comb his hair, which she did. Then along came the troll, and this time he had ten heads. "Knös, is that you?" asked the troll. "Yes," said Knös. "Haul me ashore!" said the troll. "Pay out the cable!" said Knös. And this time Knös had his sword of ten hundredweights at his side, and he cut off all ten of the troll's heads. And so the second princess was freed. But Red Peter held his sabre at the princess' breast, and forced her to say that he had delivered her.

Now it was the turn of the youngest princess. When it was time for the troll to come, Red Peter was sitting on his willow-stump, and Knös came and begged the princess to comb his hair, and she did so. This time the troll had fifteen heads.

"Knös, is that you?" asked the troll. "Yes," said Knös. "Haul me ashore!" said the troll. "Pay out the cable," said Knös. Knös had his sword of fifteen hundredweights at his side, and with it he cut off all the troll's heads. But the fifteen hundredweights were half-an-ounce short, and the heads grew on again, and the troll took the princess, and carried her off with him.

One day as Knös was going along, he met a man carrying a church on his back. "You are a strong man, you are!" said Knös. "No, I am not strong," said he, "but Knös at the king's court, he is strong; for he can take steel and iron, and weld them together with his hands as though they were clay." "Well, I'm the man of whom you are speaking," said Knös, "come, let us travel together." And so they wandered on.

Then they met a man who carried a mountain of stone on his back. "You are strong, you are!" said Knös. "No, I'm not strong," said the man with the mountain of stone, "but Knös at the king's court, he is strong; for he can weld together steel and iron with his hands as though they were clay."

"Well, I am that Knös, come let us travel together," said Knös. So all three of them travelled along together. Knös took them for a sea-trip; but I think they had to leave the church and the hill of stone ashore. While they were sailing they grew thirsty, and lay alongside an island, and there on the island stood a castle, to which they decided to go and ask for a drink. Now this was the very castle in which the troll lived.

First the man with the church went, and when he entered the castle, there sat the troll with the princess on his lap, and she was very sad. He asked for something to drink. "Help yourself, the goblet is on the table!" said the troll. But he got nothing to drink, for though he could move the goblet from its place, he could not raise it.

Then the man with the hill of stone went into the castle and asked for a drink. "Help yourself, the goblet is on the table!" said the troll. And he got nothing to drink either, for though he could move the goblet from its place, he could not raise it.

Then Knös himself went into the castle, and the princess was full of joy and leaped down from the troll's lap when she saw it was he. Knös asked for a drink. "Help yourself," said the troll, "the goblet is on the table!" And Knös took the goblet and emptied it at a single draught. Then he hit the troll across the head with the goblet, so that he rolled from the chair and died.

Knös took the princess back to the royal palace, and O, how happy everyone was! The other princesses recognized Knös again, for they had woven silk ribbons into his hair when they had combed it; but he could only marry one of the princesses, whichever one he preferred, so he chose the youngest. And when the king died, Knös inherited the kingdom.

As for Red Peter, he had to go into the nail-barrel.

And now you know all that I know.

The Blue Belt

(Norwegian)

ONCE ON A TIME there was an old beggar-woman, who had gone out to beg. She had a little lad with her, and when she had got her bag full she struck across the hills towards her own home. So when they had gone a bit up the hillside, they came upon a little blue belt which lay where two paths met, and the lad asked his mother's leave to pick it up.

"No," said she, "maybe there's witchcraft in it"; and so with threats she forced him to follow her. But when they had gone a bit further, the lad said he must turn aside a moment out of the road; and meanwhile his mother sat down on a tree-stump. But the lad was a long time gone, for as soon as he got so far into the wood that the old dame could not see him, he ran off to where the belt lay, took it up, tied it round his waist, and lo! he felt as strong as if he could lift the whole hill. When he got back, the old dame was in a great rage, and wanted to know what he had been doing all that while. "You don't care how much time you waste, and yet you know the night is drawing on, and we must cross the hill before it is dark!" So on they tramped; but when they had got about halfway, the old dame grew weary, and said she must rest under a bush.

"Dear mother," said the lad, "mayn't I just go up to the top of this high crag while you rest, and try if I can't see some sign of folk hereabouts?"

Yes! He might do that; so when he had got to the top he saw a light shining from the north. So he ran down and told his mother.

"We must get on, mother; we are near a house, for I see a bright light shining quite close to us in the north." Then she rose and shouldered her bag, and set off to see; but they hadn't gone far, before there stood a steep spur of the hill, right across their path.

"Just as I thought!" said the old dame, "now we can't go a step farther; a pretty bed we shall have here!"

But the lad took the bag under one arm, and his mother under the other, and ran straight up the steep crag with them.

"Now, don't you see? Don't you see that we are close to a house? Don't you see that bright light?"

But the old dame said those were no Christian folk, but Trolls, for she was at home in all that forest far and near, and knew there was not a living soul in it, until you were well over the ridge and had come down on the other side. But they went on, and in a little while they came to a great house which was all painted red.

"What's the good?" said the old dame. "We daren't go in, for here the Trolls live."

"Don't say so; we must go in. There must be men where the lights shine so," said the lad. So in he went, and his mother after him, but he had scarce opened the door before she swooned away, for there she saw a great stout man, at least twenty feet high, sitting on the bench.

"Good evening, grandfather!" said the lad.

"Well, here I've sat three hundred years," said the man who sat on the bench, "and no one has ever come and called me grandfather before." Then the lad sat down by the man's side, and began to talk to him as if they had been old friends.

"But what's come over your mother?" said the man, after they had chatted a while. "I think she swooned away; you had better look after her."

So the lad went and took hold of the old dame, and dragged her up the hall along the floor. That brought her to herself, and she kicked and scratched, and flung herself about, and at last sat down upon a heap of firewood in the corner; but she was so frightened that she scarce dared to look one in the face.

After a while, the lad asked if they could spend the night there.

"Yes, to be sure," said the man.

So they went on talking again, but the lad soon got hungry, and wanted to know if they could get food as well as lodging.

"Of course," said the man, "that might be got too." And after he had sat a while longer, he rose up and threw six loads of dry pitch-pine on the fire. This made the old hag still more afraid.

"Oh! now he's going to roast us alive," she said, in the corner where she sat.

And when the wood had burned down to glowing embers, up got the man and strode out of his house.

"Heaven bless and help us! What a stout heart you have got!" said the old dame. "Don't you see we have got amongst Trolls?"

"Stuff and nonsense!" said the lad; "no harm if we have."

In a little while, back came the man with an ox so fat and big, the lad had never seen its like, and he gave it one blow with his fist under the ear, and down it fell dead on the floor. When that was done, he took it up by all the four legs and laid it on the glowing embers, and turned it and twisted it about till it was burnt brown outside. After that, he went to a cupboard and took out a great silver dish, and laid the ox on it; and the dish was so big that none of the ox hung over on any side. This he put on the table, and then he went down into the cellar and fetched a cask of wine, knocked out the head, and put the cask on the table, together with two knives, which were each six feet long. When this was done he bade them go and sit down to supper and eat. So they went, the lad first and the old dame after, but she began to whimper and wail, and to wonder how she should ever use such knives. But her son seized one, and began to cut slices out of the thigh of the ox, which he placed before his mother. And when they had eaten a bit, he took up the cask with both hands, and lifted it down to the floor; then he told his mother to come and drink, but it was still so high she couldn't reach up to it; so he caught her up, and held her up to the edge of the cask while she drank; as for himself, he clambered up and hung down like a cat inside the cask while he drank. So when he had quenched his thirst, he took up the cask and put it back on the table, and thanked the man for the good meal, and told his mother to come and thank him too, and, afeared though she was, she dared do nothing else but thank the man. Then the lad sat down again alongside the man and began to gossip, and after they had sat a while the man said:

"Well! I must just go and get a bit of supper too"; and so he went to the table and ate up the whole ox – hoofs, and horns, and all – and drained the cask to the last drop, and then went back and sat on the bench.

"As for beds," he said, "I don't know what's to be done. I've only got one bed and a cradle; but we could get on pretty well if you would sleep in the cradle, and then your mother might lie in the bed yonder."

"Thank you kindly, that'll do nicely," said the lad; and with that he pulled off his clothes and lay down in the cradle; but, to tell you the truth, it was quite as big as a four-poster. As for the old dame, she had to follow the man who showed her to bed, though she was out of her wits for fear.

"Well!" thought the lad to himself, "'twill never do to go to sleep yet. I'd best lie awake and listen how things go as the night wears on."

So, after a while, the man began to talk to the old dame, and at last he said:

"We two might live here so happily together, could we only be rid of this son of yours."

"But do you know how to settle him? Is that what you're thinking of?" said she.

"Nothing easier," said he; at any rate he would try. He would just say he wished the old dame would stay and keep house for him a day or two, and then he would take the lad out with him up the hill to quarry cornerstones, and roll down a great rock on him. All this the lad lay and listened to.

Next day the Troll – for it was a Troll as clear as day – asked if the old dame would stay and keep house for him a few days; and as the day went on he took a great iron crowbar, and asked the lad if he had a mind to go with him up the hill and quarry a few cornerstones. With all his heart, he said, and went with him; and so, after they had split a few stones, the Troll wanted him to go down below and look after cracks in the rock; and while he was doing this the Troll worked away, and wearied himself with his crowbar till he moved a whole crag out of its bed, which came rolling right down on the place where the lad was; but he held it up till he could get on one side, and then let it roll on.

"Oh!" said the lad to the Troll, "now I see what you mean to do with me. You want to crush me to death; so just go down yourself and look after the cracks and rifts in the rock, and I'll stand up above."

The Troll did not dare to do otherwise than the lad bade him, and the end of it was that the lad rolled down a great rock, which fell upon the Troll and broke one of his thighs.

"Well! you are in a sad plight," said the lad, as he strode down, lifted up the rock, and set the man free. After that he had to put him on his back and carry him home; so he ran with him as fast as a horse, and shook him so that the Troll screamed and screeched as if a knife were run into him. And when he got home, they had to put the Troll to bed, and there he lay in a sad pickle.

When the night wore on, the Troll began to talk to the old dame again, and to wonder how ever they could be rid of the lad.

"Well," said the old dame, "if you can't hit on a plan to get rid of him, I'm sure I can't."

"Let me see," said the Troll; "I've got twelve lions in a garden; if they could only get hold of the lad, they'd soon tear him to pieces."

So the old dame said it would be easy enough to get him there. She would sham sick, and say she felt so poorly, nothing would do her any good but lion's milk. All that the lad lay and listened to; and when he got up in the morning his mother said she was worse than she looked, and she thought she should never be right again unless she could get some lion's milk.

"Then I'm afraid you'll be poorly a long time, mother," said the lad, "for I'm sure I don't know where any is to be got."

"Oh! if that be all," said the Troll, "there's no lack of lion's milk, if we only had the man to fetch it"; and then he went on to say how his brother had a garden with twelve lions in it, and how the lad might have the key if he had a mind to milk the lions. So the lad took the key and a milking pail, and strode off; and when he unlocked the gate and got into the garden, there stood all the twelve lions on their hind paws, rampant and roaring at him. But the lad laid hold of the biggest, and led him about by the forepaws, and dashed him against stocks and stones till there wasn't a bit of him left but the two paws. So when the rest saw that, they were so afraid that they crept up and lay at his feet like so many curs. After that they followed him about wherever he went, and when he got home, they lay down outside the house, with their forepaws on the door sill.

"Now, mother, you'll soon be well," said the lad, when he went in, "for here is the lion's milk."

He had just milked a drop in the pail.

But the Troll, as he lay in bed, swore it was all a lie. He was sure the lad was not the man to milk lions.

When the lad heard that, he forced the Troll to get out of bed, threw open the door, and all the lions rose up and seized the Troll, and at last the lad had to make them leave their hold.

That night the Troll began to talk to the old dame again. "I'm sure I can't tell how to put this lad out of the way – he is so awfully strong; can't you think of some way?"

"No," said the old dame, "if you can't tell, I'm sure I can't."

"Well!" said the Troll, "I have two brothers in a castle; they are twelve times as strong as I am, and that's why I was turned out and had to put up with this farm. They hold that castle, and round it there is an orchard with apples in it, and whoever eats those apples sleeps for three days and three nights. If we could only get the lad to go for the fruit, he wouldn't be able to keep from tasting the apples, and as soon as ever he fell asleep my brothers would tear him in pieces."

The old dame said she would sham sick, and say she could never be herself again unless she tasted those apples; for she had set her heart on them.

All this the lad lay and listened to.

When the morning came the old dame was so poorly that she couldn't utter a word but groans and sighs. She was sure she should never be well again, unless she had some of those apples that grew in the orchard near the castle where the man's brothers lived; only she had no one to send for them.

Oh! the lad was ready to go that instant; but the eleven lions went with him. So when he came to the orchard, he climbed up into the apple tree and ate as many apples as he could, and he had scarce got down before he fell into a deep sleep; but the lions all lay round him in a ring. The third day came the Troll's brothers, but they did not come in man's shape. They came snorting like man-eating steeds, and wondered who it was that dared to be there, and said they would tear him to pieces, so small that there should not be a bit of him left. But up rose the lions and tore the Trolls into small pieces, so that the place looked as if a dung heap had been tossed about it; and when they had finished the Trolls they lay down again. The lad did not wake till late in the afternoon, and when he got on his knees and rubbed the sleep out of his eyes, he began to wonder what had been going on, when he saw the marks of hoofs. But when he went towards the castle, a maiden looked out of a window who had seen all that had happened, and she said:

"You may thank your stars you weren't in that tussle, else you must have lost your life."

"What! I lose my life! No fear of that, I think," said the lad.

So she begged him to come in, that she might talk with him, for she hadn't seen a Christian soul ever since she came there. But when she opened the door the lions wanted to go in too, but she got so frightened that she began to scream, and so the lad let them lie outside.

Then the two talked and talked, and the lad asked how it came that she, who was so lovely, could put up with those ugly Trolls. She never wished it, she said; 'twas quite against her will. They had seized her by force, and she was the King of Arabia's daughter. So they talked on, and at last she asked him what he would do; whether she should go back home, or whether he would have her to wife. Of course he would have her, and she shouldn't go home.

After that they went round the castle, and at last they came to a great hall, where the Trolls' two great swords hung high up on the wall.

"I wonder if you are man enough to wield one of these," said the Princess.

"Who? I?" said the lad. "'Twould be a pretty thing if I couldn't wield one of these."

With that he put two or three chairs one atop of the other, jumped up, and touched the biggest sword with his finger tips, tossed it up in the air, and caught it again by the hilt; leapt down, and at the same time dealt such a blow with it on the floor that the whole hall shook. After he had thus got down, he thrust the sword under his arm and carried it about with him.

So, when they had lived a little while in the castle, the Princess thought she ought to go home to her parents, and let them know what had become of her; so they loaded a ship, and she set sail from the castle.

After she had gone, and the lad had wandered about a little, he called to mind that he had been sent out on an errand thither, and had come to fetch something for his mother's health; and though he said to himself, "After all the old dame was not so bad but she's all right by this time" – still he thought he ought to go and just see how she was. So he went and found both the man and his mother quite fresh and hearty.

"What wretches you are to live in this beggarly hut," said the lad. "Come with me up to my castle, and you shall see what a fine fellow I am."

Well! they were both ready to go, and on the way his mother talked to him, and asked how it was he had got so strong.

"If you must know it came of that blue belt which lay on the hillside that time when you and I were out begging," said the lad.

"Have you got it still?" asked she.

"Yes" – he had. It was tied round his waist.

"Might she see it?"

"Yes" – she might; and with that he pulled open his waistcoat and shirt to show it to her.

Then she seized it with both hands, tore it off, and twisted it round her fist.

"Now," she cried, "what shall I do with such a wretch as you? I'll just give you one blow, and dash your brains out!"

"Far too good a death for such a scamp," said the Troll. "No! Let's first burn out his eyes, and then turn him adrift in a little boat."

So they burned out his eyes and turned him adrift, in spite of his prayers and tears; but, as the boat drifted, the lions swam after, and at last they laid hold of it and dragged it ashore on an island, and placed the lad under a fir tree. They caught game for him, and they plucked the birds and made him a bed of down; but he was forced to eat his meat raw and he was blind. At last, one day the biggest lion was chasing a hare which was blind, for it ran straight over stock and stone, and the end was, it ran right up against a fir-stump and tumbled head over heels across the field right into a spring; but lo! when it came out of the spring it saw its way quite plain, and so saved its life.

"So, so!" thought the lion, and went and dragged the lad to the spring, and dipped him over head and ears in it. So, when he had got his sight again, he went down to the shore and made signs to the lions that they should all lie close together like a raft; then he stood upon their backs while they swam with him to the mainland. When he had reached the shore he went up into a birchen copse, and made the lions lie quiet. Then he stole up to the castle, like a thief, to see if he couldn't lay hands on his belt; and when he got to the door, he peeped through the keyhole, and there he saw his belt hanging up over a door in the kitchen. So he crept softly in across the floor, for there was no one there; but as soon as he had got hold of the belt, he began to kick and stamp about as though he were mad. Just then his mother came rushing out:

"Dear heart, my darling little boy! Do give me the belt again," she said.

"Thank you kindly," said he. "Now you shall have the doom you passed on me," and he fulfilled it on the spot. When the old Troll heard that, he came in and begged and prayed so prettily that he might not be smitten to death.

"Well, you may live," said the lad, "but you shall undergo the same punishment you gave me"; and so he burned out the Troll's eyes, and turned him adrift on the sea in a little boat, but he had no lions to follow him.

Now the lad was all alone, and he went about longing and longing for the Princess; at last he could bear it no longer; he must set out to seek her, his heart was so bent on having her. So he loaded four ships and set sail for Arabia.

For some time they had fair wind and fine weather, but after that they lay wind-bound under a rocky island. So the sailors went ashore and strolled about to spend the time, and there they found a huge egg, almost as big as a little house. So they began to knock it about with large stones, but, after all, they couldn't crack the shell. Then the lad came up with his sword to see what all the noise was about, and when he saw the egg, he thought it a trifle to crack it; so he gave it one blow and the egg split, and out came a chicken as big as an elephant.

"Now we have done wrong," said the lad; "this can cost us all our lives"; and then he asked his sailors if they were men enough to sail to Arabia in four-and-twenty hours if they got a fine breeze. Yes! They were good to do that, they said, so they set sail with a fine breeze, and got to Arabia in three-and-twenty hours. As soon as they landed, the lad ordered all the sailors to go and bury themselves up to the eyes in a sandhill, so that they could barely see the ships. The lad and the captains climbed a high crag and sat down under a fir.

In a little while came a great bird flying with an island in its claws, and let it fall down on the fleet, and sank every ship. After it had done that, it flew up to the sandhill and flapped its wings, so that the wind nearly took off the heads of the sailors, and it flew past the fir with such force that it turned the lad right about, but he was ready with his sword, and gave the bird one blow and brought it down dead.

After that he went to the town, where everyone was glad because the King had got his daughter back; but now the King had hidden her away somewhere himself, and promised her hand as a reward to anyone who could find her, and this though she was betrothed before. Now as the lad went along he met a man who had white bear-skins for sale, so he bought one of the hides and put it on; and one of the captains was to take an iron chain and lead him about, and so he went into the town and began to play pranks. At last the news came to the King's ears, that there never had been such fun in the town before, for here was a white bear that danced and cut capers just as it was bid. So a messenger came to say the bear must come to the castle at once, for the King wanted to see its tricks. So when it got to the castle everyone was afraid, for such a beast they had never seen before; but the captain said there was no danger unless they laughed at it. They mustn't do that, else it would tear them to pieces. When the King heard that, he warned all the court not to laugh. But while the fun was going on, in came one of the King's maids, and began to laugh and make game of the bear, and the bear flew at her and tore her, so that there was scarce a rag of her left. Then all the court began to bewail, and the captain most of all.

"Stuff and nonsense," said the King; "she's only a maid, besides it's more my affair than yours."

When the show was over, it was late at night. "It's no good your going away, when it's so late," said the King. "The bear had best sleep here."

"Perhaps it might sleep in the ingle by the kitchen fire," said the captain.

"Nay," said the King, "it shall sleep up here, and it shall have pillows and cushions to sleep on." So a whole heap of pillows and cushions was brought, and the captain had a bed in a side room.

But at midnight the King came with a lamp in his hand and a big bunch of keys, and carried off the white bear. He passed along gallery after gallery through doors and rooms, upstairs and downstairs, till at last he came to a pier which ran out into the sea. Then the King began to pull and haul at posts and pins, this one up and that one down, till at last a little house floated up to the water's edge. There he kept his daughter, for she was so dear to him that he had hid her, so that no one could find her out. He left the white bear outside while he went in and told her how it had danced and played its pranks. She said she was afraid, and dared not look at it; but he talked her over, saying there was no danger if she only wouldn't laugh. So they brought the bear in, and locked the door, and it danced and played its tricks; but just when the fun was at its height, the Princess's maid began to laugh. Then the lad flew at her and tore her to bits, and the Princess began to cry and sob.

"Stuff and nonsense," cried the King; "all this fuss about a maid! I'll get you just as good a one again. But now I think the bear had best stay here till morning, for I don't care to have to go and lead it along all those galleries and stairs at this time of night."

"Well!" said the Princess, "if it sleeps here, I'm sure I won't."

But just then the bear curled himself up and lay down by the stove; and it was settled at last that the Princess should sleep there too, with a light burning. But as soon as the King had well gone, the white bear came and begged her to undo his collar. The Princess was so scared she almost swooned away; but she felt about till she found the collar, and she had scarce undone it before the bear pulled his head off. Then she knew him again, and was so glad there was no end to her joy, and she wanted to tell her father at once that her deliverer was come. But the lad would not hear of it; he would earn her once more, he said. So in the morning when they heard the King rattling at the posts outside, the lad drew on the hide and lay down by the stove.

"Well, has it lain still?" the King asked.

"I should think so," said the Princess; "it hasn't so much as turned or stretched itself once."

When they got up to the castle again, the captain took the bear and led it away, and then the lad threw off the hide, and went to a tailor and ordered clothes fit for a prince; and when they were fitted on he went to the King, and said he wanted to find the Princess.

"You're not the first who has wished the same thing," said the King, "but they have all lost their lives; for if anyone who tries can't find her in four-and-twenty hours his life is forfeited."

Yes; the lad knew all that. Still he wished to try, and if he couldn't find her, 'twas his lookout. Now in the castle there was a band that played sweet tunes, and there were fair maids to dance with, and so the lad danced away.

When twelve hours were gone, the King said:

"I pity you with all my heart. You're so poor a hand at seeking; you will surely lose your life."

"Stuff!" said the lad; "while there's life there's hope! So long as there's breath in the body there's no fear; we have lots of time!" And so he went on dancing till there was only one hour left.

Then he said he would begin to search.

"It's no use now," said the King; "time's up."

"Light your lamp; out with your big bunch of keys," said the lad, "and follow me whither I wish to go. There is still a whole hour left."

So the lad went the same way which the King had led him the night before, and he bade the King unlock door after door till they came down to the pier which ran out into the sea.

"It's all no use, I tell you," said the King; "time's up, and this will only lead you right out into the sea."

"Still five minutes more," said the lad, as he pulled and pushed at the posts and pins, and the house floated up.

"Now the time is up," bawled the King; "come hither, headsman, and take off his head."

"Nay, nay!" said the lad; "stop a bit, there are still three minutes! Out with the key, and let me get into this house."

But there stood the King and fumbled with his keys, to draw out the time. At last he said he hadn't any key.

"Well, if you haven't, I have," said the lad, as he gave the door such a kick that it flew to splinters inwards on the floor.

At the door the Princess met him, and told her father this was her deliverer, on whom her heart was set. So she had him; and this was how the beggar boy came to marry the daughter of the King of Arabia.

How a Lad Stole the Giant's Treasure

(Scandinavian)

ONCE UPON A TIME there lived a peasant who had three sons. The two elder ones used to go with him to the field and to the forest, and helped him in his work, but the youngest remained at home with his mother, to help her in the house. His brothers despised him for doing this, and whenever they had a chance they used him badly.

At length the father and mother died, and the sons divided the property among them. As might have been looked for, the elder brothers took all that was of any value for themselves, leaving nothing to the youngest but an old cracked kneading-trough, which neither of them thought worth the having.

"The old trough," said one of the brothers, "will do very well for our young brother, for he is always baking and scrubbing."

The boy thought this, as was only natural, a poor thing to inherit, but he could do nothing, and he now recognized that it would be no use his remaining at home, so he wished his brothers goodbye, and went off to seek his fortune. On coming to the side of a lake he made his trough watertight with oakum, and converted it into a little boat. Then he found two sticks, and using these as oars rowed away.

When he had crossed the water, he saw a large palace, and entering it, he asked to speak with the king. The king questioned him respecting his family and the purpose of his visit.

"I," said the boy, "am the son of a poor peasant, and all I have in the world is an old kneading-trough. I have come here to seek work."

The king laughed when he heard this.

"Indeed," said he, "you have not inherited much, but fortune works many a change."

He took the lad to be one of his servants, and he became a favourite for his courage and honesty.

Now the king who owned this palace had an only daughter, who was so beautiful and so clever that she was talked of all through the kingdom, and many came from the east and from the west to ask her hand in marriage. The princess, however, rejected them all, saying that none should have her for his wife unless he brought her for a wedding-present four valuable things belonging to a giant who lived on the other side of the lake. These four treasures were a gold sword, three gold hens, a gold lantern, and a gold harp.

Many king's sons and many good warriors tried to win these treasures, but none of them came back, for the giant caught them all and ate them. The king was very sorrowful, for he feared that at this rate his daughter would never get a husband, and so he would not have a son-in-law to whom to leave his kingdom.

The boy when he heard of this thought that it might be well worth his while to try to win the king's beautiful daughter. So he went to the king one day, and told him what he meant to do. When the king heard him, he got angry, and said –

"Do you think that you, who are only a servant, can do what great warriors have failed in?"

The boy, however, was not to be dissuaded, and begged him so to let him go that at last the king grew calmer and gave him his permission. "But," said he, "you will lose your life, and I shall be sorry to miss you."

With that they parted.

The boy went down to the shore of the lake, and, having found his trough, he looked it over very closely. Then he got into it and rowed across the lake, and coming to the giant's dwelling he hid himself, and stayed the night there.

Very early in the morning, before it was light, the giant went to his barn, and began to thrash, making such a noise that the mountains all around echoed again. When the boy heard this he collected some stones and put them in his pouch. Then he climbed up on to the roof of the barn and made a little hole so that he could look in. Now the giant had by his side his golden sword, which had the strange property that it clanked whenever the giant was angry. While the giant was busy thrashing at full speed, the boy threw a little stone which hit the sword, and caused it to clank.

"Why do you clank?" said the giant. "I am not angry."

He went on thrashing, but the next moment the sword clanked again. Once more the giant pursued his work, and the sword clanked a third time. Then the giant got so angry that he undid the belt, and threw the sword out of the barn door.

"Lie there," said he, "till I have done my thrashing."

The lad waited no longer, but slipping down from the roof seized on the sword, ran to his boat, and rowed across the water. On reaching the other side he hid his treasure, and was full of glee at the success of his adventure.

The next day he filled his pouch with corn, put a bundle of bast-twine in his boat, and once more set off to the giant's dwelling. He lay hiding for a time, and then he saw the giant's three golden hens walking about on the shore, and spreading their feathers, which sparkled beautifully in the bright sunshine. He was soon near them, and began to softly lead them on, scattering corn for them out of his pouch. While they were picking the boy gradually led them to the water, till at last he got them into his little boat. Then he jumped in himself, secured the fowl with his twine, pushed out from the shore, and rowed as quickly as he could to the other side of the water.

The third day he put some lumps of salt into his pouch, and again rowed across the lake. As night came on he noticed how the smoke rose from the giant's dwelling, and concluded that the giant's wife was busy getting ready his food. He crept up on to the roof, and, looking down through the hole by which the smoke escaped, saw a large cauldron boiling on the fire. Then he took the lumps of salt out of his pouch, and threw them one by one into the pot. Having done this, he crept down from the roof, and waited to see what would follow.

Soon after the giant's wife took the cauldron off the fire, poured out the porridge into a bowl, and put it on the table. The giant was hungry, and he fell to at once, but scarcely had he tasted the porridge when he found it too salty. He got very angry, and started from his seat. The old woman made what excuse she could, and said that the porridge must be good; but the giant declared he would eat no more of the stuff, and told her to taste it for herself. She did so, and pulled a terrible face, for she had never in her life tasted such abominable stuff.

There was nothing for it but she must make some new porridge. So she seized a can, took the gold lantern down from the wall, and went as fast as she could to the well to draw some water. She put the lantern down by the side of the well, and was stooping down to get the water, when the boy ran to her, and, laying hold of her by the feet, threw her head over heels into the well. He seized hold of the golden lantern, ran away as fast as he could to his boat, and rowed across the water in safety.

The giant sat for a long time wondering why his wife was away so long. At last he went to look for her, but nothing could he see of her. Then he heard a splashing in the well, and finding she was in the water, he, with a lot of work, got her out.

"Where is my gold lantern?" was the first thing he asked, as the old woman came round a little.

"I don't know," answered she. "Somebody came, caught me by the feet, and threw me into the well."

The giant was very angry at this.

"Three of my treasures," said he, "have gone, and I have now only my golden harp left. But, whoever the thief may be, he shall not have that; I will keep that safe under twelve locks."

While these things occurred at the giant's dwelling, the boy sat on the other side of the water, rejoicing that he had got on so well.

The most difficult task, however, had yet to be done, and for a long time he thought over how he could get the golden harp. At length he determined to row over to the giant's place and see if fortune would favour him.

No sooner said than done. He rowed over and went to a hiding place. The giant had, however, been on the watch, and had seen him. So he rushed forward in a terrible rage and seized the boy, saying –

"So I have caught you at last, you young rascal. You it was who stole my sword, my three gold hens, and my gold lantern."

The boy was terribly afraid, for he thought his last hour was come.

"Spare my life, father," said he humbly, "and I will never come here again."

"No," replied the giant, "I will do the same with you as with the others. No one slips alive out of my hands."

He then shut the boy up in a sty, and fed him with nuts and sweet milk, so as to get him nice and fat preparatory to killing and eating him.

The lad was a prisoner, but he ate and drank and made himself as easy as he could. After some time the giant wanted to find out if he were fat enough to be killed. So he went to the sty, made a little hole in the wall, and told the boy to put his finger through it. The lad knew what he wanted; so instead of putting out his finger he poked out a little peeled alder twig. The giant cut the twig, and the red sap ran out. Then he thought the boy must be yet very lean since his flesh was so hard, so he caused a greater supply of milk and nuts to be given to him.

Some time after, the giant again visited the sty, and ordered the boy to put his finger through the hole in the wall. The lad now poked out a cabbage-stalk, and the giant, having cut it with his knife, concluded that the lad must be fat enough, his flesh seemed so soft.

The next morning the giant said to his wife –

"The boy seems to be fat enough now, mother; take him then today, and bake him in the oven, while I go and ask our kinsfolk to the feast."

The old woman promised to do what her husband told her. So, having heated the oven, she dragged out the boy to bake him.

"Sit on the shovel," said she.

The boy did so, but when the old woman raised the shovel the boy always fell off. So they went on many times. At last the giantess got angry, and scolded the boy for being so awkward; the lad excused himself, saying that he did not know the way to sit on the shovel.

"Look at me," said the woman, "I will show you."

So she sat herself down on the shovel, bending her back and drawing up her knees. No sooner was she seated than the boy, seizing hold of the handle, pushed her into the oven and slammed the door to. Then he took the woman's fur cloak, stuffed it out with straw, and laid it on the bed. Seizing the giant's bunch of keys, he opened the twelve locks, snatched up the golden harp, and ran down to his boat, which he had hidden among the flags on the shore.

The giant soon afterwards came home.

"Where can my wife be?" said he. "No doubt she has lain down to sleep a bit. Ah! I thought so."

The old woman, however, slept a long while, and the giant could not wake her, though he was now expecting his friends to arrive.

"Wake up, mother," cried he, but no one replied. He called again, but there was no response. He got angry, and, going to the bed, he gave the fur cloak a good shake. Then he found that it was not his wife, but only a bundle of straw put in her clothes. At this the giant grew alarmed, and he ran off to look after his golden harp. He found his keys gone, the twelve locks undone, and the harp missing. He went to the oven and opened the door to see how the meat for the feast was going on. Behold! there sat his wife, baked, and grinning at him.

Then the giant was almost mad with grief and rage, and he rushed out to seek the lad who had done him all this mischief. He came down to the edge of the water and found him sitting in his boat, playing on the harp. The music came over the water, and the gold strings shone wonderfully in the sunshine. The giant jumped into the water after the boy; but finding that it was too deep, he laid himself down, and began to drink the water in order to make the lake shallower. He drank with all his might, and by this means set up a current which drew the boat nearer and nearer to the shore. Just when he was going to lay hold of it he burst, for he had drunk too much; and there was an end of him.

The giant lay dead on the shore, and the boy moved away across the lake, full of joy and happiness. When he came to land, he combed his golden hair, put on fine clothes, fastened the giant's gold sword by his side, and, taking the gold harp in one hand and the gold lantern in the other, he led the gold fowl after him, and went to the king, who was sitting in the great hall of the palace surrounded by his courtiers. When the king saw the boy he was heartily glad. The lad went to the king's beautiful daughter, saluted her courteously, and laid the giant's treasures before her. Then there was great joy in the palace, that the princess had after all got the giant's treasures and so bold and handsome a bridegroom. The wedding was celebrated soon after with very much splendour and rejoicing; and when the king died the lad succeeded him, ruling over all the land both long and happily.

I know no more respecting them.

Silverwhite and Lillwacker

(Swedish)

ONCE UPON A TIME there was a king, who had a queen whom he loved with a great love. But after a time the queen died, and all he had left was an only daughter. And now that the king was a widower, his whole heart went out to the little princess, whom he cherished as the apple of his eye. And the king's young daughter grew up into the most lovely maiden ever known.

When the princess had seen the snows of fifteen winters, it happened that a great war broke out, and that her father had to march against the foe.

But there was no one to whom the king could entrust his daughter while he was away at war; so he had a great tower built out in the forest, provided it with a plenteous store of supplies, and in it shut up his daughter and a maid. And he had it proclaimed that every man, no matter who he might be, was forbidden to approach the tower in which he had placed his daughter and the maid, under pain of death.

Now the king thought he had taken every precaution to protect his daughter, and went off to war. In the meantime the princess and her maid sat in the tower. But in the city there were a number of brave young sons of kings, as well as other young men, who would have liked to have talked to the beautiful maiden. And when they found that this was forbidden them, they conceived a great hatred for the king. At length they took counsel with an old woman who was wiser than most folk, and told her to arrange matters in such wise that the king's daughter and her maid might come into disrepute, without their having anything to do with it. The old hag promised to help them, enchanted some apples, laid them in a basket, and went to the lonely tower in which the maidens lived.

When the king's daughter and her maid saw the old woman, who was sitting beneath the window, they felt a great longing to try the beautiful apples.

So they called out and asked how much she wanted for her precious apples; but the old woman said they were not for sale. Yet as the girls kept on pleading with her, the old woman said she would make each of them a present of an apple; they only need let down a little basket from the tower. The princess and her maid, in all innocence, did as the troll-woman told them, and each received an apple. But the enchanted fruit had a strange effect, for in due course of time heaven sent them each a child. The king's daughter called her son Silverwhite, and the son of her maid received the name of Lillwacker.

The two boys grew up larger and stronger than other children, and were very handsome as well. They looked as much alike as one cherry pit does to another, and one could easily see that they were related.

Seven years had passed, and the king was expected home from the war. Then both girls were terrified, and they took counsel together as to how they might hide their children. When at length they could find no other way out of the difficulty, they very sorrowfully bade their children farewell, and let them down from the tower at night, to seek their fortune in the wide, wide world. At parting the king's daughter gave Silverwhite a costly knife; but the maid had nothing to give her son.

The two foster-brethren now wandered out into the world. After they had gone a while, they came to a dark forest. And in this forest they met a man, strange-looking and very tall. He wore two swords at his side, and was accompanied by six great dogs. He gave them a friendly greeting:

"Good day, little fellows, whence do you come and whither do you go?" The boys told him they came from a high tower, and were going out into the world to seek their fortune. The man replied:

"If such be the case, I know more about your origin than anyone else. And that you may have something by which to remember your father, I will give each of you a sword and three dogs. But you must promise me one thing, that you will never part from your dogs; but take them with you wherever you go." The boys thanked the man for his kind gifts, and promised to do as he had told them. Then they bade him farewell and went their way.

When they had travelled for some time they reached a crossroad. Then Silverwhite said:

"It seems to me that it would be the best for us to try our luck singly, so let us part." Lillwacker answered: "Your advice is good; but how am I to know whether or not you are doing well out in the world?"

"I will give you a token by which you may tell," said Silverwhite, "so long as the water runs clear in this spring you will know that I am alive; but if it turns red and roiled, it will mean that I am dead." Silverwhite then drew runes in the water of the spring, said farewell to his brother, and each of them went on alone. Lillwacker soon came to a king's court, and took service there; but every morning he would go to the spring to see how his brother fared.

Silverwhite continued to wander over hill and dale, until he reached a great city. But the whole city was in mourning, the houses were hung in black, and all the inhabitants went about full of grief and care, as though some great misfortune had occurred.

Silverwhite went though the city and inquired as to the cause of all the unhappiness he saw. They answered: "You must have come from far away, since you do not know that the king and queen were in danger of being drowned at sea, and he had to promise to give up their three daughters in order to escape. Tomorrow morning the sea-troll is coming to carry off the oldest princess." This news pleased Silverwhite; for he saw a fine opportunity to wealth and fame, should fortune favour him.

The next morning Silverwhite hung his sword at his side, called his dogs to him, and wandered down to the seashore alone. And as he sat on the strand he saw the king's daughter led out of the city, and with her went a courtier, who had promised to rescue her. But the princess was very sad and cried bitterly. Then Silverwhite stepped up to her with a polite greeting. When the king's daughter and her escort saw the fearless youth, they were much frightened, because they thought he was the sea-troll. The courtier was so alarmed that he ran away and took refuge in a tree. When Silverwhite saw how frightened the princess was, he said: "Lovely maiden, do not fear me, for I will do you no harm." The king's daughter answered:

"Are you the troll who is coming to carry me away?" "No," said Silverwhite, "I have come to rescue you." Then the princess was glad to think that such a brave hero was going to defend her, and they had a long, friendly talk. At the same time Silverwhite begged the king's daughter to comb his hair. She complied with his request, and Silverwhite laid his head in her lap; but when he did so the princess drew a golden ring from her finger and, unbeknown to him, wound it into his locks.

Suddenly the sea-troll rose from the deeps, setting the waves whirling and foaming far and near. When the troll saw Silverwhite, he grew angry and said: "Why do you sit there beside my princess?" The youth replied: "It seems to me that she is my princess, not yours." The sea-troll answered: "Time enough to see which of us is right; but first our dogs shall fight." Silverwhite was nothing loath, and set his dogs at the dogs of the troll, and there was a fierce struggle. But at last the youth's dogs got the upper hand and bit the dogs of the sea-troll to death. Then Silverwhite drew his sword with a great sweep, rushed upon the sea-troll, and gave him such a tremendous blow that the monster's head rolled on the sand. The troll gave a fearsome cry, and flung himself back into the sea, so that the water spurted to the very skies. Thereupon the youth drew out his silver-mounted knife, cut out the troll's eyes and put them in his pocket. Then he saluted the lovely princess and went away.

Now when the battle was over and the youth had disappeared, the courtier crawled down from his tree, and threatened to kill the princess if she did not say before all the people that he, and none other, had rescued her. The king's daughter did not dare refuse, since she feared for her life. So she returned to her father's castle with the courtier, where they were received with great distinction.

And joy reigned throughout the land when the news spread that the oldest princess had been rescued from the troll.

On the following day everything repeated itself. Silverwhite went down to the strand and met the second princess, just as she was to be delivered to the troll.

And when the king's daughter and her escort saw him, they were very much frightened, thinking he was the sea-troll. And the courtier climbed a tree, just as he had before; but the princess granted the youth's petition, combed his hair as her sister had done, and also wound her gold ring into his long curls.

After a time there was a great tumult out at sea, and a sea-troll rose from the waves. He had three heads and three dogs. But Silverwhite's dogs overcame those of the troll, and the youth killed the troll himself with his sword. Thereupon he took out his silver-mounted knife, cut out the troll's eyes, and went his way. But the courtier lost no time. He climbed down from his tree and forced the princess to promise to say that he, and none other, had rescued her. Then they returned to the castle, where the courtier was acclaimed as the greatest of heroes.

On the third day Silverwhite hung his sword at his side, called his three dogs to him, and again wandered down to the seashore. As he was sitting by the strand, he saw the youngest princess led out of the city, and with her the daring courtier who claimed to have rescued her sisters. But the princess was very sad and cried bitterly. Then Silverwhite stepped up and greeted the lovely maiden politely. Now when the king's daughter and her escort saw the handsome youth, they were very much frightened, for they believed him to be the sea-troll, and the courtier ran away and hid in a high tree that grew near the strand. When Silverwhite noticed the maiden's terror, he said:

"Lovely maiden, do not fear me, for I will do you no harm." The king's daughter answered: "Are you the troll who is coming to carry me away?" "No," said Silverwhite, "I have come to rescue you." Then the princess was very glad to have such a brave hero fight for her, and they had a long, friendly talk with each other. At the same time Silverwhite begged the lovely maiden to do him a favour and comb his hair. This the king's daughter was most willing to do, and Silverwhite laid his head in her lap. But when the princess saw the gold rings her sisters had wound in his locks, she was much surprised, and added her own to the others.

Suddenly the sea-troll came shooting up out of the deep with a terrific noise, so that waves and foam spurted to the very skies. This time the monster had six heads and nine dogs. When the troll saw Silverwhite sitting with the king's daughter, he fell into a rage and cried: "What are you doing with my princess?" The youth answered: "It seems to me that she is my princess rather than yours." Thereupon the troll said: "Time enough to see which of us is right; but first our dogs shall fight each other." Silverwhite did not delay, but set his dogs at the sea-dogs, and they had a battle royal. But in the end the youth's dogs got the upper hand and bit all nine of the sea-dogs to death. Finally Silverwhite drew out his bare sword, flung himself upon the sea-troll, and stretched all six of his heads on the sand with a single blow. The monster uttered a terrible cry, and rushed back into the sea so that the water spurted to the heavens. Then the youth drew his silver-mounted knife, cut out all twelve of the troll's eyes, saluted the king's young daughter, and hastily went away.

Now that the battle was over, and the youth had disappeared, the courtier climbed down from his tree, drew his sword and threatened to kill the princess unless she promised to say that he had rescued her from the troll, as he had her sisters.

The king's daughter did not dare refuse, since she feared for her life. So they went back to the castle together, and when the king saw that they had returned in safety, without so much as a scratch, he and the whole court were full of joy, and they were accorded great honours. And at court the courtier was quite another fellow from the one who had hid away in the tree. The king had a splendid banquet prepared, with amusements and games, and the sound of string music and dancing, and bestowed the hand of his youngest daughter on the courtier in reward for his bravery.

In the midst of the wedding festivities, when the king and his whole court were seated at table, the door opened, and in came Silverwhite with his dogs.

The youth stepped boldly into the hall of state and greeted the king. And when the three princesses saw who it was, they were full of joy, leaped up from their places, and ran over to him, much to the king's surprise, who asked what it all meant. Then the youngest princess told him all that had happened, from beginning to end, and that Silverwhite had rescued them, while the courtier sat in a tree. To prove it beyond any chance of doubt, each of the king's daughters showed her father the ring she had wound in Silverwhite's locks. But the king still did not know quite what to think of it all, until Silverwhite said: "My lord king! In order that you need not doubt what your daughters have told you, I will show you the eyes of the sea-trolls whom I slew." Then the king and all the rest saw that the princesses had told the truth. The traitorous courtier received his just punishment; but Silverwhite was paid every honour, and was given the youngest daughter and half of the kingdom with her.

After the wedding Silverwhite established himself with his young bride in a large castle belonging to the king, and there they lived quietly and happily.

One night, when all were sleeping, it chanced that he heard a knocking at the window, and a voice which said: "Come, Silverwhite, I have to talk to you!" The king, who did not want to wake his young wife, rose hastily, girded on his sword, called his dogs and went out. When he reached the open air, there stood a huge and savage-looking troll. The troll said: "Silverwhite, you have slain my three brothers, and I have come to bid you go down to the seashore with me, that we may fight with one another." This proposal suited the youth, and he followed the troll without protest. When they reached the seashore, there lay three great dogs belonging to the troll. Silverwhite at once set his dogs at the troll-dogs, and after a hard struggle the latter had to give in. The young king drew his sword, bravely attacked the troll and dealt him many a mighty blow. It was a tremendous battle. But when the troll noticed he was getting the worst of it, he grew frightened, quickly ran to a high tree, and clambered into it. Silverwhite and the dogs ran after him, the dogs barking as loudly as they could. Then the troll begged for his life and said: "Dear Silverwhite, I will take wergild for my brothers, only bid your dogs be still, so that we may talk." The king bade his dogs be still, but in vain, they only barked the more loudly. Then the troll tore three hairs from his head, handed them to Silverwhite and said: "Lay a hair on each of the dogs, and then they will be as quiet as can be." The King did so and at once the dogs fell silent, and lay motionless as though they had grown fast to the ground. Now Silverwhite realized that he had been deceived; but it was too late. The troll was already descending from the tree, and he drew his sword and again began to fight. But they had exchanged no more than a few blows, before Silverwhite received a mortal wound, and lay on the earth in a pool of blood.

But now we must tell about Lillwacker. The next morning he went to the spring by the crossroad and found it red with blood. Then he knew that Silverwhite was dead. He called his dogs, hung his sword at his side, and went on until he came to a great city. And the city was in festal array, the streets were crowded with people, and the houses were hung with scarlet cloths and splendid rugs. Lillwacker asked why everybody was so happy, and they said: "You must hail from distant parts, since you do not know that a famous hero has come here by the name of Silverwhite, who has rescued our three princesses, and is now the king's son-in-law." Lillwacker then inquired how it had all come about, and then went his way, reaching the royal castle in which Silverwhite dwelt with his beautiful queen in the evening.

When Lillwacker entered the castle gate, all greeted him as though he had been the king. For he resembled his foster-brother so closely that none could tell one from the other. When the youth came to the Queen's room, she also took him for Silverwhite. She went up to him and said: "My lord King, where have you been so long? I have been awaiting you with great anxiety." Lillwacker said little, and was very taciturn. Then he lay down on a couch in a corner of the Queen's room.

The young woman did not know what to think of his actions; for her husband did not act queerly at other times. But she thought: "One should not try to discover the secrets of others," and said nothing.

In the night, when all were sleeping, there was a knocking at the window, and a voice cried: "Come, Lillwacker, I have to talk to you!" The youth rose hastily, took his good sword, called his dogs and went. When he reached the open air, there stood the same troll who had slain Silverwhite. He said: "Come with me, Lillwacker, and then you shall see your foster-brother!" To this Lillwacker at once agreed, and the troll led the way. When they came to the seashore, there lay the three great dogs whom the troll had brought with him. Somewhat further away, where they had fought, lay Silverwhite in a pool of blood, and beside him his dogs were stretched out on the ground as though they had taken root in it. Then Lillwacker saw how everything had happened, and thought that he would gladly venture his life, if he might in some way call his brother back from the dead. He at once set his dogs at the troll-dogs, and they had a hard struggle, in which Lillwacker's dogs won the victory. Then the youth drew his sword, and attacked the troll with mighty blows. But when the troll saw that he was getting the worst of it, he took refuge in a lofty tree. Lillwacker and his dogs ran after him and the dogs barked loudly.

Then the troll humbly begged for his life, and said: "Dear Lillwacker, I will give you wergild for your brother, only bid your dogs be still, so that we may talk." At the same time the troll handed him three hairs from his head and added: "Lay one of these hairs on each of your dogs, and then they will soon be quiet." But Lillwacker saw through his cunning scheme, took the three hairs and laid them on the troll-dogs, which at once fell on the ground and lay like dead.

When the troll saw that his attempt had failed, he was much alarmed and said: "Dearest Lillwacker, I will give you wergild for your brother, if you will only leave me alone." But the youth answered:

"What is there you can give me that will compensate for my brother's life?" The troll replied: "Here are two flasks. In one is a liquid which, if you anoint a dead man with it, it will restore him to life; but as to the liquid in the other flask, if you moisten anything with it, and someone touches the place you have moistened, he will be unable to move from the spot. I think it would be hard to find anything more precious than the liquid in these flasks." Lillwacker said: "Your proposal suits me, and I will accept it. But there is something else you must promise to do: that you will release my brother's dogs." The troll agreed, climbed down from the tree, breathed on the dogs and thus freed them. Then Lillwacker took the two flasks and went away from the seashore with the troll. After they had gone a while they came to a great flat stone, lying near the highway. Lillwacker hastened on in advance and moistened it with liquid from the second flask. Then, as he was going by, Lillwacker suddenly set all six of his dogs at the troll, who stepped back and touched the stone. There he stuck, and could move neither forward nor backward. After a time the sun rose and shone on the stone. And when the troll saw the sun he burst – and was as dead as a doornail!

Lillwacker now ran back to his brother and sprinkled him with the liquid in the other flask, so that he came to life again, and they were both very happy, as may well be imagined. The two foster-brothers then returned to the castle, recounting the story of their experiences and adventures on the way. Lillwacker told how he had been taken for his brother. He even mentioned that he had lain down on a couch in a corner of the Queen's room, and that she had never suspected that he was not her rightful husband.

But when Silverwhite heard that, he thought that Lillwacker had offended against the Queen's dignity, and he grew angry and fell into such a rage that he drew his sword, and thrust it into his brother's breast. Lillwacker fell to earth dead, and Silverwhite went home to the castle alone. But Lillwacker's dogs would not leave their master, and lay around him, whining and licking his wound.

In the evening, when the young King and his wife retired, the Queen asked him why he had been so taciturn and serious the evening before. Then the Queen said: "I am very curious to know what has befallen you during the last few days, but what I would like to know most of all, is why you lay down on a couch in a corner of my room the other night?"

Now it was clear to Silverwhite that the brother he had slain was innocent of all offense, and he felt bitter regret at having repaid his faithfulness so badly. So King Silverwhite at once rose and went to the place where his brother was lying. He poured the water of life from his flask and anointed his brother's wound, and in a moment Lillwacker was alive again, and the two brother's went joyfully back to the castle.

When they got there, Silverwhite told his Queen how Lillwacker had rescued him from death, and all the rest of their adventures, and all were happy at the royal court, and they paid the youth the greatest honours and compliments. After he had stayed there a time he sued for the hand of the second princess and obtained it. Thereupon the wedding was celebrated with great pomp, and Silverwhite divided his half of the kingdom with his foster-brother. The two brothers continued to live together in peace and unity, and if they have not died, they are living still.

Litill, Tritill, the Birds, and the Peasant Lad

(Icelandic)

THERE ONCE REIGNED A KING AND A QUEEN, and in the same country there also lived a poor old man and his wife. The king had an only daughter, called Enid, who was greatly beloved by both her father and mother. They spared no expense, and she had the best masters and governesses, and a number of servants to wait upon her; but notwithstanding that she was so carefully watched and looked after, she suddenly disappeared. The head-governess said she had left her in her room only for a few minutes practising her harp, with two of her maidens in attendance, and when she came back she found both the girls fast asleep, and the princess gone. Inquiries were made of everyone, but nothing could be heard of the princess. No one had seen her; she had vanished in the most mysterious manner. The king, in despair, sent out messengers in all directions, and spent a great part of his treasure searching for her; but all in vain. Then, at last, he vowed that he would give the princess in marriage to whoever should be fortunate enough to find her, and also give him the half of his kingdom. But though many of the knights and nobles about the court, eager to secure so great a prize, went off in search of her, they one and all returned empty-handed.

Now, the poor old man who lived outside the palace grounds had three sons. Their names were Osmond, Tostig, and Harald. The two eldest boys were greatly beloved by their parents; but Harald, the youngest and handsomest, was disliked by his father and mother, and both his elder brothers ill-treated him and made him do all the work, while they went out shooting and fishing.

When the boys were grown up, Osmond came to his parents, and said he would like to start off and see the world, and try to win fame and riches for himself.

His father and mother were quite willing he should do so, and providing him with a new pair of boots and a large bag of food, he started off on his journey.

After he had gone a long, long way, he arrived at a little hillock. Here he sat down to rest, and unpacked his bag of provisions.

Just as he was beginning to eat, a tiny little man, dressed in grey, came up to him, begging for a morsel of food. Osmond angrily ordered him away, threatening to beat him if he did not go quickly.

After he had rested, Osmond went on again a long, long way, till he came to another hillock. Here he again sat down to rest, and began to eat. But he had hardly commenced than a still smaller and shabbier little man, dressed in green, came up to him and asked him for a morsel of food. Osmond spoke angrily to him, and sent him away with a volley of abuse.

He then went on again a long, long way, till he reached a large open glade in the wood. Here he sat down on the soft, mossy grass at the foot of a big beech tree, and thought he would eat another morsel. But no sooner had he opened his bag and taken out the food, than a whole flock of birds flew down beside him; but he angrily chased them away, and then, having rested himself, went on his way, till he came to a big cave. Looking in, and seeing no one, only a lot of cattle, he thought he would go in and wait till the dawn arrived.

Just as the sun was setting, an enormously big giantess walked in. Osmond was greatly startled, but, taking courage, he went up to her, and asked whether he might stay the night there.

The giantess said yes, on condition that in the morning he would do the work she would require of him. This he promised he would do; so she allowed him to remain the night, she herself retiring into an inner cave.

The next morning the giantess told him that he must clean out the cave, and put down fresh bedding for the cattle, and that he must have it all finished before the evening, else she would take his life. With these words she went away.

Osmond took up a prong he saw standing in a corner, but no sooner did he begin to turn up the straw than the prong stuck fast in the bedding. In vain he pushed and pulled and tried to drag it out, the prong remained firmly fixed; and when in the evening the giantess came home and found that the cave had not been cleaned out, she took hold of Osmond and hung him up to a nail in the cave.

Meanwhile Tostig, the second son, thought he, too, would like to go out into the world to seek his fortune, for he felt sure his brother by this time must be quite a rich man. So he told his parents that he did not care to remain at home now his elder brother was away, and with only that stupid Harald at home; so having gained their consent, he, too, started off, provided with a pair of new boots and a big bag of provisions.

But he was not more fortunate than Osmond had been. He flouted the little men while he rested on the hillocks, he chased and killed some of the birds who came flocking round him for crumbs; and when he reached the cave, he also received leave from the giantess to remain the night, on condition that he cleaned out the cave next morning. When he went and took up the prong to throw out the old bedding, it stuck fast in the straw, and no efforts of his could move it. So the giantess coming home, and finding that he had failed to accomplish his task, took him and hanged him beside his brother.

So now there was only the youngest son, Harald, left. But though he was the only one at home, his parents did not love him any better, and the poor lad often felt that his presence reminded them of their lost sons, and that they regretted not having sent him away in their place. So he also decided to go away.

"I do not suppose I shall win riches and fame. All I hope is that I may be able to earn enough to support myself, and be no longer a burden to you."

Then his parents told him he might go; but instead of nice strong new boots, they only gave him an old pair of his brother's, and his sack contained nothing but some hard, dry crusts.

But Harald started off with a light heart, and as it chanced he, too, took the same road his brothers had done, and presently he came to the first hillock. "I think my brothers must have rested here, if they felt as tired as I do," he said, "so I will do the same." And seating himself on the hillock, he began to eat one of his dry crusts, when, looking up, he saw a little old man in grey standing beside him.

"Will you share your crust with me? I am very hungry, and have had no food today," he said.

Harald pitied the old man, who looked so feeble and tired. He begged him to sit down beside him and share his meal. When they had done, the old man got up, and, after thanking him, said, "My name is Tritill. Although I am old and feeble, if ever you are in need of help, call me, and I will come to you." So saying, he went round the back of the hillock and disappeared.

Harald then continued his journey till he came to the second hillock.

"I feel sure my brothers must have rested here," he said. "It is a long way from the last hillock. I, too, will rest here awhile." And he sat down, and opening his bag, took out another crust. Hardly had he done so when a tiny, shabby, little old man, dressed in green, came up to him and asked for a morsel of food. Harald very good-naturedly asked him to sit down beside him, and shared his crust with him. When they had finished eating, the little green man got up, and, after thanking Harald, said –

"Call me, if ever you think I can do you a service. My name is Litill." And he, too, went away, and was soon out of sight.

Harald then continued his journey until he came to the large open glade in the wood.

"I am sure my brothers must have rested here," he thought. "I will do the same." And he sat down and took out another crust. No sooner had he done so than a great flock of birds came down. They circled round and round him, and seemed so hungry and fought so eagerly over every crumb he threw them, that Harald's heart was filled with pity. "Poor little things!" he said; "they need it more than I do." And he broke up the remaining crusts and threw the crumbs among them.

When they had eaten up every crumb, the biggest bird alighted gently on Harald's shoulder and whistled softly –

"If ever you think we can do you a service, call us. We shall hear you wherever we are, for we are *your* birds." And ere he had recovered from his astonishment, they had all flown away and were out of sight.

Harald then continued his journey, until he, too, came to the big cave. Looking in, he saw it was full of cattle, and hanging from a beam in one corner he saw the bodies of his two brothers.

Startled at the sight, Harald's first impulse was to go away; but he thought he must first bury his brothers. So he took down the bodies, and seeing a spade near the entrance, he speedily dug a grave and buried them in the sand outside the cave. Just as he had finished, the giantess arrived.

Harald, who was very tired, asked her if he might stay the night there.

"You may do so, if you will promise to do what I tell you in the morning," answered the giantess.

This Harald agreed to, and he slept that night in the cave.

Next morning, the giantess, who had slept in an inner cave, told him that he would have to clean out the cave, and put down clean bedding for the oxen.

"But remember, if your work is not finished when I come home, I shall hang you the same as I did your brothers." And so saying, she went away.

Harald took up the prong standing in the corner and began his work. But no sooner had he pushed the prong into the bedding and tried to lift it than it stuck fast to the ground. In vain he used all his strength, the prong remained firmly fixed. In his despair he called out: "Oh, dear Tritill, come and help me!"

No sooner had the words passed his lips than he saw Tritill standing beside him, who asked what he could do for him. Harald showed him the difficulty he was in.

Then Tritill called out: "Prick prong and shovel spade!" and immediately the prong pricked up the bedding and the spade shovelled it away, till in a very short time the cave was all cleaned out and fresh straw put down. Harald thanked him warmly for his help, and Tritill went away.

When the giantess came home in the evening and saw that the work was done, she said to Harald –

"Oh, man, man! you have not done this by yourself! But I will let it pass!" and she retired into the inner cave.

The next morning the giantess told Harald that she had some fresh work for him to do. He was to carry her own bedding outside the cave, take out all the feathers, spread them out in the sun to air, and then put them back again.

"But remember, if when I come back in the evening there is a single feather missing, I shall hang you as I did your brothers!" And with these words she went away.

Harald carried out the great featherbed and the big pillows; and as the sun was shining warm and bright, and there was not a breath of wind, he ripped open the seams and spread out the feathers in the sun.

No sooner had he done so than a strong wind arose, and in one moment all the feathers were whirled away, not a single one remaining.

In despair Harald called out: "Dear Tritill, dear Litill, and all my dear birds – oh, come and help me if you can!" And almost before the words had passed his lips, Tritill, Litill, and the whole flight of birds came bringing the feathers with them; and while Tritill and Litill helped Harald to fill the bed and the pillows, and sew them up again, the birds flew round picking up all the stray feathers, so that none were missing. But out of each pillow they took one feather, and, tying them together, told Harald that when the giantess missed them and threatened to kill him, he was to tickle her nose with the feathers.

Thereupon Tritill, Litill, and the birds all disappeared.

When the giantess came home in the evening, she went up to her bed, and threw herself down on it so heavily that the whole cave shook. Then she began carefully feeling all over the bed, and when she came to the pillows she cried out –

"Aha, man! I have caught you – there is a feather missing in each pillow! Now I shall hang you like your brothers!"

But as she took hold of him, Harold quickly pulled the two feathers out of his pocket and tickled her nose with them.

In an instant the giantess fell back on her bed looking terribly white and frightened; but Harald laughingly gave her back her feathers, telling her he did not want to keep them.

"Ah, man, man!" said the giantess, "I know you did not do this alone; but I will let it pass this time!"

So this third night Harald also passed in the cave, and in the morning the giantess said to him –

"I have some fresh work for you today. You must kill one of my oxen. Then you must scrape and clean the skin to make a leather bag; cut up the animal in joints ready for cooking; clean all the entrails, and make spoons out of its horns. All must be finished ere I return this evening. I have fifty oxen, as you see, and it is one of these I want killed. I shall not, however, tell you which one I have fixed upon; that you must find out for yourself. If all is done as I wish when I return, you can depart in the morning and go wherever you like; and in addition, as a reward, you may choose three things from among such of my treasures as I value most. If, however, everything is not finished, or if you kill the wrong animal, then it will cost you your life, and I shall hang you the same as I did your brothers." And so saying the giantess departed.

Harald was sorely puzzled. How could he possibly decide which of the animals the giantess wished killed? Then he remembered his friends.

"Dear Tritill, dear Litill, come once again to my aid," he cried.

Hardly had the words passed his lips, than he saw them both coming towards him, leading a huge ox between them. They at once set to work and killed him, and while Harald cleaned the entrails and cut up the joints, Tritill scraped the skin and prepared it for making the bag, and Litill began fashioning the spoons out of the horns.

So the work sped along quickly and merrily, and all was ready ere the sun sank to rest.

Harald now told his friends what the giantess had promised him if he should have finished his task ere she returned.

"Can you advise me what to ask for?" he said.

Then they told him he should first ask for that which was over her bed, then for the chest which stood beside her bed, and lastly for that which was behind the wall of her bed.

Harald thanked them warmly for all they had done for him, and said he would do as they had told him, whereupon the little men disappeared.

When the giantess came home in the evening and found that Harald had finished all the tasks she had set him, she exclaimed –

"Ah, man, man! you never did all this alone; but you have conquered, so I must let it pass." And so saying she retired to rest.

The next morning, the giantess called Harald into the inner cave and told him he might choose the reward she had promised him, and that then he might go where he liked.

"Then," said Harald, "if I may have whatever I like, I choose, first, that which is above your bed; then the chest which is beside your bed; and, lastly, that which is behind the wall of your bed."

"Ah, man, man!" cried the giantess. "You have not chosen these things by yourself; but I cannot refuse you; you are too strong for me, and you have conquered, and I must give you the reward you claim."

So saying, she mounted some steps above her bed cut into the rock, and, opening a secret door, she led forth a beautiful maiden. This was none other than the fair Princess Enid, who had disappeared so mysteriously some time ago.

"Take her back to her father, and he will reward you as you deserve," said the giantess as she placed the princess's hand in that of Harald.

She then opened the lid of the chest beside her bed. This was filled with gold, pearls, and precious stones; and then moving aside the bed, she touched a secret spring, and the wall sliding back, they saw the blue sea, and anchored close to the cave lay a beautiful ship completely fitted out, her sails all set, and her pennant flying, and possessing the power of sailing wherever its owner wished, without aid of either captain or crew.

When the giantess had handed him over these gifts, she told Harald that he would henceforth be one of the happiest and luckiest of men.

Harald then carried the chest containing the gold and precious stones on board ship, and then having arranged some soft cushions for the Princess Enid, in the stern of the vessel, they quickly departed, and reached her father's country.

The delight of the king and queen on recovering their long-lost daughter can be more easily imagined than described. They never tired hearing of the wonderful adventures through which Harald had gone, and the king ordered a great feast in honour of the rescuer of his child, which ended with the wedding of Enid and Harald.

The king then made Harald his prime minister; and so well and so wisely did he rule the country, that on the king's death he was chosen to succeed him, and he and Queen Enid lived long and happily together, seeing their children and grandchildren growing up around them.

Prince Hlini

(Icelandic)

IN A FAR COUNTRY, there once lived a king and a queen. They had an only son, called Hlini, who even as a child showed wonderful talents, and grew up the handsomest, cleverest, and bravest man in all the land.

One day, the prince went out hunting with some of the courtiers. It was a beautiful morning; the sun shone with unusual brilliancy, birds and game of all kinds were plentiful; and, well pleased with their good day's sport, the whole party turned homewards as the afternoon shadows began to lengthen, when suddenly a thick fog arose, which soon completely surrounded them. They lost sight of the prince, and it was only with great difficulty that they made their way back to the castle.

When the king heard that his son had not returned, he became very anxious; and the fog having somewhat lifted, he at once sent out messengers to try and find him. But although they searched in all directions for three days and nights, they could find no trace of him – no one had heard of or seen Prince Hlini.

This sudden disappearance of his son greatly grieved the king; and when, on the evening of the third day, the messengers returned without any news of him, the king retired to his room, and, throwing himself on his bed, gave way to the deepest grief. In vain the queen tried to cheer him, telling him that Hlini was so brave and clever, he would be sure to return safely. The king would not be consoled, and said he would gladly give the half of his kingdom to anyone who would bring him back his son.

Now, not far from the palace, in the middle of a wild moor, covered with yellow gorse and purple heather, there lived an old man in a little cottage with his only child, a daughter called Signy, who was both beautiful and clever. They were very poor, but lived happily and contented on wild honey and the berries that grew on the moors. When Signy heard from the shepherds that the prince had disappeared and that the king had offered the half of his kingdom to whoever should find him, she begged her father to let her go in search of him. At first he was very unwilling to part with her, dreading the dangers she might have to encounter; but Signy said she felt quite sure she would succeed in her search. All she wanted was a pair of new shoes and some food. And so, after a little more persuasion, her father gave her his blessing and started her on her journey.

Signy wandered on for several days, resting in the evenings in some sheltered nook, and ever going towards the north. It was now midsummer, the days were long – in fact, there was scarcely any night; and on the fourth evening, just as the sun, like a huge red ball, was setting in a bed of crimson and gold, only to rise again, Signy saw some rocks in front of her, in one of which was a huge cave. Listening carefully for a few minutes and hearing no sound, Signy entered very softly, and there she saw two beds: one was covered with a beautiful blue silk quilt, embroidered with gold; the other had a crimson velvet quilt, embroidered with silver. Going cautiously forward, she saw the prince, lying fast asleep on the bed with the golden quilt.

Signy was delighted with her discovery, and went up to him to waken him; but though she shook him, at first gently and then more roughly, she found she could not rouse him. Looking up, she saw some strange letters, or *runes*, cut into the wooden headboard of the bed.

Now, though her father, who was a learned old man, had taught Signy to read runes, she could make nothing of these. She therefore determined to wait and see who the owner of the cave was, and discovering a narrow recess near the opening, she crept quietly in.

Hardly had she got safely into her hiding place, than she heard a terrible noise, like a peal of thunder. The earth began to quake, and presently two frightful giantesses entered the cave.

As they came in, the taller and elder of the two cried out angrily, "Pah! I smell the smell of a human being here!"

"Of course you do," replied her sister, "seeing that Hlini the king's son is asleep here."

They then went to the bed on which Hlini was lying, and moving the headboard, on which the *runes* were carved, to one side, out came two beautiful silver swans.

"Sing, my beautiful swans, sing, and waken Hlini," cried the giantesses.

And as the swans, obeying, sang a lovely sweet song, the prince awoke.

The younger giantess then brought him a silver tray laden with delicious fruit and wine; but the prince would not touch anything.

"Will you marry me now?" then asked the giantess.

"No, no, and again no!" cried the prince.

"Then sing, sing, my beautiful swans, that Hlini may go to sleep again," she called out angrily.

And as the swans raised their voices in a sad, plaintive melody, the prince fell back on the bed, and was soon in his magic sleep again.

The two sisters then lay down on the other couch with the silver-embroidered quilt.

In the morning they again wakened Hlini in the same manner, and offered him food, which, however, he angrily refused; whereupon the younger giantess again asked him if he would marry her; and when he refused, as before, the sisters put him to sleep by the song of the swans, and then left the cave, closing it as they went out.

After waiting a little while to make sure that the wicked sisters were not coming back again, Signy came out of her hiding place, and moving the headboard of the bed, as she had seen the sisters do, she called to the swans, and as they sang their song, the prince awoke.

He was greatly surprised to see Signy in place of the hideous giant sisters, and thanked her warmly for her help, asking how she had come there.

Then Signy told him how much his father sorrowed at his mysterious disappearance, and that she had determined to try and find him.

Hlini was very grateful, and told Signy that, after he had got separated from his friends in the fog, he had suddenly encountered the giant sisters, who, having their swans with them, put him to sleep before he had time to fight them or get away, and that they had then forcibly carried him off to their cave; and that the younger sister, as she had no doubt heard, wanted to marry him. But this he had steadily refused to do. As long as he remained firm, they could only keep him there asleep; but, he added, he would rather remain thus for ever than marry the ogress.

When he had finished his tale, Signy said, "Now the first thing we must do, is to find out the meaning of the *runes* on the headboard. When, therefore, the sisters come in this evening, do not refuse their food (for you will want all your strength to get away), but be friendly with them, and then ask them what the letters mean, and also what they do all day while they are away."

Hlini said he would certainly follow Signy's advice. Then, finding a chessboard and some men on a shelf, they sat down and amused themselves playing and chatting, till they thought it was drawing near the time when the giantesses usually returned; then Signy called the swans and put the prince to sleep, as she had seen the sisters do, after which she hid herself in her dark corner.

Soon she heard the sisters returning, and presently they entered the cave.

"I certainly *do* smell the smell of a human being," said the elder sister, sniffing angrily round the cave.

"Nonsense!" replied the younger one, who, having lit the fire, was anxious to get their supper cooked. "Of course you smell it when Hlini is here."

"But this is a different smell," persisted the elder sister; and Signy, seeing her peering about, feared she would discover her.

But the younger sister, having plucked and cleaned the birds they had caught, told her elder sister she must cook them at once, as she was about to waken Hlini; and, going up to the couch with the gold-embroidered quilt, on which Hlini was lying asleep, she called forth the swans, and wakened him.

By this time the birds were cooked; and when she asked him if he would take any food, instead of refusing, Hlini said he felt hungry, and would join them at their supper.

The younger giantess was greatly pleased, and after helping him to fruit and wine, asked him whether he would not now make her his wife.

But Hlini said he must first know more about her and her sister before he could decide.

"What, for instance, is the meaning of those *runes* carved on the bedhead?" he asked.

"Oh," replied the giantess graciously, "the words are –

'Fly, fly, oh bedstead mine,
And carry me whither I will.'

You have only to sit down on the bed and repeat those words, and immediately you are carried to whatever place you wish to go."

The prince was delighted when he heard this, as he hoped it would enable him and Signy to escape.

"And what do you and your sister do all day when you are out?" he asked.

"Well, we roam about, looking for some man, woman, or child, for our dinner, for we always prefer them to birds or animals; and then, when we get tired, we sit down under a tree and play with our 'life egg.'" replied the giantess.

"I suppose you have to be very careful when you are playing with your life egg?" asked the prince.

"Yes, indeed we have to be," answered the giantess, "for if it were broken, we should both die. But there is no fear of that," and she gave a loud laugh, "we are much too careful; it can only be broken by a human being; and whenever one of them comes near us, we soon catch him and eat him."

The prince now declared that he felt so tired, he really must go to sleep; and though, before calling the swans, the giantess again asked him to marry her, he said he could say nothing till the morning, so he was put to sleep as before.

The next morning, after the sisters had wakened him and given him some food, they asked him if he would go to the woods with them; but Hlini said he still felt very tired, and would prefer to rest, so the sisters put him to sleep again and went away, closing the cave after them.

Waiting a short time, so as to make quite sure that the giantesses would not return, Signy presently came forth from her hiding place and awakened the prince.

"Get up quickly," she said, "for we will follow the giantesses into the wood. Take with you your hunting spear which stands beside the bed, and when they begin to play at 'throw and catch' with their life ball, you must throw your spear at the egg; but keep a clear eye and a firm hand, for, remember, if you miss, both your life and mine will be forfeited."

"Never fear," said Hlini; "there is too much at stake. I will be careful." Then they seated themselves on the couch, and both repeated the *rune*.

"Fly, fly, oh bedstead mine,
And carry me whither I will."

And immediately the bed rose up, the wall of the cave opened, and passing swiftly through the air, it landed them amid the leafy branches of a huge oak tree.

Peeping cautiously down, they saw the two giantesses sitting at the foot of the tree; one was holding the golden life egg in her hand, ready to throw it at her sister, and both were laughing loudly, as the egg flew backwards and forwards between them.

Watching his opportunity, Hlini threw his spear just as one sister was poising it in her hand, and as the point of the spear hit the egg, it broke in half.

At the same instant, both giantesses fell back dead, a stream of dark-coloured poison poured from their lips, and huge deadly black and yellow fungi sprang up and speedily covered them completely.

Hlini then seated himself beside Signy on the couch, and immediately they were carried back to the cave.

Here they found, on searching round, an immense quantity of gold, silver, and jewels; and having laden both beds with these and the two silver swans, they each sat down on one, and, repeating the *runes*, were speedily transported to the hut of Signy's father, who was delighted at his daughter's safe return, and made Hlini very welcome.

The next morning Signy went to the king's palace and demanded an audience, and the king, having admitted her, asked her who she was and what she wanted.

"I am the daughter of the old man who lives in the little hut on the moor near your palace," replied Signy, "and I have come to ask what reward you would give me if I bring your son back to you safe and well?"

The king laughed good-naturedly. "I do not think I need trouble to answer that," he said. "There is not much chance of your finding him, when so many others have failed."

"But if I succeed," persisted Signy, "will you give me the same reward as you have promised to others?"

"Certainly," replied the king; "if you succeed in bringing back my son safe and well, I will not go back from my word."

Then Signy returned to the hut, and begged the prince to return with her to the palace; and together they entered the great audience hall.

When the king beheld his son, whom he had mourned as dead, alive and well, he was greatly rejoiced, and made him sit down on his right hand and relate the story of all that had happened to him since the day he became separated from his friends during the chase.

When Hlini seated himself beside the king, he begged Signy to take the seat on his other hand, and then began the relation of all his adventures – telling of his imprisonment in the cave, and how Signy had freed him, and saved his life by rescuing him from the hands of the wicked giantesses.

When he had finished, he rose from his seat, and standing before his father, asked his permission to take Signy as his wife. To this the king willingly assented, saying that no reward could be too great for her, who had restored his son to him. So orders were at once issued for the preparation of a magnificent wedding-feast; all the great nobles of the kingdom were invited, neither were the poor forgotten. There was ample provision made for all, and everyone praised the king for his right royal hospitality, for each one received rich gifts ere they returned home. Signy's father was made the king's librarian, and put in charge of the royal manuscripts; and Hlini and Signy lived long and happily together, surrounded by their children and grandchildren.

The Last Home of the Giants

(Norwegian)

VALE AND MOUNTAIN alternated in beautiful succession beneath the blue sky of Norway thousands of years ago just as they do today, and the Gulf Stream flowed then as now past its rugged coasts; yet it was a far different land. In the thick forests no axe had yet been heard felling the strong timbers that the Norwegian rivers would bear down to the sea, to float hereafter as noble ships upon the breast of the ocean; in the sheltered bays no cosy houses nestled with their neatly-kept surroundings of garden and field; no boat yet flew over the sea with nets and fishing tackle. Man had not yet sought out as a home this beautiful northern land.

A race of giants, of tall and powerful build, dwelt there. Their lifetime was measured by centuries as ours by years. They tore rocks asunder with their hands, and left the great streams a free channel. They bore huge blocks on their shoulders to the shore, and built them into castles whose turrets towered into the clouds. Their voice drowned the roar of the ocean, and scared the eagle from its nest. But this powerful race, beneath whose tread the ground trembled, were of peaceful, harmless disposition. No quarrel divided, nor envy embittered, their hearts. They lived together like the children of one great family.

Their chief was Hrungnir. His companions voluntarily submitted to his control; for he excelled them all in years, wisdom, and strength, as a father his children.

Hrungnir lived in a splendid castle by the sea. The mountains of Norway had had to yield their most precious metals to adorn the walls of his giant dwelling within and without. The chief's numerous flocks and herds roamed over miles of land, the bears of the thick forests were slain in hundreds by his hands that their skins might cover pillows for his guests, and the tables and drinking-horns gleamed with precious stones. But Hrungnir's most cherished possession was Guru, his only daughter. Her hair shone golden as the stars of the northern night, her eyes were blue as the sky of her native land, and her skin was of dazzling whiteness.

The most powerful giants of the whole country were suitors for Guru's hand, and Hrungnir promised his daughter to him who should excel in swiftness in the race, or whose arm should be strongest to hurl huge boulders. Then the mighty men came down from their castles in the mountains, where the snowstorm sweeps round the hoary peaks, and from seaside fortresses, till Hrungnir's roof could scarcely give shelter to the host of powerful suitors. The tables smoked with countless dishes, the horns of mead were filled and filled again, and from the windows the songs of the giants sounded forth so loudly that the waves fled back in terror towards the sea.

After the feast, the giants went out to the strand, broke huge masses from the rocks, and hurled them out in the sea as children would throw pebbles. Far out into the ocean flew the masses of stones, but none so far as those thrown by the hand of Andfind, the valiant youth whose castle stood amid the rocks of the storm-swept Doverfjeld, whose wealth almost equalled Hrungnir's, whose beauty bore comparison with that of Guru herself. Then when the suitors arranged themselves on the strand for the race, and the shingle resounded with their golden sandals, Andfind left all his rivals far behind, and his long fair locks floated like golden pennons on the rock that was the goal of the race, while his fellow suitors were still toiling along the course.

Andfind was victor, and Guru's heart sang for joy, for she had long loved him in secret, though she was prepared to submit to her father's wish, even if he had chosen some other for his son-in-law.

Far from grudging envy, the giants loudly applauded the conqueror, bore him on their shoulders to Hrungnir's castle, where the chief bade him welcome, and called his daughter to meet her chosen bridegroom.

The lovely Guru came dressed in a sky-blue robe with a silver-embroidered hem, which she and her maids had woven and wrought in the retirement of the women's room. Round her white neck and rounded arms lay gleaming jewels, and her locks were bound with a golden fillet. Thus she came to meet the guests. Hrungnir took his daughter's hand, laid it in Andfind's right, and then, as priest of the household, the chief united them in the indissoluble ties of marriage.

Night fell round the Castle of Hrungnir. The chief and his guests lay wrapped in deep slumbers, preparing for the enjoyment of a new day. But destruction approached them as they slept, with stealthy steps; for Odin, that crafty king, of whose origin no man could tell, came with his trusty warriors down from the mountains. They had heard of the beauty of Norway, and wished to win it for their home. They had heard that the bravest in the land were feasting in Hrungnir's castle, and they had waited till the hours of slumber that they might strike unawares the foes with whom they could not have dared to cope on equal terms.

The moonlight glided through the open windows and fell on the forms of the defenceless sleepers: the deep breathing of the warriors and the murmur of the waves were the only sounds that the ear could distinguish. But dark shadows fell in the moonlit hall, tall forms climbed in at the windows, and noiselessly, holding their weapons carefully to prevent them from clashing, they stole into the rooms. With sure aim they bathed their swords in the heart's blood of the sleepers, so that, with one last groan, each warrior yielded up his brave spirit. The pavement swam in blood, but Odin's band passed from hall to hall and never slipped on their gory path.

The death-groan, though short, reached Guru's ear. She rose and listened. No, it was no dream; there came that sound again with dreadful distinctness. She threw on her garments and sprang to the window, and when she drew aside the curtain she saw strange forms in the courtyard, bearing with difficulty a heavy burden. She looked more closely, and recognized in the clear moonlight the bloody corpse of her noble father. She stole up to Andfind's couch, and whispered, "Awake, awake, my husband, and let us fly, for treachery and death have entered our house!"

The bloody work seemed finished in the other rooms, and now the dreaded footsteps were drawing near.

Guru raised a stone from the pavement and disclosed a secret stair. She bade Andfind descend, and then quickly following him, she carefully closed the opening behind her.

By a narrow passage which led beneath the castle and the rocks to the strand they reached the sea unseen. There a boat lay rocking, which Guru and her maids had often used for pleasant sails. They stepped in. Andfind spread the sail and seized the helm, and the boat flew out into the open sea.

Odin had conquered. The noblest of the land were killed in the inglorious victory of that night, and the weak remnant of the giant race were obliged to leave their old home and seek a refuge in unknown lands. Notwithstanding this ignoble beginning, Odin's reign was one of wisdom, power, and beneficence.

Of Guru and her husband nothing more was ever heard. Whether the sea had swallowed the boat in its hungry depths, or whether the waves had borne them to happier coasts, none had ever brought back the tidings to their old home. But in the winter evenings, when the maidens sat around the blazing pine-log, and talked at their spinning about the days of the Norwegian giants, some aged dame would tell her shuddering listeners of that night of death, and of the mysterious fate of Guru and her noble bridegroom.

* * *

Odin's reign was long since ended. His wisdom and his crimes were both alike well-nigh forgotten. Olaf had many years ago brought in the knowledge of the Christian religion, and reared churches on the sites of the old altars; and to the ancient honesty and strength of the nation was added the mild spirit of the religion of the cross.

On the spot where Hrungnir's castle once stood rose now a fortress as proud, and well-nigh as strong, as that of the giant chief; the flocks that grazed around it were as great as his; and the present possessor, Sämund, like him, counted as his dearest treasure an only daughter.

It seemed almost as if the days of Guru were come back again, for Aslog's golden hair and snowy skin, Aslog's blue eyes and graceful form, attracted the wealthiest and most powerful nobles of the land to woo her.

As each noble suitor was rejected, the father's heart swelled high with pride and hope. "She will only take the best and greatest," he thought. But when the most powerful prince in the land came, and the fair one's lips said "No" to him also, Sämund no longer praised his daughter's prudence. With bitter words he reproached her for her folly, and commanded her to choose before Christmas Eve someone on whom he might bestow her hand.

Days came and went, and Aslog's cheek grew paler and her father's eye more gloomy, for her heart was given to Orm, the poor but beautiful youth whom her father had given her as page. Orm's strong arm had on lovely summer evenings rowed the boat out into the gold-flooded sea; Orm's hand had guided her over the vast snow-fields, as in snow-shoes, with points thin and supple as a beech leaf, they glided swiftly through the bracing air; and in long winter evenings, while the guests were drinking and singing in her father's halls, Orm used to sit and tell her beautiful stories as she sat by the cheerful fire.

Sämund loved the brave youth, but had anyone spoken of him as his daughter's choice he would have challenged the informant to single combat.

The lovers knew this, and it was with trembling that they awaited the decisive day.

"If she has not chosen before the time I have named," said Sämund to Orm, "I will choose her a bridegroom myself, and you shall have the honour of bearing her bridal train."

Orm gave no answer, but with trembling hand he arranged the table for the guests, and pressed his lips close together to restrain the eager words that his love prompted.

It was the night before Christmas Eve – starry and cold. A secret door opened in the side of the mountain, and two muffled figures slipped out. They were Orm and Aslog. They had brought nothing with them but a little bundle of necessary clothing, a warm skin rug, and a bow and arrows which Orm had slung across his shoulder.

On they hurried over the icy plain, swiftly and terror-stricken, like a pair of hunted doves. They reached the edge of the wide plain. Their snow-shoes were no longer of use, for their road led now towards the defiles and rocky heights of the highlands. It was bitterly cold, the wind whistled through the clefts of the mountain, and its icy breath made Aslog's frail form tremble. Long their path wound among the snow-clad mountains; then they reached a thick fir wood, in the midst of which stood a little hermit's cottage.

"It is I, Father Jerome," said Orm to the old man who came to greet them at the door.

"Welcome, my son!" said the old man, as the youth stooped to press a reverent kiss on his withered hand; "and the maiden at thy side is welcome too to the poor hospitality of the hermit's cell."

The offered rest and refreshment were eagerly accepted by the weary maiden. With pitying eyes the hermit gazed on her grief-marked features, and when Orm begged him to unite them in marriage, the old man, after short consideration, granted their request.

How different was this hour from Aslog's dreams! Not that she gave many thoughts to the splendour and festivity that should have done honour to her bridal, but she felt bitterly the want of her father's blessing.

The ceremony over, there could be no further delay. On the wanderers pressed on their weary way, till Aslog would have sunk exhausted but for Orm's supporting arm. Through the thick fir woods, over rough mountain paths, they hastened on till the first streak of dawn gleamed in the eastern sky. Then Orm pointed to a cluster of dark rocks that lay before them.

"There," said he cheerfully – "there, my Aslog, is rest and safety."

Aslog's courage rose; with renewed energy she pressed over the intervening ground, till they reached a tall jagged rock and entered a cleft in its side. They now found themselves in a cave, which, though narrow at the entrance, became higher and wider as they went on, till it formed a spacious chamber. Out of this gloomy abode Orm's care and thoughtfulness made a home for his loved one that was not wholly lacking in comfort or happiness, and here they lived in secure retirement as long as the winter blocked the mountain roads. But when spring came, and the ways became accessible, Sämund's spies were able to explore more thoroughly, and Orm could no longer go out and in freely among the mountains. But when provisions ran short, he was obliged to tear himself from Aslog's weeping embrace, and sally forth with his bow and arrows. At last, when, after weeks of mild weather, no living soul had been seen near their retreat, their fears subsided, and Orm began to lay aside caution and to venture further from the cave. Perhaps Aslog's father had grown tired of the fruitless search, or perhaps he was even cherishing thoughts of forgiveness. Aslog's heart was quick to believe what she so ardently wished, and Orm began to believe it too. One night, while his wife was sleeping, he took the path towards the valley where the hermit's cell nestled amid the woods. His breast beat high with hope that the old man might be able to give him some good tidings to take back to his loved Aslog, who, although she bore her privations even cheerfully, was yet paler and feebler every day. He drew near a jutting rock, behind which lay the path to the hermit's cottage. In his glad excitement he had forgotten all fear. His bow hung with loose string behind him, and his hand grasped his staff but carelessly. Suddenly he heard a rustling in the thick bushes beside him, and two heavy hands were laid on his shoulder. With a strong effort he shook himself free, stepped back a few paces, and swung his stick menacingly.

"It is he whom we seek," cried his assailants; "remember the reward."

Then it seemed to Orm as if all the bushes and even the brown rock behind him became alive, so great a rustling was heard on every side. Quick as thought he brought his stick down on the heads of the two who had first attacked him, and before the others could leave their hiding places he had turned and fled.

At first there was wild shouting and a sound of eager feet behind, but he never stopped to look back, and he soon passed out of sight of his pursuers. The way was long and rough, but Orm was strong and fleet of foot, and before him lay his home and Aslog. At last he was at the cave.

How different was this homecoming from his former hopes! Aslog lay in sweet sleep, with a happy smile on her lips, as if she dreamt of love and forgiveness; and Orm must soon waken her, and tell her that she must go forth once more a homeless wanderer.

"Awake, awake, beloved one," he whispered, seizing her hand, "and let us flee, for your father's men are on our track, and we must be far from this before tomorrow dawns."

Aslog opened her eyes, and gazed in speechless astonishment at her husband's lips, but when she could no longer doubt, she sprang quickly up and arranged her clothing and the soft skins which had formed her covering in a neat bundle. Without delay they crept out of the cave by its narrow entrance, and went forth, not, as they had hoped, to Sämund's castle, but to a dark and unknown future. Westward, where Aslog's home lay, danger and treachery threatened them, so they turned their steps northwards, on untried mountain paths. The air was mild, the moon shone brightly on their way, and the soft moss kept no trace of their footsteps that might betray them to their watchful enemies. Thus they wandered northwards for hours. The cave in the rock lay miles behind them, and they were far from the place where Orm had been seen by his father-in-law's men. Then at last he ventured to turn westwards, towards the sea. Their way led down towards the lowlands. The wintry mists were still hanging over the plain. Orm's keen eye could scarcely pierce their grey veil, and Aslog shuddered as she felt their cold embrace. They could no longer tell in what direction they were going, but they went on and on, hoping to come ere long to the friendly ocean. At last Aslog's pale face caught a flush of joy as she heard its distant murmur. Nearer and nearer sounded the familiar music, and soon the wanderers came to a narrow valley, at the further edge of which rose a cluster of dark rocks.

"It is the coast!" said Aslog joyously, as she almost flew along the ground.

In a little bay at the foot of the rocks lay a fishing-boat. Orm bore his wife in his arms along the sand, for on this open strand the greatest haste was necessary, lest some hostile eye might see them. He placed Aslog gently in the boat, sprang in after her, and with trembling hands spread the sail.

The wind seemed to wish the fugitives well. It swept down from the mountains and filled the white sail, so that the little boat shot out into the sea like a swan with spreading wings. The sun rose higher and higher, the cliffs of their native coast seemed now but a line of low hills; proud ships glided not far from them, and on the farthest horizon appeared a group of islands gleaming in the golden mist. As the sun sank slowly to the horizon, the great ships passed by without noticing the wanderers, and the little islands were still in the far distance. Aslog's face, that had before glowed with hope, grew pale and wan.

"What is wrong, my darling?" asked Orm anxiously.

"I am hungry," answered Aslog faintly.

Orm sighed deeply. They had had to flee without waiting to get provisions, and now they had been twenty-four hours without food, and the islands lay far, far away. The sun sank into the sea.

"Sleep, my Aslog, sleep!" begged Orm at length; "you will not feel your hunger while you are asleep, and by the time you awake, perhaps we shall have reached one of the little islands before us."

And Aslog smiled submissively, and loosing the skins from the bundle, lay down beneath their protecting warmth at the bottom of the boat. The waves rocked the little vessel gently, the oar splashed in measured monotony, and at last Aslog's eyes closed, and she fell asleep.

Orm now kept watch alone on the wide ocean. Night had come, but a warm breath of spring was still hovering over the sea. The moon rose slowly above the distant mountains of Norway, and flooded the ocean with its silvery light. The waves danced sparkling round the boat, sails and masts shone brightly, and the hair of the slumbering fair one gleamed like waves of gold.

Full of love and grief, Orm's eyes rested on Aslog's pale face. Allowing himself but short rest, and that at long intervals, he rowed on all night, and when morning dawned, a large island with blossoming trees lay before his eyes bathed in the purple light. His cry of joy woke Aslog, who rose and looked at this lovely haven of refuge, which seemed offered to the homeless wanderers. Like a guardian of their future safety a tall grey rock stood upon the shore, in form not unlike a gigantic human figure.

Orm tried to steer between the small islands that lay round this tempting spot; but the waves, which had heretofore played so gently round the shores, now foamed and roared about the boat, and drove it back into the open sea. Nevertheless Orm undauntedly plied helm and oar, only to be driven back irresistibly again and again.

Noon came, and the fruitless struggle still continued; and now the sun was inclining towards the west. Orm's strength and heroic perseverance began at length to fail. His hands bled, his arms trembled, hunger and exhaustion almost overpowered him; while Aslog, who had sunk from a state of the most eager hope into the deepest despondency, clung, well-nigh unconscious, to the mast. Orm thought her dying. Then despair gave him fresh strength. "Almighty God, pity us!" he cried aloud to heaven. Immediately the waves submitted to the holy name; the foaming billows glided gently beneath the boat; the vessel shot like an arrow through the midst of the islands, and drew near the haven where the giant rock with its dark countenance looked down on the little boat that glided past it to the smooth strand. Orm sprang out, took the exhausted Aslog in his arms, and carried her across to the dry, soft sand. He looked round for something to eat. Fruit trees waved their blossoming crowns at no great distance, but the time for fruit was not come. Orm looked still more anxiously about the beach. Then he saw a mussel right at his feet, then another and another. He lifted them, and offered them to his half-fainting wife; and so much refreshed did she feel by the slight nourishment, that she was able to walk towards the centre of the island, supported by Orm's arm, in search of some place of shelter.

The blossoming fruit trees bore evidence of some careful hand, but no path, no footprint told of the cheering nearness of human beings. They went on further through the green island, over which the sun was shedding its last golden beams. There before them they saw a clear space amid the foliage, and with hearts beating with hope and fear they approached it. Soon they stood before a house of very ancient architecture. Its walls sank deep into the earth, and towered so high into the air that the firs could scarcely stretch their dark branches over the hide-covered roof. The windows were small, and their panes made of fishes' skins. The door was made of strong planks, and firmly bound with iron. The whole house looked as if it bade defiance to the storms, and had done so for centuries.

But where were now its builders? Did they lie sleeping in the depths of the ocean? Did the tall grass of the little islands wave above their last resting-place, or did they still sit, spellbound, behind the iron-bound door and the grey walls of the dreary dwelling? Checking the slight shudder that shook his frame at these thoughts, Orm knocked at the door of the mysterious house. No sound, no footstep told him that he had been heard within. He knocked again, then a third time, but there was still no movement. Then he laid his hand on the heavy latch; the door opened, and they entered a stone-paved hall. There was no one to bid them welcome or refuse them entrance. At one side of this hall was another door. Orm knocked, and when again there was no answer he opened it, and stepped with Aslog by his side into a large and lofty apartment. There was no one to be seen, yet everything bore traces of an orderly hand. A bright fire burned on the hearth, and above it hung a cauldron with fish, the smell of which greeted the hungry fugitives with pleasant invitation.

"Forgive us, noble master of this house!" said Orm in a loud voice, yet in a respectful tone; "it is necessity, not forwardness, which makes us intruders."

They both listened breathlessly; but there was still no answer. Then Orm poured some of the contents of the cauldron into two plates, and placed them on the table. With trembling at first, but afterwards with growing comfort and courage, the wanderers enjoyed the much-needed food.

When their hunger was satisfied, and their spirits revived, they looked around them. At the farther side of the room stood two beds of gigantic size, and of an ancient, long-forgotten form. The fire below the cauldron was getting low, the evening light had ceased to fall through the windows, and the darkness was only broken by the faint glimmer of the dying embers.

Nature at last claimed her rights. The wanderers' eyes were almost closing, and, laying aside all fear, they took possession of the couches where surely giant forms had once reposed.

When they awoke the sun was shining brightly outside, but its beams could fall but dimly through the rude windowpanes. The doors were firmly fastened, and there was no trace of human footsteps, yet the fire burned once more on the hearth, from the bubbling cauldron rose a tempting fragrance, and the table was laid as for a meal.

"See, dear Orm," cried Aslog joyfully, pointing to the fire and the table, "this language is easy to understand, though it be a silent one. The unseen owners of this dwelling know our need, and bid us welcome to their hospitable roof."

When they had again partaken of the contents of the boiling cauldron, Orm and Aslog went into the hall, and found there a stair which led up to a room just below the hide-covered roof. This and the room in which they had passed the night were the only apartments of the house, but they contained all that was necessary for a life of retirement. There was no sign of any inhabitant, yet it seemed as if someone had lately been there, whose hand had lovingly arranged everything for the poor homeless ones. They understood the silent language, and they remained henceforth contentedly in the house, enjoying the sweet feeling that they had at last a home.

Orm never cast his net into the sea without drawing out a rich supply of delicious fish; the snares he set in the morning for the birds were never empty at evening. The fruit trees bore abundantly, and Aslog found plenty of employment in gathering and storing the rich harvest.

Summer passed away, and the short autumn was drawing towards its close, when a lovely baby boy came to cheer the hearts of Orm and Aslog through the dreary winter. The child was called Sämund, and seemed to his parents a pledge of future reconciliation.

One day Orm was holding his little son in his arms, and watching with delight his baby smiles, and Aslog stood at the fire preparing the midday meal, when a tall shadow passed the window, the heavy house door swung open, and a loud knocking was heard at the door of the room. Aslog let the spoon fall in terror, and even brave Orm pressed his boy closer to his heart as the visitor entered.

A gigantic woman stepped into the room. Her stature was greater than Orm and Aslog had ever seen among their own powerful nation. She wore a sky-blue robe with a silver-embroidered hem; a golden fillet bound her long snow-white hair, and on her once beautiful features centuries of joy and grief seemed to have left their traces.

"Do not be afraid," said the majestic visitor, with gentle gravity; "this is my island and my house, but I gladly gave them up to you when I knew of your distress. Only one thing I ask of you. Christmas Eve is drawing near. For that one night let me have the room for a few hours, while we hold our yearly festivity. But you must promise me two things – not to speak a word while our feast lasts, and not to make any attempt to see what is going on in the room below. If you grant this request you may live here undisturbed, and enjoy my protection until you wish to leave the island."

With lightened hearts Orm and Aslog gave the promise, then the majestic lady bowed her silvery head in gracious farewell, and passed out through the door.

It was Christmas Eve; Aslog had cleaned and tidied the room with even more than her ordinary care. The boards were snow-white, and Orm strewed them with finely cloven fir twigs. The fire burned brightly on the neatly-swept hearth, and above it hung the shining cauldron. Aslog rolled her baby in the softest of the skins that served to cover her bed, and went with Orm to the upper room, where they sat down beside the warm chimney of the apartment below, which passed of necessity through this second storey.

For a long time all was silent. Suddenly a sweet, soft sound was heard; others followed, and soon the music swelled in waves of melody through the night air.

Aslog listened entranced, while Orm went to the gable end of the roof, and, since this was not forbidden, opened the shutter which in the daytime served to let in air and light.

There was motion over the whole island. Little shrivelled forms, with grave and aged faces, were bustling about with blazing torches in their hands. They ran dry-shod over the waves, and made their way to the rock that guarded the entrance to the bay. When they reached it they placed themselves in a circle round it, and sat down on the ground in respectful humility. Then a tall form approached from the centre of the island. The dwarfs opened their circle to admit her, and Orm recognized by the flickering light the noble lady who had a few days before paid them so unlooked-for a visit. Her sky-blue robe and the gold in her hair gleamed with even more than their former brilliance. She stepped up to the rock, threw her arms round the cold stone, and remained so for a moment in a silent embrace. Suddenly the stone acquired life and motion. The gigantic limbs were freed from their petrifaction, the hair rolled down over the shoulders, the eyes began to glow once more with life. As if awaking from the sleep of death, the giant rose, seized the hand of the stately lady whose loving embrace had called him back to life, and they both turned towards the house, whither the dwarfs accompanied them with flaming torches and heart-enthralling melody. The ground seemed to tremble beneath the tread of the giants. Soon they reached the house door. Then Orm shut the shutter, and groped his way back to where his wife sat beside the chimney.

Below there was rattling of dishes and the patter of many feet; the young couple heard every sound through the wide chimney. The strong voice of the rock giant sounded like thunder to human ears, and the voice of the lady, which Orm and Aslog had heard once before, was like the powerful notes of some musical instrument.

Tables and chairs were moved, drinking-horns were knocked together; the feast was beginning, and now was heard once more that music which had before so overwhelmed Aslog with delight. Then an irresistible longing seized her to see the wondrous company which Orm had described to her. She rose and groped for a crack in the floor through which it was possible to see into the room below. Orm in silence held out his hand to check her fatal rashness, but the movement woke the sleeping babe, who, terrified by the unwonted sounds below, raised a cry that went to the mother's heart. Forgetting everything now but her child's distress, she began, as was her wont, to soothe him with caressing words. Then suddenly an awful cry and a wild tumult arose below, the music ceased, and through the door rushed the dwarfs in wild commotion. Their torches went out, the noise of their flight sounded but a few moments, then night and silence reigned over the place which a minute before had resounded with festive merriment.

In deadly terror Aslog had sunk back on her seat, tremblingly awaiting the fate that her rashness had called down on her dear ones. They were anxious hours that they spent now in the dark upper room, almost more anxious than those of their flight and of that hard struggle with the waves. At last the morning dawned. A clear sunbeam shot through a hole in the shutter and awoke the boy, who began to cry with cold and hunger. Then her love for her child overcame her fear, and Aslog persuaded her husband to go down with her and learn their fate. They descended the stairs, trembling at every step. Now they stood at the door of the room and listened. There was no sound – all was still as death. At last they lifted the latch; Aslog pressed her child to her heart and entered the room. A loud cry escaped her lips. At the far end of the room, at the seat of honour at the table, sat the mighty giant whose awakening Orm had witnessed; but life had again left his veins, and he sat there a cold, grey mass of rock. It seemed to Aslog that the stony hand which still grasped the drinking-horn might yet be raised to hurl destruction at her and her dear ones. She gazed in speechless terror at the rock-giant, her eyes passing slowly from the motionless head to the massive folds of the stone garment. Then she perceived another form, sunk motionless, as in deepest anguish, on the floor. The face was pressed against the cold stone, but the blue robe with the silver-embroidered hem and the flowing white hair told the terrified Aslog who it was.

"Andfind, my Andfind!" moaned the giant lady, raising her face at last, "thou wilt never again smile on thy faithful Guru, and rejoice with her at thy short space of life and freedom."

Aslog uttered a cry, but not, as before, of terror for her own fate, but of anguish and remorse. Her bitter sobbing caused even the grief-stricken giantess to raise her head.

"Do not weep so," she said gently, "and do not be afraid; I could indeed easily kill you, and break this house, which I gave you as your home, like a child's toy.

"It is true that your forgetfulness has caused untold anguish to me, but the revenge of the powerful must be – forgiveness! Then do not weep, for there is nothing to fear."

"Oh, that is not all!" sobbed Aslog. "The names which you named, noble lady, cut me to the heart. They remind me of a legend which I often heard when a child about Guru, the beautiful giant-maiden, who was obliged to flee from cruel Odin with her beloved Andfind. The story of their fate always touched me deeply, and I thought when I heard these names that you might perhaps be that Guru, and this thought added fresh bitterness to my remorse."

The giantess appeared sunk in dreamy meditation.

"And do they remember us still in the old Fatherland?" she said at length; "and are there yet any halls remaining of Hrungnir's castle?"

"No, noble lady," answered Aslog, "they have all long since crumbled to dust, for many centuries have passed over Norway since those days. It is true a proud castle still looks down on the foaming waves, but it is owned by Sämund, whose only child I am."

"Our fate, O daughter of my former home, is wondrously alike," said Guru; "but your life will end more joyfully than mine. We lived here in undisturbed happiness for many centuries, for it was to this island that our trusty bark bore us after that night of death. This house, which my husband's strong arm built for our home, is small and poor compared with my father's halls, but we did not miss the lost splendour. The days went by in quiet happiness, and we felt no longings after the land which drove out us and our friends. The dwarfs also, who like us had turned their backs on an inhospitable country, settled round about on the little islands, and lived there in the heart of the earth in peace and contentment. Every Christmas Eve we met in this room, and held festival as our forefathers did even before your religion had spread to these northern lands. Centuries passed away, and one evening I was standing with Andfind at the shore of our island looking out over the sea. On the northern horizon appeared a stately ship, and Andfind, whose eye was sharper than the eagle's, and had power to see into the future, recognized in the man at the prow a powerful foe of the freedom of Norway and of our authority. It was Olaf, whom you call a saint, who, not long afterwards, overcame the princes of Norway in one night, and destroyed the last vestiges of the old customs. All this my husband's prudent foresight saw, and with a mighty effort he blew the waves to fury with his breath, so that they threatened to break Olaf's proud ship to pieces. But the invader spoke some prayer such as you uttered when you approached our shores, and the raging sea grew calm. Then Andfind put forth his hand to push back the vessel as it drew near the shore, but Olaf, raising his hands towards heaven, said, in a tone of stern reproof – 'Stand thou there a stone henceforth!' Immediately the eyes in which I had been wont to read my husband's every wish were closed, the hand that had grasped mine lovingly grew cold and hard, the form so full of life and beauty turned to unfeeling stone, and my beloved Andfind stood a grey, lifeless rock upon the shore. The invaders sailed on towards the coast of Norway, and I remained in dreary desolation on the now lonely island. Only once a year, on Christmas Eve, petrified giants are allowed a few hours of life if one of their own race embraces them, and thus sacrifices centuries of his own lifetime. I loved my husband too dearly not to offer this sacrifice willingly, that he and I might enjoy yearly a few hours of intercourse. I never counted how many times he woke to life at my embrace, how many centuries of my life I yielded for his sake; I did not wish to know the day when I, as I embraced him, should likewise turn to stone, and stand henceforth on the shore one for ever with my Andfind. Now all is over," Guru concluded; "I may never more awake my beloved one, for a human eye, a human voice has disturbed the sacred festival of our spirit-race. Stone must my Andfind remain till that day when all the rocks and mountains of old Norway will perish in the ruin of the world."

She threw her arms once more round the cold stone, lifted her golden harp from the floor, and then turned to Orm and Aslog, who had listened in silent grief.

"Farewell!" she said; "I leave you my protection and my blessing. Yours are henceforth the costly vessels that adorned our festive board; I need them no more. Live still in peace and happiness in this house until you return to receive Sämund's forgiveness, and live a life of gladness on the site of my old home."

She passed out, and her sorrowing guests followed her to the door. Without once looking back, she glided away through the leafless trees; her blue robe gleamed far away over the snow-covered plain. Orm and Aslog watched her crossing the waves to the little islands; then they saw her no more.

Had she descended to the music of her golden harp into the cold billows? Or did she go to rule as queen in the kingdom of dwarfs? Orm and Aslog never knew her fate, but her prophecies of good were richly fulfilled.

Sickness and misfortune kept far aloof from their island home. They were happy in their mutual love, strong in body, cheerful in spirit, contented even in their isolation. Their boy grew daily in beauty, strength, and obedience; the trees bore double fruit, the sea yielded its tribute more freely than ever, and the bird-snares were never empty. Sunshine and the fragrance of flowers filled the air, and they drank in life and happiness at every breath. And when winter came, the storm raged round the house, and the thick snowflakes whirled through the cracking fir branches against the window, then the little family sat cosily in their sheltered home; the dry wood blazed brightly on the hearth, and at the cheerful fireside sat Aslog making nets, while Orm carved away at a new oar, and the child listened eagerly to the tales of Old Norway.

Year after year rolled away, and left no traces of care on the faces of the lonely exiles, save that when Aslog thought of her father a shadow crossed her white brow, and the old longing awoke for his love and forgiveness.

It was the beginning of spring. The fruit trees wore their wreaths of blossoms, and the sunbeams played through the dark fir branches on the roof of the lonely house. The door opened, and Orm, accompanied by Aslog and the boy, stepped out, bearing one of the precious vessels which Guru had left as a parting gift to her guests. The utensils which her motherly hand had provided had become worn out in the course of years, and Orm was going to the coast of Norway to sell the golden goblet, and buy the needed utensils with its price. He had long postponed this step, for he still feared the sharp eye of treachery and revenge; but their need was pressing, and there could be no longer delay.

The parting was a bitter one. Aslog embraced him again and again, and even Guru's prophetic words had lost their power to comfort. But Orm, although his heart was far from light, soothed her with a promise of a quick return; then he tore himself away, sprang into a boat, and pushed from the shore.

The boat flew like a seamew over the waves, through the circle of little islands, and out into the open sea. A wind as fresh as that which had favoured their flight came now from the north to swell the white sail. Orm drew in the oars and watched how his boat darted over the gleaming waves. He directed his course towards the south-east. As it was drawing towards noon the coasts of his native land appeared above the horizon; and long before the set of sun the boat sailed up the narrow waters of the Trondheim Fiord, and landed at the quay of the old royal city. Orm passed the streets with hurried steps, and with the precious vessel under his arm he entered the shop of a goldsmith.

The man seemed amazed at the rich metal and the rare and elaborate workmanship, paid without demur the price asked, and Orm hastened gladly to another building to choose his purchases. There was a great crowd of buyers, and fearing lest some old acquaintance should be among them, he turned aside, and examined the wares in silence.

"Welcome, friend! What's the news in your mountains?" said the merchant to a countryman who had just entered.

"Thanks, sir, not much good," replied the newcomer.

"What is wrong?" asked the merchant. "Is your master, rich Sämund, not well? Has he not yet submitted to his fate?"

Orm listened eagerly.

"It will soon be all over with him," replied the countryman; "his grief about his daughter is breaking his heart. He is ill, lonely, and sad. He has had it proclaimed through the whole land that he will forgive the fugitives everything if they will only return; and he has promised a great reward to anyone who will bring him the smallest tidings of them. But they seem to have vanished from the earth, and it is most likely the old man will die without one of his kin to close his eyes in the last sleep."

Orm thought no more about his purchases; he thought only of Aslog and her dying father. Without being noticed in the crowd he left the shop. Scarcely had he turned the first corner when he ran at full speed to the quay, sprang down the steps, loosed his boat, and by the last rays of the setting sun he steered skilfully along the narrow fiord among all the larger vessels, and rowed towards the ocean. His heart beat with eager longing and delight. Had not a reconciliation with the father of his loved Aslog long been the most cherished wish of his heart as well as of hers, though he had been silent on the subject for Aslog's sake?

It was night when his boat glided out of the fiord and sailed out to sea. The wind, which had blown towards land all day, had turned, and, sweeping now from the Norwegian mountains, drove Orm's boat with the swiftness of an arrow over the waters. The moon rose clear and full above his native land, and the waves dashed their silver spray against the keel. Orm could not but think of that night when Aslog lay hungry and exhausted at his feet – behind him terror and treachery – before, an unknown future. The moon's clear radiance and the sparkling waves were the same then as now, but in all else how blessed was the change!

Thus the night passed, and when the east began to glow with red his boat glided between the little islands, and when the first full beam fell on the fir tree tops he landed on the shore of his island home.

He scarcely took time to fasten the boat. Then he hastened under the blossoming fruit trees – with empty hand, indeed, yet with a richer gift than Aslog would have dared to hope for.

And now he stood beside her couch. "Awake, awake, beloved one!" he whispered as he bent over her; "I bring news of your father, the best news that your heart could wish for – love and forgiveness!"

Then Aslog awoke, and her beaming eyes, the silent tears that fell over her clasped hands, told of even deeper joy than Orm had pictured to himself as he hastened home.

Soon all was bustle in the quiet room. Once more Aslog lit the fire, once more the breakfast bubbled in the cauldron, while she adorned herself and her boy in festive garments, and Orm carried Guru's gifts of gold and precious stones down to the boat. Once more they sat together at the table enjoying the provisions of Guru's hospitable home. They gazed at the lofty walls which had afforded them shelter, and sadly looked on the stony form of Andfind, who had for years been a silent member of the little household. Then Orm seized his wife's hand; and they left the house, carefully closing the door behind them, and followed the boy, who had run on before in his eagerness, towards the strand.

"Farewell, thou lovely island!" cried Orm, as he loosed the rope; "and if ever again hunted fugitives land on thy shore, be to them as sweet a home as thou hast been to us."

The child was already seated in the boat, playing with the beautiful vessels of gold and precious stones, and Aslog sat down beside him to tell him about his new home and his dear grandfather, while Orm dipped the oars, and the boat left the strand of the 'Last Home of the Giants.'

The sun was just about to sink into the sea; its rays cast a parting glance on the windows of the lonely castle, on the rock which had once resounded with mirth and revelry. And now the splendid halls were desolate. The servants, serving not out of love but out of fear, obeyed in sullen silence the commands of their gloomy master. The daughter, the only one whom his cold heart had ever loved, was lost to him. His old age was lonely and desolate. Then his pride yielded. "What if she has disgraced my house by choosing the servant instead of the prince? Still she is my child, my only one, and dear and loving she has always been to me! Oh, bring back my daughter, my Aslog, that I may look upon her face before I die!"

Rich were the rewards offered by the sorrowing father for the least tidings of his child, but he waited days and weeks in vain. She seemed lost to him for ever.

"Take me out, that I may see the sun as long as I have sight!" said he to his servants as the evening sun looked in at the castle windows.

The servants supported his tottering steps to the edge of the rock. Then he beckoned to them to go, and leave him with his sorrow.

The sun sank like a ball of fire into the ocean, and the sea rolled in purple waves from the farthest horizon, and broke them into golden spray at the foot of the castle rock.

"Would that my old age could be calm and clear, like this sweet evening, and would that my life might sink in brightness as the sun into the sea!"

Then he heard in the distance the splashing of oars, and his eye, keen as of old, looked eagerly towards the horizon. A boat, gently urged on by the wind, was sailing from the north-west. Nearer and nearer it came, and seemed to be directing its course to the rock where the old man sat. At the helm sat a manly form, and at the prow stood a graceful woman with a boy pressed closely to her side. Her hair gleamed golden, as his daughter's used to do; and now she raised her hand, and fluttered a white kerchief as in eager greeting. Sämund's heart beat with glad presentiment, he felt his weakness no longer, but raised himself, unaided, from the stone breastwork, and fixed his gaze on the approaching boat. Now the little vessel came up to the very foot of the rock, he heard the chain rattling round the post, and the sound of familiar voices was borne up to him on the evening air. It was no dream. There were light footsteps beside him, and when he turned to look, Aslog, his lost Aslog, knelt before him, her eyes full of humble penitence, and by her side knelt a fair-haired boy, who stretched out his hands to the old man, and echoed his mother's words in childish accents – "Oh, grandfather, forgive and love us!"

The old man opened his arms, and pressed the welcome suppliants to his heart, and as he kissed his lovely grandson, he said in a voice more mild and soft than was his wont – "Thank God, I shall not die in my loneliness after all!"

And he did not die. From day to day he felt more and more of his old vigour, and when he saw how tenderly Aslog loved her husband, what a faithful husband and father Orm was, and what a dutiful son to himself, he forgot all his disappointed hopes – even the royal diadem that Aslog had rejected. The love of his children and grandchildren made his last days his brightest, and thus the wish of that spring evening was fulfilled, his old age was calm and clear, and his life sank in brightness as the sun into the sea.

Tales of Wind, Snow & Sea

Introduction

A THOUSAND YEARS after the first longships struck their way across the high Atlantic swell, Hans Christian Andersen's 'Little Match-Seller' struggled through a city's icy winter streets. No one knew better than the Vikings did the raw power of the snow and wind and rain: the elements are an elemental force in Nordic myths and tales.

Father Weatherbeard, who rides the winds ('I am at home both in the north and south and the east and the west…'), is as sinister as any troll. The parents who entrust their son to him – he promises to train him up as his apprentice – find he's nothing like as quick to give him back. As for the Sea Queen, in 'First Born, First Wed', she may be happy enough to save the stricken mariner – but she demands that he hand over his young son in return.

Human life has always hung by a thread and mythology everywhere is aware of our fragility, but the Vikings were unusually – perhaps uniquely – vulnerable. Countless lives have been lost to wind and waves in every generation in what are still seafaring nations.

Farmer Weatherbeard

(Norwegian)

THERE WAS ONCE UPON A TIME a man and a woman who had an only son, and he was called Jack. The woman thought that it was his duty to go out to service, and told her husband that he was to take him somewhere.

"You must get him such a good place that he will become master of all masters," she said, and then she put some food and a roll of tobacco into a bag for them.

Well, they went to a great many masters, but all said that they could make the lad as good as they were themselves, but better than that they could not make him. When the man came home to the old woman with this answer, she said, "I shall be equally well pleased whatever you do with him; but this I do say, that you are to have him made a master over all masters." Then she once more put some food and a roll of tobacco into the bag, and the man and his son had to set out again.

When they had walked some distance they got upon the ice, and there they met a man in a carriage who was driving a black horse.

"Where are you going?" he said.

"I have to go and get my son apprenticed to someone who will be able to teach him a trade, for my old woman comes of such well-to-do folk that she insists on his being taught to be master of all masters," said the man.

"We are not ill met, then," said the man who was driving, "for I am the kind of man who can do that, and I am just looking out for such an apprentice. Get up behind with you," he said to the boy, and off the horse went with them straight up into the air.

"No, no, wait a little!" screamed the father of the boy. "I ought to know what your name is and where you live."

"Oh, I am at home both in the north and the south and the east and the west, and I am called Farmer Weatherbeard," said the master. "You may come here again in a year"s time, and then I will tell you if the lad suits me." And then they set off again and were gone.

When the man got home the old woman inquired what had become of the son.

"Ah! Heaven only knows what has become of him!" said the man. "They went up aloft." And then he told her what had happened.

But when the woman heard that, and found that the man did not at all know either when their son would be out of his apprentice-ship, or where he had gone, she packed him off again to find out, and gave him a bag of food and a roll of tobacco to take away with him.

When he had walked for some time he came to a great wood, and it stretched before him all day long as he went on, and when night began to fall he saw a great light, and went towards it. After a long, long time he came to a small hut at the foot of a rock, outside which an old woman was standing drawing water up from a well with her nose, it was so long.

"Good-evening, mother," said the man.

"Good-evening to you too," said the old woman. "No one has called me mother this hundred years."

"Can I lodge here tonight?" said the man.

"No," said the old woman. But the man took out his roll of tobacco, lighted a little of it, and then gave her a whiff. Then she was so delighted that she began to dance, and thus the man got leave to stay the night there. It was not long before he asked about Farmer Weatherbeard.

She said that she knew nothing about him, but that she ruled over all the four-footed beasts, and some of them might know him. So she gathered them all together by blowing a whistle which she had, and questioned them, but there was not one of them which knew anything about Farmer Weatherbeard.

"Well," said the old woman, "there are three of us sisters; it may be that one of the other two knows where he is to be found. You shall have the loan of my horse and carriage, and then you will get there by night; but her house is three hundred miles off, go the nearest way you will."

The man set out and got there at night. When he arrived, this old woman also was standing drawing water out of the well with her nose.

"Good-evening, mother," said the man.

"Good-evening to you," said the old woman. "No one has ever called me mother this hundred years."

"Can I lodge here tonight?" said the man.

"No," said the old woman.

Then he took out the roll of tobacco, took a whiff, and gave the old woman some snuff on the back of her hand. Then she was so delighted that she began to dance, and the man got leave to stay all night. It was not long before he began to ask about Farmer Weatherbeard.

She knew nothing about him, but she ruled over all the fishes, she said, and perhaps some of them might know something. So she gathered them all together by blowing a whistle which she had, and questioned them, but there was not one of them which knew anything about Farmer Weatherbeard.

"Well," said the old woman, "I have another sister; perhaps she may know something about him. She lives six hundred miles off, but you shall have my horse and carriage, and then you will get there by nightfall."

So the man set off and he got there by nightfall. The old woman was standing raking the fire, and she was doing it with her nose, so long it was.

"Good-evening, mother," said the man.

"Good-evening to you," said the old woman. "No one has called me mother this hundred years."

"Can I lodge here tonight?" said the man.

"No," said the old woman. But the man pulled out his roll of tobacco again, and filled his pipe with some of it, and gave the old woman enough snuff to cover the back of her hand. Then she was so delighted that she began to dance, and the man got leave to stay in her house. It was not long before he asked about Farmer Weatherbeard. She knew nothing at all about him, she said, but she governed all the birds; and she gathered them together with her whistle. When she questioned them all, the eagle was not there, but it came soon afterwards, and when asked, it said that it had just come from Farmer Weatherbeard's. Then the old woman said that it was to guide the man to him. But the eagle would have something to eat first, and then it wanted to wait until the next day, for it was so tired with the long journey that it was scarcely able to rise from the earth.

When the eagle had had plenty of food and rest, the old woman plucked a feather out of its tail, and set the man in the feather's place, and then the bird flew away with him, but they did not get to Farmer Weatherbeard's before midnight.

When they got there the Eagle said: "There are a great many dead bodies lying outside the door, but you must not concern yourself about them. The people who are inside the house are all so sound asleep that it will not be easy to awake them; but you must go straight to the table-drawer, and take out three bits of bread, and if you hear anyone snoring, pluck three feathers from his head; he will not waken for that."

The man did this; when he had got the bits of bread he first plucked out one feather.

"Oof!" screamed Farmer Weatherbeard.

So the man plucked out another, and then Farmer Weatherbeard shrieked "Oof!" again; but when the man had plucked the third, Farmer Weatherbeard screamed so loudly that the man thought that brick and mortar would be rent in twain, but for all that he went on sleeping. And now the Eagle told the man what he was to do next, and he did it. He went to the stable door, and there he stumbled against a hard stone, which he picked up, and beneath it lay three splinters of wood, which he also picked up. He knocked at the stable door and it opened at once. He threw down the three little bits of bread and a hare came out and ate them. He caught the hare. Then the Eagle told him to pluck three feathers out of its tail, and put in the hare, the stone, the splinters of wood and himself instead of them, and then he would be able to carry them all home.

When the Eagle had flown a long way it alighted on a stone.

"Do you see anything?" it asked.

"Yes; I see a flock of crows coming flying after us," said the man.

"Then we shall do well to fly on a little farther," said the Eagle, and off it set.

In a short time it asked again, "Do you see anything now?"

"Yes; now the crows are close behind us," said the man.

"Then throw down the three feathers which you plucked out of his head," said the Eagle.

So the man did this, and no sooner had he flung them down than the feathers became a flock of ravens, which chased the crows home again. Then the Eagle flew on much farther with the man, but at length it alighted on a stone for a while.

"Do you see anything?" it said.

"I am not quite certain," said the man, "but I think I see something coming in the far distance."

"Then we shall do well to fly on a little farther," said the Eagle, and away it went.

"Do you see anything now?" it said, after some time had gone by.

"Yes; now they are close behind us," said the man.

"Then throw down the splinters of wood which you took from beneath the grey stone by the stable door," said the Eagle. The man did this, and no sooner had he flung them down than they grew up into a great thick wood, and Farmer Weatherbeard had to go home for an axe to cut his way through it. So the Eagle flew on a long, long way, but then it grew tired and sat down on a fir tree.

"Do you see anything?" it asked.

"Yes; I am not quite certain," said the man, "but I think I can catch a glimpse of something far, far away."

"Then we shall do well to fly on a little farther," said the Eagle, and it set off again.

"Do you see anything now?" it said after some time had gone by.

"Yes; he is close behind us now," said the man.

"Then you must fling down the great stone which you took away from the stable door," said the Eagle.

The man did so, and it turned into a great high mountain of stone, which Farmer Weatherbeard had to break his way through before he could follow them. But when he had got to the middle of the mountain he broke one of his legs, so he had to go home to get it put right.

While he was doing this the Eagle flew off to the man's home with him, and with the hare, and when they had got home the man went to the churchyard, and had some Christian earth laid upon the hare, and then it turned into his son Jack.

When the time came for the fair the youth turned himself into a light-coloured horse, and bade his father go to the market with him. "If anyone should come who wants to buy me," said he, "you are to tell him that you want a hundred dollars for me; but you must not forget to take off the halter, for if you do I shall never be able to get away from Farmer Weatherbeard, for he is the man who will come and bargain for me."

And thus it happened. A horse-dealer came who had a great fancy to bargain for the horse, and the man got a hundred dollars for it, but when the bargain was made, and Jack's father had got the money, the horse-dealer wanted to have the halter.

"That was no part of our bargain," said the man, "and the halter you shall not have, for I have other horses which I shall have to sell."

So each of them went his way. But the horse dealer had not got very far with Jack before he resumed his own form again, and when the man got home he was sitting on the bench by the stove.

The next day he changed himself into a brown horse and told his father that he was to set off to market with him. "If a man should come who wants to buy me," said Jack, "you are to tell him that you want two hundred dollars, for that he will give, and treat you besides; but whatsoever you drink, and whatsoever you do, don't forget to take the halter off me, or you will never see me more."

And thus it happened. The man got his two hundred dollars for the horse, and was treated as well, and when they parted from each other it was just as much as he could do to remember to take off the halter. But the buyer had not got far on his way before the youth took his own form again, and when the man reached home Jack was already sitting on the bench by the stove.

On the third day all happened in the same way. The youth changed himself into a great black horse, and told his father that if a man came and offered him three hundred dollars, and treated him well and handsomely into the bargain, he was to sell him, but whatsoever he did, or how much soever he drank, he must not forget to take off the halter, or else he himself would never get away from Farmer Weatherbeard as long as he lived.

"No," said the man, "I will not forget."

When he got to the market, he received the three hundred dollars, but Farmer Weatherbeard treated him so handsomely that he quite forgot to take off the halter; so Farmer Weatherbeard went away with the horse.

When he had got some distance he had to go into an inn to get some more brandy; so he set a barrel full of red-hot nails under his horse's nose, and a trough filled with oats beneath its tail, and then he tied the halter fast to a hook and went away into the inn. So the horse stood there stamping, and kicking, and snorting, and rearing, and out came a girl who thought it a sin and a shame to treat a horse so ill.

"Ah, poor creature, what a master you must have to treat you thus!" she said, and pushed the halter off the hook so that the horse might turn round and eat the oats.

"I am here!" shrieked Farmer Weatherbeard, rushing out of doors. But the horse had already shaken off the halter and flung himself into a goose-pond, where he changed himself into a little fish. Farmer Weatherbeard went after him, and changed himself into a great pike.

So Jack turned himself into a dove, and Farmer Weatherbeard turned himself into a hawk, and flew after the dove and struck it. But a Princess was standing at a window in the King's palace watching the struggle.

"If thou didst but know as much as I know, thou wouldst fly in to me through the window," said the Princess to the dove.

So the dove came flying in through the window and changed itself into Jack again, and told her all as it had happened.

"Change thyself into a gold ring, and set thyself on my finger," said the Princess.

"No, that will not do," said Jack, "for then Farmer Weatherbeard will make the King fall sick, and there will be no one who can make him well again before Farmer Weatherbeard comes and cures him, and for that he will demand the gold ring."

"I will say that it was my mother's, and that I will not part with it," said the Princess.

So Jack changed himself into a gold ring, and set himself on the Princess's finger, and Farmer Weatherbeard could not get at him there. But then all that the youth had foretold came to pass.

The King became ill, and there was no doctor who could cure him till Farmer Weatherbeard arrived, and he demanded the ring which was on the Princess's finger as a reward.

So the King sent a messenger to the Princess for the ring. She, however, refused to part with it, because she had inherited it from her mother. When the King was informed of this he fell into a rage, and said that he would have the ring, let her have inherited it from whom she might.

"Well, it's of no use to be angry about it," said the Princess, "for I can't get it off. If you want the ring you will have to take the finger too!"

"I will try, and then the ring will very soon come off," said Farmer Weatherbeard.

"No, thank you, I will try myself," said the Princess, and she went away to the fireplace and put some ashes on the ring.

So the ring came off and was lost among the ashes.

Farmer Weatherbeard changed himself into a hare, which scratched and scraped about in the fireplace after the ring until the ashes were up to its ears. But Jack changed himself into a fox, and bit the hare's head off, and if Farmer Weatherbeard was possessed by the evil one all was now over with him.

The Three Princesses of Whiteland

(Norwegian)

THERE WAS ONCE UPON A TIME a fisherman, who lived hard by a palace and fished for the King's table. One day he was out fishing, but caught nothing at all. Let him do what he might with rod and line, there was never even so much as a sprat on his hook; but when the day was well nigh over, a head rose up out of the water, and said: "If you will give me what your wife shows you when you go home, you shall catch fish enough."

So the man said "Yes" in a moment, and then he caught fish in plenty; but when he got home at night, and his wife showed him a baby which had just been born, and fell a-weeping and wailing when he told her of the promise which he had given, he was very unhappy.

All this was soon told to the King up at the palace, and when he heard what sorrow the woman was in, and the reason of it, he said that he himself would take the child and see if he could not save it. The baby was a boy, and the King took him at once and brought him up as his own son until the lad grew up. Then one day he begged to have leave to go out with his father to fish; he had a strong desire to do this, he said. The King was very unwilling to permit it, but at last the lad got leave. He stayed with his father, and all went prosperously and well with them the whole day, until they came back to land in the evening. Then the lad found that he had lost his pocket-handkerchief, and would go out in the boat after it; but no sooner had he got into the boat than it began to move off with him so quickly that the water foamed all round about, and all that the lad did to keep the boat back with the oars was done to no purpose, for it went on and on the whole night through, and at last he came to a white strand that lay far, far away. There he landed, and when he had walked on for some distance he met an old man with a long white beard.

"What is the name of this country?" said the youth.

"Whiteland," answered the man, and then he begged the youth to tell him whence he came and what he was going to do, and the youth did so.

"Well, then," said the man, "if you walk on farther along the seashore here, you will come to three princesses who are standing in the earth so that their heads alone are out of it. Then the first of them will call you – she is the eldest – and will beg you very prettily to come to her and help her, and the second will do the same, but you must not go near either of them. Hurry past, as if you neither saw nor heard them; but you shall go to the third and do what she bids you; it will bring you good fortune."

When the youth came to the first princess, she called to him and begged him to come to her very prettily, but he walked on as if he did not even see her, and he passed by the second in the same way, but he went up to the third.

"If thou wilt do what I tell thee, thou shalt choose among us three," said the Princess.

So the lad said that he was most willing, and she told him that three Trolls had planted them all three there in the earth, but that formerly they had dwelt in the castle which he could see at some distance in the wood.

"Now," she said, "thou shalt go into the castle, and let the Trolls beat thee one night for each of us, and if thou canst but endure that, thou wilt set us free."

"Yes," answered the lad, "I will certainly try to do so."

"When thou goest in," continued the Princess, "two lions will stand by the doorway, but if thou only goest straight between them they will do thee no harm; go straight forward into a small dark chamber; there thou shalt lie down. Then the Troll will come and beat thee, but thou shalt take the flask which is hanging on the wall, and anoint thyself wheresoever he has wounded thee, after which thou shalt be as well as before. Then lay hold of the sword which is hanging by the side of the flask, and smite the Troll dead."

So he did what the Princess had told him. He walked straight in between the lions just as if he did not see them, and then into the small chamber, and lay down on the bed.

The first night a Troll came with three heads and three rods, and beat the lad most unmercifully; but he held out until the Troll was done with him, and then he took the flask and rubbed himself. Having done this, he grasped the sword and smote the Troll dead.

In the morning when he went to the seashore the Princesses were out of the earth as far as their waists.

The next night everything happened in the same way, but the Troll who came then had six heads and six rods, and he beat him much more severely than the first had done but when the lad went out of doors next morning, the Princesses were out of the earth as far as their knees.

On the third night a Troll came who had nine heads and nine rods, and he struck the lad and flogged him so long, that at last he swooned away; so the Troll took him up and flung him against the wall, and this made the flask of ointment fall down, and it splashed all over him, and he became as strong as ever again.

Then, without loss of time, he grasped the sword and struck the Troll dead, and in the morning when he went out of the castle the Princesses were standing there entirely out of the earth. So he took the youngest for his Queen, and lived with her very happily for a long time.

At last, however, he took a fancy to go home for a short time to see his parents. His Queen did not like this, but when his longing grew so great that he told her he must and would go, she said to him:

"One thing shalt thou promise me, and that is, to do what thy father bids thee, but not what thy mother bids thee," and this he promised.

So she gave him a ring, which enabled him who wore it to obtain two wishes.

He wished himself at home, and instantly found himself there; but his parents were so amazed at the splendour of his apparel that their wonder never ceased.

When he had been at home for some days his mother wanted him to go up to the palace, to show the King what a great man he had become.

The father said, "No; he must not do that, for if he does we shall have no more delight in him this time" but he spoke in vain, for the mother begged and prayed until at last he went.

When he arrived there he was more splendid, both in raiment and in all else, than the other King, who did not like it, and said:

"Well, you can see what kind of Queen mine is, but I can't see yours. I do not believe you have such a pretty Queen as I have."

"Would to heaven she were standing here, and then you would be able to see!" said the young King, and in an instant she was standing there.

But she was very sorrowful, and said to him, "Why didst thou not remember my words, and listen only to what thy father said? Now must I go home again at once, and thou hast wasted both thy wishes."

Then she tied a ring in his hair, which had her name upon it, and wished herself at home again.

And now the young King was deeply afflicted, and day out and day in went about thinking of naught else but how to get back again to his Queen. "I will try to see if there is any place where I can learn how to find Whiteland," he thought, and journeyed forth out into the world.

When he had gone some distance he came to a mountain, where he met a man who was Lord over all the beasts in the forest – for they all came to him when he blew a horn which he had. So the King asked where Whiteland was.

"I do not know that," he answered, "but I will ask my beasts." Then he blew his horn and inquired whether any of them knew where Whiteland lay, but there was not one who knew that.

So the man gave him a pair of snow shoes. "When you have these on," he said, "you will come to my brother, who lives hundreds of miles from here; he is Lord over all the birds in the air – ask him. When you have got there, just turn the shoes so that the toes point this way, and then they will come home again of their own accord."

When the King arrived there he turned the shoes as the Lord of the beasts had bidden him, and they went back.

And now he once more asked after Whiteland, and the man summoned all the birds together, and inquired if any of them knew where Whiteland lay. No, none knew this. Long after the others there came an old eagle. He had been absent ten whole years, but he too knew no more than the rest.

"Well, well," said the man, "then you shall have the loan of a pair of snow shoes of mine. If you wear them you will get to my brother, who lives hundreds of miles from here. He is Lord of all the fish in the sea – you can ask him. But do not forget to turn the shoes round."

The King thanked him, put on the shoes, and when he had got to him who was Lord of all the fish in the sea, he turned the snow shoes round, and back they went just as the others had gone, and he asked once more where Whiteland was.

The man called the fish together with his horn, but none of them knew anything about it. At last came an old, old pike, which he had great difficulty in bringing home to him.

When he asked the pike, it said, "Yes, Whiteland is well known to me, for I have been cook there these ten years. Tomorrow morning I have to go back there, for now the Queen, whose King is staying away, is to marry someone else."

"If that be the case I will give you a piece of advice," said the man. "Not far from here on a moor stand three brothers, who have stood there a hundred years fighting for a hat, a cloak, and a pair of boots; if anyone has these three things he can make himself invisible, and if he desires to go to any place, he has but to wish and he is there. You may tell them that you have a desire to try these things, and then you will be able to decide which of the men is to have them."

So the King thanked him and went, and did what he had said.

"What is this that you are standing fighting about for ever and ever?" said he to the brothers; "let me make a trial of these things, and then I will judge between you."

They willingly consented to this, but when he had got the hat, the cloak, and the boots, he said, "Next time we meet you shall have my decision," and hereupon he wished himself away.

While he was going quickly through the air he fell in with the North Wind.

"And where may you be going?" said the North Wind.

"To Whiteland," said the King, and then he related what had happened to him.

"Well," said the North Wind, "you can easily go a little quicker than I can, for I have to puff and blow into every corner; but when you get there, place yourself on the stairs by the side of the door, and then I will come blustering in as if I wanted to blow down the whole castle, and when the Prince who is to have your Queen comes out to see what is astir, just take him by the throat and fling him out, and then I will try to carry him away from court."

As the North Wind had said, so did the King. He stood on the stairs, and when the North Wind came howling and roaring, and caught the roof and walls of the castle till they shook again, the Prince went out to see what was the matter; but as soon as he came the King took him by the neck and flung him out, and then the North Wind laid hold of him and carried him off. And when he was rid of him the King went into the castle. At first the Queen did not know him, because he had grown so thin and pale from having travelled so long and so sorrowfully; but when she saw her ring she was heartily glad, and then the rightful wedding was held, and held in such a way that it was talked about far and wide.

Why the Sea is Salt

(Norwegian)

ONCE ON A TIME, but it was a long, long time ago, there were two brothers, one rich and one poor. Now, one Christmas Eve, the poor one hadn't so much as a crumb in the house, either of meat or bread, so he went to his brother to ask him for something to keep Christmas with, in God's name. It was not the first time his brother had been forced to help him, and you may fancy he wasn't very glad to see his face, but he said:

"If you will do what I ask you to do, I'll give you a whole flitch of bacon."

So the poor brother said he would do anything, and was full of thanks.

"Well, here is the flitch", said the rich brother, "and now go straight to Hell."

"What I have given my word to do, I must stick to", said the other; so he took the flitch and set off. He walked the whole day, and at dusk he came to a place where he saw a very bright light.

"Maybe this is the place", said the man to himself. So he turned aside, and the first thing he saw was an old, old man, with a long white beard, who stood in an outhouse, hewing wood for the Christmas fire.

"Good even", said the man with the flitch.

"The same to you; whither are you going so late?" said the man.

"Oh! I'm going to Hell, if I only knew the right way", answered the poor man.

"Well, you're not far wrong, for this is Hell", said the old man; "when you get inside they will be all for buying your flitch, for meat is scarce in Hell; but mind, you don't sell it unless you get the hand-quern which stands behind the door for it. When you come out, I'll teach you how to handle the quern, for it's good to grind almost anything."

So the man with the flitch thanked the other for his good advice, and gave a great knock at the Devil's door.

When he got in, everything went just as the old man had said. All the devils, great and small, came swarming up to him like ants round an anthill, and each tried to outbid the other for the flitch.

"Well!" said the man, "by rights my old dame and I ought to have this flitch for our Christmas dinner; but since you have all set your hearts on it, I suppose I must give it up to you; but if I sell it at all, I'll have for it that quern behind the door yonder."

At first the Devil wouldn't hear of such a bargain, and chaffered and haggled with the man; but he stuck to what he said, and at last the Devil had to part with his quern. When the man got out into the yard, he asked the old woodcutter how he was to handle the quern; and after he had learned how to use it, he thanked the old man and went off home as fast as he could, but still the clock had struck twelve on Christmas Eve before he reached his own door.

"Wherever in the world have you been?" said his old dame, "here have I sat hour after hour waiting and watching, without so much as two sticks to lay together under the Christmas brose."

"Oh!" said the man, "I couldn't get back before, for I had to go a long way first for one thing, and then for another; but now you shall see what you shall see."

So he put the quern on the table, and bade it first of all grind lights, then a table-cloth, then meat, then ale, and so on till they had got everything that was nice for Christmas fare. He had only to speak the word, and the quern ground out what he wanted. The old dame stood by blessing her stars, and kept on asking where he had got this wonderful quern, but he wouldn't tell her.

"It's all one where I got it from; you see the quern is a good one, and the mill-stream never freezes, that's enough."

So he ground meat and drink and dainties enough to last out till Twelfth Day, and on the third day he asked all his friends and kin to his house, and gave a great feast. Now, when his rich brother saw all that was on the table, and all that was behind in the larder, he grew quite spiteful and wild, for he couldn't bear that his brother should have anything.

"'Twas only on Christmas Eve", he said to the rest, "he was in such straits, that he came and asked for a morsel of food in God's name, and now he gives a feast as if he were count or king"; and he turned to his brother and said:

"But whence, in Hell's name, have you got all this wealth?"

"From behind the door", answered the owner of the quern, for he didn't care to let the cat out of the bag. But later on the evening, when he had got a drop too much, he could keep his secret no longer, and brought out the quern and said:

"There, you see what has gotten me all this wealth"; and so he made the quern grind all kind of things. When his brother saw it, he set his heart on having the quern, and, after a deal of coaxing, he got it; but he had to pay three hundred dollars for it, and his brother bargained to keep it till hay-harvest, for he thought, if I keep it till then, I can make it grind meat and drink that will last for years. So you may fancy the quern didn't grow rusty for want of work, and when hay-harvest came, the rich brother got it, but the other took care not to teach him how to handle it.

It was evening when the rich brother got the quern home, and next morning he told his wife to go out into the hay-field and toss, while the mowers cut the grass, and he would stay at home and get the dinner ready. So, when dinner-time drew near, he put the quern on the kitchen table and said:

"Grind herrings and broth, and grind them good and fast."

So the quern began to grind herrings and broth; first of all, all the dishes full, then all the tubs full, and so on till the kitchen floor was quite covered. Then the man twisted and twirled at the quern to get it to stop, but for all his twisting and fingering the quern went on grinding, and in a little while the broth rose so high that the man was like to drown. So he threw open the kitchen door and ran into the parlour, but it wasn't long before the quern had ground the parlour full too, and it was only at the risk of his life that the man could get hold of the latch of the house door through the stream of broth. When he got the door open, he ran out and set off down the road, with the stream of herrings and broth at his heels, roaring like a waterfall over the whole farm. Now, his old dame, who was in the field tossing hay, thought it a long time to dinner, and at last she said:

"Well! though the master doesn't call us home, we may as well go. Maybe he finds it hard work to boil the broth, and will be glad of my help."

The men were willing enough, so they sauntered homewards; but just as they had got a little way up the hill, what should they meet but herrings, and broth, and bread, all running and dashing, and splashing together in a stream, and the master himself running before them for his life, and as he passed them he bawled out:

"Would to heaven each of you had a hundred throats! but take care you're not drowned in the broth."

Away he went, as though the Evil One were at his heels, to his brother's house, and begged him for God's sake to take back the quern that instant; for, said he:

"If it grinds only one hour more, the whole parish will be swallowed up by herrings and broth."

But his brother wouldn't hear of taking it back till the other paid him down three hundred dollars more.

So the poor brother got both the money and the quern, and it wasn't long before he set up a farmhouse far finer than the one in which his brother lived, and with the quern he ground so much gold that he covered it with plates of gold; and as the farm lay by the seaside, the golden house gleamed and glistened far away over the sea. All who sailed by put ashore to see the rich man in the golden house, and to see the wonderful quern, the fame of which spread far and wide, till there was nobody who hadn't heard tell of it.

So one day there came a skipper who wanted to see the quern; and the first thing he asked was if it could grind salt.

"Grind salt!" said the owner; "I should just think it could. It can grind anything."

When the skipper heard that, he said he must have the quern, cost what it would; for if he only had it, he thought he should be rid of his long voyages across stormy seas for a lading of salt. Well, at first the man wouldn't hear of parting with the quern; but the skipper begged and prayed so hard, that at last he let him have it, but he had to pay many, many thousand dollars for it. Now, when the skipper had got the quern on his back, he soon made off with it, for he was afraid lest the man should change his mind; so he had no time to ask how to handle the quern, but got on board his ship as fast as he could, and set sail. When he had sailed a good way off, he brought the quern on deck and said:

"Grind salt, and grind both good and fast."

Well, the quern began to grind salt so that it poured out like water; and when the skipper had got the ship full, he wished to stop the quern, but whichever way he turned it, and however much he tried, it was no good; the quern kept grinding on, and the heap of salt grew higher and higher, and at last down sank the ship.

There lies the quern at the bottom of the sea, and grinds away at this very day, and that's why the sea is salt.

The Little Match-Seller

(Danish)

IT WAS TERRIBLY COLD and nearly dark on the last evening of the old year, and the snow was falling fast. In the cold and the darkness, a poor little girl, with bare head and naked feet, roamed through the streets. It is true she had on a pair of slippers when she left home, but they were not of much use. They were very large, so large, indeed, that they had belonged to her mother, and the poor little creature had lost them in running across the street to avoid two carriages that were rolling along at a terrible rate. One of the slippers she could not find, and a boy seized upon the other and ran away with it, saying that he could use it as a cradle, when he had children of his own. So the little girl went on with her little naked feet, which were quite red and blue with the cold. In an old apron she carried a number of matches, and had a bundle of them in her hands. No one had bought anything of her the whole day, nor had anyone given here even a penny. Shivering with cold and hunger, she crept along; poor little child, she looked the picture of misery. The snowflakes fell on her long, fair hair, which hung in curls on her shoulders, but she regarded them not.

Lights were shining from every window, and there was a savoury smell of roast goose, for it was New Year's Eve – yes, she remembered that. In a corner, between two houses, one of which projected beyond the other, she sank down and huddled herself together. She had drawn her little feet under her, but she could not keep off the cold; and she dared not go home, for she had sold no matches, and could not take home even a penny of money. Her father would certainly beat her; besides, it was almost as cold at home as here, for they had only the roof to cover them, through which the wind howled, although the largest holes had been stopped up with straw and rags. Her little hands were almost frozen with the cold. Ah! perhaps a burning match might be some good, if she could draw it from the bundle and strike it against the wall, just to warm her fingers. She drew one out – "scratch!" how it sputtered as it burnt! It gave a warm, bright light, like a little candle, as she held her hand over it. It was really a wonderful light. It seemed to the little girl that she was sitting by a large iron stove, with polished brass feet and a brass ornament. How the fire burned! and seemed so beautifully warm that the child stretched out her feet as if to warm them, when, lo! the flame of the match went out, the stove vanished, and she had only the remains of the half-burnt match in her hand.

She rubbed another match on the wall. It burst into a flame, and where its light fell upon the wall it became as transparent as a veil, and she could see into the room. The table was covered with a snowy white table-cloth, on which stood a splendid dinner service, and a steaming roast goose, stuffed with apples and dried plums. And what was still more wonderful, the goose jumped down from the dish and waddled across the floor, with a knife and fork in its breast, to the little girl. Then the match went out, and there remained nothing but the thick, damp, cold wall before her.

She lighted another match, and then she found herself sitting under a beautiful Christmas tree. It was larger and more beautifully decorated than the one which she had seen through the glass door at the rich merchant's. Thousands of tapers were burning upon the green branches, and coloured pictures, like those she had seen in the show-windows, looked down upon it all. The little one stretched out her hand towards them, and the match went out.

The Christmas lights rose higher and higher, till they looked to her like the stars in the sky. Then she saw a star fall, leaving behind it a bright streak of fire. "Someone is dying," thought the little girl, for her old grandmother, the only one who had ever loved her, and who was now dead, had told her that when a star falls, a soul was going up to God.

She again rubbed a match on the wall, and the light shone round her; in the brightness stood her old grandmother, clear and shining, yet mild and loving in her appearance. "Grandmother," cried the little one, "O take me with you; I know you will go away when the match burns out; you will vanish like the warm stove, the roast goose, and the large, glorious Christmas tree." And she made haste to light the whole bundle of matches, for she wished to keep her grandmother there. And the matches glowed with a light that was brighter than the noonday, and her grandmother had never appeared so large or so beautiful. She took the little girl in her arms, and they both flew upwards in brightness and joy far above the earth, where there was neither cold nor hunger nor pain, for they were with God.

In the dawn of morning there lay the poor little one, with pale cheeks and smiling mouth, leaning against the wall; she had been frozen to death on the last evening of the year; and the New Year's sun rose and shone upon a little corpse! The child still sat, in the stiffness of death, holding the matches in her hand, one bundle of which was burnt. "She tried to warm herself," said some. No one imagined what beautiful things she had seen, nor into what glory she had entered with her grandmother, on New Year's Day.

First Born, First Wed

(Swedish)

ONCE UPON A TIME there was a king who had a three-year old son, and was obliged to go to war against another king. Then, when his ships sailed home again after he had gained a splendid victory, a storm broke out and his whole fleet was near sinking. But the king vowed he would sacrifice to the sea-queen the first male creature that came to meet him when he reached land and entered his capital. Thereby the whole fleet reached the harbor in safety. But the five-year old prince, who had not seen his father for the past two years, and who was delighted with the thunder of the cannon as the ships came in, secretly slipped away from his attendants, and ran to the landing; and when the king came ashore he was the first to cast himself into his arms, weeping with joy. The king was frightened when he thought of the sea-queen; but he thought that, after all, the prince was only a child, and at any rate he could sacrifice the next person to step up to him after the prince. But from that time on no one could make a successful sea-trip, and the people began to murmur because the king had not kept the promise he had made the sea-queen. But the king and queen never allowed the prince out without a great escort, and he was never permitted to enter a ship, for all his desire to do so.

After a few years they gradually forgot the sea-queen, and when the prince was ten years old, a little brother came to join him. Not long after the older of the princes was out walking with his tutor and several other gentlemen. And when they reached the end of the royal gardens by the seashore – it was a summer's day, unusually clear – they were suddenly enveloped by a thick cloud, which disappeared as swiftly as it had come. And when it vanished, the prince was no longer there; nor did he return, to the great sorrow of the king, the queen and the whole country. In the meantime the young prince who was now the sole heir to the crown and kingdom grew up; and when he was sixteen, they began to think of finding a wife for him. For the old king and queen wished to see him marry the daughter of some powerful monarch to whom they were allied, before they died. With this in view, letters were written and embassies sent out to the most distant countries.

While these negotiations were being conducted, it began to be said that the seashore was haunted; various people had heard cries, and several who had walked by the seashore late in the evening had fallen ill. At length no one ventured to go there after eleven at night, because a voice kept crying from out at sea: "First born, first wed!" And when someone did venture nearer he did so at the risk of his life. At last these complaints came to the king's ear; he called together his council, and it was decided to question a wise woman, who had already foretold many mysterious happenings, which had all taken place exactly as she had said they would. When the wise woman was brought before the king she said it was the prince who had been taken into the sea who was calling, and that they would have to find him a bride, young, beautiful, and belonging to one of the noblest families of the land, and she must be no less than fifteen and no more than seventeen years old. That seemed a serious difficulty; for no one wished to give their daughter to a sea-king.

Yet, when there was no end to the cries and the commotion, the wise woman said, that first it might be well to build a little house by the sea, perhaps then the turmoil might die away. At any rate, she said, no phantoms would haunt the place while the building was in progress. Hence no more than four workmen need be employed, and they might first prepare a site, then lay the stone foundation, and finally erect the small house, comprising no more than two pleasant, handsome rooms, one behind the other, and a good floor. The house was carefully erected, and the royal architect himself had to superintend the work, so that everything might be done as well as possible. And while the building was going on, there were no mysterious noises, and everyone could travel peacefully along the seashore. For that reason the four workmen did not hurry with their work; yet not one of them could stay away for a day, because when they did the tumult along the shore would begin again, and one could hear the cries: "First born, first wed!" When the little house was finally completed, the best carpenters came and worked in it, then painters and other craftsmen, and at last it was furnished, because when the work stopped for no more than a single day the cries were heard again by night. The rooms were fitted out as sumptuously as possible, and a great mirror was hung in the drawing-room. According to the instructions of the wise woman, it was hung in such wise that from the bed in the bedroom, even though one's face were turned to the wall, one could still see who stepped over the threshold into the drawing-room; for the door between each room was always to stand open.

When all was finished, and the little house had been arranged with regal splendour, the cries of "First born, first wed!" again began to sound from the shore. And it was found necessary, though all were unwilling, to follow the wise woman's counsel, and choose three of the loveliest maidens between the ages of fifteen and seventeen, belonging to the first families of the land. They were to be taken to the castle, said the wise woman, and to be treated like ladies of the blood royal, and one after another they were to be sent to the little house by the seashore; for should one of them find favour in the eyes of the sea-prince, then the commotion and turmoil would surely cease. In the meantime the negotiations for the marriage of the younger prince were continued, and the bride selected for him was soon expected to arrive. So the girls were also chosen for the sea-prince. The three chosen, as well as their parents, were quite inconsolable over their fate; even the fact that they were to be treated like princesses did not console them; yet had they not yielded it would have been all the worse for them and for the whole land. The first girl destined to sleep in the sea-palace was the oldest, and when she sought out the wise woman, and asked her advice, the latter said she should lie down in the handsome bed; but should turn her face to the wall, and under no circumstances turn around curiously, and try and see what was going on. She had only the right to behold what she saw reflected in the mirror in the drawing-room as she lay with her face to the wall. At ten o'clock that night the royal sea-bride was led with great pomp to the little house.

Her relatives and the court said farewell to her with many tears, left her before eleven, locked the door on the outside, and took the keys with them to the castle. The wise woman was also there, consoled the people, and assured them that if the maiden only forbore to speak, and did not turn around, she would come out in the morning fresh and blooming. The poor girl prayed and wept until she grew sleepy; but toward twelve o'clock the outer door suddenly opened, and then the door of the drawing-room. She was startled and filled with fear when, her face turned toward the wall, she saw in the great mirror, how a tall, well-built youth entered, from whose garments the water ran in streams to the floor. He shook himself as though freezing, and said "Uh hu!" Then he went to the window, and there laid down an unusually large and handsome apple, and hung a bottle in the casement. Next he stepped to the bed, bent over the sleeping girl and looked at her, strode up and down a few times, shaking the water from his clothes and saying "Uh hu!" Then he went back to the bed, undressed hurriedly, lay down and fell asleep. The poor girl, had not been sleeping; but had only closed her eyes when the prince bent over her. Now she was glad to think he was fast asleep, and forgot the wise woman's warning not to turn around. Her curiosity got the better of her, and she wanted to find out if this were a real human being. She turned around softly, lest she wake him; but just as she sat up quietly in bed, in order to take a good look at her neighbor, he swiftly seized her right hand, hewed it off, and flung it under the bed. Then he at once lay down and fell asleep again. As soon as it was day, he rose, dressed without casting even a glance at the bed, took the bottle and the apple from the window, went hastily out and locked the door after him. One can imagine how the poor girl suffered in the meantime, and when her friends and relatives came to fetch her they found her weeping and robbed of her hand. She was brought to the castle and the wise woman sent for, and overwhelmed with bitter reproaches. But she said that if the maiden had not turned around, and had overcome her curiosity, she would not have lost her hand. They were to treat her as though she were really and truly a princess; but that it would be as much as her life were worth to allow her to return to the neighbourhood of the little house.

The two girls were all the more discouraged by this mishap, and thought themselves condemned to death, though the wise woman consoled them as well as she knew how. The second promised her faithfully not to turn around; yet it happened with her as it had with the first. The prince came in at twelve o'clock dripping, shook himself so that the water flew about, said "Uh hu!" went to the window, laid down the beautiful apple, hung up the bottle, came into the bedroom, bent over the bed, strode up and down a few times, said "Uh hu!" hastily undressed, and at once fell asleep. Her curiosity gained the upper hand, and when she made sure that he was sleeping soundly, she carefully turned around in order to look at him. But he seized her right hand, hewed it off and cast it under the bed, and then laid down again and slept on. At dawn he rose, dressed without casting a glance at the bed, took the apple and the bottle, went out and locked the door after him. When her friends and relatives came to fetch the girl in the morning, they found her weeping and without a right hand. She was taken to the castle, where she found herself just as little welcome as her predecessor, and the wise woman insisted that the girl must have turned around, though at first she denied it absolutely.

Then the youngest, sweetest and loveliest of the three maidens had to go to the sea-castle amid the mourning of the entire court. The wise woman accompanied her, and implored her not to turn around; since there was no other means of protection against the spell.

The maiden promised to heed her warning, and said that she would pray God to help her if she were plagued with curiosity. All happened as before: the prince came on the stroke of twelve, dripping wet, said "Uh hu!" shook himself, laid the apple on the window, hung up the bottle, went into the bedroom, bent over the bed, strode up and down for a few times, said "Uh hu!" undressed, and at once fell asleep. The poor girl was half-dead with fear and terror, and prayed and struggled against her curiosity till at length she fell asleep, and did not awake until the prince rose and dressed. He stepped up to the bed, bent over it for a moment, went out, turned at the door and took the bottle and the apple, and then locked the door after him. In the morning the entire court, the girl's parents and the wise woman came to fetch her. She came to meet them weeping with joy, and was conducted to the castle in triumph and with joy indescribable. The king and queen embraced her, and she was paid the same honours destined for the princess who was to arrive in the course of the next few days to marry the heir to the throne. Now the maiden had to sleep every night in the little house by the strand, and every evening the prince came in with his apple and his bottle, and every morning went away at dawn. But it seemed to her that each succeeding evening and morning he looked at her a little longer; though she, always silent, timid, and turned toward the wall, did not dare see more than her mirror showed her of his coming and going. But the two other girls, who had lost their hands, and who now no longer lived in the castle, were jealous of the honour shown the youngest, and threatened to have her done away with if she did not restore their hands. The maiden went weeping to the wise woman; and the latter said that when the prince had lain down as usual she should say – keeping her face turned toward the wall:

"The maidens twain will see me slain,
Or else have back their hands again!"

But she was to offer no further information nor say another word. With a beating heart the poor girl waited until the prince came, and when he had bent over the bed longer than usual, sighed, then hastily undressed and lain down, the maiden said, quivering and trembling:

"The maidens twain will see me slain,
Or else have back their hands again!"

The prince at once replied: "Take the hands – they are lying under the bed – and the bottle hanging in the window, and pour some of the contents of the bottle on their arms and hands, join them together, bind them up, take away the bandages in three days' time and the hands will have been healed!" The maiden made no reply and fell asleep. In the morning the prince rose as usual, stepped over to the bed several times and looked at her from its foot; but she did not dare look up, and closed her eyes. He sighed, took his apple; but left the bottle, and went. When the maiden rose she did as he had told her, and in three days' time removed the bandages, and the girls' hands were well and whole.

Now the foreign princess arrived and the wedding was to be celebrated as soon as possible. Yet she was not fitted out with any more magnificence than the bride of the sea-prince, and both were equally honoured by the king and court. This annoyed the two other girls, and they again threatened to have the youngest done away with if she did not let them taste the apple which the prince always brought with him. Again the maiden sought the advice of the wise woman, in whom she had confidence. And that night, when the prince had lain down, she said:

"The maidens twain will see me slain,
Or else your apple they would gain!"

Then the prince said: "Take the apple lying in the window, and when you go out, lay it on the ground and follow wherever it may roll. And when it stops, pick as many apples as you wish, and return the same way you came." The maiden made no reply, and fell asleep. On the following morning it seemed harder than ever for the prince to resolve to go away. He appeared excited and restless, sighed often, bent over the maiden several times, went into the living room, then turned around and looked at her once more. Finally, when the sun rose, he hurried out and locked the door after him. When the maiden rose, she could not help weeping, for she had really begun to love the prince.

Then she took the apple, and when she was outside the door, laid it on the ground, and it rolled and rolled, and she followed it, a long, long way, to a region unknown to her. There she came to a high garden wall, over which hung the branches of trees, loaded with beautiful fruit. Finally she reached a great portal, adorned with gold and splendid ornaments, which opened of its own accord as the apple rolled up to it. And the apple rolled through the portal and the maiden followed it into the garden, which was the most beautiful she ever had seen. The apple rolled over to a low-growing tree weighed with the most magnificent apples, and there it stopped. The maiden picked all that her silken apron would hold, and turned to see from which direction she had come, and where the portal stood through which she would have to pass on her way back. But the garden was so lovely that she felt like enjoying its charms a while longer, and without thinking of the prince's words, she touched the apple with her foot, and it began to roll again. Suddenly the portal closed with a great crash. Then the maiden was much frightened, and regretted having done what had been forbidden her; yet now she could not get out, and was compelled to follow the apple once more. It rolled far into the beautiful garden and stopped at a little fireplace, where stood two kettles of water, one small, the other large. There was a great fire burning under the large kettle; but only a weak fire beneath the smaller one. Now when the apple stopped there the maiden did not know what to do. Then it occurred to her to scrape away the fire beneath the large kettle and thrust it under the little one; and soon the kettle over the small fire began to boil and the kettle over the large one simmered down. But she could not stay there. And since she had already disobeyed the order given her, she expected to die, nothing less, and was quite resigned to do so, because she had lost all hope of winning the prince.

So she gave the apple another push, and it rolled into a meadow in the middle of the garden, and there lay two little children, asleep, with the hot sun beating straight down upon them. The maiden felt sorry for the children, and she took her apron and laid it over them to protect them from the sun, and only kept the apples she could put in her little basket. But she could not stay here either, so again she touched the apple, and it rolled on and before she knew it the girl found herself by the seashore. There, under a shady tree lay the prince asleep; while beside him sat the sea-queen. Both rose when the maiden drew near, and the prince looked at her with alarm and tenderness in his flashing eyes. Then he leaped into the sea, and the white foam closed over him. But the sea-queen was enraged and seized the girl, who thought that her last moment had struck, and begged for a merciful death. The sea-queen looked at her, and asked her who had given her permission to pass beyond the apple tree. The maiden confessed her disobedience, and said that she had done so without meaning any harm, whereupon the sea-queen said she would see how she had conducted herself and punish her accordingly. Thereupon the sea-queen gave the apple a push, and it rolled back through the portal to the apple tree. The sea-queen saw that the apple tree was uninjured, again pushed the apple and it rolled on to the little fireplace. But when the sea-queen saw the small kettle boiling furiously, while the large one was growing cold, she became very angry, seized the girl's arm savagely and rising to her full height, asked: "What have you dared do here? How dared you take the fire from under my kettle and put it under your own?" The maiden did not know that she had done anything wrong, and said that she did not know why. Then the sea-queen replied: "The large kettle signified the love between the prince and myself; the small one the love between the prince and you. Since you have taken the fire from under my kettle and laid it under your own, the prince is now violently in love with you, while his love for me is well-nigh extinguished. "Look," she cried, angrily, "now my kettle has stopped boiling altogether, and yours is boiling over! But I will see what other harm you have done and punish you accordingly." And the sea-queen again pushed the apple with her foot, and it rolled to the sleeping children, who had been covered with the apron. Then the sea-queen said: "Did you do that?" "Yes," replied the maiden, weeping, "but I meant no harm. I covered the little ones with my apron so that the sun might not burn down on them so fiercely, and I left with them the apples I could not put in my basket." The sea-queen said: "This deed and your truthfulness are your salvation. I see that you have a kind heart. These children belong to me and to the prince; but since he now loves you more than he does me, I will resign him to you. Go back to the castle and there say what I tell you: that your wedding with my prince is to be celebrated at the same time as that of his younger brother. And all your jewels, your ornaments, your wedding-dress and your bridal chair, are to be exactly like those of the other princess. From the moment on that the priest blesses the prince and yourself I have no further power over him. But since I have seen to it that he has all the qualities which adorn a ruler, I demand that he be made the heir to his father's kingdom; for he is the oldest son. The younger prince may rule over the kingdom which his bride brings him. All this you must tell them, for only under these conditions will I release the prince. And when you are arrayed in your bridal finery, come to me here, without anyone's knowledge, so that I may see how they have adorned you. Here is the apple which will show you the way without anyone being able to tell where you go." With that the sea-queen parted from her, and gave the apple a push. It rolled out of the garden and to the castle, where the maiden, with mingled joy and terror, delivered the sea-queen's message to the king, and told him what she demanded for the prince. The king gladly promised all that was desired, and great preparations were at once made for the double wedding. Two bridal chairs were set up side by side, two wedding gowns, and two sets of jewels exactly similar were made ready. When the maiden had been dressed in her bridal finery she pretended to have forgotten something, which she had to fetch from a lower floor, went downstairs with her apple, and laid it on the ground. It at once rolled to the spot by the seashore where she had found the sea-queen and the prince, and where the sea-queen was now awaiting her. "It is well that you have come," said the sea-queen, "for the slightest disobedience would have meant misfortune for you! But how do you look? Are you dressed just as the princess is? And has the princess no better clothes or jewels?" The maiden answered timidly, that they were dressed exactly alike. Then the sea-queen tore her gown from her body, unclasped the jewels from her hair and flinging them on the ground cried: "Is that the way the bride of my prince should look! Since I have given him to you I will give you my bridal outfit as well." And with that she raised up a sod beneath the great tree, and a shrine adorned with gold and precious stones appeared, from which she drew out her bridal outfit, which fitted the maiden as though made for her. And it was so costly and so covered with gems that the maiden was almost blinded by its radiance. The crown, too, glowed with light, and was set with the most wonderful emeralds, and all was magnificent beyond what any princess had ever worn. "Now," said the sea-queen, when she had finished adorning the maiden, "now go back to the castle, and show them how I was dressed when I wedded the prince. All this I give as a free gift to you and your descendants; but you must always conduct yourself so that the prince will be content with you, and you must make his happiness your first thought all your life long."

This the maiden promised, with honest tears, and the sea-queen bade her go. When she was again in the castle, all were astonished at the beauty and costliness of her dress and jewels, in comparison to which those of the other princess were as nothing. The treasures of the whole kingdom would not have sufficed to pay for such a bridal outfit. And none any longer dared envy the lovely maiden, for never had a princess brought a richer bridal dower into the country. Now all went in solemn procession to the church, and the priests stood before the bridal chairs with their books open, and waited for the prince who, according to the sea-queen's word, would not come until the blessing was to be spoken. They waited impatiently, and the king finally told one of the greatest nobles to seat himself in the bridal chair in the prince's place, which he did. But the very moment the priest began to pray, the two wings of the church portal quickly flew open, and a tall, strong, handsome man with flashing eyes, royally clad, came in, stepped up to the bridal chair, thrust his proxy out so hastily that he nearly fell, and cried: "This is my place! Now, priest, speak the blessing!" While the blessing was spoken the prince became quiet again, and then greeted his parents and the whole court with joy, and before all embraced his wife, who now for the first time ventured to take a good look at him. Thenceforward the prince was like any other human being, and in the end he inherited his father's kingdom, and became a great and world-renowned ruler, beloved by his subjects, and adored by his wife. They lived long and happily, and their descendants are still the rulers of the land over which he reigned.

The Skerry of Shrieks

(Norwegian)

I

PEOPLE LIVE EVEN WITHIN THE POLAR CIRCLE, although grown-up folks are apt to think it a poor sort of life. But to boys the 'land of the midnight sun' is a veritable paradise. Every season of the year has its own kind of sport; and as schoolmasters are rare birds so far north, the boys are to a great extent left to follow their own devices until they are old enough to be sent away to school in the cities. From morning till night the air is filled with a screaming host of birds, which whirl in through the fiords like an approaching snowstorm. The eider-ducks lie gently bobbing upon the water, the black surf-scoters dive in the surf and make short work of the young whiting, and the puffins sit in long soldier-like rows on the rocks, and plunge headlong into the sea at the first signal of danger. In this glorious region the fish and fowl from all quarters of the globe seem to have appointed an annual meeting about New Year's; and the Norwegian peasants, who are dependent upon the inhabitants of the sea and the air for their living, are on the lookout for them, and hasten to the coast to give them a fitting reception.

Harry Winchester's motive, however, for visiting the Arctic wonderland was quite a different one. He had made the acquaintance of the Birk boys during the previous summer, and he had struck up a warm friendship with one of them, named Magnus. His parents, who lived in New York, had permitted him to accept the invitation of Mr. Birk to spend the winter with his sons, and Harry was so completely fascinated with the sports and adventures which every day offered in abundance that he would have liked to prolong his stay indefinitely.

Hasselrud, the estate of the Birks, was a fine, old-fashioned mansion, which peeped out from the dense foliage of chestnut and maple trees. Mr. Birk conducted a large business in fish and lumber, and manned every year several boats and sent them to the Lofoten fisheries. His three sons, Olaf, Magnus, and Edwin, were brisk and courageous lads, who had been accustomed to danger from their earliest years, and could handle a gun and manage a sail as well as any man in that region. Olaf was nineteen years old, and wore the uniform of a midshipman in the navy, and by courtesy was styled lieutenant; Magnus, who was sixteen, was a fair-faced, curly-headed lad, with frank blue eyes, a straight, handsome nose, and a singular talent for getting into mischief. Edwin was but twelve years old; but, as he does not figure conspicuously in this narrative, there is no need of describing him. But altogether the most important person at Hasselrud, next to Mr. Birk, was Grim Hering-Luck, a hoary, bow-legged fisherman, who was Mr. Birk's right-hand man and captain of his boat-guild. Grim had a stern, deep-wrinkled face, framed in a wreath of greyish whiskers. He had small, piercing eyes, and bushy, grey-sprinkled hair. On his head he wore a sou'wester. The seat and knees of his trousers and the elbows of his coat were adorned with great shiny patches of leather. The leathern girdle about his waist did not quite fulfil its duties as suspenders, but allowed the trousers to slip down on his hips, leaving some four inches of shirt visible under the border of the waistcoat. Grim was a gruff old customer, but it was commonly believed that his bark was worse than his bite. He liked the bright American boy better than he cared to confess, and therefore neglected no opportunity for quarrelling with him. In fact, everybody admired Harry's enterprising spirit and was entertained by his lively talk. Olaf was fairly dazzled by his knowledge and experience of the world, and little Edwin copied his walk and his picturesque recklessness to the extent of his small ability; but among all the family there was no one who was more ardently attached to Harry than Magnus. The two were inseparable; from morning till night they roamed about together, setting traps for hares and ptarmigan, spearing trout in the shallows of the river, trawling for mackerel in the salt water, and sometimes tacking in and out of the fiord in a furious gale. At such times, however, they were sure to have Grim in the boat, and Grim was a capital man to have in a boat in case of an emergency. Thus they spent the beautiful autumn months until the November storms began to blow, the snow began to fall, and the air, when they looked out over the fiord, was thick and the sky threatening. The great trees bent in agony and howled in the blast with voices of despair. Then Grim would begin to investigate and to mend the nets which hung in long festoons along the walls of the boat-houses, and, with his friendly grunt, he would say in reply to Magnus' queries:

"Wal, Mester Yallertop, the Lord he looks out fer them as they look out fer themselves. He puts the cod in the sea, but I never heared of his puttin' it in yer mouth fer ye. He made the land poor up here, but he made the sea rich, jest fer to make the average right in the end. He lets ye starve like a toothless rat if ye have a taste fer starvin'. But thar ain't no call for anybody to starve here north, ef he can bait a hook and ain't afeared of bein' late to his funeral."

"Being late to your own funeral, Grim!" Magnus would exclaim, in amazement; "how can a man be late to his funeral?"

"Wal, now, Mester Yallertop, that I'll tell ye. Fur that ain't no uncommon case here north. Suppose ye go out in the mornin' with the fishin' fleet, and it blows up right lively, and ye don't never come back again. Then after a week or so the parson reads the sarvice over yer name and prays fer ye, and the next mornin', likely as not, yer legs drift ashore, quite independent-like, jest because the cod found yer tarred top-boots indergestible."

"And do such things ever happen, Grim?" the boy would ask, shuddering at the ghastly picture which his friend's words suggested.

"Do they ever happen? Wal, I reckon they do. I might jest mention to ye that I ain't in the habit of tellin' no lies. My father – God ha'e mercy on his soul – he sent only his legs fur to represent him at his funeral; and my grandfather – wal, the cod turned the tables on him; he had meant to eat them, but – it ain't no use bein' squeamish about it – they ate him. It war in the great storm of the 11th of February, 1848, when five hundred fisherman cheated the parson out of his funeral fees."

"How terrible, Grim! How can you go to the fisheries every winter, when both your father and your grandfather lost their lives there?"

"Wal, now ye are puzzlin' me, Mester Magnus," Grim replied, taking his clay pipe from the corner of his mouth, and looking up seriously from his labor; "but I'll tell ye a yarn I heared when I was young. I reckon it is true, because I have never heared nobody say it warn't. Some city chap axed a fisherman purty much what ye have axed me, and the fisherman says, says he: 'Whar did yer father die?' 'Why, he expired peacefully in his bed,' said the city chap. 'And yer grandfather?' axed the fisherman. 'Wal, he had jest the same luck,' says the city chap. 'And yer great-grandfather?' 'He, too, turned up his toes in the same style.' 'Wal, now,' says the fisherman, 'if I were you I wouldn't never go to bed again, sence all yer forbears come to their death in it.' Now, I reckon that is the way with all of us. Ef the Lord wants us he will know whar to find us, wharsoever we be."

When the Christmas holidays, with all their old-fashioned hospitality and sports, were over the question was seriously debated whether the boys should be permitted to accompany Grim and the housemen (tenants) to the Lofoten fisheries. It was decided that three boats should be manned, and Grim was as usual elected captain of the whole guild. The 'tokens' had been uncommonly good this year, and a profitable fishery was expected. Mr. Birk, who well knew the dangers connected with this enterprise, was very unwilling to let the boys start out in the open boats, and suffer the discomforts which were inseparable from the life on these barren islands, where thousands of people were huddled together in booths and shanties, and quarrels and fights were the order of the day. Harry, however, argued that such an experience would scarcely offer itself to him a second time in his life, and that it was easy to avoid danger while still observing all that was interesting and instructive in the lives of the people. Olaf and Magnus, too, added their powers of persuasion to those of Harry, and in the end Mr. Birk (after enjoining a hundred precautions) had to yield, stipulating only that Edwin should remain at home. Grim promised to keep a careful lookout over the movements of the boys, but he refused to be responsible for their safety, because, as he remarked, "they were too lively a lot to be controlled by a stiff-legged old crab like himself."

It was a grey morning in January that the long eight-oared boats were made ready, the chests containing provisions and clothes were placed in the stern, and the sails with a rattling noise flew up and bulged before the wind. The sky had a peculiar whitish-grey colour, which has always an ominous look and promises squalls. Yet it was a glorious sensation to feel the boats shooting away over the crests of the waves, dashing the spray like smoke about them and yielding like living things to the slightest prompting of the rudder. Grim himself sat in the stern of the first boat, which the boys had named *The Cormorant*, holding the tiller in his left hand and the sheet in his right. Magnus had found a rather elevated seat in the prow, from whence he could observe the captain's manoeuvres and take lessons in seamanship. Harry and Olaf sat on the middle bench, watching the horizon and seeing the squalls dash down from the mountains and sweep their trails of smoke across the fiord.

"It must be dangerous sailing here, Grim," Harry observed, uneasily.

"It ain't no joke – fer goslings," answered Grim.

"I should think, on the whole, it would be more comfortable for goslings than for men," retorted Harry, carelessly. "They wouldn't mind a ducking half as much as I should."

"If ye are afeard just say so, and I'll put ye ashore," said Grim, sternly.

"Afraid!" said Harry, indignantly; "not much, old man; guess I can give you odds any day if you want to try my courage."

"I want to try ef ye can hold your tongue," was the captain's ungracious reply. "I ain't much for gassin' on the water."

Harry, thinking that perhaps the situation was graver than he supposed, failed to resent the snub, and fell again to watching the horizon. They shot away at a tearing speed over the waves, and sometimes *The Cormorant* careened heavily to leeward and shipped a sea, but Grim still made no motion to reef the sail. The other Hasselrud boats, which had kept bravely in the wake of their leader, were now falling behind, and the blinding spray often hid them completely from sight. The fiord was growing wider, and the long 'ground swell' showed that they were nearing the ocean. The storm petrel was seen skimming lightly, half flying, half running, over the tops of the billows, and her shrill scream pierced like a sharp instrument through the deep bass of the wind. The boats round about them multiplied, and a whole fleet of reddish-brown sails was seen steering toward the Lofoten Islands. The day passed without any incident, and when about three o'clock in the afternoon the darkness came rolling in like a grey curtain from the west, Grim put into port and the boys devoured between them a five-pound cod, whereupon they all crawled into the same bunk in a fisherman's lodging-house and slept the sleep of the just.

The next morning they were aroused before daybreak, and after a frugal repast of coffee and sandwiches were hurried into the boat. The wide ocean now stretched out before them, rolling with a mighty thundering rhythm against the rock-bound coast. A light mist was hovering over the water, but the wind was fair, and hundreds of boats were already scudding northward toward the rich fishing-banks. As soon as the fog rose and was scattered, the invisible sun sent a faint semblance of light up among the low clouds, and immediately thousands of gulls and auks and cormorants were on the wing, and whirled with a wild confusion of screams in the wake of the fishing-fleet. When toward noon the wind slackened a little, Magnus swung out a trawling-line and had almost in the same moment a bite which sent the line whizzing over the gunwale.

"Gracious! I am afraid I have caught a whale," he shouted, standing up in the boat, and holding on to the line with all his might; but being unable to keep his footing, he flung himself prone across the row-bench and would inevitably have been pulled overboard if Harry and Olaf had not caught hold of him by the legs and told him to let the line go.

"You remind me of the Englishman at the siege of Quebec who had caught three Frenchmen," said Harry. "I should say it was the whale who had caught you, in the present case, if a whale it is. Now I am going to try my luck," he added, seizing the wooden frame to which the line was attached just as it was about to fly overboard. He braced himself against the mast and flung his body backward, but the line cut into his hands so terribly that he had to cry for help. Then Olaf was promptly at his side, and by their united efforts they succeeded in hauling in a couple of fathoms; but it was not until one of the boatmen added his strength to theirs that they made any sensible headway. Great was their delight when, at the end of five minutes, they caught sight of an enormous halibut, weighing some forty or fifty pounds, but, as well might be imagined, it was no easy job to get such a monster into the boat without upsetting it. The only way was evidently to tire him out until he lost all power of resistance, and as he had swallowed the metal bait with tremendous vim there was no danger of his escaping.

It was well on toward evening when they put into harbour on the northern coast of Lofoten, where they were to remain while the fisheries lasted. An endless double row of boats stretched along the shore, and behind these the so-called 'Hjælder,' or drying-houses, rose in gaunt perspective against the dark sky. Thousands of boats were drawn up along the whole beach, and the smell of fish pervaded the air and seemed even to be borne in on the ocean breeze. Grim, followed by all the men from the three boats, marched up to the Hasselrud booth, which he unlocked, and ordered the temporary cook to make a fire on the hearth and to prepare supper. It was a large empty room, one wall of which was occupied by the hearth and two by rows of bunks, one above the other, resembling the berths in the steerage of an immigrant steamer. It looked cheerless, and the boys, whose expectations had pictured to them something quite different, shivered at the sight of the bare and sooty walls. Nevertheless when the fire had been lighted, and a couple of burning pine knots stuck into the wall, they took heart again and determined to make the best of the situation.

The next morning at daybreak they jumped into their clothes, pulling complete oil-cloth suits on the outside of their ordinary garments. Then fastening their yellow sou'westers under their chins, they surveyed each other with undisguised looks of admiration and began to feel like real fishermen. The breakfast was swallowed in haste, and they scarcely noticed how the hot coffee scalded their mouths, so eager were they to be off. Nevertheless, as they had no nets to draw as yet, they delayed their departure for several hours. It was a raw, cold morning, but the signals at the government station indicated fair but blustery weather. The whole fleet had already started, and the Hasselrud boats were among the last to set sail for the fishing-banks. It was glorious to see the wide ocean studded, as far as the eye could reach, with swelling sails, and the air filled for miles with a screaming host of great, white-winged seabirds. Round about the whales were spouting, shooting columns of water into the grey light of the morning: and the auks were rocking upon the waves, and vanishing, quick as a flash, as soon as a boat approached them. The fresh sea-breeze blew into the faces of the three boys, and they felt like Norse Vikings of the olden time starting out in search of fame and adventures. It was about twelve o'clock when they arrived at the fishing-banks; the sails were lowered and the nets sunk by means of lead sinkers and stones attached to their lower edge. Wooden floats, similarly attached to their upper edge, held them in position in the water. Grim sat, grave and imperturbable, in the stern, issuing his commands in a voice which rose high above the rushing of the water and the whizzing of the wind, and every man obeyed with a promptness as if his life depended upon it. The sea was so packed with cod that the nets often stopped, gliding slowly over the backs of the fishes, and being again arrested by the myriads of finny creatures below. Often the same net had to be taken up and disentangled several times before it made its way to the bottom. The water was thick with spawn, which clung in long gelatinous ropes to the blades of the oars, and doubled their weight to the rowers. The boys, leaning out over the gunwale, could see the huge male cod winding themselves onward through the dense throngs of females which stood still with their noses against the current, moving their fins, and shedding their spawn. It seemed a positive mercy to haul up a million or so of them, just to make room for the rest.

"I understand now," exclaimed Harry, "how the Canadians managed to cheat us out of so much money – six million, more or less, I think – because we had encroached upon their fishing-grounds. I would myself pay a good round sum for sport like this; and the joke of it is that you are making money at it and have all the fun in the bargain."

"And have ye fisheries in America too, lad?" Grim asked, with visible interest, as he let the last float slip from his hand.

"Have we got fisheries in America? Well, I should say we had, old man," said Harry, fired with patriotic ardor. "You just tell me what we haven't got in America. If you'll come over and see I shall be happy to entertain you."

"Ye are safe in invitin' me, lad," Grim retorted, biting a quid from his roll of tobacco. "A purty figger an old sea-dog like me would make in your ma's carpeted parlour."

Harry in his heart admitted the force of this remark, and he laughed to himself at the thought of Grim's ungainly form seated in one of his mother's spindle-legged blue satin chairs; but, for all that, he liked Grim too much to wish to offend him, and therefore stuck bravely to his invitation, insisting that it was sincerely meant. As they were amicably squabbling, the sun suddenly burst forth, and flung its dazzling radiance upon the ocean. The noise of the seabirds grew louder, making the vast vault of the sky alive with countless varieties of screams. The fishes leaped, the whales spouted lustily, the storm petrel danced over the crests of the billows; thousands of boats lay bobbing up and down on the waves, while the lines were being baited; a thousand voices shouted to each other from boat to boat; oars and rudders rattled, and the wind sang in the mast-tops. It was a scene which once seen could never be forgotten.

II

Long before the Hasselrud men had their lines set the whole fleet had rowed back toward land. But Grim's boat-guild, which had just arrived, and had as yet no nets to draw, lingered for a while eating their dinner, which they had brought with them in the boats. They chatted and told stories about Draugen, the sea-bogey, who rows in a half boat, and whose scream sounds terribly through the tempest. Any man who sees him knows that he will never see land again. Draugen is only out in the worst weather; he has a sou'wester on his head, his face is white and ghastly as death itself, and his empty eye-sockets have no eyes in them. The boys shuddered at the horrible picture which was conjured up before them, and it was a relief to them when the time came for pulling up the lines, and the great codfishes were hauled sprawling into the boat; each one had plenty to do now in cutting out the hooks and in winding the lines upon their frames. A smart gale had sprung up while they were thus engaged, and Grim began to look wistfully at the lurid sunset.

"The sun draws water," he said; "that means lively weather. Hoist the sails, lads, and let us turn our noses shoreward."

He had hardly uttered his command when a thick curtain seemed to be drawn across the face of the sun, and the sea became black as ink.

"Clew up the sail!" he shouted, in a voice of thunder; "we are in for it."

With a roar as of a chorus of cataracts the storm advanced, lashing the water into smoke which whirled heavenward, making the sky dense as night. The masts creaked, the boats tore away with a frantic speed, and the waves rose mountain-high, with steep, black gulfs between them.

"Cap'n," one of the men ventured to remonstrate, "are we not carryin' too much sail?"

Grim deigned him no reply, but, with a sharp turn of the tiller, ran *The Cormorant* closer to the wind. Forward bounded the boat, cleaving the coming wave with a blow of her bows which made her timbers groan. The spray was dashed fathoms high, and would have drenched every man on board if his oilskins had not been watertight. Of the other boats only two were visible, and it was splendid to see how they rose out of one sea, until half the length of their keels were visible, then buried their noses in the next, while great sheets of foam splashed on either side, and were torn into shreds by the gale.

"This is rather lively work, I should say," remarked the midshipman. "I think I should prefer a man-of-war to *The Cormorant* in this sort of weather."

"I confess to a weakness for Cunarders," said Harry; "yet I dare say I shall enjoy this affair well enough when we get safely ashore."

"You mean if we get safely ashore," said Magnus, quietly. "This has rather an ugly look to me. Though I dare say Grim knows what he is about."

He had scarcely spoken when a harsh voice bellowed, "Lay hold of the mast, lads!" and in the same moment they seemed to be flung to a dizzying height; a huge wave towered in front, showing a white whirling top which seemed on the point of breaking right over them. They had just time to clasp the mast when the boat, lying flat on her side, pressed down by her weight of canvas, plunged her nose into this mountain of water, but by some astonishing manoeuvre righted herself, slid down within another black hollow, and again rose high on the crest of another wave.

"All hands bail!" roared the captain.

The command came not a moment too soon; the water was rushing in from the leeward, and the flying wreaths of foam struck the boys' faces with a terrible force and made them smart furiously.

"Grim! Grim!" shouted Olaf, making himself heard with a difficulty above the storm, "you are carrying too much sail."

"Hold your tongue, gosling," Grim thundered back; "we have got nothin' but the sail fer to save us."

"What point are you making for?"

"The Bird Islands."

"I thought there was no harbour there."

"Reckon ye be right."

"Gracious heavens!" cried Olaf, turning a terrified countenance toward his comrades; "he means to wreck the boat; but he knows what he is about. There is no other chance."

He sat for a moment silent, gazing up into the cloud rack which scudded along at a furious rate before the wind. Strips of storm-riven sky, with momentary vistas of blue, were now and then visible, but vanished again, making the dusk more dismal by their memory.

"Breakers ahead!" shouted Olaf, "look out!"

"I see a black ridge against the sky," cried Harry; "now it is gone again!"

He was going to say more, but the wind came with a howling screech and forced his breath down his throat.

He gasped, and as the boat gave a tremendous lurch, diving down into a black hollow, he could only cling to the base of the mast, lest the next tumble might toss him overboard. The sound of a steady rhythmic roar rose and fell upon the air, and made them strain their eyes in the direction from which it was coming.

"Why, Grim, you are steering away from the island," Magnus screamed, pointing to the black ridge which was, once more, for a moment revealed.

"He means to land us on the leeward side," Olaf bawled in his brother's ear; "the chances are that the water is there a bit smoother."

To reach the leeward side was, however, a task which required no mean order of seamanship. The distance was too short for tacking, and moreover the water was filled with blind rocks and skerries which made the approach tenfold dangerous. It seemed to the unskilled eyes of the boys that for nearly half an hour *The Cormorant* was tumbling aimlessly upon the waves, shipping seas which it was a wonder did not swamp her, and righting herself, as by a miracle, when again and again she seemed on the point of capsizing. And yet all these wonderful feats were only the result of the coolest calculation and the most consummate skill.

Just as they were clearing the hidden skerries at the western point of the island the wind veered a point to the north, but did not fall off perceptibly. The spray rose from the shore like a dense and blinding smoke, and in the depths of every black abyss which opened before them death's jaws seemed to be yawning. Harry closed his eyes; and though he was no coward, his heart failed him.

"What is the use of fighting any longer?" he said to Magnus, who was lying at his side, clinging like him to the mast; "we are going to the bottom, anyway. The archangel Gabriel himself couldn't land us on this shore, with all the heavenly hosts to assist him."

"But Grim is a better sailor than Gabriel," Magnus replied, quite unconscious of his joke. "He knows every inch of the bottom here from the time he was a boy and used to row out here and gather eiderdown. He has told me about it often. If I were you I wouldn't give up yet."

"All right, old fellow," Harry answered, taking heart once more. "I am ready for anything. But I am an unlucky chap – a sort of a Jonah, who has a talent for getting into scrapes. I shouldn't wonder if, in case you threw me overboard, the storm would fall off and you might sail home in comfortable fashion."

"We mean to go overboard, all of us, in a few minutes," Magnus retorted, hugging Harry tightly with his left arm, which he had freed for that purpose. "Now I am going to propose something to you. Let us tie ourselves together with a rope so that each may help the other; and we may either live or perish together."

"I am afraid you would be the loser by that arrangement," his friend exclaimed. "You are a good deal stronger than I am, and you will need every bit of your strength if you are to plow your way through those awful breakers."

Magnus, instead of answering, slipped the end of a rope about Harry's waist and secured it tightly; the other end he tied about his own waist, although he came near losing his balance, and going headlong over the gunwale. *The Cormorant* had now slipped around to the leeward side of the island, where, under the shelter of the steep rock, the water was a trifle less tumultuous. And yet a gigantic surf was running and the undertow on the steeply sloping bottom seemed strong enough to take an elephant off his feet. The wind yelled and screeched from the top of the towering rock, and rushed down in thundering eddies on the leeward side. If it had not been for a momentary clearing of the sky, which showed the position of the breakers and the outline of the shore, it would have been madness to risk landing; and even as it was, the chance of being dashed to pieces against the rocks seemed altogether to preponderate. But Grim apparently took a different view of the situation; as long as the sail was whole and the boat true to her rudder he saw no cause for despair.

"Now, lads," he roared, hoarsely, "steady on yer shanks. No chicken-hearted chap among ye! Uncoil the rope! Thar's a bit of sandy beach thar – sixty or a hundred feet wide. If we be in luck we'll be thar in a minute."

The ridge of the island was now half visible against the dark horizon, but the beach below was wrapped in a dense smoke, through which came glimpses of the black jagged rock.

"Almighty Lord! thar's a skerry ahead," screamed one of the boatmen, as the retreating surf broke with a wild uproar over the hidden rock and rose like a mighty water-spout against the sky. There was a moment of breathless suspense. Each man seemed to hear the beating of the other's heart. As the boat was flung upward again on the next wave, the wind gave a frantic shriek; the mast bent forward under the terrible strain. The incoming surf buried the skerry under a mountain of towering water, and high upon its crest *The Cormorant* rode triumphant, only to be hurled from its crest, fairly shooting through the air, upon the beach.

"Jump overboard!" bellowed Grim, and seizing Magnus in his arms he leaped from the stern just as the boat struck the sand and broke into fragments. Every man followed his example; but the undertow swept them off their feet. Still Grim stood like a rock, holding with his gigantic strength the rope to the other end of which Harry was attached. Once he tottered, and if he had had sand under his feet he would have been dragged down by his double burden. But by a lucky chance he had planted his heels upon a boulder which rose slightly out of the surf. When the wildest force of the wave had been exhausted he sprang up on the beach, depositing Magnus and the half-unconscious Harry beyond the reach of the waves. Back he rushed again to his former station, just as one of the boatmen, who had momentarily regained his footing, was scrambling up toward him.

"I am tied to the rope," shouted the man; "someone is tugging at it."

"Hand it to me," commanded Grim.

The man struggled to his feet and planted himself resolutely at his captain's side. All this was the work of a moment. With the next incoming wave, which was happily much smaller than the preceding one, four men were flung up on the sand; but they seemed half dead, and made no effort to save themselves. Grim, who thought he saw a glimmer of brass buttons in the water, dashed forward and seized Olaf by the collar, just as he would have been sucked back by the undertow. He bore him up on the shore, while the boatman came dragging two of his unconscious comrades out of the roaring surf. One was still missing; but as the next wave that broke in tumult at their feet showed no trace of him, they knew that he was beyond the reach of human help.

The work of resuscitating the men was a long and tedious one; but Grim and Magnus both worked with their hearts in their throats, yet with a resolution which scorned fatigue. Harry revived the moment they had poured a glass of brandy down his throat, and he soon recovered his spirits and volunteered his help. But the midshipman was both badly battered and had swallowed a quantity of water; and it was only after long and persistent efforts on Grim's part that his breath came back to him. Their next thought was of fire; for the wind was raw and chill, and the last glimmer of daylight was vanishing. The problem, however, was a serious one, for there was not a tree growing on the island, except perhaps a few stunted juniper shrubs up in the crevices of the rocks. And to get at these in the dark was no easy undertaking. Nor was their situation in other respects an enviable one. Above them loomed the black cliff, and the surf was thundering at their feet. And there they were sitting, huddled together in a heap to keep each other warm, and yet shivering in their wet clothes, and thinking with horror of the long hours of the night which must pass before they could be rescued.

"Lads," cried Magnus, suddenly extricating himself from Harry and Olaf's embrace, "I am the only one of you who is not wet to the skin, and I am going to explore this island and see if we can't scare up some fuel. To sit here hugging each other in the dark is a dismal sort of business, and I am not so affectionately disposed as the rest of you."

"A mighty peart chap ye be, lad," Grim said, raising his tall figure out of the group; "but ye had better let me crawl ahead, and ye keep astern o' me. I know summat o' the island and ye don't know nothin'."

"I'll keep abreast of you, Grim," Magnus replied, "but your stern would obscure my view; so take your bearings and let's be off."

"Ye be a mighty lively customer," Grim grumbled, admiringly, giving the boy a caressing pat in the dark.

They had scarcely crawled fifty yards up the beach when their fumbling hands touched something cold and clammy, which felt like the nose of some aquatic animal. There came immediately a little chorus of whining barks, which was followed by a great flapping, as if something broad and wet struck against the stones.

"Thunder and lightning, Grim," cried Magnus, "what sort of beasts are these?"

"A herd of seals," answered Grim, quietly; "it was funny I didn't think o' them. Here we have got our fuel."

In the same moment a cold nose was stuck right into Magnus' face and he tumbled backward, scarcely knowing how to return the unexpected caress.

"Draw yer knives, lads," shouted Grim to the men, "a herd of seals is a comin' right upon ye."

The seals were now in full flight, rolling, tumbling, and pushing themselves on over the smooth sand. They instinctively knew, even in the dark, the way to the water, and they thus came plump down upon the shipwrecked men, who had arisen in response to Grim's call and were ready to give them a warm reception. In the storm and the fright of the sudden attack the keen scent of the animals scarcely served them at all. They rushed right down upon their enemies, and within a few minutes fully a dozen of them lay gasping and bleeding upon the beach. The rest plunged into the surf, where their plaintive bark was heard as they battled with the raging sea.

Grim and Magnus in the meanwhile pushed on, groping their way over the slippery boulders, and keeping close together so as to help each other in case of accident. But the farther they climbed the steeper grew the rock, and as far as they could ascertain by their sense of touch there was no sign of vegetation.

"Now look sharp, lad," cried Grim, warningly.

"Look sharp!" repeated Magnus. "How am I to look sharp when it is as dark as pitch about me?"

"Right ye be, lad, right ye be," the other retorted; "ye be a smart chap and a peart one. But don't ye lay hold o' nothin' here before ye know it is rock. Thar be thousands o' birds here on the lee'ard side when thar be a storm from the north; and ef ye mistook a gull or a cormorant fer somethin' solid ye might tumble down and break yer precious neck. Mark ye my word, chap, thar will be a mighty lively hubbub here in a couple o' minutes."

Grim had hardly uttered this prophecy when Magnus felt something feathery under his touch, and in the same instant there came a piercing scream and a powerful wing dealt him a blow across the bridge of his nose. Immediately there commenced a wild chorus of screams and chattering protest, as if the more sober-minded birds were deprecating this senseless uproar. Magnus thought, too, that he heard his name called from below, but the deafening thunder of the surf and the noise of the birds drowned all other sounds, and he concluded that he had been deceived. It was a terrible sensation, all these invisible wings flapping about him in the dark; unseen bodies precipitated against him and tumbling blindly about him with a murderous tumult from a thousand discordant voices. He raised his elbows above his head to protect himself from the blind assaults and the perpetual beating of wings. It hardly occurred to him to assume the offensive until he heard Grim's voice shouting to him:

"Draw yer knife, lad, and make it lively fer them screamin' rascals. Their down is worth money and they've got blubber as thick as a seal's. Give 'em no odds, I tell ye, my laddie."

Magnus followed this advice promptly. He drew his knife, and fought with a will, thrusting and striking right and left, and hearing the great birds tumbling about him down the steep sides of the rock. He had been thus occupied for a few minutes when suddenly, to his unutterable amazement, a great blaze rose from the strand below, lighting up the barren wall of the cliff, and showing him how narrow the ledge was upon which he was sitting. It was a superb spectacle, too, to see the whirling host of gulls, auks, and cormorants eddying wildly about his head, the great black cliff looming up above him, and the spray of the surf spouting, with angry brawl, high up into the nocturnal air.

"Hurrah! lad," yelled Grim, through the ear-splitting noise and confusion, "I war a blasted fool not to think on it. They be a-burnin' the wreck."

The descent was a much easier affair than the ascent; for the light of the fire below blazed up every now and then and enabled them to see where they were treading. They picked up between them several dozen birds, of nearly half as many varieties, and flung them down before the fire, where the company were now seated in comparative comfort, warming their stiffened limbs. Two of the boatmen were engaged in skinning the seals and cutting off the blubber, which, after squeezing out the blood, they flung into the fire. Soon the oil began to ooze out, and, flowing over the wood, burned with a clear and strong flame.

"I am going to make myself comfortable, fellows," said Harry, who was looking very pale and chilly after his involuntary bath; "and if you don't mind it, I'll make a scarf of this big duck. She fits very nicely about my throat, though she won't accommodate herself to the bow-knot. This little one I am going to stuff down my bosom. She feels so deliciously warm and downy! I tell you," he went on, with emphasis, suiting his actions to his words, "I mean to patent this invention, when I get back home, as an infallible cure for rheumatism, toothache, consumption, chillblains, corns, and kidney disease. I am going to call it Winchester's In-wincible Wivifier. That will sound well and catch the public eye. I was about ready to give up the ghost awhile ago, and now I feel quite jolly."

He stretched himself luxuriously on the windward side of the fire, arranged half a dozen ducks and auks under his head as a pillow, and closed his eyes. Magnus and Olaf soon followed his example, each tying a big gull about his throat, and feeling a grateful warmth creeping through their half-frozen bodies. The men had the good luck to find a bunch of driftwood large enough to keep the fire going until morning, and to satisfy their hunger they roasted a piece of seal-flesh, which, in spite of its oily flavor, tasted better than they had expected. When Grim saw that the boys were asleep he covered them carefully with his own oilskin clothes, while he himself kept marching up and down on the beach to keep his blood in motion. After midnight the wind shifted suddenly to the west and fell off gradually, the clouds were scattered, and the moon sailed calmly through the dark-blue sky.

The three boys slept soundly after their terrible hardships, and the eastern sky was already bright with the dawn when they opened their eyes. The whole screaming colony of birds were again on the wing, and whirled about the projecting crags of the cliff with wild clamour. Several sails were already visible on the horizon and, as soon as signals of distress were hoisted, steered toward the island. Harry, who was ravenously hungry, made a courageous assault upon the roasted seal-flesh, but after two futile attempts declared that he was not sufficiently acclimated to relish such a diet. If necessity compelled him, he preferred to roast his boots, and to use the seal-oil as gravy.

"What do you say you call this island?" he asked Grim, who was trotting at his side up and down on the sand.

"The Bird Island," answered Grim.

"I should rather call it the 'Skerry of Shrieks,'" said Harry; "for in all my living days I have never heard a finer assortment of varied yells than I heard here last night. It must be a jolly place in summer, when the nights are light and the weather comfortable."

"It ain't bad fer such as like it," was Grim's non-committal reply.

"And do you know," Magnus put in eagerly, "during the early fall the island is quite covered with eider-ducks' nests, so that you can hardly move your feet without stepping into them. All those little round depressions up on the slope there are such nests; and thousands of dollars have been made here in times past by gathering the down with which the eider-duck lines her nest; and it is even possible during the brooding season to catch the bird alive and pull the down from her breast; though I think that would be cruel, as she probably needs all she has left after having picked herself for the benefit of her young."

"The eider-duck must be very tame," Harry observed.

"Yes, it is very tame, indeed, because people rarely molest it," said Magnus; "the peasants have a kind of superstitious respect for it, and they won't allow anyone to kill it. It is very much the same kind of feeling as they have for the swallow. They think a misfortune will befall him who robs or pulls down a swallow's nest."

Several boats were by this time within hailing distance, and they were easily persuaded to run up and take the shipwrecked company on board. They insisted, however, upon drawing their nets before returning, and thus it happened that it was nearly noon before the party set foot on shore. They now learned that a great many boats besides their own had been wrecked during yesterday's storm, and that some fifty or sixty men had been drowned. Many dead bodies were washed ashore during the day, and some were even drawn up in the nets and sent home to their sorrowing widows. Sad, indeed, was the sight of the little fleet of boats which sailed southward that afternoon, each with a tarred pine box showing above its gunwales. The three boys, although they would scarcely have admitted that the disaster had discouraged them, concluded, after a short consultation, that the experience they had already had of the fisheries was an instructive one and would probably last them for the remainder of their lives. They therefore, without much regret, induced Grim to hoist the sails and pilot them safely home.

A Tale of the Sea

(Norwegian)

ONCE THERE LAY IN A CERTAIN HAVEN a large number of vessels. They had lain there very long, not exactly on account of a storm, but rather because of a dead calm; and at last they had lain there until they no longer heeded the weather.

All the captains had gradually become good friends; they visited from ship to ship, and called one another 'Cousin.'

They were in no hurry to depart. Now and then a youthful steersman might chance to let fall a word about a good wind and a smooth sea. But such remarks were not tolerated; order had to be maintained on a ship. Those, therefore, who could not hold their tongues were set ashore.

Matters could not, however, go on thus for ever. Men are not so good as they ought to be, and all do not thrive under law and order.

The crews at length began to murmur a little; they were weary of painting and polishing the cabins, and of rowing the captains to and from the toddy suppers. It was rumoured that individual ships were getting ready for sailing. The sails of some were set one by one in all silence, the anchors were weighed without song, and the ships glided quietly out of the harbour; others sailed while their captains slept. Fighting and mutiny were also heard of; but then there came help from the neighbour captains, the malcontents were punished and put ashore, and all moorings were carefully examined and strengthened.

Nevertheless, all the ships, except one, at last left the harbour. They did not all sail with like fortune; one and another even came in again for a time, damaged. Others were little heard of. The captain of one ship, it was said, was thrown overboard by his men; another sailed with half the crew in irons, none knew where. But yet they were all in motion, each striving after its own fashion, now in storm, now in calm, towards its goal.

As stated, only one ship remained in the harbour, and it lay safe and sound, with two anchors at the bottom and three great cables attached to the quay.

It was a strange little craft. The hull was old, but it had been newly repaired, and they had given it a smart little modern figurehead, which contrasted strangely with the smooth sides and the heavy stern. One could see that the rigging had originally belonged to a large vessel, but had been very hastily adapted to the smaller hull, and this still further increased the want of proportion in the brig's whole appearance. Then it was painted with large portholes for guns, like a man-of-war, and always carried its flag at the main-mast.

The skipper was no common man. He himself had painted the sketch of the brig that hung in the cabin, and, besides, he could sing – both psalms and songs. Indeed, there were those who maintained that he composed the songs himself; but this was most probably a lie. And it was certainly a lie that they whispered in the forecastle: that the skipper had not quite got his sea-legs. Young men always tell such stories to cabin-boys, in order to appear manly. And, besides, there was a steersman on the brig, who could, on a pinch, easily round the headlands alone.

He had sailed as steersman for many years of our Lord, ever since the time of the skipper's late father. He had become as if glued to the tiller, and many could scarcely imagine the old brig with a new steersman.

He had certainly never voyaged in distant waters; but as his trade had always been the same, and as he had invariably been in the company of others, the brig had sailed pretty fortunately, without special damage and without special merit.

Therefore, both he and the skipper had arrived at the conviction that none could sail better than they, and hence they cared little what the others did. They looked up at the sky and shook their heads.

The men felt quite comfortable, for they were not used to better things. Most of them could not understand why the crews of the other ships were in such a hurry to be off; the month went round all the same, whether one lay in port or sailed, and then it was better to avoid work. So long as the skipper made no sign of preparation for sailing, the men might keep their minds easy, for he must surely have the most interest in getting away. And besides, they all knew what sort of fellow the steersman was, and if such a capable and experienced man lay still, they might be quite sure that he had good and powerful reasons.

But a little party among the crew – some quite youthful persons – thought it was a shame to let themselves be thus left astern by everybody. They had, indeed, no special advantage or profit to expect from the voyage, but at last the inaction became intolerable, and they conceived the daring resolve of sending a youth aft to beg the captain to fix a date for sailing.

The more judicious among the crew crossed themselves, and humbly entreated the young man to keep quiet; but the latter was a rash greenhorn, who had sailed in foreign service, and therefore imagined himself to be a 'regular devil of a fellow.' He went right aft and down into the cabin, where the skipper and the steersman sat with their whisky before them, playing cards.

"We would ask if the skipper would kindly set sail next week, for now we are all so weary of lying here," said the young man, looking the skipper straight in the eyes without winking.

The latter's face first turned pale blue, and then assumed a deep violet tint; but he restrained himself, and said, as was his invariable custom:

"What think you, steersman?"

"Hm," replied the steersman slowly. More he never used to say at first, when he was questioned, for he did not like to answer promptly. But when he got an opportunity of speaking alone, without being interrupted, he could utter the longest sentences and the very hardest words. And then the skipper was especially proud of him.

However short the steersman's reply might seem, the skipper at once understood its meaning. He turned towards the youth – gravely, but gracefully, for he was an exceedingly well-bred man.

"You cursed young fool! Don't you think I understand these things better than you? I, who have thought of nothing but being a skipper since I was knee-high! But I know well enough what you and the like of you are thinking about. You don't care a d— about the craft, and if you could only get the power from us old ones, you would run her on the first islet you came to, so that you might plunder her of the whisky. But there will be none of that, my young whelp! Here we shall lie, as long as I choose."

When this decision reached the forecastle, it awoke great indignation among the young and immature, which, indeed, was only to be expected. But even the skipper's friends and admirers shook their heads, and opined that it was a nasty answer; after all, it was only a civil question, which ought not to compromise anybody.

There now arose a growing ill-humour – something quite unheard-of among these peaceable fellows. Even the skipper, who was not usually quick to understand or remark anything, thought he saw many sullen faces, and he was no longer so well pleased with the bearing of the crew when he stepped out upon deck with his genial "Good morning, you rogues."

But the steersman had long scented something, for he had a fine nose and long ears. Therefore, a couple of evenings after the young man's unfortunate visit, it was remarked that something extraordinary was brewing aft.

The cabin-boy had to make three journeys with the toddy-kettle, and the report he gave in the forecastle after his last trip was indeed disquieting.

The steersman seemed to have talked without intermission for two hours; before them on the table lay barometer, chronometer, sextant, journal, and half the ship's library. This consisted of Kingo's hymn book and an old Dutch *Kaart-Boikje*; for the skipper could do just as little with the new hymns as the steersman with the new charts.

The skipper now sat prodding the chart with a large pair of compasses, while the steersman talked, using all his longest and hardest words. There was one word in particular that was often repeated, and this the boy learned by heart. He said it over and over again to himself as he went up the cabin stairs and passed along the deck to the forecastle, and the moment he opened the door he shouted:

"Initiative! Mind that word, boys! Write it down – initiative!"

In-i-ti-a-tive was with much difficulty spelt out and written with chalk on the table. And during the boy's long statement all these men sat staring, uneasily and with anxious expectancy, at this long, mystic word.

"And then," concluded the cabin-boy at last – "then says the steersman: 'But we ourselves shall take the—' what is written on the table."

All exclaimed simultaneously, "Initiative."

"Yes, that was it. And every time he said it, they both struck the table and looked at me as if they would eat me. I now think, therefore, that it is a new kind of revolver they intend to use upon us."

But none of the others thought so; it was surely not so bad as that. But something was impending, that was clear. And the relieved watchman went to his berth with gloomy forebodings, and the middle watch did not get a wink of sleep that night.

At seven o'clock next morning both skipper and steersman were up on deck. No man could remember ever having seen them before so early in the day. But there was no time to stand in amazement, for now followed, in quick succession, orders for sailing.

"Heave up the anchors! Let two men go ashore and slip the cables!"

There was gladness and bustle among the crew, and the preparations proceeded so rapidly that in less than an hour the brig was under canvas.

The skipper looked at the steersman and shook his head, muttering, "This is the devil's own haste."

After a few little turns in the spacious harbour, the brig passed the headland and stood out to sea. A fresh breeze was blowing, and the waves ran rather high.

The steersman, with a prodigious twist in his mouth, stood astride the tiller, for such a piece of devil's trumpery as a wheel should never come on board as long as *he* had anything to say in the matter.

The skipper stood on the cabin stairs, with his head above the companion. His face was of a somewhat greenish hue, and he frequently ran down into the cabin. The old boatswain believed that he went to look at the chart, the young man thought he drank whisky, but the cabin-boy swore that he went below to vomit.

The men were in excellent spirits; it was so refreshing to breathe the sea air, and to feel the ship once again moving under their feet. Indeed, the old brig herself seemed to be in a good humour; she dived as deep down between the seas as she could, and raised much more foam than was necessary.

The young sailors looked out for heavy seas. "Here comes a whopper," they shouted; "if it would only hit us straight!" And it did.

It was a substantial sea, larger than the others. It approached deliberately, and seemed to lie down and take aim. It then rose suddenly, and gave the brig, which was chubby as a cherub, such a mighty slap on the port cheek that she quivered in every timber. And high over the railing, far in upon the deck, dashed the cold salt spray; the captain had scarcely time to duck his head below the companion.

Ah, how refreshing it was! It exhilarated both old and young; they had not had a taste of the cold seawater for a long time, and with one voice the whole crew broke into a lusty "Hurrah!"

But at this moment the steerman's stentorian voice rang out: "Hard to leeward!" The brig luffed up close to the wind, the sails flapped so violently that the rigging shook, and now followed in rapid succession, even quicker than before, orders to anchor. "Let fall the port anchor! Let go the starboard one too!"

Plump – fell the one; plump – went the other. The old chains rattled out, and a little red cloud of rust rose up on either side of the bowsprit.

The men, accustomed to obey, worked rapidly without thinking why, and the brig soon rode pretty quietly at her two anchors.

But now, after the work was finished, no one could conceal his astonishment at this sudden anchoring, just off the coast, among islets and skerries. And still more extraordinary seemed the behaviour of those in command. For they both stood right forward, with their backs to the weather, leaning over the railing and staring at the port bow. Some had even thought they had heard the captain cry, "To the pumps, men," but this point was never cleared up.

"What the devil can they be doing forward?" said the rash young man.

"They think she struck on a reef when we shipped the big sea," whispered the cabin-boy.

"Hold your jaw, boy!" said the boatswain.

All the same, the cabin-boy's words passed from mouth to mouth; a little chuckle was heard here and there; the men's faces became more and more ludicrously uneasy, and their suppressed laughter was on the point of bursting forth. Then the steersman was seen to nudge the skipper in the side.

"Yes; but then you must whisper to me," said the latter.

The steersman nodded, and then the skipper turned to the crew and solemnly spoke as follows:

"Yes, this time, fortunately, everything went well; but now I hope that each of you will have learnt how dangerous it is to lend an ear to these juvenile agitators, who can never be quiet and let evolution, as the steersman says, pursue its natural course. I yielded to your wishes this time, it is true, but not because I approved of your insane rashness; it was simply that I might convince you by – by the logic of events. And see – how did things go? Certainly we have, as by a miracle, been spared the worst; but now we lie here, outside our safe haven, our old anchorage, which we have forsaken to be tossed about on the turbulent waters of the unknown and the untried. But, believe me, henceforth you will find both our excellent steersman and your captain at our post, guarding against such crude, immature projects. And if things go badly with us in days to come, you must all remember that it is entirely your own fault; we wash our hands of the matter."

Thereupon he strode through the men, who respectfully fell back to let him pass. The steersman, who had really whispered, dried his eyes and followed. They both disappeared in the cabin.

There was much strife in the forecastle that day, and it grew worse after.

The brig's happy days were all over. Dissension and discontent, suspicion and obstinacy, converted the narrow limits of the forecastle into a veritable hell.

Only skipper and steersman seemed to thrive well under all this. The general dissatisfaction did not affect them; for they, of course, were not to blame.

None thought of any change. The crew had done what they could, and the skipper, on his part, had also been accommodating.

Now they might keep their minds at rest. The brig lay in a dangerous place, but now she would have to lie – and there she lies to this day.

Tales of the Nisse & Other Small Folk

Introduction

A WONDERFUL ARRAY of little people – nisses, dwarfs and goblins – are to be found in Nordic myth. They're mostly benign, but can be crotchety and bear a grudge. Their precise functions can vary: nisses often lend a hand with household tasks and farmwork.

Traditionally, a nisse was the surviving soul of the first man (he's always male) to live in a particular house and work its land, so he stands for continuity, providing a living link between the generations.

These beings may be strange, but the weirdest thing about them is the matter-of-factness with which their presence is accepted – in a tale like Hans Andersen's 'The Goblin and the Huckster', for example. Here a 'goblin' stays in a pedlar's home in the city 'because at Christmas he always had a large dish full of jam, with a great piece of butter in the middle'. The supernatural was never more mundane.

Tales of the Nisses

(Danish/Swedish/Norwegian)

THE NIS IS THE SAME BEING that is called Kobold in Germany, and Brownie in Scotland. He is in Denmark and Norway also called Nisse god Dreng (Nissè good lad), and in Sweden, Tomtegubbe (the old man of the house).

He is of the dwarf family, and resembles them in appearance, and, like them, has the command of money, and the same dislike to noise and tumult.

His usual dress is grey, with a pointed red cap, but on Michaelmas-day he wears a round hat like those of the peasants.

No farmhouse goes on well without there is a Nis in it, and well is it for the maids and the men when they are in favour with him. They may go to their beds and give themselves no trouble about their work, and yet in the morning the maids will find the kitchen swept up, and water brought in; and the men will find the horses in the stable well cleaned and curried, and perhaps a supply of corn cribbed for them from the neighbours' barns.

There was a Nis in a house in Jutland. He every evening got his groute at the regular time, and he, in return, used to help both the men and the maids, and looked to the interest of the master of the house in every respect.

There came one time a mischievous boy to live at service in this house, and his great delight was, whenever he got an opportunity, to give the Nis all the annoyance in his power.

Late one evening, when everything was quiet in the house, the Nis took his little wooden dish, and was just going to eat his supper, when he perceived that the boy had put the butter at the bottom and had concealed it, in hopes that he might eat the groute first, and then find the butter when all the groute was gone. He accordingly set about thinking how he might repay the boy in kind. After pondering a little he went up into the loft where a man and the boy were lying asleep in the same bed. The Nis whisked off the bed clothes, and when he saw the little boy by the tall man, he said –

"Short and long don't match," and with this word he took the boy by the legs and dragged him down to the man's feet. He then went up to the head of the bed, and –

"Short and long don't match," said he again, and then he dragged the boy up to the man's head. Do what he would he could not succeed in making the boy as long as the man, but persisted in dragging him up and down in the bed, and continued at this work the whole night long till it was broad daylight.

By this time he was well tired, so he crept up on the window stool, and sat with his legs dangling down into the yard. The house-dog – for all dogs have a great enmity to the Nis – as soon as he saw him began to bark at him, which afforded him much amusement, as the dog could not get up to him. So he put down first one leg and then the other, and teased the dog, saying –

"Look at my little leg. Look at my little leg!"

In the meantime the boy had awoke, and had stolen up behind him, and, while the Nis was least thinking of it, and was going on with his, "Look at my little leg," the boy tumbled him down into the yard to the dog, crying out at the same time –

"Look at the whole of him now!"

* * *

There lived a man in Thyrsting, in Jutland, who had a Nis in his barn. This Nis used to attend to his cattle, and at night he would steal fodder for them from the neighbours, so that this farmer had the best fed and most thriving cattle in the country.

One time the boy went along with the Nis to Fugleriis to steal corn. The Nis took as much as he thought he could well carry, but the boy was more covetous, and said –

"Oh! take more. Sure, we can rest now and then!"

"Rest!" said the Nis. "Rest! and what is rest?"

"Do what I tell you," replied the boy. "Take more, and we shall find rest when we get out of this."

The Nis took more, and they went away with it, but when they came to the lands of Thyrsting, the Nis grew tired, and then the boy said to him –

"Here now is rest!" and they both sat down on the side of a little hill.

"If I had known," said the Nis, as they sat. "If I had known that rest was so good, I'd have carried off all that was in the barn."

It happened, some time after, that the boy and the Nis were no longer friends, and as the Nis was sitting one day in the granary-window with his legs hanging out into the yard, the boy ran at him and tumbled him back into the granary. The Nis was revenged on him that very night, for when the boy was gone to bed he stole down to where he was lying and carried him as he was into the yard. Then he laid two pieces of wood across the well and put him lying on them, expecting that when he awoke he would fall, from the fright, into the well and be drowned. He was, however, disappointed, for the boy came off without injury.

* * *

There was a man who lived in the town of Tirup who had a very handsome white mare. This mare had for many years belonged to the same family, and there was a Nis attached to her who brought luck to the place.

This Nis was so fond of the mare that he could hardly endure to let them put her to any kind of work, and he used to come himself every night and feed her of the best; and as for this purpose he usually brought a superfluity of corn, both thrashed and in the straw, from the neighbours' barns, all the rest of the cattle enjoyed the advantage, and they were all kept in exceedingly good condition.

It happened at last that the farmhouse passed into the hands of a new owner, who refused to put any faith in what they told him about the mare, so the luck speedily left the place, and went after the mare to a poor neighbour who had bought her. Within five days after his purchase, the poor farmer began to find his circumstances gradually improving, while the income of the other, day after day, fell away and diminished at such a rate that he was hard set to make both ends meet.

If now the man who had got the mare had only known how to be quiet and enjoy the good times that were come upon him, he and his children and his children's children after him would have been in flourishing circumstances till this very day. But when he saw the quantity of corn that came every night to his barn, he could not resist his desire to get a sight of the Nis. So he concealed himself one evening at nightfall in the stable, and as soon as it was midnight he saw how the Nis came from his neighbour's barn and brought a sack full of corn with him. It was now unavoidable that the Nis should get a sight of the man who was watching, so he, with evident marks of grief, gave the mare her food for the last time, cleaned and dressed her to the best of his ability, and when he had done, turned round to where the man was lying, and bid him farewell.

From that day forward the circumstances of both the neighbours were on an equality, for each now kept his own.

The Goblin and the Huckster

(Danish)

THERE WAS ONCE A REGULAR STUDENT, who lived in a garret, and had no possessions. And there was also a regular huckster, to whom the house belonged, and who occupied the ground floor. A goblin lived with the huckster, because at Christmas he always had a large dish full of jam, with a great piece of butter in the middle. The huckster could afford this; and therefore the goblin remained with the huckster, which was very cunning of him.

One evening the student came into the shop through the back door to buy candles and cheese for himself, he had no one to send, and therefore he came himself; he obtained what he wished, and then the huckster and his wife nodded good evening to him, and she was a woman who could do more than merely nod, for she had usually plenty to say for herself. The student nodded in return as he turned to leave, then suddenly stopped, and began reading the piece of paper in which the cheese was wrapped. It was a leaf torn out of an old book, a book that ought not to have been torn up, for it was full of poetry.

"Yonder lies some more of the same sort," said the huckster: "I gave an old woman a few coffee berries for it; you shall have the rest for sixpence, if you will."

"Indeed I will," said the student; "give me the book instead of the cheese; I can eat my bread and butter without cheese. It would be a sin to tear up a book like this. You are a clever man; and a practical man; but you understand no more about poetry than that cask yonder."

This was a very rude speech, especially against the cask; but the huckster and the student both laughed, for it was only said in fun. But the goblin felt very angry that any man should venture to say such things to a huckster who was a householder and sold the best butter. As soon as it was night, and the shop closed, and everyone in bed except the student, the goblin stepped softly into the bedroom where the huckster's wife slept, and took away her tongue, which of course, she did not then want. Whatever object in the room he placed his tongue upon immediately received voice and speech, and was able to express its thoughts and feelings as readily as the lady herself could do. It could only be used by one object at a time, which was a good thing, as a number speaking at once would have caused great confusion. The goblin laid the tongue upon the cask, in which lay a quantity of old newspapers.

"Is it really true," he asked, "that you do not know what poetry is?"

"Of course I know," replied the cask: "poetry is something that always stand in the corner of a newspaper, and is sometimes cut out; and I may venture to affirm that I have more of it in me than the student has, and I am only a poor tub of the huckster's."

Then the goblin placed the tongue on the coffee mill; and how it did go to be sure! Then he put it on the butter tub and the cash box, and they all expressed the same opinion as the waste-paper tub; and a majority must always be respected.

"Now I shall go and tell the student," said the goblin; and with these words he went quietly up the back stairs to the garret where the student lived. He had a candle burning still, and the goblin peeped through the keyhole and saw that he was reading in the torn book, which he had brought out of the shop. But how light the room was! From the book shot forth a ray of light which grew broad and full, like the stem of a tree, from which bright rays spread upward and over the student's head. Each leaf was fresh, and each flower was like a beautiful female head; some with dark and sparkling eyes, and others with eyes that were wonderfully blue and clear. The fruit gleamed like stars, and the room was filled with sounds of beautiful music. The little goblin had never imagined, much less seen or heard of, any sight so glorious as this. He stood still on tiptoe, peeping in, till the light went out in the garret. The student no doubt had blown out his candle and gone to bed; but the little goblin remained standing there nevertheless, and listening to the music which still sounded on, soft and beautiful, a sweet cradle-song for the student, who had lain down to rest.

"This is a wonderful place," said the goblin; "I never expected such a thing. I should like to stay here with the student"; and the little man thought it over, for he was a sensible little spirit. At last he sighed, "but the student has no jam!" So he went downstairs again into the huckster's shop, and it was a good thing he got back when he did, for the cask had almost worn out the lady's tongue; he had given a description of all that he contained on one side, and was just about to turn himself over to the other side to describe what was there, when the goblin entered and restored the tongue to the lady. But from that time forward, the whole shop, from the cash box down to the pinewood logs, formed their opinions from that of the cask; and they all had such confidence in him, and treated him with so much respect, that when the huckster read the criticisms on theatricals and art of an evening, they fancied it must all come from the cask.

But after what he had seen, the goblin could no longer sit and listen quietly to the wisdom and understanding downstairs; so, as soon as the evening light glimmered in the garret, he took courage, for it seemed to him as if the rays of light were strong cables, drawing him up, and obliging him to go and peep through the keyhole; and, while there, a feeling of vastness came over him such as we experience by the ever-moving sea, when the storm breaks forth; and it brought tears into his eyes. He did not himself know why he wept, yet a kind of pleasant feeling mingled with his tears. "How wonderfully glorious it would be to sit with the student under such a tree"; but that was out of the question, he must be content to look through the keyhole, and be thankful for even that.

There he stood on the old landing, with the autumn wind blowing down upon him through the trap-door. It was very cold; but the little creature did not really feel it, till the light in the garret went out, and the tones of music died away. Then how he shivered, and crept downstairs again to his warm corner, where it felt home-like and comfortable. And when Christmas came again, and brought the dish of jam and the great lump of butter, he liked the huckster best of all.

Soon after, in the middle of the night, the goblin was awoke by a terrible noise and knocking against the window shutters and the house doors, and by the sound of the watchman's horn; for a great fire had broken out, and the whole street appeared full of flames. Was it in their house, or a neighbor's? No one could tell, for terror had seized upon all. The huckster's wife was so bewildered that she took her gold earrings out of her ears and put them in her pocket, that she might save something at least. The huckster ran to get his business papers, and the servant resolved to save her blue silk mantle, which she had managed to buy. Each wished to keep the best things they had. The goblin had the same wish; for, with one spring, he was upstairs and in the student's room, whom he found standing by the open window, and looking quite calmly at the fire, which was raging at the house of a neighbor opposite. The goblin caught up the wonderful book which lay on the table, and popped it into his red cap, which he held tightly with both hands. The greatest treasure in the house was saved; and he ran away with it to the roof, and seated himself on the chimney. The flames of the burning house opposite illuminated him as he sat, both hands pressed tightly over his cap, in which the treasure lay; and then he found out what feelings really reigned in his heart, and knew exactly which way they tended. And yet, when the fire was extinguished, and the goblin again began to reflect, he hesitated, and said at last, "I must divide myself between the two; I cannot quite give up the huckster, because of the jam."

And this is a representation of human nature. We are like the goblin; we all go to visit the huckster "because of the jam."

The Dwarfs' Banquet

(Norwegian)

THERE LIVED IN NORWAY, not far from the city of Drontheim, a powerful man who was blessed with all the goods of fortune. A part of the surrounding country was his property, numerous herds fed on his pastures, and a great retinue and a crowd of servants adorned his mansion. He had an only daughter, called Aslog, the fame of whose beauty spread far and wide. The greatest men of the country sought her, but all were alike unsuccessful in their suit, and he who had come full of confidence and joy, rode away home silent and melancholy. Her father, who thought his daughter delayed her choice only to select, forbore to interfere, and exulted in her prudence, but when at length the richest and noblest tried their fortune with as little success as the rest, he grew angry and called his daughter, and said to her –

"Hitherto I have left you to your free choice, but since I see that you reject all without any distinction, and the very best of your suitors seems not good enough for you, I will keep measures no longer with you. What! shall my family become extinct, and my inheritance pass away into the hands of strangers? I will break your stubborn spirit. I give you now till the festival of the great winter-night. Make your choice by that time, or prepare to accept him whom I shall fix on."

Aslog loved a youth named Orm, handsome as he was brave and noble. She loved him with her whole soul, and she would sooner die than bestow her hand on another. But Orm was poor, and poverty compelled him to serve in the mansion of her father. Aslog's partiality for him was kept a secret, for her father's pride of power and wealth was such that he would never have given his consent to a union with so humble a man.

When Aslog saw the darkness of his countenance, and heard his angry words, she turned pale as death, for she knew his temper, and doubted not that he would put his threats into execution. Without uttering a word in reply, she retired to her chamber, and thought deeply but in vain how to avert the dark storm that hung over her. The great festival approached nearer and nearer, and her anguish increased every day.

At last the lovers resolved on flight.

"I know," said Orm, "a secure place where we may remain undiscovered until we find an opportunity of quitting the country."

At night, when all were asleep, Orm led the trembling Aslog over the snow and ice-fields away to the mountains. The moon and the stars, sparkling still brighter in the cold winter's night, lighted them on their way. They had under their arms a few articles of dress and some skins of animals, which were all they could carry. They ascended the mountains the whole night long till they reached a lonely spot enclosed with lofty rocks. Here Orm conducted the weary Aslog into a cave, the low and narrow entrance to which was hardly perceptible, but it soon enlarged to a great hall, reaching deep into the mountain. He kindled a fire, and they now, reposing on their skins, sat in the deepest solitude far away from all the world.

Orm was the first who had discovered this cave, which is shown to this very day, and as no one knew anything of it, they were safe from the pursuit of Aslog's father. They passed the whole winter in this retirement. Orm used to go a-hunting, and Aslog stayed at home in the cave, minded the fire, and prepared the necessary food. Frequently did she mount the points of the rocks, but her eyes wandered as far as they could reach only over glittering snow-fields.

The spring now came on: the woods were green, the meadows pat on their various colours, and Aslog could but rarely, and with circumspection, venture to leave the cave. One evening Orm came in with the intelligence that he had recognized her father's servants in the distance, and that he could hardly have been unobserved by them whose eyes were as good as his own.

"They will surround this place," continued he, "and never rest till they have found us. We must quit our retreat then without a minute's delay."

They accordingly descended on the other side of the mountain, and reached the strand, where they fortunately found a boat. Orm shoved off, and the boat drove into the open sea. They had escaped their pursuers, but they were now exposed to dangers of another kind. Whither should they turn themselves? They could not venture to land, for Aslog's father was lord of the whole coast, and they would infallibly fall into his hands. Nothing then remained for them but to commit their bark to the wind and waves. They drove along the entire night. At break of day the coast had disappeared, and they saw nothing but the sky above, the sea beneath, and the waves that rose and fell. They had not brought one morsel of food with them, and thirst and hunger began now to torment them. Three days did they toss about in this state of misery, and Aslog, faint and exhausted, saw nothing but certain death before her.

At length, on the evening of the third day, they discovered an island of tolerable magnitude, and surrounded by a number of smaller ones. Orm immediately steered for it, but just as he came near to it there suddenly arose a violent wind, and the sea rolled higher and higher against him. He turned about with a view of approaching it on another side, but with no better success. His vessel, as often as he approached the island, was driven back as if by an invisible power.

"Lord God!" cried he, and blessed himself and looked on poor Aslog, who seemed to be dying of weakness before his eyes.

Scarcely had the exclamation passed his lips when the storm ceased, the waves subsided, and the vessel came to the shore without encountering any hindrance. Orm jumped out on the beach. Some mussels that he found upon the strand strengthened and revived the exhausted Aslog so that she was soon able to leave the boat.

The island was overgrown with low dwarf shrubs, and seemed to be uninhabited; but when they had got about the middle of it, they discovered a house reaching but a little above the ground, and appearing to be half under the surface of the earth. In the hope of meeting human beings and assistance, the wanderers approached it. They listened if they could hear any noise, but the most perfect silence reigned there. Orm at length opened the door, and with his companion walked in; but what was their surprise to find everything regulated and arranged as if for inhabitants, yet not a single living creature visible. The fire was burning on the hearth in the middle of the room, and a kettle with fish hung on it, apparently only waiting for someone to take it off and eat. The beds were made and ready to receive their weary tenants. Orm and Aslog stood for some time dubious, and looked on with a certain degree of awe, but at last, overcome with hunger, they took up the food and ate. When they had satisfied their appetites, and still in the last beams of the setting sun, which now streamed over the island far and wide, discovered no human being, they gave way to weariness, and laid themselves in the beds to which they had been so long strangers.

They had expected to be awakened in the night by the owners of the house on their return home, but their expectation was not fulfilled. They slept undisturbed till the morning sun shone in upon them. No one appeared on any of the following days, and it seemed as if some invisible power had made ready the house for their reception. They spent the whole summer in perfect happiness. They were, to be sure, solitary, yet they did not miss mankind. The wild birds' eggs and the fish they caught yielded them provisions in abundance.

When autumn came, Aslog presented Orm with a son. In the midst of their joy at his appearance they were surprised by a wonderful apparition. The door opened on a sudden, and an old woman stepped in. She had on her a handsome blue dress. There was something proud, but at the same time strange and surprising in her appearance.

"Do not be afraid," said she, "at my unexpected appearance. I am the owner of this house, and I thank you for the clean and neat state in which you have kept it, and for the good order in which I find everything with you. I would willingly have come sooner, but I had no power to do so, till this little heathen (pointing to the new-born babe) was come to the light. Now I have free access. Only, fetch no priest from the mainland to christen it, or I must depart again. If you will in this matter comply with my wishes, you may not only continue to live here, but all the good that ever you can wish for I will cause you. Whatever you take in hand shall prosper. Good luck shall follow you wherever you go; but break this condition, and depend upon it that misfortune after misfortune will come on you, and even on this child will I avenge myself. If you want anything, or are in danger, you have only to pronounce my name three times, and I will appear and lend you assistance. I am of the race of the old giants, and my name is Guru. But beware of uttering in my presence the name of him whom no giant may hear of, and never venture to make the sign of the cross, or to cut it on beam or on board of the house. You may dwell in this house the whole year long, only be so good as to give it up to me on Yule evening, when the sun is at the lowest, as then we celebrate our great festival, and then only are we permitted to be merry. At least, if you should not be willing to go out of the house, keep yourselves up in the loft as quiet as possible the whole day long, and, as you value your lives, do not look down into the room until midnight is past. After that you may take possession of everything again."

When the old woman had thus spoken she vanished, and Aslog and Orm, now at ease respecting their situation, lived, without any disturbance, content and happy. Orm never made a cast of his net without getting a plentiful draught. He never shot an arrow from his bow that missed its aim. In short, whatever they took in hand, were it ever so trifling, evidently prospered.

When Christmas came, they cleaned up the house in the best manner, set everything in order, kindled a fire on the hearth, and, as the twilight approached, they went up to the loft, where they remained quiet and still. At length it grew dark. They thought they heard a sound of flying and labouring in the air, such as the swans make in the wintertime. There was a hole in the roof over the fireplace which might be opened or shut either to let in the light from above or to afford a free passage for the smoke. Orm lifted up the lid, which was covered with a skin, and put out his head, but what a wonderful sight then presented itself to his eyes! The little islands around were all lit up with countless blue lights, which moved about without ceasing, jumped up and down, then skipped down to the shore, assembled together, and now came nearer and nearer to the large island where Orm and Aslog lived. At last they reached it and arranged themselves in a circle around a large stone not far from the shore, and which Orm well knew. What was his surprise when he saw that the stone had now completely assumed the form of a man, though of a monstrous and gigantic one! He could clearly perceive that the little blue lights were borne by dwarfs, whose pale clay-coloured faces, with their huge noses and red eyes, disfigured, too, by birds' bills and owls' eyes, were supported by misshapen bodies. They tottered and wobbled about here and there, so that they seemed to be, at the same time, merry and in pain. Suddenly the circle opened, the little ones retired on each side, and Guru, who was now much enlarged and of as immense a size as the stone, advanced with gigantic steps. She threw both her arms about the stone image, which immediately began to receive life and motion. As soon as the first sign of motion showed itself the little ones began, with wonderful capers and grimaces, a song, or, to speak more properly, a howl, with which the whole island resounded and seemed to tremble. Orm, quite terrified, drew in his head, and he and Aslog remained in the dark, so still that they hardly ventured to draw their breath.

The procession moved on towards the house, as might be clearly perceived by the nearer approach of the shouting and crying. They were now all come in, and, light and active, the dwarfs jumped about on the benches, and heavy and loud sounded, at intervals, the steps of the giants. Orm and his wife heard them covering the table, and the clattering of the plates, and the shouts of joy with which they celebrated their banquet. When it was over, and it drew near to midnight, they began to dance to that ravishing fairy air which charms the mind into such sweet confusion, and which some have heard in the rocky glens, and learned by listening to the underground musicians. As soon as Aslog caught the sound of the air she felt an irresistible longing to see the dance, nor was Orm able to keep her back.

"Let me look," said she, "or my heart will burst."

She took her child and placed herself at the extreme end of the loft whence, without being observed, she could see all that passed. Long did she gaze, without taking off her eyes for an instant, on the dance, on the bold and wonderful springs of the little creatures who seemed to float in the air and not so much as to touch the ground, while the ravishing melody of the elves filled her whole soul. The child, meanwhile, which lay in her arms, grew sleepy and drew its breath heavily, and without ever thinking of the promise she had given to the old woman, she made, as is usual, the sign of the cross over the mouth of the child, and said –

"Christ bless you, my babe!"

The instant she had spoken the word there was raised a horrible, piercing cry. The spirits tumbled head over heels out at the door, with terrible crushing and crowding, their lights went out, and in a few minutes the whole house was clear of them and left desolate. Orm and Aslog, frightened to death, hid themselves in the most retired nook in the house. They did not venture to stir till daybreak, and not till the sun shone through the hole in the roof down on the fireplace did they feel courage enough to descend from the loft.

The table remained still covered as the underground people had left it. All their vessels, which were of silver, and manufactured in the most beautiful manner, were upon it. In the middle of the room there stood upon the ground a huge copper kettle half-full of sweet mead, and, by the side of it, a drinking-horn of pure gold. In the corner lay against the wall a stringed instrument not unlike a dulcimer, which, as people believe, the giantesses used to play on. They gazed on what was before them full of admiration, but without venturing to lay their hands on anything; but great and fearful was their amazement when, on turning about, they saw sitting at the table an immense figure, which Orm instantly recognized as the giant whom Guru had animated by her embrace. He was now a cold and hard stone. While they were standing gazing on it, Guru herself entered the room in her giant form. She wept so bitterly that the tears trickled down on the ground. It was long ere her sobbing permitted her to utter a single word. At length she spoke –

"Great affliction have you brought on me, and henceforth must I weep while I live. I know you have not done this with evil intentions, and therefore I forgive you, though it were a trifle for me to crush the whole house like an eggshell over your heads."

"Alas!" cried she, "my husband, whom I love more than myself, there he sits petrified for ever. Never again will he open his eyes! Three hundred years lived I with my father on the island of Kunnan, happy in the innocence of youth, as the fairest among the giant maidens. Mighty heroes sued for my hand. The sea around that island is still filled with the rocky fragments which they hurled against each other in their combats. Andfind won the victory, and I plighted myself to him; but ere I was married came the detestable Odin into the country, who overcame my father, and drove us all from the island. My father and sisters fled to the mountains, and since that time my eyes have beheld them no more. Andfind and I saved ourselves on this island, where we for a long time lived in peace and quiet, and thought it would never be interrupted. Destiny, which no one escapes, had determined it otherwise. Oluf came from Britain. They called him the Holy, and Andfind instantly found that his voyage would be inauspicious to the giants. When he heard how Oluf's ship rushed through the waves, he went down to the strand and blew the sea against him with all his strength. The waves swelled up like mountains, but Oluf was still more mighty than he. His ship flew unchecked through the billows like an arrow from a bow. He steered direct for our island. When the ship was so near that Andfind thought he could reach it with his hands, he grasped at the forepart with his right hand, and was about to drag it down to the bottom, as he had often done with other ships. Then Oluf, the terrible Oluf, stepped forward, and, crossing his hands over each other, he cried with a loud voice –

"'Stand there as a stone till the last day!' and in the same instant my unhappy husband became a mass of rock. The ship went on unimpeded, and ran direct against the mountain, which it cut through, separating from it the little island which lies yonder."

"Ever since my happiness has been annihilated, and lonely and melancholy have I passed my life. On Yule eve alone can petrified giants receive back their life, for the space of seven hours, if one of their race embraces them, and is, at the same time, willing to sacrifice a hundred years of his own life. Seldom does a giant do that. I loved my husband too well not to bring him back cheerfully to life, every time that I could do it, even at the highest price, and never would I reckon how often I had done it that I might not know when the time came when I myself should share his fate, and, at the moment I threw my arms around him, become the same as he. Alas! now even this comfort is taken from me. I can never more by any embrace awake him, since he has heard the name which I dare not utter, and never again will he see the light till the dawn of the last day shall bring it."

"Now I go hence! You will never again behold me! All that is here in the house I give you! My dulcimer alone will I keep. Let no one venture to fix his habitation on the little islands which lie around here. There dwell the little underground ones whom you saw at the festival, and I will protect them as long as I live."

With these words Guru vanished. The next spring Orm took the golden horn and the silver ware to Drontheim where no one knew him. The value of the things was so great that he was able to purchase everything a wealthy man desires. He loaded his ship with his purchases, and returned to the island, where he spent many years in unalloyed happiness, and Aslog's father was soon reconciled to his wealthy son-in-law.

The stone image remained sitting in the house. No human power was able to move it. So hard was the stone that hammer and axe flew in pieces without making the slightest impression upon it. The giant sat there till a holy man came to the island, who, with one single word, removed him back to his former station, where he stands to this hour. The copper kettle, which the underground people left behind them, was preserved as a memorial upon the island, which bears the name of House Island to the present day.

Snowdrop

(German and Scandinavian)

IT WAS THE MIDDLE OF WINTER, when the broad flakes of snow were falling around, that the queen of a country many thousand miles off sat working at her window. The frame of the window was made of fine black ebony, and as she sat looking out upon the snow, she pricked her finger, and three drops of blood fell upon it. Then she gazed thoughtfully upon the red drops that sprinkled the white snow, and said, "Would that my little daughter may be as white as that snow, as red as that blood, and as black as this ebony windowframe!"

And so the little girl really did grow up; her skin was as white as snow, her cheeks as rosy as the blood, and her hair as black as ebony; and she was called Snowdrop.

But this queen died; and the king soon married another wife, who became queen, and was very beautiful, but so vain that she could not bear to think that anyone could be handsomer than she was. She had a fairy looking-glass, to which she used to go, and then she would gaze upon herself in it, and say:

"Tell me, glass, tell me true!
Of all the ladies in the land,
Who is fairest, tell me, who?"

And the glass had always answered:

"Thou, queen, art the fairest in all the land."

But Snowdrop grew more and more beautiful; and when she was seven years old she was as bright as the day, and fairer than the queen herself. Then the glass one day answered the queen, when she went to look in it as usual:

"Thou, queen, art fair, and beauteous to see,
But Snowdrop is lovelier far than thee!"

When she heard this she turned pale with rage and envy, and called to one of her servants, and said, "Take Snowdrop away into the wide wood, that I may never see her any more." Then the servant led her away; but his heart melted when Snowdrop begged him to spare her life, and he said, "I will not hurt you, thou pretty child." So he left her by herself; and though he thought it most likely that the wild beasts would tear her in pieces, he felt as if a great weight were taken off his heart when he had made up his mind not to kill her but to leave her to her fate, with the chance of someone finding and saving her.

Then poor Snowdrop wandered along through the wood in great fear; and the wild beasts roared about her, but none did her any harm. In the evening she came to a cottage among the hills, and went in to rest, for her little feet would carry her no further. Everything was spruce and neat in the cottage: on the table was spread a white cloth, and there were seven little plates, seven little loaves, and seven little glasses with wine in them; and seven knives and forks laid in order; and by the wall stood seven little beds. As she was very hungry, she picked a little piece of each loaf and drank a very little wine out of each glass; and after that she thought she would lie down and rest. So she tried all the little beds; but one was too long, and another was too short, till at last the seventh suited her: and there she laid herself down and went to sleep.

By and by in came the masters of the cottage. Now they were seven little dwarfs, that lived among the mountains, and dug and searched for gold. They lighted up their seven lamps, and saw at once that all was not right. The first said, "Who has been sitting on my stool?" The second, "Who has been eating off my plate?" The third, "Who has been picking my bread?" The fourth, "Who has been meddling with my spoon?" The fifth, "Who has been handling my fork?" The sixth, "Who has been cutting with my knife?" The seventh, "Who has been drinking my wine?" Then the first looked round and said, "Who has been lying on my bed?" And the rest came running to him, and everyone cried out that somebody had been upon his bed. But the seventh saw Snowdrop, and called all his brethren to come and see her; and they cried out with wonder and astonishment and brought their lamps to look at her, and said, "Good heavens! what a lovely child she is!" And they were very glad to see her, and took care not to wake her; and the seventh dwarf slept an hour with each of the other dwarfs in turn, till the night was gone.

In the morning Snowdrop told them all her story; and they pitied her, and said if she would keep all things in order, and cook and wash and knit and spin for them, she might stay where she was, and they would take good care of her. Then they went out all day long to their work, seeking for gold and silver in the mountains: but Snowdrop was left at home; and they warned her, and said, "The queen will soon find out where you are, so take care and let no one in."

But the queen, now that she thought Snowdrop was dead, believed that she must be the handsomest lady in the land; and she went to her glass and said:

"Tell me, glass, tell me true!
Of all the ladies in the land,
Who is fairest, tell me, who?"

And the glass answered:

"Thou, queen, art the fairest in all this land:
But over the hills, in the greenwood shade,
Where the seven dwarfs their dwelling have made,
There Snowdrop is hiding her head; and she
Is lovelier far, O queen! than thee."

Then the queen was very much frightened; for she knew that the glass always spoke the truth, and was sure that the servant had betrayed her. And she could not bear to think that anyone lived who was more beautiful than she was; so she dressed herself up as an old pedlar, and went her way over the hills, to the place where the dwarfs dwelt. Then she knocked at the door, and cried, "Fine wares to sell!" Snowdrop looked out at the window, and said, "Good day, good woman! what have you to sell?" "Good wares, fine wares," said she; "laces and bobbins of all colours." "I will let the old lady in; she seems to be a very good sort of body," thought Snowdrop, as she ran down and unbolted the door. "Bless me!" said the old woman, "how badly your stays are laced! Let me lace them up with one of my nice new laces." Snowdrop did not dream of any mischief; so she stood before the old woman; but she set to work so nimbly, and pulled the lace so tight, that Snowdrop"s breath was stopped, and she fell down as if she were dead. "There's an end to all thy beauty," said the spiteful queen, and went away home.

In the evening the seven dwarfs came home; and I need not say how grieved they were to see their faithful Snowdrop stretched out upon the ground, as if she was quite dead. However, they lifted her up, and when they found what ailed her, they cut the lace; and in a little time she began to breathe, and very soon came to life again. Then they said, "The old woman was the queen herself; take care another time, and let no one in when we are away."

When the queen got home, she went straight to her glass, and spoke to it as before; but to her great grief it still said:

"Thou, queen, art the fairest in all this land:
But over the hills, in the greenwood shade,
Where the seven dwarfs their dwelling have made,
There Snowdrop is hiding her head; and she
Is lovelier far, O queen! than thee."

Then the blood ran cold in her heart with spite and malice, to see that Snowdrop still lived; and she dressed herself up again, but in quite another dress from the one she wore before, and took with her a poisoned comb. When she reached the dwarfs' cottage, she knocked at the door, and cried, "Fine wares to sell!" But Snowdrop said, "I dare not let anyone in." Then the queen said, "Only look at my beautiful combs!" and gave her the poisoned one. And it looked so pretty, that she took it up and put it into her hair to try it; but the moment it touched her head, the poison was so powerful that she fell down senseless. "There you may lie," said the queen, and went her way. But by good luck the dwarfs came in very early that evening; and when they saw Snowdrop lying on the ground, they thought what had happened, and soon found the poisoned comb. And when they took it away she got well, and told them all that had passed; and they warned her once more not to open the door to anyone.

Meantime the queen went home to her glass, and shook with rage when she read the very same answer as before; and she said, "Snowdrop shall die, if it cost me my life." So she went by herself into her chamber, and got ready a poisoned apple: the outside looked very rosy and tempting, but whoever tasted it was sure to die. Then she dressed herself up as a peasant's wife, and travelled over the hills to the dwarfs' cottage, and knocked at the door; but Snowdrop put her head out of the window and said, "I dare not let anyone in, for the dwarfs have told me not." "Do as you please," said the old woman, "but at any rate take this pretty apple; I will give it you." "No," said Snowdrop, "I dare not take it." "You silly girl!" answered the other, "what are you afraid of? Do you think it is poisoned? Come! do you eat one part, and I will eat the other." Now the apple was so made up that one side was good, though the other side was poisoned. Then Snowdrop was much tempted to taste, for the apple looked so very nice; and when she saw the old woman eat, she could wait no longer. But she had scarcely put the piece into her mouth, when she fell down dead upon the ground. "This time nothing will save thee," said the queen; and she went home to her glass, and at last it said:

"Thou, queen, art the fairest of all the fair."

And then her wicked heart was glad, and as happy as such a heart could be.

When evening came, and the dwarfs had gone home, they found Snowdrop lying on the ground: no breath came from her lips, and they were afraid that she was quite dead. They lifted her up, and combed her hair, and washed her face with wine and water; but all was in vain, for the little girl seemed quite dead. So they laid her down upon a bier, and all seven watched and bewailed her three whole days; and then they thought they would bury her: but her cheeks were still rosy; and her face looked just as it did while she was alive; so they said, "We will never bury her in the cold ground." And they made a coffin of glass, so that they might still look at her, and wrote upon it in golden letters what her name was, and that she was a king's daughter. And the coffin was set among the hills, and one of the dwarfs always sat by it and watched. And the birds of the air came too, and bemoaned Snowdrop; and first of all came an owl, and then a raven, and at last a dove, and sat by her side.

And thus Snowdrop lay for a long, long time, and still only looked as though she was asleep; for she was even now as white as snow, and as red as blood, and as black as ebony. At last a prince came and called at the dwarfs' house; and he saw Snowdrop, and read what was written in golden letters. Then he offered the dwarfs money, and prayed and besought them to let him take her away; but they said, "We will not part with her for all the gold in the world." At last, however, they had pity on him, and gave him the coffin; but the moment he lifted it up to carry it home with him, the piece of apple fell from between her lips, and Snowdrop awoke, and said, "Where am I?" And the prince said, "Thou art quite safe with me."

Then he told her all that had happened, and said, "I love you far better than all the world; so come with me to my father's palace, and you shall be my wife." And Snowdrop consented, and went home with the prince; and everything was got ready with great pomp and splendour for their wedding.

To the feast was asked, among the rest, Snowdrop's old enemy the queen; and as she was dressing herself in fine rich clothes, she looked in the glass and said:

"Tell me, glass, tell me true!
Of all the ladies in the land,
Who is fairest, tell me, who?"

And the glass answered:

"Thou, lady, art loveliest here, I ween
But lovelier far is the new-made queen."

When she heard this she started with rage; but her envy and curiosity were so great, that she could not help setting out to see the bride. And when she got there, and saw that it was no other than Snowdrop, who, as she thought, had been dead a long while, she choked with rage, and fell down and died: but Snowdrop and the prince lived and reigned happily over that land many, many years; and sometimes they went up into the mountains, and paid a visit to the little dwarfs, who had been so kind to Snowdrop in her time of need.

The Lost Bell

(Norwegian)

A SHEPHERD'S BOY, belonging to Patzig, about half a mile from Bergen, where there are great numbers of underground people in the hills, found one morning a little silver bell on the green heath among the giants' graves, and fastened it on him. It happened to be the bell belonging to the cap of one of the little brown ones, who had lost it while he was dancing, and did not immediately miss it or observe that it was no longer tinkling in his cap. He had gone down into the hill without his bell, and, having discovered his loss, was filled with melancholy, for the worst thing that can befall the underground people is to lose their cap, or their shoes; but even to lose the bell from their caps, or the buckle from their belts, is no trifle to them. Whoever loses his bell must pass some sleepless nights, for not a wink of sleep can he get till he has recovered it.

The little fellow was in the greatest trouble, and looked and searched about everywhere. But how could he learn who had the bell? for only on a very few days in the year may they come up to daylight, nor can they then appear in their true form. He had turned himself into every form of birds, beasts, and men, and he had sung and groaned and lamented about his bell, but not the slightest tidings or trace of tidings had he been able to get. Most unfortunately for him, the shepherd's boy had left Patzig the very day he found the little bell, and he was now keeping sheep at Unrich, near Gingst, so that it was not till many a day after, and then by mere chance, that the little underground fellow recovered his bell, and with it his peace of mind.

He had thought it not unlikely that a raven, or a crow, or a jackdaw, or a magpie, had found his bell, and from its thievish disposition, which attracts it to anything bright and shining, had carried it into its nest. With this thought he turned himself into a beautiful little bird, and searched all the nests in the island, and he'd sang before all kinds of birds to see if they had found what he had lost, and could restore to him his sleep. He had, however, been able to learn nothing from the birds. As he now, one evening, was flying over the waters of Ralov and the fields of Unrich, the shepherd's boy, whose name was John Schlagenteufel (Smite-devil), happened to be keeping his sheep there at the very time. Several of the sheep had bells about their necks, and they tinkled merrily when the boy's dog set them trotting. The little bird who was flying over them thought of his bell, and sang in a melancholy tone –

"Little bell, little bell,
Little ram as well,
You, too, little sheep,
If you've my tingle too,
No sheep's so rich as you,
My rest you keep."

The boy looked up and listened to this strange song which came out of the sky, and saw the pretty bird, which seemed to him still more strange.

"If one," said he to himself, "had but that bird that's singing up there, so plain that one of us could hardly match him! What can he mean by that wonderful song? The whole of it is, it must be a feathered witch. My rams have only pinchbeck bells, he calls them rich cattle; but I have a silver bell, and he sings nothing about me."

With these words he began to fumble in his pocket, took out his bell, and rang it.

The bird in the air instantly saw what it was, and rejoiced beyond measure. He vanished in a second, flew behind the nearest bush, alighted, and drew off his speckled feather dress, and turned himself into an old woman dressed in tattered clothes. The old dame, well supplied with sighs and groans, tottered across the field to the shepherd-boy, who was still ringing his bell and wondering what was become of the beautiful bird. She cleared her throat, and coughing, bid him a kind good evening, and asked him which was the way to Bergen. Pretending then that she had just seen the little bell, she exclaimed –

"Well now, what a charming pretty little bell! Well, in all my life, I never beheld anything more beautiful. Hark ye, my son, will you sell me that bell? What may be the price of it? I have a little grandson at home, and such a nice plaything as it would make for him!"

"No," replied the boy, quite short; "the bell is not for sale. It is a bell that there is not such another bell in the whole world. I have only to give it a little tinkle, and my sheep run of themselves wherever I would have them go. And what a delightful sound it has! Only listen, mother," said he, ringing it; "is there any weariness in the world that can hold out against this bell? I can ring with it away the longest time, so that it will be gone in a second."

The old woman thought to herself –

"We will see if he can hold out against bright shining money," and she took out no less than three silver dollars and offered them to him, but he still replied –

"No, I will not sell the bell."

She then offered him five dollars.

"The bell is still mine," said he.

She stretched out her hand full of ducats. He replied this third time –

"Gold is dirt, and does not ring."

The old dame then shifted her ground, and turned the discourse another way. She grew mysterious, and began to entice him by talking of secret arts and of charms by which his cattle might be made to thrive prodigiously, relating to him all kinds of wonders of them. It was then the young shepherd began to long, and he lent a willing ear to her tales.

The end of the matter was, that she said to him –

"Hark ye, my child, give me your bell; and see, here is a white stick for you," said she, taking out a little white stick which had Adam and Eve very ingeniously cut upon it as they were feeding their flocks in the Garden, with the fattest sheep and lambs dancing before them. There, too, was the shepherd David, as he stood up with his sling against the giant Goliath. "I will give you," said the woman, "this stick for the bell, and as long as you drive the cattle with it they will be sure to thrive. With this you will become a rich shepherd. Your wethers will be always fat a month sooner than the wethers of other shepherds, and every one of your sheep will have two pounds of wool more than others, and yet no one will ever be able to see it on them."

The old woman handed him the stick. So mysterious was her gesture, and so strange and bewitching her smile, that the lad was at once in her power. He grasped eagerly at the stick, gave her his hand, and cried –

"Done! strike hands! The bell for the stick!"

Cheerfully the old woman took the bell for the stick, and departed like a light breeze over the field and the heath. He saw her vanish, and she seemed to float away before his eyes like a mist, and to go off with a slight whiz and whistle that made the shepherd's hair stand on end.

The underground one, however, who, in the shape of an old woman, had wheedled him out of his bell, had not deceived him. For the underground people dare not lie, but must ever keep their word – a breach of it being followed by their sudden change into the shape of toads, snakes, dunghill beetles, wolves, and apes, forms in which they wander about, objects of fear and aversion, for a long course of years before they are freed. They have, therefore, naturally a great dread of lying. John Schlagenteufel gave close attention and made trial of his new shepherd's staff, and he soon found that the old woman had told him the truth, for his flocks and his work, and all the labour of his hands, prospered with him, and he had wonderful luck, so that there was not a sheep-owner or head shepherd but was desirous of having him in his employment.

It was not long, however, that he remained an underling. Before he was eighteen years of age he had got his own flocks, and in the course of a few years was the richest sheep-master in the whole island of Bergen. At last he was able to buy a knight's estate for himself, and that estate was Grabitz, close by Rambin, which now belongs to the Lords of Sunde. My father knew him there, and how from a shepherd's boy he became a nobleman. He always conducted himself like a prudent, honest, and pious man, who had a good word for everyone. He brought up his sons like gentlemen, and his daughters like ladies, some of whom are still alive, and accounted people of great consequence.

Well may people who hear such stories wish that they had met with such an adventure, and had found a little silver bell which the underground people had lost!

The Adventures of John Dietrich

(German)

THERE ONCE LIVED IN RAMBIN an honest, industrious man, named James Dietrich. He had several children, all of a good disposition, especially the youngest, whose name was John. John Dietrich was a handsome, smart boy, diligent at school, and obedient at home. His great passion was for hearing stories, and whenever he met anyone who was well stored he never let him go till he had heard them all.

When John was about eight years old he was sent to spend a summer with his uncle, a farmer, in Rodenkirchen. Here John had to keep cows with other boys, and they used to drive them to graze about the Nine-hills. There was an old cowherd, one Klas Starkwolt, who used frequently to join the boys, and then they would sit down together and tell stories. Klas abounded in these, and he became John Dietrich's dearest friend. In particular, he knew a number of stories of the Nine-hills, and the underground people in the old times, when the giants disappeared from the country and the little ones came into the hills. These tales John swallowed so eagerly that he thought of nothing else, and was for ever talking of golden cups, and crowns, and glass shoes, and pockets full of ducats, and gold rings, and diamond coronets, and snow-white brides, and such like. Old Klas used often to shake his head at him, and say –

"John! John! what are you about? The spade and scythe will be your sceptre and crown, and your bride will wear a garland of rosemary, and a gown of striped drill."

Still John almost longed to get into the Nine-hills, for Klas told him that everyone who by luck or cunning should get a cap of the little ones might go down with safety, and instead of their making a servant of him, he would be their master. The person whose cap he got would be his servant, and obey all his commands.

St. John's Day, when the days were longest and the nights shortest, was now come. Old and young kept the holiday, had all sorts of plays, and told all kinds of stories. John could now no longer contain himself, but the day after the festival he slipt away to the Nine-hills, and when it grew dark laid himself down on the top of the highest of them, where Klas had told him the underground people had their principal dancing-place. John lay quite still from ten till twelve at night. At last it struck twelve. Immediately there was a ringing and a singing in the hills, and then a whispering and a lisping, and a whiz and a buzz all about him, for the little people were now, some whirling round and round in the dance, and others sporting and tumbling about in the moonshine, and playing a thousand merry pranks and tricks. He felt a secret dread come over him at this whispering and buzzing, for he could see nothing of them, as the caps they wore made them invisible, but he lay quite still with his face in the grass, and his eyes fast shut, snoring a little, just as if he were asleep. Now and then he ventured to open his eyes a little and peep out, but not the slightest trace of them could he see, though it was bright moonlight.

It was not long before three of the underground people came jumping up to where he was lying, but they took no heed of him, and flung their brown caps up into the air, and caught them from one another. At length one snatched the cap out of the hand of another and flung it away. It flew direct, and fell upon John's head. The moment he felt it he caught hold of it, and, standing up, bid farewell to sleep. He flung his cap about for joy and made the little silver bell of it jingle, then set it upon his head, and – oh wonderful! that instant he saw the countless and merry swarm of the little people.

The three little men came slyly up to him, and thought by their nimbleness to get back the cap, but he held his prize fast, and they saw clearly that nothing was to be done in this way with him, for in size and strength John was a giant in comparison with these little fellows, who hardly came up to his knee. The owner of the cap now came up very humbly to the finder, and begged, in as supplicating a tone as if his life depended upon it, that he would give him back his cap.

"No," said John, "you sly little rogue, you will get the cap no more. That's not the sort of thing one gives away for buttered cake. I should be in a nice way with you if I had not something of yours, but now you have no power over me, but must do what I please. I will go down with you and see how you live down below, and you shall be my servant. Nay, no grumbling. You know you must. I know that just as well as you do, for Klas Starkwolt told it to me often and often!"

The little man made as if he had not heard or understood one word of all this. He began his crying and whining over again, and wept and screamed and howled most piteously for his little cap. John, however, cut the matter short by saying –

"Have done. You are my servant, and I intend to make a trip with you."

So he gave up, especially as the others told him there was no remedy.

John now flung away his old hat, and put on the cap, and set it firm on his head lest it should slip off or fly away, for all his power lay in the cap. He lost no time in trying its virtues, and commanded his new servant to fetch him food and drink. The servant ran away like the wind, and in a second was there again with bottles of wine, and bread, and rich fruits. So John ate and drank, and looked at the sports and dancing of the little ones, and it pleased him right well, and he behaved himself stoutly and wisely, as if he had been a born master.

When the cock had now crowed for the third time, and the little larks had made their first twirl in the sky, and the infant light appeared in solitary white streaks in the east, then it went hush, hush, hush, through the bushes and flowers and stalks, and the hills rent again, and opened up, and the little men went down. John gave close attention to everything, and found that it was exactly as he had been told, and, behold! on the top of the hill, where they had just been dancing, and where all was full of grass and flowers, as people see it by day, there rose of a sudden, when the retreat was sounded, a bright glass point. Whoever wanted to go in stepped upon this. It opened, and he glided gently in, the grass closing again after him; and when they had all entered it vanished, and there was no further trace of it to be seen. Those who descended through the glass point sank quite gently into a wide silver tun, which held them all, and could have easily harboured a thousand such little people. John and his man went down into such a one along with several others, all of whom screamed out, and prayed him not to tread on them, for if his weight came on them they were dead men. He was, however, careful, and acted in a very friendly way towards them. Several tuns of this kind went up and down after each other, until all were in. They hung by long silver chains, which were drawn and hung without.

In his descent John was amazed at the brilliancy of the walls between which the tun glided down. They were all, as it were, beset with pearls and diamonds, glittering and sparkling brightly, and below him he heard the most beautiful music tinkling at a distance, so that he did not know what was become of him, and from excess of pleasure he fell fast asleep.

He slept a long time, and when he awoke he found himself in the most beautiful bed that could be, such as he had never seen the like of in his father's house, and it was in the prettiest chamber in the world, and his servant was beside him with a fan to keep away the flies and gnats. He had hardly opened his eyes when his little servant brought him a basin and towel, and held him the nicest new clothes of brown silk to put on, most beautifully made. With these was a pair of new black shoes with red ribbons, such as John had never beheld in Rambin or in Rodinkirchen either. There were also there several pairs of beautiful shining glass shoes, such as are only used on great occasions. John was, as we may well suppose, delighted to have such clothes to wear, and he put them upon him joyfully. His servant then flew like lightning, and returned with a breakfast of wine and milk, and beautiful white bread and fruits, and such other things as boys are fond of. He now perceived every moment more and more, that Klas Starkwolt, the old cowherd, knew what he was talking about, for the splendour and magnificence he saw here surpassed anything he had ever dreamt of. His servant, too, was the most obedient one possible, a nod or a sign was enough for him, for he was as wise as a bee, as all these little people are by nature. John's bedchamber was all covered with emeralds and other precious stones, and in the ceiling was a diamond as big as a nine-pin bowl, that gave light to the whole chamber. In this place they have neither sun nor moon nor stars to give them light, neither do they use lamps or candlesticks of any kind, but they live in the midst of precious stones, and have the purest of gold and silver in abundance, and the skill to make it light both by day and night, though indeed, properly speaking, as there is no sun there, there is no distinction between day and night, and they reckon only by weeks. They set the brightest and clearest precious stones in their dwellings, and in the ways and passages leading underground, and in the places where they had their large halls, and their dances and their feasts, where they sparkled so as to make it eternal day.

When John had finished breakfast, his servant opened a little door in the wall, where was a closet with the most beautiful silver and gold cups and dishes and other vessels and baskets filled with ducats and boxes of jewels and precious stones. There were also charming pictures, and the most delightful books he had seen in the whole course of his life.

John spent the morning looking at these things, and when it was midday a bell rang, and his servant said –

"Will you dine alone, sir, or with the large company?"

"With the large company, to be sure," replied John. So his servant led him out. John, however, saw nothing but solitary halls lighted up with precious stones, and here and there little men and women, who appeared to him to glide in and out of the clefts and fissures of the rocks. Wondering what it was the bells rang for, he said to his servant –

"But where is the company?"

Scarcely had he spoken when the hall they were in opened out to a great extent, and a canopy set with diamonds and precious stones was drawn over it. At the same moment he saw an immense throng of nicely dressed little men and women pouring in through several open doors. The floor opened in several places, and tables, covered with the most beautiful ware, and the most luscious meats and fruits and wines, placed themselves beside each other, and the chairs arranged themselves along the tables, and then the men and women took their seats.

The principal persons now came forward and bowed to John, and led him to their table, where they placed him among their most beautiful maidens, a distinction which pleased John well. The party, too, was very merry, for the underground people are extremely lively and cheerful, and can never stay long quiet. Then the most charming music sounded over their heads, and beautiful birds, flying about, sang most sweetly, and these were not real birds but artificial ones which the little men make so ingeniously that they can fly about and sing like natural ones.

The servants of both sexes who waited at table and handed about the golden cups, and the silver and crystal baskets with fruit, were children belonging to this world, whom some casualty or other had thrown among the underground people, and who, having come down without securing any pledge, were fallen into the power of the little ones. These were differently clad. The boys and girls were dressed in short white coats and jackets, and wore glass shoes so fine that their step could never be heard, with blue caps on their heads, and silver belts round their waists.

John at first pitied them, seeing how they were forced to run about and wait on the little people, but as they looked cheerful and happy, and were handsomely dressed, and had such rosy cheeks, he said to himself – "After all, they are not so badly off, and I was myself much worse when I had to be running after the cows and bullocks. To be sure I am now a master here, and they are servants, but there is no help for it. Why were they so foolish as to let themselves be taken and not get some pledge beforehand? At any rate the time must come when they will be set at liberty, and they will certainly not be longer than fifty years here."

With these thoughts he consoled himself, and sported and played away with his little play-fellows, and ate, and drank, and made his servant tell him stories, for he would know everything exactly.

They sat at table about two hours. The principal person then rang a bell, and the tables and chairs all vanished in a whiff, leaving all the company on their feet. The birds now struck up a most lively air, and the little people danced their rounds most merrily. When they were done, the joyous sets jumped and leaped, and whirled themselves round and round, as if the world was grown dizzy. The pretty girls who sat next to John caught hold of him and whirled him about, and, without making any resistance, he danced round and round with them for two good hours. Every afternoon while he remained there he used to dance thus merrily with them, and, to the last hour of his life, he used to speak of it with the greatest glee. His language was – that the joys of heaven and the songs and music of the angels, which the righteous hope to enjoy there, might be excessively beautiful, but that he could conceive nothing to surpass the music and the dancing under the earth, the beautiful and lively little men, the wonderful birds in the branches, and the tinkling silver bells in their caps.

"No one," said he, "who has not seen and heard it, can form any idea whatever of it."

When the music and dancing were over it might be about four o'clock. The little people then disappeared, and went each about his own business or pleasure. After supper they sported and danced in the same way, and at midnight, especially on starlit nights, they slipped out of their hills to dance in the open air. John used then to say his prayers, a duty he never neglected either in the evening or in the morning, and go to sleep.

For the first week John was in the glass hill, he only went from his chamber to the great hall and back again. After the first week, however, he began to walk about, making his servant show and explain everything to him. He found that there were in that place the most beautiful walks in which he might ramble about for miles, in all directions, without ever finding an end to them, so immensely large was the hill in which the little people lived, and yet outwardly it seemed but a little place, with a few bushes and trees growing on it.

It was extraordinary that, between the meads and fields, which were thick sown with hills and lakes and islands, and ornamented with trees and flowers in great variety, there ran, as it were, small lanes, through which, as through crystal rocks, one was obliged to pass to come to any new place; and the single meads and fields were often a mile long, and the flowers were so brilliant and so fragrant, and the songs of the numerous birds so sweet, that John had never seen anything on earth like it. There was a breeze, and yet one did not feel the wind. It was quite clear and bright, and yet there was no heat. The waves were dashing, still there was no danger, and the most beautiful little barks and canoes came, like white swans, when one wanted to cross the water, and went backwards and forwards of themselves. Whence all this came no one knew, nor could John's servant tell anything about it, but one thing John saw plainly, which was that the large carbuncles and diamonds that were set in the roof and walls gave light instead of the sun, moon, and stars.

These lovely meads and plains were, for the most part, all lonesome. Few of the underground people were to be seen upon them, and those that were just glided across them as if in the greatest hurry. It very rarely happened that any of them danced out there in the open air. Sometimes about three of them did so, or, at the most, half a dozen. John never saw a greater number together. The meads were never cheerful except when the servants, of whom there might be some hundreds, were let out to walk. This, however, happened but twice a week, for they were mostly kept employed in the great hall and adjoining apartments or at school.

For John soon found they had schools there also. He had been there about ten months when one day he saw something snow-white gliding into a rock and disappearing.

"What!" said he to his servant, "are there some of you that wear white like the servants?"

He was informed that there were, but they were few in number, and never appeared at the large tables or the dances, except once a year, on the birthday of the great Hill-king, who dwelt many thousand miles below in the great deep. These were the oldest among them, some of them many thousand years old, who knew all things and could tell of the beginning of the world, and were called the Wise. They lived all alone, and only left their chambers to instruct the underground children and the attendants of both sexes, for whom there was a great school.

John was much pleased with this intelligence, and he determined to take advantage of it; so next morning he made his servant conduct him to the school, and was so well pleased with it that he never missed a day going there. They were there taught reading, writing, and accounts, to compose and relate histories, stories, and many elegant kinds of work, so that many came out of the hills, both men and women, very prudent and knowing people in consequence of what they were taught there. The biggest, and those of best capacity, received instruction in natural science and astronomy, and in poetry and in riddle-making, arts highly esteemed among the little people. John was very diligent, and soon became a most clever painter and drawer. He wrought, too, most ingeniously in gold and silver and stones, and in verse and riddle-making he had no fellow.

John had spent many a happy year here without ever thinking of the upper world, or of those he had left behind, so pleasantly passed the time – so many agreeable companions had he.

Of all of them there was none of whom he was so fond as of a fair-haired girl named Elizabeth Krabbe. She was from his own village, and was the daughter of Frederick Krabbe, the minister of Rambin. She was but four years old when she was taken away, and John had often heard tell of her. She was not, however, stolen by the little people, but had come into their power in this manner. One day in summer she and other children ran out into the fields. In their rambles they went to the Nine-hills, where little Elizabeth fell asleep, and was forgotten by the rest. At night when she awoke, she found herself under the ground among the little people. It was not merely because she was from his own village that John was so fond of Elizabeth, but she was very beautiful, with clear blue eyes and ringlets of fair hair, and a most angelic smile. Time flew away unperceived. John was now eighteen, and Elizabeth sixteen. Their childish fondness was now become love, and the little people were pleased to see it, thinking that by means of her they might get John to renounce his power, and become their servant, for they were fond of him, and would willingly have had him to wait upon them, for the love of dominion is their vice. They were, however, mistaken. John had learned too much from his servant to be caught in that way.

John's chief delight was walking about with Elizabeth, for he now knew every place so well that he could dispense with the attendance of his servant. In these rambles he was always gay and lively, but his companion was frequently sad and melancholy, thinking on the land above, where men live, and where the sun, moon, and stars shine. Now it happened in one of their walks, as they talked of their love, and it was after midnight, they passed under the place where the tops of the glass hills used to open and let the underground people in and out. As they went along, they heard of a sudden the crowing of several cocks above. At this sound, which she had not heard for several years, Elizabeth felt her heart so affected that she could contain herself no longer, but throwing her arms about John's neck, she bathed his cheek with her tears. At length she said –

"Dearest John, everything down here is very beautiful, and the little people are kind and do nothing to injure me, but still I have been always uneasy, nor ever felt any pleasure till I began to love you; and yet that is not pure pleasure, for this is not a right way of living, such as is fit for human beings. Every night I dream of my father and mother, and of our churchyard where the people stand so pious at the church door waiting for my father, and I could weep tears of blood that I cannot go into the church with them and worship God as a human being should, for this is no Christian life we lead down here, but a delusive half-heathen one. And only think, dear John, that we can never marry, as there is no priest to join us. Do, then, plan some way for us to leave this place, for I cannot tell you how I long to get once more to my father, and among pious Christians."

John, too, had not been unaffected by the crowing of the cocks, and he felt what he had never felt there before, a longing after the land where the sun shines.

"Dear Elizabeth," said he, "all you say is true, and I now feel it is a sin for Christians to stay here, and it seems to me as if our Lord said to us in that cry of the cocks, 'Come up, ye Christian children, out of those abodes of illusion and magic. Come to the light of the stars, and act as children of the light.' I now feel that it was a great sin for me to come down here, but I trust I shall be forgiven on account of my youth, for I was only a boy, and knew not what I did. But now I will not stay a day longer. They cannot keep me here."

At these last words Elizabeth turned pale, for she recollected that she was a servant, and must serve her fifty years.

"And what will it avail me," cried she, "that I shall continue young, and be but as of twenty years when I go out, for my father and mother will be dead, and all my companions old and grey; and you, dearest John, will be old and grey also," cried she, throwing herself on his bosom.

John was thunderstruck at this, for it had never before occurred to him. He, however, comforted her as well as he could, and declared he would never leave the place without her. He spent the whole night in forming various plans. At last he fixed on one, and in the morning he despatched his servant to summon to his apartment six of the principal of the little people. When they came, John thus mildly addressed them –

"My friends, you know how I came here, not as a prisoner or servant, but as a lord and master over one of you, and of consequence over all. You have now for the ten years I have been with you treated me with respect and attention, and for that I am your debtor. But you are still more my debtors, for I might have given you every sort of vexation and annoyance, and you must have submitted to it. I have, however, not done so, but have behaved as your equal, and have sported and played with you rather than ruled over you. I have now one request to make. There is a girl among your servants whom I love, Elizabeth Krabbe, of Rambin, where I was born. Give her to me and let us depart, for I will return to where the sun shines and the plough goes through the land. I ask to take nothing with me but her and the ornaments and furniture of my chamber."

He spoke in a determined tone, and they hesitated and cast their eyes upon the ground. At last the oldest of them replied –

"Sir, you ask what we cannot grant. It is a fixed law that no servant can leave this place before the appointed time. Were we to break through this law our whole subterranean empire would fall. Anything else you desire, for we love and respect you, but we cannot give up Elizabeth."

"You can, and you shall, give her up!" cried John in a rage. "Go, think of it till tomorrow. Return then at this hour. I will show you whether or not I can triumph over your hypocritical and cunning stratagems."

The six retired. Next morning, on their return, John addressed them in the kindest manner, but to no purpose. They persisted in their refusal. He gave them till the next day, threatening them severely in case they still proved refractory.

Next day, when the six little people appeared before him, John looked at them sternly, and made no return to their salutations, but said to them shortly –

"Yes, or no?"

They answered, with one voice, "No." He then ordered his servant to summon twenty-four more of the principal persons, with their wives and children. When they came they were in all five hundred men, women, and children. John ordered them forthwith to go and fetch pick-axes, spades, and bars, which they did in a second.

He now led them out to a rock in one of the fields, and ordered them to fall to work at blasting, hewing, and dragging stones. They toiled patiently, and made as if it were only sport to them.

From morning till night their task-master made them labour without ceasing, standing over them constantly to prevent them resting. Still their obstinacy was inflexible, and at the end of some weeks his pity for them was so great that he was obliged to give over.

He now thought of a new species of punishment for them. He ordered them to appear before him next morning, each provided with a new whip. They obeyed, and John commanded them to lash one another, and he stood looking on while they did it, as grim and cruel as an Eastern tyrant. Still the little people cut and slashed themselves and mocked at John, and refused to comply with his wishes. This he did for three or four days.

Several other courses did he try, but all in vain. His temper was too gentle to struggle with their obstinacy, and he commenced to despair of ever accomplishing his dearest wish. He began now to hate the little people of whom he had before been so fond. He kept away from their banquets and dances, and associated with none but Elizabeth, and ate and drank quite solitary in his chamber. In short, he became almost a hermit, and sank into moodiness and melancholy.

While in this temper, as he was taking a solitary walk in the evening, and, to divert his melancholy, was flinging the stones that lay in his path against each other, he happened to break a tolerably large one, and out of it jumped a toad. The moment John saw the ugly animal he caught him up in ecstasy, and put him in his pocket and ran home, crying –

"Now I have her! I have my Elizabeth! Now you shall get it, you little mischievous rascals!"

On getting home he put the toad into a costly silver casket, as if it was the greatest treasure.

To account for John's joy, you must know that Klas Starkwolt had often told him that the underground people could not endure any ill smell, and that the sight, or even the smell, of a toad made them faint, and suffer the most dreadful tortures, and that by means of one of those odious animals one could compel them to do anything. Hence there are no bad smells to be found in the whole glass empire, and a toad is a thing unheard of there. This toad must certainly have been enclosed in the stone from the creation, as it were, for the sake of John and Elizabeth.

Resolved to try the effect of his toad, John took the casket under his arm and went out, and on the way he met two of the little people in a lonesome place. The moment he approached they fell to the ground, and whimpered and howled most lamentably as long as he was near them.

Satisfied now of his power, he, the next morning, summoned the fifty principal persons, with their wives and children, to his apartment. When they came he addressed them, reminding them once again of his kindness and gentleness towards them, and of the good terms on which they had hitherto lived. He reproached them with their ingratitude in refusing him the only favour he had ever asked of them, but firmly declared that he would not give way to their obstinacy.

"Therefore," said he, "for the last time, think for a minute, and if you then say 'No,' you shall feel that pain which is to you and your children the most terrible of all pains."

They did not take long to deliberate, but unanimously replied "No"; and they thought to themselves, "What new scheme has the youth hit on with which he thinks to frighten wise ones like us?" and they smiled as they said "No." Their smiling enraged John above all, and he ran back a few hundred paces to where he had laid the casket with the toad under a bush.

He was hardly come within a few hundred paces of them when they all fell to the ground as if struck with a thunderbolt, and began to howl and whimper, and to writhe, as if suffering the most excruciating pain. They stretched out their hands, and cried –

"Have mercy, have mercy! We feel you have a toad, and there is no escape for us. Take the odious beast away, and we will do all you require."

He let them kick a few seconds longer, and then took the toad away. They then stood up and felt no more pain. John let all depart but the six chief persons, to whom he said –

"This night, between twelve and one, Elizabeth and I will depart. Load then for me three waggons with gold and silver and precious stones. I might, you know, take all that is in the hill, and you deserve it; but I will be merciful. Further, you must put all the furniture of my chamber in two waggons, and get ready for me the handsomest travelling carriage that is in the hill, with six black horses. Moreover, you must set at liberty all the servants who have been so long here that on earth they would be twenty years old and upwards; and you must give them as much silver and gold as will make them rich for life, and make a law that no one shall be detained here longer than his twentieth year."

The six took the oath, and went away quite melancholy; and John buried his toad deep in the ground. The little people laboured hard, and prepared everything. At midnight everything was out of the hill; and John and Elizabeth got into the silver tun, and were drawn up.

It was then one o'clock, and it was midsummer, the very time that, twelve years before, John had gone down into the hill. Music sounded around them, and they saw the glass hill open, and the rays of the light of heaven shine on them after so many years. And when they got out, they saw the first streaks of dawn already in the east. Crowds of the underground people were around them, busied about the waggons. John bid them a last farewell, waved his brown cap three times in the air, and then flung it among them. At the same moment he ceased to see them. He beheld nothing but a green hill, and the well-known bushes and fields, and heard the town clock of Rambin strike two. When all was still, save a few larks, who were tuning their morning songs, they all fell on their knees and worshipped God, resolving henceforth to live a pious and a Christian life.

When the sun rose, John arranged the procession, and they set out for Rambin. Every well-known object that they saw awoke pleasing recollections in the bosom of John and his bride; and as they passed by Rodenkirchen, John recognized, among the people that gazed at and followed them, his old friend Klas Starkwolt, the cowherd, and his dog Speed. It was about four in the morning when they entered Rambin, and they halted in the middle of the village, about twenty paces from the house where John was born. The whole village poured out to gaze on these Asiatic princes, for such the old sexton, who had in his youth been at Constantinople and at Moscow, said they were.

There John saw his father and mother, and his brother Andrew, and his sister Trine. The old minister Krabbe stood there too, in his black slippers and white nightcap, gaping and staring with the rest.

John discovered himself to his parents, and Elizabeth to hers; and the wedding-day was soon fixed. And such a wedding was never seen before or since in the island of Rügen, for John sent to Stralsund and Greifswald for whole boatloads of wine and sugar and coffee; and whole herds of oxen, sheep, and pigs were driven to the feast. The quantity of harts and roes and hares that were shot upon the occasion it were vain to attempt to tell, or to count the fish that were caught. There was not a musician in Rügen or in Pomerania that was not engaged, for John was immensely rich, and he wished to display his wealth.

John did not neglect his old friend Klas Starkwolt, the cowherd. He gave him enough to make him comfortable for the rest of his days, and insisted on his coming and staying with him as often and as long as he wished.

After his marriage John made a progress through the country with his wife; and he purchased towns and villages and lands until he became master of nearly half Rügen and a very considerable Count in the country. His father, old James Dietrich, was made a nobleman, and his brothers and sisters gentlemen and ladies – for what cannot money do? John and his wife spent their days in doing acts of piety and charity. They built several churches, and had the blessing of everyone that knew them, and died universally lamented. It was Count John Dietrich that built and richly endowed the present church of Rambin. He built it on the site of his father's house, and presented to it several of the cups and plates made by the underground people, and his own and Elizabeth's glass-shoes, in memory of what had befallen them in their youth. But they were taken away in the time of the great Charles the Twelfth of Sweden, when the Russians came on the island and the Cossacks plundered even the churches, and took away everything.

Lucky Andrew

(Norwegian)

THERE WAS ONCE A RICH PEASANT who had two sons, named John Nicholas and Lucky Andrew. The oldest was one of those fellows of whom one never can quite make head or tail. He was a most unpleasant customer to deal with, and he was more grasping and greedy than the folk of the Northland are, as a rule, though it is only too rare to find them unblessed with these attractive qualities. The other, Lucky Andrew, was wild and high spirited, but always good natured, and no matter how badly off he might be, he would always insist that he had been born under a lucky star. When the eagle, in order to defend his nest, belaboured his head and face till the blood ran, he would still maintain that he was born under a lucky star, if only he managed to bring home a single eaglet. Did his boat capsize, which occasionally happened, and did they discover him hanging to it, quite overcome with the water, cold and exertion, and asked him how he felt, he would reply: "O, quite well. I have been saved. I surely am in luck!"

When their father died, both of them were of age, and not long after they both had to go out to the sandbanks to fetch some fishing-nets, which had been left there since the summer fishing. It was late in the fall, after the time when most fishermen are busy with the summer fishing. Andrew had his gun along, which he carried with him wherever he went. John Nicholas did not say much while they were underway; but he thought all the harder. They were not ready to set out for home again until near evening.

"Hark, Lucky Andrew, do you know there will be a storm tonight?" said John Nicholas, and looked out across the sea. "I think it would be best if we stayed here until morning!"

"There'll be no storm," said Andrew. "The Seven Sisters have not put on their fog-caps, so you may be quite at rest."

But his brother complained of being weary, and at length they decided to remain there for the night. When Andrew awoke he found himself alone; and he saw neither brother nor boat, until he came to the highest point of the island. Then he discovered him far out, darting for land like a seagull. Andrew did not understand the whole affair. There were still provisions there, as well as a dish of curd, his gun and various other things. So Andrew wasted but little time in thought. "He will come back this evening," said he. "Only a fool loses heart so long as he can eat." But in the evening there was no brother to be seen, and Andrew waited day by day, and week by week; until at last, he realized that his brother had marooned him on this barren island in order to be able to keep their inheritance for himself, and not have to divide it. And such was the case, for when John Nicholas came in sight of land on his homeward trip, he had capsized the boat, and declared that Lucky Andrew had been drowned.

But the latter did not lose heart. He gathered driftwood along the strand, shot seabirds, and looked for mussels and roots. He built himself a raft of drift-timber, and fished with a pole that had also been left behind. One day, while he was at work, he happened to notice a depression or hollow in the sand, as though made by the keel of a large Northland schooner, and he could plainly trace the braidings of the hawsers from the strand up to the top of the island. Then he thought to himself that he was in no danger, for he saw there was truth in the report he had often heard, that the meer-folk made the island their abode, and did much business with their ships.

"God be praised for good company! That was just what I needed. Yes, it is true, as I have always said, that I was born under a lucky star," thought Andrew to himself; perhaps he said so too, for occasionally he really had to talk a little. So he lived through the fall. Once he saw a boat, and hung a rag on a pole and waved with it; but that very moment the sail dropped, and the crew took to the oars and rowed away at top speed, for they thought the meer-trolls were making signs and waving.

On Christmas Eve Andrew heard fiddles and music far out at sea; and when he came out, he saw a glow of light that came from a great Northland schooner, which was gliding toward the land – yet such a ship he had never yet seen. It had a main-sail of uncommon size, which looked to him to be of silk, and the most delicate tackling, as thin as though woven of steel wire, and everything else was in proportion, as fine and handsome as any Northlander might wish to have. The whole schooner was filled with little people dressed in blue, but the girl who stood at the helm was adorned like a bride, and looked as splendid as a queen, for she wore a crown and costly garments.

Yet anyone could see that she was a human being, for she was tall, and handsomer than the meer-folk. In fact, Lucky Andrew thought that she was handsomer than any girl he ever had seen. The schooner headed for the land where Andrew stood; but with his usual presence of mind, he hurried to the fisherman's hut, pulled down his gun from the wall, and crept up into the large loft and hid himself, so that he could see all that passed in the hut. He soon noticed that the whole room was alive with people. They filled it completely and more, and still more of them came in. Then the walls began to crack, and the little hut spread out at all corners, and grew so splendid and magnificent that the wealthiest merchant could not have had its equal; it was almost like being in a royal castle. Tables were covered with the most exquisite silver and gold. When they had eaten they began to dance. Under cover of the noise, Andrew crept to the lookout at the side of the roof, and climbed down. Then he ran to the schooner, threw his flintstone over it, and in order to make certain, cut a cross into it with his sharp-cutting knife. When he came back again, the dance was in full swing. The tables were dancing and the benches and chairs – everything else in the room was dancing, too. The only one who did not dance was the bride; she only sat there and looked on, and when the bridegroom came to fetch her, she sent him away. For the moment there was no thought of stopping. The fiddler knew neither rest nor repose, and did not pass his cap, but played merrily on with his left hand, and beat time with his foot, until he was dripping with sweat, and the fiddle was hidden by the dust and smoke. When Andrew noticed that his own feet began to twitch where he was standing, he thought to himself: "Now I had better shoot away, or else he will play me right off the ground!" So he turned his gun, thrust it through the window, and shot it off over the bride's head; but upside-down, otherwise the bullet would have hit him. The moment the shot crashed, all the troll-folk tumbled out of the door together; but when they saw that the schooner was banned on the shore, they wailed and crept into a hole in the hill. But all the gold and silver dishes were left behind, and the bride, too, was still sitting there. She told Lucky Andrew that she had been carried into the hill when she was only a small child. Once, when her mother had gone to the pen to attend to the milking, she had taken her along; but when she had to go home for a moment, she left the child sitting under a juniper bush, and told her that she might eat the berries if she only repeated three times:

"I eat juniper-berries blue,
Wherein Jesu's cross I view.
I eat whortle-berries red,
Since 'twas for my sake He bled!"

But after her mother had gone, she found so many berries that she forgot to say her verse, and so she was enchanted and taken into the hill. And there no harm had been done her, save that she had lost the top joint of the little finger of her left hand, and the goblins had been kind to her; yet it had always seemed to her as though something were not as it should be, she felt as though something weighed upon her, and she had suffered greatly from the advances of the dwarf who had been chosen for her husband. When Andrew learned who her mother and her people were, he saw that they were related to him, and they became very good friends. So Andrew could truly say he had been born under a lucky star. Then they sailed home, and took along the schooner, and all the gold and silver, and all the treasure which had been left in the hut, and then Andrew was far wealthier than his brother.

But the latter, who suspected where all this wealth had come from, did not wish to be any poorer than Andrew. He knew that trolls and goblins walk mainly on Christmas Eve, and for that reason he sailed out to the sandbanks at that time. And on Christmas Eve he did see a light or fire, but it seemed to be like will-o'-the-wisps fluttering about. When he came nearer he heard splashes, horrible howls, and cold, piercing cries, and there was a smell of slime and seaweed, as at ebb tide. Terrified, he ran up into the hut, from whence he could see the trolls on the shore. They were short and thick like hayricks, completely covered with fur, with kirtles of skins, fishing boots, and enormous fist-gloves. In place of head and hair they had bundles of seaweed. When they crawled up from the strand there was a gleam behind them like that of rotting wood, and when they shook themselves they showered sparks about them. When they drew nearer, John Nicholas crawled up into the loft as his brother had done. The goblins dragged a great stone into the hut, and began to beat their gloves dry against it, and meanwhile they screamed so that John Nicholas's blood turned to ice in his hiding place. Then one of them sneezed into the ashes on the hearth in order to make the fire burn again; while the others carried in heather-grass and driftwood, as coarse and heavy as lead. The smoke and the heat nearly killed the eavesdropper in the loft, and in order to catch his breath and get some fresh air, he tried to crawl out of the lookout in the roof; yet he was of much heavier build than his brother, stuck fast and could move neither in nor out. Then he grew frightened and began to scream; but the goblins screamed much louder, and roared and howled, and thumped and clamoured inside and outside the hut. But when the cock crowed they disappeared, and John Nicholas freed himself, too. Yet when he returned home from his trip, he had lost his reason, and after that the same cold, sinister screams which are the mark of the troll in the Northland, might often be heard sounding from storerooms and lofts where he happened to be. Before his death, however, his reason returned, and he was buried in consecrated ground, as they say. But after that time no human foot ever trod the sandbanks again. They sank, and the meer-folk, it is believed, went to the Lekang Islands. Andrew's luck held good; no ship made more successful trips than his own; but whenever he came to the Lekang Islands he lay becalmed – the goblins went aboard or ashore with their goods – but after a time he had fair winds, whether he happened to want to go to Bergen, or sail home. He had many children, and all of them were bright and vigorous, yet every one of them lacked the upper joint of the little finger of his left hand.

The Famine Among the Gnomes

(Norwegian)

I BELIEVE IT WAS in the winter of 18— (but it does not matter so much about the time) that the servants on the large estate of Halthorp raised a great ado about something or other. Whereupon the Baron of Halthorp, who was too stout to walk down the stairs on slight provocation, called his steward, in a voice like that of an angry lion, and asked him, "Why in the name of Moses he did not keep the rascals quiet?"

"But, your lordship," stammered the steward, who was as thin as the baron was stout, "I have kept them quiet for more than a month past, though it has been hard enough. Now they refuse to obey me unless I admit them to your lordship's presence, that they may state their complaint."

"Impudent beggars!" growled the old gentleman. "Tell them that I am about to take my after-dinner nap, and that I do not wish to be disturbed."

"I have told them that a dozen times," whined the steward, piteously. "But they are determined to leave in a body, unless your lordship consents to hear them."

"Leave! They can't leave," cried his honour. "The law binds them. Well, well, to save talking, fling the doors open and let them come in."

The steward hobbled away to the great oak-panelled doors (I forgot to tell you that he limped in his left foot), and, cautiously turning the knob and the key, peeped out into the hall. There stood the servants – twenty-eight in all – but, oh! what a sight! They were hollow-cheeked, with hungry eyes and bloodless lips, and deep lines about their mouths, as if they had not seen food for weeks. Their bony hands twitched nervously at the coarse clothes that flapped in loose folds about their lean and awkward limbs. They were indeed a pitiful spectacle. Only a single one of them – and that was of course the cook – looked like an ordinary mortal, or an extraordinary mortal, if you like, for he was nearly as broad as he was long. It was owing to the fact that he walked at the head of the procession, as they filed into the parlour, that the baron did not immediately discover the miserable condition of the rest. But when they had faced about, and stood in a long row from wall to wall – well, you would hardly believe it, but the baron, hard-hearted as he was, came near fainting. There is a limit to all things, and even a heart of steel would have been moved at the sight of such melancholy objects.

"Steward," he roared, when he had sufficiently recovered himself, "who is the demon who has dared to trifle with my fair name and honour? Name him, sir – name him, and I will strangle him on the spot!"

The steward, even if he had been acquainted with the demon, would have thought twice before naming him under such circumstances. Accordingly he was silent.

"Have I not," continued the baron, still in a voice that made his subjects quake – "have I not caused ample provisions to be daily distributed among you? Have not you, Mr. Steward, the keys to my storehouses, and have you not my authority to see that each member of my household is properly provided for?"

The steward dared not answer; he only nodded his head in silence.

"If it please your lordship," finally began a squeaky little voice at the end of the row (it was that of the undergroom), "it isn't the steward as is to blame, but it's the victuals. Somehow there isn't any taste nor fillin' to them. Whether I eat pork and cabbage or porridge with molasses, it don't make no difference. It all tastes alike. As I say, your lordship, the old Nick has got into the victuals."

The undergroom had hardly ceased speaking before the baron, who was a very irascible old gentleman, seized his large gold-headed cane and as quickly as his bulk would allow, rushed forward to give vent to his anger.

"I'll teach you manners, you impudent clown!" he bawled out, as, with his cane lifted above his head, he rushed into the ranks of the frightened servants, shouting to the undergroom, "Criticise my victuals, will you, you miserable knave!"

The undergroom having on former occasions made the acquaintance of the baron's cane, and still remembering the unpleasant sensation, immediately made for the door, and slipped nimbly out before a blow had reached him. All the others, who had to suffer for their spokesman's boldness, tumbled pell-mell through the same opening, jumped, rolled, or vaulted down the steps, and landed in a confused heap at the bottom of the stairs.

The baron, in the meanwhile, marched with long strides up and down the floor, and expressed himself, not in the politest language, concerning the impudence of his domestics.

"However," he grumbled to himself, "I must look into this affair and find out what fraud there is at the bottom of it. The poor creatures couldn't get as lean as that unless there was some real trouble."

About three hours later the baron heard the large bell over the gable of his storehouse ring out for dinner. The woodcutters and the men who drove the snow-plough, and all other labourers on the large estate, as soon as they heard it, flung away their axes and snow-shovels and hurried up to the mansion, their beards and hair and eyebrows all white with hoarfrost, so that they looked like walking snowmen. But as it happened, the undergroom, Nils Tagfat, chanced at that moment to be cutting down a large snow-laden fir tree which grew on a projecting knoll of the mountain. He pulled off his mittens and blew on his hands (for it was bitter cold), and was about to shoulder his axe, when suddenly he heard a chorus of queer little metallic voices, as it seemed, right under his feet. He stopped and listened.

"There is the bell of Halthorp ringing! Where is my cap? Where is my cap?" he heard distinctly uttered, though he could not exactly place the sound, nor did he see anybody within a mile around. And just for the joke of the thing, Nils, who was always a jolly fellow, made his voice as fine as he could, and, mimicking the tiny voices, squeaked out:

"Where is my cap? Where is my cap?"

But imagine his astonishment when suddenly he heard a voice answer him: "You can take grandfather's cap!" and at the same moment there was tossed into his hands something soft, resembling a small red-peaked cap. Just out of curiosity, Nils put it on his head to try how it would fit him, and small as it looked, it fitted him perfectly. But now, as the cap touched his head, his eyes were opened to the strangest spectacle he ever beheld. Out of the mountain came a crowd of gnomes, all with little red-peaked caps, which made them invisible to all who were not provided with similar caps. They hurried down the hillside toward Halthorp, and Nils, who was anxious to see what they were about, followed at a proper distance behind. As he had half expected, they scrambled up on the railings at the door of the servants' dining-hall, and as soon as the door was opened they rushed in, climbed up on the chairs, and seated themselves on the backs just as the servants took their places on the seats. And now Nils, who, you must remember, had on the cap that made him invisible, came near splitting his sides with laughter. The first course was boiled beef and cabbage. The smell was delicious to Nils's hungry nostrils, but he had to conquer his appetite in order to see the end of the game. The steward stood at the end of the table and served each with a liberal portion; and at the steward's side sat the baron himself, in a large, cushioned easy-chair. He did not eat, however; he was there merely to see fair play.

Each servant fell to work greedily with his knife and fork, and just as he had got a delicious morsel halfway to his mouth, the gnome on the back of his chair stretched himself forward and deftly snatched the meat from the end of the fork. Thus, all the way around the table, each man unconsciously put his piece of beef into the wide-open mouth of his particular gnome. And the unbidden guests grinned shrewdly at one another, and seemed to think it all capital fun. Sometimes, when the wooden trays (which were used instead of plates) were sent to be replenished, they made horrible grimaces, often mimicking their poor victims, who chewed and swallowed and went through all the motions of eating, without obtaining the slightest nourishment. They all would have liked to fling knives and forks and trays out through the windows, but they had the morning's chastisement freshly in mind, and they did not dare open their mouths, except for the futile purpose of eating.

"Well, my lads and lasses," said the baron, when he had watched the meal for some minutes; "if you can complain of food like this, you indeed deserve to be flogged and put on prison fare."

"Very likely, your lordship," said one of the milkmaids; "but if your lordship would demean yourself to take a morsel with us, we would bless your lordship for your kindness and complain no more."

The baron, looking around at all the hopeless eyes and haggard faces, felt that there was something besides vanity that prompted the request; and he accordingly ordered the cook to bring his own plate and drew his chair up to the table. Hardly had he seized his knife when Nils saw a gnome, who had hitherto been seated on the floor awaiting his turn, crawl up on the arm of his big chair and, standing on tiptoe, seize between his teeth the first bit the baron was putting to his mouth. The old gentleman looked astounded, mystified, bewildered; but, fearing to make an exhibition of himself, selected another mouthful, and again conducted it the accustomed way. The gnome came near laughing right out, as he despatched this second morsel in the same manner as the first, and all around the table the little monsters held their hands over their mouths and seemed on the point of exploding. The baron put down knife and fork with a bang; his eyes seemed to be starting out of his head, and his whole face assumed an expression of unspeakable horror.

"It is Satan himself who is mocking us!" he cried. "Send for the priest! Send for the priest!"

Just then Nils crept around behind the baron, who soon felt something soft, like a fine skullcap, pressed on his head, and before he had time to resent the liberty, he started in terror at the sight of the little creature that he saw sitting on the arm of his chair. He sprang up with an exclamation of fright, and pushed the chair back so violently that it was almost upset upon the floor. The gnome dexterously leaped down and stood staring back at the baron for an instant; then, with a spring, he snatched a potato and half a loaf of bread, and disappeared. In his haste, the baron ran against Nils, the undergroom, who (now without a cap) was standing with a smiling countenance calmly surveying all the confusion about him.

"Now, was I right, your lordship?" he asked, with a respectful bow. "Did *you* find the victuals very filling?"

The baron, who was yet too frightened to answer, stood gazing toward a windowpane, which suddenly and noiselessly broke, and through which the whole procession of gnomes, huddled together in flight, tumbled headlong into the snowbank without.

"And what shall we do, Nils," said the baron, the next day, when he had recovered from his shock, "to prevent the return of the unbidden guests?"

"Stop ringing the great bell," answered Nils. "It is that which invites the gnomes."

And since that day the dinner-bell has never been rung at Halthorp.

But one day, late in the winter, Nils the groom, as he was splitting wood on the mountainside, heard a plaintively tinkling voice within, singing:

"Hunger and sorrow each new day is bringing,
Since Halthorp bell has ceased its ringing."

Tales of Love & Family

Introduction

THE FIGURE OF CINDERLAD crops up in a number of traditional tales across Europe, usually touting a different name ('Boots', 'Ashlad', 'Ashiepattle' – you'll see stories featuring him elsewhere in this collection) but always appearing as a supposedly idle, ash-covered youth who rises to unlikely heroism. In 'The Princess on the Glass Hill', Cinderlad is degraded by his two brothers for always lazing about in the ashes of the household's fireplace, but his efforts to help his father later lead to a surprising outcome in a challenge set by the king himself.

Familial relationships are a significant element in Norse folklore, revealing the valued place of the family in the culture of Scandinavia. Narratives of loyalty to one's kin, as well as rivalry between siblings, are spun into tales of magic and chivalry, as are the feats undertaken to win the heart of one's beloved.

The sagas and tales of Norse literature are imbued with these bonds of love, often compelling its characters to embark on great adventures, withstand bitter feuds, and undertake challenges of strength and skill in order to preserve them.

The Princess on the Glass Hill

(Norwegian)

ONCE UPON A TIME there was a man who had a meadow which lay on the side of a mountain, and in the meadow there was a barn in which he stored hay. But there had not been much hay in the barn for the last two years, for every St. John's Eve, when the grass was in the height of its vigour, it was all eaten clean up, just as if a whole flock of sheep had gnawed it down to the ground during the night. This happened once, and it happened twice, but then the man got tired of losing his crop, and said to his sons – he had three of them, and the third was called Cinderlad – that one of them must go and sleep in the barn on St. John's Eve, for it was absurd to let the grass be eaten up again, blade and stalk, as it had been the last two years, and the one who went to watch must keep a sharp lookout, the man said.

The eldest was quite willing to go to the meadow; he would watch the grass, he said, and he would do it so well that neither man, nor beast, nor even the devil himself should have any of it. So when evening came he went to the barn, and lay down to sleep, but when night was drawing near there was such a rumbling and such an earthquake that the walls and roof shook again, and the lad jumped up and took to his heels as fast as he could, and never even looked back, and the barn remained empty that year just as it had been for the last two.

Next St. John's Eve the man again said that he could not go on in this way, losing all the grass in the outlying field year after year, and that one of his sons must just go there and watch it, and watch well too. So the next oldest son was willing to show what he could do. He went to the barn and lay down to sleep, as his brother had done; but when night was drawing near there was a great rumbling, and then an earthquake, which was even worse than that on the former St. John's Eve, and when the youth heard it he was terrified, and went off, running as if for a wager.

The year after, it was Cinderlad's turn, but when he made ready to go the others laughed at him, and mocked him. "Well, you are just the right one to watch the hay, you who have never learned anything but how to sit among the ashes and bake yourself!" said they. Cinderlad, however, did not trouble himself about what they said, but when evening drew near rambled away to the outlying field. When he got there he went into the barn and lay down, but in about an hour's time the rumbling and creaking began, and it was frightful to hear it. "Well, if it gets no worse than that, I can manage to stand it," thought Cinderlad. In a little time the creaking began again, and the earth quaked so that all the hay flew about the boy. "Oh! if it gets no worse than that I can manage to stand it," thought Cinderlad. But then came a third rumbling, and a third earthquake, so violent that the boy thought the walls and roof had fallen down, but when that was over everything suddenly grew as still as death around him. "I am pretty sure that it will come again," thought Cinderlad; but no, it did not. Everything was quiet, and everything stayed quiet, and when he had lain still a short time he heard something that sounded as if a horse were standing chewing just outside the barn door. He stole away to the door, which was ajar, to see what was there, and a horse was standing eating. It was so big, and fat, and fine a horse that Cinderlad had never seen one like it before, and a saddle and bridle lay upon it, and a complete suit of armour for a knight, and everything was of copper, and so bright that it shone again. "Ha, ha! it is thou who eatest up our hay then," thought the boy; "but I will stop that." So he made haste, and took out his steel for striking fire, and threw it over the horse, and then it had no power to stir from the spot, and became so tame that the boy could do what he liked with it. So he mounted it and rode away to a place which no one knew of but himself, and there he tied it up. When he went home again his brothers laughed and asked how he had got on.

"You didn't lie long in the barn, if even you have been so far as the field!" said they.

"I lay in the barn till the sun rose, but I saw nothing and heard nothing, not I," said the boy. "God knows what there was to make you two so frightened."

"Well, we shall soon see whether you have watched the meadow or not," answered the brothers, but when they got there the grass was all standing just as long and as thick as it had been the night before.

The next St. John's Eve it was the same thing, once again: neither of the two brothers dared to go to the outlying field to watch the crop, but Cinderlad went, and everything happened exactly the same as on the previous St. John's Eve: first there was a rumbling and an earthquake, and then there was another, and then a third: but all three earthquakes were much, very much more violent than they had been the year before. Then everything became still as death again, and the boy heard something chewing outside the barn door, so he stole as softly as he could to the door, which was slightly ajar, and again there was a horse standing close by the wall of the house, eating and chewing, and it was far larger and fatter than the first horse, and it had a saddle on its back, and a bridle was on it too, and a full suit of armour for a knight, all of bright silver, and as beautiful as anyone could wish to see. "Ho, ho!" thought the boy, "is it thou who eatest up our hay in the night? But I will put a stop to that." So he took out his steel for striking fire, and threw it over the horse's mane, and the beast stood there as quiet as a lamb. Then the boy rode this horse, too, away to the place where he kept the other, and then went home again.

"I suppose you will tell us that you have watched well again this time," said the brothers.

"Well, so I have," said Cinderlad. So they went there again, and there the grass was, standing as high and as thick as it had been before, but that did not make them any kinder to Cinderlad.

When the third St. John's Eve came neither of the two elder brothers dared to lie in the outlying barn to watch the grass, for they had been so heartily frightened the night that they had slept there that they could not get over it, but Cinderlad dared to go, and everything happened just the same as on the two former nights. There were three earthquakes, each worse than the other, and the last flung the boy from one wall of the barn to the other, but then everything suddenly became still as death. When he had lain quietly a short time, he heard something chewing outside the barn door; then he once more stole to the door, which was slightly ajar, and behold, a horse was standing just outside it, which was much larger and fatter than the two others he had caught. "Ho, ho! it is thou, then, who art eating up our hay this time," thought the boy; "but I will put a stop to that." So he pulled out his steel for striking fire, and threw it over the horse, and it stood as still as if it had been nailed to the field, and the boy could do just what he liked with it. Then he mounted it and rode away to the place where he had the two others, and then he went home again. Then the two brothers mocked him just as they had done before, and told him that they could see that he must have watched the grass very carefully that night, for he looked just as if he were walking in his sleep; but Cinderlad did not trouble himself about that, but just bade them go to the field and see. They did go, and this time too the grass was standing, looking as fine and as thick as ever.

The King of the country in which Cinderlad's father dwelt had a daughter whom he would give to no one who could not ride up to the top of the glass hill, for there was a high, high hill of glass, slippery as ice, and it was close to the King's palace. Upon the very top of this the King's daughter was to sit with three gold apples in her lap, and the man who could ride up and take the three golden apples should marry her, and have half the kingdom. The King had this proclaimed in every church in the whole kingdom, and in many other kingdoms too. The Princess was very beautiful, and all who saw her fell violently in love with her, even in spite of themselves. So it is needless to say that all the princes and knights were eager to win her, and half the kingdom besides, and that for this cause they came riding thither from the very end of the world, dressed so splendidly that their raiments gleamed in the sunshine, and riding on horses which seemed to dance as they went, and there was not one of these princes who did not think that he was sure to win the Princess.

When the day appointed by the King had come, there was such a host of knights and princes under the glass hill that they seemed to swarm, and everyone who could walk or even creep was there too, to see who won the King's daughter. Cinderlad's two brothers were there too, but they would not hear of letting him go with them, for he was so dirty and black with sleeping and grubbing among the ashes that they said everyone would laugh at them if they were seen in the company of such an oaf.

"Well, then, I will go all alone by myself," said Cinderlad.

When the two brothers got to the glass hill, all the princes and knights were trying to ride up it, and their horses were in a foam; but it was all in vain, for no sooner did the horses set foot upon the hill than down they slipped, and there was not one which could get even so much as a couple of yards up. Nor was that strange, for the hill was as smooth as a glass windowpane, and as steep as the side of a house. But they were all eager to win the King's daughter and half the kingdom, so they rode and they slipped, and thus it went on. At length all the horses were so tired that they could do no more, and so hot that the foam dropped from them and the riders were forced to give up the attempt. The King was just thinking that he would cause it to be proclaimed that the riding should begin afresh on the following day, when perhaps it might go better, when suddenly a knight came riding up on so fine a horse that no one had ever seen the like of it before, and the knight had armour of copper, and his bridle was of copper too, and all his accoutrements were so bright that they shone again. The other knights all called out to him that he might just as well spare himself the trouble of trying to ride up the glass hill, for it was of no use to try; but he did not heed them, and rode straight off to it, and went up as if it were nothing at all. Thus he rode for a long way – it may have been a third part of the way up – but when he had got so far he turned his horse round and rode down again. But the Princess thought that she had never yet seen so handsome a knight, and while he was riding up she was sitting thinking, "Oh! how I hope he may be able to come up to the top!" And when she saw that he was turning his horse back she threw one of the golden apples down after him, and it rolled into his shoe. But when he had come down from off the hill he rode away, and that so fast that no one knew what had become of him.

So all the princes and knights were bidden to present themselves before the King that night, so that he who had ridden so far up the glass hill might show the golden apple which the King's daughter had thrown down. But no one had anything to show. One knight presented himself after the other, and none could show the apple.

At night, too, Cinderlad's brothers came home again and had a long story to tell about riding up the glass hill. At first, they said, there was not one who was able to get even so much as one step up, but then came a knight who had armour of copper, and a bridle of copper, and his armour and trappings were so bright that they shone to a great distance, and it was something like a sight to see him riding. He rode one-third of the way up the glass hill, and he could easily have ridden the whole of it if he had liked; but he had turned back, for he had made up his mind that that was enough for once. "Oh! I should have liked to see him too, that I should," said Cinderlad, who was as usual sitting by the chimney among the cinders. "You, indeed!" said the brothers, "you look as if you were fit to be among such great lords, nasty beast that you are to sit there!"

Next day the brothers were for setting out again, and this time too Cinderlad begged them to let him go with them and see who rode; but no, they said he was not fit to do that, for he was much too ugly and dirty. "Well, well, then I will go all alone by myself," said Cinderlad. So the brothers went to the glass hill, and all the princes and knights began to ride again, and this time they had taken care to roughen the shoes of their horses; but that did not help them: they rode and they slipped as they had done the day before, and not one of them could get even so far as a yard up the hill. When they had tired out their horses, so that they could do no more, they again had to stop altogether. But just as the King was thinking that it would be well to proclaim that the riding should take place next day for the last time, so that they might have one more chance, he suddenly bethought himself that it would be well to wait a little longer to see if the knight in copper armour would come on this day too. But nothing was to be seen of him. Just as they were still looking for him, however, came a knight riding on a steed that was much, much finer than that which the knight in copper armour had ridden, and this knight had silver armour and a silver saddle and bridle, and all were so bright that they shone and glistened when he was a long way off. Again the other knights called to him, and said that he might just as well give up the attempt to ride up the glass hill, for it was useless to try; but the knight paid no heed to that, but rode straight away to the glass hill, and went still farther up than the knight in copper armour had gone; but when he had ridden two-thirds of the way up he turned his horse around, and rode down again. The Princess liked this knight still better than she had liked the other, and sat longing that he might be able to get up above, and when she saw him turning back she threw the second apple after him, and it rolled into his shoe, and as soon as he had got down the glass hill he rode away so fast that no one could see what had become of him.

In the evening, when everyone was to appear before the King and Princess, in order that he who had the golden apple might show it, one knight went in after the other, but none of them had a golden apple to show.

At night the two brothers went home as they had done the night before, and told how things had gone, and how everyone had ridden, but no one had been able to get up the hill. "But last of all," they said, "came one in silver armour, and he had a silver bridle on his horse, and a silver saddle, and oh, but he could ride! He took his horse two-thirds of the way up the hill, but then he turned back. He was a fine fellow," said the brothers, "and the Princess threw the second golden apple to him!"

"Oh, how I should have liked to see him too!" said Cinderlad.

"Oh, indeed! He was a little brighter than the ashes that you sit grubbing among, you dirty black creature!" said the brothers.

On the third day everything went just as on the former days. Cinderlad wanted to go with them to look at the riding, but the two brothers would not have him in their company, and when they got to the glass hill there was no one who could ride even so far as a yard up it, and everyone waited for the knight in silver armour, but he was neither to be seen nor heard of. At last, after a long time, came a knight riding upon a horse that was such a fine one, its equal had never yet been seen. The knight had golden armour, and the horse a golden saddle and bridle, and these were all so bright that they shone and dazzled everyone, even while the knight was still at a great distance. The other princes and knights were not able even to call to tell him how useless it was to try to ascend the hill, so amazed were they at sight of his magnificence. He rode straight away to the glass hill, and galloped up it as if it were no hill at all, so that the Princess had not even time to wish that he might get up the whole way. As soon as he had ridden to the top, he took the third golden apple from the lap of the Princess and then turned his horse about and rode down again, and vanished from their sight before anyone was able to say a word to him.

When the two brothers came home again at night they had much to tell of how the riding had gone off that day, and at last they told about the knight in the golden armour too. "He was a fine fellow, that was! Such another splendid knight is not to be found on earth!" said the brothers.

"Oh, how I should have liked to see him too!" said Cinderlad.

"Well, he shone nearly as brightly as the coal-heaps that thou art always lying raking among, dirty black creature that thou art!" said the brothers.

Next day all the knights and princes were to appear before the King and Princess – it had been too late for them to do it the night before – in order that he who had the golden apple might produce it. They all went in turn, first princes, and then knights, but none of them had a golden apple.

"But somebody must have it," said the King, "for with our own eyes we all saw a man ride up and take it." So he commanded that everyone in the kingdom should come to the palace, and see if he could show the apple. And one after the other they all came, but no one had the golden apple, and after a long, long time Cinderlad's two brothers came likewise. They were the last of all, so the King inquired of them if there was no one else in the kingdom left to come.

"Oh! yes, we have a brother," said the two, "but he never got the golden apple! He never left the cinder-heap on any of the three days."

"Never mind that," said the King; "as everyone else has come to the palace, let him come too."

So Cinderlad was forced to go to the King's palace.

"Hast thou the golden apple?" asked the King.

"Yes, here is the first, and here is the second, and here is the third, too," said Cinderlad, and he took all three apples out of his pocket, and with that drew off his sooty rags, and appeared there before them in his bright golden armour, which gleamed as he stood.

"Thou shalt have my daughter, and the half of my kingdom, and thou hast well earned both!" said the King. So there was a wedding, and Cinderlad got the King's daughter, and everyone made merry at the wedding, for all of them could make merry, though they could not ride up the glass hill, and if they have not left off their merry-making they must be at it still.

The Lassie and her Godmother

(Norwegian)

ONCE ON A TIME a poor couple lived far, far away in a great wood. The wife was brought to bed, and had a pretty girl, but they were so poor they did not know how to get the babe christened, for they had no money to pay the parson's fees. So one day the father went out to see if he could find anyone who was willing to stand for the child and pay the fees; but though he walked about the whole day from one house to another, and though all said they were willing enough to stand, no one thought himself bound to pay the fees. Now, when he was going home again, a lovely lady met him, dressed so fine, and she looked so thoroughly good and kind; she offered to get the babe christened, but after that, she said, she must keep it for her own. The husband answered, he must first ask his wife what she wished to do; but when he got home and told his story, the wife said, right out, "No!"

Next day the man went out again, but no one would stand if they had to pay the fees; and though he begged and prayed, he could get no help. And again as he went home, towards evening the same lovely lady met him, who looked so sweet and good, and she made him the same offer. So he told his wife again how he had fared, and this time she said, if he couldn't get anyone to stand for his babe next day, they must just let the lady have her way, since she seemed so kind and good.

The third day, the man went about, but he couldn't get anyone to stand; and so when, towards evening, he met the kind lady again, he gave his word she should have the babe if she would only get it christened at the font. So next morning she came to the place where the man lived, followed by two men to stand godfathers, took the babe and carried it to church, and there it was christened. After that she took it to her own house, and there the little girl lived with her several years, and her Foster-mother was always kind and friendly to her.

Now, when the Lassie had grown to be big enough to know right and wrong, her Foster-mother got ready to go on a journey.

"You have my leave," she said, "to go all over the house, except those rooms which I shew you"; and when she had said that, away she went.

But the Lassie could not forbear just to open one of the doors a little bit, when – Pop! out flew a star.

When her Foster-mother came back, she was very vexed to find that the star had flown out, and she got very angry with her Foster-daughter, and threatened to send her away; but the child cried and begged so hard that she got leave to stay.

Now, after a while, the Foster-mother had to go on another journey; and, before she went, she forbade the Lassie to go into those two rooms into which she had never been. She promised to beware; but when she was left alone, she began to think and to wonder what there could be in the second room, and at last she could not help setting the door a little ajar, just to peep in, when – Pop! out flew the Moon.

When her Foster-mother came home and found the moon let out, she was very downcast, and said to the Lassie she must go away, she could not stay with her any longer.

But the Lassie wept so bitterly, and prayed so heartily for forgiveness, that this time, too, she got leave to stay.

Some time after, the Foster-mother had to go away again, and she charged the Lassie, who by this time was half grown up, most earnestly that she mustn't try to go into, or to peep into, the third room. But when her Foster-mother had been gone some time, and the Lassie was weary of walking about alone, all at once she thought, "Dear me, what fun it would be just to peep a little into that third room." Then she thought she mustn't do it for her Foster-mother's sake; but when the bad thought came the second time she could hold out no longer; come what might, she must and would look into the room; so she just opened the door a tiny bit, when – POP! out flew the Sun.

But when her Foster-mother came back and saw that the sun had flown away, she was cut to the heart, and said, "Now, there was no help for it, the Lassie must and should go away; she couldn't hear of her staying any longer." Now the Lassie cried her eyes out, and begged and prayed so prettily; but it was all no good.

"Nay! but I must punish you!" said her Foster-mother; "but you may have your choice, either to be the loveliest woman in the world, and not to be able to speak, or to keep your speech, and to be the ugliest of all women; but away from me you must go."

And the Lassie said, "I would sooner be lovely." So she became all at once wondrous fair; but from that day forth she was dumb.

So, when she went away from her Foster-mother, she walked and wandered through a great, great wood; but the farther she went, the farther off the end seemed to be.

So, when the evening came on, she climbed up into a tall tree, which grew over a spring, and there she made herself up to sleep that night. Close by lay a castle, and from that castle came early every morning a maid to draw water to make the Prince's tea, from the spring over which the Lassie was sitting. So the maid looked down into the spring, saw the lovely face in the water, and thought it was her own; then she flung away the pitcher, and ran home; and, when she got there, she tossed up her head and said, "If I'm so pretty, I'm far too good to go and fetch water."

So another maid had to go for the water, but the same thing happened to her; she went back and said she was far too pretty and too good to fetch water from the spring for the Prince. Then the Prince went himself, for he had a mind to see what all this could mean. So, when he reached the spring, he too saw the image in the water; but he looked up at once, and became aware of the lovely Lassie who sate there up in the tree. Then he coaxed her down and took her home; and at last made up his mind to have her for his queen, because she was so lovely; but his mother, who was still alive, was against it.

"She can't speak," she said, "and maybe she's a wicked witch."

But the Prince could not be content till he got her. So after they had lived together a while, the Lassie was to have a child, and when the child came to be born, the Prince set a strong watch about her; but at the birth one and all fell into a deep sleep, and her Foster-mother came, cut the babe on its little finger, and smeared the Queen's mouth with the blood; and said:

"Now you shall be as grieved as I was when you let out the star"; and with these words she carried off the babe.

But when those who were on the watch woke, they thought the Queen had eaten her own child, and the old Queen was all for burning her alive, but the Prince was so fond of her that at last he begged her off, but he had hard work to set her free.

So the next time the young Queen was to have a child, twice as strong a watch was set as the first time, but the same thing happened over again, only this time her Foster-mother said:

"Now you shall be as grieved as I was when you let the moon out."

And the Queen begged and prayed, and wept; for when her Foster-mother was there, she could speak – but it was all no good.

And now the old Queen said she must be burnt, but the Prince found means to beg her off. But when the third child was to be born, a watch was set three times as strong as the first, but just the same thing happened. Her Foster-mother came while the watch slept, took the babe, and cut its little finger, and smeared the Queen's mouth with the blood, telling her now she should be as grieved as she had been when the Lassie let out the sun.

And now the Prince could not save her any longer. She must and should be burnt. But just as they were leading her to the stake, all at once they saw her Foster-mother, who came with all three children – two she led by the hand, and the third she had on her arm; and so she went up to the young Queen and said:

"Here are your children; now you shall have them again. I am the Virgin Mary, and so grieved as you have been, so grieved was I when you let out sun, and moon, and star. Now you have been punished for what you did, and henceforth you shall have your speech."

How glad the Queen and Prince now were, all may easily think, but no one can tell. After that they were always happy; and from that day even the Prince's mother was very fond of the young Queen.

Maiden Swanwhite and Maiden Foxtail

(Scandinavian)

THERE WAS ONCE UPON A TIME a wicked woman who had a daughter and a stepdaughter. The daughter was ugly and of an evil disposition, but the stepdaughter was most beautiful and good, and all who knew her wished her well. When the girl's stepmother and stepsister saw this they hated the poor girl.

One day it chanced that she was sent by her stepmother to the well to draw water. When the girl came there she saw a little hand held out of the water, and a voice said –

"Maiden, beautiful and good, give me your golden apple, and in return for it I will thrice wish you well."

The girl thought that one who spoke so fairly to her would not do her an ill turn, so she put the apple into the little hand. Then she bent down over the spring, and, taking care not to muddy the water, filled her bucket. As she went home the guardian of the well wished that the girl would become thrice as beautiful as she was, that whenever she laughed a gold ring might fall from her mouth, and that red roses might spring up wherever she trod. The same hour all that he wished came to pass. From that day the girl was called the Maiden Swanwhite, and the fame of her loveliness spread all through the land.

When the wicked stepmother perceived this, she was filled with rage, and she thought how her own daughter might become as beautiful as Swanwhite. With this object she set herself to learn all that had happened, and then she sent her own daughter to fetch water. When the wicked girl had come to the well, she saw a little hand rise up out of the water, and heard a voice which said –

"Maiden, beautiful and good, give me your gold apple and I will thrice wish thee well."

But the hag's daughter was both wicked and avaricious, and it was not her way to make presents. She therefore made a dash at the little hand, wished the guardian of the well evil, and said pettishly –

"You need not think you'll get a gold apple from me."

Then she filled her bucket, muddying the water, and away she went in a rage. The guardian of the well was enraged, so he wished her three evil wishes, as a punishment for her wickedness. He wished that she should become three times as ugly as she was, that a dead rat should fall from her mouth whenever she laughed, and that the fox-tail grass might spring up in the footsteps wherever she trod. So it was. From that day the wicked girl was called Maiden Foxtail, and very much talk was there among the folk of her strange looks and her ill-nature. The hag could not bear her stepdaughter should be more beautiful than her own daughter, and poor Swanwhite had to put up with all the ill-usage and suffering that a stepchild can meet with.

Swanwhite had a brother whom she loved very much, and he also loved her with all his heart. He had long ago left home, and he was now the servant of a king, far, far off in a strange land. The other servants of the king bore him no goodwill because he was liked by his master, and they wished to ruin him if they could find anything against him.

They watched him closely, and one day, coming to the king, said –

"Lord king, we know well that you do not like evil or vice in your servants. Thence we think it is only right to tell you that the young foreigner, who is in your service, every morning and evening bows the knee to an idol."

When the king heard that he set it down to envy and ill-will, and did not think there was any truth in it, but the courtiers said that he could easily discover for himself whether what they said was true or not. They led the king to the young man's rooms, and told him to look through the keyhole. When the king looked in he saw the young man on his knees before a fine picture, and so he could not help believing that what the courtiers had told him was true.

The king was much enraged, and ordered the young man to come before him, when he condemned him to die for his great wickedness.

"My lord king," said he, "do not imagine that I worship any idol. That is my sister's picture, whom I commend to the care of God every morning and evening, asking Him to protect her, for she remains in a wicked stepmother's power."

The king then wished to see the picture, and he never tired of looking on its beauty.

"If it is true," said he, "what you tell me, that that is your sister's picture, she shall be my queen, and you yourself shall go and fetch her; but if you lie, this shall be your punishment – you shall be cast into the lions' den."

The king then commanded that a ship should be fitted out in grand style, having wine and treasure in it. Then he sent away the young man in great state to fetch his beautiful sister to the court.

The young man sailed away over the ocean, and came at length to his land. Here he delivered his master's message, as became him, and made preparations to return. Then the stepmother and stepsister begged that they might go with him and his sister. The young man had no liking for them, so he said no, and refused their request, but Swanwhite begged for them, and got them what they wanted.

When they had put to sea and were on the wide ocean, a great storm arose so that the sailors expected the vessel and all on her to go to the bottom. The young man was, however, in good spirits, and went up the mast in order to see if he could discover land anywhere. When he had looked out from the mast, he called to Swanwhite, who stood on the deck –

"Dear sister, I see land now."

It was, however, blowing so hard that the maiden could not hear a word. She asked her stepmother if she knew what her brother said.

"Yes," said the false hag; "he says we shall never come to God's land unless you throw your gold casket into the sea."

When Swanwhite heard that, she did what the hag told her, and cast the gold casket into the deep sea.

A while after her brother once more called to his sister, who stood on the deck –

"Swanwhite, go and deck yourself as a bride, for we shall soon be there."

But the maiden could not hear a word for the raging of the sea. She asked her stepmother if she knew what her brother had said.

"Yes," said the false hag; "he says we shall never come to God's land unless you cast yourself into the sea."

While Swanwhite thought of this, the wicked stepmother sprang to her, and thrust her on a sudden overboard. The young girl was carried away by the blue waves, and came to the mermaid who rules over all those who are drowned in the sea.

When the young man came down the mast, and asked whether his sister was attired, the stepmother told him many falsehoods about Swanwhite having fallen into the sea. When the young man heard this he and all the ship-folk were afraid, for they well knew what punishment awaited them for having so ill looked after the king's bride. The false hag then thought of another deception. She said they had better dress her own daughter as the bride, and then no one need know that Swanwhite had perished. The young man would not agree to this, but the sailors, being in fear of their lives, made him do as the stepmother had suggested. Maiden Foxtail was dressed out in the finest manner with red rings and a gold girdle, but the young man was ill at ease, and could not forget what had happened to his sister.

In the midst of this the vessel came to shore, where was the king with all his court with much splendour awaiting their arrival. Carpets were spread upon the ground, and the king's bride left the ship in great state. When the king beheld Maiden Foxtail, and was told that that was his bride, he suspected some cheat, and was very angry, and he ordered that the young man should be thrown into the lions' den. He would not, however, break his kingly word, so he took the ugly maiden for his wife, and she became queen in the place of her stepsister.

Now Maiden Swanwhite had a little dog of which she was very fond, and she called it Snow-white. Now that its mistress was lost, there was no one who cared for it, so it came into the king's palace and took refuge in the kitchen, where it lay down in front of the fire. When it was night and all had gone to bed, the master-cook saw the kitchen door open of itself and a beautiful little duck, fastened to a chain, came into the kitchen. Wherever the little bird trod the most beautiful roses sprang up. The duck went up to the dog upon the hearth, and said –

"Poor little Snow-white! Once on a time you lay on blue silk cushions. Now you must lie on the grey ashes. Ah! my poor brother, who is in the lions' den! Shame on Maiden Foxtail! She sleeps in my lord's arms.

"Alas, poor me!" continued the duck, "I shall come here only on two more nights. After that I shall see you no more."

Then it caressed the little dog, and the dog returned its caresses. After a little while the door opened of itself and the little bird went its way.

The next morning, when it was daylight, the master-cook took the beautiful roses that lay strewn on the floor and with them decorated the dishes for the king's table. The king so much admired the flowers that he ordered the master-cook to be called to him, and asked him where he had found such magnificent roses. The cook told him all that had happened, and what the duck had said to the little dog. When the king heard it he was much perplexed, and he told the cook to let him know as soon as the bird showed itself again.

The next night the little duck again came to the kitchen, and spoke to the dog as before. The cook sent word to the king, and he came just as the bird went out at the door. However he saw the beautiful roses lying all over the kitchen floor, and from them came such a delightful scent that the like had never been known.

The king made up his mind that if the duck came again he would see it, so he lay in wait for it. He waited a long while, when, at midnight, the little bird, as before, came walking up to the dog which lay on the hearth, and said –

"Poor little Snow-white! once on a time you lay on blue silk cushions. Now you must lie on grey ashes. Ah! my poor brother, who is in the lions' den. Shame on Maiden Foxtail! She sleeps in my lord's arms."

Then it went on –

"Alas! poor me! I shall see thee no more."

Then it caressed the little dog, and the dog returned its caresses. As the bird was about to go away, the king sprang out and caught it by the foot. Then the bird changed its form and became a horrible dragon, but the king held it fast. It changed itself again, and took the forms of snakes, wolves, and other fierce animals, but the king did not lose his hold. Then the mermaid pulled hard at the chain, but the king held so fast that the chain broke in two with a great snap and rattling. That moment there stood there a beautiful maiden much more beautiful than that in the fine picture. She thanked the king for having saved her from the power of the mermaid. The king was very glad, and took the beautiful maiden in his arms, kissed her, and said –

"I will have no one else in the world for my queen, and now I well see that your brother was guiltless."

Then he sent off at once to the lions' den to learn if the young man was yet alive. There the young man was safe and sound among the wild beasts, which had done him no injury. Then the king was in a happy mood, and rejoiced that everything had chanced so well. The brother and sister told him all that the stepmother had done.

When it was daylight the king ordered a great feast to be got ready, and asked the foremost people in the country to the palace. As they all sat at table and were very merry, the king told a story of a brother and sister who had been treacherously dealt with by a stepmother, and he related all that had happened from beginning to end. When the tale was ended the king's folk looked at one another, and all agreed that the conduct of the stepmother in the tale was a piece of unexampled wickedness.

The king turned to his mother-in-law, and said –

"Someone should reward my tale. I should like to know what punishment the taking of such an innocent life deserves."

The false hag did not know that her own treachery was aimed at, so she said boldly –

"For my part, I certainly think she should be put into boiling lead."

The king then turned himself to Foxtail, and said –

"I should like to have your opinion; what punishment is merited by one who takes so innocent a life?"

The wicked woman answered at once –

"For my part, I think she deserves to be put into boiling tar."

Then the king started up from the table in a great rage, and said –

"You have pronounced doom on yourselves. Such punishment shall you suffer!"

He ordered the two women to be taken out to die as they themselves had said, and no one save Swanwhite begged him to have mercy on them.

After that the king was married to the beautiful maiden, and all folk agreed that nowhere could be found a finer queen. The king gave his own sister to the brave young man, and there was great joy in all the king's palace.

There they live prosperous and happy unto this day, for all I know.

The Three Dogs

(Scandinavian)

ONCE UPON A TIME there was a king who travelled to a strange country, where he married a queen. When they had been married some time the queen had a daughter, which gave rise to much joy through the whole land, for all people liked the king, he was so kind and just. As the child was born there came an old woman into the room. She was of a strange appearance, and nobody could guess where she came from, or to what place she was going. This old woman declared that the royal child must not be taken out under the sky until she was fifteen years old. If she was she would be in danger of being carried away by the giants of the mountains.

The king, when he was told what the woman had said, heeded her words, and set a guard to see that the princess did not come out into the open air.

In a short time the queen bore another daughter, and there was again much joy in the land. The old woman once more made her appearance, and she said that the king must not let the young princess go out under the sky before she was fifteen.

The queen had a third daughter, and the third time the old woman came, warning the king respecting this child as she had done regarding the two former. The king was much distressed, for he loved his children more than anything else in the world. So he gave strict orders that the three princesses should be always kept indoors, and he commanded that everyone should respect his edict.

A considerable time passed by, and the princesses grew up to be the most beautiful girls that could be seen far or near. Then a war began, and the king had to leave his home.

One day, while he was away at the seat of war, the three princesses sat at a window looking at how the sun shone on the flowers in the garden. They felt that they would like very much to go and play among the flowers, and they begged the guards to let them out for a little while to walk in the garden. The guards refused, for they were afraid of the king, but the girls begged of them so prettily and so earnestly that they could not long refuse them, so they let them do as they wished. The princesses were delighted, and ran out into the garden, but their pleasure was short-lived. Scarcely had they got into the open air when a cloud came down and carried them off, and no one could find them again, though they searched the wide world over.

The whole of the people mourned, and the king, as you may imagine, was very much grieved when, on his return home, he learned what had happened. However, there is an old saying, 'What's done cannot be undone,' so the king had to let matters remain as they were. As no one could advise him how to recover his daughters, the king caused proclamation to be made throughout the land that whoever should bring them back to him from the power of the mountain-giants should have one of them for his wife, and half the kingdom as a wedding present. As soon as this proclamation was made in the neighbouring countries many young warriors went out, with servants and horses, to look for the three princesses. There were at the king's court at that time two foreign princes and they started off too, to see how fortunate they might be. They put on fine armour, and took costly weapons, and they boasted of what they would do, and how they would never come back until they had accomplished their purpose.

We will leave these two princes to wander here and there in their search, and look at what was passing in another place. Deep down in the heart of a wild wood there dwelt at that time an old woman who had an only son, who used daily to attend to his mother's three hogs. As the lad roamed through the forest, he one day cut a little pipe to play on. He found much pleasure in the music, and he played so well that the notes charmed all who heard him. The boy was well built, of an honest heart, and feared nothing.

One day it chanced that, as he was sitting in the wood playing on his pipe, while his three hogs grubbed among the roots of the pine trees, a very old man came along. He had a beard so long that it reached to his waist, and a large dog accompanied him. When the lad saw the dog he said to himself –

"I wish I had a dog like that as a companion here in the wood. Then there would be no danger."

The old man knew what the boy thought, and he said –

"I have come to ask you to let me give you my dog for one of your hogs."

The lad was ready to close the bargain, and gave a grey hog in exchange for the big dog. As he was going the old man said –

"I think you will be satisfied with your bargain. The dog is not like other dogs. His name is Hold-fast, and if you tell him to hold, hold he will whatever it may be, were it even the fiercest giant."

Then he departed, and the lad thought that for once, at all events, fortune had been kind to him.

When evening had come, the lad called his dog, and drove the hogs to his home in the forest. When the old woman learnt how her son had given away the grey hog for a dog, she flew into a great rage, and gave him a good beating. The lad begged her to be quiet, but it was of no use, for she only seemed to get the more angry. When the boy saw that it was no good pleading, he called to the dog –

"Hold-fast."

The dog at once rushed forward, and, seizing the old woman, held her so firmly that she could not move; but he did her no harm. The old woman now had to promise that she would agree to what her son had done; but she could not help thinking that she had suffered a great misfortune in losing her fat grey hog.

The next day the boy went once more to the forest with his dog and the two hogs. When he arrived there he sat down and played upon his pipe as usual, and the dog danced to the music in such a wonderful manner that it was quite amazing. While he thus sat, the old man with the grey beard came up to him out of the forest. He was accompanied by a dog as large as the former one. When the boy saw the fine animal, he said to himself –

"I wish I had that dog as a companion in this wood. Then there would be no danger."

The old man knew what he thought, and said –

"I have come to ask you to let me give you my dog for one of your hogs."

The boy did not hesitate long, but agreed to the bargain. He got the big dog, and the man took the hog in exchange. As he went, the old man said –

"I think you will be satisfied with your bargain. The dog is not like other dogs. He is called Tear, and if you tell him to tear, tear he will in pieces whatever it be, even the fiercest mountain giant."

Then he departed, and the boy was glad at heart, thinking he had made a good bargain, though he well knew his old mother would not be much pleased at it.

Towards evening he went home, and his mother was not a bit less angry than she had been on the previous day. She dared not beat her son, however, for his big dogs made her afraid. It usually happens that when women have scolded enough they at last give in. So it was now. The boy and his mother became friends once more; but the old woman thought she had sustained such a loss as could never again be made good.

The boy went to the forest again with the hog and the two dogs. He was very happy, and, sitting down on the trunk of a tree he played, as usual, on his pipe; and the dogs danced in such fine fashion that it was a treat to look at them. While the boy thus sat amusing himself, the old man with the grey beard again appeared out of the forest. He had with him a third dog as large as either of the others. When the boy saw it, he said to himself –

"I wish I had that dog as a companion in this wood. Then there would be no danger."

The old man said –

"I came because I wished you to see my dog, for I well know you would like to have him."

The lad was ready enough, and the bargain was made. So he got the big dog, giving his last hog for it. The old man then departed, saying –

"I think you will be satisfied with your bargain. The dog is not like other dogs. He is called Quick-ear, and so quick does he hear, that he knows all that takes place, be it ever so many miles away. Why, he hears even the trees and the grass growing in the fields!"

Then the old man went off, and the lad felt very happy, for he thought he had nothing now to be afraid of.

As evening came on the boy went home, and his mother was sorely grieved when she found her son had parted with her all; but he told her to bid farewell to sorrow, saying that he would see she had no loss. The lad spoke so well that the old woman was quite pleased. At daybreak the lad went out a-hunting with his two dogs, and in the evening he came back with as much game as he could carry. He hunted till his mother's larder was well stocked, then he bade her farewell, telling her he was going to travel to see what fortune had in store for him, and called his dogs to him.

He travelled on over hills, and along gloomy roads, till he got deep in a dark forest. There the old man with the grey beard met him. The lad was very glad to fall in with him again, and said to him –

"Good day, father. I thank you for our last meeting."

"Good day," answered the old man. "Where are you going?"

"I am going into the world," said the boy, "to see what fortune I shall have."

"Go on," said the old man, "and you will come to a royal palace; there you will have a change of fortune."

With that they parted; but the lad paid good heed to the old man's words, and kept on his way. When he came to a house, he played on his pipe while his dogs danced, and so he got food and shelter, and whatever he wanted.

Having travelled for some days, he at last entered a large city, through the streets of which great crowds of people were passing. The lad wondered what was the cause of all this. At last he came to where proclamation was being made, that whoever should rescue the three princesses from the hands of the mountain giants should have one of them for his wife and half the kingdom with her. Then the lad remembered what the old man had told him, and understood what he meant. He called his dogs to him, and went on till he came to the palace. There, from the time that the princesses disappeared, the place had been filled with sorrow and mourning, and the king and the queen grieved more than all the others. The boy entered the palace, and begged to be allowed to play to the king and show him his dogs. The people of the palace were much pleased at this, for they thought it might do something to make the king forget his grief. So they let him go in and show what he could do. When the king heard how he played, and saw how wonderfully his dogs danced, he was so merry that no one had seen him so during the seven long years that had passed since he lost his daughters. When the dancing was finished, the king asked the boy what he should give him as a return for the amusement he had given them.

"My lord king," said the boy, "I am not come here for silver, goods, or gold! I ask one thing of you, that you will give me leave to go and seek the three princesses who are now in the hands of the mountain giants." When the king heard this he knit his brow – "So you think," said he, "that you can restore my daughters. The task is a dangerous one, and men who were better than you have suffered in it. If, however, anyone save the princesses I will never break my word."

The lad thought these words kingly and honest. He bade farewell to the king and set out, determined that he would not rest till he had found what he wanted.

He travelled through many great countries without any extraordinary adventure, and wherever he went his dogs went with him. Quick-ear ran and heard what there was to hear in the place; Hold-fast carried the bag; and on Tear, who was the strongest of the three, the lad rode when he was tired. One day Quick-ear came running fast to his master to tell him that he had been near a high mountain, and had heard one of the princesses spinning within it. The giant, Quick-ear said, was not at home. At this the boy felt very glad, and he made haste to the mountain with his dogs. When they were come to it, Quick-ear said –

"We have no time to lose. The giant is only ten miles away, and I can hear his horse's golden shoes beating on the stones."

The lad at once ordered his dogs to break in the door of the mountain, which they did. He entered, and saw a beautiful maiden who sat spinning gold thread on a spindle of gold.

He stepped forward and spoke to her. She was much astonished, and said – "Who are you, that dare to come into the giant's hall? For seven long years have I lived here, and never during that time have I looked on a human being. Run away, for Heaven's sake, before the giant comes, or you will lose your life."

The boy told her his errand, and said he would await the troll's coming. While they were talking, the giant came, riding on his gold-shod horse, and stopped outside the mountain. When he saw that the door was open he was very angry, and called out, in such a voice that the whole mountain shook to its base, "Who has broken open my door?" The boy boldly answered –

"I did it, and now I will break you too. Hold-fast, hold him fast; Tear and Quick-ear, tear him into a thousand pieces!"

Hardly had he spoken the words when the three dogs rushed forward, threw themselves on the giant, and tore him into numberless pieces. The princess was very glad, and said –

"Heaven be thanked! Now I am free." She threw herself on the lad's neck and kissed him. The lad would not stop in the place, so he saddled the giant's horses, put on them all the goods and gold he found, and set off with the beautiful young princess. They travelled together for a long time, the lad waiting on the maiden with that respect and attention that such a noble lady deserved.

It chanced one day that Quick-ear, who had gone before to obtain news, came running fast to his master and informed him that he had been to a high mountain, and had heard another of the king's daughters sitting within it spinning gold thread. The giant, he said, was not at home. The lad was well pleased to hear this, and hastened to the mountain with his three dogs. When they arrived there, Quick-ear said –

"We have no time to waste. The giant is but eight miles off. I can hear the sound of his horse's gold shoes on the stones!"

The lad ordered the dogs to break in the door, and when they had done so he entered and found a beautiful maiden sitting in the hall, winding gold thread. The lad stepped forward and spoke to her. She was much surprised, and said –

"Who are you, who dare to come into the giant's dwelling? Seven long years have I lived here, and never during that time have I looked on a human being. Run away, for Heaven's sake, before the giant comes, or you will lose your life."

The lad told her why he had come, and said he would wait for the giant's return home.

In the midst of their talk the giant came, riding on his gold-shod horse, and stopped outside the mountain. When he saw the door was open he was in a great rage, and called out with such a voice that the mountain shook to its base.

"Who," said he, "has broken open my door?" The lad answered boldly –

"I did it, and now I will break you. Hold-fast, hold him fast; Tear and Quick-ear, tear him into a thousand pieces!" The dogs straightaway sprang forward and threw themselves on the giant, and tore him into pieces as numberless as are the leaves which fall in the autumn. Then the princess was very glad, and said –

"Heaven be thanked! Now I am free!" She threw herself on the lad's neck and kissed him. He led her to her sister, and one can well imagine how glad they were to meet. The lad took all the treasures that the giant's dwelling contained, put them on the gold-shod horses, and set out with the two princesses.

They again travelled a great distance, and the youth waited on the princesses with the respect and care they deserved.

It chanced one day that Quick-ear, who went before to get news, came running fast to his master, and told him he had been near a high mountain, and had heard the third princess sitting within, spinning cloth of gold. The giant himself was not in. The youth was well pleased to hear this, and he hurried to the mountain accompanied by his dogs. When they came there, Quick-ear said –

"There is no time to be lost. The giant is not more than five miles off. I well know it. I hear the sound of his horse's gold shoes on the stones."

The lad told his dogs to break in the door, and they did so. When he entered the mountain he saw there a maiden, sitting and weaving cloth of gold. She was so beautiful that the lad thought another such could not be found in the world. He advanced and spoke to her. The young princess was much astonished, and said –

"Who are you, who dare to come into the giant's hall? For seven long years have I lived here, and never during that time have I looked on a human being. For Heaven's sake," added she, "run away before the giant comes, or he will kill you!"

The lad, however, was brave, and said that he would lay down his life for the beautiful princess.

In the middle of their talk home came the giant, riding on his horse with the golden shoes, and stopped at the mountain. When he came in and saw what unwelcome visitors were there he was very much afraid, for he knew what had happened to his brethren. He thought it best to be careful and cunning, for he dared not act openly. He began therefore with fine words, and was very smooth and amiable. He told the princess to dress meat, so that he might entertain the guest, and behaved in such a friendly manner that the lad was perfectly deceived, and forgot to be on his guard. He sat down at the table with the giant. The princess wept in secret, and the dogs were very uneasy, but no one noticed it.

When the giant and his guest had finished the meal, the youth said –

"I am no longer hungry. Give me something to drink."

"There is," said the giant, "a spring up in the mountain which runs with sparkling wine, but I have no one to fetch of it."

"If that is all," said the lad, "one of my dogs can go up there."

The giant laughed in his false heart when he heard that, for what he wanted was that the lad should send away his dogs. The lad told Hold-fast to go for the wine, and the giant gave him a large jug. The dog went, but one might see that he did so very unwillingly.

Time went on and on, but the dog did not come back. After some time the giant said –

"I wonder why the dog is so long away. It might, perhaps, be as well to let another dog go to help him. He has to go a long distance, and the jug is a heavy one to carry."

The lad, suspecting no trickery, fell in with the giant's suggestion, and told Tear to go and see why Hold-fast did not come. The dog wagged his tail and did not want to leave his master, but he noticed it, and drove him off to the spring. The giant laughed to himself, and the princess wept, but the lad did not mark it, being very merry, jested with his entertainer, and did not dream of any danger.

A long time passed, but neither the wine nor the dogs appeared.

"I can well see," said the giant, "that your dogs do not do what you tell them, or we should not sit here thirsty. It seems to me it would be best to send Quick-ear to ascertain why they don't come back."

The lad was nettled at that, and ordered his third dog to go in haste to the spring. Quick-ear did not want to go, but whined and crept to his master's feet. Then the lad became angry, and drove him away. The dog had to obey, so away he set in great haste to the top of the mountain. When he reached it, it happened to him as it had to the others. There arose a high wall around him, and he was made a prisoner by the giant's sorcery.

When all the three dogs were gone, the giant stood up, put on a different look, and gripped his bright sword which hung upon the wall.

"Now will I avenge my brethren," said he, "and you shall die this instant, for you are in my hands."

The lad was frightened, and repented that he had parted with his dogs.

"I will not ask my life," said he, "for I must die some day. I only ask one thing, that I may say my *Paternoster* and play a psalm on my pipe. That is the custom in my country."

The giant granted him his wish, but said he would not wait long. The lad knelt down, and devoutly said his *Paternoster*, and began to play upon his pipe so that it was heard over hill and dale. That instant the magic lost its power, and the dogs were once more set free. They came down like a blast of wind, and rushed into the mountain. Then the lad sprang up and cried –

"Hold-fast, hold him; Tear and Quick-ear, tear him into a thousand pieces."

The dogs flew on the giant, and tore him into countless shreds. Then the lad took all the treasures in the mountain, harnessed the giant's horses to a golden chariot, and made haste to be gone.

As may well be imagined, the young princesses were very glad at being thus saved, and they thanked the lad for having delivered them from the power of mountain giants. He himself fell deep in love with the youngest princess, and they vowed to be true and faithful. So they travelled, with mirth and jest and great gladness, and the lad waited on the princesses with the respect and care they deserved. As they went on, the princesses played with the lad's hair, and each one hung her finger-ring in his long locks as a keepsake.

One day as they were journeying, they came up with two wanderers who were going the same way. They had on tattered clothes, their feet were sore, and altogether one would have thought they had come a long distance. The lad stopped his chariot and asked them who they were and where they came from. The strangers said they were two princes who had gone out to look for the three maidens who had been carried off to the mountains. They had, however, searched in vain, so they had now to go home more like beggars than princes.

When the lad heard that, he had pity on the two wanderers, and he asked them to go with him in the beautiful chariot. The princes gave him many thanks for the favour. So they travelled on together till they came to the land over which the father of the princesses ruled.

Now when the princes heard how the poor lad had rescued the princesses, they were filled with envy, thinking how they themselves had wandered to no purpose. They considered how they could get rid of him, and obtain the honour and rewards for themselves. So one day they suddenly set on him, seized him by the throat, and nearly strangled him. Then they threatened to kill the princesses unless they took an oath not to reveal what they had done, and they, being in the princes' power, did not dare to refuse. However, they were very sorry for the youth who had risked his life for them, and the youngest princess mourned him with all her heart, and would not be comforted.

After having done this, the princes went on to the king's demesnes, and one can well imagine how glad the king was to once more see his three daughters.

Meanwhile the poor lad lay in the forest as if he were dead. He was not, however, forsaken, for the three dogs lay down by him, kept him warm, and licked his wounds. They attended to him till he got his breath again, and came once more to life. When he had regained life and strength, he began his journey, and came, after having endured many hardships, to the king's demesnes, where the princesses lived.

When he went into the palace, he marked that the whole place was filled with mirth and joy, and in the royal hall he heard dancing and the sound of harps. The lad was much astonished, and asked what it all meant.

"You have surely come from a distance," said the servant, "not to know that the king has got back his daughters from the mountain giants. The two elder princesses are married today."

The lad asked about the youngest princess, whether she was to be married. The servant said she would have no one, but wept continually, and no one could find out the reason for her sorrow. Then the lad was glad, for he well knew that his love was faithful and true to him.

He went up into the guard-room, and sent a message to the king that a guest had come who prayed that he might add to the wedding mirth by exhibiting his dogs. The king was pleased, and ordered that the stranger should be well received. When the lad came into the hall, the wedding guests much admired his smartness and his manly form, and they all thought they had never before seen so brave a young man. When the three princesses saw him they knew him at once, rose from the table, and ran into his arms. Then the princes thought they had better not stay there, for the princesses told how the lad had saved them, and how all had befallen. As a proof of the truth of what they said, they showed their rings in the lad's hair.

When the king knew how the two foreign princes had acted so treacherously and basely he was much enraged, and ordered that they should be driven off his demesnes with disgrace.

The brave youth was welcomed with great honour, as, indeed, he deserved, and he was, the same day, married to the youngest princess. When the king died, the youth was the chosen ruler over the land, and made a brave king. There he yet lives with his beautiful queen, and there he governs prosperously to this day.

I know no more about him.

Frithiof the Bold

(Norwegian)

FRITHIOF WAS A NORWEGIAN HERO, grandson of Viking, who was the largest and strongest man of his time. Viking had sailed the sea in a dragon ship, meeting with many adventures, and Thorsten, Frithiof's father, had likewise sailed abroad, capturing many priceless treasures and making a great name for himself.

Frithiof was entrusted to the care of Hilding, his foster father, and in his care, also, were Halfdan and Helgé, King Bélé's sons, and, some years later, their little sister, Ingeborg.

Frithiof and Ingeborg became firm friends, and as the lad increased in bravery and strength, the girl increased in beauty and loveliness of soul. Hilding, noticing how each day they became fonder of each other, called Frithiof to him and bade him remember that he was only a humble subject and could never hope to wed Ingeborg, the king's only daughter, descended from the great god Odin. The warning, however, came too late, for Frithiof already loved the fair maiden, and vowed that he would have her for his bride at any cost.

Soon after this the king died, leaving his kingdom to his two sons and giving instructions that his funeral mound should be erected in sight of that of his dear friend Thorsten, so that their spirits might not be separated even in death. Then Ingeborg went to live with her brothers, the Kings of Sogn, while Frithiof retired to his own home at Framnas, closed in by the mountains and the sea.

Frithiof was now one of the wealthiest and most envied of landowners. His treasures were richer by far than those of any king.

In the spring he held a great celebration, which the kings of Sogn and their sister Ingeborg, among many other guests, attended. Frithiof and Ingeborg were much together, and Frithiof was very happy to learn that Ingeborg returned his affection.

Great was his grief when the time came for her to sail away. Not long had she been gone, however, when he vowed to Björn, his chief companion, that he would follow after her and ask for her hand. His ship was prepared and soon he touched the shore near the temple of the god Balder.

His request was not granted and Helgé dismissed him contemptuously. In a rage at the insult Frithiof lifted his sword; but remembering that he stood on consecrated ground near Bélé's tomb, he spared the king, only cutting his heavy shield in two to show the strength of his blade.

Soon after his departure another suitor, the aged King Ring of Norway sought the hand of Ingeborg in marriage, and being refused, collected an army and prepared to make war on Helgé and Halfdan.

Then the two brothers were glad to send a messenger after Frithiof, asking his aid. The hero, still angry, refused; but he hastened at once to Ingeborg. He found her in tears at the shrine of Balder, and although it was considered a sin for a man and woman to exchange words in the sacred temple, he spoke to her, again making known his love.

The kings, her brothers, were away at war, but Frithiof stayed near Ingeborg, and when they returned, promised to free them from the oppression of Sigurd Ring if in return they would promise him the hand of their sister. But the kings had heard of how Frithiof had spoken to Ingeborg in the temple, and although they feared Sigurd they would not grant the request. Instead he was condemned in punishment to sail away to the Orkney Islands to claim tribute from the king Angantyr.

Frithiof departed in his ship *Ellida*, and Ingeborg stayed behind, weeping bitterly. And as soon as the vessel was out of sight the brothers sent for two witches – Heid and Ham – bidding them stir up such a tempest on the sea that even the god-given ship *Ellida* could not withstand its fury.

But no tempest could frighten the brave Frithiof. Singing a cheery song he stood at the helm, caring nothing for the waves that raged about the ship. He comforted his crew, and then climbed the mast to keep a sharp lookout for danger.

From there he spied a huge whale, upon which the two witches were seated, delighted at the tempest they had stirred up. Speaking to his good ship, which could both hear and obey, he bade it run down the whale and the witches.

This *Ellida* did. Whale and witches sank; the sea grew red with their blood; the waves were calmed. Again the sun smiled over the hardy sailors. But many of the crew were worn out by the battle with the elements and had to be carried ashore by Frithiof and Björn when they reached the Orkney Islands.

Now the watchman at Angantyr's castle had reported the ship and the gale, and Angantyr had declared that only Frithiof and *Ellida* could weather such a storm. One of his vassals, Atlé, caught up his weapons and hurried forth to challenge the great hero.

Frithiof had no weapons, but with a turn of his wrist he threw his opponent.

"Go and get your weapons," Atlé said, when he saw that Frithiof would have killed him.

Knowing that Atlé was a true soldier and would not run away, Frithiof left him in search of his sword; but when he returned and found his opponent calmly awaiting death, he was generous, and bade him rise and live.

Angantyr vowed that he owed no tribute to Helgé, and would pay him none, but to Frithiof he gave a vast treasure, telling him that he might dispose of it as he would.

So Frithiof sailed back to the kings of Sogn, confident that he could win Ingeborg. What was his dismay, therefore, to learn that Helgé and Halfdan had already given their sister in marriage to Sigurd Ring. In a rage he bade his men destroy all the vessels in the harbour, while he strode toward the temple of Balder where Helgé and his wife were. He flung Angantyr's purse of gold in Helgé's face, and seeing the ring he had given to Ingeborg on the hand of Helgé's wife snatched it roughly from her. In trying to get it back she dropped the image of the god, which she had just been anointing, into the fire. It was quickly consumed, while the rising flames set fire to the temple.

Horror-stricken, Frithiof tried to stop the blaze, and when he could not, hurried away to his ship.

So Frithiof became an exile, and a wanderer on the face of the earth. For many years he lived the life of a pirate or viking, exacting tribute from other ships or sacking them if they would not pay tribute; for this occupation in the days of Frithiof was considered wholly respectable. It was followed again and again by the brave men of the North.

But Frithiof was often homesick, and longed to enter a harbour, and lead again a life of peace.

At last he decided to visit the court of Sigurd Ring and find out whether Ingeborg was really happy. Landing, he wrapped himself in an old cloak and approached the court. He found a seat on a bench near the door, as beggars usually did; but when one insulting courtier mocked him he lifted the offender in his mighty hand and swung him high over his head.

At this Sigurd Ring invited the old man to remove his mantle and take a seat near him. With surprise Sigurd and his courtiers saw step from the tattered mantle a handsome warrior, richly clad; but only Ingeborg knew who he was.

"Who are you who comes to us thus?" asked Sigurd Ring.

"I am Thiolf, a thief," was the answer, "and I have grown to manhood in the Land of Sorrow."

Sigurd invited him to remain, and he soon became the almost constant companion of the king and queen.

One spring day Sigurd and Frithiof had ridden away on a hunting expedition, and the old king being tired from the chase lay down on the ground to rest, feigning sleep. The birds and beasts of the forest drew near and whispered to Frithiof that he should slay the king and have Ingeborg for his own wife. But Frithiof was too fine and loyal to listen to such suggestions.

Awaking, Sigurd Ring called Frithiof to him.

"You are Frithiof the Bold," he said, "and from the first I knew you. Be patient now a little longer and you shall have Ingeborg, for my end is near."

Soon after this Sigurd died, commending his wife to the young hero's loving care. And at his own request the funeral feast was closed by the public betrothal of Ingeborg and Frithiof.

The people, admiring his bravery, wanted to make Frithiof king, but he would not listen to their pleadings. Instead he lifted the little son of Sigurd upon his shield.

"Behold your king," he cried, "and until he is grown to manhood I will stand beside him."

So Frithiof married his beloved Ingeborg, and later, so the story runs, he returned to his own country and built again the temple of Balder, more beautiful by far than any before.

The Hostage

(Norse)

I SEEK TO TELL OF A DANISH HOSTAGE, called Valgard the Fair, who in his youth was ceded to our great Alfred by the Danish king Guthrum when they two made peace together in the year eight hundred and seventy-eight.

From Denmark young Valgard came to England in the following of Ogmund Monks-bane, who was his elder brother and Guthrum's first war chief; and though no warrior of more accursed memory than this same Ogmund ever fed the ravens, it was known that toward his young brother alone of all living things he showed a human heart. Wherefore those on whom it lay to choose the hostages were swift to name the comely boy as the one pledge that might clinch the Monks-bane's shifty faith. And that nothing might be lacking, they further fixed it in the bond what would be the fate of Valgard and the eleven other hostages if they that gave them should break any part of their oath; and it was this – that the discipline of the Holy Church should take hold of them, and after that they should die a shameful death.

A snared and a savage man was Ogmund Monks-bane when they brought this word to the tent of skins in which he laired; and it saddened him besides that the boy Valgard strove to contend him, saying:

"It will be no hindrance to you, kinsman. Never will you so much as think of me when the battle-lust comes on you. And I shall bear it well."

In our king's will at London, therefore, young Valgard grew into man's estate and, contrary to his expectations, throve mightily, discovering a rare aptitude for gentle accomplishments. And for that his heart was noble as well as brave and he was as *débonaire* as he was comely, the king and the royal household came to love him exceeding well until – as the years went by and the peace held – they scarcely remembered that he might one day stand as a scapegoat for loathsomest crimes against them.

Only Valgard himself never for the span of one candle's burning forgot it. Like poison at the bottom of a honeyed cup it lay behind every honour he achieved. Yet even as he had promised his brother, he bore it well and gallantly enough – until, in the sixth year of his captivity, it fortuned to him to fall in love.

She of whom he become enamoured was a young maid in the queen's service, whose rightful name was Adeleve but whom men called Little Nun both by virtue of the celestial sweetness of her face and because of her being but newly come from a cloister school. And in this cloister they had taught her so much of heaven and so little of earth that whensoever her heart was taken by Valgard's brave and *débonaire* ways she knew neither fear nor shame therein, but continued to demean herself with the lovely straightforwardness of an angel or a child. Wherefore Valgard, who was used to women that smiled at him from under heavy lids or drew full red lips into rosebuds of enticement, might not dream that she felt more than friendship. And since in her presence he was always silent and humble as he had been before Our Blessed Lady herself, though elsewhere light speeches sparkled on his lips as bubbles on the clear wine, he wist not for a long time the true name of what he felt.

But one day at that season of the year when the king's household rode often to hunt the wild boar in the woody groves that compassed London round, it happened to Valgard to become separated from the rest and stray alone through still and shadowy glades. There in the solitude, as was ever his unhappy case, his gayety fell away and his forebodings climbed up behind and went with him heavily. Riding thus, it chanced to him to approach the spot where the queen and her maidens tarried and so to come upon the Little Nun herself, that also rode apart, following a brook which sang as it went. Then at last was he made aware of his love, for suddenly it was neither a dislike of death nor any rebellious wish to flee therefrom that possessed him, but solely the dread of being parted from her, which so racked him that he was in very agony.

Now as soon as ever Little Nun perceived that a great trouble was upon him she spoke straight from her heart, though timidly as a child knowing the narrowness of its power, and prayed him to say whether his distress were aught which her love might assuage. When he heard her speak thus sweetly and marked the angelic tenderness of her eyes under her little dove-coloured hood, lo! everything fell clean out of his mind before one almighty longing. Descending from his horse, he took her hands and spoke to her passionately, so:

"Tell me whether you love me. My heart cries out for you with every beat. Must it be as the voice of one calling into emptiness? Tell me that you return my love and my life will be whole though it end tonight."

The Little Nun's face of cloistral paleness flushed deeply like an alabaster vase into which is being poured the red wine of the sacrament, but her crystalline eyes neither fell nor turned aside.

"I love you as much as you love me – and more," she answered softly.

Whereupon he would have caught her in passionate arms, but that even as he reached this pinnacle of bliss it came back to him how he was a doomed man; and he was as one that is cast down from a height and stunned by the fall.

Anon his voice returned, and sinking to his knee he begged her in broken words to forgive the wrong he had done her in gaining her love, that well knew himself to be set aside for shame and dole and apart from the favour of woman.

To which the Little Nun listened as it might be one of God's angels, bending over the golden bar of Heaven, would listen to the wailing in the Pit. And so soon as he paused she spoke with halting breath.

"Alas, could anything so cruel happen? Ah, no! The peace has held six years – the king believes it firm – and every night and morning I will pray to Our Lady to change your brother's heart."

As she said this, her face bloomed again with her hope. But Valgard only bowed his head upon his hands and groaned; for that albeit he had faith in the Virgin, he knew the nature of Ogmund Monks-bane.

Soon after, constraining himself to hardness for her sake, he rose and drew her away and continued to speak with the dulness of one in great pain, schooling her how she must put him from her heart and forget him.

But to that, when she had listened a while with widening eyes, the Little Nun cried out piteously:

"Alas! what then shall I do with my love? It came into being before you called it – it cannot cease at your bidding. Oh, if it be God's will that we shall have a long life together, then God's will be done, but make not a thwarted useless thing out of the love which He has permitted me! Let me give it to you. Even though it be too poor to ease you much, yet let me give it! How else shall I find comfort?"

Suddenly, as their eyes met, she stretched out her hands to him with a little sobbing cry that was half piteous and half pitying. And so drew him back, *malgré* his will, until he had put his arms about her where she sat in the saddle above him, when she gathered his head to her breast and cherished it there, with little soft wordless sounds of comforting.

Thus, for that he was so well-nigh spent with struggling, he leaned a while upon her love. And it heartened him. And he lifted his head, thinking to set burning lips to her sweet mouth.

But even as he thought to do this, something in himself or her checked him, so that he kissed instead her small ministering hands. Wherefore the Little Nun remained unstartled and blessedly trustful, and raising her eyes to the blue heavens of which they seemed so much a part prayed softly to Our Dear Lady to keep true the heart of Ogmund Monks-bane.

The fourth morning after this, the queen's maiden Adeleve was wedded to Valgard the Hostage. And that day at noon did our benignant king and his housewifely queen make a marriage feast for the young pair that both of them held dear. A marriage feast, well-a-way!

It happened to the sweet bride to come to it last and alone, for that she had lingered above to pray once more to her on whom she fixed her faith. Blissfully enough she began the descent of the stairs that cored the massive wall; but ere she reached the foot, where a door gave upon the king's hall, dead was her joy. For this is what befell.

First, a quavering shriek as of an aged woman stabbed by evil tidings; and after that a deathlike stillness. Then the door opened and a girl staggered forth up the stairs, her hands groping before her as her staring eyes had been sightless, the while she moaned over and over the name of her soldier lover.

Though she knew not why, little Adeleve shrank from the groping hands and crept by them down the stairs. Whither rose these words in a man's loud voice:

"—but last week came a load of Danish pirates to the shore, reeking of slaughter and gorged with Irish spoil. And every night thereafter a band of them sat at drink with the Monks-bane, stirring his fighting lust, until—"

Here the voice was lost in the outburst of many voices, till it overleapt them hoarsely to answer a question from the king.

"The twoscore English soldiers I named to your grace; besides all the nuns of Saint Helena's that lie stark in their blood—"

Then once again the tumult rose, which now there was no overleaping, and the bride cowering against the wall saw how all heads turned toward him who stood opposite the king in the mockery of gay feasting clothes. And suddenly one called down Christ's curse on the race of Ogmund Monks-bane, and a second echoed the cry. Whereat the other Danish hostages – to show that their hands were clean – took up the shout more fierce than any, and smote Valgard so that he reeled under their fists. And the aged woman whose son had been slain flung her cup of wine in his face.

Thereafter the young wife saw only the figure of her doomed lord upon whom it seemed that the curses descended as a visible blight, withering to ghastliness his fresh beauty and blasting his spirit so that he shrank farther and farther from the damning looks and tongues till he might no longer in any wise endure them, but calling in agony upon his God strove with his hands to stop his sight and his hearing. And when presently he became aware of the Little Nun approaching, he cried out to know whether she also was come to curse him, and bent his arms around his head as against a blow.

But even as he did this, he met the anguished love in her eyes and saw how she was labouring to make of her fragile self a buckler for him against the press of crowding bodies; whereupon he caught hold of her shoulder and held to her as a man sinking into Hell might hold to the robe of an angel, until brutal hands thrust her one way and dragged him the other.

Now the sentence was that he should die at sunrise, unto which time the Church should have him to chasten. And this sentence our king might not alter, for that he was called the Truth-teller and had sworn to take the atonement of life for any breach of the faith. But this much he granted, out of the pity and love he had toward the young pair, that they might be together when the end drew near. And stranger than betrothal or marriage feast was this vigil of their wedding night!

Strange was all the world now to the Little Nun, since the arch of her Heaven had fallen about her with the destruction of its keystone, which was her faith in the Virgin. As the white dove of the Ark hovering over a changed earth whereon it might see no familiar foothold, she hung falteringly on the threshold of the king's chapel, while the bells tolled the midnight hour, gazing at the group of deathful men looming amid blended smoke and starlight and torch-glare, at the pitiless shining figure of Our Lady above the altar, at him who stood in grim endurance before it, stripped to naked feet and a single garment of horsehair.

When Valgard felt her eyes and turned his set face toward her, she fluttered to him as the dove to the Ark. But no longer to brood or minister; only to cling to him in utter helpless woe of her helpless love. And when it happened to her hand to touch his horsehair shirt where it was wet with the blood of his atonement, she screamed sharply and was like to go wild with weeping over him and lamenting that she might not bear any of his punishment on her own soft flesh. It was he that kneeling on the stones gathered her to his breast and cherished her, speaking to comfort her such words of resignation as no priest's scourge had drawn from him with his life-blood.

Lo! it was so that from the very helplessness of her love he drew his best strength, that he no longer cared anything at all for his own woe but only for lightening hers. When she cried out piteously that she must always fear Christ's Mother now her whole life long, and all the world saving him alone, he spoke with tenderest artfulness, thus:

"For my sake then, heart beloved of my heart! Be brave for my sake – because your tears are the only part of my doom that is heavier than I can bear."

Which was the one plea in all the world that had a meaning for her, so that she tried obediently to choke down her sobs.

Yet which was the easier to bear, her courage or her tears, it were hard to say. When the time of parting came and she had suffered him to loosen her clinging hands and fold them upon her breast and leave her, a little white and shaking figure at the Virgin's feet, it seemed to Valgard looking back that death was easier to him than life, and he pressed with mad haste upon those who went before him to the door.

Now in this vill it was that the king's chapel was hollowed out of the wall of the king's hall; wherefore the opening of the door permitted Valgard and those surrounding him to look down into the great dim room wherein our king kept sorrowful vigil with his knights, and to behold also a man that stood before the high seat with the mud and mire of the road yet besmirching him, upon whom Valgard's glance fell amazedly for that he knew him to be a Danish thrall and his brother's trusted slave, albeit the Monks-bane had used him so cruelly that some of his features were lacking.

As the door opened, the thrall began speaking, thus, in the dull voice of one who has neither wit nor will but only dogged faithfulness:

"This is the message of Ogmund Monks-bane, that because as soon as he got into his senses again he disliked the thought that he should cause the death of his brother whom he loved, he sends you this atonement."

Saying which, he thrust his hand under his cloak and drew therefrom, by the knotted yellow hair, a bloody head. And the ashen face on the head was the face of Ogmund Monks-bane.

Through stillness, the thrall spoke again. "Do you accept this atonement, king?"

To whom, after a little time has passed, our king answered in a strange voice: "I accept this atonement."

Then, his task being accomplished, the thrall loosed an awful discordant sound of grief; and raising the head between his palms kissed it on either cheek, crying:

"I slew you and I brought you hither because I have never dared go against your will in anything, but even you cannot hinder me from following you now!"

Wherewith he slew himself with the knife he had at his belt. And the sound of his falling body broke the spell, so that the bars of silence were let down and men's voices rushed in like lowing cattle, excepting only in the little chapel in the wall. There Valgard stood as a man in a dream, gazing on the dead face of his brother; while the Little Nun, clasping him close, yet lifted awe-filled eyes to Our Lady who thus in her own inscrutable way answered the prayer to keep alive in the nature of an evil man its one good part.

Let us all give thanks that there is such a Lady, and pray that she may harken to us in our need!

Thorwald and the Star Children

(Norwegian)

I

THORWALD'S MOTHER WAS VERY ILL. The fever burned and throbbed in her veins; she lay, all day long and all night long, with her eyes wide open, and could not sleep. The doctor sat at her bedside and looked at her through his spectacles; but she grew worse instead of better.

"Unless she can sleep a sound, natural sleep," he said, "there is no hope for her, I fear."

It was to Thorwald's father that he said this, but Thorwald heard what he said. The little boy, with his dog Hector, was sitting mournfully upon the great wolfskin outside his mother's door.

"Is my mamma very ill?" he asked the doctor, but the tears choked his voice, and he hid his face in the hair of Hector's shaggy neck.

"Yes, child," answered the doctor; "very ill."

"And will God take my mamma away from me?" he faltered, extricating himself from Hector's embrace, and trying hard to steady his voice and look brave.

"I am afraid He will, my child," said the doctor, gravely.

"But could I not do something for her, doctor?"

The long suppressed tears now broke forth, and trickled down over the boy's cheeks.

"You, a child, what can you do?" said the doctor, kindly, and shook his head.

Just then there was a great noise in the air. The chimes in the steeple of the village church pealed forth a joyous Christmas carol, and the sound soared, rushing as with invisible wing beats through the clear, frosty air. For it was Christmas Eve, and the bells were, according to Norse custom, 'ringing in the festival.' Thorwald stood long listening, with folded hands, until the bells seemed to take up the doctor's last words, and chime: "What can you do, what can you do, what can you do?" Surely, there could be no doubt that that was what the bells were saying. The clear little silvery bells that rang out the high notes were every moment growing more impatient, and now the great heavy bell joined them, too, and tolled out slowly, in a deep bass voice, "Thor – wald!" and then all the little ones chimed in with the chorus, as rapidly as the stiff iron tongues could wag: "What can you do, what can you do, what can you do? Thorwald, what can you do, what can you do, what can you do?"

"A child – ah, what can a child do?" thought Thorwald. "Christ was himself a child once, and He saved the whole world. And on a night like this, when all the world is glad because it is His birthday, He perhaps will remember how a little boy feels who loves his mamma, and cannot bear to lose her. If I only knew where He is now, I would go to Him, even if it were ever so far, and tell Him how much we all love mamma, and I would promise Him to be the best boy in all the world, if He would allow her to stay with us."

Now the church bells suddenly stopped, though the air still kept quivering for some minutes with faint reverberations of sound. It was very quiet in the large, old-fashioned house. The servants stole about on tiptoe, and spoke to each other in hurried whispers when they met in the halls. A dim lamp, with a bluish globe, hung under the ceiling and sent a faint, moon-like light over the broad oaken staircase, upon the first landing of which a large Dutch clock stood in a sort of niche, and ticked and ticked patiently in the twilight. It was only five o'clock in the afternoon, and yet the moon had been up for more than an hour, and the stars were twinkling in the sky, and the aurora borealis swept with broad sheets of light through the air, like a huge fan, the handle of which was hidden beneath the North Pole; you almost imagined you heard it whizzing past your ears as it flashed upward to the zenith and flared along the horizon. For at that season of the year the sun sets at about two o'clock in the northern part of Norway, and the day is then but four hours long, while the night is twenty. To Thorwald that was a perfectly proper and natural arrangement; for he had always known it so in winter, and he would have found it very singular if the sun had neglected to hide behind the mountains at about two o'clock on Christmas Eve.

But poor Thorwald heeded little the wonders of the sky that day. He heard the clock going, "Tick – tack, tick – tack," and he knew that the precious moments were flying, and he had not yet decided what he could do which might please God so well that he would consent to let his dear mamma remain upon earth. He thought of making a vow to be very good all his life long; but it occurred to him that before he would have time to prove the sincerity of his promise, God might already have taken his mamma away. He must find some shorter and surer method. Down on the knoll, near the river, he knew there lived a woman whom all the peasants held in great repute, and who was known in the parish as 'Wise Marthie.' He had always been half afraid of her, because she was very old and wrinkled, and looked so much like the fairy godmother in his storybook, who was not invited to the christening feast, and who revenged herself by stinging the princess with a spindle, so that she had to go to sleep for a hundred years. But if she were so wise, as all the people said, perhaps she might tell him what he should do to save the life of his mamma. Hardly had this thought struck him before he seized his cap and overcoat (for it was a bitter cold night), and ran to the stable to fetch his *skees*.

Then down he slid over the steep hillside. The wind whistled in his ears, and the loose snow whirled about him and settled in his hair, and all over his trousers and his coat. When he reached Wise Marthie's cottage, down on the knoll, he looked like a wandering snow image. He paused for a moment at the door; then took heart and gave three bold raps with his *skee*-staff. He heard someone groping about within, and at length a square hole in the door was opened, and the head of the revengeful fairy godmother was thrust out through the opening.

"Who is there?" asked Wise Marthie, harshly (for, of course, it was none other than she). Then as she saw the small boy, covered all over with snow, she added, in a friendlier voice: "Ah! gentlefolk out walking in this rough weather?"

"O Marthie!" cried Thorwald, anxiously, "my mamma is very ill—"

He wished to say more, but Marthie here opened the lower panel of the door, while the upper one remained closed, and invited him to enter.

"Bend your head," she said, "or you will knock against the door. I am a poor woman, and can't afford to waste precious heat by opening both panels."

Thorwald shook the snow from his coat, set his *skees* against the wall outside, and entered the cottage.

"Take a seat here at the fire," said the old woman, pointing to a wooden block which stood close to the hearth. "You must be very cold, and you can warm your hands while you tell me your errand."

"Thank you, Marthie," answered the boy, "but I have no time to sit down. I only wanted to ask you something, and if you can tell me that, I shall – I shall – love you as long as I live."

Old Marthie smiled, and Thorwald thought for a moment that she looked almost handsome. And then she took his hand in hers and drew him gently to her side.

"You are not a witch, are you, Marthie?" he said, a little tremblingly. For Marthie's association with the wicked fairy godmother was yet very suggestive. Then again, her cottage seemed to be a very queer place; and it did not look like any other cottage that he had ever seen before. Up under the ceiling, which was black and sooty, hung bunches of dried herbs, and on shelves along the wall stood flower pots, some of which had blooming flowers in them. The floor was freshly scrubbed, and strewn with juniper needles, and the whole room smelt very clean. In a corner, between the stone hearth and the wall, a bed, made of plain deal boards, was to be seen; a shaggy Maltese cat, with sleepy, yellow eyes, was for the present occupying it, and he raised his head and gazed knowingly at the visitor, as if to say: "I know what you have come for."

Old Marthie chuckled when Thorwald asked if she was a witch; and somehow her chuckle had a pleasant and good-natured sound, the boy thought, as he eyed her wistfully.

"Now I am sure you are not a witch," cried he, "for witches never laugh like that. I know, now, that you are a good woman, and that you will want to help me if you can. I told you my mamma was very ill" (the tears here again broke through his voice) – "so very ill that the doctor says God will take her away from us. I sat at her door all yesterday and cried, and when papa took me in to her, she did not know me. Then I cried more. I asked papa why God makes people so ill, and he said it was something I didn't understand, but I should understand some day. But, Marthie, I haven't time to wait, for by that time mamma may be gone, and I shall never know where to find her; I must know now. And you, who are so very wise, you will tell me what I can do to save my mamma. Couldn't I do something for God, Marthie – something that he would like? And then, perhaps, he would allow mamma to stay with us always."

The tears now came hot and fast, but the boy still stood erect, and gazed with anxious questioning into the old woman's face.

"You are a brave little lad," she said, stroking his soft, curly hair with her stiff, crooked fingers, "and happy is the mother of such a boy. And old Marthie knows a thing or two, she also, and you shall not have come to her in vain. Once, child, more than eighteen hundred years ago, just on this very night, a strange thing happened in this world, and I dare say you have heard of it. Christ, the White, was born of Mary in the land of the Jews. The angels came down from heaven, as we read in the Good Book, and they sang strange and wonderful songs of praise. And they scattered flowers, too – flowers which only blossomed until then in heaven, in the sight of God. And one of these flowers – sweet and pure, like the tone of an angel's voice expressed in colour – one of these wondrous flowers, I say, struck root in the soil, and has multiplied, and remains in the world until this day. It blossoms only on Christmas Eve – on the eve when Christ was born. Even in the midst of the snow, and when it is so cold that the wolf shivers in his den, this frail, pure flower peeps up for a few brief moments above the shining white surface, and then is not seen again. It is of a white or faintly bluish colour; and he who touches it and inhales its heavenly odour is immediately healed of every earthly disease. But there is one singular thing about it – no one can see it unless he be pure and innocent and good; to all others the heavenly flower is invisible."

"Oh, then I shall never find it, Marthie!" cried Thorwald, in great suspense. "For I have often been very naughty."

"I am very sorry to hear that," said Marthie, and shook her head.

"And do you think it is of any use for me, then, to try to find the flower?" exclaimed the boy, wildly. "O Marthie, help me! Help me!"

"Well, I think I should try," said Marthie, calmly. "I don't believe you can have been such a dreadfully naughty boy; and you probably were very sorry whenever you happened to do something wrong."

"Yes, yes, always, and I always begged papa's and mamma's pardon."

"Then, listen to me! I will show you the Star of Bethlehem in the sky – the same one that led the shepherds and the kings of the East to the manger where Christ lay. Follow that straight on, through the forest, across the frozen river, wherever it may lead you, until you find the heavenly flower. And when you have found it, hasten home to your mother, and put it up to her lips so that she may inhale its breath; then she will be healed, and will bless her little boy, who shunned no sacrifice for her sake."

"But I didn't tell you, Marthie, that I made Grim Hering-Luck tattoo a ship on my right arm, although papa had told me that I mustn't do it. Do you still think I shall find the heavenly flower?"

"I shouldn't wonder if you did, child," responded Marthie, with a reassuring nod of her head. "It is high time for you to start, now, and you mustn't loiter by the way."

"No, no; you need not tell me that!" cried the boy, seizing his cap eagerly, and slipping out through the lower panel of the door. He jumped into the bands of his *skees*, and cast his glance up to the vast nocturnal sky, which glittered with myriads of twinkling stars. Which of all these was the Star of Bethlehem? He was just about to rush back into the cottage, when he felt a hand upon his shoulder, and saw Wise Marthie's kindly but withered face close to his.

"Look toward the east, child," she said, almost solemnly.

"I don't know where the east is, Marthie," said Thorwald, dolefully. "I always get mixed up about the points of the compass. If they would only fix four big poles, one in each corner of the earth, that everybody could see, then I should always know where to turn."

"There is the east," said Marthie, pointing with a long, crooked finger toward the distant mountaintops, which, with their hoods of ice, flashed and glistened in the moonlight. "Do you see that bright, silvery star which is just rising between those two snowy peaks?"

"Yes, yes, Marthie. I see it! I see it!"

"That is the Star of Bethlehem. You will know it by its white, radiant light. Follow that, and its rays will lead you to the flower which can conquer Death, as it led the shepherds and the kings of old to Him over whom Death had no power."

"Thank you, Marthie. Thank you!"

The second 'thank you' hardly reached the ears of the old woman, for the boy had shot like an arrow down over the steep bank, and was now halfway out upon the ice. The snow surged and danced in eddies behind him, and the cold stung his face like sharp, tiny needles. But he hardly minded it, for he saw the star of Bethlehem beaming large and radiant upon the blue horizon, and he thought of his dear mother, whom he was to rescue from the hands of Death. But the flower – the flower – where was that? He searched carefully all about him in the snow, but he saw no trace of it. "I wonder," he thought, "if it can blossom in the snow? I should rather think that Christ allows the angels to fling down a few of them every year on his birthday, to help those that are sick and suffering; they say he is very kind and good, and I shouldn't wonder if he sees me now, and will tell the angels to throw down the precious flower right in my path."

II

The world was cold and white round about him. The tall pines stood wrapped in cloaks of snow, which looked like great white ulsters, and they were buttoned straight up to the chin – only a green fingertip and a few tufts of dark-green hair showed faintly, at the end of the sleeves and above the collar. The alders and the birches, who had no such comfortable coats to keep out the cold, stood naked in the keen light of the stars and the aurora, and they shivered to the very marrow. To Thorwald it seemed as if they were stretching their bare, lean hands against the heavens, praying for warmer weather. A family of cedar-birds, who had lovely red caps on their heads and grey uniforms of the most fashionable tint, had snugged close together on a sheltered pine branch, and they were carrying on a subdued twittering conversation just as Thorwald passed the river-bank, pushing himself rapidly over the snow by means of his *skee*-staff. But it was strictly a family matter they were discussing, which it would be indiscreet in me to divulge. They did, however, shake down a handful of loose snow on Thorwald's head, just to let him know that he was very impolite to take so little notice of them. They did not know, of course, that his mother was ill; otherwise, I am sure, they would have forgiven him.

Hush! What was that? Thorwald thought he heard distant voices behind him in the snow. He looked all about him, but saw nothing. Then, following the guidance of the star, he still pressed onward. He quitted the river-bed and traversed a wide sloping meadow; he had to take a zigzag course, like a ship that is tacking, because the slope was too steep to ascend in a straight line. He was beginning to feel tired. The muscles in his legs ached, and he often shifted the staff from hand to hand, in order to rest the one or the other of his arms. He gazed now fixedly upon the snow, taking only an occasional glance at the sky, to see that he was going in the right direction; the strange hum of voices in the air yet haunted his ears, and he sometimes imagined he heard words moving to a wonderful melody. Was it the angels that were singing, inspiring him with courage for his quest? He dared hardly believe it, and yet his heart beat joyously at the thought. Ah! what is that which glitters so strangely in the snow? A starry gleam, a twinkling, like a spark gathering its light into a little glittering point, just as it is about to be quenched. Thorwald leaps from his *skees* and plunges his hand into the snow. The frozen crust cuts his wrist cruelly; and he feels that he is bleeding. With a wrench he pulls his hand up; his heart throbs in his throat; he gazes with wild expectation, but sees – nothing. His wrist is bleeding, and his hand is full of blood. Poor Thorwald could hardly trust his eyes. He certainly had seen something glittering on the snow. He felt a great lump in his throat, and it would have been a great relief to him, at that moment, to sit down and give vent to the tears that were crowding to his eyelids. But just then a clear, sweet strain of music broke through the air, and Thorwald heard distinctly these words, sung by voices of children:

"Lead, O Star of Bethlehem,
Me through death and danger,

Unto Christ, who on this night
Lay cradled in a manger."

Thorwald gathered all his strength and again leaped into his *skees*; he was now on the border of a dense pine forest, and as he looked into it, he could not help shuddering. It was so dark under the thick, snow-burdened branches, and the moon only broke through here and there, and scattered patches of light over the treetops and on the white carpet of the snow. Yet, perhaps it was within this very wood that the heavenly blossom had fallen. He must not lose heart now, when he was perhaps so near his goal. Thrusting his staff vigorously into the snow-crust, he pushed himself forward and glided in between the tall, silent trunks; at the same moment the air again quivered lightly, as with the breath of invisible beings, and he heard words which, as far as he could afterward recollect them, sounded as follows:

"Make my soul as white and pure
As the heavenly blossom –
As the flower of grace and truth
That blooms upon Thy bosom."

Thorwald hardly felt the touch of the snow beneath his feet; he seemed rather to be soaring through the air, and the trunks of the huge dark trees marched in close columns, like an army in rapid retreat, before his enraptured vision. Christ did see him! Christ would send him the heavenly flower! All over the snow sparkling stars were scattered, and they gleamed and twinkled and beckoned to him, but whenever he stretched out his hand for them they suddenly vanished. The trees began to assume strange, wild shapes, and to resemble old men and women, with long beards and large hooked noses. They nodded knowingly to one another, and raised up their gnarled toes from the ground in which they were rooted, and tried to trip up the little boy who had dared to interrupt their solemn conversation. One old fir shook the snow from her shoulders, and stretched out a long, strangely twisted arm, and was on the point of seizing Thorwald by the hair, when fortunately he saw the coming danger, and darted away down the hillside at quickened speed. A long, bright streak of light suddenly illuminated the eastern sky, something fell through the air, and left a golden trail of fire behind it; surely it was the heavenly flower that was thrown down by an angel in response to his prayer! Forward and ever forward – over roots and stumps and stones – stumbling, rising again, sinking from weariness and exhaustion, kneeling to pray on the frozen snow, crawling painfully back and tottering into the *skee*-bands; but only forward, ever forward! The earth rolls with a surging motion under his feet, the old trees join their rugged hands and dance, in wild, senile glee, around him, lifting their twisted limbs, and sometimes, with their talons, trying to sweep the stars from the sky. Thorwald struggled with all his force to break through the ring they had made around him. He saw plainly the flower, beaming with a pale radiance upon the snow, and he strove with all his might to reach it, but something held him back, and though he was once or twice within an inch of it, he could never quite grasp it with his fingers. Then, all of a sudden, the strange song again vibrated through the air, and he saw a huge star glittering among the underbrush; a flock of children clad in white robes were dancing about it, and they were singing Christmas carols in praise of the new-born Saviour. As they approached nearer and nearer, the hope revived in Thorwald's heart. Ah, there the flower of healing was, lying close at his feet. He made a desperate leap and clutched it in his grasp – then saw and felt no more.

III

The white children were children of earth, not, as Thorwald had imagined, angels from heaven. It is a custom in Norway for the children of the poor to go about on Christmas Eve, from house to house, carrying a large canvas star, with one or more lanterns within it, and sing Christmas carols. They are always dressed in white robes, and people call them star-children. Whenever they station themselves in the snow before the front door, and lift up their tiny, shrill voices, old and young crowd to the windows, and the little boys and girls who are born to comfort and plenty, and never have known want, throw pennies to them, and wish them a merry Christmas. When they have finished singing, they are invited in to share in the mirth of the children of the house, and are made to sit down with them to the Christmas table, and perhaps to dance with them around the Christmas tree.

It was a company of these star-children who now found Thorwald lying senseless in the forest, and whose sweet voices he had heard in the distance. The oldest of them, a boy of twelve, hung up his star on the branch of a fir tree, and stooped down over the pale little face, which, from the force of the fall, was half buried in the snow. He lifted Thorwald's head and gazed anxiously into his features, while the others stood in a ring about him, staring with wide-open eyes and frightened faces.

"This is Thorwald, the judge's son," he said. "Come, boys, we must carry him home. He must have been taken ill while he was running on *skees*. But let us first make a litter of branches to carry him on."

The boys all fell to work with a will, cutting flexible twigs with their pocket-knives, and the little girls sat down on the snow and twined them firmly together, for they were used to work, and, indeed, some of them made their living by weaving baskets. In a few minutes the litter was ready, and Thorwald, who was still unconscious, was laid upon it. Then six boys took hold, one at each corner and two in the middle, and as the crust of the snow was very thick, and strong enough to bear them, it was only once or twice that any of them broke through. When they reached the river, however, they were very tired, and were obliged for a while to halt. Someone proposed that they should sing as they walked, as that would make the time pass more quickly, and make their burden seem lighter, and immediately someone began a beautiful Christmas carol, and all the others joined in with one accord. It was a pretty sight to see them as they went marching across the river, one small boy of six walking at the head of the procession, carrying the great star, then the six larger boys carrying the litter, and at last twelve little white-robed girls, tripping two abreast over the shining surface of the ice. But, in spite of their singing, they were very tired by the time they had gained the highway on the other side of the river. They did not like to confess it; but when they saw the light from Wise Marthie's windows, the oldest boy proposed that they should stop there for a few minutes to rest, and the other five said, in a careless sort of way, that they had no objection. Only the girls were a wee bit frightened, because they had heard that Wise Marthie was a witch. The boys, however, laughed at that, and the little fellow with the star ran forward and knocked at the door, with Thorwald's *skee*-staff.

"Lord ha' mercy on us!" cried Marthie, as she opened the peeping-hole in her door, and saw the insensible form which the boys bore between them; then flinging open both portions of the door, she rushed out, snatched Thorwald up in her arms, and carried him into the cottage.

"Come in, children," she said, "come in and warm yourselves for a moment. Then hurry up to the judge's, and tell the folk there that the little lad is here at my cottage. You will not go away empty-handed; for the judge is a man who pays for more than he gets. And this boy, you know, is the apple of his eye. Lord! Lord! I sent his dog, Hector, after him, and I knew the beast would let me know if the boy came to harm; but, likely as not, the wind was the wrong way, and the poor beast could not trace the *skee*-track on the frozen snow. Mercy! mercy! and he is in a dead swoon."

IV

When Thorwald waked up, he lay in his bed, in his own room, and in his hand he held a pale-blue flower. He saw the doctor standing at his bedside.

"Mamma – my mamma," he whispered.

"Yes, it is time that we should go to your mamma," said the doctor, and his voice shook.

And he took the boy by the hand and led him to his mother's bedchamber. Thorwald began to tremble – a terrible dread had come over him; but he clutched the flower convulsively, and prayed that he might not come too late. A dim, shaded lamp burned in a corner of the room, his father was sitting on a chair, resting his head in his palms, and weeping. To his astonishment, he saw an old woman stooping over the pillow where his mother's head lay; it was Wise Marthie. Unable to contain himself any longer, he rushed, breathless with excitement, up to the bedside.

"Mamma! Mamma!" he cried, flourishing his prize in the air. "I am going to make you well. Look here!"

He thrust the flower eagerly into her face, gazing all the while exultantly into her beloved features.

"My sweet, my darling child," whispered she, while her eyes kindled with a heavenly joy. "How can a mother die who has such a noble son?"

And she clasped her little boy in her arms, and drew him close to her bosom. Thus they lay long, weeping for joy – mother and son. An hour later the doctor stole on tiptoe toward the bed, and found them both sleeping.

When the morrow's sun peeped in through the white curtains, the mother awoke from her long, health-giving slumber; but Thorwald lay yet peacefully sleeping at her side. And as the mother's glance fell upon the flower, now limp and withered, yet clutched tightly in the little grimy, scratched and frostbitten fist, the tears – happy tears – again blinded her eyes. She stretched out her hand, took the withered flower, pressed it to her lips, and then hid it next to her heart. And there she wears it in a locket of gold until this day.

Ashiepattle and His Goodly Crew

(Norwegian)

ONCE UPON A TIME there was a king, and this king had heard about a ship which went just as fast by land as by water; and as he wished to have one like it, he promised his daughter and half the kingdom to anyone who could build one for him. And this was given out at every church all over the country. There were many who tried, as you can imagine; for they thought it would be a nice thing to have half the kingdom, and the princess wouldn't be a bad thing into the bargain. But they all fared badly.

Now there were three brothers, who lived far away on the borders of a forest; the eldest was called Peter, the second Paul, and the youngest Espen Ashiepattle, because he always sat in the hearth, raking and digging in the ashes.

It so happened that Ashiepattle was at church on the Sunday when the proclamation about the ship, which the king wanted, was read. When he came home and told his family, Peter, the eldest, asked his mother to get some food ready for him, for now he was going away to try if he could build the ship and win the princess and half the kingdom. When the bag was ready he set out. On the way he met an old man who was very crooked and decrepit.

"Where are you going?" said the man.

"I'm going into the forest to make a trough for my father. He doesn't like to eat at table in our company," said Peter.

"Trough it shall he!" said the man. "What have you got in that bag of yours?" he added.

"Stones," said Peter.

"Stones it shall be," said the man. Peter then went into the forest and began to cut and chop away at the trees and work away as hard as he could, but in spite of all his cutting and chopping he could only turn out troughs. Toward dinner time he wanted something to eat and opened his bag. But there was not a crumb of food in it. As he had nothing to live upon, and as he did not turn out anything but troughs, he became tired of the work, took his axe and bag on his shoulder, and went home to his mother.

Paul then wanted to set out to try his luck at building the ship and winning the princess and half the kingdom. He asked his mother for provisions, and when the bag was ready he threw it over his shoulder and went on his way to the forest. On the road he met the old man, who was very crooked and decrepit.

"Where are you going?" said the man.

"Oh, I am going into the forest to make a trough for our sucking pig," said Paul.

"Pig trough it shall be," said the man. "What have you got in that bag of yours?" added the man.

"Stones," said Paul.

"Stones it shall be," said the man.

Paul then began felling trees and working away as hard as he could, but no matter how he cut and how he worked he could only turn out pig troughs. He did not give in, however, but worked away till far into the afternoon before he thought of taking any food; then all at once he became hungry and opened his bag, but not a crumb could he find. Paul became so angry he turned the bag inside out and struck it against the stump of a tree; then he took his ax, went out of the forest, and set off homeward.

As soon as Paul returned, Ashiepattle wanted to set out and asked his mother for a bag of food.

"Perhaps I can manage to build the ship and win the princess and half the kingdom," said he.

"Well, I never heard the like," said his mother. "Are you likely to win the princess, you, who never do anything but root and dig in the ashes? No, you shan't have any bag with food!"

Ashiepattle did not give in, however, but he prayed and begged till he got leave to go. He did not get any food, not he; but he stole a couple of oatmeal cakes and some flat beer and set out.

When he had walked a while he met the same old man, who was so crooked and tattered and decrepit.

"Where are you going?" said the man.

"Oh, I was going into the forest to try if it were possible to build a ship which can go as fast by land as by water," said Ashiepattle, "for the king has given out that anyone who can build such a ship shall have the princess and half the kingdom."

"What have you got in that bag of yours?" said the man.

"Not much worth talking about; there ought to be a little food in it," answered Ashiepattle.

"If you'll give me a little of it I'll help you, said the man.

"With all my heart," said Ashiepattle, "but there is nothing but some oatmeal cakes and a drop of flat beer."

It didn't matter what it was, the man said; if he only got some of it he would be sure to help Ashiepattle.

When they came up to an old oak in the wood the man said to the lad, "Now you must cut off a chip and then put it back again in exactly the same place, and when you have done that you can lie down and go to sleep."

Ashiepattle did as he was told and then lay down to sleep, and in his sleep he thought he heard somebody cutting and hammering and sawing and carpentering, but he could not wake up till the man called him; then the ship stood quite finished by the side of the oak.

"Now you must go on board and everyone you meet you must take with you," said the man. Espen Ashiepattle thanked him for the ship, said he would do so, and then sailed away.

When he had sailed some distance he came to a long, thin tramp, who was lying near some rocks, eating stones.

"What sort of a fellow are you, that you lie there eating stones?" asked Ashiepattle. The tramp said he was so fond of meat he could never get enough, therefore he was obliged to eat stones. And then he asked if he might go with him in the ship.

"If you want to go with us, you must make haste and get on board," said Ashiepattle.

Yes, that he would, but he must take with him some large stones for food.

When they had sailed some distance they met one who was lying on the side of a sunny hill, sucking at a bung.

"Who are you," said Ashiepattle, "and what is the good of lying there sucking that bung?"

"Oh, when one hasn't got the barrel, one must be satisfied with the bung," said the man. "I'm always so thirsty, I can never get enough beer and wine." And then he asked for leave to go with him in the ship.

"If you want to go with me you must make haste and get on board," said Ashiepattle.

Yes, that he would. And so he went on board and took the bung with him to allay his thirst.

When they had sailed a while again they met one who was lying with his ear to the ground, listening.

"Who are you, and what is the good of lying there on the ground listening?" said Ashiepattle.

"I'm listening to the grass, for I have such good ears that I can hear the grass growing," said the man. And then he asked leave to go with him in the ship. Ashiepattle could not say nay to that, so he said:

"If you want to go with me, you must make haste and get on board."

Yes, the man would. And he also went on board.

When they had sailed some distance they came to one who was standing taking aim with a gun.

"Who are you, and what is the good of standing there aiming like that?" asked Ashiepattle.

So the man said: "I have such good eyes that I can hit anything, right to the end of the world." And then he asked for leave to go with him in the ship.

"If you want to go with me, you must make haste and get on board," said Ashiepattle.

Yes, that he would. And he went on board.

When they had sailed some distance again they came to one who was hopping and limping about on one leg, and on the other he had seven ton weights.

"Who are you, said Ashiepattle, "and what is the good of hopping and limping about on one leg with seven ton weights on the other?"

"I am so light," said the man, "that if I walked on both my legs I should get to the end of the world in less than five minutes." And then he asked for leave to go with him in the ship.

"If you want to go with us, you must make haste and get on board," said Ashiepattle.

Yes, that he would. And so he joined Ashiepattle and his crew on the ship.

When they had sailed on some distance they met one who was standing holding his hand to his mouth.

"Who are you?" said Ashiepattle, "and what is the good of standing there, holding your mouth like that?"

"Oh, I have seven summers and fifteen winters in my body," said the man; "so I think I ought to keep my mouth shut, for if they get out all at the same time they would finish off the world altogether." And then he asked for leave to go with him in the ship.

"If you want to go with us you must make haste and get on board," said Ashiepattle.

Yes, that he would, and then he joined the others on the ship.

When they had sailed a long time they came to the king's palace.

Ashiepattle went straight in to the king and said the ship stood ready in the courtyard outside; and now he wanted the princess, as the king had promised.

The king did not like this very much, for Ashiepattle did not cut a very fine figure; he was black and sooty, and the king did not care to give his daughter to such a tramp, so he told Ashiepattle that he would have to wait a little.

"But you can have her all the same, if by this time tomorrow you can empty my storehouse of three hundred barrels of meat," said the king.

"I suppose I must try," said Ashiepattle; "but perhaps you don't mind my taking one of my crew with me?"

"Yes, you can do that, and take all six if you like," said the king, for he was quite sure that even if Ashiepattle took six hundred with him, it would be impossible. So Ashiepattle took with him the one who ate stones and always hungered after meat.

When they came next morning and opened the storehouse they found he had eaten all the meat, except six small legs of mutton, one for each of his companions. Ashiepattle then went to the king and said the storehouse was empty, and he supposed he could now have the princess.

The king went into the storehouse and, sure enough, it was quite empty; but Ashiepattle was still black and sooty, and the king thought it was really too bad that such a tramp should have his daughter. So he said he had a cellar full of beer and old wine, three hundred barrels of each kind, which he would have him drink first.

"I don't mind your having my daughter if you can drink them up by this time tomorrow," said the king.

"I suppose I must try," said Ashiepattle, "but perhaps you don't mind my taking one of my crew with me?"

"Yes, you may do that," said the king, for he was quite sure there was too much beer and wine even for all seven of them. Ashiepattle took with him the one who was always sucking the bung and was always thirsty; and the king then shut them down in the cellar.

There the thirsty one drank barrel after barrel, as long as there was any left, but in the last barrel he left a couple of pints to each of his companions.

In the morning the cellar was opened and Ashiepattle went at once to the king and said he had finished the beer and wine, and now he supposed he could have the princess as the king had promised.

"Well, I must first go down to the cellar and see," said the king, for he could not believe it; but when he got there he found nothing but empty barrels.

But Ashiepattle was both black and sooty and the king thought it wouldn't do for him to have such a son-in-law. So he said that if Ashiepattle could get water from the end of the world in ten minutes for the princess's tea, he could have both her and half the kingdom; for he thought that task would be quite impossible.

"I suppose I must try," said Ashiepattle, and sent for the one of his crew who jumped about on one leg and had seven ton weights on the other, and told him he must take off the weights and use his legs as quickly as he could, for he must have water from the end of the world for the princess's tea in ten minutes.

So he took off the weights, got a bucket, and set off, and the next moment he was out of sight. But they waited and waited and still he did not return. At last it wanted but three minutes to the time and the king became as pleased as if he had won a big wager.

Then Ashiepattle called the one who could hear the grass grow and told him to listen and find out what had become of their companion.

"He has fallen asleep at the well," said he who could hear the grass grow; "I can hear him snoring, and a troll is scratching his head." Ashiepattle then called the one who could shoot to the end of the world and told him to send a bullet into the troll; he did so and hit the troll right in the eye. The troll gave such a yell that he woke the man who had come to fetch the water for the tea, and when he returned to the palace there was still one minute left out of the ten.

Ashiepattle went straight to the king and said: "Here is the water"; and now he supposed he could have the princess, for surely the king would not make any more fuss about it now. But the king thought that Ashiepattle was just as black and sooty as ever, and did not like to have him for a son-in-law; so he said he had three hundred fathoms of wood with which he was going to dry corn in the bakehouse, and he wouldn't mind Ashiepattle having his daughter if he would first sit in the bakehouse and burn all the wood; he should then have the princess, and that without fail.

"I suppose I must try," said Ashiepattle; "but perhaps you don't mind my taking one of my crew with me?"

"Oh, no, you can take all six," said the king, for he thought it would be warm enough for all of them.

Ashiepattle took with him the one who had fifteen winters and seven summers in his body, and in the evening he went across to the bakehouse: but the king had piled up so much wood on the fire that you might almost have melted iron in the room. They could not get out of it, for no sooner were they inside than the king fastened the bolt and put a couple of padlocks on the door besides. Ashiepattle then said to his companion:

"You had better let out six or seven winters, so that we may get something like summer weather here."

They were then just able to exist, but during the night it got cold again and Ashiepattle then told the man to let out a couple of summers, and so they slept far into the next day. But when they heard the king outside Ashiepattle said:

"You must let out a couple more winters, but you must manage it so that the last winter you let out strikes the king right in the face."

He did so, and when the king opened the door, expecting to find Ashiepattle and his companion burned to cinders, he saw them huddling together and shivering with cold till their teeth chattered. The same instant Ashiepattle's companion with the fifteen winters in his body let loose the last one right in the king's face, which swelled up into a big chilblain.

"Can I have the princess now?" asked Ashiepattle

"Yes, take her and keep her and the kingdom into the bargain," said the king, who dared not refuse any longer. And so the wedding took place and they feasted and made merry and fired off guns and powder.

While the people were running about searching for wadding for their guns, they took me instead, gave me some porridge in a bottle and some milk in a basket, and fired me right across here, so that I could tell you how it all happened.

The Comrade

(Norwegian)

ONCE UPON A TIME there was a peasant boy, who dreamed that he would get a princess, from far, far away, and that she was as white as milk, and as red as blood, and so rich that her riches had no end. When he woke, it seemed to him as though she were still standing before him, and she was so beautiful and winning that he could not go on living without her. So he sold all that he had, and went forth to look for her. He wandered far, and at last, in the wintertime, came into a land where the roads all ran in straight lines, and made no turns. After he had wandered straight ahead for full three months, he came to a city. And there a great block of ice lay before the church door, and in the middle of it was a corpse, and the whole congregation spat at it as the people passed by. This surprised the youth, and when the pastor came out of the church, he asked him what it meant. "He was a great evil-doer," replied the pastor, "who has been executed because of his misdeeds, and has been exposed here in shame and derision." "But what did he do?" asked the youth.

"During his mortal life he was a wine-dealer," answered the pastor, "and he watered the wine he sold."

This did not strike the youth as being such a terrible crime. "Even if he had to pay for it with his life," said he, "one might now grant him a Christian burial, and let him rest in peace." But the pastor said that this could not be done at all; for people would be needed to break him out of the ice; and money would be needed to buy a grave for him from the church; and the gravedigger would want to be paid for his trouble; and the sexton for tolling the bells; and the cantor for singing; and the pastor himself for the funeral sermon.

"Do you think there is anyone who would pay all that money for such an arrant sinner's sake?" inquired the pastor.

"Yes," said the youth. If he could manage to have him buried, he would be willing to pay for the wake out of his own slender purse.

At first the pastor would hear nothing of it; but when the youth returned with two men, and asked him in their presence whether he refused the dead man Christian burial, he ventured no further objections.

So they released the wine-dealer from his block of ice, and laid him in consecrated ground. The bells tolled, and there was singing, and the pastor threw earth on the coffin, and they had a wake at which tears and laughter alternated. But when the youth had paid for the wake, he had but a few shillings left in his pocket. Then he once more set out on his way; but had not gone far before a man came up behind him, and asked him whether he did not find it tiresome to wander along all alone.

"No," said the youth, he always had something to think about. The man asked whether he did not need a servant.

"No," said the youth, "I am used to serving myself, so I have no need of a servant; and no matter how much I might wish for one, I still would have to do without, since I have no money for his keep and pay."

"Yet you need a servant, as I know better than you do," said the man, "and you need one upon whom you can rely in life and death. But if you do not want me for a servant, then let me be your comrade. I promise that you will not lose thereby, and I will not cost you a shilling. I travel at my own expense, nor need you be put to trouble as regards my food and clothing."

Under these circumstances the youth was glad to have him for a comrade, and they resumed their journey, the man as a rule going in advance and pointing out the way.

After they had wandered long through various lands, over hills and over heaths, they suddenly stood before a wall of rock. The comrade knocked, and begged to be let in. Then the rock opened before them, and after they had gone quite a way into the interior of the hill, a witch came to meet them and offered them a chair. "Be so good as to sit down, for you must be weary!" said she.

"Sit down yourself!" answered the man. Then she had to sit down and remain seated, for the chair had power to hold fast all that approached it. In the meantime they wandered about in the hill, and the comrade kept looking around until he saw a sword that hung above the door. This he wanted to have, and he promised the witch that he would release her from her chair if she would let him have the sword.

"No," she cried, "ask what you will. You can have anything else, but not that, for that is my Three-Sisters Sword!" (There were three sisters to whom the sword belonged in common.) "Then you may sit where you are till the world's end!" said the man. And when she heard that she promised to let him have the sword, if he would release her.

So he took the sword, and went away with it; but he left her sitting there, after all. When they had wandered far, over stony wastes and desolate heaths, they again came to a wall of rock. There the comrade again knocked, and begged to be let in. Just as before, the rock opened, and when they had gone far into the hill, a witch came to meet them with a chair and bade them be seated, "for you must be tired," said she.

"Sit down yourself!" said the comrade. And what had happened to her sister happened to her, she had to seat herself, and could not get up again. In the meantime the youth and his comrade went about in the hill, and the latter opened all the closets and drawers, until he found what he had been searching for, a ball of golden twine. This he wished to have, and promised he would release her from the chair if she would give it to him. She told him he might have all she possessed; but that she could not give him the ball, since it was her Three-Sisters Ball. But when she heard that she would have to sit in the chair till the Day of Judgement, she changed her mind. Then the comrade took the ball, and in spite of it left her sitting where she was. Then they wandered for many a day through wood and heath, until they came to a wall of rock. All happened as it had twice before, the comrade knocked, the hill opened, and inside a witch came to meet them with a chair, and bade them sit down. The two had gone through many rooms before the comrade spied an old hat hanging on a hook behind the door. The hat he must have, but the old witch would not part with it, since it was her Three-Sisters Hat, and if she gave it away she would be thoroughly unhappy. But when she heard that she would have to sit there until the Day of Judgement if she did not give up the hat, she at last agreed to do so. The comrade took the hat, and then told her to keep on sitting where she sat, like her sisters.

At length they came to a river. There the comrade took the ball of golden twine and flung it against the hill on the other side of the river with such force that it bounded back. And when it had flown back and forth several times, there stood a bridge, and when they had reached the other side, the comrade told the youth to wind up the golden twine again as swiftly as possible, "for if we do not take it away quickly, the three witches will cross and tear us to pieces." The youth wound as quickly as he could, and just as he was at the last thread, the witches rushed up, hissing, flung themselves into the water so that the foam splashed high, and snatched at the end of the thread. But they could not grasp it, and drowned in the river.

After they had again wandered on for a few days, the comrade said: "Now we will soon reach the castle in which she lives, the princess of whom you dreamed, and when we reach it, you must go to the castle and tell the king what you dreamed, and your journey's aim." When they got there, the youth did as he was told, and was very well received. He was given a room for himself, and one for his servant, and when it was time to eat, he was invited to the king's own table. When he saw the princess, he recognized her at once as the vision of his dream. He told her, too, why he was there, and she replied that she liked him quite well, and would gladly take him, but first he must undergo three tests. When they had eaten, she gave him a pair of gold shears and said: "The first test is that you take these shears and keep them, and give them back to me tomorrow noon. That is not a very severe test," she said, and smiled, "but, if you cannot stand it, you must die, as the law demands, and you will be in the same case as the suitors whose bones you may see lying without the castle gate."

"That is no great feat," thought the youth to himself. But the princess was so merry and active, and so full of fun and nonsense, that he thought neither of the shears nor of himself, and while they were laughing and joking, she secretly robbed him of the shears without his noticing it. When he came to his room in the evening, and told what had occurred, and what the princess had said to him, and about the shears which she had given him to guard, his comrade asked: "And have you still the shears?"

The youth looked through all his pockets; but his shears were not there, and he was more than unhappy when he realized that he had lost them.

"Well, well, never mind. I will see whether I can get them back for you," said his comrade, and went down into the stable. There stood an enormous goat which belonged to the princess, and could fly through the air more swiftly than he could walk on level ground. The comrade took the Three-Sisters Sword, gave him a blow between the horns, and asked: "At what time does the princess ride to meet her lover tonight?" The goat bleated, and said he did not dare tell; but when the comrade had given him another thump, he did say that the princess would come at eleven o'clock sharp. Then the comrade put on the Three-Sisters Hat, which made him invisible, and waited for the princess. When she came, she anointed the goat with a salve she carried in a great horn, and cried out: "Up, up! over gable and roof, over land and sea, over hill and dale, to my dearest, who waits for me in the hill!"

As the goat flew upward, the comrade swung himself up in back, and then they were off like the wind through the clouds: it was not a long journey. Suddenly they stood before a wall of rock, she knocked, and then they took their way into the interior of the hill, to the troll who was her dearest. "And now a new suitor has come who wants to win me, sweetheart," said she. "He is young and handsome, but I will have none but you," she went on, and made a great time over the troll. "I have set him a test, and here are the shears that he was to keep and guard. You shall keep them now!" Then both of them laughed as though the youth had already lost his head. "Yes, I will keep them, and take good care of them, and a kiss from you shall pledge the truth, when crows are cawing around the youth!" said the troll; and he laid the shears in an iron chest with three locks. But at the moment he was dropping the shears into the chest, the comrade caught them up. None could see him, for he was wearing the Three-Sisters Hat. So the troll carefully locked the empty chest, and put the key into a hollow double-tooth, where he kept other magic things. "The suitor could hardly find it there," said he.

After midnight the princess set out for home. The comrade swung himself up in back again, and the trip home did not take long.

The following noon the youth was invited to dine at the king's table. But this time the princess kept her nose in the air, and was so haughty and snappish that she hardly condescended to glance in the youth's direction. But after they had eaten, she looked very solemn, and asked in the sweetest manner: "You probably still have the shears I gave you to take care of yesterday?"

"Yes, here they are," said the youth; and he flung them on the table so that they rang. The princess could not have been more frightened had he thrown the shears in her face. But she tried to make the best of a bad bargain, and said in a sweet voice: "Since you have taken such good care of the shears, you will not find it hard to keep my ball of gold twine for me. I should like to have it back by tomorrow noon; but if you cannot give it to me then, you must die, according to the law." The youth thought it would not be so very hard, and put the ball of gold twine in his pocket. Yet the princess once more began to toy and joke with him, so that he thought neither of himself nor of the ball of gold twine, and while they were in the midst of their merry play she stole the golden ball from him, and then dismissed him.

When he came up into his room, and told what she had said and done, his comrade asked: "And have you still the ball of gold twine?"

"Yes, indeed," said the youth, and thrust his hand into the pocket in which he had placed it. But there was no ball in it, and he fell into such despair that he did not know what to do.

"Do not worry," said his comrade. "I will see whether I cannot get it back for you." He took his sword and his hat, and went to a smith and had him weld twelve extra pounds of iron to his sword. Then, when he entered the stable, he gave the goat such a blow between the horns with it that he staggered, and asked: "At what time does the princess ride to her dearest tonight?"

"At twelve o'clock sharp," said the goat.

The comrade once more put on his Three-Sisters Hat, and waited until the princess came with the horn of ointment and anointed the goat. Then she repeated what she had already said: "Up, up! over gable and tower, over land and sea, over hill and dale, to my dearest who waits for me in the hill!" And when the goat arose, the comrade swung himself up in back, and off they were like lightning through the air. Soon they had reached the troll-hill, and when she had knocked thrice they passed through the interior of the hill till they met the troll who was her dearest.

"What manner of care did you take of the golden shears I gave you yesterday, my friend?" asked the princess. "The suitor had them, and he gave them back to me."

That was quite impossible, said the troll, for he had locked them up in a chest with three locks, and had thrust the key into his hollow tooth. But when they had unlocked the chest and looked, there were no shears there. Then the princess told him that she had now given him her ball of golden twine.

"Here it is," said she. "I took it away from him again without his having noticed it; but what are we to do if he is a master of such arts?"

The troll could not think of anything to suggest; but after they had reflected a while they hit on the idea of lighting a great fire, and burning the ball of gold twine, for then the suitor could surely not regain it. Yet when she threw it into the flames, the comrade leaped forward and caught it, without being seen, for he was wearing the Three-Sisters Hat. After the princess had stayed a little while she returned home, and again the comrade sat up behind, and the trip home was swiftly and safely made. When the youth was asked to the king's table, the comrade gave him the ball. The princess was still more sharp and disdainful in her remarks than before, and after they had eaten she pinched her lips, and said: "Would it not be possible for me to get my ball of gold twine again, which I gave you yesterday?"

"Yes," said the youth, "you can have it; there it is!" and he flung it on the table with such a thud that the king leaped up in the air with fright.

The princess grew as pale as a corpse; but she made the best of a bad bargain, and said that he had done well. Now there was only one more little test for him to undergo. "If you can bring me what I am thinking about by tomorrow noon, then you may have me and keep me."

The youth felt as though he had been condemned to death; for it seemed altogether impossible for him to know of what the princess was thinking, and still more impossible to bring her the thing in question. And when he came to his room his comrade could scarcely quiet him. He said he would take the matter in hand, as he had done on the other occasions, and at last the youth grew calmer, and lay down to sleep. In the meantime the comrade went to the smith, and had him weld an additional twenty-four pounds of iron on his sword. When this had been done, he went to the stable, and gave the goat such a smashing blow between the horns that he flew to the other side of the wall.

"At what time does the princess ride to her dearest tonight?" said he.

"At one o'clock sharp," bleated the goat.

When the time came, the comrade was standing in the stable, wearing his Three-Sisters Hat, and after the princess had anointed the goat and spoken her formula, off they went through the air as before, with the comrade sitting in back. But this time he was anything but gentle, and kept giving the princess a cuff here, and a cuff there, until she had received a terrible drubbing. When she reached the wall of rock, she knocked three times, the hill opened, and they flew through it to her dearest.

She complained bitterly to him, and said she would never have thought it possible that the weather could affect one so; it had seemed to her as though someone were flying along with them, beating her and the goat, and her whole body must be covered with black and blue spots, so badly had she been thrashed. And then she told how the suitor had again had the ball of twine. How he had managed to get it, neither she nor the troll could guess.

"But do you know the thought that came to me?" said she. Of course the troll did not.

"Well," said she, "I have told him he is to bring me the thing I am thinking of by tomorrow noon, and that thing is your head. Do you think, dear friend, that he will be able to bring it to me?" and she made a great time over the troll.

"I do not think he can," said the troll, who felt quite sure of himself, and laughed and chortled with pleasure in the most malicious way. For he and the princess were firmly convinced that the youth would be more apt to lose his own head, and be left to the ravens, than that he would be able to bring the princess the head of the troll.

Toward morning the princess wanted to fly home again, but she did not venture to ride alone; the troll must accompany her. He was quite ready to do so, took his goat from the stable – he had one just like that of the princess – and anointed him between the horns. When the troll had mounted, the comrade swung up in back of him, and off they were through the air in the direction of the king's castle. But on the way the comrade beat away lustily at the troll and his goat, and gave him thump after thump, and blow after blow with his sword, until they were flying lower and lower, and at last nearly fell into the sea across which their journey led them. When the troll noticed how stormy the weather was, he accompanied the princess to the castle, and waited outside to make sure that she really came home safely. But the moment when the door closed on the princess, the comrade hewed off his head, and went up with it to the youth's room.

"Here is the thing of which the princess was thinking," said he. Then everything was in apple-pie order, and when the youth was invited to the king's table and they had eaten, the princess grew as merry as a lark. "Have you, perhaps, the thing of which I was thinking?" "To be sure," said the youth, and he drew forth the head from beneath his coat, and flung it on the table so that the table and all that was on it fell over. The princess looked as though she had come from the grave; yet she could not deny that this was the thing of which she had thought, and now she had to take the youth, as she had promised. So the wedding was celebrated, and there was great joy throughout the kingdom.

But the comrade took the youth aside, and said that on their wedding night he might close his eyes and pretend to sleep, but that, if he loved his life, and followed his advice, he would not sleep a wink until the princess was freed from her troll-skin. He must whip it off with nine new switches of birch wood, and strip it off with three milk baths beside; first he must scrub it off in a tub of year-old whey, then he must rub it off in a tub of sour milk, and finally, he must sponge it off in a tub of sweet milk. He had laid the birch switches beneath the bed, and had stood the tubs of milk in the corner; all was prepared.

The youth promised to follow his advice, and do as he had told him. When night came, and he lay in his bed, the princess raised herself on her elbows, to see if he were really asleep, and she tickled him under the nose; but he was sleeping quite soundly. Then she pulled his hair and his beard. But it seemed to her that he slept like a log. Then she drew a great butcher's knife out from beneath her pillow, and wanted to cut off his head. But the youth leaped up, struck the knife from her hand, seized her by the hair, whipped her with the switches, and did not stop until not one was left. Thereupon he threw her into the tub of whey, and then he saw what sort of creature she really was, for her whole body was coal-black. But when he had scrubbed her in the whey, and rubbed her in the sour milk, and sponged her in the sweet milk, the troll-skin had altogether disappeared, and she was lovelier than she had ever been before.

On the following day the comrade said that now they must get on their way. The youth was ready to set forth, and the princess, too, for her dower had long since been made ready. During the night the comrade had brought all the gold and silver, and all the valuables which the troll had left in the hill to the castle, and when they wanted to start in the morning, the castle courtyard was so full they could scarcely get through. The dower supplied by the troll was worth more than the king's whole country, and they did not know how they were to take it home. But the comrade found a way out of the difficulty. The troll had also left six goats who could fly through the air. These he loaded so heavily with gold and silver that they had to walk on the ground, and were not strong enough to rise into the air; and what the goats could not carry had to be left at the castle. Thus they travelled for a long time, but at last the goats grew so weary and wretched that they could go no further. The youth and the princess did not know what to do; but when the comrade saw that they could not move from the spot, he took the whole treasure on his back, topped it with the goats, and carried it all until they were no more than half a mile from the youth's home. Then the comrade said: "Now I must part from you, for I can stay with you no longer." But the youth would not hear of parting, and would not let him go at any price.

So he went along another half mile, but further than that he could not go, and when the youth pressed him, and insisted that he come home with him, and stay there; or that he at least celebrate their homecoming, he merely said no, he could not do so. Then the youth asked him what he wished in the way of payment for his company and aid. "If I am to wish for something, then I would like to have half of all that you may gain in the course of the next five years," said his comrade. And this was promised him.

Now when the comrade had gone, the youth hid all his treasure, and went straight home. And there they celebrated a homecoming feast that was talked about in seven kingdoms; and when that was over they spent the whole winter going back and forth with the goats, and his father's twelve horses, bringing all the gold and silver home.

After five years the comrade came again and asked for his share. Then the man divided all his possessions into two equal parts.

"Yet there is one thing you have not divided," said the comrade.

"What could that be?" asked the man. "I thought I had divided everything."

"You have been blessed with a child," said the comrade, "and that you must also divide into two equal parts."

Yes, such was really the case. Then he took up his sword, but when he raised it and was about to divide the child, his comrade seized the point of the sword so that he could not strike.

"Are you not happy, since you need not strike?" said he.

"Yes, indeed, I never was happier," said the man.

"That is how happy I was when you delivered me out of the block of ice," said the comrade. "Keep all you have: I need nothing, for I am a disembodied spirit." And he told him he was the wine-dealer who had lain in the block of ice before the church door, spat upon by all; and that he had become his comrade, and had aided him, because the youth had sacrificed all he had in order that he might have peace, and a burial in consecrated ground. He had been permitted to accompany him for the space of a year, and the time had run out when he had first parted with him. Now he had once more been allowed to visit him; yet on this occasion he would have to part for all time, for the bells of heaven were calling him.

As the Norns Weave

(Norse)

THERE WAS A MAN named Thorolf; he was Thrain's son, Eric the White's son, of Norway. He kept house at Thorolfstede, in the Rangrivervales in Iceland. He was an honourable man, and wealthy in goods. His wife's name was Thorhilda, but she does not come into the story for she died the year after she was married to him. The name of their daughter was Rodny. While she was yet in her childhood, it could be seen that she was going to be fair of face, and her eyes were as blue as the sea where it is deepest.

Lambi was the name of another man, a son of Grim the Easterling. He dwelt in the east dales when he was at home, but he was more often at Thorolf's for the bond of friendship was strong between them. He was a true-hearted man, but somewhat soft-tempered. The name of his son was Skapti, and he comes shortly into the story.

Now one spring while Rodny was still a child in years, Thorolf took a sickness and died; but before he breathed his last he spoke to Lambi and asked him to see after his daughter and take in hand the care of her goods, and Lambi gave his word to do that.

So Thorolf died and was laid in a cairn in the Rangrivervales, and Lambi came to live at Thorolfstede to see after Rodny and her household. And Skapti, his son, came with him. And so they sat for ten winters, and nothing noteworthy happened.

At the end of that time Rodny was grown up, and the fairest of women to look upon. Some said that she was rather wilful in her temper, but for all that she was one of the best loved of maidens. A fast friend she was, too, and warm-hearted and generous; and the best proof of that is that she never grudged Skapti, Lambi's son, his way about anything.

Skapti was this manner of man. He was so born that one foot was withered and there was a hump on his back, and he never was large of frame or sturdy. But in his face he was the most handsome of men, and his hair hung down in long curls of good colour. It was thought that his father's rearing had not bettered his disposition. In order that his spirit should not be humbled by his deformity, Lambi praised his face and his wit and all he did, and begged everyone else to do the same; and the upshot of it was that Skapti thought there was no man like himself for dash and keenness, and was always bragging and boasting, and everyone had to give way to him or have his wrath. He had a shrewd mind, but he was so spiteful that many were afraid of him.

Now a fourth man is named in the story. He was called Hallvard, the son of Asgrim the White. He owned a good homestead in the Laxriverdales, but he lived more on his longship than on land for every spring he went a-sea-roving. He was the most soldier-like of men, and the best skilled in arms; tall in growth, too, and powerful and well-knit. Some said that his wits were rather slow because he lived so much where it was of most importance that hands should be quick; still for all that he was fair-spoken and bountiful, and better liked and more humble than any other man.

It happened one spring that he rode to the Assembly, with all his shipmates at his back. Many great chiefs were there besides, but everyone said that no band was so soldier-like as his; and a group of women that stood near the booths of the Rangrivervale men turned their heads to look after him; and one of them who knew him called out merrily and bade him stop and talk to them.

He got red in his face at that, for his mates were much given to gibes and jeering; still he would not refuse her; so he rode back and got off his horse and greeted her well, and told her all the news she wished to hear. It is told about his dress that it was of red-scarlet and very showy, and he had on his head a gilded helmet that King Sigurd had given him, and his face was brown from the sea winds.

Now the maiden that stood next to the one that had hailed him was Rodny, and no woman there was as fair as she. She was so clad that she had on a kirtle of a rich blue colour that trailed behind her when she walked, and a silver girdle around her waist. Hallvard could not keep his eyes off her as he talked, until his tongue began to blunder and say the same thing twice over. Rodny kept her feelings better in hand; still it could be seen that she listened eagerly to everything he said, and the colour trembled in her cheeks as the Northern Lights tremble in the sky.

As soon as he got a chance to speak apart with the woman he knew, Hallvard asked her what maiden that might be. The woman told him; and then she managed it so that he should talk alone with Rodny, though the others stood near and spoke among themselves. And they talked together a long time; though sometimes there were silences between them, but neither of them seemed to mind that.

At last Hallvard said: "Many strange wonders have I seen abroad, yet the thing which seems strangest to me I see here in Iceland."

"What is that?" said Rodny.

"It is that a maid like you should be unwed."

"Oh!" said Rodny.

Hallvard said: "It is easily seen that you would be thrown away on any match you should make; yet that would not hinder me from trying my luck if you thought me good enough to ask for you."

She was rather slow in answering that, but at last she spoke in a well-behaved way and said there could be no two minds about that since everyone thought him a man of the greatest mark.

"I might be all that," said Hallvard, "and still not be at all to your mind. I should be glad if you would say that you would have nothing in your heart against such a bargain."

Then Rodny could no longer keep herself altogether in hand, and she began to laugh a little and said that he was hard to deal with, and that perhaps if she should say that she had nothing against the bargain, he might answer that that was too bad because he had no mind to it. But the end of her jesting was that she broke off without finishing, for he got red in his face again, and it could be seen that he was much in earnest.

"I should have thought that the risk as to that lay all on my side," he said, "but now I will say right out that my life will never seem good to me again unless I get you to wife."

Then Rodny answered him well and straightforwardly, and said: "From what I have seen of you so far, I think I could love you well; but you must see my foster-father, Lambi, about it; though it will go as I say in the end."

After that they left off speaking together.

But the next day Hallvard came to Lambi's booth, and all his shipmates with him to show him honour, though they had gibed much when they first heard what he had it in mind to do.

Skapti sat in front of the booth entertaining himself with the antics of a tumbling-girl, that cut capers there while an old man played on a fiddle. The man's name was Kol, and his nickname was Fiddling Kol. Jofried was the name of the girl, and she was Fiddling Kol's daughter. She had on a man's kirtle, and she was well-shaped and not ugly of face, though one could tell by her mouth that she was determined in disposition. They were vagabond folk, that went from house to house and lodged where they could. Skapti always talked with the girl because she had the greatest store of gossip at her tongue's end; while on her side it could be seen that she set a value on every look he gave her.

Hallvard greeted Skapti kindly, and his mates did the same, for when they saw his deformity they thought that there was more than enough that was wanting in his life; and Skapti took their greeting well because it seemed to him that they could not but be envious of the fairness of his face. And so they talked together smoothly, for a while, and Skapti offered to give them his help about their errand – whatever it might be – and sent a man to call Lambi out, when he heard that that was what they wanted; but he himself went back to his sport with the tumbling-girl.

Lambi came out of the booth at once, and gave them a good welcome. After that they fell to talking, and Hallvard asked for Rodny, and added that he had spoken to her about it and the match was not as far from her mind as might have been expected.

Now Lambi had long had it at heart to wed Rodny to his son, and there was no bargain that he would not have been more willing to make than this one. And at the same time he knew that it would be pulling an oar against a strong current to go against Rodny's will. So he held his peace for a while, and after that he answered in this way:

"Every spring since you have been able to stretch your hand over a sword, Hallvard, you have fared abroad; and for all that we in Iceland can tell, you may have wooed a maiden in every land your ship has touched. It is said that the sea's own fickleness soaks into the bones of them who live on her, and many a man has done such things and been thought no less of. But with Rodny I will not have it so, and these are the terms I lay down. You shall sail abroad as you had the intention to do, and there shall be no betrothal between you; but if you think of her often enough while you are gone so that four times during the summer you send a man out to Iceland to greet her from you, then when you come home in the autumn the bargain shall be made. But if you do not think of her that often, it is unlikely that she would get any pleasure out of her love even if she were wedded to you, and you shall not get her."

Hallvard said at once: "I agree to those terms. And now let us take witnesses."

So they stood up and shook hands, and the bargain was struck; though Hallvard's friends murmured among themselves and said that such terms ought not to be laid down for a man like Hallvard.

Then Hallvard said: "I only make this condition – that Rodny should give me her word not to betroth herself to any other man while I am gone."

"I have no fault to find with that," said Lambi.

So he sent for Rodny, and she came thither, and with her three women. She spoke to them all well and courteously; and after that she sat down, and Lambi told her all about the bargain and left nothing out.

It could be seen from her way that she thought the terms far too strong. And when she heard what it was that Hallvard wanted of her, she answered without waiting:

"I will promise that, and more besides. I will promise that when his ship comes to land in the autumn, I will come down halfway between my house and the shore to meet him, that some honour may be done him, as too much has not been shown so far."

Hallvard said that it was honour enough that he got the right to woo her, still he would not fling back the kindness she offered him; and they made a bargain about that also. After that, they bade each other farewell, and Hallvard and his friends rode away to their booth.

Now it must be told how Skapti wearied of his pastime and came in and asked his father what it might be that Hallvard wanted, and Lambi told him of the bargain he had made.

At first it looked as Skapti could not believe it, and then it seemed as if he would never leave off scolding.

"Now," he said, "it is proved true what I have long suspected, that you are a doting old man that no longer knows how to behave with sense, when you thus give away to another man the woman that I have always had it in my own mind to marry."

So he went on, and made it known in every way that he thought he had been wrongfully used.

Then Lambi said: "You take it ill, kinsman, and there is some excuse for you. But now this is to be taken into consideration, that Rodny had set her heart on the man, and his honour is great everywhere."

"His body is great," said Skapti, "as big as a bear's; and he shall yet dance to my wit as a bear dances to a willow pipe."

Then they had many words about it, until they were both wroth; and Lambi said:

"There is no use in troubling oneself about what is done and over, but I see now that my rearing has made you crooked in your temper as well, and limping in your sense."

After that he went away; and Skapti flew into a great rage, so that there was no speaking to him; and he laid saddle on a horse and rode without drawing rein until he came to the booths of the Laxriverdale men.

It happened that Hallvard and his friends were still out of doors; and they were in a merry mood, and drank and made jesting wishes about the bridegroom; and Hallvard wore a joyful face, and took all their jibing blithely.

When Skapti rode up, Hallvard greeted him well and asked him to get down and drink with them. But Skapti began at once to talk in the most ill-tempered way, and the end of his scolding was that he bade Hallvard turn his steps and his thoughts away from Rodny from that time henceforward because he had the intention to wed her himself.

Now in the beginning of his speech it was so that Hallvard looked at him and did not know what to make of him. And in the middle of it, his temper got a little tried. But when he came to the end, Hallvard burst out laughing. And his friends began to laugh, one after the other; and no one took further heed of Skapti, but all went back to their drinking.

It is said that Skapti was so wroth, and had his temper so little in hand, that he wept. Then he went away by himself, aside from other men, and stayed so a long while. After that he rode over the plain until he found Jofried, the tumbling-girl. He talked long and low to her, and no man knew what passed between them. But when they stood up to part, Skapti said this out loud:

"So things shall take this turn, that she shall not come down to meet him when his ship makes land next autumn, nor shall he have courage enough to follow her up in her hall. And then it will be put to proof whether or not I am to be set aside and made game of."

Then the tumbling-girl spoke so as to flatter him, and said that she had never heard a plan that promised to work out better.

Skapti swelled out his chest and said: "Jofried, this is how it is, that when I look at the clods around me it seems as if it were given me to know their every weak spot; and I declare with truth that I can take their life-threads and weave them as the Norns weave, and my judgements are no more to be spoken against than theirs!"

After that, Skapti rode home. But Jofried did as he had bidden her and went down to the shore where Hallvard's ship lay, and prayed Hallvard to give her and her father leave to fare abroad with him that they might show their accomplishments to other audiences and increase their goods.

Hallvard gave them leave; and now the story follows the ship for a while.

Shortly after, they got a fair wind and sailed away to sea. Hallvard stood by the steering-oar, but Jofried sat on the deck at his feet. When they could no longer see the land, Jofried began to weep much and bemoan herself, so that Hallvard asked what was on her mind.

Jofried said: "I would give all I own that I had never come hither; and it will stand me in little stead though I get all the goods in Norway, if by going away I lose my chance of Skapti's love."

Hallvard laughed and said: "I did not know before that Skapti got on so well with women. But tell me who it is that you think is likely to rob you of his heart."

"It is Rodny, Thorolf's daughter," said Jofried. "He has always looked upon her with eyes of love, but now I can see by his manner that his love is at the harvest; and the likelihood is that they will be wedded before we get back." And as she said this, she wept.

But Hallvard looked as if he did not know whether to laugh or get wroth, and at last he said: "I think there is no need for this to look so big in your eyes, messmate. Skapti sets too much store by himself to love anyone who does not love him, and there is little danger that Rodny will ever do that."

"But she will do it," Jofried answered, "for he is the most handsome man that men ever saw; and his hair is as fine as silk; and there is so much of it that it hides his lame back like a cloak of gold."

"He is a little crooked stick with a gilded head," says Hallvard.

"You can call him that if you want to," said Jofried, "but it only proves what I knew before, that you know nothing at all about women; for with a woman, a gilded head counts for more than a great clumsy body like a dancing-bear's."

Now it had happened to Hallvard, each time he came before Rodny, to feel himself very big and clumsy and out of place; so he got red in his face at that, and went away to another part of the ship, and he and Jofried saw little of each other for a time.

But when they had been out three weeks they came to Norway, and sailed into the Bay there and made land at the King's Crag. And Hallvard went up to the town, where some trading-booths were, and bought a good gold finger-ring and sent it out to Rodny on a ship that stood ready to sail. Jofried praised the ring much, and Hallvard was so pleased at that that he answered her eagerly and said:

"It is no lie what you say of me, Jofried, that I know little about women; yet this has occurred to me which should also be borne in mind, that Rodny is different from other maidens. I know it for true that she sets great store by weapon-skill and deeds of might, and I tell you for your comfort that she will never give herself away to a man who spends his days kissing the maidservants by the fire."

But Jofried shook her head and answered: "That may well be, master; and yet Rodny is a woman for all that, and all women think alike. And the proof of that is this, that although I am no more than a gangrel woman, I have the same feelings as a maiden reared in a bower; and to me as to them, all other men look like shambling giants when Skapti, Lambi's son, is by."

In this manner she kept on speaking about Skapti's fairness until it seemed to Hallvard as if it could be no otherwise than so; and he got wroth and said that if it went as she foretold, Skapti would not be so handsome of feature after he got through with him. And after that he was very short with her for a while.

Then they sailed from the Bay out into the open sea again; and there they fell in with sea-rovers and a great fight sprang up; and they got the victory, and much goods. Among the spoil there was a necklace of fine gold and the best workmanship; and Hallvard took that for his share, and sent it out to Rodny by a trading-ship that was shaping her course toward Iceland. But before he sent it, he showed it to Jofried and said:

"Do you not think that will get me some favour in her eyes?"

Jofried answered: "Good is the gift, but methinks it would be still better if it were not dumb."

He asked her what she meant by that, and she went on: "I should think anyone could see that when Rodny has hung the necklace around her neck, she will think no further about it; but Skapti will sit by her side and be always speaking so as to flatter and gladden her, and the end will be that he will have all her thoughts; for in the whole of Iceland there is not his equal for a quick wit."

Now Hallvard knew himself for a slow-witted man, so his heart went down at this; and thereafter he took no pleasure in the gifts he sent. And from that day forth he grew very silent, so that men noticed it.

At first no one could guess what was at the bottom of it, but soon Jofried repeated everything that she had told him about Skapti.

All spoke against it, in the beginning; but the end was that they believed her. After that the matter was their daily talk, when Hallvard was not by; and the more they talked, the more wroth they became for his sake. At last they went so far as to go before him, one after the other, and beg him not to stop at the Rangrivervales as he had intended, lest Rodny should break the tryst and make a laughing-stock of them, but to hold his course north to the Laxriverdales and send a man back from there to see how the land lay.

Hallvard listened to them all without speaking, but it was easy to see that each piece of advice left him more sick at heart than before.

And now the days run on until the time comes to turn their faces toward Iceland.

Then one night when the shipmates were drinking under the tents on the forecastle, Hallvard came among them and said:

"I have taken counsel with myself about what you want of me; and though I will not sail past the Rangrivervales as you wish, neither will I ask you to ride up to the trysting-place, as was intended. But we will so manage it that we come to land after sunset, and make a night-camp on the shore; and there we will be that night and the next day. And if it happens that during that time Rodny sends anyone down to us with a bidding, we will ride up to her hall and make the excuse that we could not come before because we had much goods to see to; but if she does not send any welcome down, then – when we have camped on the shore one more night – we will weigh anchor and sail away north."

All said that was a better way than to keep the tryst and run the risk of being laughed at. And now the story goes back to Thorolfstede, and what happened there.

When Hallvard had been away six weeks, a ship came out from Norway and ran into the Rangriver, and a man that was on board came to Thorolfstede and greeted Rodny from Hallvard and gave her the gold finger-ring that Hallvard had sent. And Rodny was glad, and put it on her hand where she could see it all the time that she stood at her loom; and at night the hand that wore it rested under her cheek.

But when the next month had worn away, and that trading-ship came into the river which had on board the necklace that Hallvard had taken from the sea-rovers, Skapti went down to meet her, and sought out Hallvard's man and made him drunk and robbed him of the necklace and threw it into the river. And when the man came into his wits again and saw what had befallen him, he was so frightened that he dared not come near Rodny at all, but fled back to the ship and stayed there while she held her course northward. And Skapti came home and told Rodny that no greeting had been sent.

Rodny was rather cast down at first, for she had made sure that the ship would have some word for her. Still it was not long before she had thought of many good reasons why Hallvard might have been hindered from sending; and she looked at her ring more often than before, and was soon light-hearted again. So another month passes away.

Then a third ship came out from Norway, and on her was one of Hallvard's men that had in his keeping for Rodny a brooch of gold with four silver crosses hanging from it. But Skapti went down to meet him, and then it was the same story over again. The man leapt overboard and swam to a ship that was just pulling out for the east. But Skapti went home and told Rodny that no greetings had come.

At that Rodny held her peace for a long while; and once tears came into her eyes, and that was not her way. But still, when Lambi spoke and said that it began to look as if her lover had forgotten her, she answered quickly and said:

"If he has forgotten me, it is in doing deeds that men will praise; and so it may well be forgiven him. And besides, it will not be long now before he remembers me again." And in this way she answered all who found fault with him, and showed herself big-hearted in everything.

But when the summer had worn away till it lacked but five weeks of winter, a fourth ship came out of the east; and Rodny got no greetings that time either, for the man that was bringing a gold arm-ring to her was in such haste to take passage back again that he handed over his charge to Skapti of his own free will, and rowed out to another ship as fast as he could go. And Skapti threw the gift into the sea, and told Rodny the same lie as before.

Then Rodny could no longer speak up for Hallvard, but sat biting her lips in silence, when Lambi spoke against him and said how much better it was to make bargains with men whose lives she knew all about. Men thought that this time her pride was put to a hard trial. Yet she never spoke any ill words of Hallvard.

And now the time goes on until the last of the days before winter comes. One day at even, Rodny's shepherd came galloping up to the door and said that Hallvard's ship had sailed into the river. Skapti and everyone looked at Rodny; and first her face was as though it were all blood, and then it was as white to look on as the moon.

Skapti thought there was little risk, but that her temper would jump the way he wanted it to, and yet to make sure he spoke up sharp and quick and said:

"Now Hallvard has forgotten much, but one thing I hope he will remember, and that is that he has promised to meet you halfway between your hall and the shore; for you would get the greatest shame if you went down and he was not there."

Then Lambi said: "If you will lean on my counsel, foster-daughter, you will call up your pride and stay at home. Hallvard has broken agreements enough to set you free, and more besides; and it is even as my son says, that mocking tongues will not be wanting to shame you if you keep a tryst that your lover has forgotten."

But Rodny, when she had held her peace for a little, answered them slowly and said: "It is true that Hallvard has seemed to forget me, and that my pride has been sorely tried; and it is no less true that if he gives me fresh cause for anger, I may let my temper go as far as it will. But now you both show how little you guess what love is in a woman's breast, or you would know that while there is any chance at all that he may prove himself guiltless of meaning disrespect toward me, I care no more about mocking tongues than I do about the blowing of the wind."

After that she went away, and at first Skapti thought matters had taken a bad turn. But shortly he saw that it was unlikely that Hallvard would keep the tryst himself, and that would become a fresh cause of strife between them; and then he was merry again.

Now it must be told how Rodny rode the next morning to the trysting-place, and Lambi and Skapti and ten men with her. And when they got there, there was no one to meet them.

"What did I tell you?" said Skapti.

"It is early yet," replied Rodny; and so they sat for a while.

Then there came the noise of hoofs trampling over brush. But it was only one of Rodny's house-carles that had taken horse and come after her to tell her that he had just been up on a high hill that overlooked the river, and there he had seen Hallvard's men camping on the shore, and taking no steps to get ready to ride, but lying about on the sand and amusing themselves with the tumbling-girl.

Rodny made him tell it three times over, and then she was so wroth that no one had ever seen any woman so wroth before. She swung her horse about and was for riding home without a word, when Hallvard came out of the wood before her, red in his face and out of breath because he had come on foot from the shore while his mates thought him sleeping on the ship.

As soon as Skapti saw that, it seemed to him that he had got into a luckless state; and he slipped behind a bush and made off toward the shore to find Jofried and scold her for her great falling-off of wit. But Hallvard went up to Rodny and gave her a joyful greeting; and after a little she welcomed him with both hands.

Then he said: "I see that you dislike my tardiness, and I want to beg off from your wrath; for it is the truth that I came as fast as I could."

Rodny said: "But where are your friends, that you come alone and unattended like a man of no honour?"

Hallvard seemed to find that hard to answer, and he waited a while; but at last he said: "I will tell it just as it is and not lie about it. I did not want my mates along for fear that you would not keep faith with me, and I should be put to shame before them. And now I see that I have behaved like a great fool from the beginning; though the reason is that it seemed so wondrous a thing that you should love a man like me, that I could hardly believe it when you were no longer before my eyes."

At that Rodny was so well pleased that she did not want him to see how much pleased she was, and kept her eyes on her hands where they lay in his. But shortly he spoke again, and then his voice was a little downhearted.

"Though I see," said he, "that you did not like my gifts, since you wear them neither on your neck nor your breast nor your arm. And yet I had hoped that they would please you a little."

"Gifts!" said Rodny. Then he began to ask questions, and it came out that she had never set eyes on the pretty things.

Hallvard was so wroth that it looked for a while as if some man would have to go down before him. But Rodny took it in quite another way.

"It is to me as though I had got the three best gifts in the world," said she. "And I care not a whit what became of the gold so long as you remembered to send it."

With that, she slipped off her horse and put her arms around Hallvard's neck and kissed him; and thereafter their love ran smoothly enough.

And now all that is left to tell is how Skapti came down to the shore and began to scold Jofried, and she answered in this way:

"No more of the blame for this lies on me than on you; for it is proved by this that though you know much of men's weaknesses, you know nothing at all about the strong parts of their natures. And now you may have your choice of two things – either you shall take me to wife and give me equal rights with yourself over your goods, or I shall go to Hallvard and tell him everything about this plan, and then you will have his wrath to bear, and you know as well as I whether you would be able to stand up under that."

Because he thought he knew enough of her to be sure that she would do as she said if he did not give way to her, Skapti took her to wife; though he thought the choice a hard one. They went away into the east dales to live on a homestead that Lambi gave them; and Jofried stood up for her rights in word and deed.

And here we end the story of how the Norns wove.

The Old Hay

(Icelandic)

DURING THE LATTER PART of the reign of King Christian the Ninth, there lived at Holl in the Tunga District a farmer named Brandur. By the time the events narrated here transpired, Brandur had grown prosperous and very old – old in years and old in ways. The neighbours thought he must have money hidden away somewhere. But no one knew anything definitely, for Brandur had always been reserved and uncommunicative, and permitted no prying in his house or on his possessions. There was, however, one thing every settler in those parts knew: Brandur had accumulated large stores of various kinds. Anyone passing along the highway could see that.

Brandur usually had some hay remaining in lofts and yards when spring came, and, besides, there was the immense stack that stood on a knoll out in the homefield before the house. It had been there for many years and was well protected against wind and weather by a covering of sod. Brandur had replenished the hay, a little at a time, by using up that from one end only and filling in with fresh hay the following summer.

Brandur was hospitable to such guests as had business with him, and refused to accept payment for food or lodging; but very few people ever came to see him, and these were mostly old friends with whom he had financial dealings. Brandur was willing to make loans against promissory notes and the payment of interest. There were not many to whom he would entrust his money, however, and he never lost a penny. Whenever these callers came, he would bring out the brandy bottle.

The buildings at Holl were all in a tumble-down state; the furniture was no better. There wasn't a chair in the whole house; even the *baðstofa* (bathroom) had only a dirt floor, and it was entirely unsheathed on the inside except for a few planks nailed on the wall from the bed up as far as the rafters. The clock was the sole manufactured article in the room. But friends of the old man knew that underneath his bed he kept a fairly large carved wooden chest, bearing the inscription 'anno 1670'. The chest was heavy and was always kept locked. Only the nearest of kin had ever seen its contents.

Brandur was not considered obliging; it was very difficult to get to see him. Yet he was willing to sell food at any time for cash; hay, too, as long as there was still some remaining in his lofts. He would also sell hay against promises of lambs, especially wethers, once it was certain that the cold of winter was past. But his old haystack he refused to touch for anyone.

In this way Brandur stumbled down the pathway of life until he lost his sight. Even then, he was still sound in mind and body. While his vision remained unimpaired, it had been his habit to walk out to the old haystack every day and stroll around it slowly, examining it carefully from top to bottom and patting it with his hands. This habit he kept up as long as the weather permitted him to be outdoors, and he did not give it up even after his sight was gone. He would still take his daily walk out to the haystack on the knoll, drag himself slowly around it, groping with his hands to feel it, as if he wished to make sure that it still stood there, firm as a rock and untouched. He would stretch out his hands and touch its face and count the strips of turf to himself in a whisper.

Brandur still tilled the land, though he kept but little help and was living chiefly on the fruits of his former labours. He had fine winter pastures, and good meadows quite near the house, from which the hay could easily be brought in. The old man steadfastly refused to adopt modern farming methods; he had never levelled off the hummocks, nor drained or irrigated the land. But he did hire a few harvest hands in the middle of the season, paying them in butter, tallow, and the flesh of sheep bellies. The wages he paid were never high, yet he always paid whatever had been agreed upon.

Old Brandur had been blessed with only one child, a daughter named Gudrun. who had married a farmer in the district. Since his daughter's marriage, Brandur kept a housekeeper and one farm hand, a young man whom Brandur had reared and who, it was rumoured, was his natural son. But that has nothing to do with the story.

When Brandur had reached a ripe old age, there came a winter with much frost and snow. Time and again, some of the snow and ice would thaw, but then a hard frost would come, glazing everything in an icy coating. This went on until late in April. By that time, almost every farmer in the district had used up his hay; every one of them was at the end of his store, and nowhere was there a blade of grass to feed the livestock, for the land still lay frozen under its blanket of hard-packed snow and ice. When things had come to this pass, a general district meeting was called to discuss the situation and decide what should be done. Brandur's son-in-law Jon was made chairman of the meeting.

During the discussion it was brought to light that many of the flocks would die of hunger unless 'God Almighty vouchsafed a turn in the weather very soon,' or Old Brandur could be induced to part with his old hay. That stack would help, if properly divided among those who were in greatest need. The quantity of hay it contained was estimated, and the general opinion expressed that, if it were divided, the flocks of every farmer in the district could be fed for at least two weeks, even if they could not in that time be put out to pasture.

Jon being chairman of the District Council, as well as Brandur's son-in-law, it fell to his lot to go to the old man and ask for the hay.

So it came about that, on his way home from the meeting, Jon stopped at Holl. The day was cold and clear, the afternoon sun shining down upon the snow-covered landscape. The icy blanket turned back the rays of warmth as if it would have nothing to do with the sun. But wherever rocks and gravelly banks protruded, the ice appeared to be peeled off, for in those spots the sun's rays had melted it, though only at midday and on the south. All streams and waterfalls slumbered in silence under the snowy blanket. A chill silence reigned over the whole valley. Not a bird was to be seen, not even a snow bunting, only two ravens which kept flying from farmhouse to farmhouse, and even their cawing had a hungry note.

When Jon rode up to the house at Holl, he found Brandur out by the haystack. The old man was carefully groping his way around the stack, feeling it on all sides and counting the strips of turf in so loud a voice that Jon could hear him: One, two, three.

Jon dismounted and, going over to Brandur, saluted him with a kiss.

How are you? God bless you, said Brandur. And who may this be?

Jon of Bakki, replied the visitor – Gudrun sends greetings.

Ah, yes. And how is my Gunna? Is she well?

She was well when I left home this morning. Now I am on my way back from the meeting that was held to discuss the desperate situation – you must have heard about it.

Yes, certainly. I've heard about it. I should say so! One can't get away from talk of hay shortage and hard times. That is quite true. Any other news?

Nothing worth mentioning, answered Jon. Nothing but the general hard times and hay shortage. Every farmer at the end of his tether, or almost there, no one with as much as a wisp of hay to spare, and only a few likely to make out till Crouchmas without aid.

Too bad! said Brandur. Too bad! And he blew out his breath, as though suffocating from strong smoke or bad air.

For a while there was silence, as if each mistrusted the other and wondered what was in the air. Brandur stood there with one hand resting on the haystack, while he thrust the other into his trousers pocket, or underneath the flap of his trousers. He always wore the old-fashioned trousers with a flap, in fact had never possessed any other kind. Meanwhile, holding the reins, Jon stood there gazing at the hay and making a mental estimate of it. Then he turned to his father-in-law and spoke:

The purpose of my visit to you, my dear Brandur, is to ask that you let us have this hay – this fine old hay that you have here. The District Council will, of course, pay you; the parish will guarantee payment. We have discussed that matter fully.

When Jon ceased speaking, Brandur blew the air from his mouth in great puffs, as though deeply stabbed by a sharp pain in the heart. For a while he held his peace. Then he spoke:

Not another word! Not another word! What's this I hear? My hay for the district? My hay to supply all the farmers in the district? Do you think for one moment that this little haystack is enough to feed all the flocks in the whole district? Do you think this tiny haycock will be enough for a whole parish? I think not!

But we have calculated it, protested Jon. We have estimated that the hay in this stack will be enough to feed the flocks in the district for about two weeks, if a little grain is used with it, and if the hay is distributed equally among the farmers who need it most. There may be enough for three weeks, should it turn to be as much as or more than I expect. By that time, we surely hope, the season will be so far advanced that the weather will have changed for the better.

So! You have already estimated the amount of hay in my stack! said Brandur. You have already divided this miserable haycock among yourselves, divided it down to the very last straw. And you have weighed it almost to a gram. Then why speak to me about it? Why not take it just as it is and scatter it to the four winds? Why not? – The voice of the old man shook with anger.

No, said Jon. We will not do that. We want to ask your permission first. We had no intention of doing otherwise; we intended to ask you for the hay. And we did not mean to vex you, but rather to honour you in this manner. Is it not an honour to be asked to save a whole district from ruin?

Oh, so all this is being done to honour me! said the old man, roaring with laughter. Perhaps you believe me to be in my second childhood. Not at all! Old Brandur can still see beyond the tip of his nose.

The cold-heartedness shown by the old man's laughter at the distress of his fellowmen roused Jon's ire. He could see nothing laughable about the desperate situation in the district.

Are you then going to refuse to let us have the hay, refuse to sell it at full price, with the Parish Council guaranteeing payment? he asked in a tone that was angry, yet under perfect control. – Is that your final answer?

Yes, responded Brandur. That is my final answer. I will not let the tiny mouthful of hay I have here go while there is still life in my body, even though you mean to insure payment, and even though you actually do guarantee payment. After all, who among you will be in a position to guarantee payment if all the flocks die? The cold weather may not let up until the first of June or even later. In that case the sheep will all die. It won't go very far, this tiny haycock, not for so many. It will not, I tell you.

But what are you going to do with the hay? If everyone else loses his flocks, everyone but you, what enjoyment will there be in owning it? And what benefit? asked Jon.

That does not concern me! replied the old man. That concerns them. It was they who decided the size of the flocks they undertook to feed this winter, not I. Besides, they could have cut as much hay as I did, even more, for they still have their eyesight. Their failure is due to their own laziness and bad judgement. That's what ails them! Ruins them!

But you won't be able to take this great big haystack with you into the life eternal, said Jon. The time is coming when you will have to part with it. Then it will be used as the needs require. And what good will it do you? What are you going to do with it?

I am going to keep it, answered Brandur. I intend to keep it right here on the knoll, keep it in case the haying should be poor next summer. There may be a poor growth of grass and a small hay crop; there may be a volcanic eruption and the ashes may poison the grass, as they have done in former years. Now, do you understand me?

So saying, Brandur tottered off towards the house to indicate that the conversation was at an end. His countenance was as cold as the sky in the evening after the sun has set, and the hard lines in it resembled the streaks in the ice on rocks and ledges where the sun's rays had shone that day and laid bare the frozen ground.

Brandur entered the house, while Jon mounted again. They scarcely said a word of farewell, so angry were they both.

Jon's horse set off at a brisk pace, eager to reach home, and galloped swiftly over the hard, frozen ground. After the sun had gone down, the wind rose and a searing cold settled over the valley, whitening Jon's moustache where his breath passed over it.

Jon's anger grew as he sped along. Naturally high-tempered, he had lately had many reasons for anger since he took over his official duties. The people in his district were like people the world over: they blamed the Board constantly, accusing it of stupidity and favouritism. Yet most of them paid their taxes reluctantly and only when long overdue. Sometimes they were almost a year in arrears.

Jon reviewed the matter of the hay in his mind, also the other vexations of the past. He was sick and tired of all the trouble. And now the life of the whole district hung on a thin thread, the fate of which depended upon the whims of the weather. Jon's nose and cheekbones smarted from the cold; his shoes were frozen stiff, and pinched his feet, and his throat burned with the heat of anger rising from his breast.

Jon was rather quiet when he reached home that evening, although he did tell his wife of his attempt to deal with her father.

Yes, said Gudrun, papa sets great store by that hay. He cannot bear to part with it at any price. That is his nature.

Tomorrow you must go, Jon told her, and try to win the old man over in some way. I'd hate to be obliged to take the hay from him by force, but that will be necessary if everything else fails.

The following day Gudrun went to see her father. The weather still remained cold. When Gudrun dismounted before the house at Holl, there was no one outside to greet her or announce her arrival, and so she entered, going straight into the *baðstofa*. There she found her father sitting on his bed, knitting a seaman's mitten, crooning an old ditty the while:

Far from out the wilderness
Comes raging the cold wind;
And the bonds of heaven's king
It doth still tighter bind.

Gudrun leaned over her father and kissed him.

Is that you, Gunna dear? he asked.

Yes papa, she said, at the same time slipping a flask of brandy into the bosom of his shirt. This greatly pleased the old man.

Gunna dear, he said, you always bring me something to cheer me up.

Not many nowadays take the trouble to cheer the old man. No indeed.

Any news? It's so long since you have been to see me, a year or more.

No news everyone hasn't heard: hard times, shortage of hay, and worry everywhere. That is only to be expected. It's been a hard winter, the stock stall-fed for so long, at least sixteen weeks, on some farms twenty.

Quite true, said Brandur. It's been a cold winter, and the end is not yet. The cold weather may not break up before the first of June, or even Midsummer Day. The summer will be cold, the hay crop small, and the cold weather will probably set in again by the end of August, then another cold hard winter, and...

He meant to go on, foretelling yet worse things to come, but Gudrun broke in: Enough of that, father. Things can't be as bad as that It would be altogether too much. I hope for a change for the better with the new moon next week, and mark you, the new moon rises in the southwest and on a Monday; if I remember right, you always thought a new moon coming on a Monday brought good weather.

I did, conceded Brandur. When I was a young man, a new moon coming on a Monday was generally the very best kind of moon. But like everything else, that has changed with the times. Now a Monday new moon is the worst of all, no matter in what quarter of the heavens it appears, if the weather is like this – raging sad carrying on so; that is true.

But things are in a pitiful state, said Gudrun, what with the hay shortage, almost everyone is badly off, and not a single farmer with a scrap of hay to spare, except you, papa.

Yes, I! answered Brandur. I, a poor, blind, decrepit old man! But what of you? Jon has enough hay, hasn't he? How is that? Doesn't he have enough?

Yes, we do have enough for ourselves, admitted Gudrun. But we can't hold onto it. Jon lends it to those in need until it is all gone and there is none left for us. He thinks of others as well as of himself.

What nonsense! What sense is there in acting like that? Every man for himself, said the old man.

That's right. But for us that is not enough. Jon is in a position where he must think of others; he has to think of all the farmers in the district – and small thanks he gets for his pains. He is so upset, almost always on tenterhooks. He didn't sleep a wink last night – was almost beside himself. He takes it so hard.

So Jon couldn't sleep a wink last night! repeated Brandur. Why be so upset? Why lie awake nights worrying about this? That doesn't help matters any. It isn't his fault that they are all on the brink of ruin.

Quite true, answered Gudrun. He is not to blame for that, and lying awake nights doesn't help matters, but that is Jon's disposition. He's tired to death of all the work for the Council and the everlasting fault-finding. He has had to neglect his own farm since he took up these public duties – and nothing for his time and trouble. Now this is too much. He is dead tired of it all, and so am I. In fact, I know it was worry about all this that kept Jon awake last night. We have been thinking of getting away from it all when spring comes and going to America.

Do you side with him in this? asked Brandur, grasping his daughter by the arm. Do you, too, agree to his giving away the hay you need for your own flocks, giving it away until you haven't enough for yourselves? Do you, too, want to go to America, away from your father who now has one foot in the grave?

Yes, I do, Gudrun replied. As a matter of fact, the plan was originally mine. If our flocks die, there will be no alternative; but if our sheep live and those of the neighbours die, our life will not be worth living because of the poverty and want round about us. Yes, papa, it was I suggested our going. I could see no other way out.

On hearing this, Brandur's mood softened somewhat. I expected to be allowed to pass my last days with you and your children, he said. I cannot go on living in this fashion any longer.

Pass your last days with us! exclaimed Gudrun. Have you, then, thought of leaving Holl? Have you planned to come and live with us? You've never said a word of this to me.

I have no intention of leaving Holl. That I have never meant to do. But that is not necessary. I thought you might perhaps be willing to move over here and live with me. I could then let you have what miserable little property I have left, Gunna, my dear.

And what about the hay, papa? Will you turn the hay over to us, the hay in the old stack? Everything depends on that.

The hay! The hay! the old man said. Still harping on the hay – the hay which doesn't amount to anything and cannot be of any real help. It's sheer nonsense to think that the hay in that stack is enough to feed the flocks of a whole district. There is no use talking about it. I will not throw that tiny mouthful to all the four winds. It will do no good if divided among so many, but it is a comfort to me, to me alone. No, I will not part with it as long as there is a spark of life in me. That I will not, my love.

Brandur turned pale and the lines in his face became hard and rigid. Looking at him, Gudrun knew from experience that he was not to be shaken in his determination when in this mood. His face was like a sky over the wilderness streaked with threatening storm clouds.

Gudrun gave up. The tears rushed to her eyes, as she twined her arms around her father's neck and said: Goodbye, papa. Forgive me if I have angered you. I shall not come here again.

The old man felt the teardrops on his face, the heavy woman's tears, hot with anger and sorrow.

Gudrun dashed out of the room and mounted. Brandur was left alone in the darkness at midday. Yet in his mind's eye he could see the haystack out on the knoll. He rose and went out to feel it. It was still there. Gudrun had not ridden away with it. Brandur could hear the horseshoes crunching the hard, frozen ground as Gudrun rode off. He stood motionless for a long time, listening to the hoof beats. Then he went into the house.

Brandur felt restless. He paced the floor awhile, stopped for a moment to raise to his lips the flask his daughter had brought him, and drained it at one gulp. All that day he walked the floor, fighting with himself until night fell.

Then he sent his foster-son with a message to his daughter. Jon, he said, had his permission to haul the hay away the very next day, but it was all to be removed in one day; there was not to be a scrap of hay or a lump of sod left by evening.

But the weather changes quickly, says an old Icelandic adage. By morning, the weather had turned its spindle and the wind shifted to the south. Jon sent no message to anyone, nor did he proclaim that the old hay was available. He first wished to see what the thaw would amount to. By the following day, the whole valley was impassable because of slush and water, and the patches of earth appearing through the snowy blanket grew larger almost hourly.

Meanwhile, Brandur roamed through the house all day long, asking if anyone had come – aren't they going to take away these miserable hay scraps? About time they came and got them! – He seemed eager that the hay be removed at once.

That day he did not take his usual walk out to the stack to feel the hay. In fact, after that no one ever saw him show attachment to the old hay. His love of it seemed to have died the moment he granted his son-in-law permission to take it away.

That spring Brandur gave up housekeeping and of his own volition turned over the farm to his daughter and son-in-law. With them he lived to enjoy many years of good health. Never again did he take his daily walk out to the haystack to feel the hay. But he was able to take his sip of brandy to his dying day and repeat to himself the word of God – hymns and verses from the Bible.

Now he has passed on to eternity. But his memory lives like a stone – a large, moss-covered stone by the wayside.

Queen Crane

(Swedish)

ONCE UPON A TIME there was a poor, poor boy. He went to the king and begged to be taken into service as a shepherd, and all called him 'Sheep-Peter.' While he was herding his sheep, he used to amuse himself with his crossbow. One day he saw a crane sitting in an oak tree, and wanted to shoot her. The crane, however, hopped down further and further, and at last settled in the lowest branches. Then she said: "If you promise not to shoot me, I will help you whenever you are in trouble. You need only to call out: 'God aid me, and Queen Crane stay by me, and I will succeed!'" With that the bird flew away.

At length war broke out and the king had to take the field. Then Sheep-Peter came to the king and asked whether he might not be allowed to go along to war. They gave him an old nag to ride, and he rode into a swamp along the highway, and there the horse died. So he sat down and clicked with his tongue; but the horse would not move. And the people who rode by had their sport with him; while the youth pretended to feel sad.

When the people had all passed by, the youth went to the oak in which the Queen Crane dwelt. Here he was given a black steed, a suit of brazen armour, and a silver sword. Thus he rode to battle and got there as quickly as he could wish. Then he said: "God aid me, and Queen Crane stay by me, and I will succeed!" With that he killed all the enemy and rode away again. But the king thought that an angel had come to help him, and wanted to hold him back. The youth, however, rode quickly back to the oak, took off his armour, went down to the swamp, and once more began to click to his horse. When the people rode by they laughed and said: "You were not along today, so you missed seeing how an angel came and killed all the enemy." And the youth pretended to feel sad, so sad.

The following day the king once more had to take the field. And Sheep-Peter came to him and said he wanted to go along. So they gave him an old nag to ride, and he rode into a swamp beside the highway. Then he sat down and clicked with his tongue; but the horse would not move. When the people rode by they had their sport with him; but the youth pretended to feel sad, so sad. When the people had gone by, he went to the oak in which the Queen Crane dwelt, and was given a white steed, a suit of silver armour, and a golden sword. Thus equipped he rode to battle. When he arrived he said: "God aid me, and Queen Crane...and I will succeed!" But he had forgotten to say "stay by me," and so he was shot in the leg. But the king took out his handkerchief, and tied up his leg. Then the youth said once more: "God aid me, and Queen Crane stay by me, and I will succeed!" And he slew all of the enemy. Then the king thought he was an angel from heaven, and wanted to hold him. But the youth rode quickly to the oak, took off his armour, and then went down to his nag in the swamp and tried to get it to move, while the soldiers were passing. They laughed and said: "You were not along today, and did not see how an angel came from heaven and killed all of the enemy." The youth pretended to be very sad.

On the third day all happened as before. The king took the field. The youth was given a wretched nag and rode it into a swamp beside the highway. Then he began to click with his tongue but the nag would not go on, and the people who rode past laughed at him. He pretended to feel very sad; but when the people had passed, he went to the oak in which Queen Crane dwelt, and she gave him a red steed, a golden sword, and a golden suit of armour.

Thus equipped he rode to war, and all happened as before. He said: "God aid me, and Queen Crane stay by me, and I will succeed!" and slew all the enemy. The king thought he was an angel from heaven and wanted to hold him back by all means; but the youth rode quickly to the oak, took off his armour, and rode down to the swamp where he had his three nags. He hid the king's handkerchief, and when the people passed by he was clicking with his tongue as usual.

Now the king had three princesses, and they were to be carried off by three meer-women. So the king had it proclaimed that whoever could rescue them should receive one of them for a wife. When the day came on which the oldest princess was to be carried away, Sheep-Peter received a steed, a suit of armour and a sword from Queen Crane. With them he rode to the castle, fetched the princess, took her before him on his steed, and then lay down on the seashore to sleep. He had a dog with him as well. And while he slept the princess wove her hair-ribbon into his hair. Suddenly the meer-woman appeared, and she awakened him and bade him mount his steed. Many people had been standing there; but when the meer-woman appeared they all took fright, and climbed into tall trees. But the youth said: "God aid me, and Queen Crane stay by me, and I will succeed!" And then he slew the meer-woman. Thereupon he rode quickly back to Queen Crane, took off his armour, and herded his sheep again. But among the onlookers had been a nobleman, who threatened the princess, and forced her to say that he had rescued her. And from Sheep-Peter no one heard a word.

On the following day the second princess was to be carried off. So Sheep-Peter went to Queen Crane, who gave him a steed, a suit of armour and a sword, and with them he rode to the castle, and fetched the second princess. When they reached the seashore the meer-woman had not yet appeared. So the youth lay down to sleep and said to the princess: "Wake me when the meer-woman comes, and if you cannot wake me, then tell my horse." With that he fell asleep, and meanwhile the princess wove a string of pearls into his hair. When the meer-woman came, the princess tried to wake him; but he would not wake up at all, and so she told the horse to waken him. And the horse did wake him. The great lords, however, who were standing about, climbed into the trees out of pure fright when the meer-woman appeared. The youth took the princess on his steed, cried: "God aid me, and Queen Crane stay by me, and I will succeed!" and with that he slew the meer-woman. Then he rode quickly back to Queen Crane, took off his armour, and led his flock out to pasture. But among the onlookers had been a count, who threatened the princess, and said he would thrust her through with his sword if she did not swear he had rescued her. The princess did so out of fear; but from Sheep-Peter no one heard a word.

On the third day the same thing happened. Sheep-Peter was given a suit of armour, a sword and a steed by Queen Crane, and fetched the youngest princess. When he lay down on the seashore to sleep, he said to her: "When the meer-woman comes, wake me, and if you cannot wake me, then tell the horse to wake me, and if the horse cannot wake me, then ask the dog to wake me." When the meer-woman came, neither the princess nor the horse was able to wake him, and they had to call the dog to help them. At last he woke up, took the princess on his horse, cried: "God aid me, and Queen Crane stay by me, and I will succeed!" and slew the meer-woman. Then he rode back again to Queen Crane, took off his armour and let his flock out to pasture.

Not long after, the deliverers of the princesses were to come to the castle and be married. But first the king asked his daughters which of the three each wanted to have. So the oldest said: "The gentleman from court," and the second said: "the count," but the third said: "Sheep-Peter." Then the king was very angry with his youngest daughter; for he did not believe for a moment that Sheep-Peter had delivered her. But she insisted and said she would take no one else. The king then presented an apple of pure gold to the count and the court gentleman; but Sheep-Peter got nothing.

Now all three of them were to hold a three-days' shooting-match, in order to see which was the best shot; for the king hoped that Sheep-Peter would make a proper laughing-stock of himself, and drop far behind the others without any effort on their part. But Sheep-Peter was so good a marksman that he hit everything at which he aimed. And the very first day he shot a great deal, while the others shot but little. Then they bought the game he had shot from him, and gave him a golden apple for it. The same thing happened the second day, and thus he got the other gold apple. But when Peter came home on the evening of the first and second day, he had only a crow dangling from his blunderbuss. And when he met the king, he threw the crow to the ground and cried: "There is my whole bag!"

On the third day all went as before. Sheep-Peter hit everything at which he aimed; but the others scored no hits. Then Sheep-Peter promised them all he had bagged, if they would let him write what he chose on their necks. They agreed to the bargain, and he wrote on the neck of each: 'A thief and a rascal.' Then all three went home, and again Peter had no more than a crow to show.

At night all three of them slept together in one room. When they woke in the morning, the king came in to them, said good morning, and asked how they were. But he was much surprised to see that Sheep-Peter was keeping them company. Then the youth said: "I was in the war, and slew all of the enemy!" "Ah!" said the king, "you did not do that, it was an angel from heaven; for you were sitting in the swamp." Then Sheep-Peter drew out the king's handkerchief, and then the king recognized him. Then the herdsman said: "I also delivered the princesses!" But the king would not believe that, and laughed at him. And then the youngest princess came along and told how it all had happened.

And the youth took out the ribands of the other princesses, and the king had to believe that this, too, was true. Then, Peter continued: "I also shot all the game!" And again the king would not believe him and said: "Nonsense, why you never brought home anything of an evening but a wretched crow!" Then Peter produced the golden apples: "I was given this one for the first day, and the other for the second." "And what did you get for the third?" asked the king. Then the shepherd showed him what he had written on the necks of the other suitors. And when the king saw that, he had to believe him. And so he really got the youngest princess, and with her half of the kingdom, and after the king's death, all of it. But the two sham heroes got nothing at all, and had only their trouble for their pains.

The Widow's Son

(Norwegian)

ONCE UPON A TIME there was a poor widow who had only one son, and he was so dear to her that no one could have been dearer. All the same she was obliged to send him out into the world to seek his fortune, for they were so very poor that as long as he stayed at home they were like to starve.

The lad kissed her goodbye, and she gave him her blessing, and then off he set, always putting one foot before the other.

He journeyed on a short way and a long way, and then he came to a dark and gloomy wood. He had not gone far into it when he met a tall man as dark and gloomy as the wood itself. The man stopped the lad and said to him, "Are you seeking work or shunning work?"

"I am seeking work," answered the widow's son.

"Then come with me, and I will give you enough to do but not too much," said the man, "and the wages will be according."

That suited the lad. He was quite willing to work for the tall stranger. They set out and travelled along, and after a while they came to a great dark house set all alone in the midst of the wood. The man showed him in and told him what to do. The lad set to work, and everything the man told him to do he did so well and willingly that his master was much pleased with him. After he had done all the tasks set, his master gave him a good bite of supper and a comfortable bed to sleep in.

The next day it was the same thing over. The master told the lad what to do, and the lad did it willingly and well. So it went on for three days. At the end of that time the man said, "Now I am obliged to go away on a journey. Until I return you may do as you please and be your own master. But there is one part of the house you have never seen, and those are the four cellars down below.

"Into these you must not go under any consideration. If you so much as open one of the doors, you will suffer for it."

"Why should I want to go into the cellars?" asked the lad. "The house and the yard are good enough for me."

"That is well," answered the master, and then he mounted a great black steed and rode away.

The lad stayed at home and cleaned and polished and ate and drank. "I wonder what can be in those cellars that my master does not want me to see!" thought the lad. "Not that I mean to look, but it does no harm to wonder about it."

Every hour the lad stayed there in the house alone he grew more curious about the cellars. At last he could bear it no longer. "I'll just take a wee peep into one of them," he said. "That can surely do no harm to anyone."

So he opened the cellar door and went down a flight of stone steps into the first cellar. He looked all about him, and there was nothing at all there but a switch made of brier lying on a shelf behind the door. "That is not much for the Master to have made such a fuss about," said the lad. "I could see as much as that any day without coming into a cellar for it"; and he went upstairs again and shut the door behind him.

The next day the master came home, and the first thing he asked was, "Have you looked into any of the cellars?"

"Why should I do that?" asked the lad. "I have plenty to do upstairs without poking my nose in where it is not wanted."

"I will just see for myself whether or not you have looked," said the master.

He opened one of the doors and went down into the first cellar. When he came back his face was as black as thunder.

"You have disobeyed me and have gone into one of the cellars," said he. "Now you shall suffer for it!" He took up a cudgel and beat the lad until he was black and blue. "It's lucky for you you went only into the first cellar," said he. "Otherwise you would not have come off so lightly."

Then he sat down to supper.

As for the lad he sat and nursed his bruises and wished he had never heard tell of such a thing as a cellar.

Not long after the master said he was going on another journey. "I will be gone two weeks," said he, "and whatever you do, do not dare to look into any of the other cellars, or you will suffer for it."

"I have learned my lesson," said the lad. "You'll not find me doing such a thing again."

After that the master mounted his horse and rode away.

After he had gone the lad cleaned and polished and ate and drank, and then he began to wonder what was in the second cellar. "There must be something more than a stick to see," said he, "or my master would not be so particular about it." In the end he determined to look at what was in the second cellar, whatever it cost him. He opened the door and went down the stone steps that led to it and looked about, but all he saw was a shelf behind the door, and on it a stone and a water bottle.

"They are not much to see, and I wish I had not come," said the lad to himself. "I hope my master will not know about it"; and then he went upstairs and shut the door behind him.

Not long afterward his master came home. The first thing he asked was, "Have you been down in any of the cellars again?"

"How can you think such a thing!" cried the lad. "I have no wish for another beating."

"All the same, I will see for myself," said the master, and he went down into the second cellar. Then the lad was frightened, you may well believe.

When the Master came back his face was as red as fire. "You have disobeyed me again," cried he. Then he seized a cudgel and beat the lad till he could hardly stand.

"This should teach you to obey," said he, "but I fear as long as you live you will not learn."

Not long after the Master was going away on a third journey, and this time he was to be away for three weeks. "And if you look in the third cellar," said he, "your life shall pay the forfeit." After that he rode away into the forest and out of sight.

Well, for two weeks the lad would not look into the third cellar, but at last his curiosity got the better of him. He opened the third door and went down into the third cellar. There in the middle of it was a brazen cauldron set deep in the floor and full of something that seethed and bubbled. "I wonder what that is in the cauldron," said the lad to himself, and he stuck his finger in. When he drew it out it was covered all over with gold. The lad scrubbed and scrubbed, but he could not get the gold off. Then he was terribly frightened. He took a rag and wound it about his finger and hoped his master would not notice it. He shut the door into the cellar and tried to forget about it.

The first thing the Master asked when he came home was, "Have you been down in the third cellar?"

"How can you think it?" asked the lad. "Two drubbings are enough for anyone."

"What is the matter with your finger?" asked the Master.

"Oh, I cut it with the bread-knife."

The Master snatched the rag off, and there the lad's finger shone as though it were all of solid gold.

"You have been down in the third cellar," cried the Master, "and now you must die," – and his face was as pale as death. He took down a sword from the wall, but the lad fell on his knees and begged and pleaded so piteously for his life that at last the man had to spare him. All the same he gave him such a beating that the lad could not rise from the floor. There he lay and groaned. Then the Master took a flask of ointment from the wall and bathed him all over, and after that the lad was just as well as ever.

Now the Master stayed at home for a long while, but at last he had to go away on still another journey, and now he was to be gone a whole month. "And if you dare to look in the fourth cellar while I am away, then you shall surely die," said he. "Do not hope that I will spare you again, for I will not."

After he had gone the lad resisted his curiosity for three whole weeks. He was dying to look in the fourth cellar and see what was there, but he dared not, for dear life's sake. But at the end of the third week he was so curious that he could resist no longer. He opened the fourth door and went down the steps into the cellar, and there was a magnificent coal-black horse chained to a manger, and the manger was filled with red-hot coals. At the horse's tail was a basket of hay.

"That is a cruel thing to do to an animal," cried the lad, and he loosed the horse from the manger and turned him so he could eat.

Then the black steed spoke to him in a human tone. "You have done a Christian act," said the horse, "and you shall not suffer for it. If the Troll Master finds you here when he returns he will surely take your life, and that must not be. Look over in yonder corner, and you will find a suit of armour and a sword. Put on the armour and take up the sword in your hand."

The lad went over to the corner, and there lay the armour and the sword, but when he would have taken them up they were too heavy for him. He could scarce stir them. "Well, there is no help for it," said the horse. "You will have to bathe in the cauldron that is in the third cellar. Only so can you take up the armour and wear it."

This the lad did not want to do, for he was afraid. "If you do not," said the horse, "we will both of us lose our lives."

Then the lad went back to the third cellar and shut his eyes and stepped down into the cauldron, and though the waters in it bubbled and seethed they were as cold as ice and as bitter as death. He thought he would have died of cold, but presently he grew quite warm again. He stepped out from the cauldron, and he had become the handsomest lad in the world; his skin was red and white, and his eyes shone like stars. He went back to where the horse was, and now he lifted the armour with ease, he had become so strong. He put it on and buckled the sword about him.

"Now we must be off," cried the horse.

"Take the briar whip and the stone and the jug of water and the flask of ointment. Then mount my back and ride. If the Troll Master finds us here when he returns, it will be short shrift for both of us."

The lad did as the horse bade him; he took the briar whip and the stone, the jug of water and the flask of ointment, and mounted the black steed's back; and the steed carried him up the steps and out of the house and fast, fast away through the forest and over the plains beyond.

After a while the black horse said, "I hear a noise behind us. Look and see whether anyone is coming."

The lad turned and looked. "Yes, yes; it is the Master," said he, "and with him is a whole crowd of people."

"They are his friends he has brought out against us," said the steed. "If they catch us it will go ill with us. Throw the thorn whip behind us, but be sure you throw it clear and do not let it touch even the tip of my tail."

The lad threw the whip behind him, and at once a great forest of thorns grew up where it fell. No one could have forced a way through it. The Master and his friends were obliged to go home and get hatchets and axes and cut a path through.

Meanwhile the black horse had gone a long way. Then he said, "Look behind you, for I hear a noise; is anyone coming?"

The youth looked over his shoulder. "Yes, it is the Master," said he, "and with him are a multitude of people – like a church congregation."

"Still more of his friends have come to help him catch us," said the horse. "Throw the stone behind us, but be very sure it does not touch me."

The lad threw the stone behind him, and at once a great stone mountain rose up where it fell. The Master and his friends could by no means cross over it. They were obliged to go home and get something to bore a way through, and this they did.

But by this time the horse had gone a long, long way. Then he said to the lad, "Look back and see whether you see anyone, for I hear a noise behind us."

The lad looked back. "I see the Master coming," said he, "and a great multitude with him, so that they are like an army for numbers."

"Yes, yes," said the horse. "He has all of his friends with him now. Woe betide us if they catch us. Pour the water from the jug behind us, but be careful that none of it touches me."

The lad stretched back his arm and poured the water out from the jug, but his haste was such that three drops fell upon the horse's flanks. Immediately a great lake rose about them, and because of the three drops that had fallen on the horse, the lake was not only behind them but about them, too; the steed had to swim for it.

The Trolls came to the edge of the lake, and as there was no way to cross over they threw themselves down on their stomachs and began to drink it up. They drank and they drank and they drank, until at last they all burst.

But the steed came out from the water and up on dry land. Then he went on until he came to a wood, and here he stopped. "Light down now," said he to the lad, "and take off your armour and my saddle and bridle and hide them in yon hollow oak tree. Over there, a little beyond, is a castle, and you must go and take service there. But first make yourself a wig of hanging grey mosses and put it on."

The lad did as the horse told him. He took off the saddle and bridle and the armour and hid them in the tree, and made for himself a moss wig; when he put it upon his head all the beauty went out of his face, and he looked so pale and miserable that no one would have wanted him around.

"If you ever need me," said the horse, "come here to the wood and take out the bridle and shake it, and at once I will be with you." Then he galloped away into the wood.

The lad in his moss wig went on until he came to the castle. He went to the kitchen door and knocked, and asked if he might take service there.

The kitchen wench looked at him and made a face as though she had a sour taste in her mouth. "Take off that wig and let me see how you look," said she. "With that on your head you are so ugly that no one would want you around."

"I cannot take off my wig," said the lad, "for that I have been told not to do."

"Then you may seek service elsewhere, for I cannot bear the look of you," said the kitchen wench, and she shut the door in his face.

Next the lad went to the gardener and asked if he could help him in the gardens, digging and planting.

The gardener looked and stared. "You are not a beauty," said he, "but out here in the garden no one will be apt to see you, and I need a helper, so you may stay."

So the lad became the gardener's helper and dug and hoed in the garden all day.

Now the King and Queen of that country had one fair daughter, and she was as pretty and as fresh as a rose.

One day the gardener set the lad to spading under the Princess's window. She looked out, and there she saw him. "Br-r-r! But he is an ugly one," said she. Nevertheless she couldn't keep her eyes off him.

After a while the lad grew hot with his work. He looked about him, and he saw nobody, so he whipped off his wig to wipe his forehead, and then he was as handsome a lad as ever was seen, so that the Princess's heart turned right over at the sight of him. Then he put on his wig and became ugly again, and went on spading, but now the Princess knew what he was really like.

The next day there was the lad at work under her window again, but as he had his wig on he was just as ugly as before. Then the Princess said to her maid, "Go down there where the gardener's lad is working and creep up behind him and twitch his wig off."

The maid went down to the garden and crept up back of the lad and gave the wig a twitch, but he was too clever for her. He heard her coming, and he held the wig tight down over his ears. All the same the Princess had once seen what he was like without it, and she made up her mind that if she could not have the gardener's lad for a husband she would never marry anyone.

Now after this there was a great war and disturbance in the land. The King's enemies had risen up against him and had come to take away his land from him. But the King with his courtiers and his armed men rode out to meet them and turn them back. The lad would have liked to ride with them and strike a blow for the King, but the gardener would not hear of it. Nevertheless the day the King and his army were ready to set out the lad stole away to the stables and begged the stablemen to give him a mount.

It seemed to the men that that would be a merry thing to do. He was such a scarecrow they gave him a scarecrow horse. It was old and blind of one eye and limped on three legs, dragging the fourth behind it. The lad mounted and rode forth with all the rest, and when the courtiers saw him they laughed and laughed until their sides ached.

They had not gone far before they had to cross a swamp, and midway through it the nag stuck fast. There sat the lad, beating it and shouting, "Hie! Hie! Now will you go? Hie! Hie! Now will you go?" Everyone went riding by, and as they passed him they pointed and laughed and jeered.

After they had all gone the lad slipped from the nag's back and ran off to the wood. He snatched off his wig and took his armour from the hollow tree and shook the bridle. At once the black steed came galloping up. The lad mounted him and rode off after the others. His armour shone in the sun, and so handsome was he, and so noble his air that anyone would have taken him for a prince at least.

When he reached the battle ground he found the King sore pressed, but he rode so fiercely against the enemy that they were obliged to fall back, and the King's own forces won the day. Then the lad rode away so quickly that no one knew what had become of him. The King was sorry, for he wished to thank the brave hero who had fought for him.

But the lad rode back to the wood and hid his armour in a tree and turned the black steed loose. Then he put on his wig and ran back and mounted the sorry nag that was still stuck in the swamp where he had left it.

When the King and his courtiers came riding back there sat the lad in rags and a grey moss wig, and he was beating his horse and shouting, "Hie! Hie! Now will you go?"

Then the courtiers laughed more than ever, and one of them threw a clod at him.

The next day the King again rode forth to war with all his train. There was the lad still seated on the nag in the swamp. "What a fool he is," they cried. "He must have been sitting there all night." Then they rode on and left him.

But the lad ran with haste to the wood and took his armour from the tree and put it on. He shook the bridle, and the black steed came galloping up to him. The lad mounted and rode away to the battlefield. The King's forces were falling back, but the lad attacked the enemy so fiercely that they were put to rout. Everyone wondered who the hero could be, but as soon as the battle was won he rode away so swiftly that no one had a chance to question him and no one knew what had become of him. "If I could but find him," said the King, "I would honour him as I have never honoured anyone, for such a hero never was seen before."

But the lad hastened back to the wood; he laid aside his armour and turned the black steed loose. Then he put on his wig again and ran back to the swamp and mounted the sorry nag.

When the King's forces came riding home, there sat the gardener's ugly lad, whipping his sorry nag and crying "Hie! Hie! Now will you go?"

The courtiers looked upon him with scorn. "Why does he not go home and get to work?" they cried. "Such a scarecrow is an insult to all who see him." One of the courtiers, more ill-natured than the rest, shot an arrow at him, and it pierced his leg so the blood flowed. The lad cried out so that it was pitiful to hear him. The King felt sorry for him, ugly though he was, and drew out his own royal handkerchief and threw it to him.

"There, Sirrah! Take that and bind up thy wound!" he cried.

The lad took the handkerchief and bound it about his leg, and so the bleeding was stopped.

The next day, when the courtiers rode by, there sat the lad still upon his broken-down nag, shouting to it as if to urge it forward, and his leg was tied up with the bloody kerchief, and the King's own initials were on the kerchief in letters of gold.

The courtiers did not dare to jeer at him this time, because the King had been kind to him, but they turned their faces aside so as not to see him.

As soon as they had gone the lad sprang down and ran to the wood and put on his armour and shook the bridle for the black steed, but he was in such haste, that he forgot the kerchief that he had used to bind up his wound, and so, when he rode out upon the battlefield, he had it still tied about his leg.

That day the lad fought more fiercely than ever before, and it was well he did, for otherwise the King's forces would certainly have been defeated. Already they were in retreat when the lad rode forth upon the field. But at sight of him they took heart again, and he led them on and did not stop or stay till he came to where the enemy's leader was, and with one blow of his sword cut off his head.

Then all the enemy's forces fled back, and the King's men pursued after them and cut many of them to pieces, and the rest were glad to get safely back into their own country.

After that the lad would have ridden away as before, but this the King would not allow. He called to him and rode up to where he was, and when he saw the bloody kerchief tied about the stranger's leg he knew he must be the very one he had left sitting on the old nag in the swamp awhile back.

This the lad could not deny, and when the King questioned him he told him everything.

Then the King said, "Though you are only a gardener's lad still you are a mighty hero, and the hand of the Princess shall be yours.

"You shall marry her, and after I die you shall rule over the kingdom in my stead."

You may guess the lad did not say no to that, for he had seen the Princess sitting at her window, and just from looking at her there he loved her with all his heart.

So the King and the courtiers rode home with the lad in their midst, and when the Princess heard she was to marry him she was filled with joy, for she recognized him at once as the gardener's boy who had worked beneath her window.

Then all was joy and happiness. A great feast was prepared, and the lad and the Princess were married with the greatest magnificence. But first the lad rubbed his leg with the ointment and then it became quite well again; for it would never have done for him to go limping to his own wedding.

Now as soon as he was married he went out to the stable to tell it to the black steed. He found the horse sad and sorrowful. It stood drooping and would not raise its head or speak when he entered the stall.

The lad was troubled at this. "What ails you, my steed, that you stand there so sorrowful when all around rejoice?" asked he.

"I am sick at heart," answered the steed, "and you alone can cure me of my sickness."

"How is that?" asked the lad.

"Promise to do whatsoever I ask of you, and I will tell you."

"I promise," replied the lad, "for there is nothing I would not do for you."

"Then take your sword and cut off my head," said the steed.

When the lad heard this he was horrified. "What is this you ask of me?" he cried. "All that I have I owe to you, and shall I in return do you such an injury?"

But the black horse reminded him that he had promised. "If you do not do as I ask you," said he, "then I shall know that you are a coward who dares not keep his word."

The youth could not refuse after that. He was obliged to do as the horse bade him, but the tears dimmed his eyes so that he could scarcely see. He drew his sword and cut off the horse's head. At once, instead of a coal-black steed, a handsome young Prince stood before him. The lad could scarce believe his eyes. He stared about him, wondering what had become of the horse.

"There is no need to look for the black steed," said the princely stranger, "for I am he." He then told the lad that he was the son of the King of a neighbouring country. An enemy had risen up and slain the King and had given the Prince to the black master who had turned him into a horse and taken him away to his castle. "You have rescued me from the enchantment, and now I am free to claim my land again," said the Prince. He then told the lad that the enemy King whom he had lately slain in battle was the very one who had taken his kingdom from him.

Then the Prince went back with the lad to the palace, and was introduced to the King and the Princess and all the court.

After that the lad and his bride and the Prince rode forth with a great retinue into the Prince's own country, and his people received him with joy, and he and the lad lived in the greatest love and friendship forever after.

Biographies & Sources

Dagrún Ósk Jónsdóttir
Foreword
Dagrún Ósk Jónsdóttir is a folklorist at the University of Iceland and works for the Icelandic Museum Association. In her research, her focus has mostly been on Icelandic folklore: her BA thesis focused on cannibalism in Icelandic folk legends while her MA thesis discussed modern Icelandic accounts relating to Ouija board traditions. Her PhD thesis in folkloristics focused on women, femininity and gendered power relations in Icelandic folk legends. Her research has also included supernatural beings such as ghosts and the hidden people. Dagrún has been active in the dissemination of folklore, put on exhibitions and recently took part in a big project relating to the settlement of Iceland.

Hans Christian Andersen
Holger Danske; The Fir Tree; The Tinderbox; The Emperor's New Suit; The Little Match-Seller; The Goblin and the Huckster
Few names are more synonymous with fairy tales than Hans Christian Andersen (1805–1975). Born in Denmark, Andersen developed a passion for literature early in life thanks to his father, who read *Arabian Nights* to him. At fourteen he moved to Copenhagen to become an actor, but soon turned to writing instead. Publishing his first story in 1822, Andersen subsequently published other stories, poems, and novels to considerable acclaim. He is best known for his literary fairy tales, both retellings of traditional stories and original tales by Andersen which included 'Thumbelina' and 'The Little Mermaid'.

Jón Árnason
The Witch in the Stone Boat
Jón Árnason (1819–1888) was an Icelandic author, museum director and librarian. He is known for publishing the world's first collection of Icelandic folktales. This collection, entitled *Íslenzk Aefintýri (Icelandic Folktales)*, was published in 1852 and co-edited with Árnason's friend Magnús Grímsson. It was later republished in two volumes as *Íslenzkar Þjóðsögur og Aefintýri (Icelandic Folktales and Legends)* between 1862 and 1864. Árnason was the original collector of the Icelandic tale 'The Witch in the Stone Boat'. He also wrote biographies, served as the first National Librarian of Iceland and was the first curator of what would become the National Museum of Iceland.

Peter Christen Asbjørnsen
Prince Lindworm, East of the Sun and West of the Moon; The Twelve Wild Ducks; Bushy Bride; Soria Moria Castle; Minnikin; Farmer Weatherbeard; The Three Princesses of Whiteland; The Princess on the Glass Hill; The Master-Maid; Dapplegrim; The Seven Foals; Katie Woodencloak; The Three Billy Goats Gruff; The Giant Who Had No Heart in His Body; The Blue Belt; The Charcoal Burner; Why the Sea is Salt; The Lassie and her Godmother; Ashiepattle and His Goodly Crew
Peter Christen Asbjørnsen (1812–1885) was a Norwegian author and scholar. Born in what is today Oslo, Asbjørnsen began collecting fairy tales in 1832, launching his passion which would lead him to travel across Norway on foot gathering traditional Norwegian

folklore. He worked closely throughout his life with fellow author Jørgen Engebretsen Moe to collect and publish their work, and they became widely known as 'Asbjørnsen and Moe'. Their first collection, entitled *Norske Folkeeventyr* (*Norwegian Folk Tales*), was published between 1842 and 1843. Asbjørnsen also worked as a zoologist, traversing Norway's coasts for his research.

S. Baring-Gould
Grettir the Outlaw
S. Baring-Gould (1834–1924) was an Anglican priest, author, and scholar of multiple fields. He wrote prolifically on numerous subjects, producing novels, hagiographies, hymns, stories, song collections, and other works. Born in Exeter, England, Baring-Gould spent much of his childhood travelling throughout Europe with his family. After attending Cambridge University and teaching at Hurstpierpoint College, he took Holy Orders in 1864, becoming a curate in West Yorkshire, and later a rector in Essex. He is best known for his collections of traditional English folk songs, through which he helped preserve many songs that may have otherwise been lost.

Hjalmar Hjorth Boyesen
The Cooper and the Wolves; Mikkel; Magnie's Dangerous Ride; Big Hans and Little Hans; The Skerry of Shrieks; The Famine Among the Gnomes; Thorwald and the Star Children
Hjalmar Hjorth Boyesen (1848–1895) was born in Fredriksvern, Norway. Boyesen studied German and Scandinavian literature at the Universities of Leipzig and Oslo before moving to the United States in 1869. There he became a professor of languages at several prestigious universities. He was a prolific writer of both academic and fictional works, his most popular of which were based on Norwegian culture. His best-known work is his 1874 novel *Gunnar: A Tale of Norse Life*, which is considered the first novel by a Norwegian immigrant in the United States.

R.L. Cassie
A Tale of the Sea
R.L. Cassie was a British translator who specialized in the Norwegian language. Cassie is best known for his translation of Norwegian author Alexander L. Kielland's *Norse Tales and Sketches,* a collection of traditional Norwegian stories published in 1896. Cassie's goal in his translation work was to bring the attention of British readers to literature produced by popular Scandinavian authors of the era.

G.W. Dasent
Katie Woodencloak; The Twelve Wild Ducks; Why the Sea is Salt; East of the Sun and West of the Moon; The Three Billy Goats Gruff; The Giant Who Had No Heart in His Body; The Blue Belt; The Charcoal Burner; The Lassie and her Godmother
British author G.W. Dasent (1817–1896) was born in St. Vincent, British West Indies. After studying Classical literature at university and then serving in a diplomatic role in Sweden, Dasent discovered his great passion for Scandinavian mythology and literature. Going on to become an assistant editor at *The Times,* and then a professor of English literature and modern history at King's College London, Dasent also worked as a translator of Scandinavian folktales. Among his best-known works are *Viking Folk Tales* and *Tales from the Fjeld.*

Guðmundur Friðjónsson

The Old Hay

Guðmundur Friðjónsson (1869–1944) was an Icelandic author of short stories and poems. Born in the remote north-country valley of Aðaldalur, Friðjónsson was a farmer's son and a self-educated writer. Much of his work centred on radical social satire as well as natural realism, reflecting the breathtaking landscape of his home. He came to be highly popular and widely read throughout Iceland. He wrote his short story 'The Old Hay' in 1909, and it was later published in *Tólf Sögur* (*Twelve Stories*) in 1915.

Jacob Grimm and Wilhelm Grimm

Mother Holle; The Master-Thief; Snowdrop

Jacob Grimm (1785–1863) and Wilhelm Grimm (1786–1859) are two of the most recognisable names among the world's storytellers. Born in Germany and popularly known as the Brothers Grimm, they collected European fairy and folk tales, among which were 'Cinderella', 'Hansel and Gretel', and 'Sleeping Beauty', and many other well-known stories. They first developed their interest in German folklore while attending the University of Marburg. This coincided with revived public interest in folktales during the Romantic era of the early nineteenth century. The Brothers Grimm published their first collection in 1812, entitled *Kinder- und Hausmärchen* (*Children's and Household Tales*). Their methodology for researching and collecting tales came to form the foundation of folklore studies.

Mrs. A.W. Hall

Litill, Tritill, the Birds, and the Peasant Lad; Prince Hlini

Mrs. A.W. Hall was a translator and editor. She is best known for her editorship and translation of the collection *Icelandic Fairy Tales,* published in 1897. The collection preserved many traditional pieces of Icelandinc folklore that might otherwise have been lost. She also published under the pen-name of Angus W. Hall. Her other works include the short story collection entitled *The Giantess in the Granite Boat* (1897).

Thomas Wentworth Higginson

Harald the Viking

Thomas Wentworth Higginson (1823–1911) was an author, Unitarian minister, politician, political activist and soldier. Born in Cambridge, Massachusetts, Higginson attended Harvard College aged thirteen, and later studied theology at Harvard Divinity School. He soon left however to dedicate his time to the Abolitionist movement, supporting the Disunion Abolitionists. He also actively opposed the then-impending Mexican-American War, and later became a prominent advocate for women's rights and religious tolerance. He served in the American Civil War alongside Black soldiers, and in 1870 he published a memoir of his experiences entitled *Army Life in a Black Regiment.*

Margaret Hunt

Margaret Raine Hunt (1831–1912) was a British translator and author. Hunt was born in Durham, and later lived in London during the late nineteenth century. She is best known for her English translations of German fairy tales by the Brothers Grimm. She published a two-volume English-language collection of their tales in 1884, entitled *Grimm's Household*

Tales, featuring an introduction by Andrew Lang. Hunt also published works under the pen-name Averil Beaumont. Her novels include *Under Seal of Confession* (1874), *The Leaden Casket* (1880), and *Thornicroft's Model* (1881).

Alexander L. Keilland

A Tale of the Sea

Alexander L. Keilland (1849–1906) was a Norwegian author. He was among the group of Norwegian writers known as the 'Four Greats', alongside Henrik Ibsen, Bjørnstjerne Bjørnson and Jonas Lie. Keilland was born in Stavanger to a wealthy merchant family. With strong empathy for the less fortunate, he often incorporated critiques of society into his writing, and as a factory owner he treated his employees better than most at the time. He produced plays, novels, and short stories, often leaning towards satirical comedy. Keilland also wrote for the newspaper *Stavanger Avis* as a journalist, and later served as Stavanger's mayor.

Andrew Lang

The Master-Maid; The Story of Sigurd; Dapplegrim; The Seven Foals; The Wonderful Birch; Soria Moria Castle; Minnikin; Farmer Weatherbeard; The Three Princesses of Whiteland; The Princess on the Glass Hill; Bushy Bride

The Witch in the Stone Boat Poet, novelist and anthropologist Andrew Lang (1844–1912) was born in Selkirk, Scotland. He is now best known for his collections of fairy stories and publications on folklore, mythology and religion. Inspired by the traditional folklore tales of his home on the English-Scottish border, Lang compiled twelve coloured fairy books which collected 798 stories from French, Danish, Russian and Romanian sources, amongst others. This series was hugely popular and had a wide influence on increasing the popularity of fairy tales in children's literature. His fairy tale collections include *The Red Fairy Book* (1890), *The Lilac Fairy Book* (1910), and *The Book of Dreams and Ghosts* (1897).

Ottilie A. Liljencrantz

The Hostage; As the Norns Weave

Ottilie A. Liljencrantz (1876–1910) was an American author, born in Chicago. Of Swedish descent, Liljencrantz held a great fondness for her Scandinavian heritage and the literature and traditional stories of the region. She reflected this fondness in her writing, producing novels, short stories, and plays in the vein of fairy tales and Scandinavian subjects. Her books include *The Thrall of Leif the Lucky: A Story of Viking Days* (1902), *The Ward of King Canute* (1903), and *A Viking's Love and Other Tales of the North* (1911).

Logan Marshall

Frithiof the Bold

Logan Marshall was the pen-name of Logan Howard-Smith (born in 1883). He was an American author born in Philadelphia, Pennsylvania. Marshall graduated from the University of Pennsylvania in 1905, following which he became an assistant editor at the publishing firm The John C. Winston Co. There he both edited and authored a great number of books under his pen-name. His best-known of these was *The Sinking of the Titanic and Great Sea Disasters* (1912), which grew hugely popular due to massive public interest in the tragedy.

Frederick H. Martens

Frederick H. Martens (1874–1932) was an American author, translator, and music journalist. He is best known for his books on music; these include *Violin Mastery* (1919) and *Little Biographies Series 1: Musicians* (1922). Martens also translated numerous collections of fairy tales from various cultures throughout the world. *The Norwegian Fairy Book* (1922) and *The Swedish Fairy Book* (1921), edited by Clara Stroebe; and *The Chinese Fairy Book* (1926), edited by R. Wilhelm, are among his translations.

Jørgen Moe

(See the stories listed under Peter Christen Asbjørnsen)

Jørgen Engebretsen Moe (1813–1882) was a Norwegian author, folklorist, poet, and bishop. Born in the district of Ringerike, Moe was the son of a farmer and politician. He travelled annually throughout Norway to collect tales and traditions from the country's remote mountainous regions. Moe worked closely alongside fellow Norwegian author Peter Christen Asbjørnsen, whom he met at Norderhov Rectory while preparing for exams. Sharing a passion for folklore, together they collected and published numerous collections of Norwegian tales, and they quickly became known as the writing duo 'Asbjørnsen and Moe'. Through their work they have played a significant part in the development of the Norwegian language.

Mekkin Sveinson Perkins

Mekkin Sveinson Perkins was a translator specialising in the Icelandic language. His translation of the short story 'The Old Hay', written by the Icelandic author Guðmundur Friðjónsson, appeared in the collection *Seven Icelandic Short Stories.*

Katharine Pyle

The Magic Pipe; The Widow's Son

Katharine Pyle (1863–1938) was an American author and illustrator. She primarily wrote books for young adults, as well as works on the colonial history of her home state of Delaware. She became interested in writing and art as a child, and later attended the Philadelphia School of Design for Women. Pyle initially published poems in *St. Nicholas Magazine* and *Harper's Bazaar*, and she co-wrote the book *The Wonder Clock* (1887) with her brother Howard Pyle. She contributed to America's Golden Age of Illustration and collaborated with fellow creatives on many books as both a writer and an illustrator.

Clara Stroebe

The Isle of Udröst; Faithful and Unfaithful; Helge-Hal in the Blue Hill; Lasse, My Thrall!; The Evil One and Kitta Grau; Torre Jeppe; Murmur Goose-Egg; The Werewolf; The Secret Church; Charcoal Nils and the Troll-Woman; Finn, the Giant, and the Minster of Lund; Knös; Silverwhite and Lillwacker; First Born, First Wed; Lucky Andrew; The Comrade; Queen Crane

Clara Stroebe (1887–1932) was a German author, born in Freiburg im Breisgau. She attended Heidelberg University in 1907, followed by Ludwig Maximillian University of Munich from 1909 to 1910. Stroebe gathered and edited a number of fairy tale collections, including *The Swedish Fairy Book* (1921) and *The Norwegian Fairy Book* (1922), among several others. These books were published as part of *The Fairy Book* series produced by the Frederick A. Stokes Company. She is also often credited as Klara Stroebe.

Charles John Tibbits

The Legend of Thorgunna;Tales From the Prose Edda; The Dwarf-Sword Tirfing; The Icelandic Sorceresses; The Magician's Daughter; Origin of Tiis Lake; How A Lad Stole the Giant's Treasure; Tales of the Nisses; The Dwarfs' Banquet; The Lost Bell; The Adventures of John Dietrich; Maiden Swanwhite and Maiden Foxtail; The Three Dogs

Charles John Tibbets (1861–1935) was an English journalist, newspaper editor, and author. He attended Oxford University and married the novelist Annie Olive Brazier. Tibbets wrote prolifically on folktales and legends, publishing extensive collections. One of his most popular works is the series *Folk-Lore and Legends*, which features numerous volumes of tales from cultures and societies around the world. These include folklore of Native American nations, Scandinavia, Russia, and Scotland, among others.

Edward Oswald Gabriel Turville-Petre

The Story of Audunn and the Bear

Edward Oswald Gabriel Turville-Petre (1908–1978) was an English philologist. He was born in Leicestershire and attended the University of Oxford, where he studied under J.R.R. Tolkien. Turville-Petre specialised in Old Norse studies, and he became a professor at Oxford, teaching Ancient Icelandic Literature and Antiquities. He was also a member of the Viking Society for Northern Research. He authored a number of scholarly works about Old Norse literature and religion. He visited Iceland many times throughout his life, studying Icelandic traditions and culture.

GOTHIC FANTASY

For our books, calendars, blog
and latest special offers please see:
flametreepublishing.com